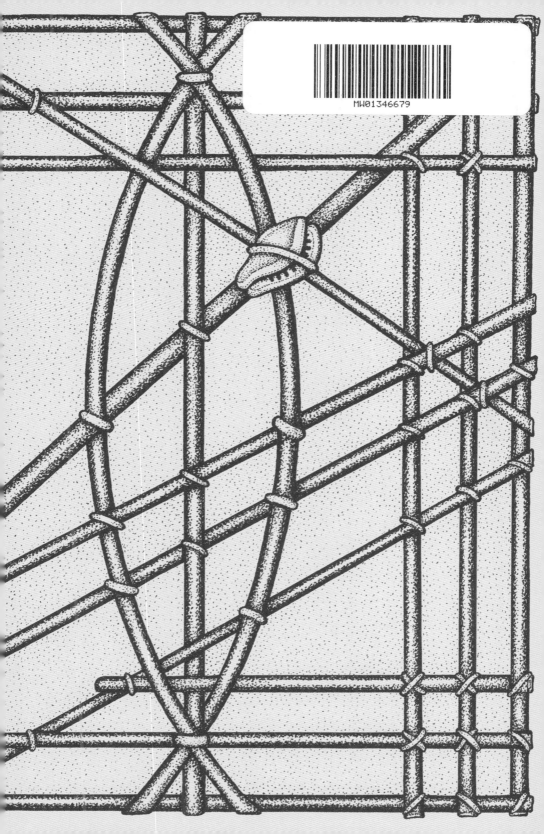

ALSO BY ADAM JOHNSON

Fortune Smiles

The Orphan Master's Son

Parasites Like Us

Emporium

THE WAYFINDER

THE WAYFINDER

A Novel

ADAM JOHNSON

MCD
FARRAR, STRAUS AND GIROUX
NEW YORK

MCD
Farrar, Straus and Giroux
120 Broadway, New York 10271

EU Representative: Macmillan Publishers Ireland Ltd, 1st Floor,
The Liffey Trust Centre, 117–126 Sheriff Street Upper, Dublin 1, DO1 YC43

Copyright © 2025 by Adam Johnson
Map copyright © 2025 by Jeffrey L. Ward
All rights reserved
Printed in the United States of America
First edition, 2025

Endpaper art by Layne Miller
Constellation art on case and in text by Layne Miller
All other art in text by rudvi / Shutterstock.com

Library of Congress Cataloging-in-Publication Data
Names: Johnson, Adam, 1967– author.
Title: The wayfinder : a novel / Adam Johnson.
Description: First edition. | New York : MCD, Farrar, Straus and Giroux, 2025.
Identifiers: LCCN 2025012951 | ISBN 9780374619572 (hardcover)
Subjects: LCGFT: Novels.
Classification: LCC PS3610.O3 W39 2025 | DDC 813/.6—dc23/eng/20250409
LC record available at https://lccn.loc.gov/2025012951

International Paperback Edition ISBN: 978-0-374-61998-5

Designed by Gretchen Achilles

The publisher of this book does not authorize the use or reproduction
of any part of this book in any manner for the purpose of training artificial
intelligence technologies or systems. The publisher of this book expressly reserves
this book from the Text and Data Mining exception in accordance with
Article 4(3) of the European Union Digital Single Market Directive 2019/790.

Our books may be purchased in bulk for specialty retail/wholesale, literacy,
corporate/premium, educational, and subscription box use. Please contact
MacmillanSpecialMarkets@macmillan.com.

www.mcdbooks.com • www.fsgbooks.com
Follow us on social media at @mcdbooks and @fsgbooks

10 9 8 7 6 5 4 3 2 1

This is a work of fiction. Names, characters, places, organizations, and incidents
either are products of the author's imagination or are used fictitiously. Any resemblance to
actual events, places, organizations, or persons, living or dead, is entirely coincidental.

For Phil & Penny

Ko e havilivili iho loungutu—
Ko koe eni.
Ko e 'one'one iho vaha'a louhi'i va'e—
Ko ho 'api eni.

The wind across your lips—
This is who you are.
The sand between your toes—
This is your home.

MANUMOTU, OR BIRD ISLAND: LOCATED IN THE SOUTHERN WATERS

KŌRERO Dreams of being her people's storyteller, but has other destinies.
KŌRERO'S MOTHER Keeper of the island's tattooing tradition.
KŌRERO'S FATHER The island's fishing captain, he's never ventured beyond the sight of land.
HINE Kōrero's best friend; her mother has died, and her father's identity is unknown.
TAPOTO A large man who becomes the island's first war captain.
TIRI Blind, she's the island's oldest woman and is responsible for healing.
HĀ MUTU The birding captain, he's the island's oldest man.
PAPA TOKI One-armed, he is charismatic and prone to dueling.
IHI The sole survivor of a neighboring island's depletion and conflict.
ARAWIWI A widowed woodworker.

TONGATAPU: TONGA'S MAIN ISLAND, THE SACRED SOUTH

THE TU'ITONGA The king of Tonga.
PŌHIVA The king's wife.
LOLOHEA The king's oldest son, groomed to become the next Tu'itonga.
SECOND SON The king's middle child, apprenticed in the study of navigation.
HAVEA A master navigator, he serves as the Second Son's supplemental father.
VAIVAO Havea's wife, daughter of 'Uvea Island's gravestone cutter.
FINAU The king's youngest son, apprenticed in the study of poetry.

NEW PUNAKE   The royal poet, he serves as Finau's supplemental father.
KŌKĪ   Finau's red-shining parrot. Kōkī has memorized all of Tonga's ancient poetry.
'AHO   The king's younger brother, 'Aho is a troubled veteran of the Fisian wars.
'OFA   'Aho's deceased wife.
MATEAKI   'Aho's son, whom 'Aho took to war with him.
THE TU'ILIFUKA   The chief of Lifuka Island, he is 'Aho's war comrade and lone friend.
SIX FISTS   From Nuku Hiva, he is indentured to serve as the king's chief of security.
MATĀPULE MU'A   The king's personal matāpule, the "face of the king's authority."
THE TAMAHĀ   The king's aunt. Keeper of the Life-Affecting Fan, she outranks all.
VALATOA   The Tamahā's reluctant chief of security.
SEVEN FISTS   The king's replacement chief of security.
TUFUGA   An old tattooist from Samoa, enlisted to ink the Tu'itonga and Finau.
VAHA-LOA   Leader of the oceanic nomads.
MOON APPEARING   Fefine Girl from the rural island of Hunga.
SUN SHOWER   Fefine Girl from Tonga's northernmost island of Tafahi.
HEILALA, KAKALA   Elite Fefine Girls from Tonga's main island of Tongatapu.

ROTUMA: AN ISOLATED, PEACE-LOVING ISLAND NORTH OF FIJI

KANIVA   The lovely daughter of the Rotuma's Mua priest.
RAHO   The young warrior who loves Kaniva.
MUA PRIEST   Spiritual leader of Rotuma, Kaniva's father.
SAU CHIEF   Chief of Rotuma.
O'HONI AUNT   The Sau chief's aunt, she holds the highest rank in Rotuma.

FISI: FIJI'S WESTERN LAU ISLANDS COMPLEX

SIGA   A war captive, she was abducted, along with her sister, by the Tuʻilifuka.

FISIAN CHIEF   He attempts to rescue Siga and her sister from Tongatapu.

VULA   Son of the Fisian chief, adopted by Pōhiva.

ANCIENT TONGAN NAVIGATORS WHO SOUGHT TO FIND LAND TO THE SOUTH OF TONGATAPU

OVAVA   Set sail from ʻAta and died in the southern waters; his story is told by his parrot.

TULIKAKI   Set sail from ʻEua and died in the southern waters; his story is told by the shark who ate him.

MĀSILAFŌFOA   Set sail from Tongatapu with his entire village and was never heard from again.

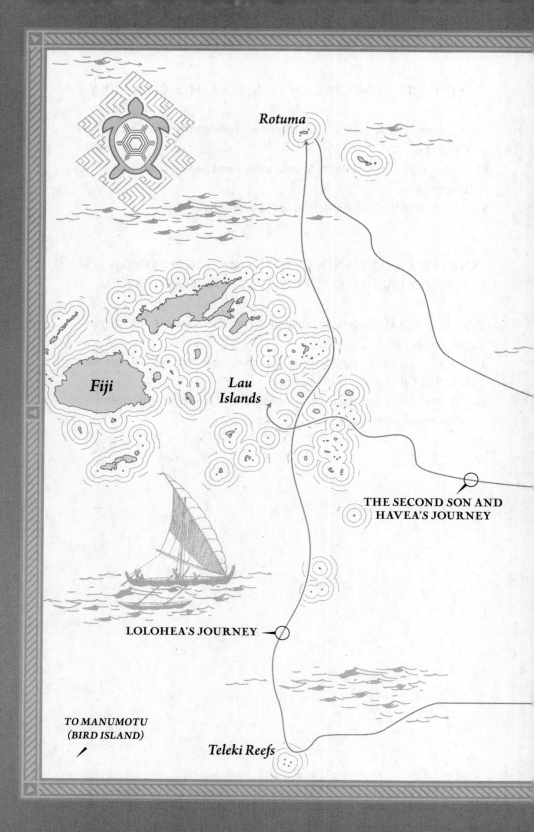

THE TU'ITONGA EMPIRE

THE WAYFINDER

ONE

KŌRERO:
THE PAST IS THE FUTURE

I'd opened my share of graves before finding something of value: a pendant in the shape of a fishhook, carved from greenstone. Greenstone only came from Aotearoa, the land our people had fled before we ended up on this island. The pendant, when held to the sun, glowed soft and green as dawn through miro trees. I was of the third generation born on this island, but the pendant was from our ancestors, from before. My father said a fishhook necklace had a special meaning: it ensured seafarers safe passage over water. To wear the pendant, I braided a cord from the inner bark of a hibiscus branch, which produced a fiber so strong, even parrots couldn't bite through it.

Unpleasant as it was, and offensive to our ancestors, I was ready to open more graves.

Still, I had other duties to perform. I was up each morning before dawn to hunt birds. Pigeons in planting season, tūī birds when the flax blossomed. This time of year, it was parrots. They arrived on our island in closely bonded flocks, and it was these social connections we'd exploit to ensnare them. When our ancestors landed on this island, it was so full of birds, they named it Manumotu, or Bird Island. If only that were still the case. These days, we'd quietly crouch all morning, ready to trigger our snares, in the hopes of catching a bird or two. The worst part was the silence. I'm the talkative type. My mother says I was born speaking, which is why she named me Kōrero. Only after hours of silent birding was I free to open graves with my best friend Hine. The two of us could talk all day.

Hine's duties, unlike mine, were endless. She'd been but a girl when her mother died and she was given to an older, childless woman named Tiri. But after a few years, when Tiri went blind, it was Hine who became the caretaker. Tiri was one of the most amazing persons in the world—I admit I only knew eighty-four people—but Hine, like me, was sixteen years old, and nobody likes it when they *have* to do something. And Hine had to do *everything* for Tiri.

After birding on the morning this story begins, I arrived at our island's cove to continue digging. Many people trapped on this island before us were buried around the cove. This was considered a good resting place because of the view and the breeze and because this was where birds landed after open-water voyages. *Where'd the birds come from?* I always wondered. *Where'd they fly off to?*

I tethered my parrots to a branch. One was named Aroha—it was she who lured the wild parrots into our traps. I'd tug on Aroha's tether, she'd squawk in distress, and wild parrots would come to her aid.

"I ohiti rā," I said to Aroha. "I ohiti pō."

This was a fisherman's adage, shortened to fit a bird's memory. *Alert by day*, the saying went. *Alert by night.* My father was a fisherman.

I knew from old stories that parrots could be made to talk, though I'd had no luck at it.

The other parrot was freshly caught. We'd named her Kanokano—the complications she caused are soon to be described.

With only a digging stick and a basket, I picked a likely spot on the upper beach and began moving sand. If only our ancestors had thought to mark their graves. But I suppose they didn't imagine being exhumed by their great-granddaughters. I ran into a lot of mangrove roots, which I hacked with the jagged edge of a mussel shell. By the time Hine and Tiri arrived, I was sweating.

"What's the ocean like today?" Tiri asked. Her pearled-over gaze was directed at nothing.

Hine rolled her eyes and helped the old woman onto a mat before handing her her weaving.

"It's blue, it's wet," Hine said impatiently. "The waves go up and down."

I described for Tiri how late-morning light penetrated the cove, illuminating the humps of mullet, how the distant reef-break frothed like coconut pulp, how sputtering waves reached up the beach before fingering all the little shells in retreat.

Hine half-heartedly stabbed at some sand with her stick.

I asked, "Did you hear the Toki brothers found an earring in a grave?"

I was arm-deep in the hole, fighting roots.

"The Toki brothers are insufferable," Hine said. She made a gesture to help me, but looking in the hole saw I was already to the point where smelly water was seeping in.

"The earring was greenstone," I said. "From the old world. I bet one of the brothers brings it to you. Will it be the big, handsome, doltish one? Or the big, handsome, inane one?"

"Don't make fun of me," Hine said. "You'll have to marry the one I reject. And have his baby."

The Toki brothers were slow-witted, trusting, and humorless. But their father was charismatic and funny, and the truth was, Hine had a parent-crush on him. It was quite possible that when the marriage ban was lifted, she'd marry a Toki brother just to become the daughter of Papa Toki.

Tiri took a breath. She always did that before beginning a story. While Hine had no patience for the old tales, I could hear them all day. Today was the story of Paikea, who was one of the navigators who discovered Aotearoa. He was from a place called Hawaiki. Tiri didn't start in the obvious places, like Paikea's departure from Hawaiki or his arrival at Aotearoa. She didn't start with Paikea sinking a canoe and drowning his seventy enemies. Nor with him being saved by a whale. Instead, she started that epic tale with a little moment: Paikea, succumbing both to vanity and shame, as he groomed his hair with a forbidden comb.

All the while, Tiri did her weaving—her fingers displaying their own kind of sight.

My hole reached the point where sand fell in as fast as I scooped it out. Hine scrunched her nose. It's probably clear that Hine's heart really wasn't into digging up graves. She could barely bring herself to touch any bones, and when she did, she was afraid they might belong to her mother, even though we knew her mother was buried up the hill, above the kūmara fields. We'd both been there when she was put in the ground. Still, one person's bones can look like another's, which can look like anybody's, which might as well be your mother's. I hoped Hine would change her outlook when she finally found something of value in a grave.

That's when my digging stick made the unmistakable knock of wood striking bone.

Tiri paused her story. I reached into the dark water and felt something in the muck. Hine winced, afraid of what I'd pull out. "I'm sorry, ancestor," I said. Then, with a sucking sound, I tugged out a dog skull. I reached back for its jaw, but the mud offered only bird bones and broken shells.

"Another junk pit," Hine said, and started pushing sand back into the hole.

I contemplated the skull. Since we'd begun digging up the dead, I'd come across many dog remains. Did they happen to die at the same time as our ancestors? Were they slain and buried alongside? Or was it something else altogether? No living person on the island had ever seen a dog, and before we started digging, it was thought that dogs had never even been here.

"What is it?" Tiri asked.

"Another dog skull," Hine said. "Look at those teeth. Who'd want to get close to one of those things, let alone share the afterlife with it?"

"Dogs had white fur, soft as tūī feathers," Tiri said. "The old stories say they'd lick your face."

"They supposedly had long tongues," I said, marveling at the skull.

Hine shook her head. "You don't believe every story you hear, do you?"

Hine knew that I did, indeed, believe every story I heard.

"There's only one thing we know for sure about dogs," Hine said. "They must've tasted good."

What interested me was the size of a dog's eye sockets. Kākā parrots also had large eyes. In fact, the eyes of a parrot were quite intelligent and expressive.

"Ancestors are supposed to be wise," I said. "But they didn't leave us a single dog."

Hine eyed its fangs. "I'm glad they're gone."

"Parrots have sharp beaks," I said. "And they're friendly."

Hine took the skull and threw it.

"One of these days, you'll lose a finger to those birds," she said.

Already, I've forgotten some stuff. That's how bad a storyteller I am. I should've mentioned that I was absolutely forbidden from teaching my parrots human words, that Hine had a father who was alive and walking around our island—we just didn't know his identity. That Papa Toki had lost an arm, with my mother and Tiri being the ones who cut it off.

But it's too late, the story's begun. Aroha looked toward the cove, spread her wings, and began screeching. We turned. Drifting in past the reef was the largest waka canoe imaginable. It had two hulls and rocked silently with the waves. Most canoes in the old stories were waka taua, war canoes. This one seemed empty—not a person or a paddle or a sail was visible. We beheld its pitched bows and soaring mast. Most ominously, the symbol of a death-bringing frigate bird was carved down its side. Then we heard it: upon the spar was a large parrot with a crimson body. It had spread its wings and was screeching back.

"What is it?" Tiri asked. "What's going on?"

"We have visitors," Hine said. She took my hand in hers, and then she screamed.

It seemed to me that, at the sound of Hine's voice, dozens of warriors would sit up in the waka and reveal themselves. I took hold of my fishhook necklace because, like the waka before me, it felt both ancient and startlingly new.

Did I mention that in all our years on the island, we'd never had a visitor?

As Hine's scream echoed off the cliffs, the hum of island life stopped. Silenced were the sounds of flax being beaten on the leeward shore and of our fathers excavating burial sites on the south-facing bluffs.

Our fathers—all the men of Bird Island—would be here in no time.

I should say the waka wasn't a total surprise. We knew something was coming. There'd been signs.

THE STORY OF THE FIRST SIGN

This happened to Tapoto, who was quite fat. Though our island had been rationing food for years, Tapoto only grew bigger. It was rumored that he maintained a secret stash of sweet potatoes.

On Aotearoa, where our ancestors came from, a chief rangatira gave the orders. You had to serve him or die. So on our island, we set things up differently. We made group decisions. Nobody told anybody what to do, and our solution to a single, all-powerful rangatira was to appoint many rangatira. Te Rangatira Ahuwhenua was in charge of farming. My father was the fishing captain. I was apprenticed to the birding captain. My suggestion of appointing a Rangatira Kaikōrero, a storytelling captain, was rejected, however. *You can't eat stories*, people said.

So if Tapoto chose to do no labor, nobody could make him do it. The strange thing was that he still wanted to be treated like a rangatira. He wanted a voice in the longhouse and ink across his forehead. Such moko carried great honor. Unfortunately for Tapoto, my mother was Te Rangatira Moko, and while you could choose to do less work than the rest, she wasn't going to let you have your ink unless you'd earned it.

On the day of this story, even though it was time to harvest kūmara, Tapoto went to the windward side of the island to sleep in the breeze. Waking from his afternoon nap, Tapoto discovered a whale on the beach. It was a grand parāoa whale, whose long jaw and large teeth were treasured.

Tapoto ran to tell the rest of us about the whale. He could be surprisingly nimble for a big man, but he was wholly depleted upon his return. And he wasn't ready for our questions. Was the whale still alive? Did it need help? How had Tapoto slept through such an arrival?

He expected us to race back to the whale, but we were exhausted. The work only got harder: because we'd cut down the trees near the shore, saltwater spray had begun destroying the crops there. To plant farther uphill, more trees had to be cut, volcanic cinders moved, and water carried. The whale would have to wait until morning.

That night, Tiri called us across the sacred space of the marae. We walked through grass toward her unseeing, pearled-over eyes. Inside the wharenui longhouse, we exchanged stories of whales. Such tales were all we had, because no whale had ever beached itself on our shores. Or if one did, the event wasn't recorded in a story, which is the same as it never happening. Tapoto knew the stories as well as the rest of us—about Tinirau's pet whale and the loyal whale Matamata. The legend of the seven whales was told twice. But Tapoto wanted a different kind of story.

"Where's the tale of how to butcher a whale?" he asked. "Where's the story that tells us what tools to take to the beach tomorrow? If a tale doesn't offer ways to preserve the meat, what good is it?"

The next morning, we all went to see the whale. There was nothing but sand. Tapoto stared at the surf in disbelief. Baffled, he waded into the water. His whale was gone. He looked at us like it was our fault.

"The whale has delivered a message to us," Tapoto said. "The arrival of a parāoa is a big event. Yet we didn't see it coming, and we didn't act quickly enough because we didn't know what to do. That's what the whale came to tell us—that we aren't prepared for things to come."

My father has a gentle soul. But he wasn't one to avoid the truth of things. Under his breath, he said, "Maybe the whale just wanted a nap."

Papa Toki joined in. "Or perhaps the whale was after sweet potatoes."

People laughed. Tapoto announced, "The whale revealed its message to *me*. I must prepare most of all."

I stood in the waves where the parāoa had been. I've been swimming and felt the loud clicks, like slaps to the back, from this whale. I've seen its plume shoot high. I'd hoped to put my forehead to its forehead and share the breath of life, perhaps its last breath.

Later, I went to Tiri and suggested this episode might make a good story.

"There's no story," she said. "The event could be reduced to a single line: One day, a whale came to the people of Bird Island. *Be ready*, it warned."

"How could you not mention it was a parāoa whale?" I asked. "Or leave out Tapoto?"

"Stories must be short as possible," she said. "That's the only rule."

It's true that my stories failed this test. I cared about every little thing. The whole reason my whale story would be long is that we didn't get to see it. We didn't run our fingers along its inky tongue or look into its lacquered eyes. We were robbed of palming its squid-sucker scars and of seeing black beaks spill from its opened belly. And what would you have me leave out of the story to come? The sound of my father using sand to remove dried blood from a greenstone war club? A boy taking the star called Rehua and placing it in my hand? The moment I land on an unfamiliar shore to kill a woman I'd never met?

The night the whale disappeared, I couldn't sleep. Before bed, all the problems of the island tended to weigh on me—the failing crops, our empty nets, the dumb, stubborn trees. The marriage ban had been in effect several years now. I was too young for a husband, I didn't even want a husband, but I didn't like being told I *couldn't* have one. Plus, our whare was infested with red flies. Even though it was chilly, my parents pulled our mats outside, where wind coming up the beach kept us from being bitten. My mother's hands were black from making her ink. My father's hands were raw from working wet rope. I brought Aroha, who ducked her head into my armpit like I was a big warm wing. We lay there, looking up.

"Can't we just return to Aotearoa?" I asked the night sky.

My parents were silent. There were endless reasons we couldn't go home. We didn't have a canoe, we didn't know how to navigate, we didn't even know where Aotearoa was. Plus, there were the reasons we'd left in the first place. My father hated everything about Aotearoa, which he considered a land of slavery and suffering. He believed our survival depended on peace, cooperation, and labor, and it was to distance himself from the warrior culture of Aotearoa that he alone refused to get his moko.

I asked my father, "Do you really think the whale had a message for us?"

He was Hī Ika Rangatira, the fishing captain. From his outriggers, he'd been close to whales many times. He lifted his hand to the stars. "See the ocean of black? And the islands of light? So it is where we live. The sea continues forever, as do the islands. The whale can visit them, while we cannot. We don't even know the direction of the nearest island. But the whale—he knows everything."

THE STORY OF THE SECOND SIGN

Hā Mutu came to get me before dawn. In the dark, with his weathered face and heavy ink, his usual sad expression couldn't be seen. Hā Mutu means

"Last Breath" and describes the final phase of the moon. He's the oldest man on the island, the only person left who saw the Great Wave, and he's Te Rangatira Manu, the birding captain.

In the spring, when Hā Mutu wakes me early to hunt kūkū pigeons, I reach for my long spear. In summer, when it's time to take tūī birds, I bring wooden bowls to place in the miro trees. The miro berries make the tūī birds thirsty—when they fly to a bowl for a drink, they do not see our snares in the water. But this was the time to catch the kākā parrots, so I fetched Aroha.

As we walked, Aroha said my name, "Kō-re-ro."

Hā Mutu responded with a look of concern.

"The bird must've heard people using my name," I told Hā Mutu.

Uphill, where the trees thickened, Hā Mutu prayed to our atua, our ancestors' spirits. He prayed that we'd catch all the birds in the forest and also that the forest would somehow replenish its stock of birds. He asked that the birds be fat, slow, and willing. He prayed I'd follow in his footsteps as the birding captain. I couldn't tell him that, though our people were hungrier than ever, I hoped the position died with him, that the taking of birds came to an end.

Rising, Hā Mutu painted mud on my cheeks and forehead to conceal my human face. His face was decorated with spirals, inked from needles made from the leg bones of herons, of which none remained. His sad eyes looked into mine. What he lamented was my coming of age in a lessened world. He lamented the marriage ban, that I might have no children because of this. But this was his concern. I wanted no husband. I wanted only to solve our eternal question: Were we blessed or cursed to be stranded on this island?

Still, I understood his deeper regret: that the times ahead wouldn't be as bountiful as they'd been for him. He saw this as a personal failure, and he was always teaching me about survival. He knew we'd need all the old wisdom, plus some new, if we were going to make it.

The first parrots were squawking when we crested the ridge. Stars were still overhead, but also a faint blue light. Here were the last big trees on the island, including one we called Kaurinui, the only tree left big enough to carve into a waka canoe. It was too large to fell with axes made of shells, and without stone adzes to hollow it out, it would be too heavy to drag to the shore. So it'd been safe all these years. There'd been other large kauri trees, but our ancestors cut them down. We never figured out how they managed to do it, and of course the structures they'd made from those trees were washed away by the Great Wave.

At a pua tree, I placed Aroha on a branch, then draped a snare loop beside her. "No human words," I whispered to her. "I don't want you to get eaten."

Around Aroha's leg was a ring called a pōria. The old stories say you're supposed to make them from the ribs of your enemy. On Aotearoa, they were often carved from rare greenstone. I made mine from turtle shell. Attached to the pōria was a long cord woven from hibiscus bark. When I pulled this, Aroha would screech. Out of concern, a wild parrot would fly in to investigate—that's when it'd become ensnared. But a wild bird wouldn't come if Aroha called human words.

Concealing ourselves in ferns, I pulled once, and Aroha made a perfect, alarmed shriek.

Right away, another kākā bird swooped in, but the snare missed its target. We reset and waited.

Hā Mutu says a bird captain needs to be observant, patient, and quiet. *You're very observant*, he was always telling me, trying to be positive. But it was true. I was neither patient nor quiet. I was also prone to nervousness, about my father being on the ocean every day, about my mother's conflict with men over their ink. I also obsessed over the cycle we were in: Because of poor harvests, more cropland was needed. For this, more trees had to be cut down, and with fewer trees, fewer fishing canoes could be built. With fewer fish to eat, we had to turn to birds, and they were disappearing. Hā Mutu had seen the loss of the koera, the whioi, the heron, the cliff owl, and even the little pihipihi. The only life we'd brought to the island were the kiore rats, and they'd attacked the eggs of the tern and albatross. Were we any better than the death-bringing frigate bird, who lived by stealing from the mouths of other birds?

I pulled the string—*screech*. A new bird arrived, and this one was easily snared.

Hā Mutu went to retrieve the bird. But instead of snapping its neck, he paused. I was worried he'd snap Aroha's neck and adopt this new non-talkative one, so I rushed to him. Here, we discovered the second sign: on the wild bird's foot there was already a pōria ring, with the remnants of a cord. And the ring was carved from greenstone, which only came from one place.

"It must've flown here from Aotearoa," I said.

Hā Mutu turned the bird, examining all aspects of it.

"No," he said. "My grandfather told me parrots from Aotearoa had gray in their feathers."

"But the greenstone, it only comes from home."

"You're right about that," he said.

Then the bird spoke. *Wa-ka*, it seemed to say.

I said, "It knows human words."

"There's a term we've nearly forgotten," Hā Mutu said. "*Kanokano*. That's when someone's been living with distant relatives."

"Kanokano," I repeated.

That night in the lodge house, we lit candlenut lamps and sat in a circle, observing the new parrot. Kanokano preened her feathers. Kanokano used her beak to climb a pole. Kanokano pinwheeled her eyes. At last, she spoke. The words were human but not entirely clear.

Tapoto heard the bird say *waka taua*. War canoe.

Papa Toki heard the bird speak the words *waka hoa*. Canoe paddle.

My father heard *toki roa*, a long adze. But he often had salt water in his ears.

Talk of an adze got people excited. While our island came with many gifts, there were no stones at all on Manumotu, nothing but volcanic cinders. The old stories speak of the usefulness of chert and flint and basalt and obsidian, none of which we had. The old stories made it sound like Aotearoa was covered with stones that were just lying around, waiting for anybody to pick them up and fashion them into prized tools. We only had pumice. Pumice and shells. Without stones, we couldn't make a single adze or ax, which my father says is the only reason we had any trees left at all. But without them, we couldn't fell a tree big enough to make a waka that could take us to a new island, one with fresh resources, a place where we could start over and try to get it right this time. An adze could change all that.

Tapoto addressed us. "What do we know?" he asked. "We know there's another island, not farther than this bird can fly. On this island are people who have a waka. In fact, they speak of canoes often enough that this bird has learned the word. To make such a waka, you need big trees and sharp tools. So these people have more resources than us. Do we agree?" The people were silent, which gave Tapoto permission to continue. "If we have discovered *them*, they can certainly find us. And as we stay up late discussing them, who's to say they are not also gathered, at this very moment, to solve the problem of us?"

"Please," my father said. "You're basing this on a bird. We don't know anything about this island. I've sailed in all directions, far enough that our island was only a speck on the horizon, and I've seen no other land."

"The fishing captain's right," Tapoto said. "We don't know anything about them. Except that they can come to our island anytime they like. We, however, have only fishing canoes. First, we need a defensive plan. Then we must construct our own war canoe. Finally, it's time for a Rangatira Taua."

"We've made it four generations without a war captain," my father said.

"If they attacked tonight," Tapoto responded, "what would you do?"

My father went silent.

"What would any of us do?" Tapoto asked. "That's how our ancestors raided, at night in blackened canoes, nothing visible but the emerald flash of their greenstone clubs."

My mother spoke up. "I suppose you volunteer to become Te Rangatira Taua?"

"If anyone else wants the job," Tapoto said, "I'll step aside."

Tapoto surveyed the room. Silence. Then, very clearly, Kanokano brought up the topic of dogs. *Kuri*, she said.

We stared at the bird and imagined war canoes, greenstone clubs, and sharp-toothed dogs, which were rumored to leap high and lock their jaws on your throat. This's how our island appointed its first war captain and gave the job to Tapoto.

The next day, while my father was on the water, Tapoto came to my mother. He stood at the entrance of our whare, eyebrows raised in an expectant way. My mother knew what Tapoto wanted. All the old stories were clear: rangatira had powerful moko.

"So you've come for your ink?" she asked.

He was a round shadow against the bright light behind him. "It's my right."

My mother had sacrificed much for our island. She volunteered to have just one child to help control our population. She'd constructed our whare from driftwood—which was why it was infested with red flies—to save trees. She learned to make inking chisels from turtle shell, in order to preserve the herons, though by then it was too late.

"Such moko speaks to people," she said. "It tells them of the challenges you've faced and the burdens you're prepared to carry."

"I know what you think of me," he said. "I've changed."

"Please tell me where you were when the new fields were cleared. And how you contributed to building the storehouse. How is it you missed the harvest and fishing duties on the full moon?"

"The whale spoke to me. Do you challenge the wisdom of the paräoa?"

My mother didn't shrink from Tapoto. "E hiki Tangaroa," she said to him.

This is the first line of a song meant to remind people that moko is on loan from the god Tangaroa, that his standards must be met.

Tapoto produced a greenstone pendant depicting a curling fern shoot. "I've brought a gift."

In the old stories, moko gifts were often family treasures—rare huia feathers or whale teeth. My mother was unmoved. "You dug that out of a grave. It means nothing to you. A true gift must be personal."

Tapoto said nothing, but I didn't like the look on his face. There are many stages to a man's moko, each swirl and ray communicating aspects of his achievement and identity. We all knew my mother should've given Tapoto his first lines long ago. Every adult male deserves this.

I spent the afternoon listening to Tiri tell stories about Aotearoa. I heard of epic mountains and crashing rivers and water so cold it stopped flowing.

What was this amazing land we'd come from? Could you feel homesick for a place where you'd never been?

The sea was good to us that night: my father's men caught several fish, so we sat in communal circles, crunching on crispy skin and savoring white, flaky meat. The firelight was on our faces. Our bellies went quiet. After three days of root broth, I left the fish grease on my fingers.

I said to my father, "Did you know that on Aotearoa there were birds bigger than people?"

Each family also got to share a sweet potato, bearded with ash from the earth oven.

"On Aotearoa," I said, "hot water bubbled up from below. And chunks of greenstone were just lying around on the ground."

"Aotearoa," my father said, unimpressed.

"If I lived there," I said, "I'd use those stones to build a lagoon of steaming water."

My mother gave Tiri a disapproving look, which the old woman couldn't see.

Still, people were listening to me. I gestured large. "I'd take baths whenever I liked. The greenstones would glow from the heat of the earth. And above, the sky would flash with the wings of countless parrots."

My father tossed his fish bones into the fire. "There are a thousand stories you don't know about Aotearoa," he said. "And that's because nobody has the stomach to tell them."

That night, I reclined on the beach with a parrot in each armpit. I stared at the stars, intermittent through clouds. Was there really another island nearby? I wondered. And on this island, was there a girl like me who was looking at the same sky, wondering where her bird had gone? Were there truly as many islands as stars? It seemed impossible, that notion. I'd only ever known this island, the one I thought of as mine, surrounded by blue, as far as you could see.

A third sign was to come. It's a simple story, but to understand it, you need to know something about us and where we came from.

THE STORY OF *THE RED CLOAK*

In the beginning, Ranginui and Papatūānuku—the sky and earth—existed in an endless embrace. When Rangi and Papa were separated by their children, humans entered the world. They settled countless islands, with Hawaiki at the center. When the islands became crowded, people wondered if there wasn't more land. Using double-hull canoes, people voyaged far to the east. They found Rapa Nui. In the north, they found islands they named Hawai'i, in honor of Hawaiki. Then Kupe sailed south on his waka named *Matahourua*. This was the most difficult journey of all. Here, he found Aotearoa, Land of the Long White Cloud. He returned with word of this place, and soon many waka followed: *Aotea, Te Arawa, Kurahaupō, Mātaatua, Tainui, Tākitimu, Tokomaru,* and so on. The peoples of each canoe founded new iwi tribes, and over several generations, these populations grew. Before long there were dozens of iwi tribes on Aotearoa. Plenitude turned to scarcity and struggle.

One year, a volcano erupted. The people who lived nearby had to flee. They'd been prosperous, owned many slaves, and were powerful in battle, yet there was no undefended land in Aotearoa. Everywhere they went, war was made upon them. Soon these people were forced to live in their canoes. They lit their fires in open hulls. In open hulls, they slept. They blackened their waka, so they could raid at night. They survived, but what honor was found in such a life? Other groups had escaped their hardships in Aotearoa by sailing to islands like Rēkohu and Rangitahua. So work began on two great canoes that would deliver them—hopefully—to a similar island.

The first double-hulled waka was called *Te Kahukura, The Red Cloak*. This canoe carried the nobles, chiefs, and warriors. From various skirmishes, these nobles had acquired many slaves from different iwi tribes. Before departure, the nobles killed most of their slaves, leaving only one from each tribe, so no group might offer resistance on the voyage. These slaves followed in a waka called *Mā Atarau, By Moonlight*, which also contained the dogs and food stock and field tools. It was a far cry from *Te Kahukura*, in which the chiefs and their royal wives wore capes of kiwi down and cloaks of fabulous feathers. Their war captains wielded greenstone clubs called mere, which, when thrust properly against the forehead, with a forceful twist of the wrist, would pop off the top of the skull, exposing the wet brain. It was with these greenstone mere that the war captains had winnowed their slaves for the journey.

During the voyage, a storm arose. The slaves cowered low in the hulls of *Mā Atarau*, while the noble warriors in *Te Kahukura* defiantly lifted their green clubs to the sky and performed, in the height of the torrent, a terrifying chant. In the dark, despite the tremendous waves, they could be heard slapping their chests, calling:

Kua mate mai i mua.	*There was death in the past.*
Kua mate mai i mua.	*There was death in the past.*
Ehara i te taru te i ora.	*Life is no light matter.*

In the morning, when the seas were calm and the storm was gone, so, too, was *The Red Cloak*. The royals and the war captains and their terrifying weapons were never seen again. We are descendants of the other ship, the slaves in the *Mā Atarau*.

THE STORY OF THE THIRD SIGN

This happened to my mother, who was at the beach, sooting candlenuts for her ink. The beach was where social labor took place—nets were mended, flax was stripped, rope was twisted. Here, Tapoto's men had begun drilling their defenses, a process that revealed how defenseless we were.

"First we become warriors on the outside," Tapoto told his men. "Then we'll become warriors on the inside." He'd taught them a routine of synchronized air-strikes, which they practiced over and over. They also wielded sticks meant to be spears, because when they'd practiced with real spears, an injury occurred.

It's true, though, that no person's born a hero. We start, like Ranginui and Papatūānuku, in darkness.

A broad-backed turtle was spotted in the surf. A tender, fat-laden, flavorful turtle. We once consumed turtles with abandon, steaming their eggs in seaweed. When they became scarce, we showed enough wisdom to make them tapu. But now—could we let any meal escape?

The turtle made its way up the sandy incline and into the mangroves, plodding along until it was stopped by a fan of roots. Then it began excavating a hole with its back flippers. My mother watched the turtle at her labors. Such work, it seemed. Such effort to survive. As the turtle dug deeper, it closed its eyes, as if ancient memory were required.

"What luck," Tapoto called out. He snapped a mussel shell to produce a jagged blade and made his way to the turtle, which had begun to drop her wet white eggs.

My mother intercepted him. "No, you don't," she said. "Turtles have been declared sacred. The taking of them is forbidden."

"Those rules were from before," Tapoto said. "They were made before we were starving."

"Are we starving?" I asked.

I was at the beach, too, weaving new leashes for my parrots.

"Of course not," my mother told me. To Tapoto she said, "But we will starve if we're stupid enough to kill the last turtles."

"And what of our enemies?" Tapoto asked. "Do you want an empty stomach when they arrive? Do you think they'd let a turtle go?"

My mother didn't have an answer for that. But when Tapoto crouched to use his blade, my mother crouched, too. "On this island, we make group decisions. To suspend tapu, we must all agree."

"I'm the war captain," Tapoto said. "My men need strength to defend this island." He looked ready to deliver a lecture on his new authority. Instead, he noticed something in the sand. Upon examination, he discovered it was a human finger bone.

My mother studied the bone. Then she got low and looked beneath the turtle. There, in the dark hole, she saw more bones and a flash of green. The turtle had begun its primordial work and couldn't be stopped. Mother lowered her head and reached under the turtle, the sand now slick with the ichor of incipient birth. Finally, she grasped the green object and brought it into the light. It was a greenstone adze blade, sharp as the day it was fashioned on Aotearoa.

"Men," Tapoto called, and ordered them to start digging.

Where, for what? they asked.

"Just dig," Tapoto commanded.

Soon we'd all be digging.

My mother took the adze to the shoreline and washed it in the frothy water.

Tapoto joined her, the two of them exchanging no words. Standing in the surf, they passed the blade back and forth, feeling its weight and design, noting how a wooden handle would slot into the blade's head. They took turns holding it emerald against the sun and basking in the glow of its mana. The axes, the blades, the drills, the chisels—all these irreplaceable greenstone tools had been in the graves this whole time. The old people, to make their afterlives more magisterial, had taken everything with them. The third sign couldn't be clearer: the key to our future would come from the past.

For me, the happiness was short-lived. That night, we pulled our sleeping mats to the beach and reclined under a cloudy sky, made eerie by the rough glow of the moon. My parrots didn't like being bound by their new leashes. They fought, they flashed their wings, they hooked their beaks.

"Are we starving?" I asked my parents.

"Of course not," my mother said. "That's a ridiculous notion."

"I'd like to punch Tapoto in the nose," my father said. "He shouldn't say such stupid things."

It went quiet again.

I asked, "Were our people really once slaves?"

My mother was on one side of me, my father on the other. I could tell they exchanged a look.

My mother said, "Those stories are from long ago."

"We aren't our ancestors," my father said. "We're free to make our own destinies."

I thought on that. "Does it still exist, slavery?" I asked. "Those people who are coming to our island, do you think they practice it? It seems impossible that one person would want to benefit from another's suffering."

"No one's coming to our island," my mother said.

I looked at her. "Tapoto's training for their arrival."

"That's just in case," she said.

"Never hurts to be prepared," my father added.

* * *

When we saw the strange waka in our cove, Hine screamed, and in the silence that followed, shimmers of baitfish breached the water, trees turned in the wind, and our cove rippled with tāniko patterns. Life is animated by unseen energies. Like the hidden hands that shape the clouds or the cold spark that ignites the moon. Have you ever felt the buzz of horizon lightning when swimming offshore? That's how the fishhook pendant felt around my neck. It was thrumming with past owners. Or maybe future ones, as the world to come sometimes reveals itself to the world that is.

From the mangroves came a rustling of undergrowth and a slashing of leaves. I turned to see Tapoto emerge, his huge body gasping for air—big as he was, he'd outrun fitter men, who appeared behind him, fists clenched around their training spears. The sight of the great double-hulled waka stopped them.

"So the day has come," Tapoto said.

He ordered a man to climb our island's volcanic peak to look for more sails. He sent others to nearby shores, so we wouldn't be flanked by multiple landing parties. Then he advanced, joining me. "Why don't they show themselves?" he wondered.

"We were digging," I reported. "We looked up, and there it was."

He sent a man for rope, then reassured Hine. "You did good to call out."

"Kōrero's the one who screamed," Hine said.

I'm not a screamer. I didn't scream. Or did I?

Instead of correcting her, I said, "I saw the waka move. There's someone in it."

Others began to arrive—the Kohimu brothers, Mama Mānunu, the Toki family, my mother. When my father arrived, he stood in awe of the great waka before us.

"Didn't I tell you?" Tapoto asked him. "Did I not predict this?"

"It's sitting high in the water," my father said. "It carries little cargo."

Soon we were all at the cove, with Hā Mutu being the last to arrive. He was the only one alive who'd seen such a waka, back when he was a boy. Tiri asked him if he recognized what he saw, but he stood silent, such were the bad memories that returned to him.

The rope arrived. "Be ready," Tapoto told his men before wading into the water.

Tiri called to the waka. She was keeper of the marae, and so performed our karanga and pōwhiri. In a high, welcoming voice, she sang, "Nau mai, haere mai."

Other women echoed her: "Nau mai, haere mai."

"I saw the waka move," I announced.

I don't know why I said this, my mouth just did it. Mother came and wrapped an arm around me.

When Tapoto reached the waka, he tried to peer over the washboards, but he was too heavy to hoist himself from the water. Instead, he threw the rope over the prow, and we began hauling it in. It took many hands to turn the waka toward us and set it in motion. While a scream had failed to rouse anyone inside, the striking of land immediately did. Sun-darkened and disoriented, a young man rose to stand on the deck. He seemed to see us and not quite see us.

"Hea koe i?" we asked him, but he didn't tell us where he was from.

He stared at us, blinking in the bright light.

"He aha tou ingoa?" we asked, but he didn't say his name.

He took a step forward, to balance himself. Tapoto's men gripped their sticks.

The young man was broad-shouldered and strong, perhaps my age. He wore only a loincloth and was inked about the waist and down one leg but not the other. Hine's eyes went wide at the sight of him.

My father asked the name of his canoe: "He aha te ingoa o to koutou waka?"

No response. My father neared and carefully placed his hand on the hull.

"Waka," he said, thumping the wood. "Waka."

"He needs water," someone said.

A gourd was handed to the young man. When he leaned his head back to drink, I could clearly see that inked on his neck was a black jellyfish, about the size of a hand.

I asked my mother, "You think he wants Kanokano back?"

She squeezed my shoulder to say, *I don't think so.*

He took a long look at us, at our number, at our spears. Then he bent down and reached for something in the hull. Tapoto's men tensed. The young man rose with a fishnet sack that contained what looked like a skeleton. Here and there, human ribs poked through the mesh.

He made his way to the bow. When he was standing above us, I could see the heavy ink covering one leg, the pattern disappearing into his loincloth. He slung the sack of bones over his shoulder. From here, I could smell them and hear flies about them. Cartilage hung from the joints, and peels of sinew, pink and brown, curled from a shoulder blade. His eyes came to rest upon me. My mother inhaled.

He leaped from the waka and made his way to me. He indicated my fishhook pendant. "A local navigator," he said. "We'll need to borrow you."

A shiver crossed my skin, like wind after water. Tiri would later tell me there was a word for such a man, a word that'd fallen from our speech for lack of use. He was an uakoao—a stranger. No stranger had ever looked at me before. I'd never been seen in this way.

"We?" Tapoto asked.

"Hold on, now," my father said. "Who are you? What're you doing here?"

"I'm Finau," he said. "What kind of island is this, where guests are met without refreshments?"

From the waka's spar, the crimson parrot spoke. Spreading its wings, it said, "Naʻe kei tahitahi e ika."

I recognized the word *ika*, "fish," but that was all. We looked to this stranger for a translation.

"These words are from a very old poem," Finau said. "They mean, *The fish is still wet with the sea.*"

Were *we* the fish? Were *they*? "Your parrot can recite poetry?" I asked.

"Kōkī isn't mine," Finau said. "He belongs to himself. But yes, Kōkī knows the old poetry of Tonga."

"*Tonga*," Tapoto repeated. This was the word we used to indicate "south."

"Don't let that word frighten you," Finau said. "We're not the Tongans you've heard about. My brother and I have nothing to do with invasions or depopulations or war."

We didn't know what to say to that.

My father indicated the sack of bones. "Have you lost someone?"

"Her fate," Finau said, "is only temporary."

The parrot named Kōkī swiveled his head and bent low, examining our island. He declared, "Toki 'alu fakamuimui e kotoa 'oku lanumata."

Finau agreed with him, saying, "Yes, this island looks green—too green."

Green? Did he mean "unripe, inexperienced"? Before I could clarify, Kōkī spotted Kanokano and flew at her, attacking her where she was tethered. Screeching, wings aflash, the two parrots battled. Kōkī grabbed Kanokano's neck with his large beak and began attempting, forcibly, to mate with her. The horrifying call she made! Risking my fingers, I ran to Kanokano and loosened her tether, allowing her to fly into the mangroves. Kōkī's wings flashed red in pursuit.

"You should leash that terrible parrot," I snapped.

Finau said, "Kōkī's as free as you and me."

I tried to see where the birds went, but I could only hear Kanokano's distant screeching. I gave Aroha many reassurances. When I looked back at the waka, another figure had roused himself. He looked a little older than Finau, though just as sea-beaten. "There's a woman here wearing a fishhook necklace," Finau told him.

While our languages were different, I could make out most words. Where we said *wāhine* for "woman," they said *fefine*. *Matau* was our word for "fishhook." *Māta'u* was theirs.

This had to be the brother. He took up his own sack of bones. Carrying these, he slipped over the side and waded toward me with a look of wary recognition, like he'd seen me before. Then we were standing face-to-face, each of us wearing a fishhook necklace, his cut from whalebone.

"He haerenga haumaru rā runga i ngā wai," I said. *Safe passage over water.*

"He haerenga haumaru rā runga i ngā wai," he repeated.

I asked, "What do we call you?"

"If I tell you our family name," he said, "you'll think less of us. I'm just a wayfinder, hoping to reach a far-off destination." This "wayfinder" then asked, "What island is this?"

"Bird Island," I said.

Uncertainty crossed the Wayfinder's face. "What island group is it in?"

My father moved to speak. I knew he'd say, *We were hoping you'd tell us.*

"Hospitality first," my mother said to our guests. "You're in need of food and water."

Finau said, "We could use some chicken or pork."

We'd heard of chickens and pigs. The old stories were filled with references to them.

My mother asked the Wayfinder what his destination was.

"She'll get us where we need to go," the Wayfinder said, looking at me.

"She's not going anywhere with you," my mother said. "We don't even know you."

Finau said, "*Kakano kehe, hui tatau.*"

I understood this line of poetry to mean, *Different flesh, same bones.* Finau was saying that, while we were from different populations, we were still peoples of the ocean.

"Speaking of bones," my mother said, "just whose remains are those?"

The Wayfinder regarded the skeleton. It was clear that, where we saw bones, he saw a person. "These are our passengers," he said. "Their lives are in our hands."

I glanced at my mother and father—they wore grave, uncertain looks.

"We're on a mission to deliver life," Finau said.

"You're delivering life?" I asked.

"What kind of island is this?" Finau asked. "Where it's impossible to get some chicken and a few dancing girls?"

"Ignore Finau," the Wayfinder said. "If you have a little brother, then you know how they can be."

"For us," I said, "children have been made tapu."

The words came out wrong. What I meant to say was, the birth of *new* children had been forbidden. Of course we had children, just none younger than me and Hine. I guess what I should've said was that *marriages* were what had been banned, and *by extension* the making of children. And only temporarily banned, that's what I really meant. It was just a temporary measure, until the crops stabilized and food was plentiful again and our people got back on our feet.

A strange look crossed the Wayfinder's face. He leaned a little bit, and then he leaned a little farther. "It's just the solid ground," he said. "We've been long at sea." When I put a hand on his shoulder to steady him, he smiled. "There hasn't been a female wayfinder since Pāintapu," he said. "And she lived so long ago, her story's probably expired."

"Stories never expire," I told him.

His eyes blurred a little. "Time is short," he said. "And these waters are unfamiliar."

I didn't know anything about Tonga or navigation or poetry. But I knew my stories. I recited a line from a tale about Tangaroa: "All waters are unfamiliar," I said, "until you make their acquaintance."

Beneath his long and untamed hair, beneath a torso salted white, was a young man who'd seen the world. "Spoken like a true navigator," he said, and began stumbling toward some shade. Others took his arms to escort him to a place where he and his brother could restore themselves.

TWO

THE BEFORE OF THE MOON

THE PREVIOUS SEASON, IN TONGA...

The king of Tonga, the Tuʻitonga, lived on the main island of Tongatapu, far in the south. From here, the Tuʻitonga presided over the hundred and sixty islands of Tonga.

Each year, the Tuʻitonga sent his matāpule to the rural islands to hold dance contests among notable young women, for there is no greater measure of feminine sublimity than the sacred tauʻolunga, a dance that requires strength, poise, and a subtle, beckoning grace. Winning contestants traveled to Tongatapu to join the royal entourage as Fefine Girls, where they were exposed to the finest protocols of Tongan life.

Māhina-eʻa, or Moon Appearing, lived on the island of Hunga, in Tonga's northern Vavaʻu chain. Hunga had a magnificent, porpoise-filled bay, and when the sun set, it did so over the volcanic island of Late to the west, whose smoking emissions purpled the sky. Moon Appearing's father was the tuʻi chief of Hunga, and as the Tuʻihunga, he ordered special lodging built for the visiting matāpule, so he wouldn't have to sleep next to the grubby-footed children of one of the island's big families.

The light was fading when the king's matāpule made landfall on Hunga's shore. He refused refreshments and ignored introductions to the heads of Hunga's families. The Tuʻihunga welcomed the visiting matāpule by describing the marvelous itinerary ahead. "Tonight we feast," the Tuʻihunga said. "Come morning, we'll tour the island. Wait till you see our refurbished sweet potato storehouses! And tomorrow evening, the dancing begins."

The matāpule walked to a flat section of beach. "The dancing takes place here, now."

"In the sand? It's almost dark," the Tuʻihunga said. "Come to our village. A feast has been prepared. The parrot meat comes all the way from Haʻamoa. And eels have been procured from Fisi. This was no easy feat. We're at war with Fisi."

For the first time, the royal matāpule seemed to notice Hunga's tuʻi chief. "Thanks for the reminder we're at war," the matāpule said. "Do you think this fact has slipped the minds of your leaders on Tongatapu?" Before the Tuʻihunga could smooth over this perceived insult, the matāpule commanded: "Build up a fire. Use coconut husks so the flame is bold."

The island's notable families could afford their own matāpule. One matāpule said, "Tradition dictates certain protocols." Another added, "There's no precedent for breaking the custom of a welcome ceremony."

The royal matāpule said, "When the constellation ʻAlo Ua rises, I make my return to Tongatapu."

People looked nervously to the sky, for the constellation Toloa was already visible.

Moon Appearing studied the king's matāpule. The matāpule on Hunga were men who called attention to every rule, protocol, and precedent. They made pronouncements, oversaw transactions, and doled punishments. They inserted themselves into every dealing, measuring portions, bickering over finer points, bending the meanings of words, and, in her opinion, prolonging as many disputes as they resolved. But here, Moon Appearing now understood, was the first true matāpule she'd ever seen. *Mata* of course means "face" or "eyes" and *pule* is the term for "authority." The man before her was the face of the king. He was the Tuʻitonga's eyes. Acting in the Tuʻitonga's interests, he could alter the destiny of any person. He could take life. Worse, he could take your afterlife. And, famously, he could even take your death.

Prominent fathers struck humble tones, for they'd expended great costs to prepare their daughters for the contest, importing sandalwood oil and turmeric powder to dust their daughters' forearms red. Several fathers had paid steep prices to import from Fisi the feathers of birds that had gone extinct in Tonga.

"Why not relax in our village?" one father asked. "Our kava is strong."

"Yes," another said. "That way our girls can beautify themselves for your consideration."

The royal matāpule pointed at Moon Appearing. "She will dance first."

The command startled her, as she rarely interacted with kehe, with strangers.

She glanced at her mother and father, who nodded.

Lacking firelight or song or even a drop of oil to glisten her shoulders, Moon Appearing brought her legs together and arched her back in a regal manner. Offering an all-encompassing smile, she began to dance. Unfortunately, she had little talent as a dancer. Her legs were strong, her hands shapely. But she lacked something the other girls had: a fluidity that conveyed the transitory elegance of a petal upon the current. At some point, one of her moves would land like the thump of a coconut in the woods. It was inevitable. She wasn't unlovely. She wasn't graceless. Until she started dancing.

Still, she clapped her hands to create a space of originality, where the world and its lineage could be brought into being, for the tauʻolunga was a storytelling dance, and the story it told was the history and nobility of the Tongan people. Foundational events were converted into arm movements, hand gestures, and the rocking proximity of the hips to the earth. She was actually doing pretty well—hands up, palms out, legs together, turn. She'd yet to mess up at all. Still, the royal matāpule said, "Feʻunga." *Enough.* He indicated the next girl.

He cycled through these girls just as quickly, allowing none to complete her movements. Then, in the diminishing light, it was her friend Laʻā's turn. Here's the truth about Laʻā: she was the better dancer, not just of the girls on Hunga, but in all of Tonga's northern islands. When it began, Laʻā's dance wasn't a series of movements but rather a confirmation that the earthly and the ethereal coexisted, for Laʻā could make realms beyond ours immediately accessible. All who beheld her motion thrummed to its dictates, nodding, lowering their eyelids, feeling the dance as much as beholding it. Laʻā's name, said various ways, could mean Sunrise, Sunbeam, Sunshine, Sunniness, and Sunset. When in motion, she was all of them, so it didn't matter that the fading light danced her into darkness, for the lamp of her dance cast its own beam.

Moon Appearing realized she'd lose her friend to Tongatapu, a place the war had yet to reach, where elites attended feasts and luxuriated in bathing ponds. The best of Hunga was already found in Tongatapu, for this was where Hunga was forced to send its finest tapa cloth, candlenut oil, and endangered birds, like Hunga's last known heron. There, La'ā would enjoy the company of Tonga's finest young women, learning the latest songs, exchanging the freshest gossip, and waiting upon Tongatapu's eligible young men.

Several mothers sparked palm spathe. As the flames took hold, the conclusion of La'ā's dance became visible. After having danced herself into a dark finality, it now seemed that with the first flicker upon her skin she'd always been dancing, unseen, in eternal darkness, and the light of human enterprise was only now revealing a grace preexisting. Moon Appearing became afraid for what awaited so pure a girl in Tongatapu, for it was said there was another side to the main island: men there took supplemental wives and exacted punishments upon rivals unheard-of elsewhere, punishments that would destabilize small islands like Hunga. And everyone knew about the king's younger brother 'Aho, who was famous for a deed he performed upon the living and the dead. He was known to leave his unsavory impression upon others, in the form of a black jellyfish. This he did in secret and in public, in broad daylight and the black of night, upon women and men alike.

When La'ā's hands came to a clasping rest, the royal matāpule continued to gaze upon her. Finally, he closed his eyes, as if this could halt the thrall of her.

A mother came running from the village, where she'd fetched coconut oil—this she began rubbing on the shoulders of her daughter.

"Don't bother," the royal matāpule said. "The contest is over."

"Over?" a father asked. "But many of our daughters have yet to perform."

"The contest cannot be over," a local matāpule said. "There is no precedent for partial evaluations."

Several mothers began imploring the king's matāpule.

"Fe'unga," he told them. "The decision's been made." Then he turned to Moon Appearing. "Make your farewells, for we depart."

Here's the truth of Moon Appearing: while among Tonga's northern islands La'ā was the best dancer, Moon Appearing's father donated the most young men to the war effort.

Her mother took her by the shoulders. Time was short, so her mother spoke directly: "You'll encounter many suitors in the Sacred South, men who speak with eloquence and grapple by firelight. Set your sights on the Tu'itonga's three sons, who are said to adorn their days with cliff-diving, poetry, and navigation. Do this or you'll end up married to one of your father's debt-holders."

Her father pulled her close and, forehead-to-forehead, shared breath with her. His eyes had misted. "Follow Tongatapu's rules. Obey the matāpule. Stay away from boys. By the time you've returned, I'll have found a husband for you."

Moon Appearing's fahu aunt arrived. As the older sister to the chief, she held the highest rank on the island and could be overruled on no matter. She was a midwife, and Moon Appearing had served as her apprentice. Together, they'd visited nearly all of Tonga's northern islands, helping deliver babies born of love, lust, war, and criminality. Her fahu aunt also handled babies destined not to be born. They referred to these babies as "red blossoms."

"I've always spoken truth to you," she told Moon Appearing. "You know the life of a young man on Hunga is worth nothing, as your father proffers them to war. I tell you this: The life of a young woman on Tongatapu is worth less. Your only concern will be making it home. Volunteer for nothing, accept no charms, and never let yourself become separated from the other Fefine Girls."

Moon Appearing could only nod.

"And if you feel a red blossom begin to bloom," her fahu aunt added, "come straight home, and I'll pluck it myself."

La'ā approached. The friends embraced, but rather than saying goodbye, La'ā offered a navigator's farewell, which suggested that partings were inevitable, as different people naturally had different destinations and navigated by different stars.

"Kuo pau ke ke 'alu," La'ā said. Meaning, *You must go.*

Moon Appearing was supposed to respond, "Pea ko koe e nofo." *And you remain.*

The first stage of moonrise is actually darkness. It's called *te'eki ha māhina*, "the before of the moon." This story begins in the *before* of Tonga, the *before* of the king, and the *before* of his three sons.

"Kuo pau ke ke 'alu," La'ā repeated.

But back then, back in Moon Appearing's *before*, she couldn't make the words.

As Moon Appearing made her way to the main island of Tongatapu, so did another figure: the Tu'itonga's younger brother 'Aho. The Tu'itonga, the king of all Tonga, had years ago sent his younger brother to fight in the war with Fisi. Now 'Aho was coming home to bury his wife.

'Aho was making this return on a double-hulled vaka canoe that belonged to the the tu'i chief of Lifuka, the Tu'ilifuka. 'Aho and the Tu'ilifuka were war comrades and had been through much together. The wind was against them, which meant endless tacking, either directly fronting the waves or cresting and dropping into their troughs.

Such voyages were opportunities to swap stories or catch up on inter-island gossip. This journey, however, was conducted in near-silence. The small Lifukan crew was troubled by a sack of bones that 'Aho had hung from the mast. 'Aho's wife had been adopted by the Lifukans and was well liked. It had been hoped she would curb 'Aho's volatile ways. And now here she was: her remains swinging overhead. Also troubling was the fact that the Tu'ilifuka brought along two war brides he'd captured in a Fisian raid, naked as the morning he'd run them down on the beach. Fisians controlled their dogs with kafa rope tethers, and this was what the war brides now wore, their leads tied to the spar. The women watched without comment as island after island took them farther from Fisi.

And, while 'Aho's son Mateaki had asked many times to return home to Tongatapu, a place he now only hazily remembered, the occasion of this journey was his mother's death. This turned every aspect of a wish come true into a somber affair—sleeping wet on the open deck, missing his mother with every breath.

The nature of the Tuʻilifuka will soon make itself known, but it must be noted that voyages were troubling for him. He and ʻAho had taken part in many raids upon Fisian islands, and it was difficult to hear the creaking of wet rope or the whistling of pandanus sails without evoking the anxiety of those attacks: the stressful anticipation of what awaited on enemy beaches and the grim mindset one later sailed home with. The Tuʻilifuka had learned many things about war, but high among them was this: the stress of war was strongest when you were far from battle, for battle was what released it. So when the Tuʻilifuka became agitated, his eyes darting about, ʻAho turned his son to gaze with him southward before the Tuʻilifuka mounted one of the war brides and forced his weight on her cold, salt-mottled skin.

They were in the open-ocean rollers, the troughs blinding them, the peaks offering views of the sea's indifference. "I've waited too long to take you home," ʻAho told his son. ʻAho had lost his front teeth in an incident a few years back, and this empty aspect of his smile amplified his every expression. When he scowled, he looked doubly menacing. When he looked uncertain, as he did now, his lip lifted a little, making him appear wayward as a child.

"They're not going to welcome us, are they?" Mateaki asked.

"Of course they will," ʻAho said. "Tongatapu's our home island."

"Won't they treat us like enemies?"

The boy had been exposed to much complaint about Tongatapu—at Lifukan kava circles where local chiefs railed against the tributes demanded by the king and on ocean crossings when Lifukan warriors lamented it was their blood being spilled for the king's war against Fisi. ʻAho understood he now had to counter some of that talk. He said, "You were born on Tongatapu, and so was I. Tongatapu is a royal island, and we have royal blood."

Mateaki asked, "Are you and the king going to fight?"

"Fight my brother?" ʻAho asked. "Do I wear my war turban? Did I bring my club?"

Mateaki looked less than reassured. "Promise me you won't battle anyone."

"I promise I have no such plans. We're here to get away from fighting."

Mateaki was silent. When a swell shouldered the canoe high, they looked into the crest line for the silhouette of Tongatapu, yet the horizon held nothing but blown froth and gray-white rain.

"Forget all the bad you've heard about Tongatapu," 'Aho said. He smoothed his son's hair, which sprang up again. "I'm going to show you the island of your birth. We'll camp upon the Liku Path and sleep beneath the chatter of peka bats. We'll contemplate the limitless southern ocean. Then, when we're ready, we'll bury your mother. A ceremony will follow like you've never seen. A thousand Tongans will spill their blood in her honor. There'll be endless feasting, and trust me, we're the ones who'll be treated like kings."

Behind them they heard the final pants and back-throat grunt of the Tuʻilifuka releasing his seed.

The morning waves rose large and see-through, with occasional fish caught bright and shining in their rolling hearts. 'Aho steered for eastern Tongatapu, away from the king's compound, which was built around his family's burial chamber. 'Aho had grown up around the grave, he'd even put his parents into it. But death, he hadn't known anything about death until he'd been sent to war. Which was why he was hesitant to face that grave. It would be no small thing to raise its massive lid, gaze at the remains of all who'd come before, and add his wife to the lifeless quid.

As they crossed the outer reef, the water warmed and calmed. Soon they were leaping into the surf to land the vaka. The crew took the opportunity after days of sailing to wade out and shit in the sea. The sun pushed sidelong into the swells, igniting their inner green and revealing the contents of their bellies—tendrils of seaweed, shimmers of baitfish, and fresh clouds of human waste being sucked into the tide.

The Tuʻilifuka opened his arms to the empty beach. "No welcome party?" he asked 'Aho. "No one to greet the great 'Ulukalala upon his return?"

'Ulukalala was 'Aho's war name. "No one here will call me that," 'Aho said.

"Whatever they call you," the Tuʻilifuka said, "you're still the brother of the king. Someone should be serving refreshments. Servant girls should be washing your feet."

'Aho studied the terrain, orienting himself. "I doubt they were expecting me."

"They knew one day you'd return," the Tu'ilifuka said.

They labored up a sharply rising beach, buttressed by the roots of lekileki and flanked by a stand of fetu'ana, or "blinding trees." The landing party consisted of four men and two women.

First, there was the Tu'ilifuka. To rule Tongatapu in the south, you had to be a royal. To rule Tonga's Vava'u island group in the north, you had to be a diplomat. But to rule Tonga's Ha'apai islands in the middle, because of the endless battles with Fisi, you had to be a warrior. Yet the Tu'ilifuka had left behind his famous war club. On Tongatapu, conflict was settled with matāpule. Club or no, the Tu'ilifuka was unmistakably a veteran of conflict: his forearms were spangled with dog-bite scars, and around his throat was a simple necklace adorned with the down of red-shining parrots, gone now in Tonga. By this band of red it was clear he'd spent his days on Fisian shores.

'Aho also bore the marks of dog bites. But he was known for two things. The first was inked on the palm of his right hand: a black jellyfish whose tentacles descended his fingers. The second was his decision to take his son, at an early age, to war with him. While the Tu'itonga's sons occupied themselves with poetry, navigation, and diving from cliffs, Mateaki had spent his youth in close proximity to combat. This experience had muted him. 'Aho hoped that, after his mother was buried, the light in his son's eyes could be restored.

Also with them were the war brides and an old man who'd been brought as a gift to the king.

'Aho tried to orient his son. "This is called the Solstice Beach. Up ahead are the cliffs of 'Utulongoa'a, famous for how they roar at night. Any of this seem familiar to you?"

Mateaki shielded his eyes from the light off the water. "Maybe."

'Aho led the way south along the tide line, examining niu trees. There was a palm trunk he wanted to show his son. Right away sand flies attacked the sack of bones, which had been stripped of flesh, but not of sinew and cartilage. 'Aho laid his hand on tree after tree, searching their trunks. "There's a small royal residence nearby. When we were kids, the king and I would escape to this place. Later in life," he said to Mateaki, "I'd bring your mother here."

He found the tree he was looking for. Burned into its trunk was the image of a jellyfish. 'Aho held up the jellyfish on his hand so they could see the images matched. In this moment, he almost looked happy. For so long, his home island had felt like a dream, but, placing his hand over the mark, feeling for himself how the two images aligned, home felt real again. He said, "When the Tu'itonga first removed a soul, he placed it into a coconut taken from this tree. That's why I marked it."

The Tu'ilifuka asked, "You've seen a soul removal firsthand?"

'Aho responded with a soft smile made malevolent by missing teeth. "Oh yes."

Mateaki asked, "How long can a soul survive in a coconut?"

'Aho said, "A soul lasts forever."

Mateaki clarified. "What happens to the soul when the coconut rots?"

"The everlasting nature of a soul," 'Aho said, "preserves the coconut."

Mateaki asked, "What does the Tu'itonga do with these souls?"

"He communes with them," 'Aho said. "The souls become his advisers."

The Tu'ilifuka asked, "And who had the honor of first losing his soul to your brother?"

"It was our uncle," 'Aho said. "He tried to kill us. He had the power to see in the dark, which made him very difficult to defeat." 'Aho addressed his son: "Your grandfather had the power of distant sight. Your uncle can remove souls, and of course I have my power," he said, raising his inked hand. "The god Tangaloa had every possible power, and as his descendants, we royals each get one." He said this in a reassuring way, to suggest Mateaki's power would eventually reveal itself.

The old man was from Ha'amoa and likely understood only part of what was said. Still, he asked, "Regarding your uncle, if you have spilled a family member's blood, have you not sacrificed your access to the afterlife? Have you not forfeited your own soul?"

"You speak the truth, grandfather," 'Aho said. "Yet my brother is very smart. The Tuʻitonga found a way around this restriction. You see, our uncle was still alive when we finished our work, and then he died by other means."

The Tuʻilifuka asked, "He remained alive without a soul?"

"You have to work fast," 'Aho said. "When the body dies, the soul departs of its own accord."

The old man from Haʻamoa asked, "By what means did your uncle die, if not by having his body opened and his soul removed by his nephews?"

An involuntary chuckle escaped 'Aho. War had changed his sense of humor. "Our uncle was the unfortunate victim of a shark attack. It happened right here." He pointed offshore. "We floated him out and together sang a shark-calling song. The next day, there were but a few bones left upon the reef. These we buried on the sacred island of ʻAta. If you don't believe me, you can visit our uncle's coconut. It resides in a ceramic bowl I made for the Tuʻitonga. This keeps Uncle's soul handy, so the king can consult him as he wishes."

Mateaki looked troubled by his father's smile.

'Aho placed a reassuring hand upon the boy's head. "Here's what's important to understand," he told his son. "Life charts a dark course into unfamiliar waters. The time to prepare for that voyage is not later but now. The Tuʻitonga was close to your age when our father died and our uncle tried to kill us. I was even younger."

In his son's eyes was a wary acknowledgment of this information, but there was little way to comprehend something like this until the day came when your own uncle tried to kill you.

'Aho's group moved along the coast until they arrived at the king's beach house in Heketā, which was surrounded by manicured gardens. When the caretakers presented themselves, they stood agog at the sight of the Fisian war brides—never had they seen women treated with such disregard for their modesty.

"Go find a matāpule," 'Aho told the caretakers. "Inform him I've arrived."

He identified himself by the jellyfish on his palm.

The Tuʻilifuka occupied the residence and began inventorying its provisions.

Mateaki asked his father, "Are you sure we should just move in?"

The Tuʻilifuka answered, "Your father's the brother of the king. This island's half his."

"That's not how it works," ʻAho told his son. "But yes, it's all right for us to stay here."

Still, ʻAho didn't fancy being inside. Over the years he'd become accustomed to sleeping on the decks of war canoes, on beaches, and even in trees when dogs were about. When he was a kid, there was a poem their father would recite called "Mohe Toto," which meant "To Sleep in Blood." The poem was about being too weary to wash away the ichor of battle before sleep, forcing one to fakaʻā toto, *to wake in blood*, before fighting again. He used to think the poem was a metaphor, suggesting one shouldn't shoulder the day's problems all the way to the sleeping mat. But the poem came to mind often now, and these days he was only interested in its literal surface: a warrior, lamenting his weariness, of what he'd done, of what he yet had to do.

In the garden, ʻAho unshouldered his wife's remains and lay down beside her. "You're home," he told her. Above, wind ruffled the leaves of futu trees. He was home, too, wasn't he? Tongatapu certainly felt familiar, but home was about belonging. Could he belong here again?

ʻAho wanted to close his eyes, but that's when troubling memories came. They weren't of combat, exactly, or even the dead. Sometimes he just thought *of* a moment, or *of* a man, not even the man himself. Memories of war could be as simple as light falling through unfamiliar trees, or the screech of Fisian parrots, like coded warnings across an island. Dappled light, a birdcall, the thump of oars—any of these could trigger the adrenal-shiver of death. Once, after landing on an enemy beach, his men realized the fighting spirit hadn't landed with them. To work themselves up, they waded out to excite their clubs by beating the surf, each man pummeling hollows into the waves. Even now, certain splashes, or a spray against the sun, could conjure the entire battle that followed. Most haunting was the mournful call of conch shells, blown to track an armada's canoes in the darkened troughs of the nighttime sea.

'Aho rolled to his side and closed his eyes. Before sleep, he saw jellyfish, parades of black jellyfish. 'Aho had the power to lay his hand upon someone and transfer his ink. When it came to powers, this certainly wasn't up there with soul-reaping. But he used his ability nonetheless. After a skirmish, he'd leave his mark upon the chests of those he'd struck down. The transfer came with the smell of burning hair, which was a timeless fragrance of war.

When the Tuʻitonga arrived, he was without an entourage or security men. He'd brought no one but his personal matāpule, whom everyone called Matāpule Muʻa, or First Matāpule.

The Tuʻilifuka disdained matāpule. 'Aho hated matāpule as well. It was a matāpule who, after their father's death, ordered the death of their mother so she might join him in the afterlife.

Matāpule Muʻa gestured for everyone to sit. 'Aho sat beside Mateaki. The Tuʻilifuka also took a seat—with a yank on their leashes, the war brides sat, too. The old man, a tātatau artist from Haʻamoa, had been sitting all along.

The Tuʻitonga was heavier than 'Aho remembered. He wore a simple vala kilt. The royal cloak, it seemed, had been retired.

"My brother, it's been too long," the Tuʻitonga said. "And you've returned with the bravest Tongan that ever lived, the Tuʻi of Lifuka, because of whom Tonga can sleep safely at night." The Tuʻitonga's eyes floated to the sack of bones. "You should have sent word. I would've prepared a proper welcome."

"It's no time for celebration," 'Aho said.

The Tuʻitonga took subtle note of 'Aho's missing teeth.

"I've returned to lay my wife to rest," 'Aho continued. "I must speak to her parents, make offerings, and attend to her burial."

"I remember your wife well," the Tuʻitonga said. "I remember the day you met her."

"She'd been dyeing tapa cloth," 'Aho said, his eyes lifting like he could see her. "She was scrubbing her hands at the well. When I chanced upon her, she covered her mouth to hide her lovely smile."

Mateaki's eyes registered no emotion.

"I'm sorry to hear of her passing," the Tuʻitonga said. "May I ask what took her life?"

"The war," ʻAho said. "And this." He grabbed some Tongan soil and displayed it for all to see.

The Tuʻitonga and Matāpule Muʻa exchanged glances.

"I'm sorry to see you've lost your front teeth," the Tuʻitonga said. "Is that injury connected to your wife's passing?"

"What? No," ʻAho said. "A Fisian club loosened my teeth. Later, when they began to fester, I pulled them myself and offered them to the sea."

"Worry not," the king assured his brother. "We'll arrange a lovely funeral for your wife. First, let's get you to the royal residence, where you can bathe, discover new garments, and reacquaint yourself with everyone. Mateaki, when did you last see your cousins?"

ʻAho shook his head. "I'm not ready to face the tomb just yet."

"Face the tomb?"

"Our parents' tomb," ʻAho said, suddenly angry. "The royal vault, where our mother had her throat drawn before being dumped inside."

The Tuʻitonga nodded, as if he were beginning to understand something.

"I was just a kid," ʻAho added. "If I'd been a little older, I would've murdered every matāpule."

Matāpule Muʻa responded with a look of alarm, but the Tuʻitonga lifted a hand in a gesture of calm. "I remember our mother's loss all too well. If it'll help, I'll be at your side when you visit the family tomb."

"Of course you'll be there," ʻAho said. "Everyone on this island will be there for my wife's funeral, for the moment we lift the lid and add her to our ancestors, for the moment every Tongan woman rakes her scalp and every Tongan man sacrifices his blood."

"Regarding the nonroyal wife of a royal," Matāpule Muʻa said, "if the royal dies first, she joins him in the grave. If she is the first to go, she must wait until his time comes."

"My wife will do no waiting," ʻAho said. "My son and I will tour Tongatapu. We'll see the sights—the Blowholes, the Pigeon Gate, the Throwing Stone of Maui. We'll speak to her parents, and when *we're* ready to let her go, she'll find her peace."

"I hear your lament," the Tuʻitonga said. "We'll have time to discuss this. For now, let's head to the royal residence and give you a proper welcome."

"There's nothing to discuss," ʻAho said. "And we'll be staying here."

"As you like," the Tuʻitonga said. "I'll have some Fefine Girls deliver fresh sleeping mats and supplies."

"I'll require coconut oil," the Tuʻilifuka said. "For the pleasure of my brides."

The Tuʻitonga tried to ignore the sinister delight in that request. "It's good that you've returned," he told his younger brother. "We'll do honor to your departed wife, rekindle our brotherhood, and before you leave, perhaps you can share some tales of your exploits in Fisi."

The Tuʻitonga offered a smile, expecting one in return.

Already the king was speaking of their departure, ʻAho thought. And what happened in Fisi, it wasn't just a story you told. How to put into words what had happened, was still happening? His time laying siege in the Koro Sea was like a giant decorator crab that kept covering itself in the broken shells of its victims, a crab that moved sideways and backward and hid when confronted. Stories were supposed to have beginnings, middles, and endings. Stories had morals, didn't they? But of his fighting in Fisi? There was certainly a *before*, followed by an endless and ongoing *during*. What even was an ending, was that what happened to his wife?

Into this awkward silence, the Tuʻilifuka asked: "Is it true that no man may touch the Tuʻitonga?"

"Any man may touch the king," Matāpule Muʻa responded. "But the man who does so receives great tapu, life-threatening tapu."

"Is this the reason why the king is the only man in Tonga without his ink?"

The Tuʻitonga nodded. "This is the reason I bear no markings."

The Tuʻilifuka asked, "Do our rules of conduct extend to other cultures? Were a Fisian to touch the king, would he receive tapu?"

"He'd be put to death," Matāpule Muʻa said.

"But would he receive tapu?" the Tuʻilifuka asked.

Matāpule Muʻa pondered this, running his mind over traditions and precedents. "No," he finally said.

"Then I offer the Tuʻitonga a gift that's long been denied him," the

Tuʻilifuka said. "I've brought a master tufuga from Haʻamoa, a man who's inked all their royalty."

The Tuʻitonga cocked his head at this development. "Him? Is he even awake?"

The Tufuga had a habit of resting his eyes.

The Tuʻilifuka patted the old man's leg. "Grandfather," he said. The Tufuga's eyes opened.

The king studied the old man, taking note of his left arm—here were constellations of dots and lines from a lifetime of testing needles on himself before proceeding with his subjects.

"He's at your disposal," the Tuʻilifuka added, "to be sent back north when he's done." The Tuʻilifuka turned to the old man. "Peʻa luga matai?" he asked in the Haʻamoan language, and pointed from his own ink to the Tuʻitonga.

The Tufuga nodded.

ʻAho could tell his brother was uncertain about the idea of endless days of pain and ink and blood, a process normally undertaken with the full grit of youth.

"He looks pretty old," the Tuʻitonga said. "Are you sure that if he starts the job, he'll live to finish it? If my ink is left incomplete, it'll be a problem."

The Tufuga had a sense of what was being said. "No tufuga ever dies," he said, "as long as one man adorned with his ink yet lives."

The Tuʻitonga rose. "Very reassuring," he grunted.

The Tuʻilifuka bade the Tufuga to rise as well.

"I'll send Fefine Girls with supplies," the Tuʻitonga told his brother. "But please, think about our offer of hospitality. There'll be a feast this evening. Tonight, Prince Lolohea completes his last test, after which he's eligible to succeed me as king."

Mateaki looked up. "Test?"

Matāpule Muʻa said, "According to custom, a prince must pass seven tests of determination and capability in order to become Tuʻitonga. Prince Lolohea has passed six of them."

ʻAho asked, "Which test is next?"

"Tonight at sunset," the Tuʻitonga said, "my eldest son Lolohea attempts the Fall of Tangaloa."

For the first time, Mateaki came to life. "Is that where it's nighttime, and you dive off a cliff to retrieve a necklace? My father taught me that one. I dove off the cliffs of Pangaimotu. It took me most of the night, but I succeeded."

The Tu'itonga regarded the boy. "Your father's been giving you tests that prepare you to become king?"

'Aho answered for his son. "In the voyage of life, one must be prepared for any destination."

The king slowly smiled. "In that, my little brother, we completely agree."

A WORD ON EMPTY-HEADEDNESS

A name can be an honor, a curse, or a destiny. No man gets to name himself, which is quite an irony, since who should know a person better? For most of us, a name is our only lifelong possession. For the lowliest, it's a sole possession.

All this is true for 'Aho, whose given name simply means Day. As the family story is told, 'Aho's mother labored all night with him. Her first son's birth had nearly killed her, and the second was worse. During the first delivery, she'd thought, *Let the child survive*. This time, she thought, *Let me*.

The torches shone orange against her sweaty abdomen. The mats were wet with her labors.

"Tuku ke u mo'ui ke sio he 'aho," she kept saying. *Let me live to see the day.*

Day came. She was still alive. Yet she didn't stop repeating the line that had kept her through the night.

When the baby came, the matāpule called him Tama Ha'a'ata, meaning Child of the Clan of the Sacred Island of 'Ata.

The mother simply said, "Kuo u mo'ui ke sio kia 'Aho." *I have lived to see Day.*

Baby 'Aho had been made unhappy by his trip through the halangatama. The journey was very long, yet he'd traveled only a short distance. This would become a theme in his life.

As a boy, 'Aho was addressed by variations of his name—Daytime,

Daybreak, Daylight, and so on. He was a sensitive boy with a big imagination. He didn't take to his martial arts training. He preferred to make pottery with his mother. It was a shock when his uncle tried to kill him. It was a hurtful surprise when his brother sent him to fight the war in Fisi.

'Aho understood neither the battles nor his role in them. But a fellow took him under wing. This was the chief of Lifuka, the Tu'ilifuka, who was known in Fisi as Mocekona, because he'd taken a club by that name from a famous Fisian warrior. *Moce* means the same as our *mohe*, "to sleep," and *kona*, of course, is "salt." In the Tu'ilifuka's hands, the club's "salted sleep" put in store rows of Fisian warriors like preserved fish.

The Tu'ilifuka helped 'Aho see that the enemy's fear was his greatest weapon, and the Tu'ilifuka tutored the younger man on battlefield brutality. In 'Aho, the old adage was proved true: sensitive men, when exposed to atrocity, become themselves the cruelest. Soon 'Aho saw his own chance to claim a notorious Fisian club, one that so loved to fight, it was said to twitch and jump when an enemy was near. The club was called 'Ulukalala. *'Ulu* means the same in Tongan as Fisian: "head." In Fisian, *ka* means "skull" and *lala* means "empty," so the club was the great emptier of heads, and by extension, this is how 'Aho became known. Sometimes the sight of 'Ulukalala and Mocekona landing on a beach was enough to scatter the Fisians into retreat, for their clubs also happily slaked Fisian blood.

The Fisian need to retake the club called 'Ulukalala would become its own occupation. 'Aho's first indication of this came after landing on one of the Lau Islands. A lone Fisian stepped forward. He had painted himself half-yellow and half-black, the colors splitting his face. Meeting such designated warriors would become of fixture in 'Aho's life.

The warrior said he was there to meet the Tongan who possessed the Emptier of Heads.

'Aho obliged him.

'Aho's father had the power of distant sight. His uncle could see in the dark. His brother could remove souls. What did 'Aho have? The ability to transfer an impression of a jellyfish. What to do with such a lesser talent? Sure, the jellyfish had its sting, but it was also blind, unfeeling, and endlessly adrift. The first time 'Aho marked an enemy was after he'd engaged the painted man, who'd been quite fierce. The contest could've gone either way. So 'Aho wanted the man's people to know that he'd fallen not to any Tongan, but to the one who wielded 'Ulukalala. He applied a jellyfish to an adversary that first time simply to say he'd personally exerted himself in this matter. Thus a symbol came to speak louder than a word, and 'Aho learned that even more powerful than a name said in fear was a name people were afraid to say.

THREE

THE SACRED SOUTH

After the Tuʻitonga finished meeting with his brother, he walked away, engrossed in conversation with his matāpule. The old Tufuga followed. He'd sailed on a cramped deck all the way from Samoa, so it was good to walk, to feel soil between his toes. The Tufuga's eyes were tired after a lifetime of fine work, so he'd often amble with his eyes half-closed, taking the occasional glimpse to check his course. He listened for the sound of a heron, the leg bone from which he'd make his inking needles. But this island was silent of such birds.

Inland, woodsmoke was heavy. The land flattened, and where he expected forest, there were only fields. So this was the Sacred South, the place that had invaded and subjugated his home of Samoa. The Fijians would likely fight the Tongans to the end. Samoans, however, were practical. They understood that when a Tongan armada arrived at dawn, it was best to serve them kava, negotiate terms, and begin paying tribute. And here he was, on the island where Samoa's harvest was sent, not to mention Samoa's comeliest daughters.

Despite all that Tonga took from its neighbors, people here were hard at their labors—Tongans digging holes, felling trees, burning brush, beating bark, husking coconuts, sluicing taro, and pounding futu nuts to make fish poison. Serious about their chores, these women wore braids to keep their hair from their work. In Samoa, women wore colorful lavalava and tuiga adorned with flowers. They smelled of wild ʻavapui. Each morning Samoan women awakened the sun with an ula dance, and at night they sang the moon into being. In between, they soothed the human heart by performing the tauʻolunga, a dance the Tongans had also taken from Samoa.

Each Tongan family had its own dwelling, which meant countless columns of woodsmoke. Samoans shared large dwellings—people lived together, ate together, and tended a single fire. It was a wonder there were any trees left in Tonga if every family fed an 'umu oven. But when these people consumed all their food, more simply appeared. When timber and supplies were needed, they magically arrived from over the horizon.

After parting ways with his matāpule, the Tu'itonga fell in stride with the Tufuga. "It's been many years since I've been to Ha'amoa," the Tu'itonga said. "Do the hills still smell of fau blossoms? Do lovely maidens still dance at every opportunity?"

The Tufuga said, "I believe Samoa's loveliest maidens end up in Tonga."

The Tu'itonga offered a knowing smile. "There are many marriage opportunities in the Sacred South."

The Tufuga thought about lowering his needles upon this king. Was he capable of leaking blood all morning and then sealing his wounds with salt water in the afternoon? There'd be many days of needles. Tongan men and Samoan men shared the same marking, from navel to knee. The Samoan term was *pe'a*, which was their word for "bat"—the bat that embraced itself in a wrap of black wings. Could the Tu'itonga endure the dark embrace?

The Tu'itonga asked, "On the voyage here, did my brother share any intelligence with you?"

"I've marked many royals," the Tufuga said. "And what is uttered before me, I do not repeat. But there's no need for discretion here—your brother didn't share the cause of his wife's death, the reason he burned his fale in Lifuka, or why he set a feather box adrift upon the sea."

"He burned his dwelling?" the Tu'itonga asked. "He cast our mother's feather box into the sea?"

'Aho had actually gently released the feather box, as if freeing it.

But the Tu'itonga didn't wait for a response—he advanced with renewed haste, and the Tufuga had to open his eyes and pick up the pace. Nearing the royal compound, structures spread like banyan limbs. At the entrance, Fefine Girls approached the king with refreshments. He ordered them instead to Heketā to supply his brother.

The Tufuga followed the king past a priest circle, a meeting of sub-chiefs, and a war council studying a shell-map of the Fisian islands. A gang of children ran past, playing scattered games of sika and knucklebones, making the Tufuga long for home. He was a simple man—his granddaughters meant everything.

At the compound's center was a massive stone tomb whose lid was cut from a single sheet of petrified reef, a slab so large the Tufuga supposed a hundred men would be required to raise it. The Tuʻitonga's wife was receiving tukituki from two young women, who, by their sour looks, must have been the king's supplemental wives, for they seemed none too happy about massaging the body of the first wife.

The king approached her. "Pōhiva," he said. "There's a problem. My brother made landfall this morning."

Pōhiva dismissed the young wives. "Who, then, is leading the campaign against Fisi? Wars don't fight themselves."

The Tufuga observed the king's face—his pained expression suggested that wars did, indeed, fight themselves.

"My brother carries his wife's remains," the Tuʻitonga said. "He aims to bury her in the royal tomb."

"Did he kill her?" Pōhiva asked. "You know he killed her."

"I asked ʻAho about her cause of death. He evaded the question."

"You know how your brother is," she said. "He'll get moody, and you'll feel bad for him. Then he'll get it in his head that he's been wronged, and suddenly someone's dead."

"He won't be here long," the Tuʻitonga said. "A few days, at most."

"Don't let his sad eyes fool you," Pōhiva said. "You must send him back to Fisi, where a pack of dogs will handle him."

"Don't say that. His wife has died. He's in obvious pain."

"Don't let him get a taste of this life," Pōhiva said. "Don't for a single—"

Here, the Tufuga was approached by a tall man who introduced himself as Six Fists. He was fully inked and was the king's chief of security. "I need to ask you some questions," Six Fists said, and led him to another part of the compound.

Six Fists's ink marked him as a warrior from Nuku Hiva, a place where priests enchanted ink to make it blade-proof, which was why this man had a breastplate of black, a skull cap of black, and a black band across the eyes.

What the Tufuga wouldn't give to learn that ink's magical recipe, to be able to armor men against knives and spear tips.

"I hear you're to give the king his ink," Six Fists said. "I need to know that if you begin the process, you'll live long enough to finish."

The Tufuga studied the exquisite inking on the tall man's face. The eyelids had been blacked, as had the lips and nostrils. "Who's to say how long a person shall live?" the Tufuga mused.

"You know what I mean, old man," Six Fists said. "Do you feel sick or anything? Do you have heart problems?"

"In Samoa, we speak to our elders with terms of respect."

Six Fists's face softened. "I'm sorry, Grandfather. In Nuku Hiva, this is also our way. This place did something to me."

The Tufuga nodded in understanding.

"Still," Six Fists said, "the issue is a serious one. In Tonga, a man whose ink is incomplete wears a mark of shame. It's assumed the ink is unfinished because he couldn't handle the pain. If for any reason the king's ink is left partial, he'll be seen as weak."

"Perhaps I should receive some royal care, to ensure my good health."

This made Six Fists smile. "All right, grandfather. Royal treatment it is. But there's someone else you'll have to ink."

Six Fists led the Tufuga to a bathing pond in which many lovely ladies were taking their leisure. Waist-deep, they chatted and braided one another's hair. Watching them from shore was a forlorn man with a leashed parrot on his shoulder. The man was somehow both lean and padded with baby fat, and he stared at the girls with such longing, he looked ready to weep.

"Him?" the Tufuga asked.

"No, that's New Punake," Six Fists scoffed. "Ignore him—he's a harmless poet."

New Punake, at the sound of his name, looked up. There were indeed tears in his eyes.

Six Fists pointed instead to a young man, perhaps sixteen, floating in the pond, his gaze directed at the clouds above. "That's Finau, youngest son of the Tuʻitonga," Six Fists said. "He's the one you'll ink."

"He's too young for needles," the Tufuga said. "The boy won't take the pain."

The parrot on New Punake's shoulder turned to the Tufuga. "Finau take pain," the parrot said.

Six Fists called to Finau and, as the boy emerged from the water, introduced the Tufuga and explained the inking that would take place. "You came all the way from Haʻamoa?" Finau asked with wonder. "I've always wanted to go there. This is my parrot Kōkī and this is New Punake, my father."

"The king is your father," Six Fists corrected.

"Why must a person have only one?" Finau responded.

"Kōkī never know his parents," Kōkī lamented. He eyed the Tufuga warily, then volunteered some old verse:

Potuʻiʻakau tētē ʻi moana,	*Driftwood on the high seas,*
ʻo ne ako a māmani kotoa pē.	*all the world it learns.*

New Punake, wiping his eyes, finished the poem:

Ka ʻi hono toe fakafoki ʻauhia ki ʻapi,	*When currents send it home again,*
kuo mateuteu ia ke tutu.	*it's ready to be burned.*

The Tufuga didn't know how to interpret these lines. Was he the driftwood? Would he be sent home? And being burned—that was a metaphor, right? He looked into Finau's eyes. The boy's pupils didn't flit back and forth, seeking information, approval, or permission. No, his eyes allowed themselves to be peered into. In there, the Tufuga saw an abiding calm. Or perhaps it was a hint of human indifference.

The Tufuga nodded. "I'll require the leg bone of a heron to make my needles."

"We're fresh out of herons," Six Fists said.

The Tufuga said, "How about the wing of a malau?"

Six Fists shook his head. "We face a general shortage of birds."

"The wing of a frigate bird will do. They're common."

"Tongans do no harm to the frigate bird," Six Fists said.

Who would revere the frigate bird, the Tufuga wondered, a bird that stole from other birds' beaks? He studied Six Fists, a fellow foreigner in this land, for some indication of how to interpret the strangeness of these Tongans, but the man from Nuku Hiva offered nothing. Again, the Tufuga marveled at how Six Fists's eyelids had been expertly inked, the black so smooth and uniform. How had the ink been applied without risking his vision, how had the curve of the eyes and the delicate nature of the eyelid been accounted for? All his life, the Tufuga had given the same tātatau, navel to knee, over and over, with the only variation being the motifs in the patterns.

Six Fists asked, "What kind of tufuga travels without his inking tools?"

"I was told that because I'd be inking a king, my needles could never have touched another man."

Six Fists said, "Looks like you'll have to improvise."

Inking needles could be cut from turtle shell and, if desperate, even boar tusk. Parrot's beak worked nicely, too. "You're a handsome bird," the Tufuga told the parrot, and true to the vanity of its species, the bird raised its head. The Tufuga tapped the parrot's beak to gauge its thickness. "Sure. I'll be able to make my tools."

Kōkī was receptive to this special attention. He fluttered his emerald flight feathers. "Can you ink someone green?" Kōkī asked. Here he raised his ruby crest. "Or a shining shade of red?"

The Tufuga was forced to concede he couldn't.

"So," Kōkī asked, "your fancy tools only make a creature . . . black?"

"The needles won't be fancy," the Tufuga told Six Fists. "But they'll get the job done."

"Not *fancy*?" Kōkī asked. "*Get the job done?*" Kōkī cocked his head toward Finau. "Rough needles is what he talk about." Kōkī laughed his parrot laugh. "What he talk about is pain!"

A WORD ON THE STORAGE OF SOULS

The Tuʻitonga believed soul-harvesting should be a natural process, so he employed no blades fashioned from human hands. The jagged edge of a broken oyster shell would do. A flap was cut around the rib cage, and once the human cavity was breached, a hand was inserted, the soul located by feel. A fresh coconut was then husked. The transfer took place inside the donor, from one dark receptacle to another. The soul was never yanked into the light to be gawked at. The Tuʻitonga would then mark the coconut, so he might not later confuse it with one containing another soul. Finally, the coconut was taken to the royal chamber and placed in a large ceramic bowl next the Tuʻitonga's sleeping mats. This bowl had been a gift from the Tuʻitonga's brother ʻAho, who'd been quite skilled at pottery when he was young.

The royal chamber was where the king retreated when troubled. Now, reclined on his side, he reached into the bowl and withdrew a coconut. It was marked with an outline of the volcanic island of Kao. Inside, preserved in a sweet, liquid eternity, was the soul of the chief of Niue, whom the Tuʻitonga consulted on all matters naval in origin. His soul had been difficult to harvest, since the removal took place on the pitching deck of a vaka, when all were still reeling from the battle of Tofua.

But the Tuʻitonga's problem had nothing to do with conflicts at sea. His dilemma concerned his brother. Why had ʻAho returned? And what had happened to the man's wife? ʻOfa was her name. She was no Fefine Girl, but ʻOfa had come from a good home. She'd taken ʻAho on as a project—he was quite fragile after their parents died and their uncle tried to kill him. The Tuʻitonga had done his part to help his brother, giving him a fresh start in the war with Fisi, where a man could make a name for himself.

The Tuʻitonga pulled another coconut from the bowl. The souls at the top were the ones he consulted most often. Regarding spiritual matters, the Tuʻitonga turned to his beloved former priest Vai-Hanga-Ki-Langi, whose name meant Pool-That-Gazes-at-Heaven. The priest hadn't exactly been on his deathbed, but by reaping his soul a little early, the Tuʻitonga granted the priest an eternity of spiritual guidance.

Deeper in the bowl were souls the Tuʻitonga referenced only for special cases. He found Hungaluopea, whose name meant Reclaimed-by-the-Sea. Hungaluopea was famous for his beguiling appeal to the female sex. In the glow of youth, before the Tuʻitonga was married, he and Hungaluopea had some escapades. Hungaluopea's appeal didn't last forever, though.

There came a time when the Tuʻitonga was forced to save him from a mob of angry women. By removing Hungaluopea's soul, the Tuʻitonga craftily satisfied the mob's demands for blood while still allowing the rake to live on. And here he was, eternal. The Tuʻitonga once turned to him for advice on matters pertaining to intimacy. Yet those days were gone. An ailment had developed deep inside the Tuʻitonga, one that made urination painful. And satisfying women—that had become unthinkable.

The issue of ʻAho was something only family could understand. So the Tuʻitonga located the soul of his uncle, the attempted murderer in question. The king now reclined on his stack of sleeping mats, all claimed from those he'd personally vanquished. Such mats, lightened by their owners' rise to the afterlife, were said to provide the finest rest. He'd long imagined his uncle as a bitter figure, a man who saw an opportunity to himself become king—all he had to do was kill a couple of nephews. But the Tuʻitonga was older now, close to the age his uncle'd been when he'd made his deadly move. What if his uncle's attack hadn't been brashly taken? What if everything in life had led his uncle down a path, a path that terminated in confrontation with a close relation?

The Tuʻitonga rested the coconut on his chest. In the lodge poles above resided the bundles of mats he and his wife had received on their wedding day. He thought about his mother's feather box, which he'd forgotten had even existed until the Tufuga mentioned it. He visualized ʻAho setting it adrift upon the waters. Memories came to him, of how his mother would open her feather box, carved from heartwood and lacquered with a distillation of beetles' wings. Of how his brother sat rapt as their mother produced feathers and told her boys stories associated with each, happy stories about islands and gifts and distant encounters.

By taking that feather box with him to war, ʻAho had brought his mother along. He'd kept her alive and by his side. To the Tuʻitonga, their mother was now like a lovely wedding mat in the rafters, a treasured thing stored so securely, it might never be viewed again. In fact, the Tuʻitonga sat daily upon the royal tomb—there he took council, heard complaints, and made proclamations—without dwelling upon the fact that his parents rotted away in the chamber beneath him. He associated the tomb not with death, but with life, his life, in all its aspects, from leadership to leisure.

But 'Aho. He'd been an emotional boy, an artistic boy. He felt deeply enough to sulk, indulge, inhabit states of total thrall. They say that's what made him such a gifted warrior. Every foe he engaged was worthy of unmitigated zeal. And here he was, back again. What to do with a younger brother? Younger brothers remembered everything their older brothers forgot.

The Tuʻitonga lifted his uncle's coconut and gently sloshed the liquid inside. It couldn't be so bad. Darkness and cool. Sweet, untroubled waters. A rugged shell, an encasing of white flesh, an endless meditative state. And if one day the king wanted to set a soul free, he'd simply plant that coconut on a friendly shore, where the soul would sprout into a lovely niu tree.

"I don't blame you for trying to kill a family member," the Tuʻitonga told his uncle. "I'm sure you felt you had no choice."

The Tuʻitonga knew he couldn't waste his uncle's time with commentary and trivial entreaties.

He had to formulate a single question.

"How did you know," he asked his uncle, "the time had come to finally act?"

The Tuʻitonga then curled to his side, pulled the coconut close, and closed his eyes. Souls surrendered their wisdom only in the realm of dream.

The king was awakened by an appearance from his aunt, the Tamahā. Of course, the Tamahā wasn't just the Tuʻitonga's aunt—she was auntie to the entire kingdom. Seeing it was she who'd roused him, the king lowered himself to the ground in deference. Everyone in the Tamahā's presence, including the Tuʻitonga, had to supplicate themselves, for she was the highest-ranking person in all of Tonga. The Tuʻitonga possessed the power. Yet the Tamahā held the rank. She could do nothing without his command. He could command nothing without her approval. The worst part of supplicating himself to her was the view of her drawn and skinny calves. No honorable woman should have such scrawny calves!

Normally, the Tamahā delighted in looming above him, but today she knelt to him. A bad sign.

She eyed the coconut he held. "I see you've been consulting my long-departed brother."

"He hasn't departed," the Tuʻitonga said. "I keep him right here."

"Might I ask the nature of your inquiry to him?"

"I consulted him about timing," the Tuʻitonga said. "I asked when life's most onerous tasks should be undertaken."

"You do make many unpleasant decisions," the Tamahā said. "About war, about tributes, about which islands go hungry. What did my brother advise?"

The Tuʻitonga could see that waiting outside was the Tamahā's entourage—her security team of nine, led by her security chief Valatoa, her trio of personal matāpule, and of course the Fefine Girls, with whom she shared educational custody. At night, the Tuʻitonga and Pōhiva taught the Fefine Girls about grace, refinement, service, and protocol. During the day, the Tamahā taught them about . . . well, who knows what the Tamahā taught those girls?

"My uncle was clear," he said. "The time to take action was *before it's too late*."

The Tamahā took the coconut and replaced it in the bowl. "One day, you'll do me the courtesy of planting this, so my brother's soul can grow free. For now, I bring important news."

"What news is this?"

"I've heard," she said, "that a vaka is on its way here from Lifuka. Your brother ʻAho is on board. He's returning to the Sacred South."

"What matter is it where my brother sails or doesn't sail?"

This was clearly not the response she was expecting. "I only share news with the Tuʻi of all Tonga, as is my duty. Though there is one other piece of news." She waited for him to beg to hear more.

"Please," he said impatiently. "Do share."

"I'm told that, trailing your brother's vaka, not a day behind, is another canoe."

"*Another canoe?*"

"In pursuit," she said. "And the canoe is manned by Fisian warriors."

He looked at her with great suspicion, for she was always up to some subterfuge.

"They sail with a pack of war dogs," she added.

"I appreciate your news, but I have news as well. My brother landed this morning in Heketā, and I assure you that no Fisian warriors were giving attack."

"Your brother's here, you've seen him? Why no welcome party, why no feast?"

He wondered if it was possible she didn't know 'Aho was on the island. Her intelligence was always keen, especially when it was used to keep him off balance.

"His wife has passed away," the Tu'itonga said. "He's in mourning and wishes solitude."

"You must warn him that he's in danger."

"This is the Sacred South," the Tu'itonga said. "No enemy has ever attacked this island."

She gave him a look of such concern that for a moment he believed it genuine.

"How can it hurt to inform him?" she asked. "Where's the harm in alerting him of danger?"

"There's truth in what you say. Trust me, I'll deliver this news to him myself."

"Make haste," the Tamahā said. "For he's your only brother." She glanced at the coconut. "I know what it's like to lose a brother."

The Tamahā then touched the Tu'itonga's face. He closed his eyes and summoned the strength to not wince as the backs of her fingers traced one stroke down his cheek.

The Tu'itonga received great tapu by coming into physical contact with the one person who outranked him. This tapu meant, among other things, that the king could not touch his food for days, that he must be hand-fed, like a baby, or take his food off the ground, like a dog. Untreated, this tapu, over time, could lead to sickness, or, for an average Tongan, death. The ritual of moemoe was the only remedy. It was a ritual the Tamahā so enjoyed, she liberally put others under her tapu.

The Tamahā extended her leg, which the king took by its sinewy calf. "You know you can come to me with your problems," she said as he placed the sole of her foot flat against his forehead. "You don't have to talk to coconuts."

The Tuʻitonga traced one slow circle around his face with her foot. Then he rose, tapu removed.

"I don't know if those coconuts answer you back," she said. "But even if you can hear my brother's voice through the liquor of eternity, you must remember that he was never a wise man. Your uncle was a second-born, while you, like your father, are a firstborn. Only one person can understand your problems, and that's me. No one else could fathom how alone you are."

The Tamahā, collecting her entourage, then shuttled away, off toward her own compound, where she kept her own court and counsel, apart from everyone.

The Tuʻitonga had much to think about. He called for kava and a girl to dance the tauʻolunga—anything to assuage his troubled mind.

It is afternoon, the sunlight diffused through the canopy. The girl summoned to dance for the king is Māhina-eʻa, Moon Appearing. She's told only that the Tuʻitonga needs a dancer to help him relax. The other Fefine Girls have been sent to deliver supplies to the king's brother. It makes sense that she didn't join them, because she's new to Tongatapu, new to the rules of the Sacred South. She's so new in fact that no one's discovered her inability to dance.

She wraps herself in tapa cloth so that it tantalizingly reveals a peek at her calves. This wrap she secures with a belt of heilala blossoms. She'd been mocked by Tongatapu girls for following a practice so rural as wearing a girdle of flowers, but those girls are gone now, and nothing so reminds her of home.

She finds the king sitting atop the royal grave, its capstone an expansive sheet of petrified reef. He's alone, holding a shell of kava. He doesn't look at her, for it's clear he contemplates a major issue. Moon Appearing's father is the Tuʻi of Hunga, a small island, to be sure, insignificant perhaps, but he's a chief nonetheless, and he often gets the same look when weighing his people's matters. In fact, when the last Tuʻitonga died, her father journeyed here to this very grave for the funeral, and Moon Appearing was weaned on stories of that ceremony, of the hundred men required to raise the dark stone before her, how every hog on the island was slaughtered, how thousands of people paraded before the grave while teams of matāpule passed out the broken shells and bamboo spikes needed to perform tuki and lafa and foaʻulu, the procession leaving in its wake footpaths clotted with blood and hair.

No one signals for her to commence. The king does not regard her. He downs his kava and leans back on his elbows. Grimace on his face, he seems to study the rise and fall of his belly as he breathes. She assumes a position of taulalo, legs together, slightly bent. Fu, she clasps her hands, which to her always suggested the man and the woman, embracing, the moment of creation and birth, and the narrative of faiva begins moving through her. She's supposed to perform a highly regularized dance, but since no one's watching, not even her audience of one, she dances her own dance, a dance that tells the story of herself to the king, starting with haʻo to, hand movements that trace the shorelines of Hunga. She tilts her head slightly to the side in a teki, which signals the next element of the dance story: a vete of hand movements opening a space in the world for her birth, the circle where the moon will appear. Teki. With a kako swirl, her hands gesture the build and release of clouds, of seasonal cycles, of how a young woman grows, billows, and blossoms, fulfilling the promise of her youth. Teki. She adds the rhythm of tongiʻone to suggest the waves and paddles of the voyage that brought her here. Teki. And with a series of fakataopasi, she signals she's brought her family stories with her, stories her father has told her, about a Tonga before this Tonga, stories her mother has told her, about a life before this life, and stories her fahu aunt has told her, about destinies still unfolding, for it was her aunt's duty to find homes for babies born of dark enterprise.

The king reclines fully, shifts one way and then the other, perhaps to scratch his back against the grit of the petrified reef. It seems ordained that the king never actually looks at her. It allows her motions, however poorly executed, to infuse everything around them, the flow of air, the foot patterns in the sand, the shadows of her arms playing across the king, and as she moves through the dance of her life, she feels that the dance is a dance without end, one that might flow forever, into another dancer, into a future daughter, or into a wind that will alter the movement of others as it blows through them.

Smiling and staring forward, she tekis from move to move until she perceives there's someone else in the garden. Near a large kotone tree is a hutch filled with lupe doves, and here, a handsome young man attends his birds, hand-feeding them as he coos and strokes their feathers. Though it breaks the rules of tauʻolunga dance, she casts her eyes to him, studies him, this handsome young man who is the king's eldest son Lolohea. He looks up, studies the sky. Moon Appearing looks up, too. Above, she sees wind-driven niu trunks twist and interlock like the necks of herons in ancient songs. She sees the green-black silhouettes of beetles doing battle on the far side of a sun-cast taro leaf. She sees kotone pollen emblazoning the afternoon light with a drifting nutmeg glow. She sees, high above, the split tail of a frigate bird choosing not to swoop down to collect the tribute of lesser birds. She sees Lolohea is the kind to take counsel in the poetry of an unfolding world.

A WORD ON THE MOON

There are several stages of the moon's nightly appearance, though average people notice the moon only when it's bright enough to help with late-night net mending. Elites on Tongatapu might speak to the moon's power to illuminate the beauty of dancing girls or supplemental wives. Such portraits ignore the other stages of moonrise. They ignore the Teʻeki ha Māhina, the "Before of the Moon," for example. The dark sky, lacking any glow, is the true beginning. Here, crouching below the horizon, the moon exists only in our imaginations, the way our own futures loom unseen. In this *before*, you can feel a human presence but cannot tell the black of night from the ink upon a man's skin, and thus cannot know if he's a brother, a lover, a rapist, or a warrior from another land.

Only after the *before* does there arrive the next stage of moonrise: Māhina Ulo, the first hint of "Moon Glow," captured in marine mist, in the faint illumination of sea-skimming clouds, in ghostly, luminous curtains of night showers upon the waves, which at their peaks reveal rafts of war dogs, set adrift by our enemies to land ravenous upon our shores.

Next comes 'Uluaki Tauloulo, a stage of moonrise most think of as the "Initial Shimmer." Here, the moon first reveals itself, spreading light like fish oil upon the water. It's enough illumination for a newly pregnant woman to pluck the abortive red blossoms of the kaute flower. And what such woman wouldn't pause to behold this soon-to-be-extinguished stage of the moon?

In the fourth stage, Māhina Hopo, the moon stands a perfect lamp upon the horizon, casting a beam of white upon the sea, a beacon that compels prawns to thrash in the shallows and commands multitudes of gleaming baitfish to strand themselves upon the shores, entire beaches of gasping fish sheened white with spore and a faint celestial light. Humans are not immune from the effects of this moon's stage—they dive from dark cliffs, take their kava graveside, and veer toward the sleeping mats of war brides.

Next comes Māhina Fekite, when the moon casts long shadows—this light is a friend to rapists who give chase down Tongatapu's sandy trails, making paths of escape confusing as they are cameoed with a bramble of shadows, from swaying fronds and the silhouetted arms of toa trees.

Following this is Māhina Tukulaumea, the stage in which the moon is marked, for when glanced at, its white surface is blackened by the wings of peka bats.

Māhina Haka has arrived. Here, the moon appears to dance. As we grow accustomed to the moon's presence, we glance upward less often, so that each glimpse reveals the moon in a new quarter, as if the moon were executing the graceful moves of the tau'olunga across the sky.

The final stage of the moon is Māhina Mate. You can say the moon dies, vanishes, or veils itself. But the moon doesn't actually go away: once we become aware of its presence, once we're used to its glow, we stop looking, and it's gone until another lovely moon, on another sweet Tongan night, arrives to take its place.

Of these stages of the moon's journey, the *before* is most important. As there is a before to the moon, there is a before of Tonga and a before for each of us, a time when we first feel the tidal pull of destiny, yet still can't imagine where the shifting current will take us. Prepared or no, we must wait in the dark for the future to cast itself like a bait net upon us. Take, for example, the story of Māhina-e'a. It's no coincidence that this young woman's name means "Moon Appearing." And her course through this humble tale will map itself onto the aforementioned stages of the moon.

Because they sailed by the stars, Havea and the Second Son slept away the daylight on the deck of a double-hulled vaka called the *Pelepeka*. Tonight, however, Havea and the Second Son would embark on a most distasteful excursion: they would set foot on land.

So, come sunset, the great navigator Havea roused himself. The sun was pressing its fire upon the western cheek of the sea. That was the exact location, Havea thought, of Fisi's Lau Islands. Though they were many days' sailing away, Havea was easily transported back to his years as the Tuʻitongaʻs military navigator. The king was skilled at keeping Tonga's conflicts far from home; it had been Havea's duty to sail into the horizon of them. The invasions, beach battles, running skirmishes—they came back in moments like this, though they weren't really memories. War was more like a broth: absorbed by your bones, it was capable of leaching sour back into your gut. For the navigator, time and distance were the same, so he reminded himself the war was far, far ago. For the last nine years, he'd been on a different journey, one that took him away from his own family and saw him installed as the supplemental father to the Tuʻitongaʻs middle boy. His mission, one seemingly without end, was to teach the king's Second Son the art of celestial navigation.

Havea nudged the boy's foot. When the Second Son opened his eyes, he winced at the orange light, saying, "Master, let me sleep. Lolohea's test isn't for a while yet."

The boy was seventeen and would sleep all night, if Havea let him. Havea had a son who was about this age and another a little older. He'd learned not to think of them, for doing so fouled every moment. But by his not contemplating their lives, his family remained fixed as he'd last seen them, like old carvings.

"Your brother's test won't be for a while," Havea said. "We'll have time to do some star work."

"It's not even dark," the Second Son said. "Just because you don't sleep shouldn't mean I can't."

The boy already knew his stars. He knew the currents and winds and weather patterns and seasonal changes to all of these. It was the large ideas he'd been slow to absorb. As Havea saw it, a mentor could only teach certain things. He couldn't simulate near misses, narrow escapes, or the witnessing of others' sorrowful fates. At some point, the sea itself was your only tutor. But the Tuʻitonga wouldn't allow the dangers of true voyaging—Havea wasn't even permitted to sail the Second Son to troubled parts of Tonga, like Lifuka, let alone to unfriendly lands.

When the boy roused himself, they raised their red sail and headed into Tongatapu's southern waters, where they'd study the stars before attending Lolohea's final test, which featured cliff-diving in the dark.

Havea and his young charge had two kinds of work—ocean work and star work. Ocean work meant night passages between the Tongan island groups. This was quiet, focused work, the kind Havea preferred. Havea never forgot a single wave he ever met. He believed the ocean would show you everything you needed to know to navigate it. Attention to the sea itself, above all, was what he tried to impart upon the Tuʻitonga's middle son. For the sea wasn't the stuff that kept the islands apart. The ocean wasn't something you survived or got across or stayed on top of. The ever-spontaneous, all-powerful, infinite expanse of the sea was the oyster liquor of existence. Those occasional specks of dryness—of dirt and tinder and dandruffy dwellings—that was the pig-shit home of man.

Tonight, because of the rough nature of the southern water, they'd do star work, which normally took place on the calm western shores of Haʻatafu. There, come dark, they'd spread shell maps. Each Tongan island was represented by a shell, with hundreds more needed to represent the vast complex of Fisi. These shells were as close as the Second Son ever got to places like Haʻamoa, Niue, Futuna, and even the peace-loving island of Rotuma. They used sticks to trace star arcs through the shells, noting zeniths and horizon lines. All it really took to understand the handiwork of the gods was a stick, a beach, and a person willing to lose some sleep.

They anchored on a stretch of white called Houma Toloa, the southernmost tip of Tongatapu. Lolohea would take his test on the cliffs nearby.

Havea and the Second Son ate 'ota ika next to an outcrop of black that fended the wind. As persons of differing rank, they were required to eat separately, but this rule couldn't be observed on the deck of a vaka, so they'd become used to eating together, something the Second Son had never done, in his entire life, with his own father.

The Second Son said, "I saw you talking to those fishermen from Lifuka this morning. Did they bring news of your wife?"

All who dwelled upon the waters seemed to have an opinion as to the fate of Havea's wife. Some said she was sick, some healthy, while others declaimed her already dead. The Tu'itonga's matāpule assured Havea that his wife Vaivao was alive and well.

The fishermen had shared a different piece of news with Havea: that the Tu'i of Lifuka and the king's brother 'Aho had arrived on Tongatapu. Havea had once sailed with these men, steering the courses for their foreign incursions. Few men had been more fierce. Few held less regard for life, including their own. And that had been nine years ago. Havea could only imagine what they were like now, having journeyed a decade further into the sea lanes of brutality.

"I know you're worried about your wife," the Second Son said. "If the news is bad, perhaps I could talk to my father about letting you visit her."

Havea cleaned his hands in the sand. He didn't like to talk about his wife with the king's boy. He especially didn't like to speak of his own sons. The only way he could still possess his family was to keep them from the royals of Tongatapu. "If the news is bad, they'll just bring me her bones."

Havea needed to initiate the Second Son as a full-fledged navigator. Once he hung an ika māta'u fishhook pendant around the boy's neck, the young man would be marked as a master pilot, one worthy of making any passage, under any conditions. Then Havea would be free. He could do it today, he could give the boy his fishhook necklace and be done with it. Except for one thing: The Second Son wasn't ready. If the boy later got himself lost or killed or, worse, imperiled his passengers, Havea's entire family would pay the price, and it wouldn't matter if Vaivao were already dead, for the Tu'itonga had ways of punishing even the deceased.

Mostly, Havea had come to believe that the attributes that made a good royal and the attributes that made a good wayfinder were antithetical. Things were probably too late, anyway. The Second Son seemed to have little notion of his father's poor health, of the perilous succession in the works, of the fact that the Tamahā would soon transfer her great rank to an as-of-yet unchosen girl. And now the two most dangerous men in Tonga—the Tu'i of Lifuka and the dreaded 'Aho—had decided to pay the king a visit, with motives unknown. The Second Son had never seen a change of leadership. He didn't know how many people died when it all went smoothly, let alone when there was chaos.

The Second Son slurped raw fish from coconut milk. With his mouth full, he said, "If I could get my father to let you visit your wife, I could come along and finally see the island of Lifuka. I could meet my brothers."

"Your brothers?"

"Your other sons."

Havea winced. Through his dwindling vision, he gazed into the southern seas. No birds flew here from the south. The waves brought no driftwood. The world below seemed a world without earthly comment, save for notions of displacement, relentlessness, and an affinity for the eternal. None of Havea's predicament was the boy's fault, he reminded himself. The boy understood nothing. And the responsibility for that was no one's but Havea's. "Can I share a notion with you?" Havea asked.

The Second Son paused. "A notion about what?"

"About disasters. When canoes go down, lives are lost. You've never seen this, but they do go down, more often than you'd think. There are reefs, rogue waves, cracked hulls, and so on. If it happens far from land, all men are lost. Sometimes, though, a man is spared. Perhaps he happened to be below the thwarts when a wave washed the others away. Perhaps he pushed a friend below the surface so that he himself might rise. Some men can go without water longer than others. Regardless, he survives. You'd think this man would be joyous, for he has lived where others have not. He is *alive*, is he not? You'd think he'd treasure this good fortune. But that's not the way of it. I've seen it with my own eyes. Often, the one whom fate spares cannot spare himself, and he lives his days as if his body had found flotation, yet his spirit had slipped beneath the waves."

The Second Son cocked his head with worry. Havea didn't talk like this.

"I want you to think about that." Havea waved his hand toward the cliffs where the royals would soon gather to watch Lolohea take his final test. "You're the only one of them who has the ability to navigate. You're the only one who can depart, if you have to. If there's to be a great wreck and fate happens to spare you, you must accept this, seize it, and embrace your fortune."

"Master, what're you talking about? What wreck?"

Havea licked the salt from his fingers and rubbed his tired eyes. He, Havea, once a great navigator, was reduced to explaining the obvious to a boy. Havea, who'd led the warships that struck Savai'i. Havea, who'd strategized the great sea battle against Niue, who'd trapped a Fisian fleet against the black cliffs of Tofua. Here was where he found himself, dropping hints to a teen. And with only one bit of wisdom gained for it: there was a danger in becoming too well regarded, for when the king wanted a navigator to raise his middle son, only the best would do, and Havea was who he turned to. Years away from his wife. Years of giving his all to someone else's boy.

"Son, I'm going to go ahead and tell you something," Havea said, then stopped himself.

The Second Son looked stricken. "Tell me... what?"

How long had Havea labored to teach the boy to see the signs around him—signs that would orient him, guide him, preserve him from danger? But of course those signs were observable only upon the sea. To survive on land, he'd need a different kind of teacher.

"It's time to attend your brother's test, that's all."

FOUR

KŌRERO:

STILL WET WITH THE SEA

Following their arrival, Hine and I led the Wayfinder and Finau to a quiet whare where they could rest. Inside were freshly woven mats and a basin of water. We had little to offer in the way of food, but we made a bowl of berries and fern bracts.

"We sleep until sunset," Finau said, dropping to a mat. "Only then do we awaken."

It was like a command, the way he spoke, lacking any gratitude or appreciation. Were we not offering them refuge after they washed up on our island?

"And then we'll need some servant girls to give us aid," he added.

"*Servant girls?*" I asked.

"*Give you aid?*" Hine asked.

"How should I know where your bathing pools are?" Finau asked. "And a man can't scrub his own back."

"You fool," the Wayfinder told his brother. "An island like this doesn't have bathing pools."

An island like this? I thought.

"Forgive my brother," the Wayfinder said. "He doesn't know anything about the world." Then he offered me a look suggesting only he and I, as navigators, possessed such knowledge. "Tonight, we'll consult the stars," he said to me. "You'll help me locate the island we seek, yes?"

I nodded because it was the easiest thing to do.

"Excellent," the Wayfinder said. "And then we'll trouble you for some supplies. When the constellation Toloa rises, we depart."

"But you just arrived," Hine said. "Tonight we'll welcome you as honored guests."

"A feast?" Finau asked longingly. "Oysters and eels?"

"Don't be stupid," the Wayfinder told his brother. "Where would these people get eels? They're in the middle of nowhere." The Wayfinder turned to me. "I apologize for Finau. Chicken is fine for me—he prefers pork."

Hine glanced at me. I glanced at her.

Though there was something angry about this Finau figure, he closed his eyes and curled to sleep like a child. The Wayfinder yawned. He swatted a couple red flies from his ankles before reclining on his own mat. "Do you know the story of Kupe and the Octopus?" he asked.

This was one of our most important tales. "You've heard of this story?" Hine asked.

"You're the Māori people, aren't you?" he asked. "From Aotearoa?"

How could he have heard of our people, when the word *Tonga* was nothing to us but a direction?

"How do you know who we are?" I asked.

"You ink your faces," he said. "And carve objects from greenstone."

My greenstone fishhook practically sang with recognition.

"Do you recognize this?" he asked, lifting a white object that hung by a cord from his neck. "This whistle was made by the Māori. It's carved from the bone of a moa bird."

The moa bird was no more. It had been extinct a long time, which made the whistle quite old.

"Is the whistle a navigation thing?" Hine asked.

"I suppose," the Wayfinder said. "It's made to call frigate birds."

"Who'd want to call a frigate bird?" I asked.

The Wayfinder said, "It can also call dogs."

The notion that our people had learned to summon dogs, it stunned me. I still couldn't quite imagine a dog, what it looked like or how it moved. But I now knew they came when called.

"You've spent time with dogs?" I asked.

"Unfortunately," he said.

But dogs meant nothing to Hine. She asked, "What else do you know of us?"

The Wayfinder placed his head on his hands. Closing his eyes, he said. "I know you're a long way from home."

Back at the cove, our people stood transfixed by the great double-hulled waka. Some dared only touch the prow, but others were wading out to run their hands down its waterline. Hine and I returned to discover Papa Toki and his boys had climbed aboard and were hoisting the tremendous sail. Tapoto's men were taking turns lifting the anchor stone, the likes of which we'd never seen. Our island was made of volcanic cinders, so we had no rocks of any kind, let alone one black as the new moon.

"Did they tell you anything?" my mother asked when she saw us.

My father asked, "Where're they headed?"

Papa Toki asked, "Did their bird really recite poetry?"

Tiri asked, "Whose bones do they bear?"

"We didn't learn anything about them," I said. "Yet they know about our people and where we're from."

Tapoto said, "I suspect these Tongans are a warrior people."

"They're just boys," my mother said.

"We must focus on what we can learn from them," my father said, "about navigation, canoe-building, other islands, the direction home."

"*This* is our home," my mother said. "We're not going back where we came from."

"They're leaving tonight," I said.

Tapoto was going to make an emphatic point but stopped. "They're leaving?"

"But . . . to where?" my father asked. "There's nowhere to go."

"Some island," Hine said. "They don't seem sure where it is."

"We can't let them go," Tapoto said. "We must convince them to stay. We must make their time here pleasant and hospitable, we must lavish attention and goodwill on them. By gaining their trust, we'll make a powerful ally."

My mother asked, "And what'll we feed them?"

Tiri stood with her hands on the bow, her clouded eyes directed toward the shimmering sound of wind through the mangroves. She could get this look on her face—it suggested that, rather than seeing nothing, she saw everything. "Tonight," she said, "we'll give our guests places of honor in our wharenui longhouse. We'll eat with them. Then we'll tell them a story, a story that contains something of who we are. They'll be obligated to return a story of their own. Then we'll discover who they are and what they intend."

"Tiri," Tapoto said—we tended to say her name before speaking, so that she might recognize our voice and know our location. "What story will you tell them?"

Tiri pointed at me. "She will select the story. She'll tell it."

Though I loved stories more than anyone—perhaps *because* I loved them so much—I tended to mess up their tellings, starting in awkward places, forgetting key elements, getting ahead of myself, exhausting everyone with detours. So nobody looked reassured that I'd be the one engaging our guests.

I waded out to get away from their lack of approval, feigning interest in the frigate bird carved down the side of the Tongan waka. I ran my fingers along the grooves that traced its swept wings and split tail. What kind of people would revere the frigate bird, a thief and a bully?

Tapoto waded out to join me. "You'll do great tonight. That Tiri has faith in you is all anyone needs to hear. These are new times," he said, placing his hand on the waka. "And new times call for new stories."

"I'm partial to the old stories," I said.

"Yes, the old tales should be cherished," Tapoto said. "We should share them with one another, even the ones with unsavory elements like conflict and servitude. We understand these stories, even if there's no proof they ever actually happened."

"Oh, that stuff happened. How else but through conflict and servitude would we have ended up on this island?"

"Do our people go around killing and enslaving one another? Tell me, have we ever sued for war?"

I shook my head.

Tapoto said, "I don't recognize us in the old stories about death and retribution. Has anyone been slain on our island? Never. Instead, we value labor, goodwill, and community."

This from a man who spent his days napping while others worked. This from the man who was dying to become the war captain.

"I don't want war and slavery to have existed, either," I said. "But why do we have words for these things if they never were?"

"Kōrero, there's not a shred of proof for those old stories."

"The stories are the proof. It's when a story is missing—that's when you should be suspicious."

"Are they proof?" Tapoto asked. "The stories tell us we're descended from a canoe filled with slaves, but were any of us there? One mistake of storytelling could change our entire sense of ourselves. What if we're the ones descended from nobles and captains?"

"That's why stories are sacred," I told him. "That's why we preserve and repeat them. That's why we're careful never to let one slip though our fingers. Since when do you care about stories, anyway?"

"Look," Tapoto said. "If you tell these Tongans we're descended from slaves, we'll look weak. We'll become vulnerable. I propose that a story did slip through our fingers—the story of our nobility. You must admit that such a story would give our people strength in times of uncertainty. And tell me it doesn't make sense? Tell me it doesn't account for how smart and resourceful we are? Yes, I believe somewhere along the line a careless hand fumbled the truth of us. But you're a better storyteller than that, Kōrero. You'll be able to carry all the stories of our people, the ones from the past, the ones to come, and the ones carelessly dropped along the way."

We weren't fish, I thought, *still dripping with the ocean we were pulled from. No, we were a people with an epic and sacred history.*

* * *

In the hunt for the wild parrot we'd named Kanokano, I enlisted Aroha. I made sure Aroha's leash was secure because I didn't want to lose her. We moved through the kata trees and up the kūmara fields where sweet potatoes were grown. We entered the last stretches of forest, low-lit and abuzz with insects moving through shafts of light. Aroha called and called, but no parrots answered. I knew that wild parrots mated all the time, and it was a screechy, beak-clashing, feather-pulling affair. But something about that Tongan parrot maddened me. I hated the way, without hesitation, it set upon a fellow of its kind. And why would someone train it to repeat those two lines—about fish being wet and things being green?

Alas, there was no sign of Kanokano. Having failed, we summited the cindery peak of the island, which offered a vista of blue in all directions. Aroha perched on my shoulder, contemplating the ocean with me. It soothed her to cup the top of my earlobe in the roof of her beak.

My father'd said there were as many islands as stars in the sky. But where were they? Out there was nothing. I knew that Kanokano had come from someplace. So had those Tongan brothers. Yet visible only was that hazy line on the horizon where sky became sea. I looked into the blue for answers, but there were only questions: How big was the world, how rare were islands, how were they found? A flock of birds swept in from the open ocean, turning with the winds that eddied into the island's lee. Was there an island, just beyond my view, upon which a girl had recently watched in amazement as a flock of birds departed into the unknown? Soon my mind was populating that island with all our counterparts.

"I thought I'd find you up here," Hine called. She was coming up the mountain, arms out for balance in the craggy cinders. She sat beside me and took a moment to feel the wind and warmth on her face.

"You fretting about which story you'll tell tonight?" she asked.

I shrugged.

"Just tell an old yawner about Maui," she said. "Maui lassoing the sun or Maui pulling up an island."

"Don't you think we should tell them a story that offers a sense of who we are?"

"I'm more interested in their stories. So don't go on and on, all right?"

"Tapoto doesn't want me to talk about where we came from and how we got here."

"Maybe he's right," she said. "Maybe that's not a story for the first night."

"What if I tell the story of the Eclipse?"

"That coincided with Tapoto's dad drowning," Hine said. "He'll be sitting right there."

"What about a story from long ago, like the Great Wave?"

"Are you kidding? Half the island died when that wave struck. Hā Mutu watched all his childhood friends get swept away. You want to see an old man cry?"

I shook my head.

"Besides," Hine said, "it's not your story to tell."

"But Hā Mutu never talks about the Great Wave. If someone doesn't tell the story, it'll be lost."

"It's not your story."

I snapped off a sprig and split it so Hine and I could suck the sweet gum inside. Our people hadn't seen Aotearoa in generations. Where we'd come from—it was only a story to me. But today, after meeting those Tongans, our home felt more real than ever. The mystery now was whether we were still like the people we'd come from. Or had we changed? If we went back to Aotearoa, would they recognize us?

"You know the story I want to hear?" Hine asked.

I looked up at her.

"I want to hear about how those Tongan boys got their legs inked and whether the black covers their asses."

"Hine," I called out. "You're a dangerous girl!"

"Look," she said. "Just talk about how we feast when the sweet potatoes are harvested. Talk about how we sing when your mother inks a woman's lips."

I nodded. I put my head on her shoulder, the wind mingling our hair. Still, I thought about weighty topics, like who we were and where we belonged. I could tell that Finau and his brother had never thought such questions, and I hated them for that.

"Your father's coming," Hine said, and sure enough, he was making his way up the peak. "You'll do fine tonight. Just keep it simple." Then she took her leave, though when she encountered my father, the two spoke a moment, at one point both turning to regard me.

When he sat beside me, I asked, "Did Mother send you up here?"

He gazed upon the sea, squinting. Years of sea-reflected sun had begun to take a toll on his eyes. "Mostly we fish the edges of the island," he volunteered. "The outer reef, the fingers, the hole. Sometimes we go out farther, when tuna are running. Once, a group of shearwaters were working some baitfish—the bonitos were striking everywhere. We followed those birds all morning—they led us to beautiful fish after beautiful fish. At some point, I looked up, and our little island was nowhere in sight. The sun was high in the sky, so east was indistinguishable from west. I hadn't really been tracking our direction. I figured we were west of our island. I knew that eventually the setting sun would confirm the direction to sail, but then how would I find our island in the dark?"

I nodded. It was a story that troubled him. He'd told it before.

"But the birds knew," he continued. "As the day went down, they ceased their fishing and all turned at once to depart. I knew that direction was home, and I didn't veer from the course they'd set. Worse than the fear was the sense of helplessness. Worst of all was the fact that the lives of others were in my hands. I was also angry. Our people had once known such things. We'd once been great navigators—we'd discovered Aotearoa. Yet we'd let such knowledge slip through our fingers."

My father went quiet. At last he said, "These boys know everything about sailing that we forgot. They seem to think you're a navigator, too. So pay attention. Listen for how they got here and how they intend to find the island they seek."

"I can't pretend I'm a navigator," I said. "I don't know anything about it."

"I'd never ask you to pretend you're something you're not. But they already believe you're a navigator. You could just, you know, allow them to think what they want. At least for a while."

Aroha closed her eyes, allowing me to stroke the downy scruff of her neck.

"Why're they carrying bones?" I asked. "I mean, whose bones are they?"

My father looked into the blue. He said nothing.

Though we'd lacked guests on our island, we still held regular pōwhiri welcoming ceremonies. This might seem strange, but a pōwhiri welcomes the living and the ancestral into your sacred longhouse. As the dead outnumbered us, we had to honor them, especially since we'd been disturbing their graves.

Finau and his brother were awakened at sunset and brought to the marae, an expanse of grass and fern that led to our communal wharenui longhouse. They'd cleaned up and donned flax kilts.

Tiri stood at the entrance to our longhouse and began singing, "Nau mai, haere mai."

The karanga—the call to guests—had begun. She welcomed the mate, the kui, and the koro. After thus greeting the elderly and the dead, she invited all to enter, singing,

E nga iwi haere mai.	*All people are welcome.*
Mauria mai te aroha	*Bring forth your love*
ki te marae e.	*into our sacred space.*

"You must announce yourselves," I told Finau. "Say who you are and why you've come."

Our people surrounded the marae, awaiting their words.

"We come not as agents of Tonga," Finau said, "but as brothers on a long journey."

Tiri asked, "And who are the dead who accompany you?"

The Wayfinder said, "They're only temporarily dead."

My mother, ever the skeptic, asked, "How can the deceased be less than fully dead?"

"They are fully dead, as you can see," Finau responded. "I assure you, however, it is an impermanent state. Recently, I found myself dead. I even visited the afterlife. Yet, as you can see, I'm quite restored."

We looked to Tiri to see how she'd respond to these unnerving declarations.

"Haere mai," she said, bidding them nothing but welcome.

We lined up to share breath with our guests, pressing foreheads, one after the other. The one named Finau smelled faintly of coconut oil and turmeric. When our noses touched, he huffed once and moved on to Hine, who waited in anticipation. My mother says you can tell a lot about a man by how he shares the breath of life: Does he want to take your breath, or does he offer only his? What did a quick huff mean?

Next was his brother, the Wayfinder. When our foreheads pressed, he closed his eyes, and together we inhaled. What I breathed seemed strangely familiar—traces of sea spray, wind-salted pandanus sails, wet rope. That is to say, he smelled like my father.

When our guests came to Tiri, she asked to touch their faces. But she wasn't really asking—already her hand was rising to their features. That they allowed this signaled something good in them.

Inside, the smell of cooking meat lifted everyone's spirits. Despite the food shortage, Tapoto had ordered the preparation of a vast meal. My father was not thrilled about feasting in lean times. It was his opinion that to truly honor someone, one should fast instead. Sacrifice, he said, spoke louder than indulgence. My mother shook her head at the sight. *Once again, Tapoto finds a way to stuff his own belly*, she muttered.

I thought Tapoto was being a good host, but a person's reputation is his least redeemable part.

After lavishing our guests with compliments and flattery, Tapoto led them to a mat, where, displayed in the light of candlenut lamps, were all the greenstone artifacts we'd recovered from our grave-digging efforts. Here were our hard-won ax-heads and adzes and chisels, along with drill bits, earrings, tiki, and pendants. It was as if our riches were so commonplace, we simply left them lying around. With the sweep of a hand, Tapoto said, "Please, take anything you like as a gift."

This outraged my father. With a glare, he admonished Tapoto.

With a look, Tapoto responded, *I know what I'm doing.*

My mother wasn't afraid to speak up. "These are our people's most important possessions."

The Tongans, fairly uninterested, did little more than glance at the objects.

Tapoto lifted the sea-green adze. It glowed with mana.

"Perhaps this is to your liking," Tapoto said, attempting to place it in Finau's hands.

Our guest declined. "I don't handle tools of the field," Finau said. "But we have seen a weapon made of this greenstone, a club capable of opening the skull. Do you have any of those?"

We knew what he was talking about, a club called a mere. Yet, long ago, all the weapons had been on the canoe called *The Red Cloak*, while in our slave waka were only tools and food stock.

Tapoto picked up a greenstone chisel. "Please, take this as a gift from our people."

Finau tried again. "Have you not heard of this club? With one strike, its sharpened stone can send a brain into the sand."

I could see Tapoto's eyes casting about. He didn't want to admit we were lacking in all manner of weapons. Instead, he said, "Perhaps it's time to eat."

I'd never seen a brain. The idea of one exposed to light or air horrified me. Picturing wind blowing across the wet surface of a human mind made my skin pimple over. And a dusting of sand? My imagination wouldn't allow sand to be placed anywhere near a naked brain.

When the earth oven was opened, we lined up for food. Our guests were placed at the front. In the old days, on Aotearoa, those of lesser birth had to eat after their more distinguished counterparts. Here, we made a point of eating together. I could smell baked sweet potatoes, bearded with ash. I could practically taste the fern roots, slow-cooked in bull kelp. Finau was at the head of the line. "At last," I heard him say. "Some chicken."

Chicken? What could Tapoto have possibly prepared? When my turn came, I got my answer. I looked at Hā Mutu, and he looked at me. The last of our protein reserves were some whioi birds we'd caught last year and preserved in their own rendered fat. Silently we watched, knowing that since we'd caught them, they'd gone extinct, making us the last people who'd ever taste them.

Still, when it was my turn, I loaded up. The birds had been basted with the purple juice of miro berries and sweetened with the nectar of flax blossoms.

We tended to sit loosely. My father asked our guests to sit near us.

Finau shook his head. "It's tapu," he said, "for us to eat with people of lesser rank."

Which meant what, that we'd prepared a feast solely to dine with ourselves? What were we honoring, if not our guests? But we were hungry, and the food was hot. So the Tongans sat on their own, the helpings went around, and the little whioi birds vanished.

I ate with my parents and Tapoto. Our island's wood-carver, Arawiwi, joined us. Her husband had died a while back, so she sat with different people every night. Right away, she said, "I heard the Tongans arguing earlier. I was walking past their whare. Through the thatching, I could make out one saying he wanted to go back. He declared he wasn't afraid of their fate back home. The other insisted they press on."

"What fate could that be?" my mother wondered.

My father asked, "What if, instead of heading toward something, they're running away?"

"The Wayfinder is the one who wishes to press on," I said. "He aims to depart this evening."

Tapoto begged to differ. "It's Finau who has fire in his eyes. Though younger, I suspect he's in control."

"Did Finau not say that he'd died?" Arawiwi asked.

My mother raised a eyebrow. "That he did."

Tapoto said, "Perhaps we could use this discord to keep them here longer."

"Letting them leave is not an option," my father said. "We have too much to learn from them."

I asked, "Why does Finau have only half his ink?"

My mother looked at me.

"What?" I asked. "Hine's curious, too. She wonders if their asses have been blacked."

"Hine is never finding out," my mother said.

"Neither are you," my father added.

It was then that Tiri called for a story. Despite her lack of vision, she managed to point at Finau.

He stood and thanked us for our hospitality, but added, "Where I come from, we value poetry over stories. I'm afraid I haven't any tales to share."

Before he could sit, Hine called out, "Tell us a poem, then."

"Our poems are old and obscure," Finau said. "Many of their words have fallen from use."

Hine implored him, "Are there no new poems?"

Finau contemplated this. "I know a recent one, composed by a poet named Punake:

Naʻa moe kakanoʻi puaka ʻoku tutue,
pea ʻikai toe ʻasi e malama o e fanga manupuna,
ko e kohu pē ʻoku matafia ehe ngāahi tafatafaʻaki langi.
Ko ha kafa haʻi manoʻo pē,
ʻoku ʻala maʻu ehe ngāahi kaungāmeʻa.
Toki ʻalu fakamuimui e kotoa ʻoku lanumata."

I tried to make sense of this poem, but could only recognize certain words.

Finau was asked what the poem meant.

"Punake was like a father to me," he responded. "His lines lament the scarcity of food in Tonga and the depletions that plague us. They also lament the fate of the poet himself."

It's hard to express how reassuring it was that people on other islands also struggled with resources.

I said, "So in Tonga, you go hungry, too?"

"Well, no," Finau said.

My mother spoke up. "But, as you said, Tonga suffers from scarcity?"

"Yes," Finau said. "Much has been exhausted."

"How can you both have enough and also not enough?" she asked.

"We struck a terrible bargain," Finau said. The way he spoke invited no follow-up.

Still, I was curious about the poet. "What was the fate of Punake, the one he laments?"

"The poet bemoans the practice of castration," Finau said.

Tapoto asked, "Do you use this for population control?"

It was said that the people of Rēkohu, in an effort to limit the number of hungry mouths, castrated every other male baby. We'd opted instead for the marriage ban.

Finau said, "Punake's castration was only the beginning of his troubles." He turned to his brother. Accusingly, Finau said, "Why don't you tell them Punake's fate! Why don't you admit what you did to him?"

"You have no sense of sacrifice," the Wayfinder said.

"Me?" Finau asked. "I went into the grave for our family."

Before things got out of hand, Tiri said, "Thank you for the lovely poem. Now Kōrero will share one of our stories."

I stood. Moving into the glow of the candlenut lamps, I beheld my people. Above were lodge poles, inlaid with our carvings. Lining the walls were mats woven with our patterns. After hearing a poem about hunger and castration, I thought we needed an uplifting and inspirational story. I decided to tell the oldest story we had of our island: how, after landing here, battered, hungry and thirsty, we discovered a nesting ground on the beach, filled with tasty tern eggs to restore us. A tree canopy offered us shade, which we'd been lacking after endless days upon the sea. And soon we discovered a tree whose roots formed a bowl that collected fresh water. But I supposed I had to start with the storm that brought us here.

"There was a terrible storm," I began, "which separated our waka from that of our enslavers." I remembered Tapoto had not wanted me to say this, so I tried to explain by backing up to Aotearoa. "You see, there was a tribe in Aotearoa that lost its land. There was no empty land left. Everywhere they went, they faced conflict. They became raiders, conscripting people from the tribes they attacked. They learned to move at night in blackened waka. Still, their numbers dwindled until they decided to escape, to sail back to Hawaiki, from which all Māori originated. That's how we ended up here." Now I could describe the lovely beach we found, with its belly-filling eggs, though I felt bound to mention that taking those eggs caused the terns to abandon the island, and the tree with the water bowl was cut down to construct our first longhouse. An ethical storyteller was obligated to mention that longhouse was then destroyed by the Great Wave.

I looked at our Tongan guests: their eyes betrayed no reaction to my words, which unnerved me. "Some people believe we're cursed. They point out those we've lost to untimely deaths." I tried not to look at Hine and Arawiwi and Tapoto and Hā Mutu, but I did, I couldn't help but glance at each of them. "But we aren't cursed, we're a blessed people. People only said we were cursed because of our isolation and crop failures and the way we lost the great vaka that brought us here, owing to the Wave I mentioned."

Though people rarely talked about the Great Wave, or perhaps *because* they rarely did, I'd re-created it in my mind from scraps: First, the sea retreated, leaving crabs to skitter across newly exposed reefs. Black shoals revealed themselves. Pink coral heads were suddenly visible. Many kids stripping flax on the beach stopped to watch, and some even advanced into the void where the ocean had been. A woman was overseeing the children. She told the smallest boy, the nimblest boy, to climb a tree to see where the sea had gone. Out past the reef, the water stopped receding. Now it was doubling up. The ocean, it was said, climbed atop its own shoulders. The woman told the children to run, but the ocean was coming fast, so they sought shelter in our great waka, which had been stored since our arrival above the tide line.

Hā Mutu's eyes were fixed upon me, which made me wonder, was I thinking these words or saying them? Was I describing, out loud, the ocean's charge, the sheets of mist blasting in the wave's advance, the brown-churning foam? Hā Mutu's face lost all expression. I was suddenly afraid that, yes, I was speaking aloud, but how could that be? The Wave lifted the waka, used it to batter down our longhouse—all the trees we'd felled to build it!—and maraud across the leeward plains. Hā Mutu, before me, started weeping, and I knew that I was actually telling this story, and it was impossible for me to stop a story before the end. Eyes wide, horrified, I began racing toward the happy part, describing how, after the sea exhausted its reach, a retreat began, the ocean taking with it everything it had grasped. As I listed all the lives the Great Wave had claimed, hands were placed upon Hā Mutu, but it brought him no comfort. Only the end of the story could deliver that. Atop a tree, one boy remained. In exchange for his safety, he had to watch a raft of his friends being towed out to sea by—

"And that," Tiri said, "concludes the storytelling portion of the evening."

"But the eggs and the water," I said. "I meant to say how fortunate we—"

"Thanks once more for the enlightening tale," Tiri said.

My father spoke up: "I'd like to hear a story from our Tongan navigator."

"I'm even less a storyteller than my brother," the Wayfinder said. He didn't bother to stand. "I live apart from the land and all its narratives."

We remained silent, pressuring our guest to speak.

"Really, I don't sit around the fire every night swapping tales," he added. "The ocean resists story. It doesn't care about morals or conclusion. It can't be captured with words."

Again, we said nothing, our faces flickering in the lamplight.

"If you'd steered the windward waves beneath the oyster-colored cliffs of 'Eua, you'd understand. If you'd encountered a ghost vaka in the Teleki Reefs, you'd know no story could contain the sea."

"What're the Teleki Reefs?" my father asked.

I could hear the hope in his voice, that we might be able to find these reefs and harvest fish from them.

"The Teleki Reefs?" the Wayfinder mused. "There, rays move beneath the surface like the shadows of clouds, and purple sea snakes rear when they sense you. It's a place unintended for people, and I was only there at the service of the prince of Tonga, who had to pass a test."

"What kind of test?" Tapoto asked.

The Wayfinder took a breath, suggesting it was too complicated to speak of. "There were many tests," he said. "They included diving off a cliff, piloting an old canoe, and, on this occasion, filling a vaka with slaves."

My mother asked, "You mean slaves, like people already in bondage, or normal people, who by being apprehended against their will suddenly become slaves?"

Tapoto asked, "How could a young man capture and subjugate many men?"

"You'd be surprised," the Wayfinder said, "how readily people enslave themselves."

Bitterly, Finau said to his brother, "Why don't you tell them your role in that adventure?"

The Wayfinder defended himself. "The navigator doesn't select the destination. The business of his passengers is not his concern. He's bound by a single duty: taking others where they need to go." Then he stood, thanked us for our hospitality, and declared, "We have preparations to make."

Was it possible they were going, that, having filled us with questions, they'd depart with the answers? My heart raced at the thought. I blurted, "You have a whistle that summons dogs. Please, what're dogs like?"

Finau shook his head. "I'm no expert on dogs. I've battled them only once. You'd have to fight a duel with dogs, as our friend Six Fists did, to truly know their character."

We didn't mean to block their exit, but we sort of were.

Papa Toki spoke up. Though he had but one arm, he was a known dueler. "You mean, fight a duel against a dog?" he asked. "Or fight a duel using dogs?"

My mother asked, "Do you two own any slaves?"

Tapoto asked, "Which one of you is the prince in the story?"

Tiri asked, "Have you ever been to Hawaiki?"

The Wayfinder shook his head. "Hawaiki? Never heard of it."

That stunned us. Everything that was, everything we were, led back to Hawaiki. Hawaiki was the place we'd been searching for when we ended up here.

Now Finau took a turn at asking questions. "Do you really have no voyaging vaka?" he asked.

We shook our heads. The story of our lost canoe was true.

"We have several fine fishing canoes," my father countered.

Finau asked, "And you honestly have no leader?"

"Of course we do," someone answered. We looked at Tapoto, whioi grease on his belly. We were feeling glad now that we had him, we were happy we had a war captain after all.

Finau then got a look that unnerved us.

He indicated Tapoto's men, with their green, newly whittled spears.

"And these are your island's only warriors?" he asked.

This question brought the final silence of the evening.

※

After Finau and his brother left the feast, they were heard arguing, and it seemed pretty clear they wouldn't be departing that night, after all. Why even leave in the dark? Why not at dawn, when the sun's up and you can at least see?

My parents and I slept on the beach that night, though sleep was unthinkable. It was one of those times when there was so much to talk about that nothing was said.

The new parrot Kanokano hadn't returned. Was she, at this moment, madly fleeing that Tongan parrot?

I lavished extra attention on my own bird, trying to teach her her name. "Aroha," I said to her. "Aroha, Aroha."

For a long time, I repeated that word, which is the word for *love*.

Finally, I couldn't take the silence.

"Is it possible," I asked my parents, "that on other islands, people are captured, they're enslaved, and it's normal, it's everyday? On other islands, do brains fall out in the sand, and it's ordinary?"

My father breathed deep.

My mother was silent.

I kept thinking about the whioi birds, about how we'd licked our fingers and wiped our faces and that was that, they were gone. In the forests, a family of whioi would nest in a bush, then post a little lookout on the trail. The lookout birds always seemed so nervous, out there alone. *Whioi*, they would call. *Whioi*, the families would answer, *whioi-whioi*, they would say, back and forth, all day long. It was that endless talk that made them easy to hunt.

"Do you think one of them was in truth the Tongan prince?" I asked.

My father said, "I wish I could say."

I suddenly remembered the flocks of birds I'd seen arriving earlier. What had brought them? Was something wrong on another island, was there trouble out there, beyond where we could see?

"Mother," I said. "Why don't you just give Tapoto his ink?"

"A man's moko isn't given," she answered. "It's earned."

We slapped at our legs. Even out here, in the breeze, the red flies were after us.

"He hasn't done a single thing to deserve it," she continued.

"He's organized a defense for our island," I said. "Our only defense."

Now I breathed deep. For some reason, I kept imagining an exposed brain. Like a person lacking the top of their skull, and they're talking and eating, yet up top, where their hair should be, was a visible, operating brain. I tried not to think of the sunlight shining on it or the breeze blowing across it, but of course that just made me think of it.

"Are people really eager to enslave themselves?" I asked.

"None of this is possible," my father said. "They're just two men. They're practically boys."

"If anything happened to you," my mother said to me, "I'd drown myself in the sea."

The evening had gotten to her. She said things like that when her heart was in the net.

"Those boys have their own voyaging waka," I said.

My father had no response.

"Can people be fooled into surrendering themselves?" I asked.

My mother changed the topic. "That was a powerful story you told. I know it wasn't easy for people to hear, but they need to hear it. Hardships happen. People need to be prepared for difficult outcomes."

My mind was racing. "How could a navigator never hear of Hawaiki? It's where an entire people are from, it's our ancestral land, it's the source of our blood and spirit and language."

I waited for Aroha to speak, but she only tugged at her tether.

"You wanna know the truth about the Great Wave?" my father asked.

We didn't answer him.

"It's the worst thing that ever happened to us," he said. "It stole a generation. If it had happened to you, if you'd been washed away in that waka, your mother and I would've joined you in the sea. With that being said, with that understood, the truth is this: if the wave hadn't come to cut our population in half, there'd have been so many of us that we'd already have starved to death."

I sat up. "Wait!"

"What is it?" my mother asked. She sat up, too.

"He's lying," I told her. "The Wayfinder said he'd never heard of Hawaiki. But he knew the story of Kupe and the Octopus. Kupe was from Hawaiki."

*   *
   *

I headed toward the whare where our guests were staying. As much as Finau's strange poem and the Wayfinder's comments had unnerved me, I became suddenly frightened that when I got to their dwelling, I wouldn't find them. What if they'd left? What if they'd jumped into their waka and we never saw them again?

Alone in the whare, however, was Finau. He lay on his side, eating from a bowl of whioi meat. His dining companion, illuminated by the light of a candlenut lamp, was a sack of bones, which he gazed upon as he ate.

"It's tapu to eat with us," I said, "but you can dine with the dead?"

He lifted his eyes to regard me. "My companion is actually of higher rank. So, it's actually tapu for him to eat with me. Tonight he seems willing to make an exception."

I took a step closer. From here, I could see Finau was actually observing a kiore rat, on its hind limbs to chew a bone.

"Can I ask whose bones they are?"

"To the rat, it might as well be anybody's," he said. "When you're dead, I suppose it doesn't matter who you were."

"I don't believe that. If people tell your story, you might become better known in death than in life."

The rat extended its yellow teeth through the mesh to gnaw some sinew.

I asked, "Why'd you teach your parrot those strange lines?"

"What lines?"

"About fish being wet with the sea and islands being too green?"

"I didn't teach those to Kōkī," he said. "He just picked them up. From Punake."

"So the poet is real?"

"Who would lie about poetry?"

"What happened to him, your poet friend?"

"Punake?" Finau asked. "He became the kind of figure people compose poems about."

The rat's teeth scraped dryly across a shoulder blade.

"You know your bird's out there terrorizing the island's parrots," I said. "Have you considered putting a tether on it?"

"I actually removed Kōkī's tether. Now he's free to do as he likes. If he prefers to be with me, he'll return." Finau took a bite of whioi meat. "I see you keep your own bird captive."

Wasn't Aroha's life with me preferable to the wild? Wasn't captivity for her own good?

Finau said, "My brother's at the cove, if you're wondering. I suppose that's who you're looking for."

"Why do you say that?"

Finau gave me a strange look. "Because you're both navigators."

I placed my hand over my fishhook necklace. "Of course."

"Don't expect me to understand it." He licked his fingers. "To me, stars are just things in the sky." Then he tipped the bowl so I could see it was nearly empty. "You got any more of this chicken? I could also use some kava. And perhaps a dancing girl. What's your friend's name?"

I'd never heard of kava, and I certainly wasn't going to utter the name *Hine*.

Finau took the last piece of whioi and, reaching out, hand-fed it to the kiore rat. Very delicately, almost humanlike, the rat reached up and placed its paws on the out-held meat.

I indicated the jellyfish inked onto Finau's neck. "What's the meaning behind this?"

"It's a gift from a relative," he said. "Or maybe *souvenir* is the right word. That's what you get to commemorate a journey, right?"

Nervously, I asked, "Are you going back to Tonga?"

"Of course," he said. "Yet it's not so simple. A soul can be pickled in coconut water. A person can visit the land of the dead. But once you've left Tonga, returning is no easy thing."

* *
*

The moon had yet to rise, so it was through full darkness that I headed to the cove—past the looming outlines of harakeke plants and the scurrying of rats through dead leaves. When I arrived, the waka was still tied off. Here I found the Wayfinder, sitting peacefully, legs crossed, on the beach.

"Hawaiki exists!" I declared.

He turned to look at me. "I'm sure it does."

"You said it didn't."

"I was asked if I'd ever been there. I said no."

"You said you'd never even heard of the place."

He was sitting in the wet sand above the tide line, among some shells, and he was facing away, so he had to turn to look at me. "That's what I said."

I walked closer. "But you mentioned the story of Kupe and the Octopus. Well, Kupe was from Hawaiki, so therefore—"

"Stop," he said, lifting a hand.

Pausing, I realized he was sitting in the center of an elaborate drawing in the sand. With a stick, he'd traced dozens of rings around himself, each bigger than the last, as if water ripples emanated from him. On each concentric circle was a shell. I'd almost walked upon his—whatever it was.

"Kupe was a famous navigator," he said. "Everyone knows he was from Tahiti."

"Tahiti? I've never heard of it."

He didn't seem to care that I'd never heard of Tahiti. Using his stick, he tapped his shells, moving each a tiny bit forward along its curving path.

"Earlier," I said, "you talked about a prince, one who had to pass tests, like cliff-diving and filling a canoe with slaves."

"Among other tests," the Wayfinder said.

"Is he you?" I asked. "Are you the prince?"

"Do I look like a prince?"

I didn't know, but I thought, *Maybe*...

He said, "How about I phrase it like this—do I look like the type to direct foreign wars? To decide which islands will be depopulated? To announce who will forfeit their souls?"

He craned his neck to survey the night sky. Then he made fine adjustments to his model.

"Why would someone dive from a cliff?"

"Because he was forced to. At first, at least."

I asked, "You mean the prince kept doing it?"

The Wayfinder nodded. "I think that beneath the waves, he could escape his problems."

"Problems like what?" Just by the way he was talking, I got a weird feeling. "The prince, is he okay?"

"He suffered a setback, that's for sure, but soon he'll be good as new."

"What happened to him?"

"That's right," he said. "You people fancy stories. Well, here's the prince's tale: His father made him demonstrate his worthiness over and over. These tests included hurting people, which the prince didn't want to do. With every test he passed, you could see he was a little less himself. But he had to pass the tests—if he failed one, everything fell apart."

"Everything?" I wondered.

"Along came a test in which he had to, you know, *more* than hurt somebody. He couldn't imagine taking someone's life. Yet if he didn't do it—"

"Everything fell apart."

The Wayfinder nodded. "And worst of all, if he did do it, the most-dreaded outcome would come to pass. He'd become king. He'd become the person charged with commanding all of Tonga's hurt."

"What happened, how'd things work out?"

"That's the thing," the Wayfinder said. "The story has no ending."

"All stories have endings. Maybe you just can't see it. Maybe you're too busy with your stars."

"The stars never steer you wrong," he said. "They're steady and loyal and predictable."

"If the stars are so fixed, why all the shells?"

He said, "There are the stars above and the stars inside your head. Doing this keeps them aligned."

I pointed to a bag of shells on the bow of his waka. "What are those shells for?"

"That's different," he said. "That's my map."

"Map of what?"

"The islands."

"All of them?"

He shook his head, like I was a child.

I studied the circles and shells. I saw that one shell was actually a shark's tooth. "That one's different."

"The girl is observant," he said dismissively. He pointed at the sky with his stick. "There it is," he added, though I only saw a bunch of stars. "This is the comet we're following. For three months it's been crossing the sky. My master said it comes but once in a lifetime. No person gets to see it twice.

You should tell a story about that—if anyone on this island survives, then the next generation will know what they're seeing."

"What makes you think we won't survive?"

He glanced at me, but it was a look I couldn't read.

"Just what are you doing on our island?" I asked.

"You sound frightened."

I didn't answer.

"You think someone would cross the ocean to attack this place?" he asked. "There isn't anything of value on this island. There isn't a single thing that anybody would want."

Suddenly I hated him. Even more, I hated that I knew so little about the world that I had no idea if he was lying or not. "On this island, people have to earn their ink. Just what did you do to earn yours?"

He ignored me.

"Since you know so much about the world," I said, "it must have been something very profound or daring. Did you enter a hot volcano or solve the riddle of the wind?"

With my toes, I moved one of his shells out of position.

"Stop it," he said.

"Perhaps you did battle with a shark. Or maybe you're the only one brave enough to venture to islands as backward and stupid as this one."

"I didn't call your island that. I only said there was nothing here anyone would want."

How I wanted to kick sand in his face!

"If you want to know about my ink, I'll tell you the truth. I wish there was some way to get rid of it. I'd scrape it off if I could. These lines, they bring you closer to being the one who decides which islands will starve, what mala'e are burned, and whose tombstones get stolen."

Almost every time he opened his mouth, something came out that scared me.

"You think you know everything," I said. "But you don't even know the end to your own story."

"It's the prince's story, not mine."

"You told it," I said. "That makes the story yours. You wanna hear its ending?"

He tapped the shells with his stick.

"The story starts with cliff-diving," I told him. "And we learn that the prince only feels free from his father's pressures when he's underwater."

"It was a temporary feeling."

"That's right," I said. "The length of a breath. In the story, the son is hopelessly trapped. He does not wish to be king, he does not want to disobey his father, he does not want to take a life, and even if he relents, he knows there will be other tests."

"So how does the story end?"

"It ends where it began, with the cliffs. The prince climbs high and dives into the water."

He looked from the sky to me. "What does that mean? Does the prince kill or not, does he live or die, does he become king or does he fail?"

"It doesn't matter, for the story can achieve what life cannot—it can conclude in a place where the young man is free."

"Unfortunately, life is not a story."

"Is the story about you?" I asked. "Are you the prince?"

He stood, stick in hand, and turned to me.

"You may know a few things about stories," he said, "but you have a lot to learn about life. No cliff is high enough to escape the king of Tonga. Nobody dives his way to freedom from him. And I told you, the story has no conclusion. In fact, it's hardly begun. What about your story?"

I had no tale—I'd done nothing story-worthy.

The Wayfinder pointed his stick at me. "I'm sorry, but there's something I must do." Slowly, he extended the tip of the stick toward me. It seemed he would poke me in the sternum. Instead, he hooked the cord that held my pendant and lifted the necklace from my skin. Then he took my greenstone fishhook in his hand and removed it from me.

"That's sacred," I said. "That belongs to our people. It came all the way from Aotearoa."

"You bet it's sacred. Only a navigator can wear it." He hung it around his own neck, so that he wore two fishhooks and a whistle made from the bone of a moa bird. "You mentioned Aotearoa several times tonight. You must have a fondness for ice and death." He selected a shell from his chart and held it out for me to take.

I hesitated to take a step closer, looking at all the intricate lines he'd drawn.

"Don't worry," he said. "I remake it every night."

With a step, I entered his sand-sketched rendering of the heavens.

"This is the star Rehua," he said, placing the shell in my hand. "It'll lead you straight to Aotearoa. If trouble is what you're searching for, this is all you need to find it."

FIVE

THE FALL OF TANGALOA

A WORD ON SLAVERY

From time to time, this ugly word is used to describe certain Tongan practices. Such suggestions are ludicrous, however. The Tongan language doesn't even have a word for slavery. There's the term *hopoate*, but this form of bondage is exclusive to war captives. There's *nofo pōpula*, which understood literally means "to dwell in lifelong darkness," though in practice the term describes how ordinary people serve Tonga through duty and sacrifice. And if the Tuʻitonga occasionally utters the word "slave," he describes only his frustration, not the fettered states of others. Proof is that he must employ the Haʻamoan word *Pologa*, as, again, "slave" and "slavery" are unknown terms in the Sacred South.

At the royal compound, Moon Appearing swept leaves while the other Fefine Girls discussed this very topic of forced labor. They, too, were supposed to be working, but the Tuʻitonga was away, so instead of tending fires and grooming the grounds, a Tongatapu girl named Heilala ordered the girls from rural islands to do the work, while she formed a gossip circle to complain about their conscription and exploitation, especially at the hands of the Tamahā, who, rather than teaching them anything to improve their marriageability, had so far compelled them to move stones, till soil, and haul water.

Sweeping leaves with Moon Appearing was a girl named ʻUha-tea, or Sun Shower. She spoke almost no words, perhaps to hide her accent, for there were Tongan islands even north of Moon Appearing's, a few isolated specks halfway to Ha'amoa like Niuafo'ou and Tafahi. Wherever Sun Shower was from, it was an island so small and distant she wouldn't say its name. 'Uha-tea was a big girl, tall and broad-shouldered, but perfectly proportioned. She had large, calm eyes, full lips, and her skin was heavenly.

As if the girls' complaints had conjured her, who should appear but the Tamahā herself. The king's sentries opened the gate, and she entered the royal compound without an entourage. She stopped only to study the war map: countless shells, representing warring islands, sprawling in the grass. Then she approached the circle of Fefine Girls. "I come to offer a word of caution," she said. "Tomorrow's tasks will be performed from your knees, so refrain from wearing any finery."

The fire crackled. The girls lowered themselves and nodded—the fahu aunt of all Tonga couldn't be questioned. The Tamahā spoke to Heilala, who was named after Tonga's loveliest flower.

"How's your father?" the Tamahā asked.

"His landholdings increase," Heilala said.

"I asked how he was."

Heilala lifted an eyebrow. "That is how he is."

The Tamahā pointed. "Why're these other girls at their labors while you are not?"

Heilala said, "Rural girls are much more proficient at manual duties."

The Tamahā stared at her.

"Also," Heilala said, "my hand recovers from a wound I sustained performing labors for *you*."

Heilala produced this wound, and the Tamahā examined it.

"There's a name for this injury," the Tamahā said. "A 'blister' is what it's called."

"Call it what you will," Heilala said. "Pain is pain."

As if nothing could entertain her more, the Tamahā smiled. "I hope your injury doesn't preclude you from being my helper for a few tasks." It wasn't a question. Heilala reluctantly rose. The two had begun crossing the royal compound when the Tamahā called to Moon Appearing and Sun Shower. "You two, holding those sweeping branches, come with us."

Moon Appearing and Sun Shower ran to catch up.

The Tamahā asked Moon Appearing, "Why do you consent to work while other girls do nothing?"

Moon Appearing didn't know if she should actually speak.

"And don't tell me," the Tamahā said, "that unlike all these fancy daughters of Tongatapu, you're used to doing your share."

"On my home island, the war accustoms us all to labor," Moon Appearing said. "Our chief has given our young men to the war. Now no one is spared from work, not even the chief himself."

"Let me guess," the Tamahā said. "This hardworking chief happens to be your father?"

The light was fading. It was the time of day when seabirds had roosted, though peka bats were yet to rouse. Three girls followed an older woman past the cooking fires to several middens of waste. Here, the Tamahā had Moon Appearing and Sun Shower use their sweeping branches to dig through a mound, the older woman watching as refuse was pulled from the pile.

Heilala lifted her hands in disgust. "Auntie, this is beneath you."

The Tamahā ignored her. "Oyster shells," she said. "Mussel shells. Oyster shells. Does the man attempt to live on shellfish alone?"

Moon Appearing came to understand "the man" was the king of Tonga.

"Eel bones," the Tamahā said. "Pig ribs. More eel bones."

Sun Shower seemed overwhelmed by what she saw. She spoke for the first time. "More meat is consumed here in one night than some islands get in a year."

"*Some islands*," Heilala said. "Strike me with lightning before I visit yours."

The Tamahā mused, "I'll outlive my nephew if he keeps eating fatty eels. Wait, what's that?" The Tamahā herself reached into the muck and lifted a bird skull. Its beak was like a spear-tip, its eye sockets downcast. A heron. "Maybe this is proof herons aren't extinct after all."

Moon Appearing thought of Hunga's last heron, sent south in tribute. "Maybe it's proof they are."

They relocated to the royal garden, which surrounded the royal grave. Though Moon Appearing had recently danced here, she'd been too nervous to take things in. Now she looked from plant to plant, tree to tree.

She'd never seen a garden cultivated solely for the sake of loveliness. This meant, however, that the medicinal was adjacent to the poisonous, the fragrant beside the foul. Pregnant women were famously averse to the scents of certain plants. When a pregnant woman enlisted the services of Moon Appearing's aunt, one of her first actions was to rid the pregnant woman's surroundings of nausea-inducing botanicals.

"You admire this garden?" the Tamahā asked Moon Appearing. "It was planted by the Tu'itonga's wife."

Moon Appearing said, "I'd wager she planted it only after bearing her last child."

The Tamahā took a moment to study this girl named Moon Appearing.

Passing the tomb, Heilala said, "There's a rumor that while we were on an important errand, an interloper danced for the king." She directed her gaze at Sun Shower, likely thinking that a girl from such a nowhere place must've been an exquisite dancer. Heilala sharpened her words. "I'm not a little plover blown here by a storm. My father cultivates the entire hihifo coast, so I've been in the Tu'itonga's company since I was a girl. I know he requires the loveliest, most sublime distractions when he wishes to relax, and no clumsy imitation will do."

Sun Shower's calm eyes returned no response to this charge.

They stopped before a kotone tree. The Tamahā spoke to Heilala. "Tell me if the base of this trunk is wet."

Heilala ran her fingers along the lower bark. "It's indeed damp. More greasy than anything."

"Your opinion?" the Tamahā asked Moon Appearing.

Moon Appearing sniffed Heilala's fingers. "The urine smells sweet."

"Urine!" Heilala said in disbelief, astonished at how she'd been used.

"This is where the Tu'itonga relieves himself each night," the Tamahā said. "But come, now, child, don't be precious." She bade Heilala's hand closer before touching her tongue to the pads of Heilala's fingertips. "Sweet as honey," the Tamahā said. "As I feared."

The Tamahā then strode toward the royal fale. The woman simply entered, as if it were her own sleeping chamber. Even Heilala, looking suddenly uncertain, fell silent. The candlenut lamps had been lit. Servant girls crouched in the corners, eternally awaiting royal necessities to fulfill.

Crossing to the Tuʻitonga's stack of sleeping mats, the Tamahā moved her hands about them. "They're damp. It's as I feared—his skin must purge what the kidneys cannot."

Moon Appearing said, "The Tuʻitonga's wife Pōhiva could be the source. Night sweats can accompany menopause."

"You're familiar with the workings of the body?" the Tamahā asked.

"The female body, at least," Moon Appearing said. "My aunt is a midwife, and I apprenticed to her."

The Tamahā shook her head. "Babies," she said. She said it like something was their fault. Before leaving, she visited the ceramic bowl where the Tuʻitonga kept his coconuts. "Here's the soul of my brother. I always visit him when I come. You see, he tried to kill my nephews. Then my nephews killed him." The Tamahā returned the coconut. "One day, I'll set my brother free." She looked from Heilala to Moon Appearing to Sun Shower. "*What's the old woman waiting for? That's what you're probably wondering.*" The Tamahā then mused to herself, "Yes, for what does she wait?"

Moon Appearing knew not to address such a question. When her own aunt spoke in this manner, it was only a method of layering the world with her observations, musings, and criticisms, so that after a while, no matter where you looked, you were forced to see things as she did.

"A human soul resides inside each of these?" Sun Shower asked. "Who are they, these people who've suffered such a fate?"

The Tamahā listed some names, chiefs and warriors Moon Appearing had never heard of. "Each coconut bears a unique mark to indicate its inhabitant."

Moon Appearing lifted one marked with a short line hovering above a longer one.

"The symbol of the floating mat," the Tamahā said. "You must know the story of Tuʻi Haʻatala."

"Tuʻi Haʻatala?" Sun Shower asked. "Hers is my favorite story. What woman did more? She visited every island, in Tonga and in Fisi, five hundred of them."

Moon Appearing had never heard of her.

Heilala said, "Who'd want to visit all those forsaken places? Unless one yearns for hunger and bloodshed and men who hump canoes."

"She did more than travel," Sun Shower said. "Tuʻi Haʻatala dueled a bolt of lightning and debated Hikuleʻo in the purple light of the afterlife."

"She achieved this and more," the Tamahā added. "All she had to do was sacrifice her life."

"How'd she end up here?" Moon Appearing asked. "What happened to her?"

"Men happened to her," the Tamahā said. "Tell me, child, would a world without men not be a world without scheming and dangerous play?"

"*A world without men?*" Heilala asked in disbelief. "Who'd protect and provide for us? Who'd fight the wars?"

"Men *are* prone to unsavory dealings," Sun Shower said.

"I don't know," Moon Appearing said. "On my home island of Hunga, women scheme against women all the time, though they enlist men to deal their blows, as when one woman recently sought revenge on another by getting my father to send the rival's husband to war."

"A topic worthy of more discussion," the Tamahā said. "Yet the hour of my next obligation arrives." She faced Moon Appearing, studying her in the low light of the royal chamber. "Hailing as you do from an island where young men have become scarce, I wonder if you've become unused to their company."

Moon Appearing was uncertain about how to take this line of inquiry.

"I'm in need of further assistance," the Tamahā said, "but the task involves a fine young man. So I must know if you're too modest to lay a hand upon a member of the opposite sex."

Moon Appearing flushed—she glanced around, feeling a sudden desire to escape this woman's company.

The Tamahā, for no reason at all, took this as a yes.

"Come, then, child," the Tamahā said. "I've a special task for you."

In the old days, royal blood was not enough. Being the son of a king did not guarantee succession. Princes had also to face challengers in combat, clashes that often ended in death. Hoping to preserve their sons, Tuʻitongas began replacing these clashes with tests designed to demonstrate a prince's strength and fortitude. Lolohea, for example, had performed time-honored feats like hefting stones, hanging from a tree, and lowering the club on a condemned man. For him, only this last test remained until he was eligible to become king.

So, on the south-facing cliffs of Tongatapu, the royals gathered at dusk to witness this test. Down the coast, the blowholes at Pupuʻa-puhi were charging, and great waves crashed beneath the Hufangalupe. In the toa trees, peka bats began to stir, first stretching their wings by hanging them low, then rubbing their teeth to sharpen them. But the royals faced the sea: the lopped edges of wave-shorn cliffs, the churning water aglow from the setting sun. Before them was the end of the world, the sea extending, landless, southward, forever.

The test was called the Fall of Tangaloa. Matāpule Muʻa addressed the assembled chiefs, sub-chiefs, advisers, and dignitaries: "As the god Tangaloa descended from the heavens to the dark of earthly waters, so, too, in one moon, must a prospective chief of Tonga."

Here, the Tuʻitonga walked his son to the cliff's edge. The light was extinguishing itself. Orange had become pink and was now a downing purple. Visible below were handholds, carved into the cliffs by the ancients. "See," he told his son, "you're far from the first to perform this deed."

An open-ocean roller heaved its shoulder into the cliff, rushing up the stone to climb high and white, like it was reaching for the crown of wind-bent shrubs at their feet. The wave then retreated into an oncoming wave, and the two rose chest-to-chest, thumping like warriors at a tournament.

Lolohea said, "You don't have to worry about me."

The Tuʻitonga placed a hand on Lolohea. "Worrying about everything. That's what it is to be king."

Lolohea surveyed the assembled spectators: there was his mother, looking forlorn, her hand resting on the shoulder of his youngest brother Finau, whose hand in turn was on the shoulder of New Punake, the boy's supplemental father. There were priests on hand to bring Lolohea back to life, should he happen to drown. Assembled also were various chiefs and dignitaries. Arriving late was Lolohea's middle brother, who was nocturnal and just awakening for the night. With him was his supplemental father, Havea.

"The Second Son sets foot on solid ground," the Tuʻitonga called before pulling his middle boy near and clapping him on the back. When the king started calling you Foha Ua, or Second Son, everyone began calling you that. When the king declared, "That slave fights like he has six fists," you became Six Fists.

"And how's the great navigator?" the Tuʻitonga asked Havea. "Have you availed my boy of the wind and the waves? Have you initiated him yet? I see he wears no navigator's necklace."

"His initiation is close at hand," Havea said.

"We're aware of your sacrifices," the Tuʻitonga told Havea. "But have you given everything?"

Havea offered no response.

Matāpule Muʻa went to Lolohea and removed his whale tooth necklace. This he lofted into the sea. In the dark froth below, there was little sign of where it might've broken the surface. Lolohea turned to face the water, took a deep breath, and dove.

It was too windy for candlenut lamps, so palm-frond torches were lit.

Young Finau broke the silence, quoting the famous poem:

Loka-foli hakau tapu. *Breakers encircle the sacred reef.*

Kōkī, wings spread on Finau's shoulder, completed the couplet:

Kolo atukuou to ki lalo. *I think of you, I who am falling.*

New Punake, Finau's supplemental father, threw the boy a rebuking look. The couplet had come from "The Song of Tukulua," a famous lament on death.

Lolohea's mother walked to the edge, but there was little to see. Below was the pounding of pumice-black waves, bruising one another in the dark. Thinking of her son beneath this torrent, she found herself not breathing.

Movement on a nearby path prompted Six Fists to level his spear.

Arriving without torches was the Tuʻilifuka, leading his leashed war brides. Not far behind was Mateaki, followed by his father, ʻAho. When ʻAho stepped into the light, the sling of his wife's bones was visible over his shoulder.

Six Fists lifted his spear. "Where I'm from," he told 'Aho, "we also bundle the bones of our loved ones."

The Tu'ilifuka ignored this entreaty. He asked the Tu'itonga, "Where'd you get this guy?"

"This is Six Fists, my chief of security," the Tu'itonga said.

The Tu'ilifuka asked, "You trust your security to a kehe, a foreigner?"

"He's capable," the Tu'itonga said.

"He looks capable," the Tu'ilifuka said of the tall man. "I asked if you trusted him."

Instead of answering, the Tu'itonga warmly hailed his brother. "Look who's decided to join us!"

"Mateaki wanted to support his cousin," 'Aho said. "What happened to your old security chief?"

"While you were gone," the king said, "Tonga continued being Tonga without you."

The Tu'ilifuka dragged his war brides to the cliff edge, where he could glimpse the sea below. He looked unimpressed. "In these violent times, shouldn't such tests be updated? Shouldn't a prince demonstrate he can lead an assault through a mangrove or face a charging dog?"

The Tu'itonga said, "Lolohea has passed all the tests put before him."

"The prince can swim in the dark, so what?" the Tu'ilifuka said. "A month of counter-raids with us would better prepare him for his future. The war, I can report, endures."

'Aho asked, "Has Lolohea even been to Fisi? There's much to test a man over there."

This comment was really directed at the Tu'itonga, who'd famously never visited a war he himself had set in motion. "My little brother, we never took any tests." Which was true. Because their father had died suddenly, the Tu'itonga had received no preparation.

'Aho said, "But we were tested by life—by battles, rebellions, invasions at dawn. We swam all night to attack Savai'i. You must admit that it couldn't have hurt for us to know how to set a village ablaze or how to get our wounded back to the canoes before the enemy counterattacked."

"Even then you're not safe," Mateaki added. "The Fisians have the fastest vaka on the sea."

"I want to know how to set a village on fire," Finau said.

Pōhiva pulled her youngest son close.

"Your boy has burned dwellings in Fisi?" the Tuʻitonga asked ʻAho. "He's been counterattacked at sea?"

"I keep my son safe," ʻAho said. "But he's witnessed a vaka going down. Once, our own hull went down, and we had to swim for it. Another time, we had to commandeer a vaka full of human cargo."

"Troubling moments, to be sure," the Tuʻitonga said. "But in the end those are exercises in endurance and calm under pressure. These, Lolohea could easily handle."

The Tuʻilifuka tugged his war brides back from the cliff. "Then why doesn't he prove it?"

The king surveyed the assembled advisers, matāpule, priests, and chiefs, all of whom averted their eyes at the notion that Lolohea had been outdone.

Matāpule Muʻa regarded the king, saying, "The corresponding tests would be swimming the Teleki Reefs and the test they call the Old Canoe." Matāpule Muʻa raised his fly whisk. When the king gave his assent, Matāpule Muʻa would lower it, and then it would be done, Lolohea would be obligated to the two extra tests. But at the sight of his son reappearing, dripping and empty-handed, the king shook his head no.

Lolohea slung back his long hair, adjusted his loincloth, and turned to face the sea. A surging mist rose from below. He took a deep breath. When you had to hang upside down from a tree all night, there was nothing but that throbbing pulse in your head. When you had to fight one of your father's warriors by firelight, each leap and feint was everything. But then it was over, it was behind you, like it never happened. So Lolohea knew the night would end. At some point, after fumbling into fire coral and sea urchin spines, he'd find his whale-tooth necklace, and then it would be done. The problem was that each successful test brought him closer to the thing that would never end: becoming Tuʻitonga.

The Second Son spoke to Lolohea. "The whale tooth was cast in that direction," he said, pointing to the constellation Humu, the Triggerfish, which was but a smudge in the sky. "Dive for Humu, and remember, as the necklace sank, the current will have pulled it to the east."

When Lolohea dove again, he dove for the Triggerfish.

One of the war brides had been watching the Second Son point to the stars. She called to him in Fisian, saying, "A kalokalo cava ena tuberi au ki vale?" While Tongan is similar enough that one can converse with people from Haʻamoa, Tahiti, and Rotuma, Fisian is as foreign as the tongue of Vanuatu.

Havea said, "She wants to know which star will lead her home."

"You speak Fisian?" the Tuʻilifuka asked Havea.

"One picks up words," Havea said. "But you don't need an interpreter to know when a girl longs for home." Havea turned to the Fisian women and started naming their islands.

Incredulous and half-laughing, the Tuʻilifuka asked, "You trying to help my wives escape?"

"Wives?" Pōhiva asked. "You can't be married to someone you stole in a raid. And why don't you cover those poor girls?"

"I cover them every morning—with coconut oil," the Tuʻilifuka said, and smiled. "Look, this is how they walk around on their own islands."

"They're not on their own islands," Pōhiva said. "This is the *Sacred South*."

New Punake quoted lines from the poem by Tangatiʻaloa, composed after he'd stolen Mulikihaʻameaʻs new bride:

Mānoa tuʻona ke hele,	*Tug at the cord to entrap her,*
maʻana teunga ki ha pō-heka.	*to adorn her for a night of dancing.*

The Tuʻilifuka smiled and shook his head. "I haven't exactly got them to dance yet."

The Fisian maidens' attention was on Havea as he named the islands of their home. It seemed to bring them solace to hear words that, after being kidnapped across the Koro Sea, were a part of them, that constructed, name by name, the place they were of.

"Moala?" Havea asked the girls. "Matuku, Lau, Kabara?"

When the girls heard *Kabara*, their eyes went wide.

"Kabara," the Tuʻilifuka said, shaking his head like it conjured a bad memory.

Havea turned to the Second Son. "What star would get them to Kabara?"

The constellations were on full display now: Maui's Burden rising in the east, the Wild Duck to the south, the Great Vaka overhead. The Second Son lifted his finger to the Two Men. "Lua Tangata," he said.

One of the girls pointed to where the Two Men would set on the horizon like she saw her home and family there.

The Tuʻilifuka asked Havea, "You trying to help them leave me?"

"In their minds," Havea said, "I'm sure they left you long ago."

The Tuʻilifuka shook his head—in disbelief, in amusement, perhaps even in admiration for the old man's cheek. "If you're looking to get a new wife and sail into the sunset, these two are taken."

"Why would I want a new wife?" Havea asked.

The Tuʻilifuka smiled but said nothing.

"Why would I want a new wife?" Havea repeated.

"Leave him alone," ʻAho said.

The Tuʻilifuka stopped smiling. "I actually feel for you, old man. I know what it's like to lose a wife. My friend ʻAho now knows this fate as well."

It was true that when Havea went to war alongside these men, he never got out of the vaka. Men like the Tuʻilifuka took up clubs and leaped into the Fisian surf. But Havea had done his part, he'd never steered them wrong. Still, it was clear how far he'd fallen. Far enough that he had nothing to fear from the Tuʻilifuka. For what prestige was to be gained from taking a life of an old babysitter like Havea?

"No one forgets what happened to your family," Havea responded. "I remember your wife, your daughter. I remember the man you used to be."

The Tuʻilifuka neared Havea. "What kind of man do you suggest I've become?"

Before things could escalate, the Tuʻitonga lifted a hand. "You just worry about initiating my son," he told Havea. "And you . . ." he said to the Tuʻilifuka, "you'll always be a father, no matter what happened to your daughter. So don't forget that these girls"—he pointed at the war brides—"have fathers, too."

"Not anymore," the Tuʻilifuka said. "We took care of that."

It was true that the Tuʻitonga lived far from the bloodshed. He knew that in the outer islands, Tongatapu was often derisively referred to as

Molūtapu, meaning "Sacred Soft." He had to acknowledge, too, that those who lived with the prospect of death also lived with greater appetites for life—for stronger kava, rawer meat, sweeter revenge, fresher wives.

In the torchlight, the Tuʻitonga stared at the rock where Lolohea had stood. Shaken-off seawater had darkened the stone, leaving a shadow where his son had been. And a lone, perfect footprint stood wet on the dark outcrop. He'd love to hang the royal cloak on Lolohea. That's all it would take to make him king. He could do it tonight. But how long could Lolohea survive? Could he force the northern chiefs to pay their tributes, could he keep the chiefs of Haʻapai from warring with Vavaʻu? Could he handle the Tamahā? Could he control men like the Tuʻilifuka? Lolohea was trusting and good-natured, and the king had fostered that. It was what he loved about the boy, about all his sons. Yet it was time for darker initiations. He'd only put it off because the flinting of his son also flinted him.

As if summoned by a father's concern, Lolohea appeared again. The Tuʻitonga went to him. In his son's eyes, he saw someone who believed a father wouldn't ask what couldn't be done, who accepted that fathers knew what was required, and that if a son accomplished those things, if he trusted his father and did what he must, all would be well. The Tuʻitonga had never held that look, at least not after his father suddenly died. The sleeping mat of his life had been torn, and he'd never know rest again, not the kind where you relent to the deepest slumber because you were under the protective gaze of your father. He knew that the Tuʻilifuka was right, that Lolohea wasn't ready. But how to get the boy ready, short of sending him into war, where things like Fisian attack dogs awaited?

"Are you all right?" he asked his son.

Lolohea nodded.

The Tuʻitonga wanted to comfort his son. He wanted to reassure Lolo that if the necklace wasn't found tonight, he'd have the matāpule reinterpret the test so that "in one moon" meant the entire month, rather than a single night. Yet he knew that even if Lolo was successful under altered rules, no feat of swimming would assuage people's concerns. Instead, he said, "Look, son, there are going to be more tests."

Lolohea, eyes red from the sea, nodded. He turned and dove again. The truth was Lolohea had felt better since the royal necklace was lifted from his neck. And the ocean was where he felt most apart from the world. Underwater, away from everything, even in the dark, was a place lacking wholly in pressures, duties, and scrutiny. He could spend an eternity there.

Peka bats, startled, lifted from the trees. The Tamahā had arrived. With her were some Fefine Girls, her personal security team, and a trio of matāpule. Everyone went to the ground.

"Is Lolohea not finished yet?" the Tamahā asked. "A feast has been prepared. Paddle dancers dance for no one. And maidens make pōmeʻe for the pleasure of nothing but firelight."

From the ground, everyone was forced to behold the Tamahā's skinny legs. The posture of the tauʻolunga was what gave Tongan women such strong and lovely legs. How but through the tauʻolunga could a woman know herself, let alone another? Who could trust a woman who hadn't been shaped by the dance that told the story of Tonga?

The Tamahā went directly to her nephew ʻAho and bade him rise. She looked to embrace him until she realized he was flanked by fly-ridden bones. "I hope your brother has been treating you like a king."

ʻAho asked in return, "Do you think I could tolerate a single day of life as a king?"

"People can get used to anything," she said.

Glancing at the Tuʻitonga, ʻAho said, "That's what they say."

"I'm sorry to hear about your wife," the Tamahā said. "Can I ask what took her life?"

"Isn't that the question?" ʻAho asked.

"Isn't what the question?"

"*What took her life?*" ʻAho repeated, his lost-tooth lisp making the words airy and forlorn.

The Tamahā nodded sympathetically, as if this response weren't cause for alarm. She turned her attention to Lolohea, rising now from the sea. "This test is but child's play," she said to Lolohea, "for one so noble as yourself."

"I'm but a humble son of Tonga," Lolohea said.

The Tamahā said, "I've brought you a gift. Moon Appearing, will you step forward?"

A Fefine Girl advanced. She was not unlovely. She stood before Lolohea, wrapped in a belt of flowers. She had large wide-set eyes that regarded Lolohea with wonder and apprehension. The Fefine Girls were trained to cast their eyes downward, so you never got a good look at them, but this one was taking in all that transpired.

Something made the Tamahā smile. "The gift is char from my servant's cooking fire."

Moon Appearing unfolded a leaf to reveal ash. Using her fingers, she darkened Lolohea's chest in sooty streaks, her eyes flashing to his. No one could miss the moment their eyes met, then darted away.

"This will lend you humility," the Tamahā said.

Coming in contact with soot from the Tamahā's firepit put Lolohea under such tapu that only the Tamahā could lift it, which ensured a personal visit to have it removed. Still, all he could think about was coming in contact with this girl, this *Moon Appearing*. Lolohea felt the linger of her, of her fingers down his chest.

"I'll let you return to your task," the Tamahā said. "Pass this final test, and you're practically king."

"Actually," the Tu'itonga announced. "After completing this test, Lolohea will face four more."

"What?" Pōhiva asked. "We've discussed nothing of the sort. I won't have my son—"

"Fe'unga," the Tu'itonga said. "Lolohea has consented. He'll swim the Teleki Reefs and helm an Old Canoe." The Teleki Reefs were hopelessly remote, ensuring Mateaki would have had no opportunity to perform such a feat. And the Old Canoe—this test alone would cure his son of his sentimentality.

Matāpule Mu'a waved his fly whisk, ordaining the tests.

"No danger at all," the Tu'ilifuka scoffed. "One requires swimming, while the other involves nothing more than sailing."

The Tu'itonga said, "The Old Canoe involves more than seamanship, I can tell you that."

"What're these other tests?" 'Aho asked with suspicion.

The Tu'itonga said, "Lolohea will also fill a Tongan Hull."

This test was ideal, as it would send Lolohea to Fisi, but not to the war.

It would entail actual combat but not battle. And no one could question the fearsome nature of the task.

"What's filling a Tongan Hull?" Finau asked.

Lolohea said, "I've never heard of this test."

Matāpule Muʻa, concern in his voice, said, "This test hasn't been performed in generations."

ʻAho looked impressed. "And what else would you have your son do?"

Watching Lolohea interact with a Fefine Girl had given the king an idea.

"Finally," the Tuʻitonga said, "Lolohea will perform the Ultimate Test."

"What's the Ultimate Test?" Mateaki asked.

ʻAho answered, "It's when you take the life of someone dear to you." He looked to Lolohea. "Your father did it when he killed our uncle. In fact, it was the act that made him king."

The Tuʻitonga smiled. "Actually, our uncle was sadly the victim of a shark attack." Here, the Tuʻitonga glanced at the bones of ʻAho's dead wife. "Have you not also passed the Ultimate Test?"

Something flashed in ʻAho's eyes. He lowered his wife's bones on the ground and took a step forward. The Tuʻilifuka intercepted ʻAho, standing between him and the king. The two had a private conversation, talking at length until ʻAho seemed to calm himself.

The Tuʻilifuka said, "I only wish I could've saved my daughter. And I know your brother would give anything to have his wife back. Loved ones, they're irreplaceable. Consider that before committing your son to this test."

"I agree," ʻAho said. "Loved ones are too precious. I only have my son left. To shelter him, to restore him—that's the reason we're here."

"Is it?" the Tuʻitonga asked. "Is that the reason you're here?"

The two brothers locked eyes, something brewing in their dangerous silence.

To end it, Matāpule Muʻa waved his fly whisk. It was done. There'd be four more tests.

The Tamahā seemed to relish these proceedings. "Let's let the prince perform his deed," she announced. Then she left Lolohea with the famous lines:

Nofo e fuifui katafa,	*Farewell flocks of tern,*
kea tuku e fonua ko māama.	*that leave the land of light.*

Retreating with her entourage, the Tamahā exited arm in arm with one of the Fefine Girls—the Tuʻitonga could never tell them apart. Still, he took note of this, for the daughter of a Tamahā would inherit her mother's great rank. To avoid surrendering her status, the Tamahā simply declined to have children. She cultivated a red flower that ensured no child of hers would ever come to term. Now that she was past childbearing age, she would have to handpick a successor or become the last of her kind.

The royal spectators began removing themselves as well. With them went their torch-fed light.

The Tuʻitonga went to his little brother. "You sure you won't join us for the feast?"

Up close, ʻAho looked more lost than angry. He shook his head.

Before turning to leave, the king asked, "You've spent many years hunting down Fisians, yes?"

ʻAho shrugged. "I don't keep accounts."

"In all those years, have Fisians ever hunted you?"

"Hunted me?" ʻAho asked. "I don't kill particular Fisians. I consider all fair game who present themselves. And when they return the favor, when they come to kill us, they take aim at any Tongan they can, be he on a vaka, in the waves, or tree-bound by dogs."

"So no Fisian has tried to kill you, personally?"

ʻAho shook his head.

"If one did try, what would happen?"

ʻAho lifted his hand to show the black jellyfish on his palm.

The king nodded and, with his entourage, began the walk back to the royal compound.

When all had departed, the prince faced the sea. Except for the turbulence below, the expansive sea seemed eminently calm. The person who passed all these tests would receive the royal cloak. He'd also receive, among the prizes bestowed upon him, ʻAho and the Tamahā and the Tuʻilifuka and a far-off, never-ending war.

Lolohea's mother Pōhiva had lingered. When he lifted his arms to dive, she couldn't help but go to him. Her palm-frond torch, when she approached, crackled in the wind and lit their faces fleetingly, like offshore lightning. She touched his cheek.

"Kuo pau ke ke 'alu," she said to him. *You must go.*

"Pea ko koe e nofo," he responded. *And you remain.*

It was the old navigator's farewell, offered when one person was departing on a sea voyage, a farewell that acknowledged that when venturing upon the waves, all possible outcomes were bad, save for one—the grace of landfall.

But to Lolohea, he was the one who got to stay and dive. He'd been diving all his life, it was how he first faced his fears, back when his father made him step, afraid, off a sea bluff as a child. No, he was strangely at home. It was his mother who had to venture into the treacherous, gossipy waters that swirled around the royal compound.

"It is you who must go," he said. "And I remain."

When his figure turned and fell from view, she placed her torch at the rock's edge, so he might see the handholds that would lead him back to her.

SIX

CELESTIAL NAVIGATION

While Lolohea continued his cliff-diving and the island's elites headed to a feast, Havea and the Second Son returned to their vaka, the *Pelepeka*, the *Tamed Bat*. Its pandanus sail was dyed red so that sentries on other Tongan islands would know the king's son from Fisian war parties.

When they pushed off, heading for the hihifo coast, it became clear the Second Son had taken the wrong lesson from his time ashore. Instead of better apprehending the nature of dangerous people, he'd somehow been enamored with the island's guests. "Lifuka," the boy said, with the awe that comes when you're seventeen and you encounter men like 'Aho and the Tu'ilifuka, men who hail from a land you're forbidden to visit, men whose scars glowed by torchlight.

"Lifuka's an island, like any other," Havea told the Second Son. "They pass the kava when you're born, they place black stones when you die."

Where moonlight had broken through clouds, the dark sea flashed like fish scales.

"Yeah, but," the Second Son said, "you saw the chief of Lifuka. You saw my uncle. Think of what they've seen. You've been to war, right? I mean, back before you retired."

Retired, that was one way to put it. "Your father apprenticed you to navigation so you won't have to see what those men have. While the navigator may sail to war, he's too valuable to lose. He never leaves the canoe."

"So you're always telling me. But—"

"No buts," Havea said. "The navigator's only duty is to his passengers. He doesn't even select the destination—he only steers the course."

"Our most famous navigators undertook voyages of great discovery. Ovava and Tulikaki and Māsilafōfoa set their own courses."

"Ovava and Tulikaki and Māsilafōfoa are dead. They got lost and never returned. Why they're so revered, I'll never know."

"At least they didn't retire," the Second Son said.

Once they rounded the cliffs into open water, the tightly woven sail crackled with the prevailing wind, and their bows rose to greet the open-ocean rollers. The Second Son sat on the navigator's perch, adjusting the sheet rope that filled and spilled the crab-claw sail. Havea worked the steering oar, allowing a dangling foot to clap the waves.

The Second Son, after a period of silence, said, "Maybe I'll still ask my father if I can go to Lifuka. It doesn't have to be about your wife. People say she's fine, anyway. Maybe if my father sees I can handle Lifuka, he'll let me go to Fisi, and then, who knows—I've always wanted to see Tahiti. What about *Vanuatu*?" This last word was said with complete awe.

Havea made no response. Leaving his family was the single hardest thing he'd ever done. He couldn't bear it twice. If he set foot on Lifuka, if he took one glance at his wife and sons, he'd grab them and run. But abandoning his mission, making an escape, that was the easy path. It required a greater strength not to act. And he knew, deep down, there was only one safe passage through his trial: the longest and most arduous one.

Passing before them were isolated beaches, patches of mangroves, and dark promontories that flashed white with wave froth. They skirted the loud and endless breakers off 'Ahononou, Havea watching the Second Son closely. The boy was a fine sailor, attentive to the varying levels of wind as it patterned the water's surface, to the draw of the current as reported by the drift of their wake froth, to the color of the water as an oracle to the reefs below. He knew the trade winds, the trusted passages, the dangerous surges of inlets. He knew all the stars you could sail by, their horizon points, progressions, and zeniths, and he could tell the whole of the sky by glimpsing a single star. He could orient by the regularity of the waves, and he could estimate his proximity to unseen land by the variety of seabirds that ventured varying distances from shore.

But being a sailor and a navigator were two different prospects. Navigation was about going to war with doubt as you held a course for weeks beneath cloud cover that rendered the sun and stars positionless. It meant giving the command to sail on when a vaka in your flotilla went missing, or calling for canoes to be swamped in a gale. It meant transporting any cargo—the dying, the dead, and the black stones to mark their graves.

The Second Son spoke. "You know what would be the greatest voyage? Pulotu, the island of the afterlife. All the stories tell us it's to the south, so we have the direction. Think of it—we could bathe in the river of life and eat from the puko tree, whose fruit is nourished by the souls of heroes."

A bitter grunt escaped Havea. "Yes, sacred Pulotu."

"You haven't lost your faith, have you?"

"My faith in the place where loved ones find reunion?" Havea asked. "I ask you, if a place exists to salve our pain and make us whole, why would the gods hide it, why place it in the southern waters? No navigator has ever found Pulotu. No navigator has even returned from the search. So get your mind off the horizon. Serious tasks lay before you. Your brother must now perform the Old Canoe. Who do you think will steer that ship of horrors? You will. And who will chart the course into enemy waters when Lolohea fills a Tongan Hull?"

"Are you mad at me?" the boy asked. "I feel like you've been mad all night."

The moon was over 'Eua now, illuminating its oyster-colored cliffs.

"I'm not angry," Havea said. "I don't know how else to say it. Only on behalf of his passengers does a navigator risk the sea."

The Second Son brightened. "But that's what I'm talking about. That's why we'd make perfect explorers. After I'm initiated, we'll be twin navigators. You'll be my passenger, and I'll be yours. Together, there'll be no challenge we can't meet."

Havea pulled hard on the steering oar, bringing the bows about.

"We're changing course?" the Second Son asked.

"I'm going to introduce you to some people," Havea said. "People who've lost so much they can't remember what they once had."

Soon they approached a secluded cove on Tongatapu's southern coast. Here, the wave-break was calmed by a ring of black cliffs that leaned over the water as if lowering themselves to breastfeed a sleeping sea. Woodsmoke was in the air, as was the smell of chickens and the singe of hog hair. Slowly, in the moonlight, they began to discern the outlines of dark hulls, tethered together.

"These are nomads," Havea said. "They follow the seasonal winds. On occasion, they pass through Tongan waters, tying off in remote places. They do some trading—then slip away." Havea explained how, having long ago lost their islands to invaders, they'd given up the need for land altogether.

"What islands? What invaders?"

Questions from a young man who'd never lost anything. Havea went on, explaining how nomads called little attention to themselves, shielding their fires and rarely setting foot ashore. He pointed out the unique design of their vaka: long double-hulls placed close together, resulting in short, cramped decks, but offering the ability to crest two ocean rollers at once.

"I recognize this canoe," the Second Son said.

Vaka of this design were carved into Tonga's oldest rocks.

Moonlight revealed bundles of root cuttings swinging from the nomads' mast, while fish traps were lashed to the stern. Hogs had adapted to life in the hulls, each pig with a thwart to its name. Fisian parrots were tethered to the yardarms, and chickens roosted in the folds of lowered sails. Carved along the hull was a lone insignia: a frigate bird, wings bent, tail split, mid-flight.

Havea produced a perfect obsidian blade, the kind you keep handy to cut a rope in a hurry. He handed this to the Second Son. "Always have a gift for the nomads. I offer them tokens of the land, since their world is water."

"Would a gift not shame them?" the Second Son asked. "For they are nobodies with nothing, and they might feel obligated to offer me, a Tu'itonga's son, an extravagant gift in return?"

Havea offered no response. There was no correcting the boy's sense of himself.

When they'd tied off, the nomads' navigator boarded and embraced Havea, the two of them touching foreheads to exchange the breath of life.

"Vaha-loa," Havea said. "It's been a season."

"You look well, my old friend," Vaha-loa said. "I didn't think I'd see you on this pass through Tongatapu. I thought you'd be in Lifuka, you know, at a time like this."

At a time like this, Havea thought. When his wife was sick.

"You know my obligations here," Havea said.

"Of course," the nomad said. "We all know your fate." He turned to the Tuʻitonga's son. "You must be the young navigator I've heard about."

"I'm not a navigator—not yet," the Second Son said, offering the obsidian blade. "A small token of appreciation from one who follows in your wake. Your generation shows us the way."

Havea nodded in approval—the boy, used to royal encounters, was good at protocol.

The nomad accepted the blade. "I'm grateful. We must sail to the volcanic island of Kao to obtain blades like this. Your father owns Kao, yes? Just as he owns all the islands in these waters. I'm told he even has an island all to himself—'Ata."

The Second Son nodded. "He has more islands every year."

"Tell your father you met a man who claims life is easier without an island to rule, let alone hundreds of them." Vaha-loa then opened a pigskin pouch. From it, he produced a human tooth, glowing in the moonlight. This he placed into the boy's hand. "Here's a gift in return."

"A tooth?"

"Everything has a story," the nomad said. He then touched the fishhook necklace hanging against his chest. "You'll soon have one of these, yes?"

"If I'm found worthy," the Second Son said before indicating the fishhook necklace around Havea's neck. "I hope to inherit my father's necklace."

Vaha-loa offered Havea a look of alarm. Havea was far from this young man's father, and his fishhook pendant was destined for one of his own sons.

The Second Son indicated the insignia on the nomad's vaka. "I see you revere the frigate bird. Tongans also honor this bird who nobly receives the tributes of lesser birds."

"I don't know about tributes," Vaha-loa said. "We admire how the frigate stays unendingly aloft, dismissing any need for land." He pointed to the last vaka. "My oldest child has a project that might interest you." There, a young woman blew a whistle that made no sound. Moments later, a frigate bird descended to a perch. Before it could fold its blade-black wings, another dropped from the sky. "There's an old story of frigate birds being trained to indicate distant land. So far, we've only got them to come when called. Have you ever fed one?"

"I've never been close to one," the boy said. "So rarely do they touch the ground."

The nomad waved him on, and quickly the boy was moving from vaka to vaka, setting each in motion as he crossed the decks. Now the men could speak in earnest.

"Ten years?" Vaha-loa asked, shaking his head.

"It's only been nine."

"If you say," Vaha-loa said with a bitter laugh. "The boy's insufferable. How can you stand him?"

"It's not his fault. His father has pawned him in favor of his older brother."

"I trust the Tuʻitonga will reward you handsomely, yes? Will you get an island?"

"I only want my freedom."

"Can't you just hang a necklace around the boy's neck and be done with it?"

"It's not so easy," Havea said.

"Yes, it is. Do it today. Your family needs you."

"Have you any word of my wife?"

"How long does she have to be sick for you to go to her? Her illness was last season's news. Regardless, your sons need you. If Vaivao dies, your boys'll be conscripted to fight in Fisi."

"What am I to do?" Havea asked. "The king's son isn't ready. He'll get himself killed out there."

"He'll never be ready. No wet-nursed boy can become one of us. How'll he find self-reliance if he thinks his father'll rescue him from any danger?"

Havea made no response.

"Have you put everything into him?" Vaha-loa asked. "Or have you held back?"

"There are things he's not ready to understand. The hardest lessons remain."

"Listen to me," Vaha-loa said. "Family is all one truly has."

The bows of the other vaka began rocking in the dark. The Tu'itonga's son was returning.

The nomad leaned toward Havea. "When your anchor becomes entangled on a foreign reef, you have to cut the line."

The Second Son returned in a state of glee. He was holding the whistle on a cord.

In the low light, Havea could see it had been polished by time to the luster of ivory.

"When I said I liked the whistle," the Second Son said, "the girl gave it to me."

"This is too generous," Havea said. "We cannot accept."

The boy's face flashed with betrayal. His father's life was a constant parade of gifts and tributes.

"Nonsense," the nomad said. "The honor is ours, but only if you accept."

"Son," Havea said, "you yourself know that whistle is part of a project to tame the frigate bird. It's a valuable object, one they need."

Vaha-loa took the whistle by the cord and hung it from the boy's neck. "Another can easily be fashioned."

Havea, with a look, relented, and the boy beamed, blowing the soundless whistle.

The nomad lifted a hand. "You must be careful. While it can summon the frigate bird, it can also bring forth dogs."

The boy now doubly admired the whistle's power.

"What'll you use it for?" the nomad asked.

"He wants to discover new land," Havea said.

The nomad's eyebrows went up. "If you ask me, we could stand to lose a little land. We lost the path to Aotearoa, and now we don't murder them, and they don't murder us."

"An entire island, lost?" the boy asked. "Did someone forget the star that leads the way?"

"We know the star," the nomad said. "It's Rehua."

"Yes, Rehua," Havea said. "The problem is, Rehua is what the people on Aotearoa call it, in the Māori language. What you would call the star in Tongan, which star it is in our sky—that's anybody's guess."

The impossible notion of losing an island was visible on the Second Son's face.

"I have a hunch," the nomad told the boy, "that if anyone can find a lost island, it'd be you. I can tell when someone has what it takes to be a navigator, and I predict you'll soon join the ranks of the initiated."

The nomad, showing a sly smile, looked to Havea, but Havea was regarding his pupil, this boy who was not his boy, but who was the closest thing.

As they sailed away, the night sky was speckled with high, tight clouds, overlit by moonlight. It gave the impression of pressing matters taking place on the clouds' far sides.

The boy pulled the tooth from his waistband. "*Everything's got a story*, that's what the nomad said."

"That's probably true."

"That nomad sounded pretty sure I'd soon be made a navigator."

Havea said nothing. The boy could right a capsized canoe ten times in a row, but canoes never capsized on sunny days in Tongatapu's lagoon.

"Why do you think he gave me a tooth? What do you think its story is?"

"No idea. It's no ordinary tooth, though. See how it holds great luster? You ever see an adult with teeth that bright?"

The Second Son shook his head.

"That shine means it's been polished in the belly of something."

The young Second Son turned the tooth in the faint light. "I really liked those nomads. It's funny how the lowliest people can be the most interesting."

"Did that girl really offer you the whistle?" Havea asked. "Or did you demand it?"

"No one forced her to give it to me."

Havea said nothing.

The Second Son asked, "How come you never told me about the nomads?"

"The existence of the nomads, that's between you and me, got it?"

"Do you think my father knows about the nomads?"

"About these nomads? No. But he knows there must be nomads. He has a feast every time an island is depopulated in Fisi."

The Second Son was quiet.

"Now you've met the people who get their islands taken. When Tongan war parties arrive at dawn, people run for the canoes. Little do they know they might never leave them. Understand that an island isn't a place, but a people. And no one in the ocean empties more islands than your father."

They sailed on in silence. The Second Son tightened the sheet to trim the wind as Havea used the steering oar to face the waves. The boy lifted the whistle to his lips, but, as advised, refrained from blowing.

"It's a lot to take in," Havea said. "You can't be expected to make sense of it all. If there's one lesson to take away from tonight, it's this: always be a friend to the nomad. Promise me you'll do that, and tonight will have been a success."

"Is that some kind of old navigating tradition?"

"It's just life, son. It's sharing the same sea. A single wind fills our sails. Plus, you never know how things'll work out. One day you might find yourself without a home, without your family. You might discover you're a nomad yourself."

The Second Son thought that was pretty funny. "Oh, Master, I'm the opposite of a nomad. I'm a son of the Tuʻitonga. All homes are my home."

"The opposite of a nomad isn't someone with a home. The opposite is a captive, and from the eyes of a captive, the nomad appears the freest person upon the sea."

A WORD ON THE NAVIGATORS OF YORE

The Story of Ovava

Ovava had apprenticed to the blind navigator Tutia, who could tell which islands were near by tasting the water that flowed between them. Ovava's own specialty was finding land by observing birds. He noted where the constellation Toloa, the Wild Duck, rose on the southern horizon each night.

Did it not follow that if *real* ducks rose and flew from *real* islands, land would be found under the rising stars that formed the Wild Duck? On this course he set sail one night from the rugged island of 'Eua. He said goodbye to his children and to his red-shining parrot named Teki. Then he turned to his wife. "You must go," she spoke to him. "And you remain," he responded. Finally, he bade farewell to the god of 'Eua, Tafakula, who advised him to bring bananas as an offering to the god of the island he discovered under rising Toloa.

Ovava wisely voyaged against the wind. This meant making long tacks and gaining little headway. But this is the prudent way to explore—if difficulty is encountered, and one is forced to turn back, the wind will bring you swiftly home. After three days Teki escaped his tether and flew across the water to Ovava, using the smell of bananas as a guide. People knew only that a man and a bird were venturing together against the southern winds, somewhere on a terrifying and inhospitable sea. Weeks passed, months. People had almost forgotten about Ovava until Teki flew home to share harrowing accounts of white floating islands, a sun that never set, and tremendous, jade-colored waves that rolled ever to the east until Ovava's vaka finally rolled with them.

The Story of Tulikaki

After many years as a navigator, Tulikaki became caretaker for the island of 'Ata, which was the personal island of the Tu'itonga. There, Tulikaki settled with his wife and small son. Yet he grew restless. A final venture called to him: the southern waters. Tulikaki had heard of the mountainous waves Ovava had faced, so Tulikaki fortified his outrigger to stabilize his vaka. After provisioning, he bade farewell to 'Ata's god Laufakana'a, whose name means "Speaks to Silence." Laufakana'a advised Tulikaki to bring a skin of hog's blood as an offering for any island he discovered. This skin he hung from the mast's stay line. Then he bade farewell to his wife. She could speak no words in her sadness. Instead, she touched his fishhook necklace, which promised "safe passage over water." His son, alas, did not see him off. In the face of the wind, Tulikaki raised sail and was never seen again. In the morning, the wife discovered her son was missing.

Seasons later, a shark was caught on the Teleki Reefs. In its belly was a rare fishhook necklace. This was taken to a priest, who successfully extracted its story. Unfortunately, the story no longer belonged to the necklace's human owner but to the shark: The shark held much prestige in the waters it patrolled. It'd been pupped in a warm atoll in Haʻapai and spent its youth gleaning the outer islands of Fisi. Springs, it preferred whale calves, still slick from their mothers, in the lagoons of Vavaʻu. In the fall, it took seals from the shores of Aotearoa. Winters were difficult. Jackfish and triggers, and, only if necessary, a human, for they were bony. But summers, summers were for the south and the endless light, for barrel-rolling in gargantuan waves—and penguins!

One day, the shark smelled a new kind of blood. The trail led him to a vaka canoe, from which hung a bag that slowly dripped. Enthralled, the shark followed the vaka. Eventually, a boy emerged from a sack of provisions, surprising the sailor. The shark was moved by their embrace. Yet they were sailing south, toward cold and peril. The shark wanted to warn them of the ice and storms ahead, yet the dripping blood made him want to eat them, too. The shark wanted to inform them that the only island around was located toward the setting star Rehua. Yet the blood made his eyes roll back in anticipation of a meal. The shark didn't like killing whale calves and seals, though they were quite tender. He ate them because it was his duty. The noble thing was to compromise. The shark decided to eat just one human, whichever was at hand when the shark heaved its jaws upon the deck. When the moment came, when the shark rose from the water and flashed its teeth, it found the two humans curled in a shivering embrace. In honor of their love, the shark locked its jaws onto both, for it knew the feeling of roaming the seas alone. The shark then rolled them into the water—father and son grasping one another—and performed its great service to the sea.

The Story of Māsilafōfoa
A military navigator from Tongatapu, Māsilafōfoa was known for getting out of the vaka and joining the battle, hence his menacing name. Though his aggression abated as he aged, his sense of himself did not. When he heard the shark's account of land under Rehua, Māsilafōfoa had a pretty good guess which star that was. To bolster his esteem, he planned a last voyage. So certain was Māsilafōfoa of his success, he departed not in an exploring

vaka, but in a great migrating twin-hull, for he aimed to start a colony in this new land. He brought his entire family, plus servants, cooks, and orphans. He also wanted to sail with the wind, for why delay success? He departed in daylight, without stars to guide him, so people could behold his fine attire. The Tuʻitonga hung a necklace of yellow coral on Māsilafōfoa, who then raised his crab-claw sails and bade his admirers farewell. Only later did he realize he'd neglected to honor Tongatapu's god, who'd protected him for so many years. Of Māsilafōfoa's fate, no word has reached us. That was generations ago.

THE STORY OF HAVEA

Havea's story is familiar to all: how he was ten years a slave, how he made the most incredible journey ever, sailing to Pulotu, the island of the afterlife. While the outcome of his oft-repeated story is well known, his *before* is also of interest.

Havea grew up in Lifuka, where his father traded in black gravestones. As the name Tongatapu means the "Sacred South," many believed our ancestors came from northern islands like ʻUvea. A grave lined with dark ʻUvean stone, the thinking went, would connect the recently departed with their forebears.

Keen navigation was needed to make landfall at ʻUvea. Luckily, Havea's uncle was a wayfinder, and Havea, being a second son, was apprenticed early to the mast. He learned to voyage on lumbering, twin-hulled barges burdened with stone. As people were often laid to rest on remote shores, Havea had occasion to make landfall at rare Tongan islands like rugged Kenutu, smoke-spewing Kao, and majestic Tofua, with its high mountain lake.

Most young navigators dreamed of making impossible journeys, like rediscovering the forgotten passage to Aotearoa. Havea and his uncle, however, hoped only to make it to the next shore. On a vaka stockpiled with stone, they were always one mistake away from making landfall on the ocean floor. Havea's uncle was slowly going wave-blind, so he was reluctant to gaze upon the daytime sea. Instead, he held a course by feeling the regularity of waves, by the wind against his skin, and even by lying on deck and gauging the angle of the sun by the warmth on his face.

Tongans of note often died far from home, so Havea had occasion to learn the navigation stars for Niue, Tuvalu, and the peace-loving island of Rotuma. Yet Havea always returned to the little island of 'Uvea. Here lived the stonecutter's daughter. She was no delicate Fefine Girl. She could heft a stone. Havea knew she was constant, and her smile—faint and revealed to few—was true.

Families conferred, offerings were made, and one winter day, Havea sailed from 'Uvea with Vaivao, for that was her name, "Dew in the Trees." Except to visit the neighboring island of Futuna, she'd never made a voyage. So it'd never registered that the demand for her father's stone was the demand of war. She couldn't have fathomed how much loss attended the lives of Tongans, especially those of Lifuka, her soon-to-be home. She couldn't know that her new husband would be sucked into war, let alone her yet-to-be-born sons. And what woman would hazard to guess that her husband would later be conscripted for a decade to raise the Tu'itonga's middle boy? Still, as she sailed away from 'Uvea, one sight hinted at her future: her wedding mats, lashed atop a stack of funeral stones.

SEVEN

KŌRERO:
YOU MUST GO

When I woke on the beach before dawn, my hand went to my chest, feeling for the fishhook necklace. It was gone—the Wayfinder had really taken it. Though I'd only worn the pendant a short time, I felt its absence profoundly.

My mother was sleeping beside me, but my father's mat was empty. I found him inside our dark whare, gathering nets by feel. He had to have his lines out by first light.

"You're awake," he said, though we could barely see each other.

"You going to fish the Boulders?" I asked.

"We were there yesterday—no luck," he said. "We'll probably put our lines down along the Fingers or maybe go around to the Blowhole."

I placed Aroha on her perch.

"Did you solve your mystery?" my father asked.

"I think so. The Wayfinder had a different word for Hawaiki—he called it Tahiti."

My father was just a shadow in the dark. "Tahiti," he said. "Hm."

"That's what he called it."

For a while, the only sounds were of him paying out cordage and carefully looping it into coils. "You were gone for a while last night," he said. "You must have found a lot to talk about with those boys."

"I mostly talked to the older one. He tracks the movement of the stars."

"We used to know all that," my father said. "But somehow we forgot."

"There's also a comet he tracks."

"Did he tell you his name?"

I shook my head.

"Did this young man speak freely with you?"

"What's that mean?" I asked.

"Did he try to make you laugh?"

"No," I said. "The opposite."

"What did he tell you about himself?"

"Not much."

"Did he touch you?"

"No, he didn't touch me," I said, since he'd used a stick to remove my necklace. I felt my chest again, and again found it bare.

My father stopped gathering his nets. I could tell he was looking at me. "Where'd your necklace go?"

"He knew I wasn't a navigator. I'm no good at pretending I'm something I'm not."

"So you gave him your necklace?"

"Sort of."

"Did he give you any tokens in return?"

"*Tokens?*" I asked. "He gave me a shell."

"A shell."

I didn't speak.

"You're not to get in that waka of his," he said, suddenly stern.

I nodded. Then my father saw something over my shoulder. I turned to look.

It was Hā Mutu, arriving at the entrance of our whare, the black moko on his face making him look half made of night. This morning, however, the swirls and circles inked on his cheeks resembled those sand drawings of the heavens.

"If we're to beat the sun," Hā Mutu said.

"All right," I told him.

Hā Mutu grabbed Aroha and stuffed her into his game pouch. I always held my finger out like a perch and let her come to me. Hā Mutu didn't hurt birds, but a lifetime of twisting their necks will make you treat them differently. "Where's the other one?" he asked.

"She didn't come back."

Hā Mutu nodded.

I turned to my father. "One more thing," I told him. "He has a map, the Wayfinder does."

"A map of what?"

"Of where the islands are."

"All the islands?"

I nodded my head.

He thought on this a moment

"No matter what," my father said, "you don't get in that canoe."

* * *

The trees were alive with newly arrived birds. From our blind, I kept Aroha calling by tugging her tether, while Hā Mutu delicately fingered the cords that tripped our snare loops. When the wind moved the trees, drops of water tapped our faces. Ants marched across our feet. And birding in the near-dark played tricks with your eyes—I kept seeing Hā Mutu's disapproving face. Even though he hadn't shown any signs of having taken offense at the story I'd told last night, I kept seeing his disappointed expressions in the dark.

Finally, I blurted out: "I'm sorry for talking about the Great Wave."

Hā Mutu didn't respond.

"I didn't mean to hurt you," I added, more quietly. "I didn't mean to tell it. The words just went there."

From the dark came only silence.

The arrival of the Tongans had made me wonder what kind of lives people lived on other islands, but this morning I became curious about what kind of lives they'd interrupted here on ours. Were our lives normal, were we living the way we were meant to live? Or was there another life we were destined for—hunting moa birds and catching river eels in Aotearoa? Were we just biding our time on this island, the way a fish swims in restless circles when trapped in a tidal pool?

This is where your mind goes when your birding partner won't talk.

We had a successful morning, catching three parrots before the light revealed our ploy. There was only one neck left to snap. You could simply twist the head around, but that looked so unnatural to me. You could also sling the bird toward the ground and jerk its head back, but that was a good way to get bird crap on your feet. Hā Mutu preferred to give a quick, hard squeeze at the base of the head, separating the skull from the neck. When you killed a kiore rat, their little black eyes blinked shut, never to open again. But it was different for a parrot. With death, their eyes opened full, their dark pupils widening, as if they had flown across the ocean to Hawaiki, and now were beholding the entrance to the afterlife.

Hā Mutu popped the last neck, then closed the flap to his game bag.

"It wasn't your story to tell," he said.

I looked down, waiting for more to come, but that's all he said.

I know I should've kept my mouth shut. I should have stared at the ground and kept nodding, but I said, "It's also the story of our people."

"It belongs to me," he said.

"But it's important. And you never would have told it."

"It's not a story," he said. "That wave wasn't made of words. I'm the only man my age because one day all my playmates climbed into a canoe and left without me. Ever since, I've been alone."

Suddenly we heard a panicked squawk. A parrot had ensnared itself on the branch beside Aroha—this was unusual because we weren't hiding or keeping quiet. "Fate smiles today," Hā Mutu said.

But when he went to bag the helpless parrot, an entire flock rushed in. There were flashing wings, screeching beaks, and in a moment, Hā Mutu was scratched about the face, and his right ear was notched. The blood was terrible. Then the Tongan parrot Kōkī swooped in—with his beak, he freed the trapped parrot, who took flight. "Not trap bird," Kōkī declared before also freeing Aroha, who didn't move. Kōkī screeched at Aroha and made some sounds, causing Aroha to fly to me for safety.

Kōkī lifted a wing and pointed. Was it aimed at Aroha or me?

"Some not ready to be freedom!" Kōkī said, and I could tell he wasn't repeating poetry.

Then the flock took wing.

※
＊ ＊
＋

Word spread that our guests had a map of the islands. By the time I returned from birding, not only did the entire island know, but Tapoto had organized some people, my parents included, to compel the Wayfinder to show us. Outside the Tongans' whare, however, we became paralyzed by our community's great flaw: discussion.

"Rouse them," Tapoto ordered, to no one in particular.

"Weren't we instructed to not wake them during the day?" my father asked.

"Is it not suspicious," my mother asked, "that they're up all night?"

Hā Mutu said, "I'm often awake all night."

"You're an old man," Tiri said.

"I'll wake them," Hine said.

"You will not," my mother responded.

"Somebody rouse them," Tapoto said, though he made no move himself.

"Shush," Arawiwi said. "They can probably hear us."

On and on we went, until Papa Toki arrived. He simply looked inside, reporting, "They're gone."

"The waka," I said, and suddenly we were heading for the cove. Luckily, the voyaging canoe was as we'd left it—tied off and rocking in the shallows. Two pairs of feet extended from the lean-to on deck. From the mast hung twin sacks of bones. And on the prow was the collection of shells, cinched in an old fishing net. Yes, they were just shells, but they were also islands, with villages and languages and histories.

"What're you doing here?" Finau asked, rousing himself. "I told you, my brother sleeps during the day."

"We hear you have a map," Tapoto said.

"What would you do with a map?" Finau asked.

We didn't have an answer to that.

The exchange awakened the Wayfinder, who stood, gathering his long hair.

Finau said to him, "They want to see your map."

"No need," the Wayfinder said. "Tell me the island you seek, and I'll tell you its navigation star."

How were we to respond? If an island hadn't been mentioned in an old story, we'd never heard of it.

Tiri said, "Aotearoa."

The Wayfinder smiled—only the blind woman wanted directions. He dropped from the hull to stand in front of me. He was proudly wearing my necklace. The smug look on his face! While regarding me, he announced, "I already told *her* how to get there."

My father looked betrayed that I hadn't shared this. Still, he humbled himself. "Please," he asked the Wayfinder. "Can you tell us where we are?"

The Wayfinder took up a stick. "You don't need a map for that," he said. We followed him to the flat part of the beach. Here, he drew two circles in the sand. "This is Ha'amoa," he said. He took two steps south, made some dots. "These are Niuafo'ou and Tafahi, Tonga's northernmost islands." He took another step south, drew a circle. "These are the islands of Vava'u. Here, our Tongan ambassadors live, for they are nearer to Futuna, Ha'amoa, Niue, 'Uvea, and the peace-loving island of Rotuma."

"I wanna go to the peace-loving island of Rotuma," I said.

"You don't," the Wayfinder responded. He took a step south, drew another circle. "These are the islands of Ha'apai, home to Tonga's warriors." He made a dot in the sand. "From the island of Lifuka, we execute the war." He took another step south and drew a final circle, larger than the others. "Tongatapu is the Sacred South," he said. "From here, the war is administrated."

"War against whom?" Tapoto asked.

The Wayfinder took several steps to the west. He drew a circle large enough to encompass us all. "Observe the hundreds of islands of Fisi," he said.

"Your small nation is at war with such a vast enemy?" Tapoto asked.

Finau said, "We occupy but a few dozen Fisian islands, the ones nearest to us. We only take what we need, and we utilize every part of the islands—there's no waste."

We stared at these markings in this sand. This was the world. This was war. My mother narrowed her eyes. I could tell she was wondering what it meant to "utilize every part" of an island.

Almost as an afterthought, almost as if he couldn't help himself, the Wayfinder placed a lone dot to the south of Tongatapu.

When Tiri was very focused, she gazed blankly into the sky. "Did he add another island?"

"Yes, beneath Tongatapu," Hā Mutu told her. "It looks like a small island."

"Don't concern yourself with 'Ata," Finau said. "It's the personal property of the king."

"An entire island?" Tiri asked. "For one man?"

"Not for a man," Finau said. "A king."

"This is all very informative," my father said, "but where are *we*?"

The Wayfinder began walking down the beach. He walked and walked, going so far, we thought he might simply walk away. At last, he drew two small circles in the sand. With the stick, he indicated one.

"That's us?" my father asked when we'd joined.

Tapoto toed the other circle. "And what island's this?"

"Don't know," the Wayfinder said. "But it's not far off. This time of year, with the wind in your favor, it's two days away."

"You've been there?" my father asked.

The Wayfinder shook his head.

My father looked perplexed. "How do you know it's there?"

"He knows," Finau said.

The Wayfinder pointed up to the white bands of mist crowning the peak of our island. "Clouds that stand still are fixed to land," he said. "Look west. There's a cloud on the horizon that doesn't move."

My father looked stunned. "An island, that close to us? All this time?"

The Wayfinder, surprised, asked, "So you've never encountered this island?"

Shame crossed my father's face. Captain of the fishing boats, yet he never sailed beyond the sight of land.

Tapoto stared at the sand, stupefied. "What's this other island like?"

"I told you," the Wayfinder said, "I've never been there."

Tapoto eyed him with suspicion. "But how do you know it's there?"

"He *knows*," Finau said. "He can read echo waves. He enlists frigate birds."

"I've only been here one day," the Wayfinder replied, "and even I've seen parrots flying in from the west."

"You have to take us," Tapoto said without warning or consultation, his voice trembling with necessity.

"Not possible," Finau said.

"My brother's right," the Wayfinder said. "We have our own mission."

My mother tilted her head. "And what might that be?"

"Yes," Tiri asked, "what's important enough to make you cross the ocean?"

The Wayfinder said, "We told you when we arrived, we're on an errand to retrieve life."

My mother indicated the bones hanging from the mast. "Looks more like you're delivering death."

Voice quavering from age, Tiri asked, "And where'll you get this 'life' from?"

"There's an island named Pulotu," the Wayfinder said. "There, the departed can find reanimation."

"And you think this *Pulotu* is nearby?" my father asked.

The Wayfinder said, "A legend tells us that once each lifetime a comet appears to guide the way."

"Legends have their value," my mother said. "But they're not real life."

"My brother's been to Pulotu," the Wayfinder said. "Tell them, Finau."

Finau looked down. If he'd been there, he didn't seem eager to recall it.

"The island exists," the Wayfinder said. "Finau made landfall, he saw the life to come."

"I didn't travel by canoe," Finau countered. "Death took me there."

"I know the island's real," the Wayfinder said. "I know someone who sailed there. He brought a loved one back to life."

"They *say* he brought her back to life," Finau pointed out. "Yet he himself never returned."

The Wayfinder regarded his brother's uncertain face. "Don't back out on me now," he said.

"I'm not backing out," Finau said. "We've been weeks upon the southern waters. And what have we found? Nothing."

I thought, *You found* us.

"It's time to accept the truth," Finau said. He, too, looked at the bones. "They're gone."

"The comet's still in the sky," the Wayfinder said. "There's time."

"Face it," Finau said. "We should turn back. Our true struggle awaits us back home."

Tapoto said, "The people on this neighboring island might know something about this Pulotu place."

"How do you know the island's inhabited?" Finau asked Tapoto. "You just learned of its existence."

"A parrot flew to us," I said. "Around its foot was a ring of greenstone."

"I hate to tell you," the Wayfinder said, "but parrots can cover vast distances."

"Greenstone?" Finau asked. "What those tools were made of? And that weapon we talked about?"

"The mere club," Tiri said. "Said to absorb a person's mana as it induces permanent sleep."

"We could use such weapons," Finau said to his brother. "With them, we could take back Tonga."

"Hold on," my father said. "These items are sacred, they belong to our people."

Finau turned to my father. Dismissively, he asked, "And what would you do with a weapon?"

The Wayfinder shook his head. "We already have a destination."

"Was this destination selected by the dead or the living?" I asked the Wayfinder. "Or by you?"

He gave me a quizzical look.

"The navigator never selects the destination," I told him. "He's bound by a single duty: taking others where they need to go."

The Wayfinder seemed to reappraise me. "How is it you don't know a star in the sky, yet you comprehend the essential rule of being a navigator?"

I didn't remind him that he'd told us this rule the night before.

Finau asked, "You really think there'll be more of this greenstone on that island?"

"It only follows," my father said.

Finau asked, "And you think there could be clubs made of it?"

Tapoto nodded. "Mind you, we've never actually seen one of these green clubs."

"Oh, I have," Finau said. "I've beheld one making entrance into the temple of the human mind."

Finau turned to his brother. "It would be a quick trip."

"One night," Tapoto said. "We'll spend one night and no more."

The Wayfinder shot me a look, suggesting this was my fault. "There'll be rules. My commands won't be questioned. And you understand that not all islands are passive like this one. People respond when you land on their beaches."

Tapoto said, "We agree in advance to your terms."

"When the constellation Haʻamonga ʻa Maui rises," the Wayfinder said, "we depart."

EIGHT

NIGHT SONGS

Pōhiva's name was formed from original terms. *Moana* was the first word. "Ocean." *La'ā* and *māhina* followed, the "sun" and "moon," which separated *'aho* from *pō*, "day" from "night." Next came *tangata* and *fefine*, "man" and "woman." *'Ofa*, "love," naturally followed. This gave reason for *me'e*, "dance," and for *hiva*, "song."

Though her name meant "Night Song," Pōhiva's evenings weren't occasions for singing. Night was when she reviewed her day and contemplated how tomorrow might go. Tonight, atop a stack of sleeping mats, she kept imagining her eldest son falling from a cliff; in her mind, he didn't even enter the water before he fell again. And now her husband had added more tests.

When they were newly married, Pōhiva and the Tu'itonga would stay up, discussing the latest intrigues and developments—who was rising at the kava circles, what marriages were in the offing, the Tamahā's latest subterfuge. Each night, she and her husband shared insights and interpretations and, before sleep, agreed upon tomorrow's course corrections.

Now, in the low light of candlenut lamps, she glanced at her husband, softly snoring. He'd become a man who no longer second-guessed his days. The future, and not the past, was his sole concern. She asked him, "Did you hear Finau declare he wanted to burn a village?"

The Tu'itonga snorted in his sleep. "Learn," he said. "The boy wants to *learn* to burn a village."

After the Tu'itonga became king, he took to the sea in a series of campaigns to stabilize Tonga. This meant subduing rebellions, unifying island groups, and dealing with defiant chiefs. Pōhiva, a new Fefine Girl, first met the Tuʻitonga as he returned from one of these campaigns. After making landfall, the Fefine Girls would garland the men to restore their fonua, their connection to their home soil. Then, to remove any residual hate in the men's hearts, a Fefine Girl danced for each of them. What was more restorative? What could better repair a man? By chance, Pōhiva danced for the new king. He was filthy from battle. He was brash and impatient, but she knew the war had done that to him, that it could be undone. She didn't alter her moves, she didn't let her eyes fall upon him, not even when he tied an ifi vine around her arm.

The next time the Tuʻitonga returned home, he stood apart from his warriors, who were weary and had been mohe toto, sleeping in blood. The king, however, appeared fresh and energized. He'd somehow found a way to bathe and adorn his topknot with feathers. Landing, he went directly to Pōhiva. Dancing before him, however, she could see the spots he'd missed in his post-battle cleanup, like blood, still crusted, inside his ears.

Now, in the low light of the sleeping chamber, Pōhiva spoke again: "Could you believe the stench of those bones? Why would ʻAho parade his wife's remains like that? Does he aim to punish us?"

The Tuʻitonga mumbled, "The man punishes himself."

After they were married, and following the births of their sons, nightly discussions about the pettiness of matāpule and the ambitions of sub-chiefs seemed frivolous. Their boys became the only topic of before-sleep conversation. Pōhiva's constant review of her sons' development had two origins. First was the fact that their mothering had mostly been taken from her. As each boy was born, a suite of servants began washing, feeding, and attending her sons' every concern. Second, as the boys grew, it became clear her sons were exposed to a corrupting influence: their father. Though the Tuʻitonga prevailed in his campaigns, he didn't stop pressing the fight, returning from distant beaches wild-eyed, brimming with energy. His manner coarsened, his humor darkened. He began displaying an indifference to the fates of others, which is not a good quality in a husband, let alone a father.

Pōhiva attempted to counter these effects of combat. When the Tuʻitonga returned from campaigns, she plied him with social activities:

dance contests, singing, and large feasts with much interaction. Next, she looked for ways to insulate her boys from their father's bloody trade. She advocated that Lolohea raise pigeons, a peaceful and meditative pastime. Finau would take up poetry. And of course second sons were born to navigate. Finally, in response to the expanding war with Fisi, she convinced her husband to deploy 'Aho, not as a strategist or a commander, but as a lead warrior, charging first up the beach with enough fire to ignite the men behind him. Eventually, Pōhiva figured, news of 'Aho's death would signal to her husband that it was time to set aside his own club. It was a good plan, except that 'Aho didn't die.

The Tu'itonga's lust for war gradually subsided. Feasts grew larger, entertainments more elaborate. But the apprenticeship of her sons to poetry and navigation came back to haunt her after her husband placed them in the custodial care of supplemental fathers. That left her with a single son and a lone topic of nightly conversation: Lolohea. It wasn't long before her husband had fatigued of this perpetual discussion.

"How can you sleep," Pōhiva asked, "while our son might be drowning?"

The Tu'itonga's eyes opened. "I'll have you know that I was in the middle of a portentous dream."

"But Lolo is—"

The Tu'itonga lifted a hand. This was his gesture for *fe'unga*.

She went quiet. She'd have to bide her time, appease him, then circle back to Lolohea. "I can tell," she said, "that it was a powerful dream."

"It carried a message I must decipher." He scanned the lodge poles above, like the meaning he sought might be found among their bundled wedding mats. "In the dream, I saw sparks lifting from a fire. They rose high and began drifting across the night sky. Then I was in the sky. I was drifting. From that height, my entire life was visible. I saw life's next installment."

Pōhiva thought on that phrase, *life's next installment*. Not long ago he was given two supplemental wives, and she wondered if they had anything to do with this dream. These fokonofo slept together like girls, for that's what they seemed to Pōhiva, girls. What could a girl know about being the mate to a great man? Still, the Tu'itonga often disappeared, just before dawn. Where else but to them?

To his credit, the king had been against extra wives. But matāpule weren't known for relenting. *Backup heirs are necessary*, they said, *should the worst occur*. So maidens were selected from rural islands. Pōhiva believed her husband when he'd said he didn't want them. But once maidens were at your disposal—well, men do have appetites. And carnality had gone missing from their own marriage.

"Sparks rose from the fire," he continued. "They led me south, across open water. Below, in the dark waves, I saw a purple island."

A purple island, she thought. Pulotu, the island of the afterlife. Perhaps it was mortality he contemplated. "Your entire life was visible?" she asked. "Could you see your birth, your . . . death?"

"My demise was there to behold. I fear the end's within sight."

"I have an irrefutable reason you're not going to die," Pōhiva said.

"What's that?"

"You have too much unfinished business."

The Tuʻitonga laughed. "So true."

"The Second Son is still uninitiated."

"Years of sailing," he said, suddenly animated. "And still Havea won't make our boy a navigator!"

"There's Finau."

"You must admit," the Tuʻitonga said, "it never hurts to know how to burn a village."

"There's the topic of your brother."

The Tuʻitonga took an involuntary breath.

Walking back from the cliffs, they'd discussed the topic of ʻAho. It was more idle talk than anything, since the notion that a team of Fisian killers might be following him, that an assassination could happen here, in the Sacred South, was so unthinkable.

"Earlier," the Tuʻitonga now said, "I'd worried that if ʻAho discovered I'd known about the attack and hadn't warned him—well, the long-dreaded clash we'd always avoided would commence. But now I consider the case in which Fisian assassins were successful. I mean, what if they killed ʻAho? What if I could've saved him but remained silent?"

Pōhiva had previously used facts to dismiss the notion of a Fisian attack—that ʻAho hadn't even been here an entire day, that no such attack had ever happened before, that the Tamahā was famous for wrong-footing them. But now Pōhiva dismissed this notion as contrary to the way of the world.

"If only life were so elegant," she said. "If only our biggest problems simply solved themselves. We should be so lucky to have the Fisians come to Tongatapu and with one stroke free 'Aho from his pain and anger. It would double the Tu'ilifuka's desire to take the fight to Fisi, it would justify a great reallocation of resources toward the war, and with the adoption of Mateaki, it would gift you with a new heir, one those fokonofo wives have been unable to provide. And if your brother died by surprise attack, it wouldn't have just been your doing, it would be ours, yours and mine together."

The Tu'itonga gave her a warm smile; it said, *I chose the right woman.*

Now was her chance to make an appeal. "And you must admit," Pōhiva said, "that when it comes to unfinished business, your most pressing concern is Lolohea."

"Fe'unga!"

"No, you can't just say *enough*. He's underwater right now. He's in those waves because he wants to please you. He wants to see himself in your eyes, but he's miserable. Leading men into battle, exacting punishments? That's not who he is."

"Was my smile real?" the Tu'itonga asked. "At his age, I had to fight the outer-island wars."

She looked into her husband's eyes. "Lolo's not like you, and you know it. Your men followed you, you won the battles. You take counsel with the extracted souls of your adversaries. That's who you are. When your son needs advice, he talks to pigeons."

He said, "First of all—"

"Admit it. We've tried to spare Lolo from brutality, and now you're expecting him to match your warrior nature. You must rescind the extra tests."

"Our son is stronger than you think," he said. "Do you forget his previous test? He stepped forward like a man to deliver his first execution. It didn't go as planned, but it was a success."

On the topic of the execution, she couldn't even speak. The test was called Tautea Mate, in which one delivers a lethal punishment. The recipient was a thief, who kept wincing in anticipation of the blow. Lolohea hesitated, requiring a second stroke to finish the task. "He changes with each test," she said. "He hardens. I'm worried the boy who finishes these tests won't be the same who started. Who would trade a son for a stranger in a feathered cloak? What's the hurry, anyway? Your father died suddenly. You were unprepared. All the more reason to show patience in preparing Lolohea. There's time. We're safe. This is Tongatapu, not Lifuka."

"Do you feel safe?" he asked her. "All the time in the world, is that what you think? That Fisi will halt their counterattacks until Lolo's ready to lead? That Ha'amoa will submit forever? You're worried, I understand. Yes, the water's turbulent. The night is dark. But these tests are about determination. And determination, Lolohea has." The Tu'itonga lifted a wooden basin. He splashed rainwater on his face. "The night my father died, my uncle came to kill us, me and 'Aho. I was younger than Lolohea."

He began topknotting his hair, a sign he'd take his leave of her, likely to visit one of his new wives.

He turned to her. "You never know the powers you possess until you're called upon to demonstrate them. There's more to Lolo than you know. In this regard, he'll surprise even himself."

She wanted to tell him there was a vast difference between defending yourself from a murderous uncle and executing a kneeling peasant, let alone filling a Tongan Hull.

But the conversation was over. The Tu'itonga stood, stomping each foot for the sake of his poor circulation, before disappearing from the light of their candlenut lamps.

The moon did indeed rise over the ancient island of 'Eua. Its glow gifted waves with white, curling beards and broadcast shimmer patterns upon the sea's trembling hillocks and skate-skin troughs. Lolohea now dove with volcanic rocks in his hands. After he broke the surface, these stones quickly propelled him to the reef shelf below, where there was light enough to see in shades of purple: urchins tumbling and reversing with the concussing waves, and sea fans bending to the fatal seduction of retreating currents. Before surfacing, Lolohea has taken to releasing part of his lungs—looking up at the bubbles, he beholds the tentacled rise of his air. Breath half spent, he becomes less buoyant and hovers, ambient in the sea, a place not at all as dark as he'd imagined: the lamp-flicker of self-illuminating jellyfish drifts like cindering palm spathe in the wind. Here, a certain present doesn't seem to exist, he sees no yellow feathers when he closes his eyes, he doesn't feel an endless ringing in his hands from the blow of a club—no one told him his fingers would ring. The now of this place contains no Tongan Hulls or Old Canoes or dog teeth. There are no matāpule in this water, no decanted souls, no tests of a person's ability to detach from the world. Down here, whale teeth belong only to whales.

Here, even the past feels like it will never come to pass.

Like the lids of langi graves will never have risen.

And women on leashes will cease ever to have been.

That the Tamahā's foot has never circled your face.

That there is no royal cloak. It never has been and never will be.

The winged shadows of oceangoing mantas fall upon Lolohea—he can see them outlined against the moon-hemmed surface above. The surface, so like the face of Hinasioata, the girl-mirror goddess herself. Except that he would drown, Lolohea feels he could rest here all night, rocked between the surface and the seabed by the cush and loll of waves heaved against stone by the buffeting warp of the sea. Though he knows he's being shuttled by oceanic currents, he's in harmony with the water around him, and for once, he feels no push or pull in any direction.

The Tuʻitonga took leave of Pōhiva. In the antechamber was Six Fists, his ever-vigilant security chief. He was tall and lean, with the sharp elbows and knees that earned him his name. And in the dim light of the candlenut lamps, Six Fists half disappeared into shadow, such did his ink befriend the night.

"Looking for Lolohea?" Six Fists asked. "Want me to check on him?"

"If he saw us checking on him, he'd think we lacked confidence in him."

"But you're worried."

"Not as a king," the Tuʻitonga said. "Only as a father."

"I'm a father, too."

Six Fists was from Nuku Hiva. In Tongan at least, *nuku* meant "home," and *hiva* was the number "nine." "Nine Homes" was probably a reference to the island cluster Six Fists was from. But hiva also meant "song," and the Tuʻitonga sometimes felt he heard his security chief's unsung *home song*. When Six Fists was captured in the east, he was given to the Tuʻitonga as an exotic gift, for the shock of his appearance, for the thrill of witnessing young Tongan warriors challenge him. Six Fists, for an entire season, was the talk of Tongatapu. When the sight of him ceased to surprise, and the battle captains demystified his fighting style, the Tuʻitonga called a halt to the combat, leaving Six Fists undefeated. Greater than his unblemished record was the loto-mālohi he possessed: he was loyal and honorable. He never bemoaned his fate. He accepted the unforeseen development of capture and servitude without bitterness or lament. He cursed nothing in this world.

The Tuʻitonga made Six Fists his security chief to put Tongans on notice: there was room for improvement in their character. The king hadn't anticipated how close he'd grow to the man, how the man's imperviousness to rumor, his indifference to entreaty, and his lack of earthly desire made him the one person with whom the Tuʻitonga could share his troubles—like how he'd begun pissing blood, the impossibility of pleasing his new wives, his vexing brother. And, being from another people, Six Fists didn't supplicate himself to the Tuʻitonga, like his sub-chiefs and matāpule. Six Fists saw the Tuʻitonga as a fellow man and was more likely to tell him the truth than anyone, save for Pōhiva.

"Something else is the matter, I can tell," Six Fists said. "Has the pain returned?"

"Yes, the pain's back. But there is something else."

Six Fists signaled for kava.

"I've had a premonition." The Tuʻitonga began describing the dream he'd just had, which began with him sitting by an evening fire, surrounded by men whose lives he'd taken. "My victims hadn't healed—their wounds still gaped. Despite their injuries, they acted normal, drinking kava and conversing."

Six Fists thought on this. "Had you joined them? Or had they joined you?"

"What do you mean?"

"Had the dead returned to the ranks of the living, or had you found membership among the departed?"

"Hmm," the Tuʻitonga said. "Was I being visited by ghosts, or had I become one? I feel the answer lies in the sparks from their fire. When they began rising, I left the men, ascending with the embers, crossing the sky toward a dark island. Awaiting me on this island was my eternity."

"I doubt the dream presages your death," Six Fists said. "Might I offer an interpretation? Central to your dream are images of those you've killed, of the fire, and of the afterlife. In your waking life, the meeting place for these three things is your bowl of coconuts, which houses the afterlives of men you've struck down, all stored in a ceramic vessel, fired by your brother."

At the mention of his brother, the Tuʻitonga felt a pain in his kidneys. "Have you heard that ʻAho has gifted me with daily needle sessions?"

"You live with much pain," Six Fists said. "Yet you flourish."

"A sharp pain, a sudden blow, those I can take. But submitting to endless needles, unable to strike back or command them to stop? Plus, I'm no longer young. When did you first take your ink?"

"My friends and I stole a canoe," Six Fists said. "We were boys and didn't know how to navigate, so we became hopelessly lost. I got my first tātatau adrift upon the sea. We used soot and bonito teeth to ink the constellation Mataliki into our shoulders, for when these stars rose on the northern horizon we knew that back home people were feasting, and we had to admit that if we weren't found, our mothers would give birth to new sons who'd be taught more respect for the sea. Then life would continue like we'd never been. That's a feeling to mark. Trust me: the needles don't hurt if the ink carries meaning."

The Tuʻitonga must've looked unconvinced, for Six Fists went on:

"The ocean's too vast to comprehend. But even the seas break down to waves, and at last waves crash into mist and are gone. If you think about the needles as they descend, the pain is a pounding surf. But if you release your mind, if your thoughts become a breeze blowing up the beach, then pain's nothing but soft ocean spray."

A girl delivered shells of kava. The king asked, "Do you think the Fisians could strike at us here?"

Six Fists was amused by this turn in the conversation. "In the royal compound?"

The Tuʻitonga smiled, too. The notion was ridiculous.

"You're a good man," the Tuʻitonga told Six Fists. "I'm really going to miss you. When the day comes to set you free, I don't know what I'll do."

The Tuʻitonga passed his supplemental wives, sleeping arm in arm on their mat. He didn't linger—just the sight of them made his groin flare with the pain of trying to satisfy them. Beyond this was a dwelling for Fefine Girls, who'd wake before dawn and head to the bathing pools. There, they'd chew mohokoi leaves, tuitui nuts, and pako into a fragrant pulp with which to scrub the bodies of royals.

On a mat beneath the stars was his youngest son Finau, who was awake and talking in hushed tones with New Punake, his supplemental father, and Kōkī, his red-shining parrot.

Finau looked up, surprised to see his father. "You worried about Lolo?"

"Of course not," the Tuʻitonga said. "He's proficient at cliff-diving."

"I liked what the chief of Lifuka said," Finau said. "About learning to fight Fisian dogs."

"Let me worry about the Fisians," the Tuʻitonga said. "And tell me if your brother returns before dawn."

"Dawn," Kōkī said, then repeated lines from an ancient poem:

I ʻolunga oe tāvani māama tautau,	*Above, the swinging lamp,*
ʻoku fungani mahofa e afi ʻihe langi.	*spills fire across the sky.*

Finau shared the line, "*The palmcrests of hahake were the first to know the sun.*"

"*Sunrise is a ripe papaya,*" Kōkī said, "*loosened from its rind.*"

In the Fisian language, New Punake recited lines concerning daybreak:

Nū cuva ra kolī osooso,	*Bow down, baying dogs,*
nū moce sara ra beka,	*sleep now, peka bats,*
e vakaroji kemunū a cabe ni siga.	*the rising sun commands you.*

The surprising sound of those foreign words gave them all pause.

Finau asked, "Do dogs really howl at night?"

"In Fisi," Kōkī asked, "is human and dog friend?"

"Just let me know if you see your brother," the Tuʻitonga told his son. He was about to take leave of them. Instead, he turned to New Punake. "Is there a poem about embers rising into the sky?"

"Embers?" New Punake asked.

"Yes," the Tuʻitonga said. "A spark from a fire that floats across the sky. I dreamed of that. At some point, I was with the ember, drifting south toward a dark island."

"There is such a poem," New Punake said, reciting, "*But once a life, celestial fires bring.*"

Finau recalled the next line, "*A spark divine, each century's spring.*"

Kōkī continued the poem, "*Southward it flies, into heaven's ring.*"

They took a moment to ponder these words.

"Is the poem about death?" the Tuʻitonga asked.

"Far from it," New Punake said. "The poem's about a comet."

"A comet?"

"Yes, it's said to appear once in a lifetime to guide the way to Pulotu, the island of eternity."

The Tuʻitonga glanced at the sky. Bats were returning to the toa trees. Stars were extinguishing themselves. The heavens were free of comet-like streaks. He told these three to claim the last of their sleep. Kōkī did as he was told and covered his eyes with a wing. Finau rolled to his side and cradled Kōkī. And New Punake cast an arm over Finau, causing the boy to close his eyes within the older man's protective grasp. There was nothing to fear, though: New Punake was a harmless poet, and, just to be safe, the Tuʻitonga had had him castrated years ago.

The hour was manupunamuʻa, the time when the first birds begin to sing, though as wild birds started to vanish, people had begun calling it ʻuʻamuʻa, rooster-crowing time. The Tuʻitonga had to piss, but he knew it'd spill orange and burning. Instead, he made his way toward Lolohea's small quarters. Inside, he studied the boy's pigeons, watchful in their hutches. When the Tuʻitonga tapped a cage, a hen ducked low to regard him with an upcast eye. The other birds fanned their wings, hoping for seeds. *Tatali, tatali*, went their call—*I await, I await*—as if they knew they were decoys, born to be tethered in front of hunting blinds with the sole purpose of luring others of their kind to their fates. It was well known that Lolohea's birds were terrible for hunting: he over-tamed them with treats, but that's perhaps why the Tuʻitonga felt his son's presence in here. He tried not to think of his son struggling beneath the dark waves, struggling not because the boy wanted to become king but because his father had asked him to.

It was time to bring the urine and get it over with. While his brother waged war daily with all of Fisi, the Tuʻitonga battled his bladder. In the first glow of dawn, he finally managed a release upon a kotone tree, activating the nutmeg smell of its sap. He didn't have to look down to know what color his piss was.

He took a seat on the family tomb, the grave as large and deep as the pool in ʻAnahulu Cave. He remembered the tomb's lid being lowered over his father, who'd offered no advice, no cautions, no warnings, no preparations. The stone was brought down, and his father was gone.

A Fefine Girl appeared with a shell of kava. He swallowed the drink—*bitter as a puddle, muddied from the rain*. Hands shaking, she waited to refill the shell. "What's the trouble?" he asked her.

She rushed to leave, but he stopped her. He could never tell the Fefine Girls apart, but he recognized her as among the group he'd sent to Heketā to supply his brother. Something was wrong. He ran his eyes over her arms and torso, looking for injuries. "What's happened to you?"

She clutched the tapa cloth that covered her hips.

"Unwrap the garment," he said. "Reveal what's the matter with you."

Slowly, trembling, the girl loosened the sheet of bark cloth. It fell away, leaving her exposed before the grave of kings. Here's what he saw: inked on her pubis was a black jellyfish whose tentacles reached into the folds of her halanga-tama. He nodded, and she made her escape.

What a way to use a gift from the gods. His father had the power of distant sight. With this, he protected Tonga from far-off plots and conspiracies. The Tuʻitonga used his gift to assemble a council of wise souls. What did

'Aho do with his power? Mark the men he'd slain, and now, it seemed, the women he'd violated.

The Tuʻitonga wondered if this was an isolated incident. Perhaps distraught, wife newly deceased, ʻAho had sought succor at the expense of another. Yet what if this was the beginning of something else? If a man will overpower a young woman, in the Sacred South, there's nothing he won't do.

Earlier, the Tuʻitonga had consulted his coconuts about the problem of ʻAho. The soul of the Malietoa of Haʻamoa, a famously diplomatic figure, thought ʻAho should be exiled to the island of ʻAta. Of course that would require relinquishing his personal island, source of the king's only relaxation. Vai-Hanga-Ki-Langi, a spiritual man, thought ʻAho should be set adrift near the Teleki Reefs, where the gods of the wind could decide his fate. And of course his uncle's soul had advocated taking direct action, though there was no scenario in which killing ʻAho would be an easy matter.

Most important was keeping the focus on Lolohea. Had the Tuʻitonga not sacrificed the raising of his other sons for this reason? And with his worsening condition, the Tuʻitonga wasn't sure how much time he had to prepare Lolohea, who still thought becoming king was a matter of cliff-diving and killing a few people. Those were good tests, they built confidence, but they were far from the reality of donning the feathered cloak. Far from what it meant to lose your father, your mother, and then discover yourself surrounded by matāpule, who ordered every hog on the island slaughtered. What follows are outer-island skirmishes, entire islands defecting, and outposts being burned on far-off islands. What to do but enlist a brother to join you in the fight? Together, you raise the sails of battle. Yes, should Lolohea become Tuʻitonga sooner rather than later, famine would be his first true test, and of course hunger's the bunkmate of war.

For the second time that day, the Tuʻitonga reclined atop the royal grave. He liked to see the peka bats return to the toa trees, the faint flashes of their translucent wings, the glisten of banana juice on their snouts. Instead, his nostrils recalled the scent of ʻAho's wife's bones. It was not unlike the smell when a blade un-hammocks the abdomen, and out looping comes a basket of shiny intestinal coils. This thought was his brother's fault, and the

Tu'itonga knew there'd be many more dark associations until the problem of 'Aho was solved.

The palest dawn lit first the white fringes of shore break. Soon the sky adopted a dim cast, faint as the blue of frigate bird eggs. The stars, one by one, began relinquishing their positions in the southern sky, and the Second Son was inclined to wonder what form of obedience made them comply with the celestial order. Why were some stars destined to climb the mountain of the sky, while to the south others turned in place?

All night, the Second Son had been occupied with the notion of nomads, of a life apart from the genealogies of land, for the sea, which kept no record, could have no history, and neither could a people who lived upon it. And living untethered from the land meant living in a realm without precedents, protocols, or matāpule, a realm in which only the wind and the tides conspired to rule you, where no force concocted undue tests for you to pass, where a father lacked any incentive to choose one son above another.

Havea, who'd been snoring, lifted a hand toward the waves. He liked to say a navigator never truly slept, but the opposite was more true: Havea was never fully awake. "Something's out there," he said.

This was one of the mysteries of Havea, how the man could barely see yet somehow knew when there was something to look at. The Second Son leaned forward to scan the waves, which were sooted with varying shades of night. Then he saw it, a lone vaka pitching in the southern troughs. He cupped his eyes and focused. "It's got a crab-claw mast, rigged forward to keep the bow low."

Soon a small crew became visible. Strands of flowers hung from the mast to call the direction of the wind. The Second Son studied the big steering paddle whose blade separated the water into twin paths, each a different side of your destiny. Only upon noticing that one hull was larger than the other did he understand this was one of Fisi's fast-attack drua canoes. "It's the Fisians," he said.

Havea, eyes closed, nodded. "Does the crew ride the smaller hull like an outrigger?"

Three men did indeed ride the hama to balance the force of the wind. The Second Son went on to describe the bow peaks, the open stern, the smoke from a cooking fire. It was said that firstborns were born to rule the land, while second-borns were born to find new land. Here was proof that the saying was true: instead of wondering why an enemy vessel was sneaking around the backside of Tonga before dawn, the Second Son instead marveled at rigging and sail shape and frothing washboards. He longed to see their shunting maneuver as they made their turn north. "Should we have a look?" he asked.

"It couldn't hurt to have a look," Havea said.

It was the time when night was gone, but morning had yet to arrive.

The Second Son lifted the anchor stone and turned the *Pelepeka* into the waves. It didn't matter that the drua was the faster craft. He just wanted to follow it for a while, if only to see how it took the upwind waves.

Only when they began to give chase did he hear the howls of their war dogs.

At first light, Lolohea made his final ascent up the stone-cut handholds. Atop the cliffs, he felt vacant, as when a bonito has fallen victim to a fish-calling song, leaving it alive but dull-eyed. In his waistband was the whale-tooth necklace. He couldn't bring himself to hang it around his neck again. Instead, he lay sideways on the rock and gazed upon the sea that'd cradled him. He could feel priests and matāpule watching him from a distance, wondering whether he'd failed or not, wondering if an injury had felled him. It was to their advantage if he'd been unsuccessful: they'd be needed to oversee a retest and to suggest the sacrifices needed to guarantee future success. An injury was what they truly desired, one that required many offerings and prayer sessions. Most ideal would be a wound that occasioned a slow death. Could there be greater proof of the necessity of matāpule? Who else could invoke the dictates of mourning? And for those lucky priests—they'd become proxies of gods.

Into Lolohea's view, a vaka appeared. His eyes absently followed it, the heavy rollers lifting it from behind, while the northerly wind dug its bows into the overtaking waves. By a string of garlands blowing from its mast, he knew it was no Tongan canoe. Then he saw, some distance behind, a smaller vaka with a red sail. This could only be his brother. Lolohea stood, understanding that both canoes were heading north toward Heketā, where his uncle was staying. If he ran fast enough, he might give his father some warning.

Lolohea ran past the astonished priests and matāpule, their hopes for his demise still on their faces. How close they must have felt to informing a king of the sacrifices necessary for his son's survival. And think how many matāpule would've been needed to oversee those sacrifices! From the slitting of hogs' throats to the proper amount of harvest to be spilled. And if those offerings were found lacking by the gods, and death ensued, those same matāpule would conscript countless men to raise the slab covering the royal tomb. Priests would then hand out sharp shells and monitor the depth and sincerity of the mourners' scalp lacerations, all before leading them through painful processions of tuki, lafa, tutu, and foaʻulu.

Lolohea imagined his funeral as he ran through rural villages. Here lived the craftsmen who would fashion the flutes to be played while his body was lowered into the grave. Farther down these paths resided the Tuʻa slaves, who would gut the countless hogs, singe their skin, and scrape free the blackened hair, before flattening them on racks for the ʻumu ovens. Once the feast was baking, the mountains of leftover intestines would be fed to any hogs that yet lived.

Lolohea weaved through countless paths toward his father, crossing one way and another, but it didn't matter which he chose: all of Tongatapu's paths converged at the royal compound, where, once inside, all courtyards opened onto the royal tomb, so that every path Lolohea might select led eventually to the grave that contained the bones of everyone who came before him.

NINE

KŌRERO:
AND YOU REMAIN

While Finau and the Wayfinder slept in our longhouse, we prepared the waka for the voyage ahead. My father's men stripped oars, bailers, and other gear from their fishing boats. People were sent to forage roots and bracts to sustain the crew on their journey. My mother led a group that filled takawai calabashes with rainwater. Hine and I wove fronds into a canopy that might offer the men shade.

On the beach, Tapoto and my father contemplated the great waka. Before, they'd regarded it with simple awe. Now, understanding that they'd be crewing it, they discussed the rigging and spars and stays. Tapoto said, "We'll make fools of ourselves if we can't maneuver it."

"Worse," my father said, "we'll prove ourselves useless."

So our men boarded the great waka to practice launching and landing. It didn't go well. Right away there were problems turning the craft to face the water. Half the men had to paddle forward, while the others needed to reverse their strokes. Yet the men hadn't agreed which direction to rotate, so they paddled from all sides, each according to his fancy. Tapoto shouted commands, the water frothed white, and the waka went nowhere.

Tiri waded out. From the water, she prayed for favorable conditions:

Whakataka te hau ki te uru.	*Divert the wind from the west.*
Whakataka te hau ki te tonga.	*Divert the wind from the south.*
Kia hau ki uta; kia hau ki tai.	*Blow, wind, over land; blow over the sea.*

Next, she taught the men a call-and-response to time their strokes.

"Hoe ki a rite," she said, and the men lifted their paddles to the ready position.

To the men in the left hull, she said, "Whakamua," and they began paddling forward.

"Katea, whakamuri," she called, and the men in the right hull paddled backward.

How could she sense these orientations? The warmth of the sun, the breeze? The difference between the boom of reef-break and the lap of shore? When the boat was turned, she said, "Tōkihi," and the men dipped their paddles, lifted them, knocked the hull, and repeated. The men circled the cove, first one way and then the other. Tapoto got the hang of it, and soon he was calling the strokes. This duty, conveniently, spared him from any labor. Still, one had to admit he got the men to sweat their paddle handles black. Exhausted, they ran the waka onto the sand.

Tiri called for us ladies to board. The men had launched by applying much muscle against the bows. Tiri, instead, had us move to the stern, where our combined weight lifted the bows from the beach. We'd learned the basics by watching the men, and what we lacked in strength, we made up for in unity. Paddle out of time, and the great waka wouldn't move, but when we worked in concert, it proved very responsive.

Rather than shouting commands, Tiri harmonized our strokes with song:

"Kupe fetched his colorful anchors," she sang.

"Tatara-a-punga," my mother responded, "me puwai-kura."

"Kupe picked his sharpest spearheads," Tiri sang.

"Kiripaka," Arawiwi answered, "me mata-waiapa."

"He steered his waka into the crests," Tiri sang out.

"From Hawaiki," I sang, "to Aotearoa."

We recited a litany of old waka songs as we circled the cove. Tiri then said, "Kia angi puku to hoe i te waito," which was the command for quiet paddling. There was no sound but the throaty draw of paddle-water.

"Aotearoa was a land of much conflict," Tiri said, her voice almost a whisper. "We were not alone in our escape. A band of people sailed east to Rēkohu. Another group escaped north. We came here. There've certainly been others."

Hine asked, "What happened to those who sailed for Rēkohu?"

"Like us," Tiri said, "they tamed their violent ways. They learned to solve their problems through discussion. They elevated their women. Soon we depart for our neighboring island. The people we encounter may not share our ways. But we must make no apologies for who we are and how we organize ourselves."

The waka surged with each communal stroke, giving the craft a pulse. Tiri made the call, *Rangimārie*, which dictated total silence. I studied Tiri, her milky gaze directed everywhere and nowhere. I closed my eyes, heard the plunge of paddles and the trickle of water between pulls. It was easy to imagine our craft on the cold mountain lakes of Aotearoa. Or the eel-filled rivers of our homeland, the smoke of Māori villages layering the air. The old stories provisioned my imagination: great forests loomed, steam rose from sulfurous springs, dogs howled in neighboring valleys.

Eyes shut, I began imagining the ocean at night. The swells were squid-beak-black, the only hint of cresting waves were lips of starlit froth. Through darkness, I paddled toward an island. Soon I saw the white of sand. On this beach was a man. Each stroke brought me closer to him. I could see his lean body, his shoulders outlined by the moon. He faced the waves, awaiting someone. Circling him was a white dog—it had fur and a tail and large ears, just as the stories had claimed. Nearing the dark shore, I realized he was the Wayfinder. A woman began walking to him. She was no girl, she was a woman, and I wanted to warn her: Didn't she know the Wayfinder hailed from dangerous waters, that he was arrogant and dismissive and remote? She placed her arm upon his shoulder. Turning, she saw me in the waves. She lifted a hand, beckoning me near, and as I closed upon the beach, I saw that she was me.

I opened my eyes as, with a hiss, the hulls struck sand—I was back on my own island, in the bright light of day. I turned to Tiri—how powerful and transporting and accursed it was to operate without sight. Being unable to perceive this world, I understood, meant existing in a dreamworld made of nothing but unfurling narrative.

After the afternoon rains, it was time to load the waka's provisions. Immediately men began bickering about who'd sit in the bows and who'd get stuck astern. We women sat waiting for their squabble to finish.

Tiri asked Hine to describe the sunset.

"It's not sunset yet," Hine said.

The men's bickering only increased.

"Is it cloudy or clear?" Tiri asked. "Can you say what the day is like?"

"One day looks like the next," Hine said. "It's sunny, and then it's less sunny."

For Tiri, I portrayed the day's decline, describing how our island's peak took on hues of maroon, and with the last canting of the sun, palm fronds seemed to cinder. The island's greens turned dark and waxy, and the sea raised its inner eyelid so that the reef was no longer visible beneath a dome of blue.

Bickering over seating arrangements soon revealed the underlying debate: which men would get the honor of going along, and which would be left behind. For the sake of our island's harmony, we decided to hold a group discussion. As usual, our process was a mixture of speeches, grandstanding, and gripe. Counterpoints were lengthy, tedious, and repetitive. But what other way was there? We managed to agree on the size of the crew—twenty—an amount deemed not too threatening to our imagined neighbors. It was also decided that our spears would be left behind, so as not to offer a bad impression.

But who would stay and who'd go? A surplus of men had volunteered, some less than capable. Such matters had to be handled delicately. Our island was small. Grievances lingered. Finally, twenty men were selected. Only then did Tapoto add, "Surely Kōrero must come. We'll need her to share the story of our adventure." If I went along, someone would have to be cut. What male would relinquish his paddle to a female?

My father said, "This is no voyage for children."

My mother didn't want me to go, either, but she raised a eyebrow, inviting her husband to determine with his own eyes whether I was still a child.

Papa Toki spoke up: "If she's going, then I'm going." With only one arm, he couldn't even work a paddle. Yet on our island, no one could tell him he couldn't come. Now two of the chosen men wouldn't go.

Several men grumbled at the idea of surrendering a seat to me. One said, "She's not even a good storyteller."

Wasn't he right? I tried to remember the name of the constellation the Wayfinder had said he'd depart by. Would a decent storyteller have forgotten that?

"She's not going," my father said. Then he brought up something that couldn't be debated: "She doesn't even have her ink."

"Perhaps we should ask Kōrero," Tiri suggested.

"Yes," Tapoto said. "Do you want to go?"

Somehow it had become night, and a fire had been lit. You know how a fire can make your world feel intimate, how there's nothing beyond the realm of its curtailed light, how inside this glow is everyone you cared about, their faces warm and alive, their gazes collected inward, focused on each other, so that a powerful sense of togetherness is achieved? I nodded.

"It's decided, then," Tapoto said.

"If my daughter goes, I go," my mother said. No man would argue with her.

Now three men would have to surrender their paddles.

Papa Toki, assured of his place in the canoe, said, "It must be pointed out that Tapoto is the size of two men. Should he not be counted twice?"

Tapoto, looking wounded, said, "I don't deny my size. People think I eat double, but that's not true. I don't know why I am the way I am."

"It's not the size of your body that offends," my father said, "but the softness of your hands."

My father didn't normally speak this way. He was upset, as we were now risking our entire family. Yet what was the alternative? Which of us would want to continue living without the others?

"Count me as two, if you must," Tapoto said. "In response, I propose we increase the expedition from twenty to twenty-four."

At last, full agreement was achieved.

I headed up the beach. From the tide line, I could see far out to sea. Black, restless water extended to the horizon, where stars were extinguishing themselves. Out there, human accord meant nothing. What had I been thinking, agreeing to venture upon such waters? We already had an island, a good island, our island.

From the trees emerged the Tongan brothers, having just awakened. The Wayfinder took advantage of the unobstructed sky to survey the stars. "It's time," he said.

"We just selected your crew," I told them.

"Our crew?" Finau asked in disbelief. "Selected by *you*?"

"*We* are the crew," the Wayfinder told me. "You people are passengers."

"Do you two even care about us?" I asked.

"Of course," the Wayfinder said. "This trip'll hopefully get us closer to the island we seek."

"And then we can finally head home," Finau said. "Weapons in hand."

I said, "Instead of separating us into *crew* and *passengers*, why don't we all work together?"

"People working together?" Finau asked, incredulous.

"These are our honored ways," I told him.

"Following *honored ways* cost me everything," Finau said. "It cost me my family and it cost me my home." His anger turned to something else. "It cost me Punake," he added, voice unsteady. "It cost me . . ." The Wayfinder put a hand on Finau's shoulder. Finau batted it away before turning down the beach, already shouting commands at people who were but outlines in the dark.

I know this sounds crazy, but only while watching Finau walk off did I notice he was carrying the bones he'd arrived with. The Wayfinder, too, shouldered his skeletal burden. I can't say why it scared me to discover they were taking their bones along. "You can leave those remains," I told the Wayfinder. "We'll safeguard them."

"That's something we can't risk," he answered. He saw me glance toward the sea. "Don't be nervous. Crossing water, making landfall, that's the easy part."

"I'm not nervous," I said, even though I was. It was more than that. Things I thought I knew, I obviously didn't, and the realm I was unaware of was growing ever vaster.

"Night is when the sea is revealed," he said. "I should've taken the time to explain it last night." He smiled faintly. "Another time, perhaps."

He said this casually, the way you'd say it if there was never going to be another time.

"Why not just leave the bones?" I asked.

"You're worried about me, I can tell," he said. "But don't be. This is a minor excursion."

Could he think of no one but himself?

"Let me teach you the navigator's farewell," he said. "You say to me, *You must go*." He'd been standing higher on the beach, so he was looming above me. Now he circled me, his back to the sea, so we were nearly eye to eye. "It's okay," he said. "You start by saying, *You must go*."

I didn't want to say it. There was no way he was going to make me say it.

"It's an old farewell," he said, "one that acknowledges that people don't want to separate, yet sometimes they must. When you think about it, separation is the first step of reunion."

"You really believe that?"

"I aim to make reunion with even the dead," he said.

I took a breath. "You must go," I said.

"And you remain," he responded.

Then he set off down the beach, following the sound of his brother's voice.

When I caught up with them, Finau was walking through the men, saying, "You and you, not you, not you, you, and you." He indicated my father and Tapoto but not Papa Toki, who stood eagerly holding a paddle in his lone hand. When Papa Toki protested, Finau asked, "How could you possibly work a paddle?"

This enraged Papa Toki. "Who're you to tell me what I can't do?"

Finau ignored him, moving through the assembled men. Some people Finau selected were less than desirable, but Finau's attitude seemed to suggest that all our men were the same to him. In just a few moments, he'd picked fourteen men. It turned out Finau had selected the younger Toki brother but not the older one. Everyone knew the Toki brothers were inseparable!

This was too much for Papa Toki. "You must take both my boys," he demanded.

"Too late," Finau said.

Papa Toki dropped his paddle to throw his arm around his dejected son. To Finau, Papa Toki said, "You're lucky you're a guest on this island. Otherwise, we'd be dueling right now."

Finau offered a wry smile. "My lucky day," he said.

"Wait," my mother said to Finau. "We've already selected our own people."

"The stars wait for no one," the Wayfinder told her.

"You can't leave," she countered. "We haven't even loaded the provisions."

Finau said, "The sea and the sky will provide."

The Wayfinder said, "We depart."

"Let's get this vaka turned into the surf," Finau called.

Nobody knew what to do. Finau looked to Tapoto. "Are you in charge of these people or not?"

"Turn the waka," Tapoto shouted, and men shouldered the hulls.

The Wayfinder climbed aboard. From the bow, he addressed the men straining below. "We'll take you to your island," he said. "But while the sun's in the sky, there'll be no noise—no singing or praying or chitchatting or joke-swapping or reminiscing. Vomit goes into the sea. Do not shit over the washboards. When you need to crap, take your business astern. Do not fall from the vaka. We do not circle back."

Having turned the waka, the men pushed it into motion, their legs kicking up white water. I could hear the thumps as, one by one, they leaped aboard to take up paddles. My father carried a torch to the bow—from here, he could guide them through the break in the reef.

The Wayfinder's instructions continued: "What you do on the other island is your business. But we'll tolerate no abductions. And no trophy-taking. We spend one night, and neither my brother nor myself will leave the beach where the vaka anchors. We depart when . . ."

A shift in the wind took his words. We could see the crab-claw masts going up, hear the knock of paddles against the hull, yet my mind couldn't make sense of it. Whenever the world got too strange, it was my father I turned to. Whenever there were more questions than answers, I gazed at the night sky with my father and we talked it through. But I couldn't talk to my father because he was straddling the prow of a canoe adorned with frigate birds. I couldn't talk to him because he was disappearing into the dark, without provisions, without the water we'd collected, without the canopy Hine and I had woven, and without any of our goodbyes.

That night, my mother and I reclined on the beach. Where my father would've been, there was empty space. Low-hanging clouds passed above. Sand blew across our feet. We listened to crabs skittering along the tide line, their claws clacking in a nightly battle over patches of shore.

"He warned me not to get on the boat," I finally said. "Father told me it was too dangerous. He forbade me. Then he went and did it himself."

My mother was quiet. I could hear her breathing.

"And you heard that story," I said. "The Wayfinder told it right to our faces. He told us about a Tongan prince who had to fill a canoe full of slaves. The Wayfinder said we'd be surprised how easily people kidnapped themselves."

I could hear the anxiety in my voice. Aroha picked up on it, too. She snuggled into my armpit.

"You won't leave me, will you?" I asked Aroha.

"Aroha," Aroha said.

"What if it's some kind of trap?" I wondered aloud. "What if an ambush has been prepared on that island, and they're heading right into it?"

"Our men are strong," my mother said. "Your father is strong."

"Or maybe there's not even an island at all. All they had was a stupid bag of shells. He drew pictures in the sand. That was all the proof we needed that this so-called island even existed. They told us they were from a rich and powerful island, that they dove off cliffs at night. And I believed it. I fall for every story I hear."

"You're upset," my mother said. "I'm worried, too. But getting worked up doesn't help."

I propped myself on my elbows and stared toward the sea. Out there was my father. I wondered if he knew where he was, or if he'd sailed too far in the dark to keep his bearings. If only we'd thought to light a signal fire. With a fire, he could at least look back and know where home was, know that we were thinking of him.

I said, "Remember how the Wayfinder said they intended to stay with the waka? What's to stop them from shoving off, from just stranding our men? What if that's how they got that waka in the first place, from slipping away in the night?"

My mother said, "You should never doubt the courage or resourcefulness of your father. He knew the risks, and he did what he had to do. Trust me, he won't be outsmarted by a couple kids."

"But that's the point. He didn't have to go. They didn't have to shove off at a moment's notice in the dark of night."

"Actually, they did have to go," my mother said. "But that's a different story."

I turned to look at her. "What story is that?"

"I can't tell you, so you'll just have to take my word."

"Can't tell me, or won't?"

"Just trust me," she said.

"No, I want to know."

My mother was quiet.

I asked, "Is it bad, this thing I don't know about?"

"Look, childhood is a special time," she said. "I want yours to last as long as it can."

That was the worst, most scary answer possible. "If I had my ink," I asked, "would you tell me then?"

She didn't answer. She didn't have to. I ran my fingers along Aroha's feathers. Was Aroha with me because she wanted to be with me, or was she simply not ready for freedom, like Kōkī said?

"When you're an adult," I asked, "do things get easier?"

"Easier how?"

"I don't know, less uncertain," I said. "Less confusing and complicated."

"I'm afraid that only gets worse," she said. "But as an adult, you can at least do something about it."

I thought about that for a while. "I should've hung my fishhook necklace on Father. It provides safe passage over water."

Mother offered her hand, and I used it to pull close to her.

"But the Wayfinder took it," I said. "He took it before he took all our men. And I let him."

TEN

TO WAKE IN BLOOD

The Tuʻilifuka slept horribly on this big, stupid island called Tongatapu. At dawn, he secured his brides and went in search of coconut oil. A man carrying a bundle of sticks directed him toward the camp of an old woman who was said to make the finest oil on the coast.

Taking the Liku Path, the Tuʻilifuka passed dwellings from which deep snores could be heard, and the well-rested Tongans he encountered were still rubbing their eyes. How he hated these deep sleepers in the slumbering south. In Lifuka, only a fool would sleep all night, for you had to keep an eye on the trees and tidal flats. You had to scan Pangai's shores for the night-glow of Fisian sails, you had to keep an ear toward the ocean, for no matter how well trained Fisian war dogs were, they couldn't help howling from canoe to canoe before an attack.

Without his war brides' sullen half strides, the Tuʻilifuka moved much faster. Because of bad dreams, mornings left him anxious. What gave him relief was thinking of the moment he'd oil down the girls' bodies and loom over their glistening torsos, leaving them to wonder, as he also wondered, which one he'd mount.

He ran across some boys wielding what he took to be spears, but on closer examination were simply poles with which to harvest hard-to-reach fruit. A team of girls came striding by with blunt clubs, the kind kids raised when they raced onto the beach to finish off enemy warriors. But, of course, these were just bark-beating mallets, carried by girls on their way to pound tapa cloth. Here, it seemed, kids didn't sleep in trees. They didn't drill escapes north across the spits to the island of Foa or south through the channel to Uoleva.

He found the woman who dealt in coconut oil. Despite her gray hair, she didn't seem old. The eyes alone aged you, what they'd seen. Her oil was warm and silky to the touch. She handed him two shells, brimming full, and there was an unspoken understanding that if he returned for more, he'd make her an offering.

So the Tuʻilifuka began walking, with small shuffling steps, holding coconut shells before his eyes to prevent a spill. When you spent much of your life concerned with war, the funniest moments turned out to be war moments. Ambling with oil was one of them, for the Tuʻilifuka had learned a few things about war.

First, it was possible to continue living without your life. The first time this happened was in the battle for Vatoa: his life flew high, then gazed—indifferent as a frigate bird—upon the conflict below. This while he himself, alone and lifeless, battled through the waves and up the beach, lowering his club upon man after man. Once your life learns it's free to wander from the flesh, it does so, and at the most surprising moments. Plucking a Fisian parrot once, he watched the red dander float in shafts of forest light, though he watched not through his own eyes, but from the upper limbs of a toa tree.

Next, battle caused the brain to leak. The eyes poured what they saw into the brain, which was the receptacle of memory. Even if, in all your battles, you escaped a blow to the head, the warrior's brain would still begin to dribble memories back into the eyes. It simply stopped working right, and the things it was designed to safeguard began coming out in visions, and not the sweet kind, like the garden you once tended when your wife was still alive or the hogs your daughter would shepherd through low tide, back when such things were safe to do, back before the Tuʻitonga pressed for the ceaseless conflicts of today.

Finally, being careful and cautious would eventually kill you. The liver was home to human courage. The more you fought, the more courage it produced, until men turned yellow with it. Discharge was the only cure. So it was that even the most stable warriors would occasionally engage in outlandish risk-taking for no other purpose than discharging an oversaturated liver. The Tuʻilifuka himself had gone on a rampage long after the battle was over. He'd once behaved outrageously during a bone-broth ceremony. Once, in a pitched battle against the men of the island of Lau, he'd thrown his war turban to the ground, loosed his topknot, and freed his kilt, so that he was naked as he advanced through the village's falling men, and he was naked when the island's women counterattacked. Amid them—women dazed, women dying, women dead, their torsos broken like oysters, their spines curled like shrimp shells—that's when a man—even a man who was once a husband and a father—was poised to do the unthinkable.

Discharge often surprised you, because how can you know when your liver has filled? It was the same way you never knew when your brain would leak a memory, of a face, of an aftermath, of a Fisian father who'd tethered his son's wrist to his, so he wouldn't lose track of his boy in a battle. There were times when the Tuʻilifuka could be sure his brain wouldn't leak. One was when he was consumed with intense focus, as when he spent hours making gifts for his daughter by weaving little figures from pure-white strips of mulberry bark. Or later, when he'd fashion necklaces out of parrot down and give them to the girls who'd been friends with his daughter, so they wouldn't forget her. Or when he was completely consumed with a task, like walking a path, focused on the clear fluid trying to crest the rims of coconut shells.

Another time was more complicated, but it began after releasing his seed deep in the manava of one of his war brides. His ule would pulse, he'd roll away, and his mind would expand outward into a cloud of well-being, an endless benign nothing that was more satisfying than anything else in his life. But even that was complicated. He'd abducted the girls out of anger, and anger was important in his use of them. He always got two shells of oil, so he could oil them both down, so they couldn't know which he'd mount, for even he didn't know until he measured the fear in their eyes. That was important, that was crucial. But at some point along the way, the girls had started reaching out to take one another's hands, a grip that didn't release until the Tuʻilifuka released. It was a grip that said, *If you take one of us, you take both of us and also take neither.* The Tuʻilifuka had to admit they were likely sisters. And at some point they would become the mothers of his children. None of which he'd imagined when he forced them into his canoe.

But the beauty of focus was not having to consider any of that. With enough focus, life came only in controlled little doses: Precious oil, cusping the lips of coconut shells. A Lifukan's shuffling steps. Glistening drops running down your fingers, thick as the water that floated the human eye. And, awaiting at the end of your path, hovering like a wing-flapping peka bat, a shuddering release.

Some Tongans passed the Tu'ilifuka. He didn't take his eyes off his shells; still, he perceived their idiotic smiles, the way they stumbled along without a care in the world. War dogs didn't roam here, kele'a alarms never sounded, and you weren't going to run across a son, lashed to his dead father as a battle raged around him, a boy wanting to cling and wanting to run and able to do neither.

'Aho was up at dawn to teach his son ceramics. He also hoped to teach the boy about fonua, though 'Aho didn't use that word the way most people did. *Fonua* meant "land." It also meant "afterbirth." The concept, as others saw it, was simple: as the placenta connects a mother to her child, so, too, is there a connection between the Tongan and his home island. This connection is solidified at birth, when a person's fonua is buried in the fonua. But 'Aho was more literal about such things. To him, fonua was the human stain. When a body was left in the sand or soil, the earth was marked. Salts and oils and minerals leached forth, altering the clay with elements that gave hue to the pottery that was fired from it. All those who'd come before had tinted Tongatapu, and this was made visible by the kiln. His wife, when buried, would contribute her pigment, and one day so would he.

Father and son set out to make a simple water vessel. First they stoked a fire in the hollow of a stump. While it burned to a bed of coals, they gathered clay from the lowlands, burial place of the least noteworthy Tongans, whose bones and blood lent the mud their meal and mineral. They drew water from a well called Tahitahi, which was unfit for drinking but whose salts would make the vessel less porous. The glaze would be made with ash from the resin-coated branches of the tuitui tree. This would streak the vessel's surface and speckle it.

'Aho and his son fanned the coals with palm fronds. He was patient with the boy, taking the time to explain the origins of ceramics. The son also was patient, listening attentively as his father paraded through Mateaki's mother's genealogies, so the boy would never forget her people.

Together, they rolled the clay and coiled it into shape, smoothing the surface with wet fingers. 'Aho was determined not to let 'Ofa's memory fade, so he spoke to his son about her talents as an artist, about how she was known for her lovely cloth, inked in the manulua design from dyes of the koka and tongo trees. Speaking of his dead wife made 'Aho sad and remorseful, and when 'Aho became melancholy, he was prone to giving name to all his faults and flaws and bad decisions and the ways in which others had paid for his mistakes, with his wife being the ultimate, though unspoken, example. On this morning, he instead listed his son's favorable attributes, all of which he'd inherited from his mother.

'Aho showed his son how to etch the interlocking triangles of his mother's manulua pattern. "Your mother lives on in you," he said as Mateaki worked the clay. "You have her attention to detail, you're good with your hands. I see in you her patience, her appreciation." Missing in this study of his son was his mother's smile and sense of humor, which had taken leave of him.

Was this the moment to talk about her death? How to speak of it?

Death and dying, those words suggested only the end of life. Killing and murdering, what more did those terms convey than one person ending another? There were so many kinds of death and killing—they hadn't been properly labeled. Was killing the same on defense and attack, for stranger and friend? Was it the same murder when you struck down a Fisian dog wrangler setting foot on your beach as when you yourself lofted a torch to Fisian roof thatching? And what of the times 'Aho and the king put down rebellions? Did you use the same word when taking the lives of Fisian strangers as fellow Tongans? What would you call it when the chief of Pangai, with whom you'd sailed west into many smoking dawns, lost his guts into the sand, and, on his hands and knees, protecting his wet organs from the sun, invited you to finish him? What was the word for that? What of the Lifukans who, after battle, raced onto the beach to beat the heads of the Fisian dead and dying alike? Wasn't the swing and the bash the same for both, was it *killing* to kill someone already dead? And what if you yourself were dead when you took the life of another? The Tu'ilifuka often said he wasn't alive when he entered battle, that his soul left him at those moments, and 'Aho knew the feeling. Could you call it killing when you took the life of another, yet you yourself weren't alive? Which led him to his wife. What if someone you loved suddenly seemed like a stranger? What if you weren't even yourself in that moment? And what if the other person you were, that stranger, didn't even feel alive? And what if that stranger, that dead other person, took the life of this other stranger, and somehow, impossibly, at the same time, took the life of the person he loved most in the world? There were names for all the fish and the stars. If only there was a word for what happened that morning by the spring, 'Aho could simply muster the will to say it aloud, to speak that word to his son, and so much suffering would be over.

These are the things 'Aho talked about and didn't talk about as he and his boy fired a vessel designed to connect them to one who was no longer with them.

Each morning at dawn, the Tuʻitonga received updates from his chiefs and priests and matāpule. Over kava, he heard reports, news, and requests for aid from the outer islands. Chiefs with the pettiest complaints clamored to speak first.

The chief of Tofua reported that volcanic eruptions on the nearby island of Kao had emptied their fishing nets. Two shipments of sweet potatoes were requested.

The chief of Kotu reported that a barge of Fisian war dogs had landed on their beach, forcing his people into the trees. During the day, the dogs could be hunted, but in the dark the roles were reversed. Three shipments of sweet potatoes were requested, along with some very long spears.

The reports on crops, hogs, and timber were, as usual, disappointing.

The chief of boat-building declared that efforts to copy the Fisian vaka design were going exceedingly well, which of course meant the opposite.

Local matāpule began listing tapu infractions committed on Tongatapu, including members of unequal rank caught eating together and a woman discovered secretly harboring an infant dog.

"Feʻunga," the Tuʻitonga said, halting this parade of complaints.

When the circle went quiet, the powerful chief of Vavaʻu spoke. "The Fisians have burned our storehouses in a night raid. Three guards died defending the food, but all was lost. There will be no tributes this year. We've retaliated against the Fisian island of Mualevu, taking life there."

"How much life?" the Tu'itonga asked.

"All of it," the Tu'ivava'u said.

The Tu'ivava'u was a cautious chief, inclined to diplomacy. Why would he escalate tensions with neighboring Fisian islands? At play was a motive the Tu'itonga couldn't discern. If only the Tu'ilifuka had attended this morning, he might have brought some wisdom from the field.

"And the report from Lifuka?" the Tu'itonga asked.

All could see the Tu'ilifuka was not in attendance.

"Is the state of Lifuka one of happiness and bliss?" the Tu'itonga wondered.

All were silent.

"Perhaps in Lifuka," the Tu'itonga said, "life's wonderful enough that an appearance before the Tu'i of Tonga is not necessary."

Into this awkwardness, Lolohea appeared, breathing heavily. The whale tooth was visible in his waistband, but before the king could order dancers to celebrate the boy's success, Lolohea said, "A Fisian attack canoe lands to the east. I saw it rounding the island."

"Fisians?" Matāpule Mu'a asked. "On our coast?"

Six Fists grabbed his spear. "To the beach!"

The Tu'itonga lifted a hand for calm. He downed a shell of kava while visualizing the bones of the woman his brother had likely murdered. "Such an attack has never happened," the Tu'itonga said. "Perhaps you saw one of the canoe chief's new prototypes."

The canoe chief shook his head.

"I saw what I saw," Lolohea said. "Think of the unsuspecting Tongans who reside near that shore."

"The morning light is well known to play tricks on the eyes," the Tu'itonga suggested.

Lolohea said, "It had a crab-claw mast, and the windward hull was smaller than the lee."

"That's a Fisian drua," the canoe chief said.

"If there was trouble, the kele'a horns would've sounded," the Tu'itonga said. "Let us not be disturbed by false alarms. What's important is that the prince share with us the story of his achievement, for he has successfully completed the Fall of Tangaloa. Come, regale us, my boy, and don't leave anything out."

"No," Lolohea said. "I must go help my brother."

"Your brother?"

"The Second Son, his vaka's in pursuit."

With that, Lolohea began running once more.

Six Fists turned toward the king, waiting for him to give the order.

The king at last nodded, and Six Fists began organizing the counterattack.

Morning light spear-tipped the sea, bluing the peaks of waves, while the ocean below remained dark. Along eastern Tongatapu, open-ocean rollers pressed shoulder-to-stern against a lone Fisian vaka. The wind, in conspiracy, stacked the waves, topknotting them white with curls of froth that trailed down their faces.

When the Fisians made landfall, the crew turned the canoe, positioning it to reenter the waves in a hurry. Dogs leaped from the hulls to pace the tide line and piss out a perimeter. From this scene, a Fisian chief and his son began running inland. They were tethered at the wrists so they couldn't become separated. The boy was only twelve. The chief had tied vines around his son's upper arms to make him look Tongan. The chief had sooted his own legs to appear from a distance that he wore Tongan ink. The son was proficient with a bola, which he wore wrapped around his waist. His father's weapon told a different story. While Fisians have been known to carry flathead clubs, eight-barbed spears, and owl-face lances, this warrior-chief carried a weapon previously unseen in Tonga.

The two had never set foot on Tongatapu. The paths twisted one way and another, through groves and thickets. The father kept the sun at his back and his boy at his heel. Relying on scant intelligence, they had only this plan: to slay a pair of kidnappers and rescue two daughters of Fisi. To give himself strength, the boy wore a garland of vesi leaves. To give the girls strength, he'd brought a clutch of dawa fruit, small and ripe and tasting of the hills of Kabara. The father felt no need of a talisman.

They ran side by side, dodging trees together. The Fisian chief had expected to see grand longhouses adorned with elaborate carvings and legions of elites bedecked in whale-tooth necklaces. Didn't the Fisian people's food and resources, stolen in raid after Tongan raid, go to support a land of riches? Did he not bring his son to witness firsthand such opulence? Yet, when they encountered Tongans at their morning tasks—stoking kilns and stripping mulberry bark—these people seemed as average and unadorned as anyone from home. Racing down paths, they glimpsed skinny children and weary old men. Here, the trees had already been gleaned, and the endless chatter of birds was nearly absent. They ran past servant girls carrying great burdens and men using staves to aerate fields of cuttings. Columns of woodsmoke told the true story of this place: Tonga was raiding other islands not because of a greedy elite but because there were thousands of people populating an island nearly depleted.

Rounding a bend, they got their only look at the kind of Tongan they'd expected: lying in the path was a young man in conversation with a leashed parrot. The boy wore a royal feathered necklace and reclined like the entire island was his. Startled, the Fisian father and son leaped over the boy and his bird.

Finau and his parrot Kōkī were sprawled on the ground. New Punake said there was one hour each day when the poet didn't have to contemplate poetry. During this hour, the first hour, the world *was* poetry. Around them, ants rustled under pandanus leaves. Horned beetles battled to summit slick plops of pig shit. Canopy green was reflected in puddle green, and cambers of light levitated palm spathe. Umbered clouds, splotched hogs, butchering stains shadowing the earth. All this poetry vanished with the morning's first hunger pang. It dissolved in the first drop of sweat.

Speaking of poetry: two humans leaped over them!

Dropped on the ground were small fruits, the likes of which Finau and Kōkī had never seen.

Finau and Kōkī regarded one another in wonder.

"*Mist forms at the volcano's dome,*" Finau said.

"*Clouds lift, drop their gifts, return home,*" Kōkī responded.

The fruits each opened to reveal a curl of slick, translucent meat, tasting of a faraway land.

"They're getting away," Finau said. "You with your glorious wings, you must follow them."

Kōkī shook his head. "Don't offer Kōkī freedom, only to tie Kōkī up again."

"You're no captive. We're best friends."

"If friends, why Kōkī restrained?"

"Because I care about you. I can't afford to lose you."

"If love Kōkī, free Kōkī," Kōkī said. "Promise no leash."

"You must promise me back," Finau said. "Promise you won't ever leave me."

"*Nea*," Kōkī said, and to seal their agreement, the two, nose to beak, exchanged the breath of life.

Thus Finau loosed Kōkī's leash and tossed the parrot into the air.

Parrots had gone extinct on Tongatapu. Roasted and eaten, every last one. So the island was Kōkī's as he swooped though the fading blossoms of siale shrubs. The canopy was his, as were the sticky, beak-staining seeds of kotone trees! In spirals of joy, Kōkī flew to the top of an uhi tree, where, fanning his wings, he felt the blood hot in the quills of his flight feathers.

Far below, Finau kept shouting, but who could listen to a ground dweller when the sun was warm on your beak? Who'd entertain pleas from the earthbound when a tropical breeze tickled your breast? "*Nea-nea*," Kōkī called to other parrots. He cocked his head and listened for a response—nothing.

A rock sailed through the foliage, snapping a leaf.

Looking down, Kōkī saw Finau hurl another.

So Kōkī took flight, falling through the canopy in the direction of the runners. Before long, on a sandy path, he encountered the Tuʻilifuka, walking slowly, meditating deeply on two coconut shells of oil. Kōkī knew where the Tuʻilifuka was taking the oil, to the females from Fisi. Kōkī knew what the oil was for. He'd unfortunately, more than once, seen humans mating. With their close-set eyes and hairy heads—they were so hard to look at! All that exposed skin, those denuded expanses! And what act of genuine love could be performed without a beak? Kōkī hadn't actually experienced parrot love. Still, it resonated deep within him: he could hear the frequency of two beaks scraping, feel the vibrations of beaks hooking and knocking and shifting for position. He knew this profoundly, and it didn't matter that he'd never encountered the female of his species.

Kōkī hovered, tail feathers fanned, to observe the Tuʻilifuka's slow shuffle, his eyes transfixed by the shells of oil before him. And then the Tuʻilifuka fell, his precious oil now sloshed upon the ground. The Tuʻilifuka closed his eyes in self-admonishment, but when he tried to stand, he found that he hadn't simply tripped—his ankles were wrapped in the weighted ropes of a bola. And then the running man and his son were upon him, binding the Tuʻilifuka's hands and dragging him to the side of the path where they forced him astraddle the trunk of a downed tree.

Here, the special weapon was produced. There was a flash of green, and the cap of the Tuʻilifuka's skull popped off, his brain sent tumbling down the path, hot ropes of blood lifting with each turn until the lobes coated themselves completely in sand. The brain stem came to rest in a patch of morning light.

With that, the chief and his son were gone.

Kōkī landed and parrot-hopped to the brain, which throbbed yet with life. Kōkī then inspected the Tuʻilifuka, who appeared like he'd only had one too many shells of kava and had simply paused for a rest. Except that his skull was open and vacant, like a gourd used to catch rainwater. While the Tuʻilifuka's eyes hadn't fallen from their sockets, their cords had snapped, making the eyes bulge heavy and low as if he were in deep contemplation of his necklace below. And here was the sad part: the necklace was woven with parrot feathers. They weren't flight feathers or tail feathers or even expressive crest feathers. No, the necklace was tufted with a simple ring of breast feathers, plumage designed to warm a small and fast-beating heart.

Kōkī hopped close and ran his beak along the red down. Was this plumage from a female of his kind? Was this as close as he'd ever come to a mate? He flew to the top of a toa tree. "*Nea,*" he called. "*Nea-nea.*" All he heard in response was the distant pounding of surf and shearwaters bouncing their calls off wet cliffs.

Kōkī had only the vaguest sense of where he came from. And no true memories of his parents—they were just a scent, a temperature, a reassuring shade. He couldn't even recite their call. *Nea-nea,* he always said, but was that even parrot talk? His head was filled with human words, and, truth be told, his earliest memory was of the human hands that lifted him from the nest, held him close, that sailed him across a sea to this forlorn, parrotless domain.

He tried to call again, but all that came was human talk. He recited a line from a Ha'amoan poem about a queen who, upon learning of her son's death, understood her entire line had passed:

Se tau manu vao mai Tongatapu,   A flock of wild birds from
                                                                 Tongatapu,
leai se kōkī na felo i le ta'aga.   *no parrot was among them.*

Kōkī was only five years old—seventy more years of pain and isolation to go.

When Kōkī returned to Finau, Finau asked him what he'd seen.

"Kōkī not want to talk about it," Kōkī said.

"Talk about what? What'd you see?"

Kōkī tucked his head beneath a wing.

"Tell me, you stupid bird," Finau said. "What happened?"

But Kōkī could feel nothing, see nothing beyond that downy ring of red. Finau pulled his parrot close. "I'm sorry I called you *stupid*."

"Were you the one who took Kōkī from Kōkī nest?" Kōkī asked.

Finau shook his head. "You were an offering from a sub-chief."

Kōkī's eyes pinwheeled. It was so hard to process, that he could be nothing but a gift.

"How long do humans live?" Kōkī asked.

"Do you mean me, how long will I live?" Finau could tell the bird was troubled. "Don't worry. I'm a Tu'itonga's son. I'm destined to have a long and comfortable life."

Finau then cradled Kōkī, and here Kōkī was again, warm and safe in human hands.

From somewhere on the island, a kele'a horn sounded, and one by one, other security teams echoed the alert. Then past them ran the Fisian father, his son, and the liberated war brides, all racing best speed for the beach.

"Kōkī see a flash of green," Kōkī said. "Kōkī watch a brain take wing."
Finau repeated those words, savoring them.
New Punake was right. Mornings, the world was poetry.

Lolohea had been running all morning, it seemed. He arrived, exhausted, at the coast at Heketā, breaking through the tidal brush to discover a skirmish under way. Four Tongan sentries were fighting club-to-club against two Fisian warriors, their backs to the surf. Men from both sides lay headbroken in the sand. From the Fisian vaka came calls to depart, but the Fisian warriors held their ground, knowing that Tongans attacked only with overwhelming forces. It was true—waiting for reinforcements, the four Tongans feinted, doing little more than knocking tips with the Fisians' clubs.

Lolohea halted, breathing hard. He'd been in many physical contests, but here was combat. His eyes lowered to the men who'd already fallen. He knew the island's sentries, but these men, crumpled, were unrecognizable. Lolohea had seen clubbing victims before. It's eerie to behold their faces, for even after death, the eyes fill with blood, tissues swell, and the broken plates of the face continue to shift. Such is the power of a club to warp our intimate features. A strike across the center of the face, for example, turns the eyes downward, making one appear to gaze in disbelief at the wound below. A club to the back of the head angles the eyes outward, lending a look of wariness, much like that of a grouper fish. And a downward blow bulges the eyes, dislodging the cheekbones, evoking an expression of eternal surprise.

Not far away, four people emerged from the tongolei mangroves. They struggled through the futu and kola and onto the beach. Lolohea recognized the war brides from the night before. There was also a Fisian chief connected by a rope to a boy. The boy was Tongan, judging from the bands on his arms. It was one thing to repatriate two women—it was another to kidnap a child. Still, it wasn't until a Tongan sentry noticed Lolohea and called for help that he found himself taking up a club from one of the dead men and advancing into the fray.

The Fisian chief cut the tether, sending the boy and the women running for the vaka. Then he joined his mates on the beach to make a fighting retreat to the waves.

"Take the women and go," Lolohea told the Fisian chief. "But leave the boy. We won't allow a kidnapping."

Five Tongans haltingly advanced as three Fisians shuffled backward toward the water.

"Tongans don't allow kidnapping?" the Fisian chief responded. "How do you think I learned your grubby language?"

When the Fisian chief saw a red-sailed Tongan vaka advancing from the south, he called to his crew, "Raise the anchor stone!" Then he drew a jade club from his waistband and made it clear that death would come to those who intended to thwart his escape.

Lolohea had never seen someone brandish a stone weapon. It was shaped like a paddle, the jade glowing green. When the Fisian chief lifted it, sunlight burnished its leading edge. The Fisian chief didn't swing the green paddle, but thrust it forward in snapping motions. "I'll fight all of you myself. If you have the honor to engage me one at a time."

"Honor?" Lolohea asked. "This from a people who attack at night, armed with slings and darts?"

As he said this, Lolohea understood this was the first Fisian warrior he'd ever beheld, that the unnerving calm in the man's eyes suggested nothing Lolohea had heard about these people might be true.

"But it's the Tongan who lacks honor," came the response. "Attacking only when you outnumber us. Where's the prestige in that?"

"What honorable people fight with dogs?" Lolohea asked.

"You burn our spirit houses," the Fisian chief countered. "On Yagasa, you disinterred our dead." The Fisian chief advanced a step. He feinted one way, but thrust another, striking a Tongan sentry in the temple. Without a sound, the man went down, the stone weapon putting him to sleep. "Even as you question our honor, even as you have superior numbers, you don't attack. Instead, you stall for reinforcements."

Had that flash of green come for him, Lolohea wouldn't have had the reflexes to dodge it, that's how stiff he was with fear. He *was* stalling. He couldn't shake the feeling that the next lick of green would come for him, that he'd suddenly go down, and he wouldn't get up again. This feeling had gripped him the night he'd held the club above the thief. Though the thief was bound, kneeling, weeping even, Lolohea had the feeling that the action he was about to take was going to wound himself more, that the fear he harbored would become visible, and the charade that Lolohea was of kingly material would suddenly collapse. Mostly, he didn't want to crack the skull of a man who'd stolen sweet potatoes. While he'd held the club high, he thought about the sound it would make: Like the crisp snap of a taro rind? Or the creaking tear of a tuber root? It turned out it wouldn't be the sound that haunted him, but the feel, the ringing in his hands and the sense that in taking another's life, he was somehow taking his own.

Lolohea decided to strike with words. "Where's the honor in sneak attacks?"

"We seek nothing more than true battle," the Fisian chief said. "One in which Tongans and Fisians die not by ambush or deception or overwhelming attack, but by falling together across broad beaches under the balancing light of the sun. Our two peoples will clash forever, until you fight us this way."

"What about peace?" Lolohea asked. "Have you ever considered that?"

At this question, the Fisian chief lowered his club, figuring there was perhaps no real fight to be had. "Now that you know how we make war, I'll tell you how we make peace. Peace comes after the survivors from both sides share a broth simmered from the bones of the fallen." Then he and his men made for the waves.

The Tongan sentries looked to Lolohea for a sign of what they should do.

He hesitated, but it was no matter. Over the dunes came Six Fists with a fleet of warriors who kicked sand toward a Fisian vaka hemmed in by the Second Son.

They say Old Punake wasn't very old when he died. They say he was in his prime when the end came. New Punake never met his predecessor. Still, he owed the man a debt for starting a tradition: each morning, Finau was encouraged to explore Tongatapu, seeing it as a poet would—the natural beauty, the ancient wonder, the daily rhythms. Old Punake had cleverly figured a way to get himself some personal time, and New Punake inherited this. Being free of babysitting, even if briefly, was the only thing that helped him survive his fate.

So Finau was up at first light, roaming the island with a poet's eyes. It's true the boy was drawn to darker things: wasps injecting larvae into living caterpillars, pigs eating the still-steaming guts of newly slaughtered pigs. Yet Finau *saw* the world, which was unusual for a royal. In New Punake's experience, royals tended to see nothing, not the slaves who served them, not the warriors who died for them, not the suffering behind every luxury. While the boy had much to learn about poetry, he had a decent memory and could compose a fair line, which would go a long way toward keeping New Punake from becoming the next Old Punake.

New Punake spent his precious time at the freshwater baths. Here, Fefine Girls scrubbed the bodies of Tongatapu's important women. Each morning, the maidens spread fresh mats at the bath's entrance and floated flower petals upon the water's surface. Men who followed the fakafefine life were allowed access to the women's bathing pool, and sadly, because of his condition, so was New Punake. That's how he thought of what'd happened to him: his condition. He'd composed in his mind a thousand bitter poems about the ironies of now being able to bathe with Tonga's most lovely virgins. Uttered aloud, though, they'd be nothing but comical.

Morning light set the canopy aglow. New Punake floated on his back and gazed into the foliage above. The blossoms had been picked, the fruit had been picked. Someone had even harvested nonu from the branches extending over the water. On the small island he was from, nonu—bitter and stinky—was a food of last resort, when the only thing left was green.

The thought occurred for a poem he'd call "Lanu-mata." *Green*. His home island of Ha'ano was awash with color, with flowers and fruit and butterflies. There were all manner of vibrant birds: the maroon-winged tū, the purple-bellied kalae, the rainbow manuma'a, the crimson-crowned kulukulu, and the bright yellow hengehenga, whose laughing call was like children at play.

The trees hung heavy with golden faina, orange lesi, and fat bunches of yellow fusi. But in the Sacred South, the birds had been eaten, the trees picked clean, and if shipments of tribute and raided goods ever stopped arriving, there'd be nothing left but green. On a small island, the signs you were about to starve were easy to see. Too much green. You couldn't eat green.

Another word turned in his mind—*fe'unga*. "Enough." Were words enough to capture life, could language portray the experience of being? Less and less he was sure about the power of words, and words were all he had. He was from a little island, where everything seemed enough, enough for those who'd come before and those who were to come. But only here did he understand he was ultimately a citizen not of Ha'ano, but of Tonga. What was enough for Tonga? Were all the islands enough? Was the world enough for Tonga?

The last to go is green, New Punake thought.

A kele'a conch shell sounded. The Fefine Girls huddled in the bath, speculating about the source of the alarm. New Punake kept floating on his back. He was less fearful since his "condition." He believed the worst thing that could happen already had, though that was an illusion. If any misfortune befell Finau, the Tu'itonga would have New Punake staked to the beach or set adrift on a raft of dogs. He never exactly heard how Old Punake went—Finau had obviously cared for the man and never spoke about it—but his own fate would certainly be worse.

A kele'a sounded from the royal compound. There were more alarms from the beach. New Punake waded ashore and pulled back his wet hair. Something was happening, and it was time to locate the boy. It was then, though, that Finau found him. Kōkī was on Finau's shoulder, and in Finau's hand was a brain.

"Look what I came across," Finau said. "It's still warm."

New Punake stared at the brain, dusted with sand. He had the impulse to ask Finau what he was holding, but it was obvious what he was holding. "Where'd you get that?" he asked.

"Kōkī find," Kōkī said. "Tu'ilifuka lose."

"I thought I should rinse it off," Finau said. "It's a very personal item—doesn't seem right that it's dirty."

Only once before had New Punake so lost his words. "How'd the Tu'ilifuka die?"

Finau crouched to submerge the brain in water, the sand falling away. "Kōkī saw it."

Kōkī looked up from Finau's shoulder. "He die of green," Kōkī said.

Interacting with Kōkī was dangerous. He could say anything to anyone, without repercussion, because he was a bird. Spending his time with Finau also made Kōkī think he was a royal. And Kōkī seemed to believe that being the last of his kind gave him special status. But there were too many poems attesting to the tastiness of parrots to think Kōkī would get far in life.

"Green killed him?" New Punake asked.

Kōkī bobbed his head at the sad truth of this.

Finau turned the brain underwater. Bubbles rose. This Finau found curious. He lifted the brain and held it high. All three of them watched water and blood dribble tacky and pink from the severed arteries. "It's kind of like those are his thoughts, draining away," Finau said before submerging it again.

"Were you in any danger?" New Punake asked. "Does your father know you're okay?"

Finau gave New Punake a sweet and innocent look that said, *You're my father.* Then he indicated the brain, glowing in the warped light of the water. "Those are the eye cords," he said. "They snapped off. And that's the spinal stump."

When the bubbles stopped, Finau lifted the brain again. This time the water ran clear.

New Punake got a chill from the sight. The brain seemed rinsed of any personality, like it could be anybody's, like it no longer possessed anything of the mind it once harbored.

"I saw the killers," Finau said. "It was a man and a boy. They were tethered together. It was a natural metaphor, like for you and me."

Protecting Finau was New Punake's primary mission, but it always posed a dilemma. Was it safer to take Finau to the beach, where the boy's father and uncle would soon be gathering, along with Six Fists and the Tamahā, and their security teams? Or was it safer to head the other direction and keep as far away from them as possible?

But New Punake didn't have to think too hard. As usual, there was no real choice: moving through the trees, he could see the tops of the Tu'itonga's feather poles, marking the royal entourage's procession toward shore.

A WORD ON CASTRATION

In Tongatapu, this procedure is rare, used only by priests treating kiatolo and certain cases of spiritual possession. Things are different in the rural islands, where population control and conflict management are essential—a few too many mouths to feed or a string of revenge killings might be all it took to depopulate an island.

Perhaps the case of New Punake might illustrate the process. He was from Ha'ano, an island prosperous enough to have specialists, people who could dedicate their time not to fishing or farming, but to pursuits like reciting verse, which he did with great flair. His poems flattered the chief and championed his deeds. His rhymes made slaves smile and matāpule weep. His go-to move was leaping high before delivering the final line.

A visit from the Tu'itonga was a rare event, so the poet composed his most spectacular verse. It was received with great approval. In fact, the Tu'itonga invited him to Tongatapu! But the poet was innocent about life. He didn't understand that when the Tu'itonga wanted to punish an enemy, he sent a fleet of warriors. When the Tu'itonga wanted to punish a friend, however, he paid that friend a visit, obliging him to provide feast after feast, to the point of depletion. The Tu'iha'ano had been getting a little too powerful, but when the Tu'itonga sailed away, Ha'ano was on the brink of collapse: bereft of food, missing its virgins, and absent the one person who sang the chief of Ha'ano's praises.

On the voyage south, the poet imagined his awaiting life: orating at the grave of kings, enthralling audiences before fires that licked the sky, offering private recitations to lovely maidens. He couldn't know his days of discourse were over, that after landing, he'd meet a man named Six Fists, who'd make him embrace a niu tree and bind his hands on the trunk's far side, rendering him unable to prevent, let alone observe, what happened below. Six

Fists had a special cord for the task. Woven from hibiscus bark, it had beads at each end to ensure a good grip. Six Fists grasped the poet's ball-sack, securing tight loop after tight loop around the scrotum, each wrap cinched tighter than the last. Pain took the poet's words—he tried to protest, beg, question, and expound on the topic of celestial mistakes. But only nonsense came out. Six Fists silently went about his work, finishing off with a bonito knot. Then he left the poet to his experience.

An afternoon rain shower. Lengthening shadows. A poet alone, tied to a tree. From afar, it would be impossible to know what transpired inside this man: an internal pillar of fire, fire as from the mouths of Fisian dogs. Fire followed by an internal shouting, expressed in a tongue known only to flesh. Throbbing next, like the clacking of funeral stones. Finally, a buzzing sleep. Worst was how New Punake had to imagine it, for the poet, bound cheek to tree, could confirm nothing of what took place below.

When Six Fists returned to free his hands, the poet's balls hung cold and still. Six Fists said three things to the poet: "Yes, the Tuʻitonga decreed this. If you loosen the cord, the dead blood will return to your heart and kill you. When it's over, you must return the cord to me."

So began the young poet's first month on Tongatapu. There would be swelling and shrinking and ghost feelings. Because of the chilly and inanimate way his balls played against his skin, not a moment passed when he wasn't aware of the dead tissue courting him. Eventually the scrotum would darken and desiccate, turning black and hard as bull kelp in the sun. The hand of gravity would perform the final tug.

Many effects of castration are known. But one less spoken of is silence. Oh, there was plenty of, *Yes, Tuʻitonga*, and *No, Tuʻitonga*. And a cascade of poetic advice to a child. But inside, in his mind, something had gone quiet, quiet as the moment New Punake approached Six Fists with a closed grip. Six Fists extended a cupped hand, and when the transaction was made, when the beaded cord, still looped tight, dropped from one palm to another, nothing was seen and nothing was said and nothing was heard.

ELEVEN

KŌRERO:
RED FLOWERS

Hā Mutu came for me early. In the dark, it was easy to imagine that everything was as it had been, that Finau and the Wayfinder had never landed, that they hadn't sailed off with the island's men. Hā Mutu led the way up the hills, using the giant kauri tree's silhouette as our guide. Before dawn, we had Aroha in position and were hidden in heavy ferns. This morning I was comfortable with the silence. All was still except for beetles struggling beneath dry leaves. All was quiet except the air through Hā Mutu's nostrils and the squawk of Aroha when we tugged her leash.

With dawn, we could see the Tongan parrot Kōkī in the great kauri tree, presiding over our parrots, including the one with the greenstone ring we'd named Kanokano. The flock had only about a dozen parrots left. They were playful, social, and curious, like people, and that's what got them killed. Stray parrots flitting about must have been from the other island.

When the first of these strays was snared, it cried out loudly, which was good, as its sounds of distress would lure even more birds. Quickly, I went to it, but instead of killing it and stuffing it in the game bag, I let it go. I can't say why I did this. I just released it.

When I reset the snare and returned to the ferns, Hā Mutu said, "Looks like that one got away."

I didn't say anything.

"Don't feel bad," he told me. "It happens."

As I waited in the dark, my mind traveled across time and water. I imagined we were on Aotearoa, living as we were meant to live, as our people always had. There, Hā Mutu wasn't a lonely, distant man whose grandparents had been enslaved and whose mates had been dragged out to sea. He might've been a revered man, one of great status, rather than one who quietly twisted the necks of birds in the dark.

And me, on Aotearoa, who would I have been?

The next bird we snared wasn't loud. When I neared, it gazed at me, bewildered, its pupils large and pinwheeling. It couldn't fathom what had happened. Being held in human hands was something that had never befallen any of its ancestors, so it had no instinct to tell it how to behave in my grasp. I let it fly away.

Hā Mutu approached me. "You're worried about that other island," he said, looking into my eyes for confirmation. "You shouldn't be. I've always known it was there. Our birds have always flown off to this unseen place. I don't believe the people there are dangerous. They're just like us, with the same words and ways. They even share our appetites. The only difference is they go too far, they over-hunt the birds."

I shook my head. "No, it's us. We're the ones."

Hā Mutu reached for my shoulder with his weathered hand. "Only hunger is to blame. If we don't eat the parrots, the people on the other island will."

I started to cry. Not for the birds, but for everything.

"It wasn't easy for me, either," he said. "Watching our men disappear in that waka."

"I've never spent a night away from my father. I've never awakened to find him not there."

Hā Mutu looked away.

My eyes, wet, had lost their focus. The world seemed a shifting pattern of green. "Something's happening on our island, isn't it?" I asked. "Something no one's talking about?"

"The oldest tales are tales of survival," he said. "You should know that."

* *

*

I took Aroha up to our island's peak. From here, we could see in every direction. To the east, dark clouds were developing into open-water squalls, the rain heavy enough to flatten the ocean and sit shiny atop the surface. Wherever my father was, he and the others might be bailing, but they weren't thirsty. Still, I was worried they'd encounter hostility when they landed on this other island. Not all peoples, the Tongans would have us believe, were people of peace. So I developed a plan: If a bird could fly to our island with a message, why couldn't Aroha return with one?

To Aroha, I began repeating the phrase, "Ka haere mai ngā tāne i runga i te rangimārie."

I looked into Aroha's eyes and said this phrase over and over, *Men come in peace, men come in peace*. I ruffled her feathers. I stroked her wings. "Aroha," Aroha answered.

All morning and into the heat of the day, I told her that our men came in peace.

"Aroha," she said, thinking this word was the source of her special attention.

I hadn't eaten anything. Still, I let my stomach growl because from below, I could smell the steam from the earth ovens—today's meal would be baked fern cakes, which this time of year you could only half digest.

I tried to simplify the phrase to "men" and "peace," but Aroha only said *Aroha*.

Thirsty and light-headed, I was ready to admit defeat.

That's when Kōkī flew in. He really was a formidable parrot, with a grand wingspan and a crimson nape. He let loose a series of squawks and screeches. "Kōkī learning parrot talk," Kōkī declared.

"Do all parrots speak the same language?" I asked.

Almost wistfully, Kōkī said, "Kōkī not know. Kōkī not meet other parrots."

"No other parrots?" I asked. "What happened to them?"

"People happened!" Kōkī said.

"Sorry," I said, and I meant it. I was sorry for every parrot we'd eaten.

"Kōkī see you teach your parrot human talk," Kōkī said. "Good luck! Rural parrot not sophisticate." Here, Kōkī shook his head in disgust. "Kōkī try to teach them Tongan classic, like 'Song of Vava'u' and 'Dawn in 'Eua.' Rural parrot not seem to care."

"I'm trying to get Aroha to deliver a message," I said. "I want her to tell the inhabitants of our neighboring island that our men come in peace."

"Ha!" Kōkī said. "Men not peace. Men drown alive. Men bury alive. Men use banana to trick Kōkī!"

I leaned close to Aroha, whispering, "Men, peace."

"Maybe Kōkī help," Kōkī said.

"Can you?"

Kōkī nodded. "But you must protect parrot. You must no kill."

I think I'd already decided this, but hadn't known it until now. I agreed.

Kōkī approached Aroha, then seized her neck in his powerful beak.

"Stop!" I said.

Kōkī released Aroha. "Parrot must *feel* word," Kōkī said. "That how parrot learn." Kōkī once more took hold of Aroha's neck and began making a series of sounds I couldn't interpret. Before long, Kōkī released Aroha, who said, if you listened closely, *Men, peace.*

The two birds screeched in each other's faces and bobbed their heads.

Cautiously, I removed Aroha's tether. She flew off, swooping down the mountain, across our meager crops, and out over the open water, indifferent to the storms ahead.

"Parrot freedom," Kōkī said.

Watching Aroha go, I had an idea. I lined up a series of black cinders to indicate the exact direction she took over the water. Then I turned to Kōkī. "How is it you speak human talk?"

"Ancient poetry," Kōkī said.

I asked, "Why'd the Wayfinder and Finau leave Tonga?"

"Tonga? Kōkī tell you Tonga," Kōkī said. "In Tonga, Kōkī ask a simple question, *Who blow the wind?* One question, and people die."

Was it possible to learn too little and too much at the same time? I looked for Aroha, but she was already out of sight.

* *
*

That afternoon, Hine came to get me. It was time to bathe Tiri, something I regularly helped with. It took two people—one to scrub Tiri while the other steadied her, lest she topple in the surf.

"Where's your bird?" Hine asked.

I explained the bargain I'd made with Kōkī, the mission Aroha had gone on.

Hine asked, "Won't the people on that other island just eat her?"

This question contained hunger, my father, that other island, and Aroha. I wanted to change the subject, but there weren't other subjects. When we reached the beach, I gazed at the spot where the Wayfinder had mapped the heavens. Erased by the tide were his star charts and shells. With few men around to take out the fishing boats, they sat listless above the tide line. And Tapoto's training spears were uselessly stacked at the base of a tree. This sense of absence was new to me. I looked to Hine, who was opening a coconut so we could make some body scrub. She seemed to take no notice of these changes. Having lost her mother, this was perhaps an everyday feeling for her.

We walked Tiri knee-deep into the surf while chewing coconut meat into a pulp, which we spit into our hands and used to scrub Tiri's thin frame. After Hine's mother died—and with her, the identity of Hine's father—we all worried about Hine. After Tiri went blind, our family invited them into our whare, but Tiri, newly sightless, was accustomed to navigating her own dwelling. I, wanting to keep my own family to myself, stopped us from moving in with them.

"Tell me what the sea looks like," Tiri said to Hine. "And don't tell me *it's blue*."

Hine defended herself. "I do my best," she said. "But a wave's a wave."

Tiri directed her pearled-over eyes my way.

"The sea's kind of tamped down," I said. "Not really flat, but the waves aren't sharp. It's like they don't have the will to crest. And with the gray sky, the sea isn't flashing."

"Keep going," Tiri said. "More about the sky."

"Well, there are low clouds, fat and floating along," I said. "Above them, the sky is sprawling and still. Imagine the sky napping after a heavy meal."

Tiri sniffed the air. "Smells like rain."

After Tiri's sea bath, we would rinse her with fresh water—an afternoon rain shower might take care of that.

I lifted Tiri's arm and scrubbed her side with the sweet-smelling pulp. I asked, "Is it true the oldest stories are stories of survival?"

Hine widened her eyes, imploring me not to get Tiri going.

"Who told you that?" Tiri asked. "It must've been a man. Love is the only enduring topic. For what is the point of surviving if you have no one to live for?"

Hine sighed a sigh of impatience, one that said, *You didn't grow up with a marriage ban.*

"Previous to the world, there were two gods, one male and one female," Tiri said. "They were Ranginui and Papatūānuku, who clasped one another in eternal embrace. That was the only narrative: male, female, love. There was no land, sea, sky, or time. There was no death. Only when humans entered the world—mortal, mortal humans—did talk of survival begin."

Hine rolled her eyes. All day, she heard such talk. I, however, lived for it.

Tiri asked us, "The real question is: Which of those Tongan boys do you think is most handsome?"

We both shrieked in outrage.

Tiri stood in the shore break, being moved this way and that as we tended her. "But why would I waste my breath speaking of love to a couple of girls?" she asked aloud, as if to herself. "You two are only girls, aren't you?" Here, Tiri felt the air until she located our jaws, as if she could tell by feel whether or not our lips had been inked.

"Or are you women?" Tiri playfully asked as she pinched Hine's side.

Hine screamed, "Stop, you're impossible."

I found myself also calling out as Tiri pinched my hip.

"Which is it—are you girls or women?" Tiri asked, Hine and I jumping in the shallows to evade her blind hands, all while having to hold her close and steady.

* *
*

Though rain had seemed imminent, it never reached us. Instead, clouds hung offshore, tendrils dark as strangler vines. We'd just rinsed Tiri and were dressing her when my mother arrived. "Tiri," she said. "Concerning these two. Are they girls or women?"

"It remains to be seen," Tiri told my mother.

Hine threw me a look. I asked, "Just what is going on?"

"Come," my mother said. She led us up the beach and along the line of scrub to a flowering bush. Here, she plucked a blossom and placed it in Tiri's hand. Tiri felt it, took in its fragrance. "Five rounded petals, wavy in texture?" Tiri asked. "Red petals surrounding a red cup, yes?"

"That's right," Hine said. "Red petals and a red center."

"And serrated leaves," my mother said. "That'll confirm you have the right flower."

"There's no need to utter its name," Tiri said. She smelled the flower and got the strangest look on her face. Was it longing, sorrow? "How'd my life be different without such a blossom?" she asked.

Hine and I knew this flower, the paurangi. Its varieties—white and pale yellow and even sapped pink—grew wild about the island, and we adorned ourselves with them all the time.

"How could a flower make a girl into a woman?" I asked my mother.

"It must be this variety," she said. "Red petal, red cup, yellow pollen."

My mother had us pick every blossom and bring them to the central fire. Upon these coals, a kōhua of water had been placed. We added these flowers to the boil, my mother kneeling to stir. "Smell that?" she asked. "Both sweet and mineral. Don't forget that smell."

Hine glanced at me, her look wondering whether everyone on our island had gone crazy.

The water darkened from pink to red to an umbilical scarlet.

"A weak brew actually has certain medicinal values," Tiri said. "It can strengthen hair or quiet an angry kidney. A strong concoction, however, has but one result."

The light was fading, yet no one surrounded the central fire. I knew where most of our men were. Where were our island's women?

My mother said, "Knowing how to use this when the time comes. That's something a woman understands that a girl does not." She slid the kōhua from the coals, the brew continuing to darken, even as it cooled.

"Controlling marriage only partly controls population," she continued. "So we have this."

"This allows you to put love first," Tiri said. "Without sacrificing survival."

Carefully, my mother touched the cooling tincture. She brought a drop to her lips. "Come, learn the taste."

Hine licked a drop, an uncertain expression on her face. Then I did. It was alkaline on the tongue, as when you make lime powder from coral by baking it in the fire.

"You don't have to drink much," my mother said. "A coconut shell's worth. First, you feel the cramping. Later come contractions. Within a day, it's over."

"You've consumed this?" I asked my mother.

She didn't answer.

"Has this kept me from having a little sister?" I asked.

My mother spilled the brew into the sand. "This isn't something to be left lying around."

"Did my mother know about this flower?" Hine asked.

"Of course," my mother said.

"So she could've chosen not to have me? But she didn't, she wanted me?"

My mother offered a warm, sad smile to this motherless girl whose father was a mystery.

"Is this flower the secret I wasn't supposed to know about?" I asked.

"What secret's that?" Hine asked.

"One secret at a time," my mother said.

※

In the twilight, the four of us walked toward the wharenui longhouse. There was an unsteadiness inside me. I felt like I'd actually consumed that brew, like something beyond my control was taking its course. Normally I'd talk about such a development, but I didn't know what to say. So I began describing things for Tiri, unimportant things, average things. "The sun's almost down," I announced. "From branches hang fishing nets. A pile of driftwood dries by the fire it's destined to feed."

My mother was studying me. I could tell she was trying to determine whether I was indeed old enough to understand what I'd been shown. Tiri revealed she was thinking the same thing:

"Don't miss the point," she said. "The blossom puts love first."

My mother said, "And the blossom puts the children you have before nonexistent ones."

"Still," Tiri said, "in order to continue as a people, we've ceased having children. But without them, we're more doomed than ever."

Hine asked, "If our people must procreate, why show us the flower?"

"So you can decide your fate," my mother said. "And, ultimately, everyone's."

Inside the longhouse, the candlenut lamps had been lit. Two mats had been prepared. Between them were my mother's inking tools. The lamps had been lit for Hine. They'd been lit for me. And here were gathered our island's women, at the ready to transport—with litters of song, storytelling, and genealogy—two young women over the peaks of pain.

I'd assisted my mother enough times to know what was to come. Hine and I would recline, our heads in the laps of our island's aunts, who'd stretch our skin and wipe the blood. My mother, between us, would be able to shift back and forth, maintaining a steady flow of ink as each of us, in turn, relented to the pain. She'd test her needles a last time by sinking them into her own skin. Then the needles would move to our lips. There'd be an initial strike, a breaking of the skin. There'd be the sooty taste of ink, and the shark-liver flavor of blood. Lips would be blacked. Moko would scroll down the chin, a mark struck in connection to all the women who came before.

A song had begun, one about Niwareka, the beautiful maiden who brought tā moko to earth from the world of darkness, the world of pō. The mats awaited. Our mouths were soon to swell. This would be our last chance to speak for some time. Hine turned to me. I had a feeling she'd use her last words to say something about Finau. I could see the way she was drawn to him, and we were, strange as it was to say, about to become women. Hine opened her mouth, but words didn't come. Instead, she fell into tears, something she almost never did. In this moment it was clear that no mother was here to aid her. Her mother wasn't, and would never be, able to take Hine's hand.

When the inking was over, my mother invited Hine and Tiri to sleep with us, but they declined. Did we invite them for their sake or ours? The thought of the two of them—one blind, one mute—clasping one another in the dark, it broke my heart. My mother could see the distress on my face. She talked to me while she spread our mats on the beach. "Don't worry about Hine," my mother said. "Though you're the same age, in many ways she's older than you, more resilient. In others, she'll forever be younger."

I looked at my mother, as if to ask, *In what ways?*

"The world teaches us soon enough," she said. "There's no need to take early lessons."

Mother blotted my lips with a medicinal infusion. We lay on mats under the stars but couldn't sleep. I was aware of everything, of waves breaking over the reef, of rats scurrying through the palm caps, of the clicking beaks of night birds, of humming beetles flying through the dark. Even the stars were too bright, each pinpoint overly insistent. The red flies bit me one after the other. It's funny, but the bites that used to hurt were now just things my skin took note of.

"You need to sleep," my mother said, though she, too, was wide awake.

The pain came in waves. It forked like lightning down my chin, as when bright bolts branch into the sea. My face hadn't even begun to swell. That would come in the morning. Later would be crusting. Finally, scabs.

For now, not being able to talk was driving me crazy. Was my father upon the sea, in a storm, landing on disputed shores? Was Aroha flapping across open water? And what of the Wayfinder, who'd left not a single thing behind, who'd not one reason to return to our nothing island? I wanted to ask my mother about these things, but I couldn't.

Mother must've sensed this. "Shh," she said.

The only place I could speak was in my dreams. In one, Aroha flew to me—now she could speak as freely as any human. We had a long conversation about what she'd seen on that other island, but when I woke, I could remember none of what she'd said.

Then I dreamed I was climbing our peak by moonlight. From this vantage, I beheld the entire island and the sea beyond, a cascade of pearl-crested waves, diminishing to the edge of the world. I saw a distant figure silhouetted against the sea. He stood where the cliffs plunged down to the Blowholes. His arms were outstretched, like he was trying to absorb the moonlight. It was the Wayfinder. He lifted his limbs high and soared from the cliffs toward the unseen surf below. In the dream, I walked to the cliff and looked down to the cinder-dark sea but saw no sign of him. I finally found him on the beach, tapping shells around his elaborate sand drawing. I told him I'd seen him dive, but he denied it. Can you believe that? He denied it.

The prince of Tonga is the one who dives from cliffs, he said. *Not me.*

I reached out and took up his long hair.

If you're not the prince of Tonga, I asked, *then why's your hair wet?*

TWELVE

LOCATING THE HUMAN SOUL

A WORD ON LOYALTY

When 'Aho was young and was first sent to the Fisian wars, few warriors were inclined to trust him. He was from Tongatapu, a place where deeds mattered less than words, where warfare was political and the weapons people fought with were matāpule. On Tongatapu, every man fought alone. But things worked differently in Lifuka and the enemy territories. Before their vaka kissed the sand of foreign shores, warriors would pass their final moments making pacts. A pair of men would agree to fight back-to-back. A vow would be taken between warriors to retrieve a comrade's body, should one happen to fall. There were pacts about quickly finishing a mate who was mortally wounded, and there were revenge pacts in which two men agreed at all costs to exact vengeance on any Fisian who should happen to bring one down. Men would pledge to care for one another's families, to adopt wives and children. Oaths would be taken to personally deliver a notice of death.

Young 'Aho had never felt such trust. He'd never had such faith placed in him. Such pacts often bound a man to nearly certain death should his partner fall. But rather than making 'Aho feel more vulnerable, invincibility is what he experienced, for the bravest men in Tonga volunteered their lives to him, and he his in return. The safest 'Aho ever felt was inside the swarm of battle, beside the men who'd sworn reciprocal death with him. There's a word for this feeling, *mateaki*, which means "loyalty." It's a word so thrown about today that a person can forget its composition. *Mate* means "to die" and *aki* can mean "for," "with," or "reciprocally."

When his son was born, 'Aho had his first opportunity to give a name, to bestow destiny. Right away, he called the boy Mateaki. There are other virtue names, such as Honor or Patience, but they're much different than Loyalty. Being honorable was always a virtue. Patience was generally good. But being loyal *in general* was the opposite of loyalty. You had to be loyal *to* something or someone. Your loyalty had a benefactor, with whom you made a binding agreement, to the exclusion of all else. So the duty of the loyal man was the search for what his life was worth.

The Tu'itonga was huffing when he arrived at the eastern beach. The morning sun was flashing off the water. At the shoreline, a skirmish was under way. He shielded his eyes, but the situation was hard to discern. A Fisian vaka was rocking in the shallows. His son's canoe, red sail luffing, blocked any escape through the reef. Dogs could be heard. A shoal of loud gulls was hovering, likely a sign that a canoe's provisions had spilled. He looked for Lolohea in the melee, scanning the men and circulating dogs. Six Fists, he knew, would be by his son's side.

Instead of advancing, the Tu'itonga held up, feeling light-headed. Hands on hips, he stood in the shade of a feta'u tree, whose yellow-and-white blossoms had always pleased him, and whose flesh, like a man's, was red. A servant began fanning him. "Finally, relief," he said. "Tell me, what's going on down there?"

The servant looked to the beach. "There are many dogs. They circle the spears of our men. Dogs leap from the bows of the vaka to attack our..."

"What?" the Tu'itonga asked.

"One of our men has been brought down."

The Tu'itonga asked, "Do you think the Fisian vaka is arriving or departing?"

"The enemy is certainly trying to escape," the servant said.

"I wonder," the Tu'itonga mused, "if they've done what they came to do."

"Who?" the servant asked. "The enemy?"

The Tu'itonga was no longer listening—he was thinking of his brother, how he'd found him yesterday, sprawled in the grass with the bones of a woman. Had 'Aho really killed his wife? Why had he returned, and why now? Did he think he was owed something, was he seeking shelter from the war? Or did he want, as he claimed, to simply restore the light in his son's eyes? Now, it seemed, Tuʻitonga might never know. He was the only one capable of looking past his brother's surface—past the hot-tempered "emptier of heads"—to the moody, sweet-natured teen who'd made ceramics with their mother.

Not prone to reviewing the past, the Tuʻitonga recalled the part he played in the making of 'Aho. It was the day their uncle tried to kill them. Though they'd subdued Uncle three times, three times he rose again. The Tuʻitonga thought, *I'll have to take the man's soul to finally finish him*, and in that instant he knew he could do it, that's how his royal power announced itself. He took hold of an oyster shell and a coconut, and, straddling his uncle, told 'Aho to put his knees on their uncle's arms, to pin him while the Tuʻitonga ran the shell's edge through his flesh. The man made much complaint. 'Aho's face changed at the sight of his uncle's still-pulsing insides. To protect 'Aho, the Tuʻitonga said, *Don't look at this business—look into his eyes*. That's how 'Aho began gazing into the eyes of a man being opened alive. That's how 'Aho began conversing with a man whose soul was leaving him. After, his little brother was never the same. And it was no one's fault but the Tuʻitonga's. It'd been his job, his mother always said, to shelter what was special in 'Aho.

The Tamahā arrived at the beach. The Tuʻitonga and his entourage lowered themselves. Here, they were forced to view her legs. Name an honorable woman with such skinny legs!

With the Tamahā were three personal matāpule, the Fefine Girls, her security team, and her security chief Valatoa. Though Valatoa had nine men at his command, they didn't join the combat—their loyalty being exclusive to the Tamahā's protection. Knowing they would not actually fight, the men begged to take up arms against the Fisians. Denied, they then leaned on their spears, watching.

The Tamahā approached the Tuʻitonga. "What is the nature of the situation?" she asked for the benefit of all. "Could anyone have predicted this surprise visit by foreign warriors? Could anyone have known there'd be an enemy attack?"

So insufferable. Her influence was visible on the Fefine Girls, who stood bored and sullen, hair still wet from the bathing pool. Just the feathers they wore cost a fortune, not to mention the sandalwood oil and turmeric powder. But did the Tamahā do anything, did she contribute in any way? The Tuʻitonga couldn't even shake his head in disgust because his aunt so outranked him.

"From where does the enemy hail?" the Tamahā asked aloud. "What was their target? It's probably too early to tell."

"You're right," he said. "It's too early to tell."

"If only there'd been some kind of alert," she said, "some way of knowing in advance that our people were in danger."

"The alarm was only just sounded."

"That's right," she said. "We only now got the warning. Maybe that's how we'll forgive ourselves if we've suffered a loss."

She neared the Tuʻitonga, her voice now hushed and personal. "If my nephew ʻAho has perished, you will have made a fateful decision."

The Tuʻitonga said nothing.

"Only less fateful than if . . ."

"If what?" he asked.

The Tamahā said, "Than if he lives."

Six Fists, limping, returned from the waves. Blood leaked from dogtooth punctures to his calf.

The Tuʻitonga wanted to throw an arm around his friend and help him to the shade, but everyone was watching, and the man, after all, was technically a slave. The Tuʻitonga clapped his hands. "Come, let's poultice this warrior's wounds."

The Tamahā took the opportunity to show the Fefine Girls which botanicals stanched blood.

Seeing Six Fists in pain, thinking of Lolohea in jeopardy, the Tuʻitonga understood he'd made a mistake with his brother. He should have warned ʻAho about the Fisian threat. Loyalty was what mattered, and if anyone could help ʻAho, it was his older brother.

The Tuʻitonga went to Six Fists. "How are your wounds, my friend?"

"What you really want to know," Six Fists said, "is whether Lolohea fights well or not."

"Nonsense, you're my only concern," the Tuʻitonga said. After a moment, he asked, "Does he?"

Six Fists winced in pain. "Your son stands tall while lesser men, like me, fall to the side."

ʻAho and Mateaki had just placed their ceramic vessel in the fire when the sentry alarms sounded. Hands wet with clay, they made their way toward the matter. Locals were fleeing the beach, shouting, "Invasion!" This was unlikely. When Fisians took an island, they struck in multiple places to amplify the chaos.

They discovered a lone Fisian vaka rocking in the waves. A skirmish was taking place at the tide line. ʻAho approached his brother and aunt, their attendants recoiling at the bones hanging from his shoulder. Death and loss, it seemed, were unknown to these people.

But the Tuʻitonga didn't wince at the sight of ʻOfa's remains. Instead, he offered a sudden and surprised smile before embracing ʻAho. "Little brother," he said, squeezing.

"Big brother," ʻAho said, separating. He nodded at the waves. "So the war makes your acquaintance."

The Tuʻitonga continued to inventory ʻAho, looking him up and down. "You're healthy? Uninjured? And your son, no harm has come to him?"

This question though Mateaki stood before him, perfectly fine.

"What're the Fisians doing here?" ʻAho asked. "Why've they come all this way with but a dozen men?"

From the beach came the gurgling howl of a dying dog, but when they turned to behold the sight, they saw a human had actually made the sound, a Tongan warrior with a dog about his neck.

Six Fists cringed at the sound. "They have twenty war dogs!"

"Dogs aren't as formidable as they appear," ʻAho said. "A person can learn to dispatch them."

Six Fists said, "If you mean to teach us a lesson, do it before it's too late."

"We leave the battlefield behind," 'Aho said.

The Tu'itonga's youngest son appeared, along with his parrot and the poet who served as his replacement father. 'Aho remembered Finau as a child, but here, in daylight, he was muscled and nearly a man. "There's been a development," Finau said to his father. In the teen's eyes, 'Aho saw a longing to be recognized, the hope of approval. That look alone exposed the impossibility of replacing a father.

'Aho observed that Finau was wearing a necklace of downy red feathers.

"I must deliver fateful news," Finau said. "I—"

"Where'd you get this necklace?" 'Aho interrupted. "What became of the man who wore it?"

"I didn't actually see it happen," Finau said. "Kōkī did."

"Take it off," 'Aho snapped. He turned to the bird. "What'd you see?"

Kōkī raised his wings. "Tu'ilifuka live!" Then Kōkī dropped his wings. "Tu'ilifuka die."

'Aho sucked air through his missing teeth. "Who did it?"

"*Nea*," Kōkī said. "All human look alike to Kōkī."

"I need you," 'Aho said, "to fly to the person who killed him. I'll do the rest."

"The one who kill Tu'ilifuka," Kōkī said, "he kill with green."

Even the parrots on Tongatapu were worthless. 'Aho took the necklace, tied it around his own throat, then glanced toward the ocean. One of the men on that vaka had killed his friend. The only way to ensure he avenged the Tu'i of Lifuka was to take lethal inventory of them all.

The Fisians were famous for bringing their boys into battle, for keeping what was most dear under their constant protection. This was something 'Aho'd learned from his enemy, though 'Aho never brought his boy into *actual* conflict. When the time came to *truly* fight, 'Aho would stow Mateaki away from danger—in the canoes, on a sandbar, even a decent tree would do. They had a routine: before each campaign, before 'Aho left his son for the fight, they exchanged meet-up plans, contingency plans, and emergency plans. They agreed who Mateaki should turn to, should the worst occur. That person had foremost been the Tu'i of Lifuka.

Kneeling before his son, so that Mateaki was taller, 'Aho said, "I have a duty to fulfill. If something goes wrong, if I don't return, you need to know who to turn to." Though this was his home island, all were strangers to the boy. 'Aho glanced toward his brother, his nephew Finau, Six Fists. "If my fight takes me to the afterlife, you go to the Tamahā. Seek her protection."

"But you promised," Mateaki said. "No fighting on Tongatapu."

'Aho softened his tone. "I said I made no plans for it." He tried to muss Mateaki's hair, but the boy pulled away. "Look, I have an obligation to fulfill. The Tu'ilifuka and I, we made a pact."

"We have a pact," Mateaki said. "You said you wouldn't fight."

"The pledge I made with him, it's much older. In the event of the Tu'ilifuka's death, I agreed to salt the sleep of the man who slayed him. He swore the same to me."

"But he wasn't even a good man."

"Loyalty isn't the measure of a man," 'Aho said. "It's the measure of those loyal to him." He gave that notion a moment to sink in. "Besides, you didn't know him before he lost his family. And remember that he saved me more than once. So his personality doesn't matter. He and I made vows, and in Lifuka, no death goes unavenged."

"You agreed to see the man who killed him dispatched," Mateaki countered. "That doesn't mean you have to do it—you just need to *see* that it's done."

Six Fists, overhearing this, spoke up. "Rest assured, my men will finish off those Fisians, though we could use some help with the dogs."

'Aho thought about letting the Tu'itonga's men handle his obligation. It was far from what a person imagined when making a revenge pact, which was simply this: that after a man struck you down, when he's walking away, self-satisfied, slaking your blood from his club, you reach to him from beyond death, via your friends, and take comfort in vengeance's lone satisfaction: the dealing of the final blow.

"Show me how to fight dogs," Mateaki said. "You said you've been meaning to."

Allowing his son into the fight was the opposite of what he'd hoped for from this trip. But one thing made the decision for 'Aho: Mateaki was beaming at the prospect, and 'Aho couldn't remember a time since 'Ofa's death that his son had been excited about anything.

'Aho stood, undoing the wrap of his kilt, leaving him naked save for a loincloth. "To defend against dogs, you must retire your garments, as they give easy purchase to bring you down. Then, to combat the dog, you must first take the hand of death." So 'Aho relinquished his wife's bones, and without weapons or coverings, walked with his son not toward the battle at the beach, but to the two Fisian warriors and the Tongan sentry who'd fallen earlier in the fighting.

Looking down at the three bodies, Mateaki said, "Maybe we should make a vow, you and I. You know, in the event that anything happens to one of us."

"Vows of loyalty are made by comrades," 'Aho said. "With family, it's implicit, it's in our blood. If anything happens to you, I act."

"What if something happens to *you*?"

"Nothing will happen to me, not on this island. Plus, it doesn't work that way. I protect you. Your duty, when the day comes, is to protect *your* son."

How had New Punake come to find himself so close to conflict? At the tide line: littered bodies, an unfolding battle between man and dog. He'd never even touched a dog. Look at the dead, haphazard in the sand! And the chaotic shrieks of seabirds! Poems flowed naturally, they moved sensibly through their topics—you could trust in poetry's guiding hand. Even the most shocking turn in a poem wasn't really a surprise, as the poem had been preparing you all along. But life! What was this stuff called life?

After 'Aho and Mateaki's all-too-happy departure to fight dogs, the Tu'itonga turned on New Punake. "My son arrives holding the brain of a killer? This is how you protect Finau? I swear that if—"

"I wanna learn to fight dogs," Finau said.

"This is unadvisable," New Punake said. "Too many poems attest to the dangers of this four-legged menace." But before New Punake could quote a single poem as proof, Finau had dropped his kilt, handed the poet a brain, and set off after his cousin.

The Tu'itonga stared at New Punake until New Punake understood that he, too, was about to learn to fight dogs. But Finau had been right about one thing: the idea of setting a brain in the sand seemed unthinkably wrong. The poet placed a broad leaf under the brain. Yet the sight of it in sunlight unnerved him just as much, for weren't brains brined in darkness? He moved it to the shade, but what was to be done? Before long, ants would begin probing its furrows—at some point, what matter a human mind?

When he caught up to Finau, the boy was standing with his cousin and uncle over the dead Fisian warriors and a Tongan sentry. Serenity occupied the sentry's face, as if he were only having a good sleep. *If you had to go*, New Punake thought, *that's the look you'd want to wear.*

"The kuli dog has but one weapon," 'Aho said. "Occupy that, and he's defenseless."

Down at the shoreline, ten Fisians fended off twice as many Tongans with the help of an ever-circulating current of dogs. New Punake wanted to dispute that the dog's lone weapon was its mouth, for even from here he could see that dogs used their claws and could jump quite high.

"The human, however, possesses two weapons." 'Aho pointed to the conflict. "Look how our comrade levels his spear toward a dog. He'll never touch that quick-footed dog with a spear tip, so the fool wastes both his weapons."

It was obvious to New Punake that the Tongan wasn't attacking dogs with a spear but defending himself from them. "Just to be clear, the human's two weapons are his hands?"

'Aho ignored this. "Check these bodies for knives," he said, producing one from his own waistband, a little utility knife, obsidian blade no bigger than a thumb. Mateaki and Finau each found a small knife in the Fisians' waistbands. When New Punake opened the kilt of the Tongan sentry, he discovered only an erection.

"To defeat the dog," 'Aho said, "you must turn to death for a helping hand."

'Aho then demonstrated: he lifted a dead Fisian's arm. By kicking the elbow the wrong way, he broke the joint. Then 'Aho circled the elbow with his knife, severing the muscle and tendons. With a sharp tug, the forearm came free. 'Aho held it up. "This is irresistible to a dog. When the dog clamps down on this severed arm, his mouth is occupied, and he's defenseless. Strike then, and the dog is yours."

Right away, Mateaki and Finau set out to break and remove the arms of the other two Fisian warriors. The cousins, rougher and lacking practice, had to make up with zeal. Watching them reminded New Punake there were much worse fates than his "condition." Only as Mateaki and Finau began walking toward the fight—each with a forearm in one hand and a blade in the other—did New Punake understand he'd have to join them. He lifted the Tongan sentry's arm, but when he kicked the elbow joint backward, the man screamed. His eyes opened, but he seemed not to see New Punake, who leaped backward and trotted away, leaving the man to roll in agony. That's how the poet found himself entering combat without a knife or an arm or anything at all.

When he caught up to Finau, the skirmish was all around them. What even was the objective, why were people fighting? He kept moving side to side to keep his distance from Tongans and Fisians alike. 'Aho was giving advice about confronting dogs, but his words were difficult to make out. Was he saying one should always confront a dog head-on? Or was he saying to never do that?

"You'd do well to drop that kilt," 'Aho told him.

New Punake had his reasons for being loath to appear in a loincloth. "I'll take my chances."

A dog raced out to meet them. 'Aho offered the animal a dislocated arm, which was accepted with delight. The beasts truly loved sinking their teeth into human tissue! By shaking its head, the dog made ribbons of flesh! A single slashing gesture from 'Aho sent the animal running—after a certain distance, the dog slowed before, almost lazily, dropping to its side. Mateaki advanced to replicate the maneuver—after he struck the dog's throat, it raced full speed into the surf, where it met a folding wave, and the foam burst pink. Finau was rougher in his execution—it took more effort to send the dog into retreat, but the satisfaction was clear on the boy's face: he was ready for more. It was New Punake's job to protect Finau from the world, but who would protect the world from Finau?

New Punake tried to absorb the whole of the skirmish—but his mind could only take in aspects. The dogs, white and stocky, cutting sideways across his vision. Angry gulls roiling the air as they attacked an unseen meal. Tongans had taken one of the canoe's hulls, the men like paddle dancers as they advanced along the thwarts, spears and clubs used as much for balance as striking. Between the warring parties, the Fisian sail, raised for escape, clapped the time by snapping full and luffing free. Above, billowing clouds advanced in an epic flotilla, passing over Tonga toward a destiny only the sky could comprehend. New Punake saw a spear sink into a Fisian's chest at the same time he heard the boil of surf break, and that's how death now sounded to him, like water being tossed upon a fire—a sudden hiss, a lifting mist, and then the dark and quiet of sleepy time.

The battle had turned against the Fisians. Their chief called from the deck of his vaka, "Lako mai!," which brought many dogs to him, and by this New Punake understood that dogs could be commanded with words, that this must be the order to return to the Fisian canoe. When a pair of dogs took an interest in him, New Punake deployed the power of language. "Lako mai!" he shouted at them, but to his horror, instead of running to the vaka, the dogs came to him, growling, their eyes fixed on his every move.

'Aho was engaged with his own four-legged challengers. He shouted to New Punake, "If a dog locks onto you, drag it into the waves, where it must release you or drown."

But New Punake wasn't defenseless. He possessed the power of poetry. He recalled the Fisian lines he'd recently uttered:

Nū cuva ra kolī osooso,	*Bow down, baying dogs,*
nū moce sara ra beka,	*sleep now, peka bats,*
e vakaroji kemunū a cabe ni siga.	*the rising sun commands you.*

New Punake summoned his skills of oration. "Nū cuva," he called to the dogs. "Au vakaroji kemunū!"

Both dogs went to their haunches, awaiting the next order.

'Aho took note of this. With amazement, he asked, "What'd you say to them?"

"I commanded them," New Punake said, "to bow down to me."

Pōhiva arrived at the beach after some sort of scuffle had concluded. She found her husband issuing commands from under a feta'u tree. Despite the shade, he was sweating. "A Fefine Girl's been assaulted," she told him.

He closed his eyes and nodded.

"You knew?" she asked.

"The assailant stands among us." He indicated 'Aho, who was talking with Finau, their eyes wild as they relived the skirmish.

Pōhiva said, "The girl would give no details."

"He marked her!" the Tuʻitonga exclaimed, as if this aspect were designed solely to antagonize him.

In the distance, the last Fisians were being subdued. Already in custody were the Tuʻilifuka's war brides. Poor things. So roughly handled. Yet, was it not better that two girls should suffer inordinately, rather than let a man like the Tuʻilifuka spread his corruption around an entire island? In no time, such a man could sully an entire generation, for once a girl knew what was worst in men, she'd never look for their best, she'd never be able to inspire or elevate her people. That's why those girls from Fisi would have to go. It was why that poor Fefine Girl would have to go, too, for a man's debasement of one girl could continue to spread to the rest—through fear, distrust, innuendo, and blame.

The Tuʻitonga shook his head in disgust. "How much trouble can follow one man home?"

"Tongatapu's no longer his home," Pōhiva said. "He's no longer one of us."

"You go too far," the Tuʻitonga said. "He was born here, same as us. Yes, his nature is troubled. He's a project, I admit."

"*A project?*" Pōhiva asked. "Observe the fire he kindles in Finau."

Her husband, having had enough of this talk, began barking orders. "Bring the captives before me. And take those last dogs alive—I want a look at these creatures."

Pōhiva went to the Tamahā, who'd positioned the Fefine Girls like a chorus under a neighboring tree. "Why must you expose these young women to such unsavory undertakings?" she asked the Tamahā.

"They must know Tongatapu's true nature," the Tamahā said.

"This isn't our island's nature," Pōhiva said. "Such an attack has never happened before."

"To which attack are you referring?"

It was so like the Tamahā to deflect in this manner. As if she herself weren't 'Aho's aunt and in some measure responsible for the harm done by him. And this from a woman who'd abandoned motherhood so she wouldn't have to relinquish her rank to a daughter. Yes, to keep her coveted title, all she had to do was forswear men and live alone in a compound with nothing but a fan for friendship.

"Their sensibilities must be guarded," Pōhiva said, aware the Fefine Girls were listening. "Our mission is to refine these girls, to elevate them, so they might learn to elevate their future husbands, and thus all of Tonga."

"Oh, is that what they're for?" the Tamahā asked. "I was under the impression they served Tonga by other means."

Pōhiva saw Lolohea returning alone from the fray. He was nursing a dog-bit hand and appeared shaken and inward. How Pōhiva's heart went to her son in this wounded state. She took several steps toward him, yet stopped. If she went to him, he'd push her away, admonishing her for fussing. And since her husband had resolved to show him no special attention, lest he be seen as sheltered in the eyes of others, Lolo seemed eternally alone. She decided to go to him anyway, knowing he'd rebuff her, but then she saw 'Aho approach him. The two talked a moment before 'Aho put a hand on Lolo's shoulder. Lolohea showed his uncle his wound. Together, they nodded about something. Visible now was another of 'Aho's dangers to them. Before long, 'Aho was escorting Lolo, Finau, and Mateaki back from combat, all of them smiling, until Mateaki caught sight of his mother's bones.

Pōhiva took her place beside the king as Six Fists's men brought the Fisians forward. There were the twice-captured war brides. Also a Fisian warrior, looking wild-eyed and uncertain. And an old Fisian navigator, marked by his fishhook necklace. Last came the Fisian chief and his son, a boy younger even than Finau. The father was speaking to his son in a calm manner, reassuring him. Arriving behind the captives were Havea and the Second Son, who kept their distance, as if conflict were other people's business.

"Those poor Fisian girls have had enough," Pōhiva told her husband. "Can't we send them home?"

The Tu'itonga shook his head. "In their escape, they took up arms against us. Perhaps they once were victims of war, but they're bystanders no more."

"Then handle them with finality," Pōhiva said.

The Tu'itonga gave her a smile—he liked this side of her.

Valatoa, the Tamahā's security chief, retrieved the jade club that Six Fists's men had captured and presented it to the king as if Valatoa had had a hand in securing it. Valatoa was a formidable-looking figure, especially in his bloodstained kilt, but that garment came with the position, and its red decorations were from his predecessor's combat. "Our men were struck down with this," Valatoa said.

The Tu'itonga took the green club, felt its weight. He held it up to examine the jade.

The Fisian chief said, "You must be the Turaga Levu."

"*Turaga Levu?*" the Tu'itonga asked.

"It's their term for great chief," Havea said.

The Fisian chief said, "Look, you've captured this warrior and myself. Why not let the old navigator take the girls and the child home?"

"What manner of weapon is this?" the Tu'itonga asked the Fisian chief.

"That's an item I picked up," he said, "on an island called Aotearoa."

"Aotearoa," the king said, sounding the word. He asked Havea, "You know this place?"

Havea said, "I've heard rumors. People there are said to ink their faces, carve weapons out of greenstone, and tell a story called Kupe and the Octopus."

The Fisian chief said, "As in Tonga, the people of Aotearoa consumed all their ready food. But unlike Tonga, they lack neighbors to attack, so the people of Aotearoa turn on each other."

The Second Son asked, "In what waters can this island be found?"

"Take my word, this is a land of ice and death," the Fisian chief said. "But back to the women and the child, would it not be honorable to let them—"

"What's ice?" Finau asked.

"Tell us the star that takes us there," the Second Son said.

Pōhiva interrupted. "Don't you dare name that star."

The Fisian chief lifted a hand to acknowledge a mother's will, and that's when Pōhiva noticed a leash leading from the father's wrist to the son's. "Why do you tether the boy?" she asked.

"Obviously," the Tu'itonga said, "he's brought his son along to school him in the ways of war. How will we defeat an adversary who tutors his boy, nipple to grave, in murder?"

"Do you really know nothing of us?" the Fisian chief asked. "Or how your attacks force us to live?"

"Hostilities would cease," the Tuʻitonga said, "if your people would simply relent."

To Pōhiva, the Fisian chief said, "I bind myself to my son so he's never beyond my protection."

The idea of leashing a child outraged Pōhiva. It was the opposite of love, wasn't it? But then she visualized a rope connecting her to her sons. Truth be told, a tether would've prevented them from being taken by nurses, by supplemental fathers, and now by Tonga itself. And, while she'd never have towed her boys into danger, anytime they went upon the seas or up against dogs, she would've been brought along to help them. Actually, the more she thought about it, the more she saw the simple beauty of the practice.

ʻAho neared the Fisian chief. "Are you the one who took the life of the Tuʻi of Lifuka?"

"What's it to you whether another man lives or dies?"

"He was my friend," ʻAho said.

"You'd count such a man as a friend?"

ʻAho displayed the black jellyfish on his palm.

The Fisian chief registered the mark, recognition spreading across his face. "So you would."

ʻAho kicked the Fisian chief to his knees. "I have a pact with the Tuʻi of Lifuka."

"I've died many times already," the Fisian chief said. "Another demise is nothing to me. But I ask that you spare the others. The girls have harmed no one. My son is but a boy. This navigator can take them home."

"We can't free the boy," ʻAho told the Tuʻitonga. "It's lamentable, but if we take the father's life yet spare the child, he'll return one day a greater menace."

Pōhiva looked to her husband, who favored any notion that might ensure Lolo's future as king. "You can't seriously be discussing killing a boy?" she asked him.

"Is he not a combatant?" the Tuʻitonga asked.

"The boy can't be called a combatant," Pōhiva said. "He was physically roped into battle."

One of the Tamahā's matāpule said, "An unwilling combatant would be subject to a life of servitude."

"Did he not throw a weapon?" Matāpule Muʻa asked.

Matāpule Muʻa would always take the king's side, whatever side that might be.

The Fisian chief had certainly, for the sake of his son, been keeping his composure. Now it cracked a little. "Servitude, then, if it must be one. Just spare him, and please, spare him the sight of my fate."

The Fisian boy, not knowing what his father was saying in Tongan, still knew his father's anguish, for he began weeping.

"We're Tongans," Pōhiva said. "This is the Sacred South. We don't harm children."

ʻAho regarded Pōhiva. "You can't pretend innocence about what takes place in your war," he told her. "This is but a sample of things done daily in Fisi."

Pōhiva asked, "So you'd have the boy witness, as the last thing he beholds, the death of his father?"

"We can take the boy first," ʻAho said.

"Have you not stated," Pōhiva asked ʻAho, "that witnessing your mother's death was the worst thing that ever happened to you? Did that moment not chart the course toward what you've become?"

ʻAho asked, "What do you mean, what I've *become*?"

"Feʻunga," the Tuʻitonga said. "Discussing the act has become more burdensome than the act."

Six Fists signaled one of his men, who took up a club.

"I adopt him," Pōhiva announced.

"Pōhiva," the Tuʻitonga said, in a way that invited her to come to her senses.

"I place him under my protection," she said. "I have that power."

The Tamahā gifted Pōhiva with a most delicious smile, for she understood what others were yet to realize: if for some reason one of the Tuʻitonga's own sons couldn't don the royal cloak, the king of Tonga would become a Fisian. Or the title would go to Mateaki.

The Fisian chief, knowing he had little time, requested a banana leaf, which he crumpled in his right hand until it was sticky with green juice. The Fisian chief then placed this hand over the son's heart, leaving a glistening handprint there. He said, "I transfer my prestige to you. I house my life force inside you." Then, in Fisian, the father told the son, "I Vula na luvequ, au na bula tiko ga vei iko. O na sega ni sese, ni na tuberi iko tu ga na ligaqu."

While the father said his farewells, Pōhiva spoke to her husband in a hushed tone. "If your brother is allowed to dispatch this Fisian chief, it might lend him much esteem. It's been some time since you've reddened your hands, has it not? And think of the value of having an enemy soul to consult when prosecuting the war."

Pōhiva then approached the Fisian father. She said nothing to him. From his knees, he regarded her deeply, looking for signs of her character, perhaps, or confirmation of her worthiness to caretake his son. She extended her hand. Then he slipped the rope from his wrist and looped it around hers.

Walking away, Pōhiva paused by Havea's side. "Did I hear him call the boy *Vula*?"

The navigator looked deeply pained to have understood a father's last words to his son. He nodded. "The father assures the boy he will never be lost, for the father will always be there to guide him."

Pōhiva began walking Vula toward the royal baths. She'd need to wash this horrible morning off him. The boy fought this development, making much fuss, with many tears being shed and much calling out in his language, all of which was proof of how much he needed her.

This morning, Lolohea had faced combat, grappled with dogs, and stormed an enemy vaka in the surf. Now his father, for the benefit of all, asked him, "Do you think Fisians possess souls?" His father's actions lately had but one goal: making him appear more kingly. But the kingly response eluded him.

Six Fists answered for Lolohea. "*Do Fisians have souls?* There's only one way to find out."

"The Fisian's life is mine to take," 'Aho said. "I have an oath to fulfill."

"Where was this oath made?" Matāpule Muʻa asked ʻAho.

"Somewhere in Fisi," ʻAho said. "I don't recall the island."

"Sadly," Matāpule Muʻa said, "foreign agreements hold no weight on Tongatapu."

"I swore to avenge a friend," ʻAho said.

"I only wish to decant the Fisian chief's soul," the king announced. "His life I leave for ʻAho to take."

"I won't have my prize stolen from me," ʻAho said in response.

Six Fists announced, "I shall deal the knockout blow, making the matter about neither brother." Then the inked man from Nuku Hiva struck the Fisian on the back of the head, slumping him face down in the sand. The other Fisians called out at the shame of it.

A circle narrowed around the downed man. "He claimed he'd died many times," Lolohea said. "What do you suppose he meant by that?"

"I know what he meant," ʻAho said.

"Me, too," Six Fists added. "I'd say the question isn't how many times a man can die—it's how many times he can die and still call himself a man."

Six Fists rolled the chief face up. Sand stuck to the man's lips.

The Tuʻitonga called for a green coconut. Then he and Lolohea knelt beside the chief from Fisi. In a hushed tone, he told his son, "We'll use this moment to elevate us both." The king snapped an oyster shell, producing an edge. Starting at the sternum and following the rib cage around to the base of the liver, the shell made jagged work of the tissue. It was no light business. Muscle and membrane had to be jerked free. Drops of sweat fell from his father's nose into the cavity. Soon the viscera was revealed.

"You can't think of this as death," his father said. "Seen one way, it's akin to birth."

His father moved the intestines. Once scooped into the sand, they slowly undulated of their own accord, like blind fetal pigs. Lolohea thought he heard the man attempt to speak.

"Check his condition," his father said.

Lolohea fingered open an eye. He wasn't sure what he was looking for.

"Has he vacated?" his father asked.

The eye didn't track him, but there was life in there. "He still resides," Lolohea said. Sand from his hand dusted the eye's wet surface.

At last, the Tuʻitonga placed a husked coconut inside the man's cavity.

Until then, Lolohea had been but a witness. His father now took his wrist and placed his hand inside, gripping the coconut. "When the transfer takes place," his father said, "you'll feel the conk."

Shoulder to shoulder with his father, each with a hand on a submerged coconut, Lolohea looked up, into the eyes of Six Fists and his men, the Fefine Girls, his brothers, and the Tamahā, who gazed at the process without expression. He looked beyond them, into the green of the Liku Path and then off to the blue-white of the shore. Gulls wheeled. Shearwaters echoed off the waves. Wind turned inside the branches above. Things were charged with immanence. Then he felt it, the conk of a soul.

His father's smile confirmed their success. "My rarest soul so far has been that of Tuʻi Haʻatala, the only female in my collection. But this one, a Fisian chief, may be my most valuable. We must acknowledge there was something to admire in the man, that despite his rough appearance, he possessed some manner of nobility." He removed his hand, leaving Lolohea to grasp the coconut alone. "When you loft the coconut," he whispered to Lolohea, "your hands must tremble with the power of the deed. The weight of the soul must be visible, and you must declare to your people what they're witnessing."

With that, Lolohea stood, lofting the coconut. Blood ran down his forearm. A murmur of awe swept the assembled Tongans, and there was a new look on Lolohea's face as he absorbed this adulation. "Behold," he said. "The soul of a Fisian chief."

Finau came forward to receive the coconut, his response suggesting it was no longer ordinary, but a thing that'd been burnished by the umbra of eternity.

ʻAho was left gazing upon an emptied cavity. More than one matāpule would be needed to support the case that the Fisian chief was still alive.

"He's yours," the Tuʻitonga said. "Your pact is ready to be fulfilled."

"You've taken something from me," ʻAho said. "Something I won't forget."

The Tuʻitonga smiled. "How many times, when we were young, did we take turns getting the better of one another?"

"The last time you got the best of me," ʻAho said, "I went to war for a decade. Now my loyalty has been taken. Do you really want a brother without loyalty?"

It was not the lot of servants to join in celebration. Instead, they began dragging the dead off the beach. The Fisian corpses would be fed to the hogs, and the local Tongans returned to their families. For Tongan warriors born on other islands, only their bones would make the voyage home.

Two servants came for the Fisian chief, each grabbing an arm.

"Take this one to my compound," the Tamahā said. "And bring along that Tongan warrior as well, the one who was killed by the green club."

The Tuʻitonga glanced at her. "Interrogating the dead again?"

"People speak with greater liberty," she said, "once they're finally free."

When the bodies were taken up, the Tuʻitonga spoke to Lolohea. "Observe the chaos of the scene," he said, pointing to the blood in the sand and the haphazard footprints surrounding the Fisian chief's corpse. As the servants hauled off the lifeless figure, the king went on, "Now look at the way a dragged body leaves behind a smooth path for you to follow. Violence is like this, chaos and mess. But afterward lies a smoother way, one you couldn't see before."

Lolohea nodded.

"Four tests remain," the Tuʻitonga said. "One of them, the Old Canoe, we could complete right now. We could use this momentum and get it over with. The Old Canoe doesn't require you to do anything. You must only bear witness, without interfering, to the fates of others."

The test being proposed was one Lolohea didn't even know how to dread because he couldn't quite imagine it. But, trusting, he nodded. His father wouldn't ask of him something he couldn't do.

As if by design, Six Fists asked, "What about these other Fisian captives?"

"I'll handle them," Lolohea declared. "Get me an old canoe."

Men were sent searching the coast for old canoes abandoned because of cracked hulls or dry rot.

Finau joined Lolohea. In one hand Finau held the jade club; in his other was the bloody coconut. Together, the brothers watched the dead being hauled off through the sand. Lolohea saw his father was right: as each corpse was dragged away, a path was left behind, fresh as the day the islands were fashioned from the sea.

Finau quoted the old poem:

'I hono maumauʻi e lanu oe ʻoneʻone	*Where the sand is stained*
mei he felihaʻa ae tangata,	*from human exposition,*
tō ha fuʻu niu.	*plant a niu tree.*

As the Tamahā had little occasion to leave her compound, she was rarely upon these eastern beaches. She happened upon a patch of sea daisy, whose leaves prevented infection. And she discovered the unmistakable footprints of a heron. *So they aren't extinct.* Also, there was much driftwood, which was the only fuel she burned—she'd have the Fefine Girls carry it back. Her true motive for wandering the scene, however, was scanning for overlooked Fisian warriors, something her security man Valatoa hadn't done. Not only had he presented the green club to the Tuʻitonga, rather than to her, he'd ordered his men to help Six Fists locate an old canoe.

The Tamahā stopped Valatoa. "Your men are supposed to be protecting me."

"I assure you the danger has passed," Valatoa responded. "You've nothing to fear."

"I'm not afraid. But neither am I assured. Have your men secured the area? Or have you been leaning on your spears?"

"Your safety's guaranteed," Valatoa said. "I warrant it."

She pointed at the greenstone club, now in Finau's possession.

"I need you to understand two things," she told Valatoa. "First, that object is my property."

Valatoa didn't wait to hear the second thing. He made his way to Finau, who was scrubbing dried blood from the club. When Finau looked up, Valatoa held out his hand.

Matāpule Muʻa, seeing this, spoke on the Tuʻitonga's behalf. "The jade weapon belongs to the king."

"The Tamahā has made a claim to it," Valatoa responded.

One of the Tamahā's three matāpule said, "It's tradition for gifts from foreign dignitaries to be received by the Tongan of highest rank, which is the Tamahā."

Matāpule Muʻa asked, "You'd characterize that Fisian killer as a foreign dignitary?"

Another of the Tamahā's matāpule added, "He's the highest-ranking Fisian to travel to our shores, and it's not our place to pass judgment on his mission as an emissary."

"This was clearly an attack," Matāpule Muʻa said, "and as such, the spoils of war go to the Tuʻitonga."

The Tamahā's first matāpule countered with the example of a visit from the Haʻamoan ambassador, which had devolved into a killing, yet the Tamahā had retained his welcome gift.

"*Welcome gift?*" ʻAho asked, suddenly taking an interest. "Are you seriously suggesting this wasn't a campaign by Fisians killers to murder a Tongan hero? Are we to believe they were instead on a voyage of cultural exchange? And how can you call a war club lifted in combat a gift?"

The Tamahā's second matāpule said, "Gifts from foreigners often take the form of spears, clubs, and shields."

Since the Fisian chief attempted to leave with the club, Matāpule Muʻa said, it could not be considered a gift. "As a spoil of war, the club belongs to the Tuʻitonga."

The Tamahā's two matāpule looked to her third, whose eyes often twitched under pressure.

He said, "I regretfully conclude that Matāpule Muʻa is correct."

Her other two matāpule closed their eyes in resignation.

The Tamahā regarded the words of her matāpule with expressionless wonder, for it was the man's job to ever champion her will. Men, when advocating for other men, never seemed to confuse their loyalties.

Now that Finau was allowed to keep the weapon, he handed it to his father.

The Tuʻitonga, hefting the stone club, wondered after the Tamahā's motive for wanting it. Perhaps, by attempting to characterize the Fisian attack as diplomacy gone wrong, rather than as a premeditated murder, one the Tuʻitonga had foreknowledge of, the Tamahā was gifting him with a cover story for not warning his brother.

"Maybe the jade weapon *is* a product of failed diplomacy," the Tuʻitonga said. "And shouldn't a gift of great prestige be received by the Tongan of highest rank?"

"Has the island gone mad?" ʻAho asked. "We're talking about the weapon used to murder the chief of Lifuka, a man whose blood still dampens the sand."

The Tuʻitonga brought the jade club to the Tamahā, who accepted it with disdain.

"Of what use is a club to me?" she asked. "Weapons belong in the hands of warriors." She handed the club to ʻAho.

And thus the Tuʻitonga realized he'd been outsmarted again, as the Tamahā had managed to get this weapon into the hands of his brother, the one person on the island who'd best know how to wield it.

"Of what use," the Tamahā asked aloud, "is a matāpule who, despite his expertise on precedent and protocol, has lost his sense of loyalty?" She turned to Valatoa. "Make room in the old canoe for another passenger."

"But, Tamahā," he countered, "this mistake can be fixed, this is a learning opportunity for a young matāpule."

"And of what use," she added, "has your security been to me?"

"Excuse me?" Valatoa asked.

She said, "Tongans were killed this morning, and your team had no idea a threat even existed."

"I assure you, Tamahā, at no time were you in danger."

"How many Fisians attacked us?" she asked him.

"We'll get a body count directly," he said.

"You don't know, do you? So you don't know if all the Fisians are accounted for. You don't know if one's in the bushes, ready to strike. Or which islands they hailed from. Or their intended targets."

"I believe they only intended to rescue the girls."

"You *believe*?"

Valatoa held his tongue. He could only refute the Aunt of Tonga so much.

"Select one of your men to join the matāpule in the old canoe," she told him.

"Tamahā, there's no need for this."

"People must pay for their lapses."

"No harm has come to you," Valatoa said. "We never left your side."

"Do you want to see my brain rolling in the sand?"

"We'll make adjustments," he answered. "We'll redouble our efforts."

"Do you want to see a boy handling my brain like a plaything?"

The security chief closed his eyes and absorbed the Tamahā's words.

"I was in peril," she told him. "If I'd been targeted, I'd have fallen as easily as the Tuʻi of Lifuka because you've never taken your service to a woman seriously. Select your man."

Valatoa faced his team. They immediately offered protests, counterarguments, and examples of exemplary service. They tallied their children, cited connections to powerful people, and soon they were nakedly outbidding one another with offers of sweet-potato stock, garden plots, and even daughters.

Kōkī had been watching from above. He hopped to a lower branch and offered some ancient poetry to the deliberating men:

Ko e havili ʻoku ne halu e ʻulu louniu,	*The breeze strips niu trees,*
pea hae ehe matangi e ngāahi lā fala loʻakau,	*wind tatters pandanus sails,*
ka kohai ʻoku puhi e matangi?	*but who blows the wind?*

"Yes," the Tamahā said. "*Who blows the wind?*"

"What's that mean?" Valatoa asked. "*Who blows the wind?*"

ʻAho approached. In his hand was the greenstone club. "Who blows the wind," he mused, his breath hollow through missing teeth. "Isn't the person in charge of the wind responsible for fallen leaves? Isn't a leader in charge of his men?"

The Tamahā asked Valatoa, "Are you an honorable man?"

Valatoa reluctantly nodded.

ʻAho asked, "Wouldn't an honorable leader select himself?"

"Do you select yourself?" the Tamahā asked.

"I have wives. I have children," Valatoa said. "Where's the honor in leaving them without a provider?"

"So you don't select yourself?"

Valatoa shook his head.

"Then I rise to the task for you," the Tamahā said, confiscating his life and his honor together.

Solemnly, Valatoa's men bound his hands, and they showed little relief that they'd escaped his fate.

THIRTEEN

KŌRERO:
RUSH THEM IN THE WAVES

When Hā Mutu came to get me in the morning, I shook my head no. "I understand," he told me. "Your lips are swollen." But that wasn't it. With a hand gesture, I told him I was through with birding. I could tell he didn't exactly understand. Still, he got the message. Without a partner and a decoy parrot, Hā Mutu couldn't hunt, either. He left looking as if something other than birds had been taken from him.

Work got me through the days ahead—net-mending, fire-tending, roof-thatching. There was all the women's work, plus much of the men's, which included clearing a new sweet potato field. At a place where runoff had cut into the soil, I discovered a rib bone. I held it to my side. Had this belonged to a great-aunt I'd never met?

For dinner, we baked pandanus heads, which were covered in thick kernels, hard as teeth. Everyone groaned, but it wasn't so bad. When they came out of the oven, you needed a sharp rock to break off each kernel. These you pounded against another rock. Yes, they were fibrous and hard to chew, but if you used your imagination, they could taste sweet or juicy, or whatever you wanted. When I tried to take a bite, a flare of pain dropped the food from my mouth.

After dinner, I showed my mother the rib. A look of determination crossed her face. She grabbed a torch and had me take her there. With planting sticks, we loosened the soil. A shoulder blade soon revealed itself. "Men took their coveted tools to the grave," she said. "But what did the women take? We remembered where the prominent men were buried, but where were our island's women put to rest? How've we forgotten that?"

Visible in the soil were finger bones.

My mother said, "There are other kinds of treasure, things a man wouldn't think to value."

I unearthed another bone, one I couldn't identify. My mother brought the torch closer. It killed me that I couldn't talk! I gave her a look that said, *What're we searching for?*

She said, "Our stories mention things that can't be located, things that should've been handed down."

My stick hit something in the soil.

"In the waka that brought us here, there was a conch shell trumpet," my mother said. "That's how they communicated between canoes. Where'd that go? And we have a song that mentions a—"

My mother hushed as I removed an object from the dirt. It was the size of my forearm and wrapped in layers of rotting flax blades. They fell away to reveal an old feather box. The wooden lid was carved with swirling rauponga patterns. Inside was a lone feather, black with a white tip. It'd come from Aotearoa's revered huia bird. Huias mated for life, and supposedly you only needed to trap the one for the other to surrender itself.

My mother marveled at the feather. "The selfishness," she said. "The shame of it. These things belonged to all of us. And what about you?" she asked, self-accusation in her voice. "What about your life, and all we've stolen from you?"

There wasn't much moon that night, but it was enough to climb our island's peak. I enlisted Hine to help me carry driftwood to the top. Over dinner, I hadn't even glanced at her, because to look at her swollen, discolored face was to look at my own. But I needed Hine, she was the only one who understood what I was going through, and besides, neither of us could talk.

Together, we sparked a fire at the island's peak. Exposed to the wind, a long tail of embers swept away from us. I gave her a look that said, *Father told me they'd only spend one night on that other island.*

Hine gave me a look that said, *My father's likely on that waka, too.*

Why've they been gone so long?

Even if my father returns, Hine's eyes said, *I'll never know it.*

Hine stretched out, placing her head in my lap. She was looking up at me, while I was looking out at the ocean, following the arrow of stones I'd lined up to mark Aroha's path to the other island. I noted the setting of stars in relation to that point on the horizon. Some of the stars I knew. Any idiot could see the Dolphin leaping over the sea. And who could miss the constellation called the Fish Trap, or Te Waka O Rangi? All year the Great Waka circled the north, scooping up the souls of the dead. Then it sank below the northern horizon. When Matariki rose again, a new year of soul-harvesting would begin.

Later, the Great Whale made its hours-long dive into the western sea, and just when it disappeared, I saw the star I'd been waiting for: the tip of the Whale's fluke was formed by the star Atutahi. That's where my father was now—where Atutahi touched the horizon.

Hine had been snoring. She had a cute snore that was all hers. When I looked down, though, I saw her eyes were partly open. I could see flying sparks reflected in them, which meant that her view of me included a river of embers. I knew what she was thinking: *I'm lucky to have Kōrero as a sister.* I knew that because I was thinking: *I'm lucky to have Hine as one, too.*

* * *

Mornings, a team of women walked the shore, gathering driftwood, palm husks, rotten coconuts, rafts of sea nettles—anything that would burn. Then we'd sing a driftwood-calling song so there might be more tomorrow. If you think fish-calling songs are haunting and forlorn, imagine how sorrowful it is to sing for scraps of wood. We beseeched the empty-handed waves, imploring them to pity us. While I couldn't sing, I joined in, beckoning with my arms.

My mother and I opened graves in silence. We uncovered a pāua-inlay necklace. Then we found that conch shell. With some cleaning up, it was ready to blow. Everyone took turns sounding long, deep notes, which my mother said could be used as an alarm in case of trouble. To blow it, however, was to commune with the past, it was to become a figure in an ancient song. So people got pretty carried away with it.

My pain flared, vanished, returned like the sun.

Nightly, I watched a whale composed of starlight dive into the sea. The wind turned my signal fire into a swept and crackling beacon. Yet on the fifth night, despite my hope, despite my efforts, Father did not return. Neither did he return the next night. Nor the next. It was all people could talk about. It repulsed me to hear on the lips of others the fearful scenarios rattling around in my own head. *The men got lost. They were attacked. It was a trap. They sailed into cursed water.*

The next morning, my mother led me uphill to where we stored the kūmara sweet potatoes. An excavated chamber kept them cool and protected. On our island, there were squabbles and jealousies and the like, but we had no problems with thievery. Still, when my mother revealed an empty chamber, I thought, *Who has made off with our food?*

"Your mouth has healed," my mother said. "You can speak if you like."

I stared at the empty pit and shook my head.

"The harvest gets worse each year," she said. "And now we're faced with a choice. When we harvest this season's kūmara we can choose to eat it, leaving us no stock to plant with next season. Or we save it all to plant, which means no food for many months."

"But, aren't we preparing a new field?" I asked.

"It gives hope," my mother said. "It keeps people busy."

I sat in the dirt. It was hard to imagine that, not long ago, what I cared about most were stories and songs and which Toki brother would next pick his nose. The whole time, hunger had been looming.

My mother sat beside me. "We're resourceful," she said. "The sea provides. We'll increase our birding."

I gave her a look to tell her what I thought of that.

"We're hoping," she said, "that the people on this other island can help."

I started breathing funny, a sign I might cry. My mother pulled my head against her shoulder.

"So this is the secret?" I asked. "I'd thought it would be a good one, like which people were secretly in love or perhaps someone was pregnant."

My mother pulled the hair from my face. We heard the conch shell blow in the distance.

I stared at the empty chamber. I'd been happily eating sweet potatoes all season, gobbling them at dinner without a care in the world. I said, "The Wayfinder wished there was a way to get the ink off him. It sounded impossible when he said it. Now I know what he means."

"Our people have made it through worse," she said. "I'm not worried. There's coconut meat."

"Which makes you sick, if that's all you eat."

"Hush," she said. "The miro berries will ripen in a couple weeks."

We'll need those to catch birds, I thought.

The conch blew again, sounding even more melancholy for all my newly acquired knowledge.

My mother stared at the ground, silent. I'd never seen her at a loss for words.

"There's always bull kelp," I said. "That can be steamed."

"That's the spirit," my mother said, wiping my eyes, though she looked ready to cry, too.

"And you can do a lot with fern roots."

"Yes," my mother said. "We're going to make it, you'll see."

"Some tree sap is edible," I added.

"Of course it is. And there's plenty of it."

Together we rose and walked arm in arm out of the chamber. The morning light was bright through the trees. Mother held my arm too tight, but I didn't say anything. A couple of women scrambled past, headed uphill.

"What's going on?" my mother called after them.

"Didn't you hear the alarm?" one shouted back.

Then we heard it again, a long conch-shell blast from the island's peak.

We followed the others, racing uphill to discover everyone gazing out to sea. Here's what they saw: A double-hulled canoe was headed our way, taking a line against the wind. Some distance behind was another large double-hull, accompanied by four smaller single-hulls.

"They're running our men down," a woman said. "And they won't stop when they reach our shore."

"Our day has come," another woman said. "If the old stories are true, we know what they'll do to us."

"We must run or hide," someone said. "What about the fishing boats? We could escape to the sea. Some of us, at least."

"All our suffering," a woman said. "All our hunger. For what, to have it end like this, taken like turtles on the beach?"

My mother flinted her gaze. "None of that's going to happen," she said. "We'll meet our men at the cove. Together, we'll face our foes. Their legs will be stiff from the journey. They'll be heavy and off balance when they enter the surf. That's when we attack."

* * *

Violence being unknown to us, on an island that had never seen a killing, we gathered at the beach to mount a defense. Tapoto's practice spears were taken up. As were planting sticks and flax-pounding mallets. Hā Mutu had his birding spear, which was long and bendy. I took hold of my mother. She was my weapon.

Before us, a double-hulled waka turned from the open sea toward the break in the reef. The other canoes were closing the distance. "We don't let them get ashore," my mother said. "We rush them in the surf."

As the waka approached, I could tell it wasn't the Wayfinder's. This waka was of a different design—wider, heavier, darker. With its sail billowing, it was hard to see the men on deck.

Papa Toki held a stick of firewood in his lone hand. I'd sometimes been less than kind to him, but I was filled with admiration as he advanced into the water. "We go at them together," he said.

I looked to Mother, but her eyes were fixed on the approaching craft. None of it felt real. It was like being in an old tale, with no way to stop it or change its direction. Old stories went where they had to go, and there was nothing you could do about it.

From the lead waka came a beastly noise, a howling I hadn't heard before. The hulls struck sand, the pandanus sail fell, and leaping from the waka was a creature that ran a semicircle around us before pausing to urinate in the sand. Its fur was off-white, the color of a fledgling albatross. Its nose fearlessly sniffed everything—feet, fists, spear points. Then it ran off.

I looked to the waka. In the bow was the Wayfinder. "Quite a welcome party," he called to us.

I was thrilled at the sight of him. He'd just crossed to another island and found his way back—like it was nothing. "Was that a dog?" I asked him. "Did you really bring back a dog?"

The Wayfinder squinted at me—I realized he was taking stock of the new ink on my face.

"I figured you'd like it," he said. "One of the first things you asked me was whether I'd seen a dog."

"Are you in danger?" my mother asked. "Are people in pursuit?"

The Wayfinder looked mildly amused. "Danger?"

Tapoto appeared from among the thwarts. He didn't look amused.

"Did you make it to the other island?" Hā Mutu asked him. "Did you meet the people there?"

"Yes, were they friendly?" Arawiwi asked. "Did they have food?"

Tapoto looked shaken. Voice rough, he said, "It's later than we thought."

"What's later?" someone asked.

Tapoto swung his legs over the side—lacerations were visible on the bottoms of his feet. He lowered himself into the knee-deep water and looked upon our island as if seeing it for the first time.

Arriving next was the waka with the frigate bird carved down its side. Here were Finau and my father, hair wild from salt and wind. Looking graven, my father limped across the deck, for his feet had also suffered cuts. Mother and I rushed to him, helping him through the surf.

"What happened?" she asked.

"They're gone," my father said.

"What happened to your feet?" I asked.

"We were too late," was all he said.

"We'll speak no more of this," Tapoto said. "I declare it tapu to talk about that other island."

Only Finau seemed pleased with the results of the trip. He pulled two heavy baskets of greenstone from the waka and tipped them into the sand. Here were the war clubs called mere, each cut from green jade and charged with the mana of countless surrendered lives.

Hā Mutu said, "These were the weapons of our captors." He advanced to the stone clubs, which were blotched with dirt. He took one up, rubbed it with sand, and I somehow understood that it was actually dried blood they were stained with. "This is what they used to control us."

Tiri came forward. With Hine's help, Tiri stood before the new waka. "Tell me, is it black?" she asked.

"It's black," Hine confirmed.

"Is this not the chariot of our oppressors?" Tiri asked. "Is this not *The Red Cloak*, the waka with which our overlords raided in the dark?"

"But how's that possible?" my mother asked. "This waka would have to be a hundred years old."

"They stored it in a canoe house," Finau said. "It hasn't seen water in ages."

"It's worthless," the Wayfinder said. "I'm surprised it made the voyage. One hull is cracked, while the other suffers dry rot. We brought their fishing canoes along to rescue us in case it sank."

In Tiri's cloudy eyes was a mix of fear and excitement. She put a hand on the waka's dark prow, touching it the way you might touch a wild parrot, a thing that was beautiful and rare yet might also draw blood. "It's not a story, Kōrero," she said. "Our past is not a tale. This is the creature that stole us." She turned to face me, the creases in her cheeks as dark as her moko, yet there was something bright and animated in her unseeing eyes. "It's returned to us," she said. "In the parade of generations, we're the ones alive to witness it!"

I placed my hand upon the hull. Tiri was right. *The Red Cloak* had been but a story. Yet here it was, making landfall from the seas of narrative. I could feel the waves our ancestors had crested. I heard the bellows of their conch shell at night. In a canoe such as this one, our children were swept away. It made fact of certain beliefs: That, regardless of our current predicament, worse fates were possible. That, convenient as it was to blame others, *we'd* lost our dogs, *we'd* mismanaged our resources, *we'd* forgotten how to voyage.

My mother asked, "If the royals have been nearby this whole time, how come they never visited us?"

The Wayfinder said, "This vessel's far from seaworthy. We had to weave new sails and re-lash the entire deck. And to build a new canoe, you'd need a tree. Of which they had none."

"No trees at all?" my mother asked.

The Wayfinder said, "What happened to that island is sadly quite common."

"What did happen?" my mother asked.

"Enough," Tapoto barked. "I've declared it tapu to speak of that island."

Finau seemed to have run out of patience for Tapoto. "Your tapu means nothing to us."

The Wayfinder turned to my mother. "They depopulated themselves," he said. "The whole journey was a waste—not a soul was left to point us toward the island we seek." As an afterthought, he added, "I suppose we did get a dog out of it." The Wayfinder blew his whistle, and bounding in from the mangroves came the dog, ears flopping, tongue lolling. "It's okay," the Wayfinder said, crouching down. "This one's been tamed."

At first the little beast was hesitant, but soon its tail was turning in circles. I was amazed at the way it panted, at the way its ears could lift and swivel. I crouched beside the Wayfinder, both of us stroking the dog's fur. The Wayfinder seemed at ease, and I liked his appreciation and wonder for the beast, even though dogs weren't new to him. He carried many burdens, not the least of which was a sack of bones. But, playing with a dog, he seemed a normal young man.

"They can be trained to do anything," the Wayfinder said. "And a dog'll defend you to the end."

The dog placed its face in my hands. How strange to know a thing first by its bones, and then to see it fleshed with life. The dog's eyes were wet and brown and thoughtful. "What've you seen?" I asked him. "Who've you been defending?"

FOURTEEN

WHO BLOWS THE WIND?

An old canoe was found, abandoned in the mangroves. Its bow was honeycombed with dry rot, its lashings frayed. Still, the canoe would serve nicely. It had six thwarts, and its mission, after all, was to sink.

The Tu'itonga spotted Lolohea standing mid-beach, warily regarding the canoe's preparation. Before the king could make his way to his son, however, he was intercepted by Valatoa's two wives and the woman married to the doomed matāpule.

"Our husbands are innocent," one implored.

"Stop this madness," another said.

"They've done nothing wrong," the third beseeched.

The Tu'itonga lifted a hand. "Your issue's with the Tamahā. Those were her men."

"Those *are*," one said. "Our husbands *live*."

The Tu'itonga looked for Matāpule Mu'a. What was the point of matāpule if they weren't around to deal with this kind of thing?

One woman had been pulling her hair, which now stood wild. "Our children will be fatherless."

"The Tamahā outranks us all," the Tu'itonga said. "Even me."

He began moving toward his son, the women hindering his way as much as they dared. Then one of Valatoa's wives stopped in the sand, blocking him.

"You're the lord of all Tonga," she said. "At your word, islands rise and fall. You have the power."

The Tu'itonga cut the air. "Fe'unga!"

The women understood any utterance after this could prove fatal. They dropped to their knees and began silently, violently throwing sand at the Tu'itonga's ankles, for this was a time-honored form of protest.

'Aho approached, smiling at the sight. "Enjoying the privileges of being king?"

"Wanna take my place?" the Tu'itonga asked.

"Defeating people is one thing. Ruling them's another. I'll stick with what I'm good at." 'Aho watched the sand pelt the king's shins. "Speaking of service, Mateaki would like to offer Lolohea his assistance during the upcoming trial."

"You'd think Mateaki had designs to be king, such is his dedication to royal tests."

"The point of the tests is to develop character and leadership. That's the reason my son takes them."

The Tu'itonga said, "Do thank Mateaki for his offer, but it's not necessary."

"You owe me too much to start telling me no."

Some sand from the protest sprayed upon 'Aho's legs. He turned his attention to the offending woman.

"Have I wronged you?" 'Aho asked her.

The woman fixed her eyes on the great slayer of Fisians.

"You think I don't know what it means to be a widow?" 'Aho asked her.

The Tu'itonga wondered if this was a joke. He asked, "Isn't being a widow the situation in which the wife lives while the husband does not?"

'Aho ignored this. He bade the woman rise, and when she did, he moved close. "Do you know what my wife'd give to have me by her side? You know what she'd be willing to do?" 'Aho shook his head in disgust. "More than tossing sand, I assure you. Yet she has no choice. She's forced to wait for me, completely alone, with no man to protect her, counting the days until she gets her husband back."

"Leave the widow be," the Tu'itonga said.

Trembling, in almost a whisper, the woman said, "I'm not a widow. My husband yet lives."

"There's only one way," 'Aho told her, "to forever live by someone's side."

With those words, the women made their escape.

The Tuʻitonga took Lolo's hand to examine the dog bite. "Foul beasts," he said, articulating the fingers and expressing the palm. "Salt water," the king said. "A good soak in the sea is all this injury needs."

In the shallows before them, the older Fisian girl, hands bound, was being lashed in the bow. Lined up, waiting their turns to be tethered, were the younger Fisian girl, the Fisian warrior, the Fisian navigator, Valatoa, and, in the stern, the young matāpule.

Trying to be positive, the Tuʻitonga said, "It'll be a fine day for sailing. Clear skies, crisp wind."

"*Sailing?*" Lolohea asked.

Some debate was taking place at the shoreline, so the Tuʻitonga sent a Fefine Girl to get a report. Then he returned to his son. "You still up for this?"

"I've yet to run."

"That urge passes," the Tuʻitonga said. "Soon, quitting and running will no longer be options. When you become king, such thoughts simply disappear. It's quite liberating when they're gone."

Lolohea had no response to that.

"I was just speaking with your uncle," the Tuʻitonga said. "It seems he's become confused about what it means to live and what it means to die."

Lolohea sucked the heel of his hand and spit red. "They say you're never more alive than when you're closest to death. Maybe with enough combat, the two can blur."

The Tuʻitonga gave this notion its due. "You have some distasteful deeds before you. But once they're over, things'll change, you'll be insulated from the ugliness."

"I'll still give the orders."

"A man either gives orders, or he carries them out."

In the distance, they'd begun lashing the younger Fisian girl to the canoe, and even from here, just by the lift of her shoulders, the Tuʻitonga could tell she was weeping. He had the urge to tell Lolo to look beyond the surface of the test at hand, to see past the tears and laments and complaints to the bigger truth that his uncle ʻAho was now circling, that his cousin Mateaki had taken up position, that the Tamahā's tentacles were extending. He wanted to tell his son to look past the slumped figures in the canoe and understand that this was life-and-death for him, too, for his mother, for his brothers, for all of them, that there was a possible future in which they were passengers in the next old canoe. But he saw the heat in his son's eyes and decided on a different approach.

The Tu'itonga shifted his bloodied coconut so he could place a calming hand upon his son's shoulder. "This is the easiest test," he said. "To pass it, you simply do nothing. The test measures your ability not to act, so that in the future you'll maintain your poise when the ground shakes, the storm rages, when squid ink darkens the waters. There's nothing to fear. Your brother will sail you upon the proper waters, a canoe will sink, and you'll return in time for lunch."

"They're going to plead and beg," Lolohea said. "They're gonna writhe."

"You don't know the future. And you can't know a person's character, not truly know it, until you've watched him die."

Lolohea looked more rattled than ever.

"Just don't interfere with their deaths," the Tu'itonga said.

The Fefine Girl returned with news, but the Tu'itonga halted her.

"Think of it another way," he told Lolohea. "Take your mind off death as a thing that's deserved or not, that should come at a certain time or in a certain way. It comes for everyone, and for most it comes too swiftly and without warning. These six people get the rare thing—a long calm with which to ponder their individual conclusions. They get to sift through the cooling ash of the past for whatever survived life's fire. They get to rise, shoulders back, of their own accord, from the seat of life. Sure, they can choose instead to slump, whimper, or bemoan—as they see fit. Either way, it's like that old poem about how people, in death, *forever seal their truest selves in the cave water of our minds.*"

The king could tell Lolohea was listening, though he remained focused on the condemned being loaded into the canoe. His eyes were reddening.

The Tu'itonga turned his attention to the Fefine Girl. She looked familiar, but they changed every year, and he'd given up on keeping them straight.

"I report that Havea," the Fefine Girl said, "believes the Fisian navigator's hands are bound too tightly, that they should be loosened out of respect for the man's vast knowledge and the fact that he's neither a warrior nor an assassin but merely a student of the stars who shuttles his superiors across the sea."

The Tuʻitonga listened in exasperation. "So our assassins are uncomfortable, is that it?"

"I also report," the Fefine Girl continued, "that Valatoa requests, as the highest-ranking Tongan in the canoe, that he be positioned in the bow."

The Tuʻitonga shook his head at this ridiculous notion.

"When you're king," the Tuʻitonga told his son, "you'll discover that every stump, rock, and tree has a damned opinion." He then turned to the girl. "Learn to ignore the entreaties of the condemned, and you'll go far. But yes, tell Havea to act as he sees fit." The Tuʻitonga then held out his blood-slicked coconut. "Most important, you're to take this coconut to the royal compound and place it in the bowl in my chamber."

The Fefine Girl took the coconut. Before leaving, she stole a glance at Lolohea's wet eyes.

Moon Appearing, bloodied coconut in hand, returned to the waterline, where the condemned were being bound to the old canoe. Havea asked her, "What'd the king say?"

"*Act as you see fit*," she reported.

Havea untied the Fisian navigator's purpled hands. He re-tied only one wrist. "Navigators aren't prone to jumping ship," he said.

The Fefine Girls shared much gossip about the men of Tongatapu. Of Havea, it was said his wife had died, but no one would tell him for fear he'd take his life or, worse, he'd chart a voyage of no return with the Tuʻitonga's son.

"What about me?" Valatoa called to Moon Appearing. "What said the king of my request?"

They'd stripped Valatoa of his war kilt—he'd go naked into the afterlife.

As directed, Moon Appearing ignored his entreaty. She looked back to the Tuʻitonga, who was in conference with Six Fists. Some girls said Six Fists was a man of little regard in his own society, that he chose not to escape his Tongan bondage because he'd return to a lower station. Moon Appearing gazed upon the man's powerful bearing, at how he stood taller than even the king. Some rumors could be dispelled with a single glance.

"Am I to be ignored by a Fefine Girl?" Valatoa asked the heavens. "Is it not enough that I'm to die? That my life will be bought at no price at all? Now a dancing girl sees through me?"

Moon Appearing glanced at Valatoa with contempt.

"Ah, I have your attention, lovely lady," Valatoa said, changing his tone. "If I could have but a moment with the Tuʻitonga, I'm sure this confusion could be resolved. Could you do that for me, could you convey the message that I humbly seek an audience?"

"How many wives do you have?" Moon Appearing asked him.

"Wives?" Valatoa asked. "What matter is it how many wives I possess?"

Moon Appearing turned away.

"Two!" Valatoa said. "I have two."

The vaka was pointed east, toward the open sea, and, while the stern rested firmly upon sand, the rest of the canoe was afloat and rocking. Moon Appearing waded into the water to wash the blood from the coconut. This gave her opportunity to observe the calm and meditative Fisian warrior, the grizzled navigator who used his free hand to hold his fishhook necklace, and then there were the poor girls. Steadying the bow was New Punake, who stared nakedly upon the girls, at the ink adorning their curves, at the flex of their ribs as their breathing clutched. The way New Punake looked at the Fefine Girls each morning was laced with lust, longing, and self-pity. The look he gave the Fisian girls was different. There was outrage in his eyes, outrage at the waste of what he was seeing, for he seemed in utter disbelief that perfectly good women were being destroyed when he himself had no woman at all, when in fact every woman had been taken from him.

Some girls claimed New Punake kept his dried testicles in a pigskin pouch, that he would pull them out from time to time and weep over them. The girls also said that being the royal poet was such a lousy position that the previous poet had taken his life by eating the red-and-black seeds of the moho plant. Moon Appearing wasn't so sure about these things. What she did know was that for every man who got two wives, there was a man who got none. This wifeless man would get restless, resentful, troublesome. These were among the men her father sent to war, and the truth was that New Punake had all the makings of being a womanless man with an unhappy fate, even if he'd never been castrated.

Though the bow of the vaka was rotten, stones placed in the stern would ensure the rear sank first, drowning them all, one at a time, starting with the matāpule in back and ending with the woman beside her, who was oddly serene as she squinted seaward. Moon Appearing wondered if the Fisians had such a practice of group drownings, and if not, did this girl even know what was happening?

The Fisian girl addressed Moon Appearing, which startled her.

Havea translated. "She wants you to lift the coconut to her ear."

"What, why?" Moon Appearing asked.

Havea said, "It contains the spirit of the man who crossed the sea to save her."

Moon Appearing asked, "What's her name?"

Havea spoke to her, then translated to Moon Appearing. "Siga. It means 'Sun.'"

Moon Appearing rinsed the coconut and extended it to Siga, who leaned her ear to it. Listening, she closed her eyes. All fell silent to observe a young woman taking counsel with the man who'd sacrificed all to free her.

Two children suddenly splashed into the waves, a boy and a girl. Each taking a hind leg, they dragged a dead dog through the water and onto the sand, where they started running down the beach with their prize. Moon Appearing had almost forgotten a battle had taken place here, that a short while ago the wave froth was pink with it.

"How do you say farewell?" Moon Appearing asked.

"Moce," Havea said.

"Moce, Siga," she said.

Siga didn't respond. She returned her gaze to the waves. Havea spoke to the condemned girl, and though Moon Appearing couldn't tell what was being said, she knew his words were consoling.

Moon Appearing asked Havea, "Do you think the Fisian chief was Siga's father?"

Havea put this question to Siga.

When she responded, everyone turned to Havea. "She says he was just a man." There was a look of bitter disgust on Havea's face. "This," he said. "This is why I never come ashore."

Moon Appearing took the king's coconut and headed toward the royal compound. She tried to push from her mind thoughts of people drowning. Last night, before sleep, Sun Shower had told Moon Appearing the story of Tuʻi Haʻatala, a rural girl whose spirit went to all the islands, no matter how small, to discover their charms. Eventually, she became a great chief. "There are other paths," Sun Shower said, "than the one laid out for us."

Moon Appearing only knew of one story in which women lived as they chose. Off the coast of her home island of Hunga was another island, one too small to support a village. Most people called it Hungatoetoenga, the "Leftovers of Hunga." But her grandmother called the island by a long-ago name: Motutahamāamafefine, the "Island of Women Who Shared the Light." Her grandmother told the story of two women who'd run from their husbands to live apart from others. She claimed that on certain nights, if you looked across the water, you could still see the torches of these women as they fished at night. There was always a moment when the two women joined forces and tied their torches together. Moon Appearing's mother said this story was foolish, that no woman could live without a man. But today, Moon Appearing knew the story was true, that real lives were needed to make stories endure.

Moon Appearing was starting to learn the place names of Tongatapu. She crossed the beach named Manutuʻufanga for the birds found there and climbed a rise named Matangavaka, the "Place of Watching Canoes." She would take Tukungaʻalafia, the "Path of Easy Accomplishment," to Halanukonuka, the "Path of Sweet-Scented Shrubs." There, she'd find the Halamotuʻa, the "Old Road."

In the Tuʻitonga's sleeping chamber, Moon Appearing lifted the coconut that contained the soul of Tuʻi Haʻatala. "A girl from a rural island needs to hear your story," Moon Appearing said. "Please let it be true." Then, with much hope and fear, Moon Appearing held the coconut to her ear.

THE STORY OF TUʻI HAʻATALA

Tuʻi Haʻatala was no tuʻi chief. She came from a poor family. Her parents, having little to offer their nine children, gave them high-sounding names like Tuʻi and ʻEiki and Hau to hopefully improve their standing in life. Following Tuʻi Haʻatala's parents' deaths, her siblings began dying, all by lightning strike. After the five eldest were struck, Tuʻi Haʻatala decided to have a word with Hikuleʻo, god of the afterlife. So she went out in a storm to catch herself a bolt. There was a bright flash, and her spirit left the flesh. "Let no one bury my body," her spirit told her remaining siblings.

Before confronting Hikuleʻo, however, Tuʻi Haʻatala decided to go traveling, for she knew nothing of the world but hunger, funerals, and the island of her birth. So she made it her business to see all hundred and sixty islands of Tonga and the three hundred islands of Fisi. Having no body, it was easy, for she traveled upon a mat made of wind. She swam the underwater caves of ʻEua, bathed in the four springs of Niuafoʻou, and paddled a vaka of vapor across the crater lake of Tofua. But it wasn't just geography she exposed herself to. She drank a bone broth of truce in Vanuatu, went fara on the peace-loving island of Rotuma, and, because she was a virgin, rubbed oil on the muscled chests of the strong men of Haʻamoa, none of whom complained about their invisible encounters.

The time came to confront her god. She broke off a branch from the uhi tree, which delivered her to Pulotu, island of the afterlife. She found Hikuleʻo's dwelling empty, though in the god's oven a sweet potato was cooking. Coming from hunger, Tuʻi Haʻatala could not resist partaking. When Hikuleʻo appeared, Tuʻi Haʻatala saw this god was both a man and a woman, blind and all-seeing. She'd once been ashamed of her lowly state, but seeing the world taught her that scarcity, poverty, and powerlessness were everywhere. "I've made my life forfeit," she told Hikuleʻo, "to press you on the suffering of Tongans, for it goes unaddressed."

"I make few interventions in human affairs," Hikuleʻo said. "Human doings alone account for the lowly state of humanity."

"Perhaps you should claim godliness of another people, if you perform so few duties on our behalf."

"Bold is the woman who steals sweet potatoes."

"I make no apology for hunger," Tuʻi Haʻatala said. "Will you account for my murdered siblings?"

"I work at the behest of your island, which is exhausted by you. So I make my culls, and why not the impoverished, for your lives seem least favorable?"

"Our own island wants us gone?"

Hikuleʻo glanced into the distance. "I see your siblings bury your body."

"I told them not to bury me!" Tuʻi Haʻatala exclaimed.

"Without a body, I cannot send you home."

Tuʻi Haʻatala thought of the islands she'd yet to see. Of the foods she'd yet to taste. Of the muscled men of Haʻamoa. "You must send me back!"

"You'd have to inhabit another body," Hikuleʻo said.

"Whatever it takes," Tuʻi Haʻatala responded.

"One is just now coming available," Hikuleʻo said. "It's the body of a man, a chief."

When Tuʻi Haʻatala agreed, Hikuleʻo floated her in the river of life. Looking up, she saw stars glowing lavender against a purple sky. She forgot that her island had conspired against her, that her god was one of indifference. Yes, there was hunger and conflict and suffering. But the world was worth knowing, she decided. Life was worth experiencing. "A man," she mused, closing her eyes. "A chief."

Tuʻi Haʻatala woke in Tongatapu's royal compound, sprawled on the ground. She found herself looking up at the Tuʻi of all Tonga, who exclaimed, "Though we've just executed you, you awaken! I promise the next blow will be more substantial."

"Wait," Tuʻi Haʻatala said. "You can't kill me, for I've achieved much understanding of the lives of women and the poor and overburdened islands."

"Hand me a club," the Tuʻitonga said. "I'll finish this myself."

Tuʻi Haʻatala said, "I've eaten a sweet potato from Hikuleʻo's fire and found buoyancy in the river of life. I've visited every island in Tonga and Fisi and eaten wild parrot with the lords of the Lau Islands."

"You know Fisi's Lau Islands?" the Tuʻitonga asked. "You know Lakemba and Fulaga? Do you know their defensive structures?"

Tuʻi Haʻatala described the fortress Lakembans had built on their southern promontory and revealed the location of a secret cave on Fulaga where refuge was sought during Tongan attacks.

"You'll be a welcome addition to my council of advisers," the Tuʻitonga said. He called for a fresh coconut. Then he picked up an oyster shell. Breaking it produced a jagged edge.

The *Pelepeka* wasn't built to carry six, but its sturdy twin hulls did their best. The Second Son sat upon the navigator's perch, with Havea at the steering oar. The small deck held Lolohea near the bows, followed by Mateaki and Finau, and of course at Finau's side was New Punake.

It'd been difficult to tow the old canoe past the reef, as there was little room to maneuver, and the red sail, often luffing, could only baby-sip the wind, but finally they were in the open rollers that funneled between Tongatapu and the island of ʻEua. Behind them, the old canoe would disappear in the waves, then rise up high. The matāpule, who'd been quiet before, found his voice and was shouting about precedents and traditions, citing examples of the sacrifices matāpule made for those they served: ". . . another matāpule who willingly took a spear for his king was . . ."

"Let out more rope," Lolohea said.

New Punake released the last two coils. "There's no more."

Finau was rarely upon the water. He gazed ahead at sun-mirroring waves cresting the bows, and then turned to behold their heavy blue shoulders rolling from the stern. He admired how white beards of albatross shit ennobled the faces of now-distant cliffs. He gazed below the waves, at chains of yellow starfish clinging to abalone-blue boulders, at the shadows of schooling fish turning in tide-hollowed reef bowls. From his back, Finau studied the sky. He let a foot dangle into the sea, upwelling with deep, cool water. "What makes a wave rise?" he asked. "I mean, what compels it?"

"The wind," the Second Son said. "No wind, no waves."

New Punake also reclined. "Maybe a wave isn't compelled. Maybe it wants to rise."

"Yeah," Finau said. "What does a wave yearn for, what's it desire?"

The Second Son was fine-tuning the rope that trimmed the sheet. To do this, he had to gauge the spray from the crests ahead. "Seriously," he said. "The wind pushes the water. It's pretty simple."

"Maybe the sea wishes to escape its low-lying life," Finau mused.

"Perhaps the sea is jealous of the land, of its permanence," New Punake added. "Or maybe it's the sky's elusive indifference that drive the tides."

"Tides are different than waves," the Second Son said. "Tides have to do with the moon."

Finau countered the poet. "But the sea has both the power to make land and take it. And one look at the horizon shows the sea and the sky become one."

Havea asked, "Do they always talk like this?"

"Yes," Lolohea and the Second Son said in unison.

"In Fisi," Mateaki volunteered, "what waves yearn for are the hard-to-reach bodies, lodged high on the beach."

"*Nea-nea*," came a call, bouncing off the water. Soon Kōkī's blue-green wings were wide and flapping as he came to rest upon the deck. "Kōkī scared of water," Kōkī said before quoting an old poem:

Liku Tonga, liku tapu,	*Tonga's seashore, sacred seashore,*
ai he nganganā kōkī,	*where the fallen parrot,*
kuo toli 'e peau.	*is plucked by the waves.*

Finau ruffled the feathers of his beloved bird. "Kōkī, what makes a wave rise?"

"Enough of this talk!" Havea said. "You wonder why a wave behaves the way it does? What choice does anything have in this world? A wave's duty is to rise when called. And the reason it bows down is simply because it must."

For a moment, there was nothing but the crackle of the sail and the wind-dampened complaints of the matāpule at the end of the rope.

"One doesn't have to understand a wave to capture it in words," New Punake said. "That's what poetry's for. What is the sun, what is silence, what's the nature of the sea? I don't know—it's beyond my reckoning. But with words, I can place the sun in your hands. I can seal the idea of silence in the 'umu oven of your mind."

"Enough of this blathering," Havea demanded. "The navigator has no need of talk. To cross the sea, you must leave the land of words. You think the ocean cares about poems? Poetry doesn't even exist out here. Light, sky, current, sun, all come speechless. Stars extinguish themselves one by one as they touch the horizon. That's the definition of silence."

New Punake cast a glance at Finau, to suggest his point had been proven, but Havea didn't see this. He continued working the steering paddle, eyes closed against the sun, only occasionally lifting a hand to peer at the world through a slit between his fingers.

Finau said, "Silent is the vaka that sets sail below the surface."

Kōkī said, "Silence is the answer to the last parrot's call."

New Punake said, "Silent is the voice that once kept you up at night."

Silence, Lolohea thought, *is a feathered cloak hanging in the dark of a royal chamber*.

"Silence," Mateaki said, "is the thing that carries your mother away."

The Second Son was focused on the sea. He felt the current change, the water flatten.

Below, purple sea urchins were laboring up submerged volcanic outcrops, while others freely tumbled back down. Then everything changed color, and nothing was below. They'd reached the dropoff.

They loosened the sheet and secured the sail. Now they were drifting. Havea and New Punake began hauling in the tow rope, though they seemed none too eager to actually land their catch. The old canoe was low in the waves and lumbering—with no one able to bail, it'd taken on water, which meant the *Pelepeka* was mostly pulling itself to them. It was three crests away, then two. They didn't throw ropes or lash hulls, which, for the Second Son, felt eerily wrong. All vaka, meeting on the open water, hold fast to one another.

The matāpule, as he neared, grew quiet again. "There's no precedent for this," he mumbled.

The moment Valatoa was sure he could be heard, he resumed his appeals. "Look, noble friends, let's not let the tensions between the Tuʻitonga and the Tamahā play out upon us. Why should their feud become ours?"

Lolohea leaped from the deck of the *Pelepeka* into the bow of the old canoe. The younger Fisian girl let out a shriek. She began speaking rapidly as Lolohea used a rock to gouge the hull, opening a hole in the dry rot the size of a fist. The gurgling spring made the girls gasp as water ran across their feet, headed for the stones in the rear.

The Fisian warrior offered a rough comment, and Lolohea looked to Havea for a translation.

"He wants you to make the hole bigger," Havea said. "To get it over with."

Lolohea studied the people before him. The older Fisian girl called Siga took in the brocade of his ink, as if the truth of the man killing her were to be found in the pattern on his legs. The girl behind her was now breathing too rapidly to speak. The Fisian warrior, eyes closed, seemed to inhabit his own realm. The Fisian navigator focused on Lolohea, as if awaiting the destination he'd steer as his final course. Valatoa resumed his entreaties: "Prince Lolohea," he said, as the matāpule desperately looked on.

Lolohea then extended a foot and pulled himself aboard his brother's canoe. He'd overseen the condemned as they were lashed. He'd towed them into deep water and broken open their hull. But it was this step, taken from one vaka to another, that made him feel like he'd killed these people. He got to leave, and they didn't. It was that simple.

"Prince Lolohea," Valatoa called again. "You're soon to be the most powerful person in Tonga. But have you considered how powerful you already are? You have the power to call for someone's death. And you have the power to call for life."

The matāpule chimed in, "There are many examples of princes exerting great authority."

"Shut up," Valatoa told him, then offered Lolohea a warm smile. "It's time to start thinking about what kind of Tuʻitonga you'll be—will you be a just one? We've clearly done nothing wrong. The Tamahā gives more thought to the feathers in her hair than to our deaths. Is that the kind of king you'll be, one who tolerates arbitrary killing? Is that the kind of prince you are now?"

Siga looked to the sky, said a phrase, and then, eyes closed, began repeating it.

"What's she say?" Lolohea asked.

Havea said, "I'm done translating."

Water had been at the matāpule's ankles, and then his calves, and it was nearing his knees when a swell swamped the back of the canoe. A great confusion appeared on his face as he found himself without anything to separate him from the sea. Several half coconut shells floated freely around him, and he gazed upon their lolling and bobbing as if they possessed everything he'd lost.

"I have a child," the matāpule said. "Our first child has just arrived."

"Do you know how many children I have?" Valatoa snapped at him. "But, Prince Lolohea," he said, his voice warm and ingratiating, "your father's sick. You'll soon be Tu'itonga. You're going need your own security chief, one loyal to you. I can be that person."

"Our father's not sick," Lolohea said, then regretted engaging him.

The Second Son asked, "What'd he say?"

"Don't listen to him," Lolohea told his brother. "He'll say anything."

"His kidneys are dying," Valatoa said. "The Tamahā knows it. You'll soon be king, and you'll either have to endear yourself to the Tamahā or find a way to outsmart her."

"My father's not sick," Lolohea insisted.

"I could be useful," Valatoa said. "I know everything about her. And you can trust me, I'm loyal, loyal to the grave. You'll see, I won't insult you, I'll offer no invectives."

The canoe's bow lifted as the stern started going down. The matāpule's shoulders were going under, and it was dawning on him that his chin would be next. "You don't just murder me," he said. "You murder my child. You are killers of children." And then the invectives began. While the Fisian will invoke curses upon a person's future, and the Ha'amoan will invite the gods to do you harm, the Tongan favors the imperative. "Go lie down in the shit fields of 'Umutangata," the matāpule commanded. "Go hump your sisters with sandy pricks and—"

Valatoa tried to retain the prince's attention as his own chest lowered into the water. "I know the Tamahā's plans," he said. "I know how to thwart her. Now, if you want to acquiesce to her, if you want to succumb to her powers, then I apologize for speaking out of turn. But if you desire to avoid that fate—"

"Feʻunga," Lolohea said.

"No," Valatoa countered. "This is my death. You need to hear—"

A swell put both their heads underwater. The matāpule emerged wide-eyed, hyperventilating. He bent his head back as the sea began to circle his face. Finau moved to the edge of the *Pelepeka*'s deck so he could gaze upon the moment water erased his features.

Valatoa addressed Mateaki. "Son, I could be of service to your father, too. If he remains on Tongatapu, he'll need help navigating the inner workings of this island. Did you know, for instance, that the assassin this morning was here to kill your father as well, that the Tuʻitonga knew this yet offered your father no warning?"

Mateaki asked Lolohea, "Is that true?"

"You can't listen to a doomed man," Lolohea said.

"I heard this from the Tamahā's lips," Valatoa said. "You can ask her matāpule, for he was there." When Valatoa looked to the matāpule for confirmation, he was gone. This was when his own eyes went wide. He began taking deep breaths. "My last act in life," he said to Lolohea, "will be a gift to you, the gift of knowledge: the Tamahā will outlast you and your father and all those around you. I know this as fact."

"How could you know that?" Lolohea asked. He leaned forward.

Valatoa ignored him. With his last breaths, he began naming his children. The water circled his face, and then he was under.

Finau kept his vigil at the edge of the deck. The matāpule gazed up at him through the water, his eyes lacking focus and expression. Valatoa, barely under, was looking side to side, as if now that he had nothing more to fear from the killers above, he was on the lookout for threats from below. Finau had the urge to reach into the water to loosen the man's topknot, so that his hair might be free.

"Don't interfere," Lolohea told Finau, somehow knowing his thoughts.

A cluster of bubbles floated up from the stern. The matāpule was gone.

The water was now swallowing the Fisian navigator, who used his free hand to steady himself in the waves. The Second Son joined Finau so he might bid farewell to the old navigator, who wore a look of beguiling satisfaction. The Second Son loved the idea that a navigator might die more nobly, that he was at home in the sea, though it was such a waste—the man knew the stars for every island in Fisi.

The water was up to the old man's neck when the Second Son offered him the navigator's farewell.

"Kuo pau ke ke 'alu," the Second Son said to him, meaning, *You must go*.

The Fisian navigator was supposed to respond, "Pea ko koe e nofo." *And you remain*.

Instead, stretching his lips to keep them above water, he said, " 'Ikai, kuo pau ke ke 'alu." *No, you must go*. And then his face slipped under. Looking upward, as if through the birth ichor of the womb into the light that is life, he removed his navigator's fishhook necklace, and with his free hand lifted it above the water. The Second Son reached for the necklace, and then Finau reached for it, which triggered Mateaki to reach as well.

"No!" shouted Havea.

New Punake leaped to block Finau's arm.

Leaving Mateaki to get to the necklace first. But instead of the boy seizing his prize, the old Fisian navigator took hold of his wrist, jerking him into the water and pulling him under.

Finau scrambled to rescue Mateaki, but Lolohea stopped him, saying, "It's not for us to interfere."

They could see a frantic struggle below, bubbles rising to the surface, Mateaki jerking his arm one way and then another. Beside this struggle, the Fisian warrior was going down. Ignoring the underwater battle beside him, he gazed only at the water before him. At the last moment, he exhaled all his air and went under.

At last, Mateaki freed himself. When they pulled him aboard, he was shaking and had lost access to language. He held his wrist and glared at his fellow Tongans as if they'd tried to kill him.

Finau saw bubbles rise from the shadow that was Valatoa. Grabbing two coconut shells, Finau submerged them, preparing for the man's final belch of air.

New Punake said, "There's no way he held his breath that long."

But, lo, a trellis of bubbles rose, and Finau was there to trap the man's last breath. Lifting them from the water, he cupped the shells together and bound them with a strip of old lashing. "How many people have their final breaths preserved?" he asked. "How many people get that courtesy?"

The old canoe was completely submerged now, and all that was visible was a girl from the shoulders up, trying to give solace to a girl visible only above the neck.

Siga kept repeating a phrase in Fisian.

Lolohea looked to Havea for a sign of what these words might mean. Havea looked away.

"Such big waste!" Kōkī screeched. "Kōkī have no mate. These boys have no mate. Havea lose his mate. Even Punake deserve somebody!"

"What's that bird talking about?" Havea said. "I have a wife."

"Kōkī alone. Us all alone. And, *nea*, we kill women."

Then the younger girl went down. The second her lips submerged, she screamed in horror, and Finau reached with coconut shells to catch the breath that left her lips. When she found herself without air, her eyes went wide, and she breathed the salt water. Her throat clutched, her entire body kinked, and then she was still, eyes unfocused but slowly roaming, one slow sweep of her limited horizon, and then her arms went weightless, all while her hair floated yet at the surface. Her death, start to finish, was shorter than a misi bird's call.

Siga focused only on her breathing, taking deep breaths, then a series of short, choppy ones. All that remained of the entire endeavor was her head above water. A wave rolled over her face, shocking her eyes wide. When her features cleared the surface again, snot and water sprayed from her nose, and you could tell her focus had now shifted from hoarding air to finding the exact moment to snatch a last breath, which came quickly. She stole a final breath and went down. As the old canoe began to sink in earnest, it caught the northerly current and seemed to set sail.

Lolohea realized that he, too, was holding his breath. He stared at the water where the canoe had been. Only a submerged shadow remained. It was less than that, a feeling, a memory. Finau lifted his coconut, like he was about to share a philosophical thought. Kōkī was raising his crest feathers, a sign he was about to make a smart-ass comment.

"Shut up," Lolohea told them.

For a moment there was only water lapping the hulls, and the calls of shearwaters, clipped short when they turned. Then there was a shout upon the waves. All turned toward shore. A vaka was paddling toward them, someone in it calling out.

Lolohea cupped his hands. "What?" he called back.

That someone shouted, "Save the . . ." but the rest was taken by the wind.

"Save who?"

"A girl," came the call. "Save one of the girls. The king wants someone to take the story back to Fisi."

Lolohea dove. He could see the canoe—lighter against the backdrop of the abyss. Warping shafts of light struck it, its human sails billowing. Since he only knew canoes to travel on the surface of the sea, he had the illusion he was pulling big strokes downward from the sky as the Fisian navigator's free-floating arm beckoned him.

Siga perceived him. She turned to watch him swim to her. When he reached the bow, he looked into her eyes. There was a calmness to her face. She seemed to be on the other side of what had happened to her. In her eyes was no real regard for him, as if he were just a shadow, cast from a world she'd left behind. Weightless hair obscured half her face. Siga then turned from him to face forward, as if she'd chosen to embark, as if she herself had called the course. Lolohea knew what she was feeling: underwater, you were beyond obligation, duty, expectation, and destiny.

Suddenly someone was beside him, there was a burst of fiber as ropes were cut, and then three people were racing upward for air. On the surface, Lolohea could see his middle brother had freed Siga.

"You're the perfect hero," the Second Son said. "Except you didn't save the girl."

"I was working on it," Lolohea said.

Siga surfaced, gorging air. "Taci-qu," she implored. "Taci-qu."

"*Taci-qu*," the Second Son said. "Could that be like our word *tehi-na*?"

"Little sister," Lolohea said. He turned to Siga, but she was already swimming back down.

FIFTEEN

RETREATING WAVES

A WORD ON MATĀPULE

Has the Tuʻitonga shown weakness by sparing the Fisian girl? Has his resolve wavered like a reed on the weather coast? The case for the Fisian girl's death is clear: as a spoil of war, she was the property of the Tuʻilifuka. Plus, she was quick to cast her lot with his assassins. Most irrefutable, her heart pumped with the blood of the peoples who so bedevil us. So how could her life be spared? Has the Tuʻitonga flopped like a mullet in a warm lagoon?

The Tuʻitonga has plans for the Fisian girl, so don't be outraged by this little act of mercy. What's truly outrageous is the degree to which matāpule have become a burden upon society, dominating every exchange and interaction, insinuating themselves into every aspect of our lives. What happens when the face of authority becomes authority itself? Take Matāpule Muʻa, for instance. If the Tuʻitonga wields the power and the Tamahā possesses the rank, it's Matāpule Muʻa who gathers the wealth. He determines if sufficient tributes have been paid. He disburses parcels of land and approves marriages and allocates burial ground. Are gifts not necessary for favorable outcomes in all of these matters?

Thus we find a situation in which the matāpule is richer than his master. While all of Tonga may belong to the king, it's Matāpule Muʻa who harvests the best groves and bathes in the sweetest pools. Yes, the king has personal possession of the sacred island of ʻAta. Yet his matāpule received as a gift the island of Fatumanga, with its pleasant view of lovely Late, whose volcanic smoke bloods the setting sun. Has the Tuʻi of Huʻunga not gifted Matāpule

Muʻa with a pair of islands whose spirits are said to offer good fortune? Even the Malietoa of Haʻamoa gave him the island of Apolima to facilitate access to the king.

If action had been taken long ago, perhaps the matāpule of today wouldn't have become the great parasitic class we now face. Today, a man can't shit in a field without two matāpule debating the property line and arguing which way the stink will blow. Today, average people must rent or borrow matāpule if they have official business. And of course some matāpule are so powerful they employ their own matāpule. Matāpule with matāpule! How far we've strayed from our ancient, noble selves! Are there enough old canoes in all of Tonga to fix the matāpule problem now plaguing us?

The old Tufuga from Haʻamoa slept under a tree outside the royal compound. He often dreamed he was inking skin. In his sleep, he'd endlessly watch himself tap patterns into others. The meanings of the dreams, like messages from the spirit world, were received in the unfolding patterns, patterns he didn't know he was going to create until he did. This night, he dream-inked not the usual wave crests or tuna fins, but the disorderly and dangerous tentacles of the feke octopus.

In the morning, steamed taro was brought to him, and though he'd been told that herons had gone extinct, several bones of this bird were also delivered. So he spent the early hours fashioning his needles, shaping and shaving the bones with a blade, then sooting his ink by burning the husks of tuitui nuts.

Before long, he heard the calls of keleʻa horns. Then there were more. They seemed to fancy blowing lots of alarms on this island. Later, some vicious dogs were roped to a tree not far from him. They sat, frothy and red-snouted, panting at him. Then bodies began arriving. They'd been dragged a great distance, judging by their condition. Finally, one of the naked Fisian women was tied to a nearby tree. She was in terrible condition—looking worse than when she'd been tethered to a mast by the chief of Lifuka. *Good morning, Tonga,* he thought. Who had concocted such a place? He made it his goal to see as few Tongan dawns as possible.

Then Six Fists, limping, came to him. Grimacing, he said, "This afternoon, the Tuʻitonga and Finau will take their ink."

"I'll be ready," the Tufuga said.

"Do you forget your pledge to complete the Tuʻitonga's inking?"

The Tufuga shook his head.

"By striking the first mark," Six Fists said, "you agree to strike the last."

"Have you been bitten by dogs?"

Six Fists said, "No matter what, the king's ink won't be left incomplete."

Was he being asked, should the occasion arise, to ink a dead man? How would the skin respond, and would blood still run? Without pain to limit the sessions, would the black be struck all night, racing the tones of decomposition? *Good morning, Tonga,* he thought. *Good afternoon, good evening.*

Ahead, Havea helmed the Fisian attack vaka. The Second Son followed as they journeyed around Tongatapu's coast to the calm lagoon. There, they'd tie off and finally get some sleep. The Second Son wanted the day to disappear. He wanted to feel their vaka rock in the shade of the mangroves, to see Havea roll to his side and begin to snore. Then, waking at sunset, maybe things'd be normal again. He'd rouse his master by patting his weathered hand. He'd wash the salt from Havea's feet. There'd be no one else, just him and Havea, a son and his supplemental father.

But the Fisian vaka was very fast. Knifing through the water, its outrigger glistened when it lifted. Soon Havea's sail was visible atop only the highest swells. Why didn't Havea spill his wind a little? Why race for the horizon? Unless he intended to keep going, to Lifuka, to his sons and beyond, beyond the reach of the Tuʻitonga, if there was such a thing. The pain on Havea's face had been visible all day: When forced to translate the words of a condemned father to the son he'd leave behind. Repeating the testament of drowning girls. Hearing once again that his wife was gone.

The Second Son kept seeing the Fisian navigator's hand, extending from the water. Only Havea had stopped him from grabbing the necklace. What a child he'd been, to focus on the pendant and not the man, a man never again to behold the stars, to feel his hulls lift, to make reunion with his loved ones.

Worst was the look on Havea's face, his repugnance at the needlessness of it. And here he was, slipping from view.

As he dropped into the hollows, one after another, the sea felt newly unsteady to the Second Son. When he closed he eyes, he saw people drowning. Death had once been safely housed in stories and poems. Not anymore. People could slip below the waves, and nothing of them was left behind.

If Havea was indeed derelicting north to Lifuka, who were the boys he'd be sailing toward, his "real" sons? Had Havea watched a thousand star-rises with them? Had they seen surging rivers of bonito running silver beneath them? Had Havea and his boys witnessed the drifting purple clouds that marked the calving of whales?

Turning into Tongatapu's lagoon, all was as it should be. Wind riffled the beards of palms. Dragonflies mated midair. Dolphins hunted the tannic waters, their rolling blowholes and clicking bursts making fish breach in fear. Nothing he could remember was separate from Havea. Havea had pointed out the loveliness of rainwater pooling upon the lagoon's brackish surface, how the lens of it bent the afternoon light. Havea'd shown him how a mooring knot could save your life and how to gauge properly made rope by the creak of its twisting. *Tighter,* Havea would say. *Rope can never be twisted too tight.*

Perhaps all that people leave behind is their voice inside your head.

He remembered a day back when he was a boy. His father took him for a walk to the lagoon. Here, his father pointed at a man under a niu tree. He was rolling cord for rope. "You see that man?" his father asked. "He wears a navigator's pendant. One day, you'll wear the same."

The boy looked at the man, who tugged the cord, length by length.

"He'll teach you many things," his father said. "He's sworn to never leave you."

"Where'll you be?" the boy asked. He was seven.

"Right here," his father said. "You'll see me all the time."

"But who is he?"

"Just go to him," the father said. "He'll impart upon you a wisdom few possess." The father took the boy's shoulders and pointed him at the man. With a pat, the boy began walking.

The man was alone. Except for his necklace, he fancied no adornments.

His skin was sun-toned, and it was clear from the salt on his arms that he'd recently been at sea.

When the boy reached the man, the man took a long look at him.

"Ever made rope?" he asked.

The boy shook his head. This was before the *Pelepeka*, before they'd felled the trunks and adzed out the hulls and seasoned the mast and drawknifed the curving yardarm. The rope he was coiling, though, it was the beginning, it would lash the decks, serve as batten and stay, affix the broad sail.

"Then that's where we'll start," the man said, offering the boy some cordage.

The boy didn't know if he should accept. Even at his young age, he understood there were many protocols to the giving and receiving of things. He turned to his father for guidance, but the father was gone.

When Havea made it to the lagoon, the sun was high, the light dampened by mangroves. He reclined on the Fisian vaka, closed his eyes. The deck smelled of dogs, of blood and piss, of cooking fires and gutted fish. To him, these were the smells of war. Today'd brought it back. The before-battle bargains, curses, laments, farewells. The lift of hulls as warriors leaped into the surf. The sounds of distant clashes while Havea turned the vaka, preparing for escape. There was no sound like clubs meeting full-force. There was no silence like men running for the canoes.

When he watched the drownings today, something came clear to Havea: the Tu'itonga's need of him would never cease. As long as Havea was of use, he'd be used. Next would come a Tongan Hull, and even after he initiated the boy, there'd be some new pressing mission. It'd been foolish to think the Tu'itonga would honor a deal made years ago, one he likely didn't even remember.

For the first time in years, Havea considered the possibility he might see war again.

Before long, the *Pelepeka* came about, the Tu'itonga's son leaping aboard, kneeling over him, a smile upon his face. "Havea," he said. "Havea."

"What're you so happy about?"

"Nothing," the boy said, suppressing a grin. "Just glad to see you."

"It's no happy day, son, for today we discover the life of a navigator is worth nothing. We're disposable, like sticks used to stir the coals before they themselves are fed to the flames."

"Of course," the young man said, smiling broadly. "It truly is a terrible day!"

What cheery thing could the boy have taken from a group drowning? Havea once shared the story of Ovava with him, hoping to impart the lesson that even seasoned navigators could make foolish decisions. Instead, the boy came away determined to bring a parrot when he made his own epic journey. And after hearing the story of Tulikaki, the boy seemed not to register the lesson that it was better for family members to die together, rather than apart. Instead, he marveled at a necklace's power to retain a narrative, even in the belly of a shark.

"You're upset," the Second Son said. "You're worried about your wife. Don't believe what Kōkī says. That bird doesn't know anything."

They both knew the truth, that Kōkī sat at the shoulder of all the kingdom's gossip.

"I've heard nothing about your wife," the Second Son said. "I'd tell you. It wouldn't be easy, but I'd find a way." He offered a reassuring smile.

"How is it you're in such good humor?" Havea asked. "Does the Old Canoe not haunt you?"

"I reached for that necklace," the boy said. "But you saved me. Without you . . . I would've been pulled under. Can't I be glad of that? And most important, we're together."

Havea said nothing.

The Second Son said, "*The ones whom fate has spared must learn to spare themselves.* You told me that. One canoe sank, while we got to sail away."

Havea only wished to find his sons, and, if the rumors were true, if that stupid bird was right, bury his wife. "I own those words. But spared for what? Don't you see? Today was only the beginning. There'll be other tasks, more onerous ones. When we help your brother fill a Tongan Hull, the people we kidnap, they'll know they're destined to be slaves. Their laments won't last a few moments as they slip beneath the waves. They'll curse us over days and weeks, as we cross great expanses of water. Their hands'll work unseen against their bonds. With looks and gestures, they'll conspire. When our eyelids lower, they'll move against us."

This sobered the young man. He looked like he wanted to say something to ease Havea's concerns—but what solace could a boy offer?

"I remember when your father sent a matāpule to summon me to Tongatapu," Havea said. "He must've been superstitious, for he was hesitant to approach a property stacked with funeral stones. He shouted, *Havea must come south.* I remembered thinking that all my service to the Tuʻitonga had paid off, that my family would leave the realm of war and take up residence in the Sacred South. I called to my wife, saying, *Gather the boys, for we leave this dangerous life behind.* The matāpule corrected me. *Only you are called upon,* he said. *The others must stay behind.* And I did it, my boy. I did the unthinkable. I obeyed."

The Second Son lowered himself to the deck, where he, too, lay on his back. They looked into the mangroves above, these trees that spent their lives half-submerged until, at last, they died that way.

"So she's gone," Havea said. "My wife's gone, and no one's told me. It's okay if you knew. I have no blame for you."

The Second Son moved to speak, but Havea stopped him.

"It doesn't matter," Havea said. "What matters is that I determine the state of my sons and whose hands they're in."

Above them, the mangrove leaves were large and hand-shaped. Depending on the breeze, they sometimes beckoned, sometimes warned you away. When the wind was warm from the north, like now, they called upon you to bow down.

"You know that feeling when you've missed the tide?" Havea mused. "It means everything you meant to do will have to wait. Well, I've missed the tide of my life."

"Havea," the Second Son said.

The navigator rolled his head to look the other way.

"You never left me," the Second Son said. "You never let me down."

Havea closed his eyes. He nodded.

Finau and his father took their ink in the royal garden: fruit trees, scented paths, the family tomb. Finau's gift to the Tufuga was a string of iridescent beetle wings. The Tuʻitonga offered a vessel of sandalwood oil.

The son and the father lay on their stomachs, on either side of the Tufuga, so he could shift between his subjects, inking one while the pain subsided in the other. Finau could hear Lolohea's pigeons, cooing in their cages. He could smell food being prepared: grilled eel, baked night birds, oysters in their brine.

Finau held the coconuts containing the final breaths of Valatoa and the younger Fisian girl. He had an urge to part her shells, to breathe her. What wouldn't a person give to have their final breath back? Would it revive a person, Finau wondered, if you could somehow return their breath? But had he actually captured it? He unlashed the shells containing Valatoa's last exhalation, took a tentative sniff. It did smell acrid, manly. He studied the Fisian girl's shell. *Yes*, he thought. *She's in there.*

His father asked, "What've you got?"

"It's the breath of that girl, the one we drowned."

"You captured her breath?"

"I'm safekeeping it," Finau said.

Finau hadn't seen his elder brothers' inking sessions. Lolohea had sailed to the island of ʻAta, just him and the artist who inked him. The Second Son had taken his ink at sea, the rocking of the vaka aiding the placement of the ink. Still, Finau knew how it would go. First came the peka, a pure black, bat-shaped emblem on the lower back. This would expand with patterns that wrapped around the torso, so that an upper band girded the body at the navel, and then, in successive inkings, the artist worked the ink through the groin, around the buttocks, and, in long, spiraling sessions, down the legs to halt above the knee. Today was about the bat.

The Tufuga's inking adze was tipped with a heron-bone blade whose edge had been fashioned into needles. These he dipped into candlenut ink, then tapped them into the Tuʻitonga's back.

"What're you using!" the Tuʻitonga called out. "Stingray barbs?"

More softly this time, the Tufuga struck again. The king visibly winced.

"Some dancers would help," the Tuʻitonga said. "But of course the

Tamahā has the Fefine Girls this time of day. What does she do with them? What goes on inside that compound of hers?"

When a normal Tongan took the ink, family and friends gathered to recite genealogies, sing songs, and summon ancestors to help him through the trials. Group clapping was known to drown the endless tapping. A single flute could also serve as a beacon, a signal fire to light the way for a man alone upon a sea of pain. But the Tuʻitonga had no friends. He had no extended family. And since no Tongan could touch the king, this was all an experiment: he was the first Tuʻitonga to take the ink.

Kōkī flew into the scene, eating some banana. His tongue made wet smacking sounds while the king grimaced. "Get that bird out of here," the Tuʻitonga said.

"You better go," Finau told Kōkī.

Kōkī seemed content to finish his banana.

The Tuʻitonga threw a bowl at the bird. There was a squawk, a rush of wings, banana on the ground. The Tufuga resumed, but after a few more taps, the king shook his head. "Give the boy a turn."

The Tufuga repositioned himself to face Finau. Then he began.

Finau: The first strike drew a veil upon his sight. There was only dark, with needles letting in the faintest light. And then the tapping drew the focus of his mind, a regularity, a rhythm not unlike poetic lines. The tapping incremented the moment, like a measurement of time, each tap in cadence with the last, the harmonics of an ancient rhyme. The pain was singular, focusing, the only fire of its kind. Existing beyond language, it was the attentive, repeating pressure of the sublime.

The Tufuga paused. "You doing all right?"

"Don't stop," Finau said. "Keep going."

While Finau was taking his ink, New Punake was graced with a free afternoon, his first in years. Though he could do anything with this time, he found himself where he spent his morning stints of freedom—the women's bathing pools. He sat at his usual spot, yet everything felt different. The sideways morning light, which illuminated the forest's understory, was replaced with an overhead glow, casting everything in shadow. And, of course, the Fefine Girls were gone, off at the Tamahā's compound this time of day. Perhaps it was better without them and the ever-present irony of his access to them, the torture of watching them wash each other's glistening arms, of how, even when they emerged to coat one another's shoulders with coconut oil, his sleepy little ule snoozed on. He kept seeing certain images over and over. They weren't of dead men on the beach or the faces of those as they drowned. What he kept seeing, what he kept feeling, was rope cinching around the victims' wrists in loop after ever-tightening loop.

Only two souls were in the pool: Pōhiva and the Fisian boy, Vula. She was talking to him as she ran her fingers through his hair, as she washed a departing father's handprint from his chest.

Kōkī landed beside New Punake. "Tu'itonga kick Kōkī out!" Kōkī said.

New Punake asked, "How'd you get off your tether?"

"Freedom is negotiable," Kōkī said. "With Finau, Kōkī strike deal."

A bird could bargain for his liberty? New Punake wondered. Yet he himself remained in servitude. "What made you think of that poem? The one you recited to Valatoa?"

Kōkī cocked his head, pinwheeling an eye.

"You know the poem," New Punake said. "The one that asked, *Who blows the wind?*"

"Kōkī only repeat human words," Kōkī said. "Birds not make poems."

"Those words got a man killed."

Kōkī took a step away. "Kōkī, bird," Kōkī said. "Good bird."

That's how Kōkī spoke when he felt agitated or afraid.

"What d'you think happened to the rest of your kind?" New Punake asked.

Kōkī bobbed twice and took another step away. "Birds lost," Kōkī said. "Kōkī find."

New Punake returned his attention to the queen as she bathed the boy.

The moment seemed designed for no one but him. It made his mind travel beyond the cage of this island and the person he'd become, beyond the ridiculous "poetic" performances he once rendered in praise of the people who fed him. He remembered back to his home island of Ha'ano, to his family, to his grandmother, who by the fire taught him songs she'd learned on faraway islands, songs she repeated for their beauty alone, as they were from places the boy would never visit and composed by people he'd never meet.

Kōkī began climbing, beak over foot, up a shrub beside New Punake, so the two were soon eye to eye. "Ruffle Kōkī's feathers?"

Absently, New Punake ran his fingers along the parrot's neck and crown. But he couldn't take his eyes off a mother attending to another's child. Pōhiva cupped some water. She lifted this and poured it out. "Vai," she told the boy. "Vai." Pointing toward the disc of the sun, she repeated the word "laʻā," and, lifting a broad leaf from the surface of the pool, she indicated its color, "lanumata." Green, she taught him. Green.

Words, he thought. Words had once been everything to him, but today he wondered what they even were. Were they capable of anything? He recalled what had been uttered by the Fisian warrior, by the occupants of the condemned canoe. Could words save a person, bring someone back, could they so much as grant an extra breath? Could a poem about a mother bathing another mother's child ever be the measure of the act itself?

Suddenly he felt the sharp claws of a parrot stepping onto his shoulder. He batted the bird away.

Kōkī squawked loudly and, with a flash of feathers, arrested his fall.

"I'm not your perch," New Punake said. "I'm not Finau."

I'm not Finau, he thought. *I'm not this place. I'm not a part of how it works here.*

These notions came like liberation itself. Suddenly he thought of the line from this morning, *the last to go is green*. He realized it wasn't the first line of a new poem, but the final one. And just like that, his mind started composing again.

Kōkī, before waddling away, offered the poet a brief, direct look. "Beak, sharp," was all Kōkī said.

Lolohea retreated to the southern cliffs, where no one would find him. Here was a grove of bamboo, the stalks shushing one way and another with the wind. Nowhere in sight were the matāpule and priests who tracked his movements. He lay on a bed of dry, papery leaves and looked up the rising green poles. His eyes were tired and irritated, but when he closed them, he saw the old Fisian navigator, free arm beckoning to the depths. Lolohea wondered how deep the ocean was, whether the vaka had come to rest or if it was sinking still.

Salted light fell through the grove. He'd heard there used to be a variety of pigeons that roosted here. He wondered what it'd sounded like. Was there a way to preserve an extinct bird's call? Perhaps a flute could be tuned to the notes of its song. He'd never really thought about it before, what remains after something disappears. But now it was all he could think about, the look in someone's eyes, the way water circled their faces, filled their features, and then, once they were under, replaced their faces with yours, reflected on the surface. Closing his eyes made it worse, for suddenly there'd be a green weapon striking a temple, a sea-frothed pink, or the unnatural float of a woman's hair before her face.

His hand was stiff from the dog bite. The punctures wept a clear fluid. The pain, it brought his mind around. Valatoa's death couldn't have been arbitrary, he saw that now. The Tamahā must've had good reasons for wanting him tied to that canoe. Perhaps he did know too much about her. And Lolohea acknowledged that he'd known, at least on some level, that his father was sick. Always giving leadership advice, always focused on the future, always talking about that feathered cloak.

He took a deep breath, closed his eyes. Now there was just the pulse of the sun through lowered eyelids. It was a clean, focusing glow. Nothing else could wash the footprints of the day from the beach of his mind.

He heard movement. From the blur of swaying bamboo, he saw a young woman standing at the cliffs. Below her: ocean booming, mist afurl. He remembered her from last night, the girl whose fingers sooted his chest. Moon Appearing. As if somehow sensing a presence, she turned toward him. Around her: gnarled trees bent on escaping the reach of the sea. Beyond her: a deep, glowing blue.

"The Tamahā sent me," she called. "I'm told you have a wound."

He left the bamboo. Nearing her, he felt the ocean exhaling in concussive breaths.

"How'd the Tamahā know where to find me?" he asked.

Moon Appearing shrugged.

He shook his head at the futility of escape. "How far does one have to go to be free?"

"Does the prince of Tonga lack liberty?"

"Not *free*, I suppose," he said. "Free *from*."

She produced a leaf, which, unfolded, revealed a medicinal balm. "I'm to attend to your wound." She glanced up and down his limbs, gave his torso a quick study. She raised her eyebrows, as if to say, *Where're you hurt?*

He offered his hand, asked, "Do you know what you're doing?"

"I've treated many people," she said. "Well, I've *assisted* in the treatment of many people. To be honest, I've never actually treated a man." She studied the marks in his palm. "What'd you tangle with, a dog?"

"It tangled with me."

She dipped her finger into the salve. "I was told to make sure the medicine fills the wound."

He winced as she pressed.

"Do you remember me? Or do all Fefine Girls look alike to you?"

"Would I forget the woman who rubbed soot on me?"

"I didn't *rub* it. I *applied* it." She turned his hand to treat the other side. "And it wasn't my idea. The Tamahā obviously enjoys taunting new arrivals."

"Arrival from where?" he asked.

"Trust me, you've never been there."

"I suspect the island has a tall, central mountain."

She paused, looking at him, wondering how he could know this.

"Your name is *Moon Appearing*," he said. "Only from certain peaks can one look down upon a dawning moon. Islands like Tofua or 'Eua or 'Ata."

"You mean your private island, 'Ata?"

"It's my father's island."

"I'm actually from Hunga. It's not a place you'd want to go. For young men, it's a shortcut to war." Though his punctures were quickly treated, she continued to fuss with them. "Those killings this morning. Do things like that happen all the time?"

He didn't answer.

She asked, "Are matāpule to blame?"

"It's them, certainly," he said. "But it's more, it's complicated."

"Can't you order them banished?"

"The matāpule?" he asked. "When I give orders, people don't seem to listen."

"Isn't giving orders what kings do?"

He offered a fatalistic smile. "I wouldn't expect you to understand."

She glanced up at him. "What wouldn't I understand?"

"The situation I find myself in," he said. "You're a Fefine Girl, so you've won the dance contests. You've probably been groomed your whole life for it. I'd bet your mother was a Fefine Girl, too. Which means this all comes naturally to you. So I doubt you'd know the feeling of having to do something you're no good at, of being forced down a path that will lead to . . . I don't know."

"To being found out for what you really are?"

"Or aren't."

Moon Appearing studied him a moment, assessing him. "If the wound darkens, the Tamahā says you should see her directly." Then she gave him the strangest look, one he couldn't read at all, before taking her leave of him.

SIXTEEN

KŌRERO:

THE HORIZON IN HER EYES

After the men returned to our island, my mother and I tended to Father's cut-up feet, cleaning the lacerations and applying an extract of wai kōwhai. Concerning his wounds, he only said this: he'd walked across a field of volcanic rock, sharp as obsidian. My parents kept looking at each other in a certain way but said nothing. My mother turned to me. "Go fetch Tapoto. His feet also need tending. And I suppose the time's come for his ink."

I hesitated. I could tell they were about to have a discussion, and I didn't want to miss anything. But they stared at me until I left.

I checked a few places Tapoto was known to nap—in the cool sand below the cliffs, amid the breezy foliage of the lava dome. No luck. I'd seen him sometimes contemplate our lone, large kauri tree, like it was a problem to be solved, but when I circled the tree, hoisting myself over its waist-high roots, he was nowhere to be found.

It turned out he was on the beach where the whale had appeared. He seemed shaken and unsure, like he'd spent his whole life carrying out the traditions of a people and only now had gotten a glimpse of who they really were.

"My mother sent me to get you."

"The whale warned us trouble was ahead. It said we weren't ready."

I wrapped his feet in disinfecting horopito leaves, securing them with strips of flax.

I asked, "Is it true what the Wayfinder said, that the other island depopulated itself?"

"There were some signs of conflict. Mostly, the island looked empty, like they'd sailed away. But their canoes were at hand, and they wouldn't leave without..."

"Without what?"

He didn't answer. Then, like something had occurred to him, he let out a sardonic laugh. "You wanna know how desperate they were at the end? They'd started opening the graves of the dead."

"Isn't that what we're doing?"

He looked at me, his eyes saying, *There you go.*

I helped him to his feet. "We're not at the end."

"Is that you talking, or your parents? It's their duty to fill you with hope." He said this last part bitterly.

Tapoto's father had drowned. One day, his fishing canoe washed ashore without him. And Tapoto's mother, with no obvious cause, succumbed soon after. He was just old enough to not be raised by another family. His laziness, or perceived laziness, was a state that simply continued on from his grief. He'd had no one to champion him, challenge him, or admonish him when he acted outrageously.

"I'll tell you this," Tapoto said. "Those Tongans didn't look too happy about what they saw over there. But they'd clearly seen it before."

When we entered our whare, Tapoto looked timid as he met my mother's eyes. "I have no gift," he said.

"No need," my mother answered.

He seemed to remember a satchel hanging from his neck. "I do have this."

From a cord hung a fresh leaf that'd been folded into a pouch. When my mother opened the leaf, she discovered a shift of sand. "Is this from the other island?"

Tapoto nodded. Whereas he'd done nothing to earn his previous offering of greenstone, for this sand he'd made a great journey and suffered personal wounds.

My mother opened her feather box and placed the pouch inside.

Tapoto lowered his large body to the mat. My mother contemplated him, his feet wrapped in leaves, belly sprawling. She must've felt certain that he'd exhibited bravery and leadership, for after testing the needles on the back of her hand, she began inking rays across his forehead—lines that indicated the rank of a rangatira captain. While she worked, Tapoto stared at the roof thatching, but his focus seemed farther away.

There was no one to sing as Tapoto took his ink. He had no one to recite genealogies. There was only me, assisting my mother, stretching skin and wiping blood and ink. When Hine came by for something, I implored her with my eyes to help. Reluctantly, she sat, allowing Tapoto to place his head in her lap. Looking up at her, tears in his eyes, he smiled. Hine and I sang the usual moko songs. We repeated some tapping chants. Then Tapoto quietly began naming his ancestors. He didn't get far before he stopped. "I have these names in my head, going back generations, but I don't know who they are anymore. Were they my people, or were they *them*? Is our story even our own, or just an episode in someone else's tale?"

I tried to think of a story to tell him, one that would offer solace. None came to mind.

"When I heard about that island," Tapoto said, "I thought that by going there, we'd finally become the people we were meant to be." He shook his head, suggesting the opposite had happened.

"Hush," my mother said.

Tapoto said, "I want you to know we did everything we could to save her."

"Save who?" I asked.

"Hush," my mother said.

With that, Tapoto closed his eyes and let the pain take him away.

※

In the purpled twilight of the setting sun, the Wayfinder and Finau joined us for dinner. The pair sat amid us but not among us. We prepared the finest meal we could: fire-wilted fern buds and rata shoots that'd been pounded into balls and steamed with rimu. The problem with rimu wasn't the taste—I kind of liked seagrass—it was the texture. Also, half an oarfish had washed ashore, so everyone got a taste of meat.

Our Tongan guests nibbled here and there. Their faces betrayed no opinion regarding the meals they were served. Still, Finau marveled at the way others devoured their dinners. I had the eerie feeling he was truly seeing us for the first time. The Wayfinder fed his fish to the dog, an act that was missed by no one.

Tapoto—feet bandaged and forehead wrapped—thanked our new friends for their help and declared Tongans the friendliest people of the sea. He understood our guests were soon to depart, so he got to the point. "Now that we have our own voyaging canoe, please, tell us the next island we should visit."

"How about Hawaiki?" someone called.

"Or a Fisian island," Arawiwi said. "You said there were hundreds. Surely they can spare one."

"Any island'll do," Tapoto said. "Just name the star, and we'll handle the rest."

Finau held a greenstone club in each hand. He was rubbing them together, polishing them. This made a resonant, droning sound that bored into your ears. To him, these were merely weapons. To us, they were taonga: objects of great meaning that linked us to our past. Yet these clubs had been used to dominate us, to take our ancestors' lives. What'd it mean when your inheritance had indentured you?

Finau said, "There's no such thing as perfect little islands, just waiting to be found."

"We found this one," my father said.

"Folks like telling the story of discovering new islands," Finau said. "The story of killing the people who were already there, not so much."

I looked to Tiri, who chewed her fern shoots. Her face showed no expression, none at all.

"Forget about that old voyaging canoe," the Wayfinder told Tapoto. "It's not seaworthy. I've watched an old canoe go down. I've seen what it looks like when all on board perish."

Tapoto, whose father had drowned, asked, "This is something you witnessed?"

"Were you able to lend aid?" my mother asked. "Surely you saved a life or two?"

The Wayfinder was silent.

"I saved their breath," Finau volunteered.

Hā Mutu asked, "How does one preserve human breath?"

"With coconut shells," Finau said. We waited for him to elaborate, but he didn't.

Hine asked, "You rescued not the people but their air? Isn't air what drowning people need above all?"

Tersely, Finau said, "They relinquished it." To further his defense, Finau quoted an old poem:

Ko e ngāahi peaua oku tahifo maʻu pē,   *Where waves ever crest,*
hoku laumālie oku i api.   *that's where my soul resides.*

The poem's lines continued, but I wasn't really listening. My mind was attempting to assemble these elements: a canoe, coconut shells, Finau, and a person in the water, struggling. Would the two people not be close enough to gaze into one another's eyes, to touch each other's cheeks? I thought of Tapoto's father, treading water alone, soon to slip beneath the surface. I thought of Hine's mother, slowly wasting to nothing, I thought of my little sisters-to-be, each one rinsed away by a tincture of red tea.

"Please understand," the Wayfinder said. "What my brother describes isn't typical. You see, Tonga's traditions are . . ." Here he paused. "When it comes to order, we—"

"We do our duty," Finau snapped. "We make our sacrifices. Tonga isn't a place where people go about doing whatever they please, listening to any old person who's appointed himself in charge of something."

My mother listened to this young man indict our way of life. Then she asked, "And how much Tongan order would one have to violate to merit being drowned?"

Finau didn't respond.

Father said, "You use the words *duty* and *sacrifice* in the same breath, yet are they not opposites? A duty is mandatory. Sacrifice, however, is voluntary, it's personal."

Tiri struck a conciliatory tone. "I can tell you boys are troubled by the events you describe. The bones you carry, are they victims of that sunken canoe? Are you on a journey of redemption for not saving their lives?"

"What?" the Wayfinder asked. "No. And they weren't victims. They were—"

"You don't understand the first thing about Tonga," Finau said. "We're at war. People lose sons and daughters. They lose souls. You can lose even more than nature has given you. Anyone who's lost two fathers can attest to that. And our uncle 'Aho, taken alone, is as menacing as an entire nation."

Hā Mutu asked, "Was it your uncle who drowned those people?"

Frustrated, the Wayfinder said, "No, that was our father's doing. And our great-aunt. I suppose our brother had his role. As if you people have no need of discipline."

We shook our heads. I said, "When we have problems, we simply talk about things."

"And when that doesn't work?" Finau asked.

"We talk some more," I said.

"For truly intractable circumstances," Tiri volunteered, "we retain the option of the duel."

"Ha!" Finau said. "As I thought."

"About this 'Aho fellow," Tiri said. "Have you tried listening to him? Has anyone asked him what he wants?"

"Anything he wants, he takes," Finau said.

"Perhaps he has unmet needs," Tiri suggested. "He might have a grievance that can be resolved. Or he might be wounded, deep down. If all of you came together, you could heal him."

The Wayfinder said, "The deepest wounds are self-inflicted. That's what my mother says." A pained look crossed his face. "That's what she used to say."

Mention of a lost mother ended the discussion.

A bowl of nonu fruit was passed. The nonu was yellow with ripeness, which meant it smelled horrible—think vomit—and tasted bitter, but with a little imagination you could be eating anything. All you had to do was dream of your ideal food and just get to chewing. A mango, which I'd never encountered except in stories, was what I chose to enjoy. A quiet fell over us as we masticated our nourishment.

Here, something surprising happened. The nonu bowl was attacked by Kōkī and a band of raiding parrots. There were clashing screeches. Wings flashed against the firelight. People were scratched. Taking our fruit in their talons, the parrots flew high into the branches, where they sank their beaks into the yellow flesh.

"Human not eat parrot food!" Kōkī demanded. Kōkī then flew off, all the parrots following but one. This parrot shuffled its green wings. It looked at all of us and none of us. "Kākā whakaaio," it said. *Parrot, peace.* This was Aroha, and I understood that now, to her, I was just another human.

※

When the Wayfinder left dinner, he took a torch with him, something he hadn't done before. My father had used a torch to find the break in the reef, so it struck me that this was the moment—the Wayfinder was leaving. I caught up with him on the path. He turned to face me, seemingly unsurprised to see me.

"I understand something happened to you in Tonga," I said. "I know you lost people."

With a resigned look, he acknowledged this.

I said, "You don't have to handle everything on your own."

"I've got my brother."

"Have you considered that it doesn't exist, this island you're after? Or maybe you're just punishing yourself."

"Punishing myself for what?" he asked.

I didn't know. "Suppose you find this island, then what?"

"Then we'll resurrect the people who can save Tonga."

"In a community, it's never about one or two people, it's about everyone. You're never stronger than when you stand with your family and your people."

"What happens when your people are no longer yours?" he asked. "What if you lose your family?"

"Maybe I don't know much about the world," I said. "But family isn't something you're necessarily born with, it's something you can make. And when you stand with people, any people, they stand with you."

"You don't even know us."

"I know those green clubs won't solve your problems."

He didn't have an answer to that.

I asked, "You wanna end up like your uncle?"

He indulged me. "What do you propose?"

"Use words," I said. "Words are the answer to everything."

"This is a most unusual island. I just might miss it."

The torchlight was shifting in his eyes. I asked, "Are you really going?"

"I see you took your ink," he said. "After I took mine, my skin felt strange, it felt new." He leaned forward to look at me. "A light breeze or a blade of grass, it was like I'd never felt those things before." He extended his hand in the wavering light. Ever so gently, he ran the pad of his finger across the face of my lips. It was delicate, his touch. I felt it before he even made contact. I felt it after.

He studied me a final moment. "I'm sorry about what happened to your people," he said.

Then he took his torch and left me in the dark.

I joined my parents on the beach. It was chilly enough that we scrunched together. When it got a little colder, the red flies would disappear, and we'd sleep inside again. Down in the cove, some women were night fishing with palm-spathe torches whose gold-black flames would hopefully lure fish to their gigs.

We were quiet, our little family, each of us turning our own problems in our minds. In my mind I saw two coconut shells trapping a human breath. I envisioned our people, long ago, first landing on this island, while a group of earlier inhabitants welcomed us from shore. I saw a great wave, an empty sweet-potato pit, the black-and-white feathers of a long-ago bird.

"Father," I said. I was looking at the sky. "Remember when you told me not to let the Wayfinder touch me?"

My parents sat up. For a moment they just stared at me, like they were inspecting me for damage.

"What'd he do to you?" my mother asked.

"He touched you?" my father asked. "Where?"

"On my lips," I said.

"With his lips?" my mother asked.

I said, "With the tip of his finger."

"What were his intentions?" my father asked.

"It wasn't romantic or anything," I told him. "At least I don't think so. It was more philosophical."

My mother harrumphed. "A *philosophical* touch of the lips?"

"He's leaving, you know," I said. "Tonight."

"When he touched you," my mother said, "how'd it feel?"

I exhaled. "I have nothing to compare it to."

I didn't mean for it to sound sad, but it sounded sad even to me.

My parents reclined again. Above were the outlines of clouds. "Father," I said. "How'd he do it? How'd he make it to that other island?"

"The kid has confidence, that's for sure," he said. "And he knew his stuff. Like the range of every bird—with that, he could tell the distance to land he couldn't see. And he was sensitive to the *feel* of the sea. He perceived the slightest variations in the waka's motion against the swells."

I asked, "If we could've gotten to that other island earlier, might we have saved some of them?"

My father exhaled. "It was no one's doing but their own. They'd depopulated themselves. Except for the child."

In disbelief, I asked, "Child?"

My mother was silent. She'd obviously heard this.

"I think it was a girl," my father said. "We never got close enough to be sure."

"There was a girl, all alone, and you left her?" I asked.

My father was quiet. He looked to my mother, who said nothing.

"You brought back a dog? But left a child?"

"We tried," he said. "For days we tried. But we couldn't catch her."

"A group of strange men chasing her?" I said. "Of course she ran."

"Your father did everything he could," my mother said. "The girl knew the island. There were caves. And petrified lava. Your father hurt his feet going after her. So did Tapoto."

"I believe you," I said. "But we have to rescue her. She's out there right now, all alone. How's she supposed to survive? Who'll protect her?"

"No one's at fault," my father said. "We just got there too late."

"All she needed was a girl to reach out to her," I said. "I could bring her back." I looked at my parents, who said nothing. "If you can't help me, I'll find someone who will."

"You have your moko," my father said. "You're adult enough to make your own decisions. But you're also adult enough to accept certain truths. We did everything possible. We could do no more."

Out of respect for my father, I didn't counter his self-serving assessment. I stood and dusted off my legs.

"They did all they could," my mother said. "As an adult, there are truths you just have to swallow."

I gave my mother a wicked look. *Like red tea*, I thought.

"There's one more thing," my father said. "Stowed in the hull of their waka is another set of bones."

"More can be done," I said defiantly. Then I began making my way to the cove.

My mother called after me, "You do make a habit of running off to him."

* * *

As I walked to the cove, the wind was off the water. Flax blades fluttered, rain smelled imminent. I pictured the Wayfinder in his usual spot, shuffling shells around. I'd been pretty impressed when I first saw him tend his star chart, but now the idea seemed quite lonely—sitting up all night, obeying the sky's minor advances.

I found the Wayfinder with his brother, preparing their waka for departure.

When the Wayfinder saw me, he paused, rope in hand. "One farewell wasn't enough?"

Was that what we'd done? Had touching my lip been a goodbye?

"We have to go to that island," I said. "There's a girl there who needs rescue."

Finau smiled in disbelief. "We just got back from that place."

"She got left behind," I said. "She's all alone."

"We didn't leave her," the Wayfinder said. "Tapoto did that. Your father, too."

"At least they tried."

The brothers exchanged an exasperated look.

The Wayfinder said, "Your people pleaded with us to bring that canoe back."

"Begged," Finau said.

"Yeah, begged," the Wayfinder said. "We spent days re-lashing the thing. It needed new yardarms and stays, and there weren't any trees. Have you ever woven a sail? I didn't have time to chase a kid around. I never even saw her."

"You're talking about canoes," I said. "I'm talking about life and death."

An enraged look crossed the Wayfinder's face. "Come," he said. He walked me not thirty steps down the beach. Here sat *The Red Cloak*, one of its hulls completely submerged. "Don't tell me we didn't risk our lives for you people."

"What happened to it?" I asked.

He looked at me like I was an idiot, then went back to coiling rope on his waka.

"She still needs to be rescued," I said. "We have to go get her."

"*We?*" he asked. "You're forgetting this fact: the girl ran from everyone who tried to help her."

"They were trying to capture her," I said. "I would've run, too."

"Fair enough," he said, then pointed at his comet. "It wanes. It'll only guide us to Pulotu for so long."

"No," Finau said. "We're going back to Tonga."

"After we sail for the afterlife," the Wayfinder corrected.

"We'll figure things out on the water," Finau said, loading a basket of greenstone war clubs.

The Wayfinder turned to me. "When we first landed, I was hoping we could take on provisions. Now I wish we had some to leave you." Sprawled in the sand was the white dog. It had a tether around its neck. The Wayfinder handed me the lead. "Feed him, and he'll be loyal. He can live on fish heads."

I said, "He belongs to that girl."

The Wayfinder gave me a disappointed look.

Luckily, I knew how to make him help me. I said, "I know that as a navigator, you're duty-bound to take people where they need to go. I declare my need to go to that island."

"That request has been fulfilled," he responded.

"If you won't help me," I told him, "I'll go there myself."

Finau groaned. "God, she's a Fefine Girl!"

"Fefine Girl?" I asked.

"Causing trouble," Finau grumbled. "Enacting dramas."

The Wayfinder asked me, "And how'll you get to this island you've never seen?"

I told him, "I'll aim for the star Atutahi."

This got the Wayfinder's attention. "And before Atutahi rises? What about after it sets?"

"The Whale constellation takes all night to set," I said. "Atutahi's simply the last star in the fluke."

The Wayfinder studied me. "And on a cloudy night? And if there's a current or contrary winds or a storm?"

I mimicked what my father had said. "Birds will tell me the proximity of land. I'll attune myself to the regularity of the waves."

"And how'll you return?" he asked. "Under what rising star is your own island located?"

I didn't have an answer.

He said, "Sounds like you know just enough to get yourself into danger."

I lifted my eyes to his. As sweetly as possible, I said, "I'd prefer to go with you."

Finau was loading green palm fronds. "You're not taking her," he told his brother.

The Wayfinder ignored him. He pointed to the Milky Way. "See that cloud of stars, the large one? We call that Ma'afu Toka."

Through a part in the clouds, I saw the constellation. "We call it Tīoreore."

"That's how you get home," he said. "Depart before sunset, and that should keep you on course."

This news deflated me. I'd really thought I'd be able to talk him into taking me. Hadn't I just preached that words could make anything happen? Action was my last option. I pulled the dog to my father's fishing canoe and tied its tether to the mast. Then I began the nearly impossible task of pushing the waka toward the water.

"There she goes," Finau said.

"You going to bring any food or water?" the Wayfinder asked.

"*The sea and the sky will provide*," I said. It felt great to turn their own words back on them. But wouldn't I need food and water?

"How about leaving the dog," Finau said. "No need to risk its life."

I strained, making an unlovely grunt as I heaved the canoe forward.

Finau said, "Remember the Fefine Girl who 'hurt her ankle' so Lolohea would have to carry her?" They both had a laugh at that.

This infuriated me. "I'm at least headed someplace," I told the Wayfinder. "You're running away."

Finau said, "And remember the one who pretended to drown so Lolohea would 'save' her?"

"Who's Lolohea?" I asked.

"This is truly unadvisable," the Wayfinder told me. "You'll get yourself killed."

"Aw, let the Fefine Girl go," Finau said.

"You don't have to do this," the Wayfinder told me.

I reached the water, where the waka's bow lifted. "Someone has to do it."

Finau approached. He tossed some palm fronds onto the fishing waka's little deck. "You'll thank yourself for the shade," he said before tying a calabash of water to the mast.

"Is there any stopping you?" the Wayfinder asked.

I thought, *You, you could stop me.*

"Okay, then." Sounding resigned, he said, "You must go."

Not without some spite, I said, "And you remain."

I climbed aboard my little waka and began paddling toward the break in the reef. I hadn't brought a torch, but I didn't need one: I could see large waves bowing down, their backs breaking white before me. Glancing at shore, I saw the Wayfinder watching me go—his expression couldn't be read. The boiling reef then took my focus. Suddenly I was in the big swells. They took my words.

SEVENTEEN

THE HIGH CHILD

The Tamahā had long ago planted a chain of coconuts around her compound, so that over the decades there grew a living wall of niu trees. Vines, trained up the trunks, prevented any glimpse inside. Few even approached, because in the surrounding plots the Tamahā grew rare botanicals. Many of these were curative, like akataha and lala tahi. Then there were more alarming plants. Who would cultivate an upas tree, used by warriors to poison their spear tips? Or the deadly toto tree? What sane person would plant moho, whose red-and-black seeds were the most fatal known? And then there was her bed of kaute, whose red blossoms, when ingested by a pregnant woman, offered a remedy both singular and irreversible.

In addition, the Tamahā used her great rank to forbid the entry of men. Even her security team and matāpule were forced to reside beyond her gates. This prohibition was fodder for the male imagination, already alight with rumors about her famous aviary, terraced fishponds, and floating sleeping chamber. On occasion, she admitted a man or two, but only if they were deceased.

After the Fisian attack, the Tamahā was teaching the Fefine Girls to process turmeric. From their knees, the girls pounded the root until their hands were orange with it. Most were chiefs' daughters, sent to serve the Tuʻitonga for a year, a time during which they might adopt refined protocols and hopefully acquire a noble husband. But the Tamahā got them for a portion of each day, and she had other things to impart. Most Fefine Girls had never known work, and she had need of much labor. The Tamahā had no power or income, and while she received many gifts in honor of her high rank—gifts like custom-cut stones and engraved lodge poles—she had only the Fefine Girls to haul said rocks and raise such timbers, to maintain the entire compound and harvest all the food, for she was completely self-sufficient.

These girls had previously occupied their days with dancing, serving kava, and extolling the deeds of great Tongans through song. Of course these great Tongans were exclusively male, so the Tamahā offered an alternate history of notable Tongan women. Today, the Tamahā told the story of Ate:

"This story concerns a Tu'itonga whose home island was Nomuka," the Tamahā said as she examined the girls' work. "Once a year, this Tu'itonga would return to Nomuka to pay tribute to his ancestors' grave. This grave was on the island's highest ground, surrounded by lovely groves that he'd made tapu. Upon his arrival, he called for a great fire to be built up. All the young women of Nomuka were brought into the light. One by one, the Tu'itonga asked the girls to step back until only Ate stood in the glow. He ravished her that night, and the Tu'itonga liked that she struggled and writhed. It brought him extra pleasure. Even her bruises served as tokens of his delight. In the morning, the Tu'itonga said he'd make Ate one of his supplemental wives. She didn't want to become a spare wife, but the ceremony would happen that day, after which she'd step into the king's vaka and leave her family for Tongatapu. Now—how did she avoid this fate?"

Since some of these girls dreamed of becoming supplemental wives to the king, they eyed the Tamahā with suspicion. The girl named Kakala suggested, "Ate quickly married another man."

"But wouldn't this betray the king, since Ate was already betrothed to him?" the Tamahā asked. "The Tu'itonga would slay this other man, and Ate's family would lose its standing."

The girl named Sun Shower said, "She disfigured herself, so she'd no longer be attractive to him."

The Tamahā said, "Ate's looks first attracted the Tu'itonga, but it was her suffering that truly appealed to him. Wouldn't more suffering, especially inflicted on his account, draw him closer?"

The girl named Heilala, confident of her answer, said, "This is a trick question, for Ate's duty is to accept the Tuʻitonga's will."

Kakala tried again, saying, "Ate has but one honorable path, the taking of her own life."

"Which of you two is the most stupid?" the Tamahā asked. "Do I tell you stories in which women end up defiled, destitute, or dead?"

The Fefine Girls looked at one another, as if to say, *All your stories are about women who end up defiled, destitute, or dead.* But they were silent.

"Use your minds," the Tamahā said. "What does Ate know about the Tuʻitonga that she can use to her advantage?"

Moon Appearing said, "He is reverent."

Finally, the Tamahā smiled. She approached Moon Appearing and ran a thumb down her cheek, which obligated her to later come have this tapu removed. "Yes, he's reverent. That's something Ate can use."

Before the story's conclusion, several girls turned to look at something. Servants were dropping off a pair of bodies in the ferns outside the gates. These were the corpses of the Fisian chief and the Tongan warrior, dragged from the weather coast. The lowborn servants then sprawled in exhaustion, using the moment to peer through the famed gates, their eyes studying the lovely Fefine Girls, the serene fishponds, and the delicious-looking flightless birds.

The Tamahā indicated Kakala. "Take those men some water. Then get rid of them."

To Moon Appearing, the Tamahā said, "You, to the fishponds."

Moon Appearing frowned but obeyed. Because of its seeming futility, the girls considered circulating pond water a punishment.

The Tamahā entered her fale, which was a simple structure, though well-appointed with mats gifted to her from the regents of great islands. The dwelling, despite its treasures, had fallen into disrepair. Her lodge poles were from the chief of Suva, yet they supported a roof that leaked. Still, the place was hers, open to inspection by no man.

Her floating bed, suspended by ropes, was as impressive as people imagined—the slightest breeze set it swaying. Upon the bed's platform was a humble mat, made by a Fefine Girl several years ago. The Tamahā had given this girl the nickname Muʻamui, "First and Last." In all the Tamahā's years of working with Fefine Girls, Muʻamui had been the first true candidate for inheriting the Fan. Until the king found out.

Upon a peg hung the Fan. The key to wielding the Life-Affecting Fan was moving no unintended air. It should be handled like a knife, so that you cut through the air. You never pushed air unless you were ready to dole life—or confiscate it.

Heading toward the gates, the Tamahā passed Moon Appearing, sweating, hair loose, carrying a skin of water from the bottom tier of the fishpond up the path to the top. Water had to be circulated, though the girls saw it as an exercise concocted to drain them of poise and dignity, for as soon as the water was poured, it began overspilling from one plant-filled pond to the next so that when the girl walked back down, the water was waiting for her again.

"Did you attend to Prince Lolohea?" the Tamahā asked.

Moon Appearing wiped her brow and nodded.

"How was he?"

"There was something forlorn about him, sad even," Moon Appearing said.

The Tamahā quoted a poem: *"Whenever a person's life appears easy, look again."*

Moon Appearing had a question. "How is it the baby fish reside in the top pond, far from the parent fish in the bottom? Shouldn't the little fish be found in the lowest pool, where the water would wash them down, with the bigger fish residing in the higher tiers, since they alone can leap?"

The Tamahā smiled; she loved to see a girl's mind at work.

"And I notice you cultivate the red blossoms of the kaute plant," Moon Appearing added. "My aunt also tends this plant."

"Your aunt, the midwife?"

Moon Appearing nodded. A sad recognition passed between them.

The Tamahā said, "I look after threatened birds, vulnerable fish, and, on occasion, an endangered girl."

The flesh of the dead men had been much abraded, and of course the Fisian chief's intestines had been hastily returned to him. After the Fefine Girls hauled them inside the compound, the Tamahā said, "See if they possess anything of value."

The girls started with the Fisian, removing a necklace carved from dolphin teeth. Unwrapping his loincloth, they discovered a small pigskin pouch.

"The necklace was probably his wife's," the Tamahā said, extending a hand for it. "And the pouch will carry the dried umbilical cords of his children. Men do that, bring talismans of women and children when they set sail to kill other men."

The girls were less comfortable stripping a Tongan man. Lifting the fold of his loincloth, they discovered that, despite his dead and cooling body, his ule was erect.

Kneeling down, the Tamahā indicated his scrotum. "This is where the seed is made." Then she took hold of the stiffened ule. "This is what he uses to punch the baby into your belly. If I stroked it a couple times, even now, you'd see it burp its spore. That's all it takes, a few strokes." She released the thing and, standing, offered her hand to the girl named Heilala. "Smell," the Tamahā demanded.

Tentatively, Heilala took a sniff.

Her recoil was all the other girls needed to know about erections.

The Tamahā knelt. She opened the Tongan's mouth, and with her Fan, wafted air inside. He opened his eyes. He looked at the lovely girls, at the fishponds. He tried to speak, but couldn't. The Tamahā fanned another breath into him.

"I can see the loveliness of the next world," he said. "Is this the island of the afterlife?"

"Soon," the Tamahā said. "First, a question. You fought alongside Lolohea this morning."

"Yes," he said.

"Did he show fear?"

"Inside, all men are afraid."

The Tamahā rewarded this truthful response with an extra waft.

"How is it," she asked, "that he's alive, and you are not?"

"Am I not alive?"

"Sadly, no."

His eyes lost a little focus. "I feel alive."

"What I need to know," the Tamahā said, "is whether Lolohea ran from the fight. Did he show cowardice or abandon you to the enemy?"

"What keeps a man from running?" he mused. "Isn't that what he ought? Wouldn't I be alive if I'd fled? I'm no longer alive, you say?"

The Tamahā shook her head.

"The only reason some men don't run is because others don't. It's because other men, men like Lolohea, choose to enter the battle and stand beside you. It's because others believe in you that you believe in yourself."

The Tamahā rolled his head so he could behold his neighbor, the dead Fisian chief.

The Tongan warrior studied the man who'd taken his life. "If they're all like him . . ." he said, shaking his head at the impossibility of winning the war.

The Tamahā pulled two breaths from him, drawing closed his eyes.

He was in the dark again. "About my children," he whispered.

"Hush," the Tamahā whispered back.

She palmed his mouth shut and pinched his nose. After a brief spasm, he was still.

Moving to the Fisian chief, she paused, addressing the Fefine Girls.

"Perhaps I was in error earlier," she said. "I shouldn't leave you repulsed by a man's genitals, for they're items you'll have to contend with. They can be useful, for they can reveal a man. There was once a young woman, soon to be married, who was concerned her future husband wouldn't treat her well. Before the ceremony, she secreted herself into his fale. She asked him if he'd always treat her tenderly. *Yes*, he said. She asked if he trusted her. When he nodded, she reached under his vala kilt. In a great display of bravery, for she needed to look him in the eye, she gently clasped his balls. She needed to know if he would wince, widen his eyes, or make a hostage of her flesh. Would he hurt her to assuage his fear of being hurt? Or would he do as a true man would, and endow her with his faith?"

Heilala asked, "Did she end up marrying him?"

"She didn't have a choice," the Tamahā said. "She just needed to know her future."

The Tamahā studied the girls as they offered her favorite look—heads cocked and leaning forward. Cocked in uncertainty. Leaning forward to hear more. They'd never met a person like her, and they never would again, unless one of them, before it was too late, became her.

"What was that girl's name?" Moon Appearing asked.

"It doesn't matter," the Tamahā said.

The Tamahā approached the Fisian chief. "And now we face a lamentable truth about men," the Tamahā told the girls. "Here's proof they are rash, foolish, and observe the world from the shade of bad judgment. Having captured an enemy chief, a supreme piece of intelligence, does our Tu'itonga ask him how he evaded our security? How large his infiltration team? If he had other intended victims? If he'd received aid from any of our people? If his mission was part of a larger scheme? No, our king inquires after none of this. Instead, in a grand display, he removes the man's soul." She shook her head. "Now we must do the king's work for him."

She opened the Fisian chief's mouth and wafted her Fan. His eyelids fluttered, his focus drifting from face to face, taking in those who gazed down upon him. He'd seemed handsome earlier, in his own sort of way, but now, lacking any blood, his features were drawn. "Water," he said.

Placing her Fan before his chest, the Tamahā pulled forth strokes of air, causing his torso to rise until he was sitting upright. His arms hung limp at his sides, so the drinking gourd was held to his lips.

He drank in long, quenching pulls.

Then he looked down—the water was running from his open abdomen. "I've left so much incomplete," he said. "My comrades will be waiting at the meeting point. I alone possess the counterattack signal. The dogs are trained on my command. And my wife, she'll never know my fate. Or whether our son yet lives. He lives, yes?"

"He lives," the Tamahā said.

"You can't let him see me like this."

The Tamahā nodded. "Yet you did make a battle companion of him."

"At your side, that's where a loved one is most safe."

"What about those girls you came to free? If they were so special, how come they'd left your side?"

"Who said they were special? How special must one be to merit rescue from the Tongans?"

"You made much effort," she said, "and paid a steep price."

"You're surrounded by young women," the Fisian chief said. "Wouldn't you mount a rescue if one were stolen by a big-bellied Tongan?"

Something in this question elicited a smile from the Tamahā. She wafted more life into him, widening his eyes. He discovered he could now lift a hand to wipe the dirt from his face.

The Tamahā said, "All these girls are going to be stolen by big-bellied Tongans. I have the power to save only one."

The Fisian chief asked, "Do you have the power to save me?"

"Yes, but I can't heal your wounds. You'd just die again."

"Why do you speak truthfully to me?"

"Because you're only briefly visiting. And soon to depart."

"*Briefly visiting,*" he mused. "*And soon to depart.* This is the normal state of Fisian affairs since Tonga attacked. Normal is smoke on the horizon, announcing which islands have fallen. Normal is attending the graves of other people's ancestors because your own island has been inventoried and loaded onto barges."

"So you've lost your home island?"

"*My island is the shore where I rest until dawn,*" he said. "*My home is the sand I unroll my mat upon.*"

This quoting of Tongan poetry made the Tamahā smile. "If your people are in disarray, who then orders your attacks?"

"Counterattacks," he corrected. "Let me ask you a question. This girl you plan to save from the big-bellied Tongans, how will you know which one is worthy of your efforts?"

The Tamahā looked not at the Fefine Girls surrounding her; instead, she looked beyond her gates, toward greater Tonga. "How will I ever?" she wondered.

The Fisian chief asked, "Will you look after my son?"

The Tamahā shook her head. "I concern myself solely with the fates of women. But if Tonga wins this war, there'll be a place for a young man who knows both worlds."

"Wins what?" he asked. "The Tongans don't occupy or administrate.

They don't direct the planting or the harvest. They take the birds, the hogs, the boats, the timber. They raid the storehouses, grab some survivors, light their fires, and leave."

The Tamahā acknowledged this. "Our conversation draws to a close."

"One more question, if I may," he said. "What'll happen to me?"

"To your body?" she asked. "You'll be fed to the hogs."

He nodded, contemplating that.

"I have a final question as well," she said. "Do you know that you're missing your soul? Can you feel the lack of it?"

"Missing my soul? Where might my soul be?"

"Right now?" she asked. "Inside a coconut."

"A coconut?"

"Don't take my word for it. These girls witnessed its removal. That's why your belly is thus."

The Fisian moved his eyes across the Fefine Girls, who regarded him with silent horror.

"Where's this coconut?" he asked. "How do I get my soul back?"

"I don't think you do," she said, and drew, with her Fan, some life from him.

His eyes went wide. "Death, I've no fear of death. But without my soul, how'll I make my reunions?"

The Tamahā pulled some life from him, and then elegantly reversed the Fan, pushing his chest lower to the ground; she drew life and lowered him, drew life and then he was on the ground, reclined, eyes closing.

"How'll I commune with my wife?" he asked. "How'll my son find me?"

And then, with a flash of her Fan, he was snuffed.

She turned to the Fefine Girls, who'd gone silent.

"Snack time," she said. "And then back to pounding turmeric."

None of the girls moved.

Moon Appearing asked, "Is he gone?"

The Tamahā only smiled.

Sun Shower asked, "But what's the answer to his question, how'll he make his reunions?"

The Tamahā lowered her Fan. "It seems he won't."

The Tamahā's snacks were universally received as loathsome. Sometimes she baked the hard, green heads of the pandanus tree. Others, it was fao seeds, bitter but edible. Today, she passed out green clumps of steamed limu. The girls had been trained to smile, and they made the gestures of eating, but little seagrass disappeared. If the Tamahā didn't teach them which foods to turn to in famine, who would? Every night, they feasted, savoring poached sea turtle eggs, salted river eel, and always some variety of exotic bird, the closer to extinction the better. There was only one Tamahā in the world. She knew what it was like to live at the edge of extinction.

The girls set their food aside and began discussing the dances they'd perform that night and who'd be highlighted with solos. They bickered over the order in which they'd perform the tauʻolunga, who'd stand in positions of prominence for the lakalaka, and, concerning the māʻuluʻulu, who'd be relegated to the wings.

The Tamahā ate her limu and watched them bicker. It was hard not to hate them. Here they were in a sanctuary, safe from the world of men, and all they could talk about was who might receive a ribbon from Lolohea tonight, for that was their goal, to dance with such allure that he'd rise in the firelight and grace one of them. "You know those dances aren't even Tongan," the Tamahā said. "We took them from the Haʻamoans."

They waited for her to elaborate, and when she didn't, they returned to synchronizing their movements.

The Tamahā asked, "Is there a single dance the men perform for your pleasure?"

Again, as ambassadors of politeness, they paused the appropriate amount of time.

The Tamahā, Fan in hand, moved closer to them. "A dance is supposed to say something, it's supposed to express who you are. What does your dance say but—*pick me*? I ask you, what dance would you dance if there were no men?"

"No men?" Kakala asked. "At all?"

"What dance would you dance if you danced only for each other?"

Their faces were blank, which meant they were purposefully not looking at her like she was crazy.

"What dance would you dance for yourself?"

Heilala asked, "Why would someone do that?"

The Tamahā lifted the Fan to her face, obscuring her features. Then, using the Fan's blade, she cut a slow circle around herself. Bending a knee and extending a leg, she turned with the Fan, moving just behind it, as one would trail a partner. She lifted the Fan high and brought it low, turned with it, and then allowed the Fan large, free arcs before bringing it close again. Quick gestures sent plumes of dust down the path before her. High wafts shimmered leaves in the boughs above. The Fan flashed at an empty patch of sky—a great crack was heard, followed by a rolling boom. The Tamahā floated over to the dead Tongan warrior and, circling him, coaxed him from the ground with graceful pulls. The man's torso would rise, falter, start to descend again, but another pull of the Fan kept him hovering. He rose and rose, nearly upright, yet still leaning perilously back. Taking the warrior's hand, the Tamahā leaned back as well, so they were both defying the pull of the earth as they turned, the living and the dead, hand in hand. His eyes opened, and for a moment they gazed at one another. Then she spun him slowly down, releasing him to his previous recumbency, the Fan extinguishing him again.

The Tamahā turned to the Fefine Girls, their eyes wide at the impossibility of what they'd seen.

"All that matters is that the dance is yours," she said. "Now, get these dead men out of here."

"Wait," Moon Appearing said. "What's the end of the story? How did Ate outsmart the Tuʻitonga?"

"Ah, Ate's story," the Tamahā said. "She was very crafty in her defeat of him. Knowing he was reverent, she asked a priest to wed her to the Tuʻitonga's ancestors. In this way, she technically married into his family. There was a brief ceremony, and she met the Tuʻitonga's family grave in wedlock. The Tuʻitonga was forced to acknowledge the sanctity of this union."

Moon Appearing shook her head. "Didn't Ate defeat herself? She was now married to a stone vault, to a bunch of bones. She'd never have a husband. She'd never create a family."

The Tamahā made a show of reappraising Moon Appearing for the worse.

"The grave was situated on the island's best property, filled with bountiful groves," she told them. "And no person could trespass upon it. All she had to do was tend an old tomb. For that small price, no man would violate her again." The Tamahā directed her Fan at the bodies in the sun. "Seriously, get them out of here. And then go, dance your fancy dances."

In the afternoon, the Tamahā made an infusion of nonu juice, which had once helped her with hot flashes. Though she was past that stage in life, she still took comfort in the drink. In the shade of her compound's entrance, surrounded by the glow of sunstruck ferns, she waited for visitors to come have tapu removed. It was customary to receive a gift for this service, and gifts were what she lived on. *Tama* was the word for "child" and *hā* meant "on high." This was what she often felt like, a high child, with all the benefits accorded a favored child's status, yet in the end a child still, living on what was given her.

With one sweep of her foot around their features, she removed the tapu of three villagers. One had wandered into a restricted grove, another had been touched by the blowing hair of his chief, while a third drank from a forbidden spring. He was thirsty, he said. If serious tapu was left unattended, the kind that came from graves or persons of high rank, ailment and death could ensue.

Afternoon rain clouds traced the coast. It was the time when doves would hail one another, back when there were doves enough. The Tu'itonga came ambling up the path, his entourage lingering behind. She'd been expecting him, since only she could remove the tapu she'd placed on him that morning. She'd prepared an elixir of vai kahi for him, which cleansed the kidneys. When he sat—wincing—he gifted her with a conch shell, which could be made into a valuable kele'a horn. He took a moment to study her, with her graying hair pinned with frigate bird feathers. Then he performed the duty he considered so odious, lifting her foot and tracing a path around his face.

"That wasn't so bad," she said.

He snorted and took the vai kahi from her, drinking deep. Then he turned to show her the ink on his back. "More pain," he said. "My brother's gift to me."

She had him lie face down, then gathered leaves from her matolu vine.

These she squeezed so their milk drizzled across his lower back. "If it's any consolation, the ink work is very fine."

While she tended him, he gazed through the gates into her compound.

"What do you see in there?" she asked.

"Looks peaceful. No one to bother you."

"A refuge?"

He asked, "What did you learn from your chat with the Fisian chief?"

"The man was both a father and a chief. From the father, there was only a lament of how much he'd left unfinished."

"And from the chief?"

She asked, "How many islands are in Fisi?"

"Havea puts the number at three hundred."

"From our chat, I came to the conclusion that you'll have to defeat the Fisians three hundred times. They need defeat you only once."

"Don't get me going on the war," he grumbled. "You goaded me into starting it."

Her role in starting the war was regrettable. She lamented it, especially since the spoils of war had turned the war into a quest for more spoils. Calling for the fighting had been an emergency maneuver, at a time when she was cornered and had no other options. On the bright side, it did keep the dangerous and unpredictable 'Aho off Tongatapu for a dozen years. And it had diverted the king's attention, sapping his abilities for just as long.

He changed the topic. "Did you have to kill the matāpule?"

"Sending that fool to the afterlife was quite refreshing, actually."

"You shouldn't favor my brother."

She was silent.

"You know he already violated one of the Fefine Girls."

"What?" she asked. "Which one?"

"I can't tell them apart. He left her with a keepsake, though: a black jellyfish. She'll find no husband now, and I'm the one who'll have to pay her family."

She reviewed the day, recalling the girls' faces, trying to remember a sign, a look, any unusual behavior. "Your brother aims to tour Tongatapu with his son. You're the one letting him feel our soil between his toes."

"What would you have me do with him?"

When everything ran smoothly, the powerful men of Tonga turned their attention toward her—why did she have such fine property, why must they bow down before her, what did she contribute? So these men had to be constantly diverted, disrupted, thwarted. Each concession she wrung from the Tuʻitonga conditioned him to her will. Each time she wrong-footed him, his danger was directed elsewhere. Distraction, interference, confusion—when you had no real power, this was all you had.

"I find myself wondering about those bones," the Tamahā said, "and who they might belong to."

"The bones ʻAho carries? Are they not his wife's?"

"Certainly that's what he claims. But do you have any proof? Could they not be anyone's bones? Have you received any official word from Lifuka that his wife has passed?"

"No," he said. "But there's a war going on—confusion reigns in Lifuka."

"Has ʻAho recounted her death to you, or has he left that a mystery?"

"It remains a mystery," he conceded. "But why claim someone else's bones as his wife's? Why travel all this way to bury a stranger?"

"Why indeed," she mused. "He insists on placing those bones inside the royal vault. What if that's his real goal, opening the family tomb?"

"But why would he want the royal vault opened? How would that benefit him?"

"Oh, I have no idea," she said. "I just find myself wondering."

The Tuʻitonga stood, awkwardly, regarding her a moment, before walking unevenly away.

Before long, one of Valatoa's widows came by. She'd accidentally come in contact with the king during her sand-throwing protest and now was under tapu, the kind only the Tuʻitonga or the Tamahā could remove. Such was her dilemma, to submit to the woman who'd requested her husband's drowning or the man who gave his consent. She found herself here because the Tamahā was the one who couldn't kill her. Not directly, at least.

"I'm happy to slowly die under tapu," the widow announced. "But I'm a mother, and I don't have the luxury of thinking only of myself."

The Tamahā had limited patience for the outrage of a Tongatapu wife.

This woman had once been a Fefine Girl. She'd married an elite and sat upon a throne of wedding mats the day she was betrothed. She'd shared the gossip, eaten her fill at the feasts, birthed the favored babies, and taken her share of the spoils when her husband Valatoa made forfeit the lives of others.

The Tamahā said nothing. She merely lifted her foot.

Despite the woman's anger and indignation, her hands trembled as she performed her task.

"And now your gift," the woman said. She handed the Tamahā something small, wrapped in a leaf.

"Thank you," the Tamahā said, and set it aside with the other offerings.

"Please," the widow said. "Do me the honor."

Unfolding the leaf, the Tamahā discovered two teeth.

"I saved them," the widow said, "so I might one day bury them with my husband, so he'd be complete in the afterlife. But there'll be no burial now, since his body is at the bottom of the sea."

"I shall put them to good use," the Tamahā said. "For teeth, once ground up, make excellent fertilizer."

"I'll have you remember that my husband lost those teeth in a duel with Six Fists, defending your will against the Tu'itonga's."

"What I remember of your husband," the Tamahā said, "is that he thought it beneath him to serve the interests of a woman. Yet he could attain no better station. That duel was undertaken by Valatoa as an opportunity to eliminate Six Fists and audition for his role. He was lucky to escape with only a crooked smile as a keepsake of his failed ambitions. The truth of Valatoa is that it shamed him to be loyal to a woman, so I can only speculate on what kind of husband he was."

Tears welled in the woman's eyes. She stood to leave. "He was the noble kind. And yes, when it comes to love and husbands and families, you can only speculate."

By the time Moon Appearing had finished her chores, her hair had fallen and she smelled like pond water. It was evening, and the light from the west lit the thorny ribs of palm fronds and set the pale green ferns aglow.

She found the Tamahā sitting at the gates to her compound, examining the gifts she'd received that afternoon—some kava, a conch shell, sandalwood. Fine gifts, though the Tamahā handled them as if the air of charity were about them. "Did any of the girls seem different today?" the Tamahā asked.

"Different?"

"Acting different, talking different."

"Those girls don't confide in me," Moon Appearing answered.

"Were any withdrawn?"

Moon Appearing shook her head. Tonight she'd have to dance with the other girls at the feast, and it would become obvious how little aptitude she had for it. She cringed at the humiliation in store. She could hold all the steps in her mind, she could keep the rhythm, yet the moves came out awkward and halting.

"You seem reluctant to return to the Tu'itonga's compound," the Tamahā said. "Is there something you're avoiding?"

Moon Appearing shook her head. She could see how the evening would play out—firelight, drums, a line of lovely girls moving in unison. And then there'd be her—struggling, exuding frustration.

The Tamahā asked, "So, you don't dawdle here in hopes of avoiding a threat over there?"

"A threat? I linger because I'm a lousy dancer."

The Tamahā dismissed this. "The dances the king promotes, they're made by men, for the pleasures of men. As long as your body wriggles, they'll be happy."

"Can you not assign me some task that would excuse me from tonight's activities?"

"You're not a bad dancer," the Tamahā said. "You're just not dancing your own dance."

Dancing your own dance—Moon Appearing remembered the Tamahā twirling with a corpse.

The Tamahā said, "If what was in your mind right now traveled through your body, if what you felt became movement, what manner of dance would this be?"

"It would be the dance of an imposter, of a person who doesn't belong."

The Tamahā lifted her eyebrows, as if to say, *Have you not answered your own question?*

Moon Appearing shook her head. "That'd be no kind of dance, at least not one anyone'd want to see."

"Depends on who you're dancing for. A girl could dance for big-bellied men. She could dance for the audience in her head, the one she imagines is judging her. Better, she could dance for herself. Or she could dance for all the women who came before her." Here, the Tamahā's tone lightened with possibility. "What if she danced for the ones to come?"

Moon Appearing thought on that. Evenings on her home island were bluer, clearer. Here, clouds—maroon and moody—clung to the island. She felt like the only example of her kind.

"Do you know the story of Lolongo?" the Tamahā asked. "Lolongo's father, to protect her from suitors, sent her to the afterlife, where no living man could hurt her. As the only person alive in the spirit world, she was constantly aware she didn't belong. At every turn, she felt like an interloper. Then she found love. She now had a reason to act, and act she did. Here's a dance ready-made for you, Lolongo's dance."

Moon Appearing could imagine aspects of the story, Pulotu's purple light, the specters of dead heroes, the feeling of being completely alone. "Can you teach me these steps?"

The Tamahā laughed. "Child, the dance doesn't exist. It's yours to invent."

Moon Appearing groaned. "But I can't dance."

"Not even for yourself?"

Moon Appearing looked up. She heard someone approaching.

The Tamahā spoke with urgency. "Never let anyone isolate you, understand?"

"Isolate me?"

"And if something happens," the Tamahā said, "you come directly to me."

Moon Appearing was caught off guard. She could only nod.

"I promise you," the Tamahā said. "If someone's hurting girls on this island, I'll destroy him."

Rattled, Moon Appearing stood. Lolohea came around the bend. He smiled at the sight of her, but she studied him the way you'd study a figure on a moonless night, when it's too dark to tell if he's a friend, a lover, or the man who will kill you.

The Tamahā welcomed Lolohea. The light was fading, and the young man glanced down the path that Moon Appearing had taken, concern on his face.

"She's fine," the Tamahā assured him.

"She didn't look fine."

"She's just . . . have you ever felt you must dance someone else's dance? That the steps ahead are predetermined?"

"She feels that way?"

The Tamahā took his hand, examined his dog bite. "Since I humbled you with soot from my fire, you've done well. You retrieved your royal necklace. You battled Fisians. And you helmed a canoe of no return."

He moved to speak, but she cut him off.

"Don't tell me you're but a humble son of Tonga," she said. "These are real achievements. Your dream of becoming king is on the horizon. When that happens, you and I will work together often."

He all but winced at this depiction of his future. "I really have to go. Perhaps you could remove the tapu you placed upon me?"

"Of course. Have you brought an offering?"

His eyes closed in frustration. "I forgot."

Her goal was to see if Lolohea could be worked with, if he was subject to influence. "I have a little task I can't handle. And here I have a strong man." She invited him to follow her through the gates.

"Is this place not tapu for me?" he asked.

"Lolo, are you not here to have tapu removed?" She'd heard his mother call him that, Lolo.

He followed her through the living wall, the two of them advancing side by side, Lolohea trying to take it all in—fruit trees brimming, a canopy of slitted banana leaves, the dark green of taro, and a field of 'atiu vine. He indicated the flock of flightless birds. "What variety are these?"

"These are malau. They follow me everywhere."

"Are malau not extinct?" Lolohea asked.

"The creature survives on a small Tongan island, one we don't trifle with because there's no profit in it. That's where I got the eggs."

"Do they taste as good as the old poems suggest?"

"I've never eaten one."

"Then why raise them?" Lolohea asked.

"Why indeed?"

He indicated a mound of sand.

"That's where I incubate sea turtle eggs."

"What kind of place is this?" he asked.

"*This*," she said, "is what Tonga used to be. Or my approximation of it."

Lolohea's gaze fell upon the terraced ponds, formed from black stones. With the light fading, and under heavy canopy, the aquatic lilies and cress were more charcoal than green, the fish nothing but swirls in shadowy water.

"Come," she said. "I need your muscle."

Inside her fale, the main beam was in danger of slipping off its post and bringing down the roof. "It happened in a storm," she said. "I can't get up there to fix it."

"That's a big job. Many men would be needed to lift the roof while the lodge beam is adjusted."

"You adjust the pole. Let me handle the roof." She took up her Fan.

"Can it do all they say?" he asked. "Fill sails, fell trees, lighten men of their hides?"

She only smiled.

"How'd you come to possess it?"

"I suspect you know the answer to that, but I like that you ask questions. I inherited it."

He positioned himself to shimmy up the post but paused. "Did you have to kill those men? I'm no matāpule-lover, and Valatoa was a perfectly unlikable fellow, but they'd done nothing to deserve death."

"I might remind you that you're the one who called for an old canoe, and you're the one who actually killed them. But I take the question—what's the value of a life, and whom should we entrust to curtail the affair of living? I notice you don't ask about those Fisian women who were condemned without a thought."

"One was spared."

"But you take my question, yes? What's the value of a woman? Did you know there was going to be a new Tamahā, just a few years ago? I'd chosen her to inherit the Fan. But when your father found out, the girl disappeared. Simply to undermine me, an innocent girl met her fate."

"My father wouldn't do that."

"Ask him."

Lolohea climbed the post, if only to escape this accusation. With wafts of her Fan, the Tamahā made weightless the roof, and Lolohea easily slid the timber into place.

Outside, they made their way to the gate. The malau followed the Tamahā, anticipating their nightly feeding.

"You don't cage these birds?" Lolohea asked.

"They're free to leave. If I make life here preferable, they'll remain."

The young man looked adrift. She wondered if his parents knew how alone he must be feeling.

The Tamahā often felt she'd be a good mother to a son. Of course, it hadn't been worth the risk of having a child, for it could've been a girl, and to her, adept or no, the Tamahā would've had to pass the Fan. No, she'd leave nothing to chance. Still, if she'd had a son, she would've shielded him from the impulsive ways of men. The way they acted brashly, taking needless risks. The way they succumbed to foolishness, like rushing into battle or standing ground when all was lost. The Tamahā was pretty sure she could spare a boy the folly of becoming a man. With her help, he'd stealthily advance, quietly dispatching rivals, heading off opposition, and fulfilling whatever destiny he was meant for. Studying Lolohea, she saw there was an openness to his face. He was still becoming. No, he was not too grown for mothering.

"You know you can share your problems with me," she said. "Your father speaks to me about his."

"I very much doubt that."

"Ask him," she said. "Ask him about our talks."

Passing through the gate, he turned to her. His eyes were soft and vulnerable.

She extended her foot. "Isn't this what you came for?"

He knelt and performed his tapu removal, circling her foot once around his features.

She still couldn't tell what kind of king he'd be, and whether she'd be able to work with him. She decided to unbalance him to see how he responded. "If I could direct your attention to the future," she said.

Imperceptibly around them, ferns were folding closed for the evening. "Yes?" he asked.

"Your father has burdened you with more tests. You'll have to swim around the Teleki Reefs. You'll have to fill a Tongan Hull. Then there's the Ultimate Test. You probably haven't imagined what it'll be like to take the life of someone you care about. Don't listen to the matāpule, who'll say it must happen in the most public of places, between roaring fires. The old poem that guides us sets no terms. My advice is this: Set your own terms. Design the event as you wish—just you and the victim, perhaps. You might perform your task by light of day or in the dark, a dark like this, with just enough light to do the deed. You could take that life on the beach, so the wind steals the victim's pleas. Or it could take place in a meadow of soft ferns, like these ferns, on a night like this night, with the person you care about kneeling, mostly obscured by tender, arching fronds, nothing but her soft breathing and the moonlight falling on her trembling shoulders. Perhaps you already know the girl who'll be the candidate. My advice is to release her from your heart. Imagine a nobody kneeling amid the ferns, an anyone. Don't look down to her wet eyes. Close your mind to her choked goodbyes. Listen instead to the insects droning. Hear the call of an extinct bird's song, focus on the coolness rising from the green. Only then should you tighten your grip and raise the club that'll spill the liquor of her mind."

Lolohea rose, stumbling as he backed up. Saying nothing, he turned to go.

Though the dark, she could hear the pace of his footfalls. Soon he was moving full speed.

THE STORY OF LOLONGO

Lolongo was the beauty of Tongatapu and daughter to the great warrior Sinilau. Word of Lolongo's loveliness spread through the islands, and soon handsome young men began arriving to make their introductions. These suitors were brave and strong, yet Sinilau found them inferior.

Evenings, these young men waited along moonlit paths to regale Lolongo with their crooning. Mornings, they enchanted her bathing pool with poems from Ha'apai. While she ate dinner, they oiled their torsos and grappled for her benefit.

To protect Lolongo from these bachelors, Sinilau sent her to Pulotu, the island of the afterlife, which is ruled by the god Hikule'o, who is both male and female, blind and all-seeing. There, Sinilau figured, Lolongo would be tutored in the appraisal of true Tongan heroes, for the afterlife is stocked with no other sort. She indeed learned to recognize the emblems of greatness.

In time, she became an assistant to Hikule'o. She greeted newly arrived souls by anointing them with lolohea, oil from the sacred hea tree. She also dipped water from the soul-refreshing stream Vaiola so she could hallow the bodies of warriors who'd died in battle. She was even allowed to fetch Hikule'o's Life-Affecting Fan, which was capable of wafting existence itself.

Still, being the only mortal on the island of the departed, she was lonely.

A parrot resided in the groves of Pulotu. Lolongo often shared her woes with Teki, the parrot who'd journeyed with Ovava into the southern seas. Hearing of Lolongo's forlorn status, Teki crossed vast waters to deliver this news to Sinilau, who was distressed to hear of his daughter's loneliness. To lift his daughter's spirits, Sinilau resolved to find her a suitable husband. He discovered a candidate on the island of 'Eua. The young man's name was

Tokelau. He was brave and handsome and infused with essential skills—combat arts, punake, and reverence for his aunts.

"Please deliver a message to my daughter," Sinilau told him. "Tell her I'm ever in mind of her."

"Deliver this message how?" Tokelau asked. "Where is this beautiful woman I'm to wed?"

"Close your eyes," Sinilau said. "When you next open them, she'll appear before you."

When the young man closed his eyes, Sinilau struck him down.

When Tokelau opened his eyes, a beautiful woman placed a drop of lolo on his forehead.

"This oil is from the sacred hea tree," Lolongo said.

Tokelau said, "I'm sent by your father to become your husband."

Lolongo, because of her time among heroes, recognized the man's great qualities. Yet, reaching to take his hand, she found only vapor, for he was no longer among the living.

"If you trust me," Lolongo said, "close your eyes."

When Tokelau did so, Lolongo rolled his soul inside a taro leaf.

She then stole Hikuleʻo's Fan by slipping it from his girdle. This act Hikuleʻo saw and didn't see. Using one of Teki's flight feathers, Lolongo traveled to ʻEua, where she found Tokelau's still-warm body. She unfurled his soul, and with a few wafts, coaxed Tokelau's essence into its former residence.

When Tokelau rose, it was clear he'd swum through surfs eternal and stroked beyond the reefs of the dead. His soul had been loosed by murder and repaired by the breath of the sublime. Their glorious wedding, both glistening with sandalwood oil, is still spoken of. Lolongo's ability to appraise a true Tongan is lauded to this day. And Tokelau's willingness to die for love is ever a model.

Yet the idyllic portion of this story was soon to expire. Lolongo's uncle ʻOfamaikiatama would eventually cause trouble, and Tokelau was soon to lose his life in a dispute over a necklace wagered in a game of tolo. But the careful listener will have heard how, despite this story's noble elements, the tale is a dark one, as no Tongan alive could celebrate the separation of the Life-Affecting Fan from its rightful owner.

EIGHTEEN

BLACK JELLYFISH

In the royal compound, Moon Appearing was adorning herself for the upcoming performance. By candlenut light in the Fefine Girls' fale, she ringed a girdle of flowers about her waist, and she didn't care if it marked her as a rural girl. All that mattered was not making the others look bad by dancing terribly. She could hear them out in the garden, practicing their steps—Heilala was calling the moves, and Moon Appearing followed along in her mind as she rubbed sandalwood oil on her shoulders and reddened her forearms with turmeric.

Her aunt was fond of saying, *The female body knows how to give birth. It's the mother who doesn't know how to have a baby, and the baby who doesn't know how to be born.* So much of midwifery was keeping the mother from hindering what came naturally and keeping the baby from delays, wrong turns, and changes of heart. This wisdom Moon Appearing tried to apply to herself, but in visualizing the dance steps they were to perform, she also imagined ways to mess up. Why weren't there midwives for dancing?

Placing a final feather in her hair, she decided she was as ready as she'd ever be. That's when she heard raised voices. Then shouting. Outside, she found Heilala, backed by several girls, confronting Sun Shower. "You've got the wrong girl," Sun Shower said. "Stay away from me."

But Heilala wasn't retreating. By torchlight, she said, "I'll put an end to these rumors." Then she seized Sun Shower's hand. With the help of several others, the strong girl from Tafahi was taken down.

"What's going on?" Moon Appearing asked. "What're you doing to her?"

"It's not me!" Sun Shower shouted. "I'm not the one!"

But with five girls subduing her, Sun Shower was quickly overcome.

Heilala took hold of her ankles, spreading Sun Shower's legs.

What Heilala saw disappointed her.

"I told you," Sun Shower said. "I told you it wasn't me."

"Have you gone mad?" Moon Appearing asked Heilala.

Yet Heilala's attention had already settled on another girl, Kakala, who wilted under their collective gaze. When they went to her, she went limp. When she was on the ground, her eyes rolled shut, and she offered no resistance as her legs were spread. It was as if the assault were happening all over again. Everyone went quiet as they beheld the black jellyfish.

"What's that?" Moon Appearing asked in horror. "What's happened to her?"

No one would answer.

At the nightly feast, the Tuʻitonga and Six Fists sat at their own fire. It was tapu for people of differing ranks to consort, so priests dined with priests, sub-chiefs ate with sub-chiefs, and so on. Much humor and conversation drifted in from the other fire circles, but, as none could match the king's rank, he ate alone, without even his family. Only Six Fists, being from Nuku Hiva, was exempted. Without him, the king would've cut a forlorn figure. He likely would've abandoned all things social, as the Tamahā had.

Tonight, the Tuʻitonga suffered from a deep and mysterious pain. His spirits lifted only when the food arrived: pigeon in taro pudding, poached sea-turtle eggs, and, most sumptuous: tiny triller birds, grilled whole, ten to a spit. The Tuʻitonga drew a triller off the skewer with his teeth. It was a single, perfect bite—the joy of crunching down its salty bones!

"Where'd we find these delicious birds?" the Tuʻitonga called to a circle of matāpule.

Matāpule Muʻa was also satisfying his mighty appetite. A little wing extended from the corner of his mouth. "Why, they are courtesy of our friends the Fisians!"

The Tuʻitonga turned to Six Fists, that he might share the humor, but the man didn't smile. He stared into the fire with inward-looking eyes. The Tu'itonga knew the problem. The man had started to doubt he'd ever make it home. Despite all the king's promises, Six Fists, over time, had convinced himself he'd never see his shores again. This created the irony by which the ruler of all Tonga had to regularly offer assurances to a slave. It was apparently part of Six Fists's beliefs that it wasn't enough to send one's bones back to the shores of his birth. No, Six Fists believed that to reach the afterlife, he actually had to *die* on the island he came from. This meant Six Fists must still be alive when he gained his freedom. But on which of Nuku Hiva's islands was Six Fists born, how was it found, what even was Six Fists's real name? No, Six Fists didn't make it easy for a king to solve his problems.

In a comforting tone, the Tu'itonga asked, "Would some dancing cheer you up?"

"I prefer whatever you prefer," Six Fists said.

The poor man was really down. This called for something special. The Tu'itonga knew that in Nuku Hiva, poetry was highly valued. So he shouted to New Punake's dining circle, which was quite distant, for the poet took his food with lowly sorts. "Punake," he called. "Let's have a poem. One of your dramatic ones, or better yet, a funny one."

The poet looked startled. He lowered a morsel of pigeon. The king had just called him "Punake," so now he was Punake. The poet must certainly have been thinking that the transition from New Punake to Punake put him closer to the transition from Punake to Old Punake. "It has been some time since my last recitation," Punake responded. "I'm not sure what poems I have at my disposal."

"Nonsense," the Tu'itonga said. "You're the royal poet."

Punake made his way to the central fire, apprehension on his face. Without greeting the crowd or invoking ancient poets, he began:

Na'a moe kakano'i puaka 'oku tutue,	*When even the pork is lean,*
pea 'ikai toe 'asi e malama o e fanga manupuna	*when shining birds go unseen,*
ko e kohu pē 'oku matafia ehe ngāahi tafatafa'aki langi.	*smoke is what the horizons glean.*

Ko ha kafa ha'i mano'o pē,
'oku 'ala ma'u ehe ngāahi
kaungāme'a.
Toki 'alu fakamuimui e kotoa 'oku
lanumata.

*A tightening cord
is what friends afford.*

The last to go is green.

Not realizing the poem was over, the Tu'itonga sat waiting for it to begin. Punake stared at the Tu'itonga, and the Tu'itonga stared at Punake. The Tu'itonga lifted his hands.

"That's it," Punake said.

"What's it?" the Tu'itonga asked.

Punake asked, "Shall I recite it again?"

"That was the poem?" the Tu'itonga asked. "No leaping? No, you know..." He made big gestures with his hands. "What about the voices and faces? Where were all the words?"

"It's a different kind of poem," Punake said.

Exasperated, the Tu'itonga stood. There was a sharp pain in his gut. In his hand, he discovered three empty skewers. Those little birds had bewitched him into eating thirty in a row! "Dancing girls," he called.

When he turned, he was faced with his brother, eyes orange with firelight. With him was that foul set of bones. The Tu'itonga smiled broadly. "You decided to join us. I knew you'd—"

"I am made to believe," 'Aho said, "that the Fisians this morning were here to murder me."

"Trying to guess the mind of a Fisian would be like trying to—"

"I'm further told you had foreknowledge of this," 'Aho said.

"You've been talking to the Tamahā."

"It's also said you kept this knowledge from me. As if you wanted them to kill me."

"I don't need foreigners to do my bidding."

"So you'd have me dead?"

"Come, my brother. You get yourself excited. Kava's being made. Dancing's to come."

"And my son tells me," 'Aho said, "that upon your order, one of the prisoners in the Old Canoe was left unbound. This condemned man tried to drown my son, and your boys did nothing to help."

"A lamentable affair. What matters is that Mateaki is fine."

"He's not fine. He was certain he was going to die. He just lost his mother."

"Membership aboard that canoe was voluntary. Plus, the nature of the excursion wasn't the fostering of inter-island cheer. And what else is tested by the Old Canoe than one's ability to not interfere? Lolohea passed that test, and some might argue Mateaki did not."

"My son isn't trying to pass tests," 'Aho said. "I brought him home after a loss to refresh the Tongan spirit in him, but, sadly, I find the Tongan spirit here lacking. And no one seems to value the proper burial of a loved one."

"I've given my word that your wife'll find her place in the family tomb. Our only dispute is the occasion. Why can't she wait? Eternity's in no hurry. When your bones are placed in the grave, hers, having safely been stored, will join you. Is it not ideal to enter the afterlife together?"

'Aho pointed west, toward Fisi. "Do you know what's happening out there? Have you any idea how many of us surrender our souls on foreign shores, bones never to be recovered? I won't gamble my wife's afterlife on the unlikely recovery of me. I'm going to walk around this island with my son, and then she'll be properly laid to rest."

A drum began beating. The Fefine Girls were taking their places.

"If it helps in any way," the Tuʻitonga said, "I swear that, should anything befall you, I'll stop at nothing to ensure your bones are placed in the royal vault, along with your wife's."

'Aho said, "I pledge to do the same."

"Do the same what?"

"Should anything befall you, my older brother. If your time comes before mine, I pledge to assist you in your voyage to the afterlife."

The Tuʻitonga's pleasant demeanor fell away. "Nothing's going to happen to me, I assure you. There's no possibility of my demise, except, it seems, in your imagination."

'Aho flashed his toothless grin. "I make no plans for my downfall, either."

The Fefine Girls were summoned to dance, halting the hunt for more jellyfish. Hustling to the dining grounds, Moon Appearing tried to call no attention to herself. Apprehension was building in her. She didn't have a name for this fear. It felt like the look on women's faces before they first gave birth.

Two great fires had been built up, and when the girls arrived at the dining circles, their oiled bodies echoed the yellow of the flames. A few old-timers were singing an almost-forgotten song:

Ta hifo ki liku o toli kakala,	*Let us pluck the seaside flower,*
'o ka teitei tō e la'ā.	*when the sun is near to setting.*

The girls, in unison, began to dance. Their collective hands reached and, fingers turning inward, beckoned. They were supposed to gaze horizonward, their focus landing on nothing, which served as an invitation to be gazed upon—for the savoring of oiled shoulders and the contemplation of heavenly calves.

But Moon Appearing was too agitated to look at nothing. She stole glances at Kakala, who'd somehow recovered and now moved perfectly. Kakala seemed to study an ever-receding distance where bad things didn't happen to pretty girls. You'd never know, by her faultless smile, that moments ago she'd fainted as if into death. Fear and uncertainty also guided Sun Shower into a realm of careful mastery. And Moon Appearing discovered that her body, without thought or effort, operated as it ought.

Her eyes landed upon the Tu'itonga, who stood with his brother 'Aho, the two exchanging serious words. When they parted, 'Aho's angry attention turned to the dancers. He approached the nearest fire circle, forcing men of lesser rank to excuse themselves. Sitting alone, he lifted his chin to take in the girls, none of whom dared regard him.

The old men repeated the chorus, and 'Aho, in his lisping, childlike voice, sang along:

Toli e kakala, ki mu'a	*Pluck the flowers*
pea ngangana honau matala	*before their blossoms fall.*
Tutu ho'omou tūhulu, pea mou ōmai.	*Kindle your torches and come.*

After several beckoning motions, the dance called for a halting gesture. The girls flashed their palms in unison. A foot slap followed, and the tease continued as the girls turned, showing the audience their backs before coyly beckoning again.

'Aho smiled nakedly, delicious pleasure on his face. His eyes locked on no single girl; instead, his study perused them all. He reached dirty-handed into an oyster bowl before raising several high and slurping them raw, one after another. As the last oyster slid into his mouth, Moon Appearing saw that beneath the briny sheen of his hand was a tentacled black jellyfish. At that moment, his eyes flashed sideways to her. She must've revealed something. She must've acted in a way that caught his notice. All she could do was close her eyes, but the image lingered: his inked hand feeding oysters into an open mouth. She knew this would be her abiding image of him, the one she'd never stop seeing.

As the song progressed toward conclusion, it became apparent that 'Aho favored a longer recital. Disappointed, he stood and began clapping faster, increasing the rhythm, so the girls were forced to quicken their movements. That's when his smile returned, when he realized how easy it was to control the entirety of them.

Remarkably, Moon Appearing's body kept up. There was nothing elegant or graceful about it, but she flubbed none of the steps, even as she moved faster and faster. The other girls seemed not to see 'Aho at all. They seemed to behold no one, performing as if for an audience beyond the horizon.

When 'Aho had them rapidly dancing, at the edge of stumbling, he paused to enjoy them racing through their moves, sweating, breathing hard, collectively unsure if they were allowed to stop. He admired his handiwork, and then left while they were moving full speed, his self-satisfaction the last part of him to recede.

Only when Moon Appearing came to rest did she feel the hot streaks of tears down her face. She wanted to be away, from the firelight, from these people, from this place called the Sacred South. She began moving toward a toa tree, where she wouldn't be seen, summoned, or thrown to the ground and inspected. But Lolohea intercepted her, amazement on his face. He was marveling at her. Had he not seen what'd happened? Did he not understand what had just taken place, right in front of him? She shook her head, to stop him from speaking, so, without words, he tied an ifi vine around her arm.

Before sleep, the Tuʻitonga made a final tour of the royal compound. The outer gates had been shut, the watchmen posted. He came across some cooks, quietly eating in the dark. He strolled past the family grave, through the royal gardens, and along a night-fragrant path. The entire time, a boy followed with a broom, sweeping away the king's footprints and his own as they made them.

Candlenut lamps were glowing in Lolohea's fale. Entering, he saw his son opening pigeon cages. Some birds had flown off, while others paced atop their hutches.

"What're you doing, son?" he asked.

"Freeing my birds."

"You've raised them by hand," the Tuʻitonga said. "You dote on them."

"If they prefer to be with me, they'll stay. If they miss me, they'll return."

"They can't live without you. They've been tamed. Out there, they'll be easy meals."

Lolohea unlatched the last bamboo door. "Not if they fly far enough."

"I don't understand. Do you want them to remain, or do you want them gone?"

"I want them to do as they wish."

"What's got you thinking like this?"

Reaching for a reluctant bird, Lolohea rolled it into the bowl of his hand and ran a finger along its breast. "I never liked that they were hunting decoys, used to lure others to their deaths."

The Tuʻitonga didn't quite understand, but he nodded.

"I talked to the Tamahā today."

"Ah," the Tuʻitonga said. "The situation clarifies."

"Did you kill a girl, the Tamahā's successor, a few years ago?"

"What? I don't go around killing girls. I had her married to a chief in Vanuatu."

"Why must I do extra tests?" Lolohea asked. "Why the Ultimate Test?"

"The Tamahā talked to you about this, too, did she?"

"She had this way of making me feel like I was doing it."

"Son, you must come to me with your concerns. And if you speak to her, be very careful. Everything you reveal, she'll use against you."

"Don't you confide in her?" Lolohea asked.

"She's my aunt. It's my duty to seek her advice. Yet I'm careful around her. She's like a shark who determines if you're tasty by taking a bite."

Lolohea set the bird atop its cage, offered it seed from his palm. "Why does anyone have to die? Why would anyone be asked to kill someone they cared about?"

"When you rule," the Tuʻitonga said, "people must believe that, should an enemy spear sink into your chest, its tip would be blunted by the flint of your heart." The Tuʻitonga placed a hand on his son's shoulder. "Once you become king, you won't ever have to harm anyone again. You'll simply express your will, and others will do what needs to be done."

"Sometimes you say things like they're reassuring, but they're the opposite."

"Don't worry. I have a plan to get you through the Ultimate Test."

Doubtful, Lolohea asked, "Yeah?"

"What we'll do is convince people you care about someone."

"Who's this someone?"

"It doesn't matter. Anyone. It'll be a person you barely know, a person who's nobody to you. We'll let the word get out that you're sweet on her."

Lolohea looked at his father with an expression that suggested the only thing worse than taking the life of someone you cared about was taking the life of an innocent stranger.

"Is there someone you're sweet on?" the Tuʻitonga asked. "A girl you walk with in the moonlight?"

Lolohea said nothing.

"Good, good," the Tuʻitonga said. "For this to work, you can't reveal your heart to anyone. Don't go around tying ribbons on girls. That's how a girl gets killed. And if the Tamahā finds out you're secretly sweet on someone, she'll make sure you have to hurt her, just because that's how she works."

The Tuʻitonga held out some seed for the pigeons. When one stepped onto his hand, he ever so gently lowered it into a cage, latching it shut.

"Let's save some of these birds," the Tuʻitonga said. He lifted another bird and looked into its small, dark eyes. "Son, I want you to understand that a man isn't one person. He can be a person who's tender toward pigeons. And he can be a person who must drown an enemy. He can be both these things, even on the same day. And, while a man can be more than one person, a king must be many. Most of the people I've had to be, you've never even met. You never got to meet the frightened, uncertain boy I was the day my father died. You've never gazed upon the me who led men into battle. There was a me that even I hadn't met. You, Lolohea, only know this person before you, the me who presides over a stable Tonga, who makes toasts, officiates weddings, and says solemn words at funerals. The man who did the deeds that made all this happen, you never even glimpsed him. But that man, he's still in me. He's in you, too. And it's time, like it or not, to make his acquaintance."

The Tuʻitonga woke before dawn. His wife Pōhiva was nowhere to be seen. A pain was inside him, one he hoped was urine. He headed outside, toward his kotone tree, where the piss was most likely to flow. On the way, he encountered Six Fists, standing guard in the dark. "Your middle son came to see me," Six Fists said. "He wanted to enlist my help in allowing Havea to visit his wife and sons."

"What'd you tell him?"

"I told him the truth, that Havea's wife was dead and that his sons had been conscripted into the war as gravediggers on the island of Matuku."

"You did the right thing. It's best the boy knows the truth."

"Your son had another question," Six Fists said. "He wondered, if a man weren't free to visit his dying wife, if he weren't free to bury her, if a man couldn't see his sons before they went to war, well, your son asked if Havea shouldn't be considered less than free."

"Did you tell him it was an honor to tutor the son of a king? Did you remind him that for the system to work, everyone must be of service, that Havea, by doing his duty, was merely paying his tribute to Tonga? Did you tell my boy that Havea should stop his moping and do his damned duty like the rest of us?"

"I didn't tell him those things," Six Fists said. "Here, you and I have differing opinions. I'd argue that the unfree are better placed to define the terms of bondage."

So Six Fists's motive in bringing up this topic revealed itself: the man was fishing for yet another assurance that his freedom was on the horizon. How many times did the king have to guarantee it? "Six Fists, my friend, I promise I'll release you of your service."

Six Fists blankly regarded him.

"I'll do it the day my son becomes king—I swear."

Instead of acknowledging this pledge, Six Fists asked, "Do you intend to let your brother bury his wife?"

"Sadly, I don't think it's wise."

"If I may," Six Fists said. "Why not let the man lay a loved one to rest? Yes, there's a rule against it, but you're the king. Aren't the rules yours to make?"

"If he only intended to lay his wife to rest. But burying her is just a pretense. He wants the tomb opened for a different reason."

"What reason could that be?"

"That's what I'm trying to figure out."

Reaching the kotone tree, he leaned his forehead against the bark. Waiting for the urine, waiting for the fire. Better to not fight the waves of pain. Instead, he used the crests to appreciate all that he had, and the troughs to begin letting go of what he must lose.

Then, like a vision, Pōhiva was beside him, the rope around her wrist tethering the Fisian boy. "I've been looking for you. Your supplemental wives said they hadn't seen you, they said they never see you. Is this where you disappear to in the mornings? Is this the condition you're in?"

"The Tamahā says it's my kidneys. She asked if my father was similarly afflicted. I didn't have an answer. I saw him so little, and then he was gone.

I've tried to be a better father. I've kept Lolo at my side. And to our other sons, I've given individual fathers, so they might never lack for attention, as I did. My poor brother, he had it worse. To 'Aho, a second son, our father paid no mind at all. How could a father do that? How could he ignore one of his sons?" The Tu'itonga placed his hand on the tree—instead of sensing its great age and nobility, he apprehended only its destiny to one day be felled.

Hearing her husband speak in this reflective manner changed Pōhiva's face. It was perhaps the only diagnosis she needed. She took a breath, absorbing her husband's state. When his time came, so would hers, and joining her departure would be her attendants, leaving many additional people unprovided for. Now she'd added a boy to the mix. She must've been worrying about her sons more than she knew, feeling her ability to protect them slipping away. "I didn't mean to adopt him," she said.

In Pōhiva's eyes he could see the future had taken up residence. "We'll see he's cared for."

"There's much planning to do," she said. "Will you work with me? Can we agree to do this together?"

The Tu'itonga felt a sudden and profound love for his wife. It was a warmth, moving through his entire body. He nodded.

"Then come with me," she said. "Another pattern has entered the weave."

Pōhiva left the Fisian boy in the compound. Taking up a torch, she led the Tu'itonga through the gates. Outside, they passed the Tufuga, sleeping next to his inking tools. Next came the war dogs, tethered to a tree. Their eyes were open, studying the passing torch. Beyond them was a steaming patch of ground where, below, the body of the Tu'ilifuka was baking, so his bones could be removed for their journey home. At last, they came to the Fisian girl, tethered to her own tree. She was naked, face down in the dirt. The Tongan attire she'd been given was heaped in a mess to the side.

"What's wrong with her?" the Tu'itonga asked.

Pōhiva used a foot to jostle the girl into rolling over. When she did, the ink of a jellyfish was visible between her legs. The girl gazed at them with contempt before returning to her former position.

The Tu'itonga shook his head in disbelief. "I was just with 'Aho at dinner.

Now, with his wife's bones in hand, he commits another assault? What am I to do with him? I can't kill him without sacrificing my soul, and if someone else does it, the Tamahā will simply bring him back to life."

They took a moment to absorb such a thought.

Then, reluctantly, the Tuʻitonga made a confession. "I've agreed to grant Six Fists his freedom."

Pōhiva's eyes widened. "You'll have to rescind that. We'll need him to protect Lolo from your brother."

"I can't go back on my word. We're speaking of my honor."

"What's honor if you're dead? What's honor if it costs you a son?"

The Tuʻitonga said nothing.

"I've changed my thinking," Pōhiva said. "You were right. We must make Lolo as strong as possible, as quickly as possible."

"There's an ideal pace. It's not about whether he can commit certain acts. It's about his ability to come to terms with them."

"He'll have to be strong if he's to contend with the Tamahā when we're gone."

"She's already undermining us in support of ʻAho. I tell you, she'll have regrets if he prevails."

"She doesn't really support ʻAho," Pōhiva said. "She strengthens herself by weakening the both of you. If she felt you'd fallen too far by her designs, she'd start undermining him."

They gazed upon the Fisian girl.

"Imagine it," Pōhiva said. "Tied to a tree. Hair still wet from the old canoe. Then you're visited by him, his oyster breath, missing teeth, dirty fingers. He's adorned with the skeleton of the last woman he murdered. Then comes the assault, not just by him but by her, her bones swinging from his shoulders, the rotting smell of her. He cradles the two of you in a single embrace. Then he gifts you with an indelible memento. He makes everlasting the stain of his seed."

"Such a wasted opportunity," the Tuʻitonga added. "The girl was rare. I beheld her calm when they tied her to the old canoe. And death, they say, was something she nobly faced. I was going to have her schooled in our traditions so she might serve as a go-between, something we'll need if we ever hope to broker a Fisian surrender. Now that plan's no more. Siga, that's what they say her name is."

Pōhiva also lamented this outcome. "It's best to put her out of her misery."

"No, I'll have her returned instead. The Fisians have struck at our people, on our own shores. She can still serve as a messenger. Perhaps the sting of 'Aho's jellyfish on a daughter of Fisi is the proper response."

NINETEEN

KŌRERO:
COMETS WAIT FOR NO ONE

The dog was licking my face, that's what woke me. The sun was up, the sea had flattened. I stood on the deck of my father's canoe, which seemed orphaned without the island it was made to circle. Still, I felt my father's presence—him paddling between fishing spots, watching birds work the water, pairing himself with the light before dawn.

Before I'd left, all I could think about was a little girl. Last night, however, there was no time for that: each dark swell had to be confronted. Sometimes the moon would edge the rising waves, giving me a chance to turn into them. Others, there was only the sound of them hissing as they rolled. When I heard heaving thumps in the distance, I knew those were the ones that could've swamped me. And there was no one but me. Who else to trim the sail, without which I had no speed, and without that, no ability to steer? Who else to bail or anchor the outrigger? So I wasn't thinking about a girl. The last thing on my mind was a star.

Now there was nothing but a featureless blue scape, the sun a complete cipher. Last night I'd felt panic, fear, self-pity, and despair. Daylight brought the shame of having acted like a fool in front of the Wayfinder and the regret of having rebuffed my parents. Such emotions leave you tamped as the late-morning sea. I found myself newly appreciating how my father kept his hope and resolve alive, how my mother, fierce and protective, never lost focus. How she did everything for me, even if it cost her another child.

Feeling so alone made me think of Tapoto differently, how he'd had to negotiate the world without anyone to look out for him. And then there was Hine, whose situation was perhaps worse: She'd lost her mother. Yet her father walked the same paths as her, took his meals near her, perhaps right beside her, all without revealing himself, let alone claiming her. "But you know all about it, don't you?" I asked the dog. "You were the last dog on your island. For all I know, you're the last of your kind." Of course, I thought of that little girl. If something happened to her, there'd be no people on her island at all. In essence, they'd be extinct. That idea had never occurred to me, that a people could cease existing. The word *depopulated* had been thrown around, but only now, in solitude, did I understand how possible such a thing was. I'd been imagining this girl as a lost sister, but now I understood her as the most remote and forlorn girl in the sea.

You'll never feel more turned around than when the sun's directly above you. Reflected light flashes from all directions, allowing the horizon to conceal its features. I recalled paddling with Tiri, how, when I closed my eyes, my imagination ran wild without reference to the real world. *This is what it's like to be blind*, I'd thought. But now I knew what sightlessness must be like. It wasn't about darkness or rampant imagination. It was knowing there was an entire world out there, none of it able to reach you.

Several birds flew overhead—noddies and terns. I adjusted course to follow them. Before long, I detected a distant patch of white, and, with a following wind, approached a submerged reef. The water got colder, which meant it was welling up from deep before spilling across the reef, creating a current that drew me closer.

Shearwaters took turns folding and diving. Not far off my outrigger, the water thrashed as vast schools of baitfish shot glimmering above the surface, many into the waiting beaks of hovering birds. In spray after spray, the little fish erupted, with nothing but the occasional slashing fin to suggest the fates of those below. Quickly, I tossed a couple of my father's trolling lines into the water—bonito lures that shone with abalone shell. The sea began drawing our little waka faster, rushing us across the reef. Our sail was full, the water frothing, and racing past below were purple fans, bright yellow tubes, and marbled outcrops of brain coral looming grayer and more ghastly than any human mind.

Moments later, we were off the reef and subject again to the regularity of the waves, yet our lines were taut: one with the silver-blue shimmer of mackerel, one heavy with a thick-cheeked fish I didn't recognize. Soon the dog and I were savoring still-twitching chunks of mackerel tail, silver-pink, translucent, and sweet.

If myths could be made from the lives of girls—of average girls from neglected islands—if a person like me could be the stuff of legend, then such a story would contain rare moments like this: eating fish on a small canoe in the middle of the ocean as one girl heedlessly set out to rescue another. Epic tales, I realized, weren't told about girls who talked a lot. They were reserved for those who'd decided to act.

The dog waited patiently for each bite I gave him. I realized he'd been hand-fed. He favored flesh over guts, gnawing the head over flesh, and crunching semi-clear spines above all else. As I thought of bones, some mid-ocean clarity came to me: the bones Finau carried must belong to that poet named Punake. Finau was clearly upset that something horrible had happened to the man, and Finau seemed to blame his brother for the poet's outcome. Why else quote so much poetry? Why say he knew what it was like to lose two fathers?

And what of the remains that occupied the Wayfinder's attention? Now that I thought about it, they had to belong to a beautiful girl, perhaps one of those Fefine Girls. Why else be so determined to reach a magical island, except to reanimate a girl he'd loved?

The dog stopped chewing. His ears lifted, swiveled. He sniffed the air once, twice, and then he began barking like mad.

※

A double-hull canoe marked with frigate birds soon came astern. The white dog jumped from waka to waka, sniffing and greeting everyone. "You idiot," Hine screamed, leaping onto my deck for a hug. "We nearly lost you!"

"Kōrero!" I looked up in time to see Tapoto's great frame launch from the Wayfinder's bow—his impact submerged our outrigger, nearly pitching us into the sea. He wrapped me tight. "I thought we'd never see you again."

I'd never been so happy to see his big face. "Would I disappoint our war captain?"

The Tongan brothers regarded us from their tall bows. In wonder, or perhaps disbelief, the Wayfinder said, "You managed to hold a steady course. If you'd veered at all, we never would've found you."

"Maybe this navigation stuff isn't so hard," I told the Wayfinder.

This suggestion scrunched his mouth. I could tell he was holding back a dismissive comment.

Hine said, "Maybe there was a wayfinder in you all along, and you just needed to meet her."

Despite being completely lost, I said, "Yeah, I just needed to meet her." A swell lifted our overburdened fishing canoe—because it was riding so low, water sloshed in our hull. When my ankles got wet, I let out a yelp of fear. Now the Wayfinder smiled. I saw his waka was outfitted for voyaging, with calabashes hanging from the mast. "So you're going, then?" I asked him.

"Comets wait for no one," he said.

"We could use your help, you know."

"Looks like you've got it handled."

I nodded toward a sack of bones. "That Fefine Girl must be pretty important."

"What would you know about her?" the Wayfinder asked.

"Why're you so set on serving the dead," I asked, "when there are living people, right in front of you, who need your help?" To Finau, I said, "I'm sorry Punake's gone, but we're not."

The young man turned white before my eyes. "He's not gone, we can bring him back! That's why we have to go back to Tonga, not some mythical island."

"Don't set my brother against me," the Wayfinder told me.

"First we get Punake," Finau responded. "He'll help us."

"A melancholy poet?" the Wayfinder asked. "As if he could help us defeat our uncle."

Defensive, Finau said, "He's much more than that, and you know it."

"We'll get him," the Wayfinder told his brother. "First things first, though. We've sailed a long way, and Pulotu must be close." Finau said nothing, which the Wayfinder took as agreement. He turned to our small, overburdened fishing boat. "If I were you, I'd drop sail and heave-to until nightfall. Wait for Atutahi to rise, and then chase it down."

"Thanks for the advice," I said. "But I know where I'm headed." Then I pointed in the wrong direction.

"They're turned around," Finau said. "Outrigger underwater. Hull half-swamped. They'll die out here."

The Wayfinder studied us. He shook his head. "How'd we happen upon your impossible island?" he asked of no one. "How'd your people become our responsibility? How've you survived this long, when you're clearly the most incompetent people in the sea?" To his brother, he said, "Throw them a towline. We'll get them to their stupid island."

We tethered our two-man fishing canoe behind their great voyaging waka. When the Wayfinder took my hand and helped me aboard, I said, "My father told me never to get on a boat with you."

"A wise man," he said.

※

That night, our large voyaging waka chased a star called Atutahi. The troughs cradled us and wave-backs gave us hope. Lashing crests, however, imposed the sea's discipline. Behind us, my father's empty fishing canoe bucked and pitched. I paid attention to the Wayfinder, how he marked the current, how he reached through the dark to gauge the tension on his ropes. When the torches burned out, he didn't seem to mind.

Deep into the night, there were squalls at our back, so that lightning illuminated our waka's deck and the sea before us. In flashes, I saw Hine and Tapoto sleeping together, Hine turned into Tapoto's bulk for warmth. The dog had wedged itself against Tapoto, too. I was prone to imagining the sea as a monster, with ever-looming wave-faces, but flashes of light showed fields of ash-colored water, not churning with danger, but motionless in halting glimpses.

"It won't be long," the Wayfinder said. "We'll land at dawn."

How he'd determined this, I had no idea. But with him in charge, I could appreciate the vaulting stars, the rhythm of the waves, the sheer vastness of it all, which last night had terrified me. Last night, I'd had to perceive the world one swell at a time.

The Wayfinder said, "I made this passage with the men of your island. Right here, just before dawn, they became talkative. They didn't discuss what might be awaiting come landfall, but what they'd left behind. They talked about their wives and families. Your father talked about you, about your good judgment and your calm under pressure. He said you were his greatest achievement."

I wondered if my father still believed that, now that I'd disobeyed him and recklessly taken to the sea, now that I was on the Wayfinder's waka.

"You are a confounding people," he said. "You're leaderless, defenseless, passive. You insist on doing everything the most difficult way imaginable. But then I see you eat together, truly together, without regard for status or bloodline or rank. Then I see your family on the beach at night, talking and gesturing and looking at the sky. That never happened once in my life. I never shared a single meal with my true father. And I'm pretty sure he wasn't singing my praises when I wasn't around."

"You don't know that," I said. "You might give the man some credit."

"Praise isn't the point. All I'm saying is, meeting your people helped me feel certain I was sailing in the right direction, that it wasn't possible to get far enough from home."

"And yet, after you find this island, this *Pulotu*, you're returning to Tonga?"

"Where am I to go?" the Wayfinder asked. "Should I become a nomad?"

"You mentioned your *true* father. Might that mean that, like Finau, you have a second one?"

The Wayfinder was silent. I thought he wasn't going to speak. Then he said, "Had."

"Sorry to hear that."

"At least I think he's gone. Havea was his name. I last saw him on a Fisian island named Matuku."

I couldn't make out the Wayfinder's expression, but I could hear the loss in his voice.

"My father told me you have a third set of bones."

"Yes, we have another member of our party." He pointed at a dark shape in the bottom of the hull. "His bones weren't easy to get. We had to make quite a detour to retrieve them."

"Whose are they?" I asked.

"They belong to the man who's going to protect us when we return to Tonga. In combat, no man ever defeated him."

Yet he'd become a sack of bones.

"So you are going back?"

"What choice do we have? Live out here?" The Wayfinder gestured at the dark water. "No, we'll go home, but we'll return with someone who can fight, someone who can give orders, and someone willing to wield the Fan."

"*Fan?*" I asked.

"The Life-Affecting Fan," he said. "That'll be the Fefine Girl's job. At all costs, we must resurrect her, for, of the tasks ahead, hers is most important."

It was dawn when we approached the island. The rising sun imbued the surf with an amber-green glow and cast our shadows long across the beach break. Except for one volcanic peak, the island was low and flat, and, lacking trees of any sort, the morning breeze was lifting ribbons of dust, which drifted off the island's lee. It was clear that without trees, this island, over time, would largely blow away.

We stood on deck, marveling at this sight, which inspired some reverie in the Wayfinder. "In Fisi," he said, "they rise each morning and make their way to the beach. There, they sing the sun into being. Each night, they sing it down again."

I loved that image. I tried to imagine those voices conjuring the light.

Hine asked, "Aren't you at war with Fisi?"

The Wayfinder didn't respond.

"Only because they refuse to submit," Finau said.

"Is Tonga at war with all its neighbors?" Tapoto asked.

Finau said, "Our neighbors select their own fates."

Before our hulls kissed sand, the dog leaped into the surf and swam ashore.

Without trees, we couldn't tie off and were forced to bury our anchor stones. Tapoto lowered himself carefully to the beach, as his feet hadn't fully healed from the last visit. When my feet first touched this new island, I could feel the difference right away: I was used to fine, squeaky sand. Here, it was gritty, darkened with the tint of ground lava. Charcoal and ash marked the high-tide line, a sign that great fires had carried embers and ash out over the water, only to have the sea return them.

"We don't chase her," I announced. "This'll only work if she comes to us."

I grabbed my fat-cheeked fish, and the five of us began walking inland. There was much brush and flax, but nothing grew above chest-high. Vines creeped blindly down paths, in search of nonexistent trees to suckle. Much of the land looked purposefully cleared, but if people had been farming, there was no evidence. Most surprising were how few signs of life there were—there was no bark-beating log, no rope-twisting stand, no kelp-drying racks or canoes under construction. When at last we encountered a dwelling, it'd been burned and was nothing but a scorch on the ground. Near it was a turtle-shell comb, a single strand of hair in its teeth. Hine bent to pick it up, then changed her mind.

We continued inland, coming across a hole in the ground, perhaps knee-deep. In the bottom were a few bones I took to be human. "Look familiar?" the Wayfinder asked me.

I'd opened my share of graves. "That's not what you think it is," I said.

Finau said, "A hole with human bones is the definition of a grave."

"What is it, then?" the Wayfinder asked.

"I don't know," I said. "But no one digs a grave this shallow."

"Maybe for your enemies," Finau said.

"How could these people have enemies?" I asked. "Where would they come from?"

I turned to Tapoto, who looked down. There was something he wasn't telling me.

A dusty haze obscured much of the land. Tall grass rose and fell in waves. Absent the sounds of human life, there was only the dry rustle of flax blades, the lonely flapping of sea wattle leaves. Though we passed more dwellings, all reduced to stains on the ground, it seemed more like people had never lived here, rather than that they'd gone missing.

At last, we found the longhouse, burned but still standing. It was a large structure, made to serve many. Nearing, I could see its beams had been hand-carved, the chisel marks preserved in the charred surface. Hine touched the lintel. Her hand came away black.

"There she is," Finau said.

We lifted our eyes to the volcanic dome. Visible on a lower ridge was a human figure and a white dog.

Tapoto said, "She outran or outsmarted every one of us."

I said, "Let's see who's hungry for breakfast."

To block the wind, we sat in a tight circle, feeding twigs and grass into a fire. Once skewered, the fish's fins were soon blackening in the flames. "To rescue her, we'll have to work together," I said. "Think of what she's been through."

In a flat voice, Hine said, "As if you know anything about it."

It was true. By definition, the girl had lost everyone, and I'd never lost anyone.

The Wayfinder said, "Better to have no sibling than to have one and lose him."

"And lose him for no reason," Finau said. "None at all."

I wanted to say I was sorry about their brother. I wanted to know his name. But what could I say?

The Wayfinder gazed at the little fire. "You assume you know your brother, but it's only later, when you think back on your conversations, that you understand the things he was trying to tell you. It's only later, after he's gone, that you get to know the person you lost."

That kind of loss was only an idea to me, but Hine and Tapoto went quiet at these words. I looked up to the girl on the ridge—she was gone. Soon enough, I spotted her watching from the brush nearby. I caught Tapoto's eye and nodded toward the girl. Soon we were all aware of her.

"That fish sure smells good," Tapoto announced. "But I'm full, I don't know if I'll be able to eat my share."

"Yes," Hine declared. "Looks like we'll have extra."

When the juice, once milky pink, ran clear down the stick, I knew the fish was fully cooked. I lifted it from the fire and pulled free a chunk of white meat, blowing on it to cool it down. I held out the piece of fish, offering it in the direction of the girl.

With great trepidation, she neared us. I could tell she was looking at the ink on my face. Then her eyes went to the familiar moko on Hine. She couldn't have been more than ten, and though she was fairly dirty, her hair had recently been tamed, or I wanted to think that. Maybe I was hoping she hadn't been alone too long. When she was a few steps away, she said, without inflection, "You brought my dog back."

I extended the morsel of fish. The girl reached, and just as she was about to take it, she instead snatched the stick from my other hand and raced off with the entire meal, the dog leaping with joy by her side.

"Once her belly's empty," I said, "she'll be back."

Hine said, "There are other things a person gets hungry for."

We continued trekking, noting the darkened patches where families had once dwelled. Without any canopy, the sun was always on us, and the wind through the tall grass was pressing. Why had they cut down their trees, what did they use them for, where did they grow crops? Things only started to become clear when we came to a fence, erected as an imposing barrier.

The look on Tapoto's face suggested it was worse to encounter it the second time. He said, "It stretches from one end of the island to the other."

I said, "The old stories say that back on Aotearoa, Māori tribes would build vast defensive structures called pā." I put my hand on the timbers, to confirm they were real. "But who would these people be defending against?"

"On Aotearoa," Hine asked, "who were the Māori tribes defending against?"

I looked both ways, the wall receding in each direction. "Other Māori tribes."

There was a place where, by some great force, the wall had been breached. After we slipped through this gap, things only got stranger, because, not twenty steps away, there was another wall, running astride the first wall, as far as we could see. We slipped through this wall, and here was the other half of the island, complete with burned dwellings, and as we neared, a second wharenui longhouse, this one collapsed from fire.

"Two longhouses?" Hine asked.

"Two villages," Tapoto lamented.

"Two chiefs," the Wayfinder said.

"There can only be one chief," Finau said.

"Or, in our case, none," I said.

Finau said, "Well, there certainly can't be two."

We wandered this side of the island, no different in essence than the other. There were occasional burn marks and human leftovers. Most eerie were personal items scattered about, items no family would let out of its sight, like a death mask, carved to preserve a grandfather's moko.

Still, I couldn't get over the impossibility of it. How could all the forests be gone, how could they not save a single tree? How could people rob themselves of bark to make cloth, or candlenuts to light the dark? An island was such a rare thing in the vastness of the sea—how could anyone strip it bare? And the people—what people could erase themselves, or, worse, leave behind but a single delegate? These people were also us, which left me wondering if this might be our fate, too.

Ahead, the remainder of the island ran bereft to the sea. We stopped walking. From the dirt, Hine took up a bleached parrot's skull. She looked at me but didn't say anything.

Finau squinted into the forlorn landscape. "Is this what you saw in Fisi?" he asked his brother.

The Wayfinder's face gave little away. "Something like it."

Tapoto tried to be positive. "If we made this place tapu for long enough, our grandchildren would return to find it teeming with birds and trees and turtles."

It made me sad to think we'd have to clutch our stomachs and smile for another generation.

Even sadder was the notion our children would also have to scavenge to survive.

Finau spotted a group of dead people. The men went to investigate. They wanted to determine who had died and how and why. Hine and I stayed behind. It wasn't death that kept our distance. People died on our island. We prepared them and lamented them and said our farewells. And it wasn't decay. Hine and I were no strangers to human remains. What we weren't ready to face was the notion of violence. We could see, even from where we stood, that one of the forms wore a flax skirt, which rustled in the wind. She was long gone, dry skin over white bones. But she hadn't died of natural causes. She'd been murdered.

TWENTY

THE OUTSKIRTS OF WAR

The Second Son was tasked with returning the girl named Siga to Fisi. While she was being lashed to the Fisian vaka, he made his farewells. Pōhiva offered her son three gifts that might ensure his safe return. The first was an enchanted keleʻa shell. "When this horn is blown, it'll be heard by my priest, no matter how many seas lie between." Next was a set of whale teeth, with which her boy should buy his freedom, should he encounter dangerous actors. The third gift she adorned him with personally: a headdress of boar tusks that ringed his crown so that each tooth rose up and pointed outward at aggressive angles. "You've started dressing like Havea," she said, indicating Havea's loincloth and battered navigator's cloak. "Should you encounter persons of high station, this headdress will signal your kinship with them."

In his defense, Havea said, "I dress like any other navig—"

Pōhiva lifted a hand. "I've given the Fisian girl a Tongan garment and tried to make her presentable. The poor thing. She didn't learn the tauʻolunga or make a single proper acquaintance. Instead, she was exposed to nothing but unwholesome affairs. Judging by her case alone, one might think rough treatment is all that could be expected from Tongan hands."

"Won't my father be seeing me off?" the Second Son asked.

"I bid farewell for the both of us," Pōhiva said.

"Kuo pau ke ke ʻalu," Pōhiva said to her son. *You must go.*

"Pea ko koe e nofo," he replied. *And you remain.*

They placed their foreheads together. Pōhiva inhaled to recall the life she'd given him, and in exhaling gave him more. Then she departed, before losing her composure.

Finau also offered his farewells. "I'd give anything to join you on this mission," Finau said, handing his brother the coconut containing the last breath of Siga's sister.

The Second Son savored the word *mission*. He envisioned himself in the future, recalling by firelight this very scene. *I undertook a mission with the great navigator Havea*, was how the story would begin.

Exiting Tongatapu's lagoon, the Second Son looked back at the *Pelepeka*, at its red sail, at the way it stood too high in the water without a ballast of passengers, provisions, or purpose. Leaving it behind, this craft he and Havea had built and lived upon—it was the end of something.

On the open water, they turned before the wind at Pangaimotu, Fafá visible to the north. The crown of boars' teeth sat heavy on his head. When the vaka rocked, the tusks made a clacking sound. Yet he knew he looked quite grand to the boys waving from Ha'atafu's beach.

Havea seemed no longer his teacher. Together, they helmed a mission. And after they dropped off Siga, it would be just the two of them. They'd be free to explore the northern Lau Islands, even head up to Ha'amoa. Whatever they fancied.

Proof this voyage was different: Havea was not withdrawn and sullen-seeming. He began conversing with Siga in Fisian, and it was nice to hear the man animated and engaged.

Siga said something, and Havea responded with a single cynical laugh.

"What'd she say?" the Second Son asked.

Havea said, "She merely shared an observation."

Siga openly glanced his way, and he could tell the topic was him. She spoke and then Havea spoke. How was it these two—a lowly war captive and a famous navigator—had such a rapport? Havea spoke and then she spoke. What could they possibly have in common? She said something pointed, and then Havea fell silent. At last he said, "Vosota a caravou. Sa qai yabaki jinikalima."

"What're you two talking about?" the Second Son asked.

Havea said, "She asked your age, and I told her you were only seventeen."

Only? What did his age have to do with anything? And why'd Havea speak like he was making an excuse?

"Hand her this," Havea said. From the stern, he passed forward a knife. When the Second Son hesitated, Havea said, "No need to worry. She knows that if she kills us, she'll never find her home."

"If she kills *you*," the Second Son said. "If she kills you, she'll never make it home."

For the first time, Havea smiled. "Point taken," he said.

He handed Siga the blade. First, she cut the tether, and in a spray of fiber, sliced the rope from her wrists. Free, she tore the garlands from her shoulders and the wrap from her body, tossing them into the sea. Then she pulled the plaits from her hair and shook it loose.

Havea said to him, "And you, too, should feel free to remove—" Here, Havea gestured a circle at his own head. "Your . . . thing."

Shame beset the Second Son. Only in removing the headdress did he realize how hot and itchy his scalp had become.

Siga, standing tall, regarded the Second Son. The look she gave made him nervous. She returned the knife by tossing it to him, taking satisfaction at the panic on his face as his mind scrambled to figure out how to safely catch it.

A WORD ON OLD FISI

Toward what manner of place were Havea and the Second Son sailing, and why was their passenger so prone to discarding her attire? Was it true that Fisian women went about careless as to whether their bodies were covered? Did vicious dogs really patrol the shores ahead?

We ask these questions because the Fisians of today are people with whom we trade canoes, share kava, and exchange daughters in marriage. These things wouldn't be possible without some esteem for one another. So, why do we continue to share unsavory tales about our neighbors, the

Fisians? How many times have you heard a story about Fisi begin with, "In the old days," only to be followed by depictions of murder, mayhem, and titillation?

Why do old stories bend toward the violent horizon and take place in the lurid tableaus of firelight, wet jungle, or moonless dark? And don't these tales tend to feature nude females, breasts unbound and hips accessible to any willing listener? The women of Fisi no longer wander about uncovered. Did they ever? And if Fisian women have been made naked in our narratives, for what purpose has their modesty been omitted? And what of the men, often depicted without regard for their lives? They fight on in our tales with broken limbs and open head wounds. Amid torture, they call out for more torture, often of higher quality.

Why do we thirst for such stories? Certainly those stories were once told to justify the harm done to our Fisian neighbors. And, of course, the more fearsome we depicted our enemies, the more fearsome we made ourselves in facing them. But why do *we, today*, still repeat such salacious tales? Some say we've gone soft, that life-and-death stories connect us to our more vital, previous selves. Others say such stories prepare us for arduous futures we know are in store.

Can we trust accounts of old Fisi? To answer this question, we must ponder the origins of such stories. One source was the Fisians themselves, who shared portraits of their homeland after they were captured, kidnapped, or enslaved. At our mercy, might they not have told us stories we wanted to hear? Which again raises the question of our desire for lurid tales.

There's another source of such stories: Tongans who made passage to the Fisian islands and returned with firsthand accounts. Shouldn't these tales be considered most trustworthy? Yet who were these eyewitnesses, these men who waded ashore—seasick, eyes reddened with salt and sand and sweat—to fight up the beaches, all while shaking off dogs and dodging darts? The men who survived these assaults often discovered, after catching their breath amid the strewn bodies, that the dart-hurlers had been women and the dog-handlers children. What man wouldn't burn that village, scorching all trace of what'd happened? Which leaves the storytelling to ancillary figures, like the men who stayed with the canoes or the ones who dug the graves.

If the old stories about Fisi are to be met with suspicion, what about the stories of old Tonga? Would it surprise you to learn that some of our old stories are repeated by firelight in Fisi, especially the tale of 'Aho'eitu, who was butchered by his brothers? Or the story of Moon Appearing, which is still whispered, late at night, from one Fisian virgin to another.

The larger question is this: Who were we? Do we recognize ourselves in the old stories, and if so, must we not admit that those aspects yet reside in us, that we, today, are still capable of such dark trade? And if we don't recognize ourselves in such tales, why do we repeat them? If we don't own those stories, if we say these figures from long ago are not us, then who, exactly, is it that we are?

The answer perhaps lies in missing stories. We like to think we're above associating with creatures like the dog, yet recently uncovered middens of dog bones suggest we once shared our lives with them. Where did tales of the Tongan and the dog go? Carved into our oldest rocks are depictions of migrating canoes. Yet, where's the story of the island we came from? What dire circumstance made us flee our old home? What was it like to take to the canoes and face the open sea? Where's the account of our arrival and the possibility we felt when setting foot on new land?

There is reason for hope when it comes to recovering missing stories: it's well-known that women, when they gather beyond the purview of men, tell stories, too, and it has long been suspected that their versions are different than the official ones. Perhaps if one day women can be cajoled into violating the sanctity of their gossip circles, some of our questions about the past might be answered.

What, finally, is the truest way to tell a story? Storytellers, we see, are a problem. So are listeners. Poetry, for sure, is more loyal to its duty. But is the truest way to tell a story not the motion of the human body? Can hips dissemble? Could the fluidity of the human form ever tell anything but the truth? Can we not agree that if we left all important communication to the realm of dance, the world would be a more peaceful and informed place, one where longing was achingly palpable, where war could never be glorified, and all the stories that can't be told—of love and wounds and loss—would finally come pouring out?

In the morning, 'Aho and his son Mateaki washed their faces in bowls of rainwater. They rolled their sleeping mats and said farewell to the little fale that had sheltered them. Before departing on their sightseeing trip around Tongatapu, they took a last look at the Tu'ilifuka's possessions. Upon his tattered mat were a few scattered items. Mateaki took up a little pouch that contained the baby teeth of a lost daughter. 'Aho examined the man's downy red necklace.

"Want any of it?" 'Aho asked.

"I don't need a reminder of that guy."

"He wasn't all bad," 'Aho said. "He was loyal. You'd want him on your side in a fight."

That only two qualities could be said for the man only ratified Mateaki's low opinion of him.

"He wasn't always the way he turned out," 'Aho said. "There was a time when he was generous. When he had a sense of humor and was carefree. He was once the kind of guy to make necklaces for his daughter. And don't forget: I wouldn't be alive if it weren't for him, which means you wouldn't be here, either."

Mateaki shrugged.

"And remember—he didn't set out to become the man you met. It just happened, over time. I wish you could've known him from before." 'Aho removed his own necklace, made from dog's teeth, and dropped it on the mat. "I suppose I'm a different man, too," he said, taking up his wife's bones.

On the rocky shore, they began stripping pandanus blades, long and green, from fā trees, so they might weave a nice basket for 'Ofa's remains, one that would serve as a vessel when they lowered her into the family grave.

Above were heavy clouds, mists spitting below. Only glimpses of 'Eua

Island were visible across the water. 'Aho was in a philosophical mood. He wanted to speak his heart, but he had no practice at it. "The only thing that matters to me is you," he told his son. "You're the only reason I make it home from the fight."

Using thorns, they stripped the serrated edges from long blades of fā.

Mateaki asked, "Where'd you go last night?"

"You know how the Tu'ilifuka always had to have the last say in things?" 'Aho asked. "Well, he's not around anymore, so I had to do it for him."

"Did it have to do with that Fisian woman?"

'Aho rolled the strips into a tight bundle and tied them off. "I made a pledge to the Tu'ilifuka," he said, "to act as his hand from beyond the grave. So it wasn't really my hand. It wasn't my act."

They waded into the sea, submerging the bundle with rocks. Over the next few days, the salt water would soften the strips, making them pliable. In the waves, 'Aho's mind roamed the past. He remembered a comrade from long ago. His name was Malupo, from the Tongan island of 'Uiha. They were raiding a Fisian island one night. In the name of stealth, they swam ashore. Malupo happened to cut his foot on the reef, and because of adrenaline or perhaps the water temperature, the man had no sense of the severity of his cut. By the time they reached the shore, he'd bled to death. His last words were, "Is it bad?" For some reason, they made fun of him. For the longest time, whenever someone was wounded, they cracked each other up by asking, *Is it bad? Is it bad?*

A swell rolled up 'Aho's chest, wetting the bones, making them stink anew.

He recalled a warrior from Niuafo'ou—what was his name?—who'd lost his life in waves like these because he didn't know that dogs could swim.

And then there was that guy—Pome'e, that's what he was called—who surrendered his life when a Fisian woman threw a cast-net over him and began jabbing him in the waves with a fishing gig.

"This one time," 'Aho said, "we were sailing all night to attack the Fisian island of Tobua. We planned to land at dawn. We didn't know that the Fisians had been sailing all night from Tobua to attack us. We met in the blackness of the open water. Things like that remind you life's a comedy."

"What happened?" Mateaki asked.

"The only thing that could happen."

Mateaki had his hands out, to steady himself in the surf. "Do you have to carry her bones everywhere?"

"I wish I had the words to explain it," 'Aho said. "We lived at each other's side. It was my duty to protect her. And I failed."

His son waited for more.

"I know you can't understand," 'Aho said. "It's also . . . I'm just not ready to set her down. The time will come. And when it happens, it'll be for good."

As the night progressed, the sky clouded, and the Second Son sailed into an expanse of weather. The sea flattened and sheened over. When the rain came, heavy and straight, they couldn't hear one another speak. There were several lightning strikes, each making Havea's dull eye glow white. Gusts of wind shed water from the sail in claps. Siga, shivering, curled up. When Havea offered his cloak, she disappeared inside, leaving the old man uncovered in the downpour.

When the weather finally cleared, the heavens shone with ultimate clarity.

Above was the new star they'd heard about.

"Ha fetu'u fuka," the Second Son mused. *A comet*. His first.

Havea said, "Si'i fetu'u fuka." *The comet*. He used the emotional article, which imbued the declaration with feeling, making his words mean, *The longed-for, once-in-a-lifetime comet*.

"Do you think it truly points the way to the island of the afterlife?" the Second Son asked.

"What other purpose would a comet have?"

The morning light was clear and penetrating, reflecting the world in each drop that dripped from the spar. Though the day warmed, Siga did not return the cloak. Instead, she braided strips of palm into a visor, which she placed on Havea's head. Then she made Havea a collar of frill to protect the man's shoulders from the sun. To the Second Son, Havea now resembled the lowliest slave, the sort who almost daily improvised fresh attire from cast-asides or the raw offerings of nature.

During this process, a conversation began between Siga and Havea. The Second Son and Havea tended to discuss things that were sailing-related. Other than that, they sailed in silence. With Siga, however, Havea spoke as free and casual as if they were bathers in a royal pool.

"What're you two talking about?" the Second Son finally asked.

"You really want to know?" Havea responded. "The girl's uncertain and afraid."

"*Afraid?* She's alive. She's free."

"She wonders what awaits her at home, and whether her people will want her back."

Siga lay sideways in the shade of the sail, watching them discuss her.

"How could they not want her back?"

Havea said, "She returns without her younger sister. And her freedom was bought at quite a price."

"My father says she must be royal. Otherwise, why would her people mount such an effort to retrieve her?"

"She's no royal. Does she act like the world exists for her? Does she assume others are there to serve her? No, she's just a girl who was walking down the wrong beach. And her people mounted a rescue when her father, dead at the hands of the Tu'ilifuka, could not." Here, Havea's tone turned bitter. "Would the average Tongan not do the same? If a Tongan father were dead or held against his will many years, would a fellow Tongan not do everything he could to help the man's wife and sons?"

The Second Son heard the criticism. "Things are eventually made right. In the end, sacrifices are rewarded."

"*Sacrifices are rewarded,*" Havea echoed. "Thanks for your wisdom."

The Second Son now wished he'd opted for silence. "All I'm saying is, if she's but a typical Fisian girl, as she claims, all the more reason her life should return to normal."

"The girl has also been . . ." Here Havea searched for the right words. "Poorly handled. Perhaps I can put her case another way. Let's say a Tongan girl is kidnapped by the Fisians. She's gone a long time. Perhaps her funeral has taken place. Suddenly she reappears. She cannot speak of what happened. Or if she can, she's smart enough not to reveal much. But she's marked, making her ill treatment obvious to everyone. How's this girl received upon her return to Tongatapu, how would we welcome such a child of misfortune?"

"With open arms, that's how we'd receive her," the Second Son said. "First, the mothers of Tonga would embrace her, they'd cleanse and purify her. The sisters of Tonga would attend to her beauty and rebuild her esteem. The grandmothers, with song, would help her put the past behind."

"Perhaps the women would embrace her," Havea said. "But what of the men? There are brothers who'd say that, while they love the girl, her misfortunes came through her own carelessness. There's always an uncle who'll suggest the girl must've favored rough treatment and the kind of men who gave it. There are men who'd argue that it was no harm to damage a girl who'd already been damaged. Of course her father would welcome her back, but what of other fathers? Wouldn't they fear a girl who'd seen the dark hearts of men, a girl who knew what men were capable of, even men like themselves, nice fathers who, once they'd crossed the Koro Sea, did as they pleased? Wouldn't they fear this knowledge about men could be transferred to their own daughters, whom they considered innocent? Wouldn't a time come when these fathers blacked their faces and entered the night? Might they not seek this girl and wordlessly subdue her, one man sitting upon her chest, so she hadn't the air to call out, as other men pressed each upon a limb? Then, wouldn't but one hand be needed—the hand of any father would do—to squeeze closed her nose and mouth? Isn't that how some people *put the past behind*?"

Unchanging in Tonga is the custom that one may partake of the meal of another, simply by sitting at his fire. Midmorning, Mateaki and 'Aho came across three men cooking taro in a field. The men made room for their guests and portioned the food into equal amounts. The men took note of the bones hanging from 'Aho's shoulder.

"You headed to a funeral?" one asked.

'Aho shook his head.

"Your destination isn't a burial?" another wondered.

'Aho said, "We're here to take in the beauty of this island."

The third man asked, "Which is your home island?"

"This is our home," 'Aho said. "But we've been away, and much has changed. I remember a grove of toa trees to the north."

"Those trees," a man said, "were cut for the Tuʻitonga's new residence in Lapaha."

"Yes, he conscripts us to build it," another said. "You'll encounter no one on the path today, for everyone must move earth for the king's foundations."

The third man added, "And each village must pay for the privilege. Along with workers, each chief must deliver a tribute of hogs and sweet potatoes."

'Aho asked, "Would you have your king live out of doors?"

Perhaps they expected a more sympathetic response.

"They already take our sons for the war, and our daughters as servants," one said.

"Things are no longer as you remember them," another man told 'Aho. "We once paid tribute to the Tuʻitonga, offering him the first fruits of our harvest. Now he commands the entire harvest. After taking his share, he offers the remainder to his sub-chiefs and matāpule. They take their shares and offer the remainders to the village chiefs. Then we must proffer gifts for a meager portion of what we ourselves have grown."

"Every matāpule has a hand out," the final man said. "Soon we'll have to pay for the right to piss in the sand."

'Aho reached for the water bowl, and when he did, the jellyfish on his palm became visible. Understanding who he was, the men removed themselves from the fire, for they were forbidden from consorting with a person of 'Aho's rank.

'Aho asked, "Have you yourselves grown the taro we eat?"

None spoke.

'Aho asked, "How is it you've avoided the Tuʻitonga's earth-moving details?"

The three men glanced warily at one another.

"And have you gentlemen served in the war?"

Cautiously, one offered, "If farmers are sent to war, the nation will not eat."

"Yes," 'Aho said. "And if sweets-makers are sent to war, there'll be no dessert."

When 'Aho stood, a great fear filled his hosts' eyes. He had an urge to beat them with the bones of his dead wife. There was a rightness to that, something that deeply appealed to him. Disrespectful to 'Ofa's memory, of course, but a delicious notion nonetheless. Then he saw the fear on his son's face. 'Aho took a breath and checked himself. He left these three with a simple question: "If a Tongan doesn't do his duty, may he still regard himself a Tongan?"

Father and son made their way south along the Liku Path. They passed the tract of land called Ha'alakovaka, named after a family that once washed ashore there. They passed Finehika, "Place of the Woman Whose Hair Is Straight," named for wives who kept watch in the wind for husbands returning from 'Eua.

'Aho had avoided conflict with those men. Still, he felt he'd moved things in the wrong direction. He knew how to assert, to lay claim. Direct engagement, that's what he understood. Being easy with his son, appealing to his inner nature, drawing him out—these skills eluded him. He didn't think he lacked tenderness—he had tender thoughts all the time, ones that threatened to bring him to tears. He'd kept his son close, unlike his brother, who'd farmed fatherhood out. Yet his efforts didn't convert to the warmth he knew was possible between him and Mateaki. Perhaps if he lived a life of leisure, if he had all day to pigeon-hunt with his son, like the Tu'itonga and Lolohea, maybe they'd be closer. But somebody had to face the Fisians. Somebody had to meet them on the beach. Compared to his brother's life of politics and pettiness, 'Aho was pretty sure his was the favorable path. He'd been upon the seas. He'd gazed upon the enemy, studied their nature, and even learned from them—about honor and bravery and strategy. He'd even learned something about parenting from the Fisians: foremost, it was best to keep your loved ones under your close protection. Not "Fisian close," of course. He could never get over the sight of a father and son charging into battle, tether taut between them. But the guiding principle was true. By taking your son to war, you could assess the enemy with your own eyes and know the safest place to stow your child while an engagement was in play. Mateaki usually tended the canoes, keeping them nosed into the waves for emergency departures. There was always a pre-established meeting point, a fallback meeting point, an escape plan, and a contingency escape plan. There was always a designated warrior that Mateaki should turn to in the event that a father and son did not find easy reunion or should the unthinkable occur: that a father made no return. By this system, no sad outcome had ever come to pass, unlike many tales of warriors who returned home to discover that everything they'd fought for was gone, as was the case with the Tu'ilifuka. And 'Aho would argue that taking your young son to war required thought and attention, consideration and careful planning. It required devotion. It required love. Leaving your child unattended, like a seed in the wind, with no way to lend him aid or defense, with no way to reassure him or take his hand and tell him things would work out—well, that was no kind of parenting at all. And if 'Aho had it to do over, he would've brought his wife along as well. They would've been a family, together. If 'Ofa had come to war with him, she'd have understood him better, she wouldn't have become afraid of him, and maybe she'd still be alive.

The next night, the comet was again visible. The Second Son lay on his back, contemplating the heavens. When the wind gusted, and he felt the outrigger lift, he loosened the sheet before cinching the sail tight again. All this he did without taking his eyes off the stars. "What's to stop us from sailing that comet down?" he asked.

Havea was but a shadow in the stern.

"We've got time," the Second Son said. "The comet will take an entire season to cross the sky. After releasing the girl, we could follow it south. Imagine finding the island of the afterlife. Imagine planting your feet in supernatural soil."

"Returning safely to your father," Havea said. "That's your only task. And

I keep telling you—the navigator never sets the destination. His passengers do that. He only steers the course."

The Second Son heard Havea, but his imagination was already over the horizon. "What if we brought back a ghost parrot from the afterlife? It'd be made of vapor and would fan its wings from our shoulders."

"I'll visit the afterlife soon enough," Havea said. "All I need do is forfeit this world, and my wife and I will reunite." Havea began singing a forlorn 'Uvean song. His timbre was rough and wavering but infused with feeling. The song was about a father who must depart from his family in the morning. He cannot sleep, and when he does, he dreams he is paddling, already paddling away from them.

About halfway through, Siga joined, singing Fisian words to the same melody. It was deeply haunting, this duet of different languages and lyrics, sung in lamenting harmony, especially the last note, trailing and dissonant.

"If I could live my life over," Havea said, "I'd do it different, every bit of it."

"What?" the Second Son asked. "How could you say such a thing?"

"Yes," Havea said. "I'd do none of it the same."

"Master, you mustn't speak like this. You're the most praiseworthy navigator alive. You saw our people through the greatest battles we've faced. Without you, would we have subdued Ha'amoa? No is the answer. You're counselor to kings, tutor to princes. You're as a father to me. You mustn't speak this way. You can't say such things."

Against the night-glimmer of the sea, Havea was only an outline.

It was Siga, looking west at dawn, who spotted the caravan of Tongan sails. Spoils-laden, the vaka were returning from Fisi, the large double-hulls taking a line against the wind. The lead craft was small and nimble, so it might move freely among the lumbering barges.

This craft made its way to them. On board was an older, heavyset supply captain and a young navigator, younger even than the Second Son. The boy wore a fishhook pendant, the sight of which made the Second Son flush with jealousy and resentment. Quickly, he donned his boar's tusk headdress.

The supply captain puzzled over them. "Tongans heading west, on a Fisian canoe?"

Havea, as was his custom, first addressed his navigating counterpart. Though the navigator seemed but a child, Havea hailed him with an honorific, formally calling him *Tangata poto 'i he faka'uli*. "I'm Havea, and the boy helping me is—" When he glanced at the Second Son, Havea's eyes went wide at the sight of the boar's tusk headdress, and with that, the introduction was over.

Behind the lead vaka, a vast barge of hogs slowly passed. Normally social creatures, the animals were sprawled low and unmoving on the deck, for pigs were notoriously prone to seasickness. The crew was busy grilling pork, making the most of lost cargo.

Of the young navigator, Havea asked, "What're the conditions of the seas behind you?"

"Occasional squalls," the boy said. "Last night, we lost a vaka."

"No emergency call," the supply captain added. "This morning, it was simply gone."

Havea nodded, acknowledging that such things happened.

The supply captain said, "That vaka carried our most precious cargo. It was stacked high with fine Fisian wedding mats."

Behind him passed a barge laden with magnificent lodge poles, each having served as the main beam in a Fisian family's home. Siga stared in disbelief at what was before her, and only now did the supply captain seem to notice a Fisian girl standing before him. "What's your business upon these waters?" he asked Havea.

Had the supply captain not realized he was talking to Havea, *the* Havea? That all the water of the world was Havea's business? "We're a special envoy to Fisi," the Second Son said. "And I'll have you know this man is none other than—"

Havea lifted a hand to stop the Second Son.

The supply captain asked, "An envoy, you say?"

The Second Son said, "Our mission is to free the girl before you."

"Do you know how hard Fisians are to catch?" the supply captain asked.

The Second Son said, "Our orders come from the Tu'itonga himself."

The supply captain snorted. "Ah, the Tuʻitonga. The figure who makes our lives thus, the man for whom we sail nonstop—warriors from Lifuka to Fisi, spoils from Fisi to Tongatapu, and empty barges from Tongatapu to Lifuka. For that is Tongatapu's only export, empty barges."

The Second Son asked, "Would you rather it worked the other way, that the Tuʻi of Tonga let our treasures sail away from Tongatapu? Would you rather Tongans paid tribute to foreign rulers?"

The supply captain smiled at the novelty of defending the system on display before them. "The war is older than my boy here," he said. "The Koro Sea's been his only cradle. As a consequence, he knows almost nothing of life on dry land. You tell me—is he Tongan? Can a person be said to be *of* a place if he knows nothing of that place? And if you doubt whether Tongans pay tribute, I assure you we make the highest possible offerings, and I'll leave you to guess whom we pay them to."

It was then that Siga made a blood-slaking scream, the kind she'd refrained from even at the event of her own death. Sailing past them was a barge laden with dark stones.

The supply captain glanced at the slabs of black, stacked carefully to distribute their weight. "Is it not an irony that a load of featherlight wedding mats goes to the bottom, while a vaka laden with stone sails on?"

Havea, stunned at the sight, asked, "You're harvesting their funeral stones?"

The supply captain seemed surprised to be receiving criticism. "This is the finest stone available. It comes from the sacred island of ʻUvea."

Havea studied the passing stones, perhaps wondering if he himself had long ago delivered them to grieving families in Fisi. "Come," he told the Second Son. "We've exchanged enough news."

The supply captain asked, "What care a stone if it consecrates a Tongan grave or a Fisian?"

The Second Son raised sail, and the two vaka began drifting apart. He recalled Six Fists telling him that Havea's boys had been made gravediggers on the Fisian island of Matuku. He called to the supply captain, "These barges, do they hail from Matuku?"

On the supply captain's face was a curious look, one puzzling over how a stranger could know the origin of a stone just by looking at it. Siga then found her voice and began berating the supply captain across the water. He shook his head in disbelief, as if now he'd seen it all.

Siga, eyes filled with contempt, turned to the Second Son. The look terrified him. He had to force himself to hold her gaze. She scrutinized him the way one would inspect a thorn, still wet, that'd been pulled from a wound. Then she clapped him hard with an open palm. The strike swung his head and tipped his headdress into the sea. He heard the splash but didn't dare turn from her to see it go down.

'Aho and Mateaki spent the day walking through hills chest-high with kava and fields tangled with sweet potato vines. Along ditches, children were spreading copra to dry, and through low brush, teenage girls moved hogs, for their war-aged brothers were gone.

Come nightfall, they saw an old couple ahead on the path. Their sleeping mats were unfurled, their fire had burned to coals. 'Aho concealed his inked hand with a wrap of banana leaf. Greetings were exchanged. It turned out the old couple were journeying to the coast to meet a new grandchild.

"Are you visitors to the island?" the old woman asked.

She didn't gawk at the bones 'Aho carried.

"We're taking in the sights," Mateaki said.

The woman nodded. "My husband thinks the Blowholes capture the majesty of Tongatapu."

The man said, "My wife has always been partial to the underground baths at 'Anahulu."

In the coals was a single sweet potato. The man used a stick to turn it, honeyed steam escaping.

"For me, Tongatapu is found in little things," the woman said. "Our soil is different. It's darker, redder. It holds a footprint."

"For me," the old man said, "it's the southern waves. They've come from the end of the sea. It was their life's labor to reach us. Then they arrive. With their last breaths, they rise, they reach, they expose their pale blue hearts, and then they fall."

"My husband favors the poetic expression," the woman said.

"The gods gifted us with words," the man replied. "We'd be remiss not to use them."

When the sweet potato was ready, the man divided it four ways.

"When we were young," the woman said, "we never took food with us. You could pluck your dinner from any tree."

"Yes," the man said. "Set a snare anywhere and you'd soon be roasting a bird for dinner. Now they say the Tuʻitonga owns more decoy pigeons than there are wild pigeons left to hunt."

"We were told the war would fill our bellies," the woman said as she accepted her meager portion.

As they quietly ate, ʻAho could feel their scrutiny.

"I see the bandage on your hand," the woman said. "Are you hurt?"

"Have you returned from the war?" the man asked.

ʻAho said nothing, but Mateaki said, "Yes."

"When I was young," the man said, "the conflict was to subdue Niue. Certainly it was a smaller war, against one island, just a series of battles, really, nothing like what's happening in Fisi. But the people of Niue speak a language we understand. When they uttered their last words, they were words you were going to hear for the rest of your life."

ʻAho said, "In Fisi, plenty of dying Tongans utter final words that refuse to be forgotten."

"Survivors say stuff, too," Mateaki said. "They're wounded. There's blood in the bottom of the canoe. And the things they say, it sticks in your head."

There was a silence. ʻAho changed the subject. "Is it a boy or a girl?"

"We have a granddaughter," the man said. "I'm curious to see if the child shows signs of my wife's stubbornness."

The woman looked at her husband. "If she babbles, we'll know who she gets it from."

Their smiles quickly faded. "Our son does his duty in Fisi," the man said. "This is why his wife moved back with her parents. This is why we're on the road."

"Our son," the woman said, "he's our only child."

"You've seen the war," the man said to ʻAho. "Might it end soon, in your opinion?"

"The war's first decade was a difficult one," 'Aho said. "Still, I believe that in the decades to come, we'll gain the upper hand. What's important is that we never relent."

The man and the woman were quiet a moment. Then the man said, "My friend, I hope you don't mind if I say something fatherly to you. It's your duty to desire the end of war. You have a son, and he's all that matters. You must spare him what you've been through. Your concerns can only be of him."

"The war's end is what matters, in this we agree," 'Aho said. "But there's only one way to finish it, and I've seen it with my own eyes."

The woman studied the look on Mateaki's face. "Has he seen it, too?"

Something deadened in 'Aho. He sat there, bones over his shoulder, looking at the fire. Even he didn't know what he might say or do. It could be nothing, nothing, nothing, or something. Things were known to happen without his foreknowledge or permission.

The old couple exchanged a nervous glance. Before anything could happen, the man said, "It's been an honor to share our meal with you, but we are old and need our sleep. You should be on your way if you're to make any kind of camp before the light completely fails."

TWENTY-ONE

BEING MADE AKIN

The Second Son had noticed over the years that after certain human encounters, Havea retreated into the sea. Silence would overtake him, and he'd become denatured, attuning himself only to the elements—registering his existence by his hindrance to the wind and submitting himself to the clarifying gestures of the sea, for, while the sea was neither just nor fair, while it was indifferent to the desires of men, it operated wholly without subterfuge or betrayal or false hope. It might aid in your demise but would make no profit by it. The ocean might confound and torment but took no joy in such measures. On the contrary, if you were attentive, the ocean revealed its all to you. If you submitted to its vastness, its complexity leavened away, for its mysteries were never of motivation and purpose, but only of spontaneity, eternity, and the simple fact of being. And the supply captain couldn't have been more wrong: the ocean gave nothing for the notion of irony.

Siga began attending the horizon. Perhaps she sensed these waters were her waters, that the wind had become the wind of Fisi. In the afternoon, she spotted a dullness in the waves, something limp, and bade Havea to steer for it. What they found was a Fisian wedding mat. After retrieving it, the Second Son spread it across the deck to dry. Siga gazed at the mat like she knew the couple who'd been betrothed upon it. The Second Son scanned the water for other signs of the sailors who'd gone down, but there was nothing.

In the evening, though no shorebirds had been spotted, Havea claimed he could hear breakwater. Rather than risk a reef in the dark, they dropped sail and heaved to. When the sea was dark as octopus ink, they heard something out there, snorts and simpering cries. Then the Second Son spotted it, just off the outrigger—Siga leaned out and plucked from the sea a squealing piglet. She offered it water from her cupped hand, let it curl in her lap.

At last, the Second Son billowed the sea anchor. Now he could get some rest—not naps or nod-offs, but true sleep. He lay on his side, placing his head upon his arm. His face stung where he'd been slapped. He wondered how long the piglet must've been swimming and how long it could've kept going. Had it lasted longer than the men crewing the vaka of wedding mats? Would fate allow the rescue of a pig, yet leave men treading in the dark? He wanted to ask Havea about such things, but Havea hadn't spoken to him since the flotilla that morning. When the Second Son had asked about a course adjustment, Havea glanced at him in a manner that truly scared him. The look said, *Sail as you damn well please.*

With dawn, they discerned the dark outline of an island, nestling in the shadows of cloud cover. It took the entire morning to make their way to it, but as they neared, they discovered it'd been darkened not by shade but by fire. The pitiful island was stubbed with charred tree trunks, and, because there wasn't any ground cover, the wind lifted soil in gusts, stacking it in leeward dunes before carrying it off over the sea.

The Second Son imagined his shell map, spread across the beach of his mind. This island was likely Ogea Driki, which placed them farther south than he'd predicted. The next island would be Fulaga—hopefully a more hospitable place to leave Siga.

But when Havea spotted a break in the reef, he steered toward the blackened beach.

"We can't leave her here," the Second Son said. "There's surely no water or food."

"Her people will find her," Havea said.

The Second Son asked, "Where'll she shelter? How'll she provide for herself?"

"Our task is to deliver the girl, nothing more," Havea said. "If you think the destruction before you is special, you're wrong—there are many more islands like it."

"We've traveled a great distance. Can't we try the next island? It must be safer."

"If by safe you mean inhabited, I remind you that Fisians are precisely what make an island unsafe."

"Our duty is to return her, not abandon her."

With disbelief, Havea said, "What do you know of duty?"

"We take her to the next island."

Havea held the steering oar steady.

The Second Son loosened the sail so it began to luff in the wind.

"Does my bondage never end?" Havea asked before steering for Fulaga in the distance.

Frigate birds hovered above Fulaga's shores, and smoke from cooking fires rose through the foliage. People were likely to make their homes on the sheltered shores, so Havea made for a windswept beach that lacked signs of industry. The surf was heavy. Just before the swells began to crest, Havea said, "She can swim from here."

The Second Son didn't loosen the sail.

"There's no wisdom in making landfall," Havea said. "To depart, we'll have to launch into the waves, against the wind."

The Second Son sailed on.

There was nothing for Havea to do but keep the vaka square as they entered the chaos of shore break. And, of course, long before the bow kissed sand, Siga jumped and swam for it. But they couldn't turn without swamping. The Second Son took up his own paddle to keep the hull from laying into the waves. And when the water was shallow enough, he leaped into the boil to hand-escort the bow.

Siga was waiting on the beach, dripping and breathing hard. Her hands were out, like she might defend herself or, at the slightest sign, flee in any direction. She stood like that, staring at them, catching her breath. Then she bolted their way, snatching from the hull the rolled-up wedding mat and the little pig, which was woozy when placed on solid ground.

Siga looked up and down the beach, perhaps trying to decide which direction to run.

"Wait," the Second Son said to her.

From the vaka, he produced the coconut containing the last breath of Siga's sister. He took a step toward Siga, extending it. The sight of the coconut gave her pause. Cautiously, she accepted it. Instead of fleeing, she reached down and took up some sand, holding it like she never thought she'd touch home again. With reverence, she extended it to him. This, he now understood, was the truest souvenir, not any kind of treasure, but a portion of a person's home, offered in gratitude for deliverance. As the son of a Tuʻitonga, he knew a thing or two about gift reception. He lowered his gaze, bowed slightly, and offered his hands, cupped in acceptance. That's when Siga whipped the sand into his eyes and hurled the coconut at Havea, who, being nearly blind in one eye, couldn't avoid the impact. Siga then scratched the Second Son, digging her nails into his cheek, before launching a campaign of cries for help.

The Second Son stumbled into the waves, but splashing his eyes with salt water gave little aid. He had no way of knowing if men, at that very moment, were responding to Siga's call, so he placed his shoulder against the bow. When a wave lifted the hull, he pushed for all he was worth.

It was dark when ʻAho and his son unfurled their sleeping mats. They made no fire. Above, the stars were blocked by canopy. ʻAho thought about the old couple they'd met, about the fatherly tone the man had adopted, his easy way. Mateaki must have liked them, too, because he said, "I wish I had grandparents."

The night was warm and still.

"You have grandparents," ʻAho said. "You'll see them when we reach your mother's village."

Mateaki said, "I don't remember those people."

They heard the chatter of peka bats. They smelled the soft exhalations of the soil.

"You said you gave a last word to that Fisian girl," Mateaki said. "The Tuʻilifuka's last word."

"It was more of a story I told her."

"What story could you tell her? You don't speak her language."

'Aho wanted to remind his son that the Fisians had come and murdered the Tu'ilifuka. That 'Aho had taken an oath of retribution. He wanted to explain that there was no joy in what he did to the girl from Fisi, but certain things had to be done. Yet, he couldn't say any of that in a fatherly tone.

Mateaki said, "She didn't do anything to anyone."

"Most people think war takes place far away, that it doesn't happen in quiet meadows, like this one."

Mateaki asked, "Is the war happening for you, right now?"

"I'm afraid it's happening for you, too."

"So that girl, whatever you did to her, you'd call that war?"

'Aho looked into the black under-cupping of the leaves above. "I'm glad you don't understand. You're just a kid. This isn't supposed to make sense to you."

Mateaki was silent. 'Aho could hear him snapping twigs.

"Do you think there's a place," Mateaki asked, "where there aren't bad things, where killing and war are unknown?"

Even though he couldn't see the sky or hear the sea, 'Aho felt them out there, expanding in all directions. "If such an island exists, I'd like to know the star that takes you there."

Deeper into the night, a sound roused 'Aho. In the moonlight, he saw a piglet, snout inside the webbing that held his wife's bones. The piglet's tongue licked here and there, its little teeth scraping.

'Aho became aware of a presence. He was being watched, he could feel it. The outlines of trees were traced by the moon. Fine-leafed shrubs thrummed with soft light. Yet he saw no one. He stilled himself, opened his senses to the night. Eventually, he perceived a figure. When 'Aho rose, the figure took a step back. When the figure ran, 'Aho gave chase.

The night was the blue-black of mid-ocean. 'Aho ran with an arm out, parting vines and undergrowth. The figure was moving fast and erratically, it was difficult to get a look at him—bushes and saplings would part, and 'Aho might glimpse a shoulder or an arm before the branches snapped back. Who was this person, how could he run so fast? They moved briefly into the open, through the high scrub of a fallow field, then back into the tricky roots of 'ovava trees. Finally came the groan of a stumble, and 'Aho was upon him. Rolling him to his back, 'Aho sat astride his belly. Here, he understood that beneath him was a young woman, slapping at him, scratching his arms. He grabbed her collarbone, digging his fingers into the hollow. Wincing, she relinquished her struggle, but he didn't let go.

"Why were you watching me?" he asked.

"I'm just looking after our pigs," she said. "Are you new here? I don't recognize you. You should know that on this island, all pigs are the Tu'itonga's pigs. If anything happens to them, if he loses even one, he'll be very angry. Let me go, and I won't say anything."

"Yes, the Tu'itonga," 'Aho said. "Let me tell you about him. If he could feel what it was to truly lose something, something he couldn't afford to lose, then he wouldn't rule as he rules. Of course, it'd have to be taken from him, this something. It would hurt, but in time he'd see it was for the best. If I gave him some hurt, then we'd share hurt in common."

The girl was silent.

'Aho leaned back and studied her. Her hair was tied with a rough piece of cord. Her wrap looked handed down through many sisters. He felt for her and her hard life. "I'm sorry," he said.

Her eyes moved across him, trying to determine his intentions.

"I'm sorry, but something's about to happen," he added. "And there's nothing to be done about it."

His words were a variation of something once said to him, long ago, on the night his uncle came to kill him. His uncle arrived unannounced at the royal fale, and finding 'Aho alone said, "Understand that I don't want to do this." He was a reluctant man, a sad man, one who had to work himself up to do anything. "Still, it's going to happen," Uncle added. "And there's nothing to be done about it." 'Aho didn't know what the man was talking about, he didn't know what "it" was, yet some part of him had already begun to accept that "it" would soon be taking place, and whether he fought or relented didn't matter. He was only fifteen. The thing about being choked from behind is how alone you feel. You're close to someone—there's an elbow at your throat, you're pulled into a human chest, heart beating—but you can't see anyone, and when you try to reach back, you grab only air. Instead, you gaze upon the emptiest things: thatching, a water bowl, a single flame from a candlenut lamp. Your eyes start fluttering shut. There's breath, forceful, on the back of your neck, but your own breath, where'd it go? Of course, things turned out differently. "It" never happened. Instead, your brother entered the fale and thus began the night's long, moonlit struggle.

But his uncle had put a feeling in 'Aho, an inevitability, and it lodged deep. He'd been one person, and then he was another. The old him—carefree, trusting, hopeful—became a stranger, and the new him was a person he'd spend the rest of his life getting to know. But after, he could look at people and tell if they'd ever felt what his uncle had made him feel—that life was about to freight upon you its ugly cargo, and there was nothing to do but accept the burden. That cargo could be loss, mayhem, even death. But the burden was the feel of it, the knowledge of it, that things happened, that there was nothing to be done. Cargos got delivered, but a burden was something you could never set down. He knew at a glance if someone's life had been similarly burdened. Burdens marked people in a way that 'Aho could see and others could not—that mark made folks akin to him. When 'Aho marked people with a black jellyfish, it was just a way of helping the world see what to him was obvious. The world's capacity to not grasp obvious truths amazed 'Aho. For instance, other Tongan warriors noted with bafflement a certain phenomenon: when they set a Fisian island ablaze, the survivors would flee in their canoes not toward untouched Fisian islands, but to ones that'd already been decimated, where there was no food, no shelter, nothing but dazed survivors. But what could be more simple, more human, than seeking out those who'd been through what you'd been through, who'd become what you'd become?

The girl scratched at him again, with sharp, digging swipes.

"Think of this as a story I'm going to tell you," he said to her.

"Just let me go," she said. "My father's a matāpule. He's very powerful. He has his own security detail."

These half-hearted lies were uttered in a failing voice.

"It's an old story," 'Aho said. "One that gets told and retold. The settings change, the details."

She screamed, loud and long, and when she stopped, she seemed surprised that nothing had changed.

It was said in Lifuka that 'Aho killed men and attacked women for sport, that he marked them for pleasure. These charges were untrue in every regard. 'Aho was the one who'd first felt the jellyfish's sting, a mark that'd been burned onto him by the gods. He was the one who'd looked into a killer's eyes and found familial recognition. And he'd never taken a life that wasn't war-related, though people needed to understand that war wasn't what they thought it was. As for his other encounters, the ones with women, it wasn't physical exchange he was after, but kinship, and sometimes you had to make someone akin to you.

"I just want to open your eyes to something," 'Aho told her. "Something about the world."

He lowered his face to hers, so their foreheads were touching.

When she exhaled, he inhaled. And she couldn't help but take in his breath.

It was deeply satisfying, this comingling, this reciprocity.

After his uncle's attack, 'Aho assumed for a long time that the man must've hated him. But as 'Aho aged, he came to see the attack wasn't about him at all. There wasn't even anything his uncle could do about it—the path of the man's life had simply led him there.

"Are you ready for the story?" he asked her. "The tale is old, yet each telling is different. Every ending is new. Even I don't know the endings."

She looked away, exposing the white and vulnerable sides of her eyes.

It was then that he heard a searching voice. It was his son, calling, "Father, Father."

'Aho contemplated the girl. "I don't have enough time," he told her. "If I could've made myself known to you, then next time, we wouldn't be strangers in the dark."

'Aho stood, allowing her to scramble away.

He turned to see, some distance away, the outline of his boy moving through dark foliage.

"Mateaki," he called, and began walking his son's way.

"What's happening?" Mateaki asked. "I heard someone call out. I woke and you were gone."

'Aho put a hand on his shoulder, turned him, began walking him toward their sleeping mats.

Mateaki looked back. "Is someone over there? Is someone in trouble?"

"Yes," 'Aho said. "Someone's over there. Someone was."

"Who is it? What's going on?"

'Aho kept them walking in the direction of their camp. "There was a stranger," 'Aho said. "Someone out in the dark. For a moment, it seemed like we might recognize one another. For a brief while, I thought it would turn out that we knew each other. But in the end, no."

After Siga struck at them, they made their escape from the island of Fulaga. Havea lay on the deck, his injured eye swollen shut, his opaque eye open and unblinking in the sunlight.

"Don't worry, Master," the Second Son said. "I'll get you home. Before you know it, you'll be safe on the shores of Tongatapu."

The Second Son rigged a line so he could adjust the sail from the steering oar in the stern. He hadn't figured a way to shunt the canoe by himself, so he was forced to tack against the wind, dangerous when the outrigger was to the lee. "My father's priests will heal you. Soon you'll be back to normal."

Havea said, "You're sailing the wrong way."

"Yes, we're rigged all wrong. When we're off the Koro Sea and out of danger, I'll figure a way to shunt the spars on my own."

"No. You're sailing in the wrong direction."

"I assure you, Master, we head east, toward home."

"Remember that Fisian chief?" Havea asked. "The one your father opened alive?"

The Second Son didn't like this turn in the conversation.

Havea said, "I've been thinking about the way he'd tethered his son. He said it was safer to have his boy at his side, where he could offer protection. But shouldn't it work the other way? Instead of bringing a boy to war, shouldn't a father join his son in battle? No matter how old or infirm, this father could still receive a spear meant for his son. Such fathers would fall with the knowledge that their sons still stood."

"You've suffered quite a blow," the Second Son said. "Don't focus on such weighty things."

"You wish me restored for your own sake. You keep me around to pass the time because your own father—"

"You're injured," the Second Son interrupted. "You're not making sense."

"After your initiation, do you intend to free me?"

"You're free right now, I assure you. You've always been free."

"If I ask you to promise me something," Havea asked, "will you swear to it?"

"Master, you're making me nervous."

"Promise me you'll leave me on one of these islands."

"Are you joking? The Fisians would find you. They'd make a slave of you."

"After ten years of what Tongans call freedom, I'll take the Fisian way."

"I can't dump you on a foreign beach. You think I'm capable of abandoning you blind to the enemy?"

"I'm afraid I've come to a conclusion," Havea said.

A pulse of fear shuddered through the Second Son.

"I no longer believe I can initiate you."

"Is this because I insisted on taking Siga ashore? That was a mistake, one I regret, as the price has been paid by you."

"It's not that."

"The headdress, then, right? It was a gift from my mother. Still, I shouldn't have worn it."

"It's not you," Havea said. "You're a good boy, I mean that. You're smart, you've absorbed all I had to teach you. All except the most important thing: There's no prestige in navigation. To be the one who finds the way is to be a servant of those who seek safe passage. It makes you the lowliest person in the vaka, the one whose needs and safety come last. I've told you countless times—the destination isn't yours to set, you only steer the course."

"That's not fair. You wanted to dump Siga on an island without food or water. What care had you for her safety?"

"She wasn't my only passenger," Havea said. "I was responsible for your safety, too."

Now the Second Son was silent.

"Answer me this," Havea said. "Tell me who your passenger is."

"We delivered her. We have no passengers."

"Who's your passenger?"

The Second Son looked at Havea, sightless, flat on his back. "You are."

"That's right. Does your passenger share his needs? Does he tell you where he wishes to go?"

Reluctantly, the Second Son said, "Yes."

"My remaining duties lie in Fisi. So, to the nearest island, then. The blackened one will do."

The Second Son closed his eyes. He held the steering oar in one hand, the sheet rope in the other. "I know where you need to go."

What was this state called wakefulness? What did it mean to sleep? Could the two trade places, or become one? When the Second Son nodded off, the dreams came instant and vivid, yet when he slapped his face and shook his arms, life felt dulled over, each moment eliding the next. The sea and the sky took no breaks—strong currents circled the island of Kabara, wind shadowed the peaks of Totoya. When conditions were right, the Second Son lashed the steering oar to tend his mentor, but beyond food and water, little comfort could be given.

So he would become no navigator. When his mind finally grasped this thought, he waited for the next thought, but there wasn't one. There was the comet and its wake across the celestial sea. There was the steering paddle in his hand, wood darkened by Havea's grip. He began, without realizing it, to sail long stretches with his eyes closed. When he was young, Havea often blindfolded him, to make him feel the wind, hear the birds, and orient by the regularity of the waves. As a boy, eyes bound, he saw only scary blackness. Now, eyes closed, there was much to behold, for when you saw without your eyes, you saw the wind, you gazed beneath the waves, and of course night was no impediment.

On the third day, Havea said, "It's daytime, is it not? I perceive the color red."

With this, they knew that beneath the swelling, the eye still worked.

Havea asked, "Have you known all along where my sons were?"

"I learned their location the night before we left."

Havea nodded. "It's okay that you withheld this from me. Forces act beyond your control. My fate is my own, and none of it's your doing."

The Second Son wondered about the degree to which these statements were true.

"Are my boys all right?" Havea asked. "Have they been in combat?"

"You'll see for yourself. We should reach them in the morning."

Havea showed no relief. "What if I don't recognize them? Worse, what if I'm nobody to them?"

"Nothing could be further from the truth," the Second Son said. "You're their father."

"Wouldn't you hate a father who left you when you needed him, who remained elusive when he could've come to you?"

"No," the Second Son said. "It only makes me want him more."

His vision went blurry as he said this.

Even without sight, Havea seemed to know the young man's eyes were misting.

"Your father did what he felt he had to do. I'll say this now, and then there'll be no more talk of it." Havea turned his way, and it didn't matter that Havea couldn't see him. "I'm not your father, but you've been as a son to me. At times, I've been too blind to see it, but it's clear to me now."

They set their anchor stones at a Tongan outpost on the Fisian island of Matuku. Several barges were preparing for the journey back to Tongatapu. One was loaded with curved Fisian clubs. They were lashed into bundles, the deck stacked with them. The Second Son asked the loading foreman what use Tongans had for foreign weapons.

The foreman shook his head. "Souvenirs. Every family in Tonga must have one."

"Souvenirs of battle?" the Second Son asked. "For those who haven't been to war?"

"Last year, everyone wanted lali drums."

When asked about two brothers from Lifuka, the foreman pointed to a pair loading a vaka with ceremonial yaqona bowls, *yaqona* being the Fisian word for "kava."

With a hand on Havea's shoulder, the Second Son steered him toward his boys.

"Sons of Havea," the Second Son called out. "Your father has arrived."

Havea's eye, ringed with scarlet, had only partly opened, but he could somewhat see.

After a moment of bewilderment, the two young men advanced. They took careful steps before rushing Havea with a full embrace. Then the questions began coming, questions asked so fast there was no time for responses: *Is it truly you? How'd you find us? Did you get our messages? Have you heard about Mother?* One of the boys indicated the Second Son. "Is this your mate?"

Havea turned toward the Second Son. "Think of him as a brother from another family."

As they continued their reunion, the Second Son found himself studying the young men, noting the way they shared Havea's jaw and cheekbones. He found himself scrutinizing them, comparing what he saw as their strengths and weaknesses to what he perceived as his, and he didn't like this feeling. Plus, this moment was about family, and he was something other than that.

High above the tide line were beached Fisian canoes, their hulls sleek, their spars swept. He made his way to these, admiring their design, running a hand along their contours. He could feel the lives of the men who'd crewed them. Ahead, some Tongans were unlashing these vaka, breaking them down to their elements. There were piles of outrigger arms and masts and decking.

"What're you doing?" he asked.

One Tongan barely glanced his way. "We're stripping them," he said. "For firewood."

"But these are very fine vaka, the finest on the water."

"People say they're hard to sail."

"Sure, they require more attention, but they're twice as fast as ours."

The Tongan now looked at him. "What's your hurry? Are you late for the next invasion?"

Before he could answer, the Second Son heard a cry of agony. He ran to find his mentor on the ground, weeping over a basket of bones. Kneeling, he placed a hand on Havea's shoulder. "Master, what is it?"

One of Havea's boys spoke. "These are the remains of our mother. We've been carrying them, with no opportunity for proper burial."

"She's truly gone," Havea said, his voice shuddering.

"Master," was all the Second Son could say. He'd never met the woman.

Havea looked at him, his eye angry. "Her death was kept from me. *She was kept from me.* I was allowed no farewells, my wife died with no husband at her side."

"Father," the boys kept saying. They didn't know how to console him, either.

Havea pulled the basket onto his lap. "Vaivao, you're the dew on my tree." Then, as if berating himself, he looked up, lamenting, "What if I could've done something, what if I could've saved her?" Tears flowing, he said, "I'd have done anything." Then the look on his face shifted. He held out his hands so his sons could raise him to his feet. "What if something can be done? What if she can still be saved?"

Havea's boys regarded him with unease. "Father," one said, "what're you talking about?"

"There's a way," Havea said. "She can be restored."

The Second Son knew what he was talking about. "Take me with you. You'll need me."

"No, it must be us," Havea said, indicating his boys. "By restoring her together, we'll restore ourselves. We'll become a family again."

One of his boys asked, "What do you mean, *restore*?"

Havea began to explain the comet and the island of the afterlife.

The Second Son ignored the selfish thoughts that came to him. He quelled the urge to imagine himself voyaging to Pulotu. Instead, he made his way to the vaka to retrieve two items, which he then pressed into Havea's hands. "You can't present yourself to the god Hikule'o without an offering," he said, consigning the whale teeth to his mentor. "And here's a conch shell horn. It's charmed by the Hau priest of Tonga—its call can cross any sea. If you blow it, I'll come."

"I'm not good at saying things," Havea said. "It's easier for me to tell a story and let it stand for what I mean. But there's no time for that. I should tell you that I'm sorry. That I'm grateful. And that I'm proud."

"Those things," the Second Son said. "They're also how I feel."

Havea pulled him close. Foreheads touching, they exchanged breath.

"Where will you go?" Havea asked.

The Second Son lifted his shoulders.

"The winds favor a passage to Ha'amoa," Havea said. "You've always wanted to visit Tahiti."

"I guess I'll go," the Second Son said, "wherever people need to be taken."

Havea gave him a look he'd never seen before. The man had to tilt his head to study him through his scarlet eye. Then Havea removed his fishhook necklace and hung it on the Second Son.

"That's right," Havea said. "You'll go where people need to be taken."

This image of Havea—head cocked, one eye pearled, the other erupting red—is how the Second Son would always remember him.

The Second Son walked the beach. He felt a sense of nothing, and at the same time, he felt a new *something*. He looked at his vaka, the one he and Havea had crossed so much water upon. It looked foreign to him, it didn't seem like his anymore. But then, looking at the dozens of Fisian vaka above the tide line, he sensed they were in need of someone, anyone, who might respect them and the wisdom that'd fashioned them.

Piled nearby was an assortment of Fisian steering oars, wood darkened from handling. He wondered how much water they'd cut in the world. He noticed on the ground a scattering of pouches that had once been tied to masts. They contained the little battle charms Fisian warriors had taken to sea, now tossed aside.

The Second Son looked up to the towering ridge that dominated Matuku.

He called to the foreman. "Just how many people lived on this island?"

"They live here yet," the foreman said. "We're still finishing off the last villages on the other coast."

The Second Son took up one of the pigskin pouches. He knew what was inside—a dried coil of umbilical cord or some baby teeth, perhaps, the kind of thing a man had fought for, the thing he hoped might bless him and preserve him. The pouch was sacred, he understood, and wasn't his to open. It didn't belong to him. Yet there was no one to return it to. It wasn't his to keep, though he couldn't toss it aside as others had. Ignoring the truth of these lives seemed like the biggest crime. So the Second Son felt bound to the pouch, bound to a stranger who belonged to the past. The feeling was akin to sailing stories he often retold but hadn't actually lived—they were a part of him but were in no way his. He supposed he could tie the pouch to his next mast until he figured out how to honor it. A thing he'd learned from sailing with Havea was this: At some point in every voyage, the familiar water around you became unfamiliar. But only by sailing onward did the unknown seas join the ranks of the known.

For the next few days, 'Aho and his son traveled Tongatapu's southern shores. Masked terns nested in shorn cliffs. Billowing clouds baby-crawled the horizon. Fish trapped in tidal pools were gigged, steamed in seaweed, and eaten with sunrise.

Turning north, they traversed fallowed plots and fields stippled with saplings. Reaching the island's inner lagoon, they marveled at its vibrant green.

"Bamboo-shoot-green," Mateaki said.

"Beetle-wing-green," 'Aho suggested.

"The green of steamed limu."

Mateaki skipped a rock across the surface. *Puck, puck, plunk.*

'Aho unshouldered the burden of his lost wife and took up the challenge, bouncing a few rocks himself. The rocks pattered along until—seeming to pause on the surface—they slipped beneath the green. The father and the son forgot their concerns as they took turns, throwing together, double-throwing, throwing left-handed, and watching in awe as an occasional fish struck at the bouncing stones. They spoke of nothing serious. This was the moment of normalcy and ease 'Aho had hoped to achieve. He ran a hand through his son's hair. One day, their troubles might be behind them, 'Aho felt. One day the ordeal of his wife's loss might be over.

When the light had changed, 'Aho said, "I suppose we should pay your grandparents a visit."

Mateaki said nothing. He didn't move.

"There's nothing to be afraid of," 'Aho said. "They're your grandparents."

"What're we going to say to them?"

"You don't have to say anything. I'm the one who has the talking to do."

They continued walking toward the sleepy village of Kolomotu'a. They crossed the low-lying area called Talalo, whose thick mangroves obscured the lagoon. They waded through Vai-ko-Puna, the Leaping Stream, and came to Tufumāhina, where people watched the moon rise over the brackish water. To let his wife's parents know what happened to their daughter, he was going to have to let himself know.

At last, in the late-afternoon light, they approached a simple fale with a well-tended garden. Before them was 'Ofa's mother, carrying a skin of water for the hogs. When she saw 'Aho, she set the skin down, where it flattened and emptied. She must've made some sound, for 'Ofa's father appeared, calling, "What is it?"

'Ofa's mother said nothing. She simply stared at the bones adorning her son-in-law.

"We've been on a long journey," 'Aho said. "A journey to bring your daughter home."

With fear in her eyes, 'Ofa's mother said, "But where is she?"

"Finally, I can set her down," 'Aho said. "On her own soil, at the place of her birth."

'Ofa's parents watched him lower the bones, dirty and fly-covered.

"Is that our little girl?" 'Ofa's father asked.

"She's been taken," 'Aho said. "Sadly, her life has been cut short. We've returned to share this woeful news and lay her to rest."

'Ofa's mother beckoned Mateaki to her. The boy looked at his father, uncertain, before moving slowly to the woman, who, when he was close, clutched him protectively.

'Ofa's father asked, "How . . . in what way was she was *taken*?"

"Unfortunately," 'Aho said, "it was by means of violence."

'Ofa's mother's eyes lowered. She seemed to be looking through the bones, into the earth, into time, history, memory. She looked like she might collapse. "Our little girl," she said.

"Violence?" 'Ofa's father asked. "You mean someone hurt her? How could someone hurt her?"

For a moment, no one spoke. Then 'Ofa's mother raised her eyes to her son-in-law. "By what means did the end come for her?"

'Aho closed his eyes. "Well, it was morning. The light was clear and sideways. 'Ofa was at a spring. She'd crouched to wash her hands. She was so beautiful. There was dye on her fingers, and she was at pains to cleanse this from her skin. She'd been patterning tapa cloth, and when she smiled, she lifted an inked hand to cover her mouth, and—"

"Stop," 'Ofa's mother said. "We know this story. This is the story of when you and 'Ofa met, of when you first laid eyes upon one another. I ask about her last moments."

'Aho was confused. When his heart asked his brain for the memory of her death, this was what'd come.

"Perhaps," 'Ofa's father said, "you can tell us of the man who hurt her."

'Aho nodded. "He was a good man, though he was troubled. He kept getting confused about certain things. He had a good heart, though, and 'Ofa was determined to help him. She thought that with some guidance, he could be made whole again."

"This man," 'Ofa's father said. "He must be hunted down. Have the chiefs in Lifuka been notified? It wasn't so long ago that I myself was a sub-chief. I still hold some sway. If you know where to find him, you must reveal it."

Before 'Aho could respond, 'Ofa's mother asked, "This man, what was he confused about?"

"This man," 'Aho said, "he burned one too many dwellings in Fisi. Lifting his torch to yet another roof, he got it in his head that it was his own fale he was setting ablaze. Later, a similar thing happened. They'd sailed all night, and at first light were ready to attack a Fisian village, but when this man looked from the bow, he saw his own village. He'd never been so certain. He recognized the gardens before him, the middens, the meeting house. *Those pigs on the beach are my pigs*, the man thought. He berated the navigator for getting them turned around and nearly causing them to attack their own people. 'Stars do not dissemble,' the navigator said. When the battle came, when the man waded ashore and depopulated the island, he saw up close how wrong he'd been, for they weren't his people at all."

"I can tell you know this man," 'Ofa's father said. "I see you're inclined to him. But you can't shield him. He must be held to account."

'Ofa's mother regarded 'Aho with studied blankness. "But the man, he came home from the war, didn't he?"

"Yes, you understand," 'Aho said. "When he returned to Lifuka, he discovered the opposite could happen. Sometimes the water tasted of fire. Even though it'd run from his own roof into a ceramic vessel that he himself had made, the water tasted of ash, as if it'd fallen through the smoke of Fisian skies. He'd wake in the night, itchy and uncomfortable, thinking he was sleeping on the mat of a Fisian he'd killed. Other times, when a woman approached too quickly or startled him, he became certain she must be Fisian, that she was about to avenge the loss of her family upon him. For why should he have a family while she should not? How could he have a spouse and son while others had lost theirs? Who could blame her for trying to kill him? Didn't he deserve it? He would say, *Are you Tongan? Tell me if you're of Tonga!* to test whether she responded in the alien tongue of Fisi. If, in such a moment, this woman did not offer him the reassuring speech of our people, anything could happen."

This story seemed only to enrage 'Ofa's father. "Who's this man you speak of? Is he still at large?"

"He walks free," 'Aho said. "That's the worst part. He goes about his life while 'Ofa cannot."

"Tell us now," 'Ofa's father demanded. "Tell us how we find him!"

'Aho didn't speak. He cast his gaze to the ground. As he did so, tears spilled.

"I believe," 'Ofa's mother said, "the man has found us."

'Aho, weeping, dropped to his knees. He lowered himself, placing his forehead to the soil.

"I do not shield myself," he said. "I do not defend him."

It was here that the son went to the father, and, crouching beside him, placed a hand upon 'Aho's trembling back.

TWENTY-TWO

KŌRERO:

THE LAST OF YOUR KIND

Hine and I wandered this lonely island, gathering twigs and brush for a fire. The sun, unbroken by trees, was ceaseless. The wind buffeted us. The way it hissed through the grass unsettled me. We came across the remnant of a sleeping mat. The pattern of its weave, I discovered, was our pattern. I'd never felt so dislocated, and I assumed Hine was experiencing this, too. "So familiar," she said.

"I know," I said, thinking of the hands, not unlike Tiri's hands, that had woven it.

I picked it up, imagining the little family that lowered their heads upon it each night.

"I'm not talking about the mat," Hine said. "This place is familiar."

I studied her, trying to understand.

"Not the place itself," she said. "Just the feel of it."

I knew we had to leave this island. We needed to lure that girl into our company and depart. I suggested we could draw her near by having lots of fun. Hine was skeptical, saying "fun" wasn't what the girl was after.

"Trust me," I said.

So the five of us built up a fire of grass and brush. The Wayfinder surprised us by volunteering a song called "Flea and Nit Go Fishing." While Finau slapped out a rhythm on his thighs, the Wayfinder clapped his hands. "Kutu mo liha, faʻu hona vaka," he sang. "Pea ʻuli ki moana, fusi ena ika." The song didn't make much sense—the flea and the nit catch a magical fish—but it was bouncy, and before it was over, Tapoto nudged me to indicate a certain girl was watching.

Hine asked Finau to show us a dance from Tonga.

"Only one dance matters where we come from," he said, "yet it's danced only by women."

"You know the dance, though?" I asked.

Finau nodded. "Every night, women dance the tauʻolunga."

"So you could show us, then?" Hine asked. "Tapoto's an eager learner."

Both men looked affronted. "It's for a little girl," I admonished them.

Reluctantly, they stood, the pupil and the master. It was quite a sight: Tapoto's great bulk next to the compact and hard-muscled Finau.

The Wayfinder got into the spirit. "First, we must adorn these dancing maidens," he said. Pulling up some creeper vines, we wrapped bands of green around their foreheads and midsections, which unflatteringly highlighted Tapoto at his widest. Then, behind the right ear, each man received a pink blossom.

The Wayfinder began singing a song called "Flowers of Lifuka," whose tune was slow and sad and lovely. Thus they began. Finau bent his knees and gathered his hands before him. So did Tapoto. Soon Finau's subtle gestures were being echoed by Tapoto, who was surprisingly light on his feet. "Imagine you're a lovely Fefine Girl," Finau advised Tapoto, as both men let the dance flow through their arms and hips. "Your moves soothe the elites, who are exhausted after a long day of ruling Tonga."

Finau clapped once and tapped a heel—a moment later, Tapoto did the same.

"Your mother was also a Fefine Girl," Finau said. "Her tauʻolunga was capable of captivating kings." Finau then accented his posture and hand placement. "So your gestures must beckon," he told Tapoto. "Your head must lilt invitingly."

It was astonishing how smoothly Tapoto rotated his frame, how gracefully he lowered himself to the ground and raised himself up again.

"Yet you're more than a lovely diversion," Finau said. "Your dancing gets the prince's attention. He's so enraptured by your mystique that he rises and ties a ribbon around your delicate wrist."

Tapoto offered his wrist to this imagined prince. Tapoto gazed longingly into this prince's eyes. He offered what he believed to be an enticing feminine smile, but it was when he batted his eyelashes that Hine and I lost it, and we all burst into laughter, including an unseen girl in the bushes.

Appearing insulted, Tapoto pulled off his vines. "Let's see you try it," he told Hine.

After composing herself, Hine folded her hands and began to sing. "Katia ō karu, e taku kōtiro," she plaintively called. "Ko te moe hei whaea mōu." Her voice was low and restrained, for this was an old lullaby, one that asked a girl to close her eyes and let sleep become a surrogate mother. "Moe mai tonu," she sang. "Moe mai tonu." *Keep sleeping, keep sleeping.*

My lips moved silently along. My mother had sung me this song. Were there fonder memories than looking up to her, her face comprising the entirety of the world, singing, "Kia oho mai koe, hei konei ahau," *When you wake, I will be here*?

Hine tried to sing the second verse, but after her voice began to quaver, the tears came. She wiped her eyes, snorted. I could tell she was upset with herself, for this was the opposite of the lighthearted effect we'd desired. But when you have sorrow in you, everything leads to sorrow.

Hine tried to sing again, but her throat clutched, and she fell into sadness. I placed my hand upon her shoulder. Tapoto knelt and did the same. Surprisingly, the Tongan brothers extended their touch. And then, upon Hine's arm, a little hand appeared.

Hine caught her breath and turned to the girl. "Do you know that song?"

The girl shook her head.

"It's a lullaby," Hine said. "Did you mother sing you those?"

The girl nodded.

"Do you know where your mother is?" Hine asked.

"She left in a canoe," the girl said. "She went after the others."

"Did she leave you all alone?"

The girl paused. "She left me with my grandfather."

"Can you take us to him?" Hine asked.

The girl said nothing.

After a moment, Hine put her hand on the girl's arm. "I'm sorry about your grandfather."

"I know what you're after," the girl said.

"We're not after anything," Hine said. "Will you tell us your name?"

The girl gave no response.

"We have to call you something," Hine said. "Can I give you a name, something we can use until you share your true name?"

The girl didn't say no.

"Do you know the word *ihi*?" Hine asked. "It's that feeling you get when something amazing happens. It fills your whole body. That's what we felt when we saw you. Can we try that, Ihi?" When the girl didn't resist, Hine asked, "So what do you think we're after?"

"It's what everyone was after," Ihi said. "It's what the whole war was about."

* *
*

What could provoke a war? If something justified killing a girl in a flax skirt and leaving her body to decompose in the sun, I didn't want to know what it was. Plus, to see this "thing that everyone was after," we'd have to cross the lava field that'd cut the feet of Tapoto and my father. The Tongan brothers, however, insisted.

"You have to step in the right spots," Ihi instructed as she entered the field of dark rock. One by one, we followed her movements—the Tongans, Tapoto, Hine, and me. You had to place your feet in awkward and unexpected places. Still, there was a way through the jagged rock. I took a breath, reminded myself that it wasn't enough to be a woman of words. Life required action. Arms out for balance, I followed the others.

Hine asked, "How'd you find this place?"

Ihi said, "It's where people hid when they ran away."

"Ran away from what?" Hine asked.

Ihi didn't answer. She was fast—her feet had memorized the safe places to step. We kept asking her to slow down. I thought of my father, navigating these dangerous rocks. Even though I found myself in the same situation,

I couldn't imagine what he must've felt because I'd always had someone to show me the way.

I heard the screech of parrots. They were swooping across the island toward the volcano's dome, where they crested the rim and disappeared inside. I wondered if within its bowl there wasn't a little forest, just like on our island. "Are there trees up there?" I asked.

"It's tapu to enter the dome," Ihi said.

"But if there are parrots, there must be trees," Hine said. "That could mean fruit and berries."

"It's not like we'd hurt them," I said. "I love parrots."

"There's no sign of food on this island," Tapoto said. "If there might be fruit, we must look."

"There's plenty to eat," Ihi said. "You just have to find it."

"Where you're taking us," Hine said, "is that where the food is? Is food what they fought over?"

"No," Ihi said. "People started hiding food from each other. Eventually it all got buried."

"How do you know where to dig?"

"I don't," Ihi said. "My dog sniffs it out."

I shuddered at the thought of Ihi digging up rotten limu and worm-eaten sweet potatoes. And then I understood that by taking her dog, we'd doomed her to true hunger.

Tapoto must've been thinking the same thing. "Your tapu wouldn't apply to us," he said. "Maybe we could simply look to see if there are fruit trees. Together, we could even lift the tapu."

"Disobeying tapu," Ihi said, "that's one of the things they fought about. The nobles decided they wouldn't obey our tapu, and we paid no mind to theirs."

"Were the nobles on the other side of the island?" Hine asked. "Is that what you called them?"

"That's what they called themselves," Ihi answered. "They said they were of noble blood. And that we weren't."

"But you all came from the same waka," I said. "*Te Kahukura.*" The Red Cloak.

Ihi glanced back at me, in disbelief that I could know this. We were in the last stretch of rock, which was particularly treacherous.

"Do you know who we are?" I asked Ihi. "We were on the sister waka. *Mā Atarau.*" By Moonlight.

"That's right," Hine said. "We're the other half of your people."

At last, we found ourselves free. Only now could I see how stressful it had been for Tapoto. Ihi looked up at me. "What'd you call your canoe again?"

"Don't you remember the story?" I asked. "Two canoes fled Aotearoa, but there was a storm, and they got separated. You ended up on this island, with all the weapons. We ended up on a nearby island, with all the tools."

Ihi shook her head. "You're thinking of a different story. There was no other waka. There was no storm. Destiny brought our canoe here."

So they'd stopped telling our story. Or perhaps they never did. All these years, I'd thought about our counterparts in *The Red Cloak.* Yet we never occurred to them.

The cave was a single chamber, shallow enough that torches weren't needed. The first thing I noticed was a haphazard pile of spears. These were nothing like Tapoto's freshly cut training spears. Instead, they'd been fashioned from heavy, dark wood, likely from trees fortified by the soils of Aotearoa. Something told me they'd many times done their duty.

The Wayfinder found a conch shell and took it up. The deep bell of its sound brought the chamber to life.

There was a hand-carved lintel on the ground and several lodge poles, but Ihi went to a garment draped over a rock. "Here it is," she said, indicating a cloak adorned with kiwi quills. The way Ihi gazed at it suggested an invisible history. "Wanna try it on?" she asked Hine, who shook her head. Tapoto also declined. Though he'd campaigned to become our war captain, he wanted nothing to do with a garment that gave permission to distribute death and servitude without reservation. I wondered how we'd have turned out if that cloak had ended up on our island. Would there have been a war? Would we still exist?

Only the Wayfinder touched its feathers. "Our brother spent his life avoiding a cloak like this."

"You mean Lolohea?" I asked.

The Wayfinder said, "Yet everything he did brought him closer to the day it'd be draped across his shoulders."

"Why, then?" Finau said to his brother. "Why try to make him wear it again? He didn't want to be king. And he certainly didn't want a second life. All he wanted was to live the life he had, in whatever way he wanted."

The Wayfinder released the feathers. "That's what I'm trying to give him."

"Isn't this about Havea?" Finau asked. "He made his greatest journey without you, and you can't stand it."

"It's not about finding an island, but finding the afterlife. Havea proved it could be done."

"But Havea didn't make it back," Finau said, trying to talk sense to his brother. "The comet dims more every night. And you keep waylaying yourself to help these people." He gestured toward us. "Let Lolohea rest. We have to fight our own battles. You can't recruit the dead to do it for us."

"How'll we defeat our uncle?" the Wayfinder asked. "He killed you once already."

Finau said, "Resurrecting Six Fists isn't the answer."

"And how do we combat an all-powerful Fan?"

"I don't know," Finau said. "That's something we have to figure out. But Lolo's gone. It's not right that he was taken from us, but he was. You've got to face that."

The Wayfinder turned and stared into the cave. His emotions were running high, and I wondered if he was hiding tears. But his voice didn't quaver when it echoed back. "*You're* the one who wants to go home," he told Finau. "*You're* the one who misses Tonga. I'm just trying to help *you*. And I'm trying to find a way that doesn't involve losing you, too."

✦ ✦

Sunset hung itself sea-urchin-yellow in a sky streaked pancreatic-pink.

We recrossed the lava field before the shadows grew too long. It was even more confusing going the opposite direction, but this time I was behind the Wayfinder. I put my hands on his shoulders and stepped where he stepped. I kept thinking about how the Wayfinder and Finau had debated their next course of action. What they didn't realize, what they didn't even question, was that they had any choices at all.

Once free, the Tongans went to fetch a calabash from their waka. Tapoto started a fire.

I was used to stretches without eating, but something about this island made me famished. I could even hear Hine's stomach. So when the dog caught scent of something, I was ready to follow it toward any kind of meal. But what happened was this: Ihi looked at Hine, and Hine looked at Ihi. Then the two gave chase, leaving me behind.

It was twilight. An upper blue light was cut with a pale, pale white. Already, stars were visible. Without trees, I could see horizon-to-horizon, and even though people surrounded me at various distances, even though I could hear a dog out there somewhere, it was not hard to imagine myself as this island's last human.

When the Tongan brothers returned, we took long, satisfying pulls of water.

"Where do you think the girl's mother went?" Tapoto asked.

The Wayfinder said, "To leave her daughter behind, she must've been desperate."

"She wouldn't have left the girl," I added, "unless it was more dangerous to take her."

"Which was the dangerous part?" Tapoto wondered. "The voyage, the destination, the company?"

Finau asked me, "You think you can convince the girl to leave?"

I looked into the modest fire. "Hine will. The girl's drawn to her."

The Wayfinder asked me, "When we found you on the waters, were you as lost as you appeared?"

I remembered, not without some shame, pointing the wrong direction. "Well," I said. "When I focused on where I was supposed to go and how I should get there, I felt pretty lost. When I forgot all that and just sailed, I seemed to go in the right direction."

The Wayfinder's smile suggested he understood this all too well. He pointed east, to darkness, to the great band of the Milky Way, rising into view. "The journey home'll be easier," he said. "The wind'll be against you, but Ma'afu Toka is a strong target in the sky."

He indicated a glowing cloud in the Milky Way we called Tīoreore.

"Won't we be sailing together?" I asked.

In lieu of an answer, he tipped his head to the side.

"But that little fishing canoe," I said. "It's only made to carry two people."

"It might take you more than one trip," he said. Then he joined Finau and Tapoto in reminiscing about their dance earlier. The Wayfinder offered a comment, and whatever he said made them laugh.

Scary as it'd been to venture alone across the ocean, the idea of being responsible for others terrified me.

From the dark peak above, we heard parrots squawking as they settled for the night. Parrots often caused the biggest ruckus just before sleep.

Tapoto, hearing them, said, "I love grilled parrot. Crisped over an open fire—those tiny wings, those juicy thighs!"

"Is it true you've never tasted pork?" Finau asked Tapoto. "Wait till you try eel, straight from Fisi. They grill it with honey and—"

"Who's *they*?" I asked.

Finau gave me a strange look. "I don't know. People. Cooks, I suppose."

"And how does the eel get from the cooks to you?"

"No special way," Finau said. "People just bring it."

"Servants bring it?" I asked. "Slaves?"

Over the course of a day, I'd developed a growing resentment for the Wayfinder and his brother. It was pretty clear that even without civil war and deforestation, our island would still go the way of this one. But the Tongans—they'd just sail on, back to their empire, where girls danced for their betters, where men feasted at the bathing ponds.

"Hold on," the Wayfinder said. "The Tongan language doesn't even have a word for slavery. It's true that people must make themselves useful. And different people are born to different fates, but—"

"*Different fates?*" I asked. "Is that like *duty* and *sacrifice*? Being *of service*?"

The Wayfinder gave me a disappointed look.

"Tell me," I said. "If I was in Tonga, if I was *making myself useful* by serving your meals, would you know my home island? Or that I liked stories? Would those things matter to you, would you be aware of them?"

"The Tongan people form one great family," Finau said.

"Would you know my name?" I asked.

The Wayfinder said, "We've obviously offended you in some way. If I said the wrong thing, or if—"

I lifted a hand to stop him. "If I was in your service, would you even notice me? Or would your pork just seem to appear?"

"You're being very unfair," the Wayfinder said.

"Do your royals thrust themselves upon servant girls? Is that part of the tribute girls pay?"

The Wayfinder's face turned serious. "That's not who we are."

"So, who are you, then?" I asked.

"We're the ones who left Tonga."

"You said that before. It means less now that you're going back."

"Who said we're going back?" the Wayfinder asked.

"We're going back," Finau asserted.

Tapoto asked, "Do you have any place else to go?"

The Wayfinder's confident demeanor faltered. At a loss, he glanced at the fire. "I admit I'm not as good a navigator as Havea. He found the island of the afterlife, while we washed up on your shores. I suppose it's unlikely we could resurrect Lolohea and Six Fists. And unless we revive Moon Appearing, there's no point in returning."

"*Moon Appearing?*" I asked. "That's the Fefine Girl's name?"

"What happened to her?" Tapoto asked.

Flatly, Finau said, "She was murdered."

Tapoto hesitated before asking, "How'd your brother die?"

The Wayfinder said, "If you're asking about the forces that conspired to take his life, there were many. If you're asking what actually killed him, that's simple."

I raised my eyebrows.

Finau said, "Our brother's cause of death was a meteor."

Tapoto asked, "The kind that streaks across the sky?"

"Does this make you," I asked the Wayfinder, "the prince of Tonga?"

The Wayfinder said, "In my mind, that title will always belong to Lolohea."

"Your friend Six Fists died, too?" Tapoto asked.

"And our parents," Finau said.

"You shouldn't be sailing around on your own," Tapoto said. "This is a difficult time. You need support. You should stay with us. We can help."

The Wayfinder turned to me. "There's no bondage in Tonga," he said. "I need you to understand that. But I'll admit there are different kinds of free."

The dog trotted up and sprawled by our fire. In its mouth was a dog's skull, which it gnawed with calm pleasure. Hine appeared, followed by Ihi, who had a newly excavated bundle in her hands. Hine saw the sober looks on our faces. "What'd I miss?" she asked.

Ihi sat, placing before her a filthy bundle of bull kelp. The outer layers were hard and dirt-crusted. As those were pulled away, a smell began emanating—it was the vinegary stench of entrails. When she removed the last layer of kelp, a gray organ was exposed. Was it the stomach of a dog? The gullet of some sea creature?

I'd chipped barnacles off the reef and eaten them raw. I'd eaten the little fish that spilled milky from the gutted bellies of big fish. But certain things were not meant to be consumed. Hine must've been thinking the same thing. She put a hand on the girl's shoulder and said, "Sometimes hunger is better."

The dog, sensing an opportunity, snatched up this dinner and made for the dark.

"There's food on our island," I told Ihi. "Do you want to come share meals with us?"

She shook her head.

Hine said to her, "You're worried about your mother, right?"

Ihi nodded.

Hine pulled her close. "I understand," she said. "You want to be here when she gets back."

I asked Ihi, "Do you know which direction she went?"

Ihi seemed uncertain. "It had to do with a star."

"Was it Rehua?" I asked.

She didn't know.

"Wanna to know where our island is?" I asked her. When she nodded, I rolled a chunk of pumice into the open. Tapoto helped me place another so they lined up with the constellation Tīoreore, rising now above the horizon. I explained that by sailing toward the place where Tīoreore rose in the night sky, you'd run into our island. Ihi understood, I could tell. With gravel, we made the heavens, starting with the Milky Way, which the Tongans called Kaniva. We marked the small cloud-like cluster Tīkatakata. Then Tapoto hung Pūtara in the sky, Hine set a stone for Pekehāwani, and I placed Rūhī where it belonged.

The Wayfinder surveyed our work. "Not a bad map," he said.

Hine said, "It'd be easy to let someone know you'd gone to that island." With gravel, she made an arrow pointing from this island to the other one.

Ihi asked, "But how would my mother know I was there?"

The Wayfinder knelt to Ihi's level. "Did your mother give you this necklace?" he asked. When she nodded, he lifted it from her, and hung it from the rock that represented our island. Ihi looked uncertain, apprehensive. The Wayfinder didn't reassure her—he just looked into her eyes. Could a girl's eyes be both hopeful and blank? Could they yearn for the most important, irreplaceable love in the world, and also be flat and empty? When the Wayfinder beheld those eyes, I knew he'd end up taking us.

"How would my mother get there?" Ihi asked. She glanced at Tapoto. "He stole our waka."

"We happen to have a spare canoe," the Wayfinder said. "We could leave it for her."

The girl looked to Hine for approval. Hine managed to let none of the sadness of the moment cross her face. She revealed none of her personal loss or longing. She gave away nothing of what was really happening, that a decision was being made for the good of a child that would likely ensure her mother, if alive, would never be seen again. When I realized this was the same decision Ihi's own mother had made, my eyes started to mist. Hine, instead, offered a reassuring nod.

✶ ✶
✦
✶

The moon that night was birthed between our bows. Everyone was at ease with the Wayfinder at the helm. Hine slept on a mat with an arm around a girl who had an arm around a dog. Tapoto's frame blocked their wind, his snore soft as the coo of a kererū bird.

We were headed home, all of us safe, with the girl we'd hoped to retrieve. But home to what? All I thought I'd known—of who we were, where we were from, and what we might become—now felt like ash, ash from the fire of a depopulated island.

I sat beside the Wayfinder as he made his adjustments. He was not unlike the sea at night: ever in motion, yet somehow at rest. "I can't imagine losing my parents," I said.

"Neither can I," he said, though he had.

Newly risen, the moon illuminated the far sides of waves so only their edges shone white.

I said, "That girl who was killed, Moon Appearing."

"Yeah?"

"You said your brother loved her?"

He nodded. "What drew them together was simple: she didn't want to be a Fefine Girl, and he didn't want to be a king."

"So, if they'd managed to avoid their fates, they might not've come together?"

"They were never going to avoid their fates," the Wayfinder said. "My father was single-minded about Lolo becoming king. And Moon Appearing fell under the protection of the Tamahā."

"The what?" I asked.

"She's the aunt of our people. She can't be touched. And she has an all-powerful Fan. So she's nearly impossible to kill."

"Kill? Your aunt?"

Instead of responding, the Wayfinder inspected the sail.

He'd interrupted the discussion of a dead young woman to suggest the murdering of an older one. How was it I felt safe around him? How was it I was worried he'd leave us as soon as we landed?

"Am I going to see you again?" I asked.

"The ocean's not so big."

I knew he didn't have another destination. Was wandering preferable to spending time with us? Without him, could I go back to normal life? How was I to recline on the beach at night, wondering about the world, now that

I knew about other people and places and customs? Now that I was aware there were paths across the sea. And people who traversed them.

"You owe me a story," I said.

"What story would that be?"

"When we met, you said there was a female navigator."

"Ah, Pāintapu," he said. "She was from an atoll named Tarawa. That's up north, near Tuvalu. Her father was a famous navigator, and, having no sons, he secretly taught his daughter to steer by the stars. In their tradition, the navigator lies on the deck and observes not the sea but the heavens. Come, try it."

The Wayfinder reclined on the deck. I leaned back beside him.

"By sighting up the mast, Pāintapu could position herself by zenith stars and steer by the regularity of the swells. Can you feel them now, how our bows greet the rollers?"

The Wayfinder paused, I suppose, to let me feel what he was saying.

What I felt was this: the sea rocking us together, treating us as one.

"The king of Tarawa was getting on in years. When he embarked upon war, he enlisted his son Ruki to command the battles. Pāintapu's father, also being older, he sent his daughter instead. Ruki, vain and superstitious, was loath to discover he'd be guided by a woman. He thought a woman's presence would doom his expedition. Before his departure, Ruki berated Pāintapu before all his men. Yet he had no other navigator.

"Thus Pāintapu boarded the lead canoe. When she reclined to observe the stars, Ruki accused her of sulking. For most of the night, he commanded her to rise and do her duty. Yet she remained on her back, calling the steering adjustments. Exasperated and certain he could do better, Ruki had Pāintapu cast into the sea. He promised death to any who might rescue her. Ruki then changed course to suit his own estimation. A hundred vaka passed Pāintapu in the water. Only the men in the last canoe, warriors of lowest rank, were willing to pull her aboard. In gratitude, she shared with them the proper course. The other hundred vaka were never seen again."

I sighted up the mast to the heavens. I noticed how the mast's tip traced slow revolutions, drawing circles around our zenith star. The Wayfinder sat up, took measure of the conditions, and altered his course. The thing was—I could *feel* that change in direction.

I asked for more stories about navigators, Tongan ones.

"You're asking for sad stories," the Wayfinder said, "since the great Tongan navigators all sailed south, none to return."

Perhaps to avoid the topic of Havea, he told the stories of other Tongan explorers. One's story was only known because a parrot survived to tell the tale. Another concerned a father and son who died together, confirmed by the shark who ate them. Then the Wayfinder told the story of Māsilafōfoa, who, in a yellow coral necklace, headed south with his entire village, never to be heard from again.

Our people had been blessed, on occasion, to receive signs of things to come. The story of Māsilafōfoa, it would turn out, was the most important sign yet.

TWENTY-THREE

RECIPROCAL STRIKING

The Tuʻitonga's morning briefing was of the usual sort—land disputes, village feuds, and, since the Fisian incursion, rumors of enemy attacks, including one against a young woman tending her family's pigs. Also, a comet had been spotted.

Updates from the outer islands were no better. When the various food and supply shortages were laid out for the Tuʻitonga, his war chiefs waited for the inevitable response. He felt a sudden pain course through his veins. "Go ahead," he said. "Take another Fisian island."

But there was good news: an emissary from Haʻamoa had a gift for him, a shiny rock. When he received it, he understood it was no ordinary stone—the object weighed more than he could believe.

"We've heard you had a premonition regarding a comet," the emissary said. "So we bestow upon you, as a token of friendship between our peoples, a meteor."

Turning the object in his hands, the Tuʻitonga beheld its lustrous metallic surface.

"It was more of a dream than a premonition," he said.

"For the Tuʻi of Tonga," the emissary said, "dream is destiny."

The king really did like these Haʻamoans. Invading them had been one of his better moves.

"How'd you come by a piece of the sky?" he asked.

The emissary told the story, while the Tuʻitonga focused on the meteor. It'd once glowed with fire, yet now was cool to the touch. Though it had been liquid, nothing could appear more solid. It had streaked the heavens.

Now it rested in human hands. He wondered which of these was the meteor's natural state.

After, he found Finau in a patch of sun near where they'd take their morning ink. The boy looked very alone. The Tuʻitonga sat beside him. "Where's that parrot of yours?"

"I set him free," Finau said. "Now he comes and goes."

"You released your parrot?" he asked. "Why? What's gotten into everyone?"

"I freed Kōkī because he asked me to."

"And where's Punake? Don't tell me you freed him as well."

Finau asked, "Is Punake not free?"

"Of course he is, my boy. Free as any man alive."

Some Fefine Girls began practicing songs to accompany the inking session. Singing would hopefully lift the men over the peaks of pain. Last night, the king had dreamed that while taking his ink, he let loose a howl of agony, one that stopped the entire island. His dream about the comet had come to pass. What if this one did as well?

The Tuʻitonga waved Six Fists over. "Is it right that the Tufuga, much our senior, should make the journey to us? Is he not our elder, should we not make our way to him?"

Six Fists studied the Tuʻitonga, trying to make sense of this statement, for the king did not make it his habit to convenience others. "You'd do the old fellow much respect."

"And why make an old man submit to all the scrutiny found here?"

"Yes," Six Fists said, seeming now to understand. "Let's spare our guest unwanted attention and make our way to him."

So it was that Finau, Six Fists, and the Tuʻi of all Tonga exited the royal compound, leaving behind the transcendent sound of virgins singing "Falaʻolongo."

The leaf-lined path glowed brown-gold before them, and in the morning light, waist-high foliage was inner-lit with green. Six Fists gripped his spear as they passed the Fisian dogs, snarling and straining at the end of their tethers. Before long, they came across the open hole where the Tuʻilifuka's skeleton had been baked from his flesh. Bones harvested, the discarded material had become but a stain where the hogs had feasted.

"What good's the afterlife if pigs have eaten the eyes that would've beheld it?" Six Fists asked the grease-darkened earth. "Delivering my bones to Nuku Hiva will give me no aid. I must die on my home island."

Weary of this talk, the Tuʻitonga said, "I don't forget our agreement."

The Tufuga, when they found him, was making ink from candlenut soot. "I was about to head your way," he said.

"Today, we do you the courtesy," the Tuʻitonga responded.

Morning light hovered beneath the canopy, illuminating things in exceptional detail. The Tufuga took the opportunity to inspect his previous day's work: for Finau, waves of shark's teeth rounding a hip, and for the Tuʻitonga, black bands along the spine. And as if he couldn't help it, he cast his gaze at Six Fists. "If only I could meet the man who applied your blade-proof ink."

Six Fists said, "My ink was the work of Nuku Hiva's highest priest."

The Tufuga studied the tall man's chest, layered in so many protective patterns that it'd become solid black. He asked, "And your ink's resistance to weapons, it's been battle-tested?"

The Tuʻitonga answered for Six Fists. "His ink has proven impervious! No blade can wound him."

"What about a shark bite?" the Tufuga asked Six Fists. "Would such a tooth cut you?"

The Tuʻitonga said, "As if he goes around fighting sharks."

"Have you never cut yourself on coral or stepped on a sharp shell?" the Tufuga asked.

"Do you think there's ink on the soles of his feet?" the Tuʻitonga asked.

"I am a man," Six Fists said.

The Tufuga nodded. "So blood can be drawn from you."

Mats were spread, and the king elected to go first. The Tufuga blacked his needles, then sank them into his own forearm. He licked away the excess, and, approving of the mark, began inking the king's flank.

The king's eyelids twitched with every delivery. His nose began to run. When the king thought of these daily pain sessions, it was his brother who came to mind. His brother was responsible for the way he must daily drop to the ground and submit. His brother was the reason his skin seeped blood. His brother was why the Tuʻitonga kept dreaming of needles, so that the cursed process never seemed to stop.

On the mat beside him, Finau stared up at the stiff boughs and weepy limbs of a toa tree. "To be weapon-proof," he said. "Now, that would be a power. I wonder which divine ability I'll receive. I hope it's a good one, like remote sight."

"There's no way of knowing," the Tuʻitonga said. "As royals, we're descendants of Tangaloa, who was all-powerful. He could travel the skies, read minds, command birds, reconstitute life. His gifts were endless, as are the possibilities for the power you'll inherit."

"Please don't let it be a stupid one," Finau said. "No offense, but transferring jellyfish is not much of a gift."

The king's eyes drifted to the tree where the Fisian girl'd been lashed. He felt the ugliness of what'd been done to her, the way she'd been desecrated by his brother's mark. "It's not the gift, but what you do with it." Then he quoted the old poem:

Nāmuʻi e laukau poʻuli,	*Smell the night flower,*
vakai ki he kapakau o e manu kai niu.	*observe the beetle's wing.*
Ngāahi meʻaʻofa tuʻu kimuʻa	*Are the greatest gifts*
kia koe, kaʻikai maʻu?	*before you, unreceived?*

Before long, Kōkī appeared. After landing, the red-shining parrot rolled to his back and sprawled, colorful wings spread across the ground. With his little legs in the air, he gazed at the sky from whence he'd come. "Today, Kōkī lose his virginity."

"Have you found another of your kind?" Finau asked.

"Sadly, no," Kōkī said, and let out a moan. "Oh, Kōkī's ule is sore! Kōkī never imagine it could hurt so much." He bent a wing to fan the feathered region between his legs.

"How's this possible?" Finau asked.

"Kōkī do what Kōkī must do," Kōkī said. "Love, loneliness, extinction. They'll drive a bird to do unimaginable things, unforgivable things."

"I take it back," the Tuʻitonga said. "You were right to let the bird go."

Finau asked, "Has Kōkī been a bad bird?"

"Bad bird!" Kōkī said.

"What'd Kōkī do?" Finau asked.

"Kōkī need love."

"What did Kōkī do?" Finau repeated.

"This morning, Kōkī saw a lupe dove," Kōkī said. "It just happened, Kōkī was loving her. And suddenly Kōkī was with a misi bird and then a kulukulu and then a jungle hen, and she was three times Kōkī's size!"

"Those poor, confused birds," Finau said.

Kōkī stared at the sky. "Everywhere Kōkī look, Kōkī see their drab feathers, their beady eyes! A skinny-legged pigeon? It isn't the same," Kōkī lamented. "It's nowhere near the same."

"The same as what?" Finau asked.

"Exactly!" Kōkī squawked. "That's the cruelty of Kōkī being the last of Kōkī's kind."

"Last of your kind?" the Tufuga asked. "I've seen many parrots of your variety in Samoa."

Kōkī lifted his head. "Does the old man speak the truth to Kōkī?"

The Tufuga said, "I might even say your kind is common."

Kōkī's eyes pinwheeled. "*Common?*" He flashed his brilliant plumage. "*Nea*, Kōkī is the rarest specimen. There is but a single he. And having nobody"—Kōkī let his wings droop—"is Kōkī's tragic fate."

"Kōkī has Finau," Finau said.

The Tuʻitonga rolled his eyes.

Dejected, Kōkī walked to Finau's outstretched hands. When Finau shaped them into a bowl, Kōkī nestled inside. "It's not easy being wild," Kōkī said. "Kōkī doesn't know if Kōkī wants to be free. After Kōkī's bad day, Kōkī came looking for Finau, but with all the commotion in the royal compound, Kōkī couldn't find him. Kōkī was scared. Kōkī was lonely. But here we are, together again."

The Tuʻitonga asked, "What sort of commotion was this?"

Before the bird could answer, Six Fists rose to his feet. "Warriors approach," he said, and sure enough, two sentries, spears in hand, were racing toward them. Out of breath, one warrior said, "We have a situation."

"What sort of situation?" the Tuʻitonga asked.

The other warrior said, "It's your brother."

When the Tuʻitonga returned to the royal compound, the virgins were no longer singing.

Chiefs and matāpule stood in the company of servants and sentries, all gazing upon a scene: One of Six Fists's security men was on the ground with his arm bent backward. Several priests were treating the injury with cave water and soot from a cooking fire. At the royal grave stood ʻAho, explaining to Mateaki how the tomb's great stone would be raised. He didn't seem bothered that a man had been maimed.

There was a groan of agony as Six Fists reset the sentry's arm.

Joining the king, Matāpule Muʻa said, "He'll survive."

"And his arm?" the Tuʻitonga asked.

Matāpule Muʻa said, "As one would expect."

Pōhiva came to her husband's side. Tied to her wrist was the Fisian boy.

"It looks like today's the day," the king said.

"It doesn't have to be today," she responded.

"One day or another," the Tuʻitonga said, "my brother has to be dealt with."

"Our goal," Pōhiva said, "is Lolohea."

"I'm thinking of Lolohea," he said. "Where is the golden boy, anyway?"

"Off somewhere, being Lolo."

The Tuʻitonga studied his brother. "Someone has to handle him."

"Let him do what he came to do," Pōhiva implored her husband. "Then bid him good riddance."

If only it was that easy, the Tuʻitonga thought.

Flanked by Six Fists and Matāpule Muʻa, the Tuʻitonga approached his brother, who was running a hand along the tomb, illustrating its attributes.

A freshly woven basket was in Mateaki's hand—it contained human bones. And in the waistband of 'Aho's kilt was the green club.

'Aho surprised the king with a smile. "I'm sorry about that fellow of yours. He tried to stop us from approaching the tomb. I explained that it housed my ancestors. He wouldn't listen."

"So you broke his arm?"

"The matter was unfortunate. You know violence isn't my preference."

"What, exactly, is your preference?"

"I prefer people not place their hands upon me."

"I'm told he has children. What's he going to do now? What's a one-armed sentry worth?"

"What's a sentry need but eyes and ears?"

"I'll remember that when I'm compensating his family," the Tu'itonga said.

"I've been doing some thinking," 'Aho said. "Walking around this fine island of yours, I realized my demand for a ceremonial funeral was misguided. 'Ofa was a modest woman and wouldn't want a big display. Allow us to lower her remains into the family tomb, and we'll be on our way."

"You claim the tomb is also yours," the Tu'itonga said. "Why not open it yourself? This is your home island. If you can find enough friends, you have my blessing to inter your wife yourself."

"A generous offer," 'Aho said. He raised his voice so all might hear. "I need some Tongans to come to my aid." He began circulating, so he might speak directly to those assembled. "Don't we pride ourselves in helping those in need? Don't we offer much support for those who mourn?" 'Aho lingered before each chief and matāpule as if gauging his honor and, sadly, finding it lacking. "Am I not a son of Tongatapu? And wasn't 'Ofa one of Tongatapu's sweetest daughters?"

The Tu'itonga leaned toward Six Fists. "Could he be more condescending?"

"Let him bury his wife," Six Fists said. "Then we'll be rid of him."

"What, open the tomb?" the Tu'itonga asked. "And fall for his ploy?"

'Aho raised his voice, so he might be heard by all. "What d'you say? Might a widower count on his fellow Tongans to help lay a beloved wife to rest?"

The assembled chiefs and matāpule cast glances toward the Tu'itonga, searching for clues as to how they should respond—when the king offered no reply, neither did they.

'Aho returned to the Tuʻitonga. "I'm sad to discover no Tongans of honor."

It was then that the Tamahā arrived, Fefine Girls in tow. People lowered themselves at her approach. The Tamahā bore her Fan, something she rarely carried. Her first action was to embrace her nephew 'Aho.

"Hear some advice from an old friend," Six Fists whispered to the king. "Allow the burial and walk away. Take some dancing girls to the coast. Drink kava and admire the cliffs of 'Eua until sunset. When you return, your brother will be out of your life."

"He defeats me only if I defeat myself," the king whispered back.

When the Tamahā's matāpule bade everyone rise, the Tuʻitonga spoke. "I'll allow the burial," he told his brother. "I'll solicit volunteers to raise the stone right now. All I ask is that you share one piece of intelligence with me."

"And what's that?" 'Aho asked.

"Just reveal the real reason you want the family vault opened."

"What reason would I have, other than to lay a wife to rest?"

"Can you establish these bones actually belong to your wife?"

Anger flashed in 'Aho's eyes. "What're you accusing me of?"

The Tuʻitonga stood silent, as if awaiting a great confession.

"Do you think I mistake the woman I love for another?" 'Aho asked in disbelief. "Do you think I want her in a tomb, rather than by my side? Or that I enjoy returning to this fat, lazy island? Do you think I want to teach you what I have to teach you?"

"You, little brother, have plans to educate me?"

"A tutorial is long overdue," 'Aho said.

"Enlighten me."

"The lesson will be simple," 'Aho said. "Here in the Sacred South, you take no risks, endure no setbacks, suffer no losses. You've no occasion to look into the eyes of the enemy, let alone return the stare of the sand-covered dead. You do not regard the outcomes of your commands. Today I endeavor to restore your gaze."

"*Restore my gaze?*" The Tuʻitonga snorted. "What're you talking about?"

"I'm going to show you something. After that, our brotherhood will be stronger, and you'll no longer be afraid of me."

"No one on this island's afraid of you. Except girls caught alone in the dark."

"It'll hurt," 'Aho said. "But after, we'll have hurt in common. We'll share that."

"Did you teach your wife this lesson?" the king asked. "Did you share some hurt with her?"

'Aho remained calm. Mostly, he looked disappointed. "I was planning to take someone from you, someone close. But now I see that's not enough." He closed his eyes and said, "Fetā'aki."

The Tu'itonga was caught off guard by this word, which, though rarely uttered, speaks for itself: *tā* is the word for striking, *'aki* suggests togetherness, and *fe* implies acts of a reciprocal nature. Was his brother truly challenging him to a duel? "Enough with your games," the Tu'itonga said.

"Fetā'aki is a time-honored way of settling disputes, and it seems we have a dispute."

"This is ridiculous," the Tu'itonga said. "Save your showmanship for the firelight, when you have dancing girls to intimidate. Besides, what you suggest is impossible. He who takes a family member's life forfeits his soul. The defeated may lose his life, but the victor loses the afterlife. Whatever our differences, my brother, an eternity awaits us in Pulotu to work them out."

"I fear I've already relinquished my soul," 'Aho said.

"That's not true," the Tu'itonga said. "I know it's not."

"Either way, I'm prepared to settle this once and for all. If I win, the tomb'll be opened for my wife's burial. Of course, if I win, the tomb'll be opened for your burial."

"Would that tableau bring you pleasure?"

"You've no idea how the notion pains me," 'Aho said.

"And if I prevail?"

"Then you'll find the thorn that is your brother finally pulled," 'Aho said. "And my desire to be interred with my wife is fulfilled."

"Where's your son in this formulation? Would you casually make an orphan of him?"

"You speak in hypotheticals," 'Aho said. "My demise is not on the horizon. It's your death we discuss."

"What's in that tomb?" the Tuʻitonga asked. "What's so important, that you'd take your brother's life?"

"You think a man of honor wishes to duel with you? Dear brother, look at your bloated body, look at your yellow hue."

The Tuʻitonga's back was killing him. His groin throbbed. He looked upon the faces of those assembled. When his eyes landed on Pōhiva, he saw her not as she was, a mother, eyes red with worry, but as she'd once been, a lovely young woman whose smile was finally opening to him. He saw Finau not as he was, but as the man he'd one day become, broad-chested, hotheaded, a student of the past, an instrument of the future. His thoughts turned to his middle son, upon the waves that very moment to return the Fisian girl. He was a boy who'd make his way. And where was Lolohea? Poised on a clifftop, perhaps. The Tuʻitonga had to admit it took great courage to plunge from those heights. He imagined Lolohea at the island's terminus, arms out, feet together, eyes closed. The ocean below white with churn. Exhales of mist curling up the cliffs. Yet the boy has his balance, his focus. In, out, he breathes. He won't leap until he imagines the perfect dive—the reach, the arc, the plummet, a final streamlined entrance. It also took great strength not to dive, to remain composed above the chaos. To hold one's stance against such buffeting takes focus, poise, power. Yes, the leap is the lesser act—a single decision followed by inevitability. But at some point, the leap must be taken. One can't stand on the ledge forever.

"No need to trouble yourself with departure plans," the Tuʻitonga told his brother. "I accept your challenge."

"Father!" Finau shouted. "Don't do it. Let me fight him."

Pōhiva ran to her husband. "You can't duel ʻAho. Lolohea needs you, we all need you."

The Tuʻitonga offered a reassuring smile. "Have a little faith in the old king."

Six Fists also protested. "There are other paths. For the honorable, all paths lead to honor."

Even 'Aho implored him. "Come, now, I've no desire to take your life. Just let me bury my wife."

The Tamahā began walking their way. "I don't want to lose a nephew. Please, let the matāpule settle your differences."

Pōhiva blocked her approach. "You foment their difficulties," she said to her. "You've concluded you'll take no profit from a duel—thus, with feigned concern, you intervene."

The Tamahā looked disappointed by such talk. "You understand," she cautioned Pōhiva, "that arguing against me is arguing for your husband's possible demise."

"You must always be argued against," Pōhiva said.

The king ended this bickering by declaring, "I accept. Fetā'aki it is."

Matāpule Mu'a waved his fly whisk. "It's done. The challenged party has the right to choose the weapons, along with the time, place, and manner of the contest."

With great solemnity, 'Aho placed a hand on his older brother's shoulder. "Don't make me do this. There are ways out. You can select hibiscus blossoms as our weapons. You can set the duel ten years into the future."

The Tu'itonga felt his brother's sincerity. Though 'Aho's face had hardened over the years, in his eyes was the vulnerability of a boy who'd long ago suddenly lost everything. "No," the king said. "We'll see this to its conclusion."

'Aho released his grasp. "As you wish."

The Tu'itonga turned to Six Fists, so they might privately confer. "He wouldn't want to fight you," the king said. "You're undefeated, you're coated in blade-proof ink."

Six Fists cautiously listened.

"Consider this the day of your freedom," the Tu'itonga said. "Losing your friendship, your loyalty, your good counsel, it's something I can barely imagine. But if you accept this challenge on my behalf, I'll put you on our swiftest vaka home. When the stars rise tonight, you'll embark."

"*Freedom*," Six Fists said, tasting the word.

"That's the spirit," the Tu'itonga said. He turned to Matāpule Mu'a. "As the challenged party, I opt for a surrogate."

'Aho said, "Already, you maneuver to steal my prize?"

The Tu'itonga said, "I only follow the rules bequeathed to us."

"I'm here to teach the oldest lesson of all," 'Aho said. "As to the pupil, I suppose I'm indifferent."

"Six Fists will fight in my place," the Tu'itonga announced. "He will set the terms of the duel."

"Wait," the Tamahā called out. "I loan my visiting nephew the use of a matāpule."

She ignored the dismay on 'Aho's face, for he famously disliked matāpule.

Immediately, the Tamahā's matāpule spoke: "If the challenged party adopts a surrogate, the right to select weapons and set terms reverts to the challenger."

'Aho began walking in a slow, deliberate circle. "Set terms?" he asked.

"Time, place, manner," the Tamahā's matāpule said.

"When's the proper time to do battle with a brother?" 'Aho asked aloud. "Should we have fought long ago, when the stakes were lower? And what's the proper place? Where we'd roust about as boys? Where we'd pass time with our mother? Certainly one place is as bad as another when brothers fight."

"Another speech," the Tu'itonga moaned. His enlistment of Six Fists had emboldened him. "Does our guest from Lifuka make delays?"

"Here's as good a place as any, and why not now?" 'Aho turned to the Tamahā's matāpule. "What's meant by *manner*?"

"A duel can conclude when one fighter relents," he said. "Or it can terminate with death."

"That's the one I want," 'Aho said. "Now, here, death."

This audacious declaration was met with gasps from many in attendance.

"Now, what're my choices for a weapon?"

Matāpule Mu'a looked nervously toward Six Fists. "Typically, this might include items like spears or clubs. Some opt for bare hands."

"When it comes to weapons," the Tamahā's matāpule said, "history offers no restriction."

"Any implement I select?" 'Aho mused.

"Don't waste your time," the Tu'itonga said. "Your opponent is weapon-proof."

'Aho turned to the Tamahā's matāpule. "You said *weapons*. Does that mean I can choose two?"

"Just go," the Tu'itonga said. "Depart already."

"Two *different* weapons?" Matāpule Mu'a asked.

"Take your leave of us," the Tu'itonga said. "I'll ensure you suffer no dishonor."

The Tamahā's matāpule said, "There's no precedent against multiple weapons."

"None of this has to happen," the Tu'itonga said.

"Then relent," 'Aho said. "Or let me finish my business."

"Fine," the Tu'itonga said. "We agree to your terms. Select any weapons you desire."

Nothing seemed to make 'Aho more angry than this. "The first weapon is the war dog."

Six Fists's resolve visibly wavered.

"The dog's a Fisian weapon," the Tu'itonga said. "There's no safe way for a Tongan to deploy it."

"We recently captured several dogs," 'Aho said. "They're tied to a tree not far from here. I'll let my opponent select the dog of his choice. I'll select from the remaining ones."

The matāpule quietly conferred. With great reluctance, servants were dispatched to retrieve the dogs.

"And the second weapon?" Matāpule Mu'a asked.

"A bowl," 'Aho said.

"This is madness," the Tu'itonga said. "He's playing us for fools."

"The second weapon," 'Aho clarified, "is the ceramic bowl in the Tu'itonga's sleeping chamber that houses the coconuts of reaped souls."

"Now you're being petty," the Tu'itonga said. "You made that bowl for me. It keeps me in mind of you."

"You never think of me," 'Aho snapped. "You couldn't live if you were in mind of people like me."

The Tamahā's matāpule asked, "Which combatant gets possession of the bowl?"

Without taking his eyes off his brother, 'Aho said, "Neither."

Soon five wary handlers arrived with five agitated dogs. Each man held a rope, tethered around a dog's neck. Each also employed a stick to keep the beast at bay. This struggle between holding a dog back and keeping it away occupied their full attention.

Six Fists, dread visible on his face, could barely look at them.

To Six Fists, 'Aho said, "Perhaps I was thoughtless when I dictated the terms. I should've asked if you preferred to fight now or perhaps another day."

Six Fists attempted to speak.

"He'll fight right now, thank you," the Tu'itonga said.

"And concerning the place," 'Aho said, "I didn't even consult you—do you prefer hard-packed soil, or the shifting sand of a sloping beach? That's what I'm used to."

"I do prefer the solid ground," Six Fists said.

'Aho turned to the Tamahā's matāpule. "I now prefer to fight on the beach."

"Six Fists'll fight you anywhere," the Tu'itonga said. "On dirt, in sand, or beneath the sea."

The matāpule conferred. "If both parties agree," they announced, "then sand it is."

Six Fists appealed again to the king. "Why not let the man bury his wife?"

"Keep your focus," the Tu'itonga said. "We gain our advantage by selecting the most vicious dog."

It wasn't easy to present the dogs for inspection—they chewed their tethers and snapped at the sticks that kept them at bay. "The first pick is yours," 'Aho said.

The Tu'itonga had never taken the study of a dog. Their coats were generally white, with tufts of gray. Their ears were notched from fighting, and their muzzles were streaked with scars. "It looks like their greatest enemy is their own kind," the Tu'itonga said.

"Is that not true of ourselves?" Six Fists asked.

"Stay focused," the Tu'itonga implored. "You can get philosophical later, when you're victorious and the kava's being passed."

One dog was shaking from hunger or perhaps illness; still, it snapped at the slightest provocation. Three dogs made moans of frustration as they bucked at their handling. The final dog made no lunges. It faced forward, stance wide, growling, the fur on its back alternately rising and settling.

"That one does not attack its handler," Six Fists said. "I think I could manage that one."

"No, no," the Tuʻitonga said. "Your dog must be fierce."

"How'll I use a dog to fight my opponent, if the thing is fighting me?"

The Tuʻitonga appealed to Six Fists. "You're my friend. I can't afford to lose you. We must use our wits, for ʻAho slays people day by day. He kills so much he gets life and death mixed up."

If Six Fists had looked concerned, even fearful, these words made him doubly so.

The Tuʻitonga returned to the dogs. "We must concentrate on these three."

"The people ʻAho kills, his victims—"

"I don't like the one with the nipped-off tail," the king said. "For clearly he has lowered his guard and allowed an attack from the rear."

"Were they Tongan or Fisian?" Six Fists asked.

"What? You know the answer to that. He'll kill anyone. His own wife, even." The Tuʻitonga then crouched to get closer. "This one here, with the different-colored paws, he has the fewest scars on his nose, which means he must be getting the better of clashes with his mates."

"Him, then," Six Fists absently said. "You've made a wise choice."

"*We*," the Tuʻitonga said. "*We've* made a wise choice. Even though you do the actual striking, we fight him together."

After sending a servant to fetch some pork, ʻAho made a certain whistle through his teeth. The sick dog and the scared dog ignored this, but the two aggressive ones obeyed by sitting back on their haunches. ʻAho held up the meat. This he moved into the space between them. When one dog tried to take the morsel, the other popped its teeth, taking the morsel for itself. ʻAho then fed the dog who'd lost out, so both got a taste.

"The one dog doesn't wish to prevent the other from eating," ʻAho explained. "It's just the order that matters. Their adherence to rank is even more rigid than ours."

'Aho selected the dominant dog. Its coat was splotched like the down of albatross chicks.

The great bowl was retrieved, wide as a man's shoulders, its salt-and-ash glaze glistening ocher in the sun. 'Aho placed his greenstone club and his wife's bones atop the family grave. The party then made its way toward the beach, the brothers walking side by side.

"You're enjoying this," the Tuʻitonga said.

"Before conflict," 'Aho said, "that's the time to relax."

"Don't most take pleasure *after* the battle's over?"

'Aho asked, "But what if, after the battle, you find yourself not alive enough to rejoice?"

Alive enough, the Tuʻitonga thought. As if being alive wasn't something you were or weren't but gradations of sunset. He pondered the way his brother saw the world, how time was elusive, how pain wafted from the same fan as joy, how waking was but a shallow state of slumber. And perhaps, to 'Aho, death itself was just a deeper sleep.

"Besides," 'Aho added, "after a battle, all you can think about is the battle. Do you remember the stories Mother would tell about the Mat of Forgetting? Arriving in Pulotu, you'd recline on this, and all your earthly problems became things you couldn't recall."

"Yes, the Mat of Forgetting," the Tuʻitonga repeated. "To partake of its effects, one need only surrender his life."

"Is it such a steep price for a fresh start? I've been thinking about retiring to the islands of Fisi."

"You must be joking."

"Their people are not as different as we'd like to think. I've heard Fisians playing flutes in the forest, and their tunes are much like ours. I've heard their maidens sing the moon into the sky. And the old men wade into the sea each morning to awaken the blades of their adzes with sprays of seawater and the recitation of sacred words."

"They'd kill you on sight."

"Maybe," 'Aho said. "Do you know they believe in an afterlife called 'Burotu,' an island located in the same direction as our Pulotu?"

Through the palms that lined the path, white strips of beach became visible.

'Aho asked, "And did you know that in Fisi, dogs are actually friendly, that they bow down and lick your hand?"

The Tu'itonga gave his brother an incredulous look.

"It's true," 'Aho said. "They're not born as you see them. The Fisians separate some pups and train them to be ruthless. Believe me, normal dogs are as tame as decoy pigeons. It's just the ones that are made into war dogs that you have to watch out for."

"It's hard to believe that Fisians allow these beasts near their wives and children."

"On that point you're right," 'Aho said. "War dogs, when they've served their purpose, can never return. All they know is inflicting hurt. That's why the Fisians abandon them on our shores."

The late-morning wind had switched direction. Above the leeward coast, clouds had started to tower.

"I can tell you care about your security guy," 'Aho said. "It's a bad feeling, missing someone."

"It's not too late to stop this nonsense," the Tu'itonga said.

"It's not too late to come to your senses."

"You know who I'm going to miss?" the Tu'itonga asked. "You."

When an expanse of beach was selected, the spectators formed a circle. Here were Fefine Girls, the royal council, various matāpule, chiefs, sub-chiefs, and all available servants, for servants were vital witnesses of the deeds of their betters, and it was important they repeat such stories in their labor gangs, taro sluices, and hog wallows.

'Aho addressed these people: "Today, for the pleasure of the king, a foreigner will duel an outcast."

The Tu'itonga, standing next to Six Fists, asked, "Can you believe 'Aho's cheek? Depicting himself as an outcast, rather than a royal?"

"I request only that no one intervene," 'Aho continued, "for I stand alone, with no one but my boy to sponsor me."

"There'll be no interference," the Tamahā affirmed.

'Aho raised the ceramic bowl before slamming it flat upon the sand. A spray of flakes burst from the impact. What remained was a rough circle of knifelike shards. "The Tuʻitonga's man will position himself there," ʻAho said, pointing. "I'll stand opposite. The ceramic daggers will be between us. We'll each have our chosen dogs."

The Tuʻitonga walked Six Fists to the shards. "Your arms are long, so you'll have the advantage when it comes to snatching a dagger. Though having him grab a dagger first would be delicious, too. Imagine the look on his face when it broke upon impact with your skin."

Six Fists gazed at the jagged shards with dread. "That was just a story I told."

"What was?" the Tuʻitonga asked.

"That my ink was enchanted. That blades can't hurt me."

"Nonsense," the Tuʻitonga said. "I've seen with my own eyes how your skin repels weapons."

"We see in the weave of the world the pattern of our own minds," Six Fists said. "Which came first: my invincibility or the story of my invincibility?"

"It doesn't matter. Your perfect record speaks for itself."

"I held my resolve when I was taken captive. I didn't despair when I was brought to the Sacred South. But when I realized I was to fight every warrior on the island, I invented a story, a story that said you couldn't hurt me. That story became my only weapon, a weapon my opponents used against themselves."

The Tuʻitonga contemplated this. "Well, blade-proof or not, you're the greatest warrior I've seen. In fact, removing the element of magic makes you even more formidable, for all your victories are not by divine aid but by your own hand. Plus, your opponent still believes you're blade-proof. He won't even try to stab you."

Six Fists looked across the sand to ʻAho's dog. "I'm not sure today's the day I want my freedom."

"Don't falter. With this single deed, you'll free yourself. With one act, you'll gain your liberty and repay your debts."

"What *debts*?"

The Tuʻitonga looked surprised. "When you came to me, you were but a curiosity in ropes. I unbound you. I elevated you. I gave you the trust and confidence of a king. I gave you friendship and respect."

"Is it not more true to say that I set aside my anger at the ill treatment I received by Tongan hands? Did I not swallow my need for revenge? Was I not initially hung naked by my heels so that all might prod me before forcing me to fight for sport? Yet, despite these indignities, did I not follow your commands, I who am of another people? Did I not offer you *my* loyalties?"

'Aho joined them at the broken bowl. It was clear he perceived their tension, and it made him smile. "You're wise to study the blades and make your selection beforehand. That long shard looks deadly." 'Aho pointed to the ground, where Six Fists seemed to glance for the first time. "But long blades can break. No, I'll take that medium-sized shard in the middle—unless you get to it first."

"You waste your breath," the Tu'itonga told 'Aho. "For my friend is impervious to blades."

'Aho then gave the king the gaze one offers before departing on a long journey. "I'm sorry, my brother, but something's about to happen to you."

"And what's that?" the king asked.

'Aho tipped his head to the side.

"You get it wrong," the Tu'itonga said. "I'll be fine. I'll be watching from the shade."

To Six Fists, 'Aho said, "I lament that we must clash, for I don't know you well, and I certainly have no feud with you. I guess it's just our fate."

"What is fate," Six Fists asked, "but the things we must submit to?"

The Tu'itonga took leave of his man. What more could he do? He'd offered advice, encouragement, cautions, and incentives. He'd given and given and given some more. Once in the shade, he realized he could feel his heartbeat in his skin. His vision skipped with his pulse.

The Tamahā appeared beside him. "You gift us with the fearsome sight of Six Fists in action again. I've not seen him fight since his defeat of Valatoa. What a battle that was. People speak of it like it happened yesterday, though really it's been, what, six years? I'm sure you've had many opportunities to see Six Fists demonstrate his ferocity since then."

The Tu'itonga thought about that. When *was* the last time he'd seen Six Fists fight? In the years since his clash with Valatoa, he could recall nothing. He glanced at the tall man, who stood stiff and nervous beside his white dog. The Tuʻitonga wanted to shout at the man, tell him to take deep breaths, to loosen up, but he knew Six Fists already held too many instructions in his head.

"And your brother," the Tamahā said. "The fight has yet to begin and already he's injured."

"What's this?"

"You don't see his wound?" she asked.

He looked across the sand to his brother, who was speaking with his son. "*Wound?*"

The Tamahā offered the Tuʻitonga a sweet smile—it was the kind she'd give a Fefine Girl who'd said something especially innocent or stupid. "Tell ʻAho to see me after the contest. I'll apply a salve to prevent infection."

"Should he be fortunate enough to survive, you mean."

"Just tell him," she said before rejoining her entourage.

Of course, the Tamahā was just tying his mind knots. Still, he studied his brother's torso and limbs. He watched as ʻAho went to his knees so he could look into the eyes of his son, as ʻAho took his son's hands and began speaking to him. The words were indiscernible, but really, they didn't matter, for here was a father, eyes focused solely on his boy, and even from here, it was obvious ʻAho was speaking in a register of comfort and reassurance. Before long, Mateaki was nodding and standing straighter.

The Tuʻitonga had been making plans for his own family's transitions. He'd been preparing his sons for the day he would no longer be king. But had he prepared them for the day he'd no longer be their father? The Tuʻitonga called Finau over.

"What?" Finau asked.

The Tuʻitonga stared at him. What language gave solace to a boy before your departure, not from a chiefly position, but from his life? Even though it'd happened to the Tuʻitonga himself, even though his own father had died when he was young, he lacked the words. So he ruffled his boy's hair and pulled him close.

Matāpule Muʻa stepped forward and waved his fly whisk—the fetaʻaki was under way.

ʻAho squatted beside his dog, one hand on its pigskin collar. Six Fists's eyes flashed from his opponent to the ceramic daggers between them. And then it began. Six Fists abandoned his dog and dashed for the blades, sand kicking behind him. Two things happened at once. 'Aho's dog, seeing Six Fists advance, advanced itself, bounding forward. And Six Fists's dog, seeing Six Fists flee, gave chase. The white dog took Six Fists from behind. Securing an ankle, it brought him down. This knocked Six Fists's vala kilt open, leaving him naked as the day he'd arrived in bondage. 'Aho's dog seized a forearm, and both beasts began to hazard the tall man from Nuku Hiva, heads shaking, throats agrowl, their tails whipping gleefully. Six Fists was still able to sit upright, though his body jerked one direction and then another with the tug of dog teeth.

The Tuʻitonga broke the silence. "Grab its throat," he shouted.

"Attack the eyes," another man called.

If Six Fists heard these commands, he made no such attempts. Writhing, he tried to twist free. At last, in an effort to dislodge the dogs, he attempted to roll, but the move left Six Fists flattened in the sand. Now the dogs began tugging in opposite directions.

"There's no honor in this," one of Six Fists's men shouted.

"This isn't the Tongan way," another called.

The Tamahā's matāpule said, "Both parties agreed to the terms."

It was then that 'Aho's dog locked onto Six Fists's throat. The man's eyes went wide with horror. He took hold of the dog's coat but did little with this purchase, for it was likely that his every action resonated through the dog's teeth back into his own neck.

A restless, hand-wringing silence settled over the spectators.

At last, the dog deepened its bite, sank its nails into the sand, and began to shake.

"Six Fists!" a warrior called before running, spear raised, at the dog.

The Tamahā cracked her Fan at the warrior, whose skin flashed from his body, stopping him in his tracks. The man beneath was made plain—tendon, vessels, striated tissue. The entire whites of his eyes were visible, giving him a look of sad surprise, yet without lips or eyebrows his true expression could not be read. Turning, he saw his skin hanging in ribbons from branches of a tongolei tree. He took two steps, went to his knees, and fell forward in the sand.

For the first time, 'Aho moved. He didn't select a dagger from the broken bowl. Instead, he made his way to Six Fists, where, with great dispassion, he regarded the scene below. "The man's eyes lose focus," 'Aho declared. "It's done." With a whistle, he called off the dogs.

"Six Fists!" the Tu'itonga shouted. He raced forward and dropped to his knees. "How've I allowed this to happen? I blame myself!"

Several sub-chiefs contradicted the king, assuring him that each man makes his own decisions.

Six Fists gazed blankly at the sky. He could make only a swallowing sound.

"I can't lose you," the Tu'itonga said. "What'll I do without you, without your advice, without your friendship?" The Tu'itonga placed his hands on his friend's ink-darkened cheeks, but how could he issue more life into him? The man's ribs still expanded with breath, and the Tu'itonga's tears, when they tapped down, made circles in the dust on Six Fists's chest. The Tu'itonga let his eyes drift toward the Tamahā, who, with her Fan, regarded the tableau before her. A few wafts could save his friend. But, *No*, the Tu'itonga thought. *I couldn't ask her that. I couldn't owe her that.*

The Tu'itonga patted Six Fists, as if to rouse him. "Would you like me to save you?"

Six Fists swallowed hard.

"I can save you, Six Fists. I'm sure I can, but I'll have to work fast." The Tu'itonga shouted, "Get me a freshly husked coconut and an oyster shell."

Six Fists's eyes, though lost, went wide.

"Don't worry, my friend," the Tu'itonga said. "Though it may be too late for your body, your spirit can still be preserved."

'Aho crouched beside them. "Save your energy," he told his brother. "The man fades."

"The opposite is happening. He's about to live forever." Then the Tu'itonga yelled, "Where's that oyster shell?" In a softer tone, he said, "It's okay, Six Fists. I'm here. Your long sojourn is almost over."

"So you agree to open the tomb?" 'Aho asked.

"Yes, the tomb'll be opened. But not now. Can't you see my friend is dying?"

This answer seemed to satisfy 'Aho, who noticed something in Six Fists's hand. He peeled back the man's fingers to discover a little pigskin pouch.

Opening it, 'Aho found a braid of hair and some baby teeth. "These must've belonged to his wife and children," 'Aho said. At last, out poured a sprinkle of sand.

"From the beaches of his home island?" the Tu'itonga asked. "How'd he keep it all these years?" The king glanced at his brother, and it was from this position that he spotted 'Aho's injury. "You're wounded."

With more curiosity than concern, 'Aho examined himself. Sure enough, low on his shin, a flake of pottery was lodged against the bone. "It must've happened when I smashed the bowl. I never even felt it."

There'd been no bleeding until 'Aho removed it. Then it was clear the flake had gone deep, for it was the size of a shark's tooth. Once it was removed, the cut stayed open, a runnel of blood issuing.

"You should go to the Tamahā," the Tu'itonga said. "She can tend to that."

'Aho laughed. "You think I'd trust her?"

Making eye contact, two brothers acknowledged a truth.

An oyster shell was delivered. The Tu'itonga looked down at his friend, who was fading fast. There was a small tātatau, just nine dots representing the constellation Mataliki. This was Six Fists's first ink, which he'd given himself when his vaka drifted so far that he had to acknowledge he might never find home.

The Tu'itonga broke the oyster shell, exposing a jagged edge.

Six Fists, blind now, winced at the sound.

"You're not alone, Six Fists," the Tu'itonga said. "Your old friend's by your side. And you're no longer adrift, for I know the way. Liberation, at last, is at hand."

TWENTY-FOUR

THE SACRED ISLAND OF 'ATA

Though it was midday, the Tuʻitonga reclined upon his pile of sleeping mats. Scattered around him were the coconuts containing the souls he'd reaped. All except for Six Fists's soul, which rose and fell in the coconut against his chest. When he closed his eyes, he saw Six Fists's torn throat. He saw the blade of an oyster shell sailing through flesh. Baby teeth, tipping into the sand.

Pōhiva reclined beside him. Together, they gazed at their wedding mats stored in the lodge poles above.

"I agreed to open the tomb," he told her. "I managed to put it off a bit, to buy us some time."

They both knew that only gave ʻAho more time to make trouble.

Pōhiva asked, "Do you think ʻAho would respect the sacredness of ʻAta?"

"Do you propose that after he slays my friend, I invite him to my private island?"

"If he doesn't respect the sanctity of ʻAta," Pōhiva said, "then he respects nothing."

"And if it turns out he respects nothing?"

"You know that's not true," she said. "Believe it or not, he holds much regard for you. And he values the Tongan way, as well as all things ancient. He'll behave himself on ʻAta. Meanwhile, we'll figure a way to outsmart him."

"For the sake of our sons, we must locate his weakness."

"Or locate our strengths," Pōhiva said.

"I suppose that if he were to cause trouble on ʻAta, he'd have to answer to the island's god, Laufakanaʻa."

"And 'Ata is near Teleki," Pōhiva said, "whose reef Lolohea must swim."
"After that, only two tests remain."

Pōhiva sat upright. "The Tongan Hull is next-to-last. For that test, Lolohea may select his crew. The Second Son could navigate while Finau provides support."

"Which would put them out of harm's way while I deal with my brother." The difficulty of that task made the Tu'itonga philosophical again. "But how to handle him? If his life is taken by my hand, I lose my soul, and if another does the awful work and the Tamahā finds him, she'll simply resurrect him."

"One task at a time. First we focus on getting our boys safe. Then we turn our attention to your little brother."

The Tu'itonga let his eyes roam the thatching above. "All right. I'll tell the matāpule. Tomorrow, we'll sail for 'Ata."

It was midday, the lagoon a calm expanse of green. Dragonflies etched the water's surface. Sullen clouds signaled afternoon rain. At the king's dock, a flotilla of canoes was being prepared for the voyage to 'Ata.

The Tu'itonga, much to the consternation of his matāpule, was personally overseeing these preparations. Or, rather, he went about unpreparing others making the journey with him, for what was the point of going to 'Ata, if not to return to the austere ways of their ancestors? Upon inspecting the vaka belonging to the chief of Kolomotu'a, the king discovered several pigs. "Remove these animals," he commanded. "On 'Ata, we'll take our food raw." And on the vaka of another chief, the king found a pillow, which he kicked into the water. "The soil of 'Ata will provide our comfort," he shouted. The Fefine Girls had made themselves lovely for the trip, rubbing turmeric on their forearms, feathering their hair, and coating their shoulders with oil. "Ladies," the king told them, "the point of the trip is to unadorn the self, to naturalize." They were dunked in the lagoon.

Into this situation, the Second Son arrived, wearing but a loincloth and a banana leaf for a visor. The boy's skin was salted, his chest flecked with fish scales. Pulling him close, the father gave his breath and breathed his son's in return. The Tuʻitonga regarded the fishhook necklace around his son's throat.

"Safe passage over water," the father said.

"Safe passage over water," the son repeated.

"The boy departs a middle child," the Tuʻitonga proclaimed. "He returns a man, a wayfinder. No," he corrected himself. "*The* Wayfinder. My son is *the Wayfinder*."

Matāpule Muʻa lifted his fly whisk. With a wave, it was done, the Second Son was now the Wayfinder.

"And what of Havea?" the Tuʻitonga asked.

"He's at his liberty," the Wayfinder said. "He intends to make reunion with his wife."

Is the woman not dead? the Tuʻitonga wondered. Still, he said, "Havea was a kindly fellow who served us well. I didn't get a chance to thank him."

"Serving his king," the Wayfinder said. "That's reward enough for any Tongan."

The king clapped his son on the back. "Now you're getting it. Come, you've arrived just in time to lead our flotilla to ʻAta."

The Wayfinder shook his head. "I must rest. It's been a long journey."

"Rest? What is sailing but an endless holiday?"

For a moment, the Wayfinder looked as if he'd lodge a complaint. Instead, he said, "We must leave quickly if there's to be light left when we make landfall tomorrow."

"There's the spirit."

The Wayfinder surveyed the progress toward departure. "Where's Six Fists?"

The king shook his head. "I ask myself."

Right before departure, the Tuʻitonga hastened into the trees, hiking his kilt for one last attempt to make urine. An initial spray raised his hopes, but this was followed by dribbles and pain. When he lifted his eyes, he was startled to discover the Tamahā.

"Can I find neither relief nor privacy?" he asked.

There was no point in trying now. He lowered his kilt.

She handed him a gourd filled with vai kahi. "I made it this morning. I added olovalo leaves and fau bark. They'll help with your symptoms, but the disease is beyond my reach." She took his hand, checking for coolness in the fingertips. "Are you better or worse?"

He drank deeply of the thick and bitter fluid. "I'm ever as you find me."

She pulled down a lid to inspect the color of his eye. She pressed a thumb into his shoulder to see how the fluid returned.

"Well?" he asked.

"Be faithful to your medicine," she said.

"That bad?"

"And unless you want to spend eternity half inked, tell that tufuga to hurry."

"When my earthly work is finished, I'll happily retire to the next world."

"Ah, the afterlife," she said, "where your enemies await."

She gave him a look, and he knew what must be done.

He lowered his bulk to the ground to remove the tapu he'd acquired from coming in contact with her. After circling her dusty foot once around his face, he said, "You're not getting any younger yourself."

She shook her head and walked away.

The two kept no tradition of parting words.

A line of canoes journeyed south, led by the Wayfinder, who sailed alone. The royal vaka followed. Then came canoes for the Fefine Girls, for various chiefs, and for matāpule. The Tuʻitonga had tried to leave the matāpule behind, but they countered his arguments with exceptions, precedents, and, most maddeningly, past pronouncements he himself had made. Finally, there were several vaka of servants. Why—why!—did it require more servants to live in a rural fashion than a regal one?

As the sun advanced, the sails' curved faces glowed orange. Tongatapu slipped from view, then gone were the oyster-colored cliffs of ʻEua. When the range of shorebirds was surpassed, the flotilla was, as they say, "upon the sea." On the royal vaka, there was no talk of Six Fists, whose recently liberated bones, in a basket, were lashed to the mast. They refrained from discussing the Tamahā, even though she was absent—she never spent a night outside her compound. And with 'Aho and his son present, no one mentioned Tongatapu's recent spate of assaults. It was good that these topics took their rest. In fact, the Tu'itonga could feel, with each swell they crested, his problems recede. The bickering, the disputes—they'd soon be gone. Gone would be the sounds of war dogs and Six Fists's last breaths. Gone already was the royal grave, which of late had come to feel like a family member: someone you were bound to, someone who'd always welcome you, someone who didn't necessarily wish you well.

The servants shucked oysters, passing them on the shell. First, they went to the Tu'itonga, who'd yet to pass one along, himself downing a dozen in a row. Though he'd already regaled everyone about his son becoming a navigator, he again raised the topic. "Did you see how modest my middle son was? I tell you, becoming a wayfinder is no small thing."

His other boys were silent: Lolohea at the bow, feet dangling, and Finau, face down, taking his ink.

What the Tu'itonga truly felt was this: *A son is safe, I've gotten one to safety. Two more to go.* Still, when the lead vaka crested waves, he was troubled by the distant sight of his middle boy, sailing alone.

Belly full, the king at last passed an oyster to 'Aho. He knew his brother would pass it along, not taking one for himself until everyone had their fill. Then he'd call for the oyster bucket to be placed beside him, where he'd untether his appetite.

The Tufuga timed his strikes to the beat of the swells.

Finau said to him, "I hope my father and I receive the finest ink in the world."

"I've inked many royals," the Tufuga said. "Perhaps I flatter myself, but I believe you're the beneficiary of my best work."

"So you improve at your trade?" Finau asked. "Each tātatau is better than your last?"

The Tufuga, being modest, didn't directly answer. "Some might say."

"I wonder where your talent resides," Finau mused. "In your sense of rhythm? Or your vision, perhaps?"

The Tufuga said, "My eyesight fails a little, but the ink still finds its home."

"Do your fingers possess the talent?" Finau asked. "Could you still work if you lost a digit or two?"

An involuntary laugh came from the Tufuga. "I can't say the thought's entered my mind. I suppose I could make do."

"What about your thumbs?" Finau asked. "Could you still ink if you lacked thumbs?"

The Tufuga paused. He seemed to grasp something. "I'm old and have long planned to retire," he said, voice unsteady. "Truth be told, I've resolved that yours will be my greatest work as well as my last. Yes, after your ink is complete, I swear I'll never take up my needles again."

"Forgive the boy his speculations," Pōhiva said. "Perhaps you should continue tomorrow, as the light abandons us, yes?"

"Yes," the Tufuga said. "The light abandons us."

The look on Punake's face suggested he was wondering what kind of poet he'd be without his tongue. He ventured a question to the king. "It's wonderful to hear the Wayfinder has completed his training. Any news of his supplemental father, Havea?"

"Old Havea," the Tu'itonga said, as if he and the navigator weren't the same age. "I hear the man journeys to make reunion with his long-absent wife."

'Aho asked, "Does the man not know she's dead?"

Finau raised himself to a sitting position, so servants could wipe the blood and ink from his back. Perhaps feeling for the old navigator, Finau quoted the ancient poem:

Iha fakataha ko ha fakamāvae,	*When a reunion is a farewell,*
ko e ulo e afi pongipongi	*the morning fire is lit*
ehe malala tamatemate oe po'uli.	*by the night's dying coals.*

"Who wouldn't give everything for a reunion?" Mateaki asked. "Even if a little late."

'Aho placed a hand on his son's shoulder.

That gesture, of a father comforting his son, struck at the Tu'itonga. He wanted to reach out to his own boys, and even to 'Aho, troubled after many years of war. It felt natural to have 'Aho around, so natural it was easy to forget he was the source of all the king's problems.

Punake, tentatively, asked, "So when Havea's service was complete, he was free to go?"

There was an awkward silence. Kōkī laughed, then quoted a poem about dashed hopes:

Ihe a'u ki langi e laumālie oe peau,	As the wave's spirit reaches skyward,
ko e ngāahi maka, oku ui hono hingoa.	the rocks call its name.

The Tu'itonga, impatient, said, "Havea sacrificed everything for Tonga. That prerequisite met, the man's fate, as he should've known all along, was my son's to decide."

Punake stole a look at Finau's face, but the boy didn't seem to be listening.

Under his breath, Punake said, "Maybe Havea didn't sacrifice *everything*."

The Tu'itonga pretended not to hear this. Sometimes the lowly needed their say.

"Tātatau," Pōhiva said to the Fisian boy Vula. She indicated the black patterns on Finau's torso. "*Tātatau.*"

Vula, at the end of the tether, said nothing.

The meteor was on deck. The Tu'itonga had brought it, hoping to discover the object's natural state—cool or hot, earth or sky. Pōhiva touched this, saying, "Fetu'u tō, fetu'u tō." *Falling star.*

The Fisian boy was silent.

"Does he show any inclination to our words?" Lolohea asked.

Pōhiva said, "What makes a person want to learn a language except by being drawn to the people who speak it? If the boy's given love, the words will follow."

'Aho said, "That's the danger in learning an enemy's language. If we come to know their words, we'll come to know them. Then how'll we fight our war?"

"If you hand-feed the boy Tongan words, he'll spit them out," the Tu'itonga said. "But if he thinks he'll need our language to survive, he'll devour every syllable."

"If I could humbly posit," Punake said, "it's only through poetry that he'll come to love our language. For, if he doesn't love our Tongan words, if he doesn't see their beauty, he'll learn our language as a slave learns to farm our fields, knowing he'll never taste the food he grows."

"Punake's right," Finau said. "You must cherish words to remember them. I still remember the day my father presented Punake to me. The poet looked at me, just a boy, and said, *The fish is still wet with the sea*. It was my first line of poetry. I was scared, I thought my father was giving me away to a stranger. But the words comforted me, and I realized my father was instead giving the man to me."

"Kōkī wish he knew parrot talk," Kōkī said. "Kōkī's parents made sounds, but Kōkī not recall them." Kōkī dropped his feathers in sadness. "*Nea*, do parrots even make poems?"

Finau pulled his bird close. "In the afterlife, you'll find your parrot language restored." Then Finau quoted the old poem:

Ko e ngāahi matapā hū'anga ki Pulotu, 'oku ava,	*The gates of the afterlife do open.*
Ma'u pē ki loto a 'enau avangia.	*Ever inward do they swing.*

The Tu'itonga regarded Finau. Fire and language, that's what the boy was filled with. Was there a more potent combination? The Tu'itonga contemplated how his middle son had finally been initiated, how his older son was only a few tests away from becoming king. The Tu'itonga wondered if, in his remaining days, he might get rid of Punake and devote his efforts to raising Finau himself. The thought brought him great solace.

Vula said something in his own language.

One of the vaka's crewmen said, "I know a little of his talk. He asks the Tongan word for *need*."

Smiling, Pōhiva turned to Vula. She said, "Fie, fie."

The boy and the crewman spoke again.

"He wishes to know our word for *home*," the crewman said.

The Tu'itonga said, "Tell him our word for home is *Tonga*."

The crewman spoke to the boy, and the boy spoke back.

"He asks," the crewman said, "if *Tonga* truly is our word for home."

"As far as he's concerned," the Tuʻitonga said, "yes."

The crewman said, "He now wants to know our word for *mother*."

The Tuʻitonga turned to Vula. "*Pōhiva*. It's Pōhiva."

The Fisian boy contemplated these words. "Fie Tonga Pōhiva," he said. "Fie Tonga Pōhiva."

Tears came to Pōhiva's eyes. She hugged Vula tight.

Fie Tonga Pōhiva, the Tuʻitonga thought. Never had a child had it so right.

"You should reward the child by removing his tether," the king told his wife. "There's nowhere for him to go, anyway."

With darkness came the firmament, the ten heavens of Tonga. The flotilla kept formation via keleʻa calls, the Wayfinder blowing a conch shell and listening for the other canoes to sound off.

A volley of laughter, followed by clapping, rose from the vaka carrying the Fefine Girls.

From the servants' vaka, the Tuʻitonga heard low singing, the kind that gives solace to those whose fate is servitude.

The Tuʻitonga, reclining, gazed at the comet: it mirrored him, sailing its own celestial sea.

The gates of the afterlife do open.

He barely slept anymore. When he closed his eyes, there was a throbbing in his veins that didn't let him rest. He thought of the Fisian chief, the man's son now relegated into adversarial hands. The Fisian chief's abiding thought, even after death, the Tamahā had said, was how much he'd left unfinished. Yes, the Tuʻitonga thought, there was so much left to do.

Ever inward do they swing.

Again, the Wayfinder sounded the keleʻa horn. He'd blow it all night, as the others comfortably slept. The feeling his son was likely having, the feeling that ahead were nothing but challenges, himself the first to face them, while in his wake was all that was precious—that's what it felt like to be king.

The next afternoon, they found 'Ata towering before them, a rock of an island whose greenery resided on a high plateau. 'Ata had no lagoon, no protective reef, no natural harbor, no beach. It was cliff and sea, with the only possible landfall being a field of black boulders, slick with green, assailed by waves as dangerous in retreat as they were in advance.

Assembled beyond the breakwaters, the flotilla's canoes lifted and fell as their passengers watched the Tu'itonga—a man at each shoulder to steady him—brave the surf. Once ashore, the king supplicated himself to make offerings to 'Ata's god Laufakana'a.

Offshore, Lolohea watched from the royal vaka. When swells lifted, he got glimpses of his father upon his knees, uttering sacred assurances. When they lowered, Lolohea regarded the dark cliffs, the entire island like a massive funeral stone. 'Ata was where, a few years ago, he'd isolated himself to take his ink. Laufakana'a was no minor god. His name meant "Speaks to Silence," and it was true—the quieter you were, the more the island communicated its essential nature to you. His father had given him exclusive use of the island on the condition that he refrain from speech. For a month, the island's only inhabitants were Lolohea and the young tufuga who tapped ink into him. Without people to sustain, 'Ata was abundant in fruit and wild with jungle hens. Scattered artifacts—pottery shards and broken blades—suggested people had lived here from the very beginning. Strewn among the tree roots were the bones of these previous inhabitants, disinterred by rain. Luckily, they'd left behind a cistern for fresh water. Its lid was a sheet of dark stone, and every time Lolohea drew a ladle, it was like drinking from a grave.

At first the quietude was unnerving. On Tongatapu, mornings were scored by the beating of bark, while afternoons echoed with warriors at their training. Porters chanted to coordinate heavy lifting. Rope binders repeated their twisting tunes. 'Ata, however, rang only with silence. Slowly, Lolohea learned to hear anew. Wind whistled through casuarina wisps. Drizzle fell through branches, the drops striking different notes on banana leaves and fau blades and the dry wings of cordia seeds. Only after taking his ink for several days did he notice the tapping of inking sticks echoing off promontories, sounding like the island itself was being blacked with his pattern. The forest, he discovered, could breathe. And one day, he stopped in his tracks:

the surrounding foliage seemed to speak to him. When he listened closely, the canopy above was whispering back his thoughts, as if the curving dome of the forest were an expansion of his mind.

The only words on 'Ata were uttered by birds. At dusk, along cliff faces, shearwaters returned after hunting the sea. Once home, they didn't land right away, preferring instead to hover above their nests, males and females reuniting by sharing their singular call—*ooo-er, ooooo-err*. In these simple duets, the shearwaters established the island's sole language, and by these sounds alone managed to convey everything mates might share on the subjects of constancy, parenting, survival, and the injustice of frigate birds who stole from their beaks.

Now, across the waves, Lolohea saw his father turn and give the signal for all to come ashore. It was time for their party to brave the surf before soldiering single file up the steep cliffs. Soon his father would be calling commands, issuing challenges, and administrating their every moment with his ever-present voice. The last thing anyone would find on this island was quiet.

By the time the Fefine Girls made it onto 'Ata's high plateau, they were miserable, wet, and ragged. Their feet smelled of bird shit. Moon Appearing's hands, after tugging on clumps of grass to help her up the steep trail, were green. And glancing down to the crashing sea had left her light-headed.

The Tu'itonga addressed his guests: "The ancients of 'Ata constructed no seawall, landing platform, or burial vaults. They needed no more than the nature you see before you. While we cut our trees in favor of fields, they preserved the forest. Birds we drove to extinction, they managed to save. For the first Tongans, Tonga was enough. Let's let 'Ata be enough for us, too. Let's shed our modern ways and robe ourselves in nature."

Matāpule Mu'a waved his fly whisk, and people began entering the trees.

Moon Appearing knew what this exercise meant: farewell to her soft tapa-cloth wrap, traded in favor of rough leaves and exposed skin. All around, the trees were thick, without obvious trails, and the canopy was dark under afternoon clouds. Suddenly the other Fefine Girls scattered.

Then she saw what'd made them flee: the man they'd nicknamed "the Jellyfish." His arm was on his son's shoulder, as if the man were truly fatherly, and not the dark figure responsible for the boy's spooked eyes and muted nature. All she could think of was Kakala, who'd gone limp and fallen to the ground, eyes rolling to some distant place as she allowed other girls to spread her legs. Turning, Moon Appearing caught sight of Lolohea, who waved her near. She tried to straighten her wrap so it might hide her figure, but, wet, it clung to her. When she glanced back at the Jellyfish, his eyes were directed at her. So she made her way to Lolohea, and together they entered the 'ovava trees.

"I'm not the kind of girl who secrets herself into the shade with young men," she said.

"I only thought you'd like to freshen up. I meant no inference."

She felt her hair, which was unkempt. She wiped her cheek, leaving a streak of green. "There's always an inference."

Lolohea brought his hands together. "Then I apologize. I hope to see you at sunset, when we gather to watch the birds." He turned to walk deeper into the trees.

She looked back to the clearing but saw no sign of the Jellyfish, which was the only thing worse than seeing him. "Wait, where are you off to?"

"I have to wash the bird shit out of my hair." He turned so she could see the dropping in his topknot.

She scratched her arms. "Why aren't others washing up?"

"They're welcome to," he said. "But perhaps they don't know the island as well as I do. I've spent some time here."

"Why did you select me, and not some other?"

"Select you? You turned to me, distress on your face. And did you not attend to my dog bite? Am I not in your debt?"

"You have the Tamahā to thank for that."

"So I do." He paused, waiting for something. When it didn't come, he said, "Well, I'll see you this evening, and I hope you dance again. You're the only one who can truly move."

"My father visited Tongatapu once. He found flattery to be the sole occupation in the Sacred South."

Lolohea smiled. "Your father's a wise man."

She had to admire that, using flattery to defend a charge of flattery. "I don't like being lied to. I know I'm an awful dancer."

"Anyone can memorize dance steps. I said you could *move*."

She looked farther down the path. "So, what's out there, a bathing pond?"

"A cistern," he said. "It's small, but the water's pure."

They advanced through strangler trees, stepping over roots that wove through the forest floor. The canopy also interlocked, dimming the light and washing the path of color.

Moon Appearing said, "When your father described how simply the ancients dwelled here, I blushed at the thought of my home island. I'd bet nothing's changed on Hunga in a thousand years."

"My father doesn't exactly make the rounds of Tonga. So his notions don't always match reality."

"Still, there's something to what he said. On Hunga, people marry, rethatch their roofs every year, and when they die, their graves are marked with nothing but black sand."

Lolohea said, "What's it matter how you live, if you're happy? Some lupe pigeons prefer the comforts of captivity, while others wish to fly free."

Moon Appearing scrutinized Lolohea. *Lupe* was a base term for a virginal woman. Men were always boasting of the lupe they were hunting, the one they'd recently snared or the unattainable pigeon that made their mouths water. She didn't think Lolohea meant anything by the reference, which meant there was something innocent about him.

"And 'Ata's former inhabitants weren't undeveloped." Lolohea indicated a low, broken wall of stone, almost completely reclaimed by roots. "Birds didn't make this wall. Stacking stones—that's what people do when they clear fields. Where we walk, crops were once grown. Only after the people were gone did the island reclaim itself."

"Where'd they go, the people of 'Ata?" Moon Appearing asked.

"Where do people go when they disappear?" he wondered in an eerily casual way.

Moon Appearing looked back toward the clearing. There was only heavy foliage. She wondered whether, if she called out, her voice would carry or be smothered by trees.

The cistern was at the foot of a dark massif. The rain it absorbed was filtered as it seeped down. Lolohea knelt and pushed aside a stone lid, revealing a bowl cut from the rock. "No matter how much we take," he said, "tomorrow it'll be full again." He took up the ladle and offered her a drink.

She sipped, the water tasting of mineral and mist.

On the ground was a flat black stone. "Here's where people washed themselves. You can see the impressions their feet have worn into the rock." He shook his head in wonder. "It's hard to imagine, stone worn down by human flesh. It's like time has become visible, like generations have shown themselves." He waved her closer, then poured a ladle upon the stone.

"What d'you think?" he asked.

"Think of what?"

"This is one of my favorite sounds," he said. "Water clapping against this stone."

He poured another ladle, and this time she could hear it, the slap and clatter, the echo of the splatter off the outcrop, and the pitter of spray against pebbles.

"Stand here," he said. "In the depressions."

She complied. He ladled water over her forearms and hands before scrubbing them, gently, with coconut fiber. He didn't speak, just washed and rinsed her hands. There was only the sound of water falling at their feet. Letting a man touch your inner wrist was one thing. Letting him handle your calves was another. She imagined her mother at her age, standing awkwardly and unable to see her feet because she was already baby-bound. Only the war, and the loss of boys her age, had spared Moon Appearing that fate. Still, she found herself allowing Lolohea his will. Here was the prince of Tonga running his thumb along her ankles.

"You haven't done this before, have you?" she asked. "Attended maidens at your special well?"

He looked up with surprise. "I lived alone on this island. I took a vow to make no speech while in residence."

"And did you?"

Offended, he asked, "Did I break my vow?"

She placed a hand on his shoulder so she could lift her feet, one by one, to allow him to run his palm along her soles. When he worked his fingers between her toes, her stomach dropped. No man had ever touched her in such a remote and vulnerable place.

"That's enough," she said, taking a breath. "I'm clean."

"Refreshing, yes?"

She nodded.

"Excellent," he said. "I'll take but a moment. The sun declines, and still we must make our garments." Lolohea stepped onto the stone. She did not lay hands upon him; instead, she poured water as he quickly and roughly scrubbed his arms and hands.

"How much time did you spend on this island?" she asked.

"Not enough." She ladled scoop after scoop upon him. When he was done, he stomped his feet to shed the excess water. "Shall we be on to the next endeavor?" he asked.

"Haven't you forgotten something?" She pointed at her own hair.

"Oh yes," he said. "That."

"I can help," she said, and when he crouched, she released his hair, which was surprisingly long, before pouring several ladles to remove the worst of it.

"On this island," he said, "if you're quiet, you'll start to hear your thoughts. After a while, you can even hear the island's."

"Island's what?"

"Thoughts."

It didn't take long to wash the offense away. Yet her fingers lingered in his hair.

He said, "My father has me completing a series of challenges. 'Tests,' he calls them. I hate them, trust me. Remaining silent on 'Ata was the only one that one benefited me."

"Perhaps I'll try my hand at some of this silence."

"Ha!" Lolohea barked.

Using his hair, she swiveled his head to see his expression. He was smiling!

"A Fefine Girl, silent?" He laughed again. "All you girls do is bicker and gossip."

"I'm not like those girls."

Still laughing, he said, "I know, I know, you're not like them, I'm sure of it. It was just the *idea* of a Fefine Girl being quiet. Of course you're not like them, not at all." He rose to his feet and faced her. He tried to speak some more, but before he could get the words out, he laughed again.

"Do you not know that women have been taught their entire lives not to speak their true minds?"

Chastened now, he nodded.

"They speak of trivial things because topics of consequence invite dangerous scrutiny."

Soberly, he said, "I hear you."

"And I'll have you know I could hold my tongue as long as I liked. Forever, if it pleased me!"

"I apologize. It's just that I've spent my life around those girls. My mother was one."

"Trust me," she said. "Becoming like them—that's the last thing I'd want."

"So what do you want?"

"I'd like to not be mocked and insulted, thank you."

He lifted his hands to declaim his innocence.

She regarded him until she was assured of his sincerity. "What is it *you'd* like?"

"That's easy. I already got what I wanted, which is returning to 'Ata. I'd live here if I could." He poured two ladles of water across the black rock. "I like to leave the stone clean."

"For the next person, on an uninhabited island?"

"We're here, aren't we?" He gave her a sideways look. "You evaded the question of what *you'd* want."

"You think a girl shares her desires with any boy who comes along with bird shit in his hair?"

"Well, then, the man who gains your confidence will be of a rare breed." He knelt to replace the stone lid. "The cistern has always looked like a grave to me," Lolohea said as he heaved it shut. "I can't help thinking of it as a vaitupu putu." *A funeral well.*

"No," she said. "It's life-giving. It's special. I'd call it, he vaitupu fufū." *The secret cistern.*

She'd used the word *fufū*, a secret kept between two people, rather than *me'a fakalilolilo*, a secret kept to oneself, or *me'a fakafufū*, a secret possessed by a group.

"I like the sound of that," he said. "*Si'eta vaitupu fufū.*" Our secret cistern. He'd added the word *our* and used *si'eta*, its emotional form. He replaced the ladle on its peg. "Shall we set about on our tasks?"

Moon Appearing hadn't missed that he'd linked them with a pronoun. Like his reference to lupe pigeons, she set it aside. "All that time you were silent on this island—what'd you think about?"

Lolohea put up his wet hair and tied it off. "I suppose I didn't think so much as listen. I meant what I said—this place gives you back your thoughts."

Moon Appearing wondered what thoughts would roam 'Ata if freed from her mind: Feeling endlessly, woefully inadequate? Her queasiness at being married off to an old man? Her fears of facing an assailant without front teeth? That's one thing she didn't worry about on Hunga—she knew every man on the island and feared none of them.

Some look must have come to her face, for Lolohea said, "It's not a bad thing, communing with this island. You should try it."

"You mean, like now?"

He shrugged. "It'll be dark before long. We could try silence until then."

"Silence," she said, testing the sound of it.

Moon Appearing and Lolohea hadn't declared any intentions to remain silent; they just stopped talking. Then neither seemed willing to be the first to speak. So they moved wordlessly about the island's high plateau, which was ringed by volcanic cliffs and promontories of basalt. These escarpments affected how sound moved, echoing noises, refracting them, making them seem to come from untrue directions. Moon Appearing and Lolohea paused to point things out: birds located by their calls, tree limbs creaking in the wind, feral chickens clucking unseen. Moon Appearing pointed to a patch of bamboo, though what she really pointed toward was a shimmering whisper.

As the pair walked on, tuitui trees seemed to form a chain littering the ground with candlenuts, their brown husks cracked by rats' teeth. In the limbs above, she heard her aunt's voice: *Never let yourself become separated.* She noticed a lone kaute bush and wondered if the ancient women of 'Ata had cultivated it for its abortive powers, or whether it was an innocent plant, blossoms striving for pollination on an isolated island.

Lolohea lucked into the company of some sī plants. He harvested a bundle of their bladelike leaves for the kilt he'd make. Moon Appearing stopped before a fau bush. She communicated "belt" by pantomiming a ring around her waist. Lolohea handed her a little knife, which he kept in his waistband. Its blade was no bigger than a fingertip and worked perfectly for stripping the inner bark of fau, which when woven made the strongest cordage. Using it, she couldn't help thinking of the little knife the Jellyfish had used to fight dogs on the beach. Had he pressed that blade to the necks of the girls he'd violated, or did he prefer bare hands? She could still see oyster liquor running down his hand, the firelight in his eye. She could hear him clapping, clapping, see his eyes, his delight.

Lolohea saw the look on her face. His eyebrows went up in question and concern, but she only shook her head. The novelty of silence had worn off. Instead of hearing the island in some essential way, instead of connecting to the ancients, she heard her own thoughts, projected everywhere. She thought of Ate, who had to marry a grave to avoid her fate, of Lolongo, who was only safe in the land of the dead. And she kept imagining *him* behind trees, down paths, camouflaged by undergrowth. If only she had the Tamahā's Fan—with a waft, these woods could be denuded and nefarious figures exposed. She kept seeing her abiding image of him: smiling his missing-tooth smile, reaching dirty-handed into the oyster bowl before raising several high and slurping them raw, one after another, from a dripping, tentacle-inked palm.

They came upon a fā tree, the ground below littered with its dry blades.

Moon Appearing tried to clear her head with the task at hand. Making a proper skirt, one that's full and fluffy and therefore concealing of the female figure, was a long process that only began by selecting the finest blades of fā and soaking them in the sea. But there was no time. Moon Appearing and Lolohea harvested the dry, fallen blades, which they then rubbed in long strokes over volcanic stones to soften them and give them volume. She kept thinking of Sun Shower. *It's not me!* the girl had shouted. *I'm not the one!* She remembered Kakala going limp, her eyes rolling away.

They began assembling their garments, he stringing green blades of sī, she knotting gray strips of fā. Lolohea finished first. She turned from him, this being their only recourse to privacy. Looking the other way, she saw a puko tree, whose sweet-scented berries, when you came in contact with them, revealed their unpleasant surprise. Her eyes focused deeper into the woods, searching for a man she couldn't see. She heard Lolohea's vala kilt drop to the ground, and she knew the prince wore nothing but ink. There was a rustle or two, and a moment later, he clapped, making her flinch.

When she turned, he was something to behold. The green kilt rested low on his waist, revealing the points of his hips. His stomach muscles were defined, and they led into a valley of suggestion.

Now it was her turn. He faced away, but she didn't turn her back on him—she felt she must monitor him for attempts at stealthy glimpses. This made disrobing herself more nerve-racking. A modest girl, her mother always said, circles her body twice with tapa cloth. Now she was exposed, in these strange woods, before a young man. The moment was both more than real and less than real, like when a storyteller conjures a long-ago tale—you find yourself inhabiting it, even as you're aware it's but a vapor of words.

She donned her skirt, which, rather than softly shushing, rustled like the dry beards of palms.

He turned. No man had ever beheld her bare midsection, and this was where his eyes fell. Now she was glad they'd agreed not to speak, for she was afraid of what he'd say.

He'd also made a belt for her, woven from yellow hibiscus blossoms. It was clear he wanted to place this upon her. Should she offer him her back, so that he'd reach around her body from behind and tie it at her stomach? No, she faced him as he advanced. For him to extend his arms around her, they had to get close, cheek-to-cheek close, and it was in this proximity that she smelled oysters on his breath. She recoiled, stepping back. She didn't think, she was suddenly just gaining some distance, and when, with concern, he neared her, she found herself backing up more. And then she was running, one arm across her chest to secure herself.

She sprinted past a spooky cave, she dodged trees and vines, vaulted great roots. The soil was dark and lacked footprints. She truly heard everything, birds, wind, waves, a pounding in her head, and the heave of her breathing. She glanced back to see Lolohea in pursuit.

She was pretty sure she could outrun him, at least for a while.

She knew she wasn't even running from him. She was just running, and it was only now, darting through the brush, that she saw disinterred bones mingling in the roots. She thought of the story of Tui Ha'atala, who'd visited every island. Why had Moon Appearing romanticized this notion? Dodging vines and running down fallen trunks, she wondered why, why would someone set foot on an island that wasn't their own? Some islands were best left unvisited, she was sure of that now, for on some islands unspoken practices were certain to thrive.

"Moon Appearing," Lolohea called. "Wait, stop."

She didn't part the underbrush but pushed through it. She glanced back to see Lolohea, who issued an end-of-the-world shout to "Stop!"

To arrest herself, she grabbed a branch.

He caught up to her. "What's going on?" he demanded. "What's the matter?"

She said nothing, she couldn't catch her breath.

"No more silence," he said. "Just tell me what's going on. Are you okay?"

When she didn't speak, he took her by the hand and walked her but a few paces farther down the path, where several sea daisy bushes stood. When he parted them, a frigate bird hovered before her eyes. They stood at the absolute edge of a perilous cliff. Moon Appearing looked down, farther down than she'd ever imagined. From this height, the waves were but wrinkles on a grandmother's hand.

Lolohea exhaled. He kind of laughed, but it wasn't a real laugh. "We almost lost you. On the same day I get to know you, you were nearly taken."

Moon Appearing looked out upon the sea she'd almost joined. Off the island's coast was the lone pinnacle of Manupuna Maka. Beyond it, the downing sun. She thought of the Fisian girl, lashed to an old canoe. On the cusp of death, she only wanted to hear the voice of the chief who'd tried to save her. And now Moon Appearing felt she could hear what the Fisian girl had heard when she put her ear to that coconut: a voice saying, "The next world is visible from this one."

She took a chance. "You know what's happening to us, right?"

"*Us*, meaning you and me?"

She shook her head. "You have no idea, do you?"

"Idea about what?"

"Something's happening to us, one by one."

It was clear he noted the concern in her voice. "What is it? You can tell me."

"I don't think I can." She took his hand. Turning up his palm, she drew a jellyfish's bulb and traced its tentacles down his fingers.

TWENTY-FIVE

KŌRERO:

IN OUR BEFORE

For two days, we sailed toward home. Then, before dawn, the Wayfinder woke me. I looked up into his eyes. "There's a light," he said.
  I don't know if I'd been dreaming or what, but I pictured a single flame, about to go out, and maybe I was still kind of in the dream, because I visualized our hands, cupping the tiny flame from the wind. "You and I will save it," I told him. Confused, he pointed to the horizon, where a distant light flickered. It was a signal fire, lit for us.
  In the pink-gray glow of morning, the outline of my island emerged. And what a little island it was! With its cone peak and gentle slopes, its sheltered cove. As soon as we could discern its finer features, a far-off conch shell blew. The Wayfinder responded with our newly acquired shell. Shortly, we were on the beach, making our reunions. If my parents were cross with me, they didn't show it. Instead, they showered me with hugs. I could smell on them the smoke of the signal fire they'd been tending. Instead of pressing me with questions, they alternately held me and stared at me with wonder.
  While Finau unloaded his haul of battle-proven spears and additional greenstone clubs, Ihi was coaxed onto shore, where she clung to Hine's side as an entire island lavished attention on its youngest member. Tiri went to her knees, arms open in joy. "Is it so?" she asked. Her clouded eyes misted over, and she trembled to be in the presence of a child again, even a silent one she couldn't see. I saw Hā Mutu watching from the edge of the circle.

He'd never married, never had children, this man who preferred to crouch quietly beneath his bird snares—even he marveled at the sight.

Most evident was this: we weren't meant to not have children around. To be *us*—the people we came from and had to stay true to—we'd need to change.

My father approached the Tongan brothers. Wordlessly, he grasped them by the backs of their necks, one in each hand. He pulled Finau close to share the breath of life. Then he exchanged breath with the Wayfinder.

"You brought her back," my father said.

Finau shrugged in modesty.

"I didn't do anything," the Wayfinder said. "I only held the steering oar."

Released, the Tongans looked like boys, their faces overcome to have a father take them in hand. In that moment, they seemed ready to do anything for him.

Ihi appeared overwhelmed to be surrounded by so many. Hine took the girl's hand. "It's time for a bath," Hine said. Tiri took Ihi's other hand, and the three began walking toward the longhouse. The sight brought tears to people's eyes: three generations, hands entwined. A simple story, yes, yet an epic one, a tale so ancient and human it didn't need words.

No one spoke while they departed, and after they were gone people remained quiet. For too long.

"What?" I asked.

Papa Toki turned to my parents. "Are you going to tell her?" he asked.

My mother nodded. "There's been a development," she said.

They took me to an open grave at the edge of a clearing. I remembered the dog had been digging here before we'd left. The soil had been excavated, but bones lay undisturbed at the bottom, forming the general outline of a human. Visible among the ribs were remnants of a necklace made from yellow coral. There was no such coral around these parts. There were no stories of yellow coral in Aotearoa.

Tapoto asked, "Strangers have set foot on our island?"

The Wayfinder knelt to peer into the grave. Leaning down, he strained to reach deep inside. With his fingertips, he fumbled through the coral and ribs until he retrieved a fishhook pendant. Showing it to us, he said, "This is the tomb of a Tongan navigator. This is the body of Māsilafōfoa."

"You know this person?" my mother asked.

"I know his story," the Wayfinder said. "I begged my master countless times for Māsilafōfoa's tale."

I asked the Wayfinder, "Is this the navigator who set sail with his entire family?"

"Māsilafōfoa famously embarked with an entire village," the Wayfinder said. "This would have included servants, matāpule, laborers, and even a priest or two. Perhaps forty people."

"Forty people," my father said. "That's more than we started with."

"Forty people?" Tapoto asked. "Where'd they go?"

Papa Toki pointed into the grave. "He didn't go anywhere."

I still didn't understand the significance of what I was seeing. I was only thinking about stories. I said to the Wayfinder, "Those other Tongan navigators—the one with the parrot, and the other with his boy—they found no land at all. And Māsilafōfoa, he went no farther than here. You've gone as far south as any navigator known."

"Havea made it farther," he said.

"But he didn't live to tell," I said.

Hā Mutu understood what he saw. "There was a people here before us, and we didn't even know it."

"They lived entire lives," my mother said. "They probably got married, had kids."

My father said, "Maybe they founded a society, maybe they expanded, grew, lived, and died out."

Finau said, "Maybe they got tired of this place and simply moved on."

"Or maybe they starved to death," Papa Toki said.

"We thought this island was empty," my mother said. "It was just depopulated."

Not far away, the dog started digging.

Papa Toki said, "Looks like he found another Tongan."

Dinner that night was a somber affair. Clouds descended, shrouding us in mist. It dampened the firelight. It whitened spiderwebs, making them visible.

Hine introduced Ihi, describing what she knew of the girl—that Ihi liked song and dance, that she was resourceful, nimble, and athletic. "Ihi will be staying with us until her mother comes to retrieve her," Hine said, smiling, though her sad eyes signaled the unlikeliness of this.

Arms clean, freshly skirted, Ihi could've been any little girl. You'd never guess she'd been found scavenging an island of the dead. She held a rope that terminated around the dog's neck. I didn't know if the dog was tethered to provide Ihi comfort or to keep it from digging up more graves.

Our meal, while lacking substance, at least had variety: portions included various berries, shoots, bracken, and roots. It wasn't like we were reduced to eating bark or anything. When we did eat bark, it was just to supplement a meal, to stretch it a little. And it was actually the *inner* bark you boiled, which was white and flavorless, easily edible. Only later, in the middle of the night, did you wake with intestinal cramps.

My father was in a good mood. Despite the fact that we'd discovered a previous people had gone extinct on our island, despite what that meant for our own futures, his daughter had been safely returned to him. He kept glancing at me, like he might suddenly share stories of when I was a baby. That's how I knew some part of him had believed I'd been lost.

My mother addressed the Tongan brothers. "You once said there were no available islands out there. I don't doubt your words. But people push islands from abundance to scarcity, yes? Must there not be places that are left fallow?"

"No islands are freely surrendered," Finau said. "They must be fought for."

The Wayfinder offered Finau an impatient look, one suggesting Finau hadn't actually experienced this. "Yes, islands become depleted," the Wayfinder said. "But why relocate to a place that's used up?"

Arawiwi was carving a little flute for Ihi. She said, "All I'd want are a few fruit trees, the kind you can pluck whenever you're hungry."

Hā Mutu said, "A place where birds still roost."

"Where there's fish enough to bother dropping a net," my father said.

"We're not hoping for abundance," my mother said. "Just a little less depletion."

"We're nice people," someone said. "What're islands made for, if not folks like us?"

"Why're islands so delicate?" someone asked. "Why don't they sustain us?"

"Why are they so far apart?" another asked.

Tapoto asked, "What if we went to Tonga and got some of those pigs and chickens you mentioned? Might that make this island livable again?"

"The journey you're talking about," the Wayfinder said, "you have no idea how long it is."

"When we leave," Finau added, "we don't return."

"Yet you don't seem to leave," my mother said.

"They're in the same situation as us," Tiri said. "They have no island to go to, either."

"At least we're aware of our situation," Finau responded. "We're not fooling ourselves."

What were people talking about? Leaving our island was an impossible idea. Anywhere else, we'd no longer be us. Our island was what made us us. I picked at my food. Of course, I'd eaten the berries first, followed by the green shoots. When I looked under the flax roots for something good I might've missed, I discovered some white, fibrous pulp, which'd been boiled.

"We're happy to tell you what you want to hear," Finau said dismissively. He gestured large. "We could describe an island just waiting to be found, one that's ancient and uninhabited, one that's mystical and bountiful, an island kept pristine for generations because it's so sacred."

That struck me as a particularly cruel thing to say. The Wayfinder gave Finau the strangest look.

"What?" Finau asked him.

"Well, that particular island . . ." the Wayfinder said, "it does exist."

People stopped chewing. Eyes lifted.

"Not as far as they're concerned," Finau said.

"What island is this?" my father asked.

"My brother's right," the Wayfinder said. "To your people, this island might as well not exist. It's the personal property of the Tuʻitonga. You can't even anchor off its coast without the king's permission."

"But it's bountiful?" my father asked.

The Wayfinder allowed that this was true. "Birds in the tens of thousands," he said.

Finau said to my father, "The island of ʻAta is an impossibility. For you to even set foot there, my brother here would have to become the king of Tonga."

"What kinds of birds?" Hā Mutu asked.

"And for that to happen," Finau said, "for my brother to become king, someone would have to kill the Tamahā." He lifted his eyebrows to suggest that was a discussion-ending notion.

"The Tamahā is the aunt of all Tonga," I explained.

"Why would you have to kill her?" Tiri asked.

"Technically, we'd only need her blessing," the Wayfinder said.

"Trust me," Finau said. "Murder would be easier."

"Yet we're forbidden from taking the life of family members," the Wayfinder said. "We're among the few people in the world who could never kill her."

There was a moment of quiet. Then my mother asked. "Could someone else kill her?"

I threw her a look. "*Mother*," I said.

"The Tamahā is as old and frail as her," Finau said, nodding toward Tiri. "But she has much power."

I thought, *If you only knew how powerful Tiri is* ...

The Wayfinder said, "Still, the Tamahā's a trifle compared to the real problem."

"There's someone else who'd have to be dealt with," Finau said. "Our uncle ʻAho."

With the mention of that name, the spirit drained from our Tongan visitors.

I asked, "What kind of blessing would your aunt bestow?"

The Wayfinder said, "It would take the form of a fan."

"A fan that gives and takes life," Finau added. "Among other things."

We didn't ask what the other things were, but the Wayfinder shared some. "It can denude, it can deform, it can amputate. It can blow a man so far across the water that he'd have no hope of ever swimming home."

"This fan sounds quite unpleasant," Tiri said. "Yet it also gives life?"

"It can revive," the Wayfinder acknowledged. "It can summon wind, animate trees, invite rain."

Tapoto cleared his throat. "This island," he said. "It's truly pristine?"

"The island exists as the first islands did," the Wayfinder said. "Back before people."

Tapoto stood. "You've mentioned this 'Aho figure before. He sounds like quite the troublesome fellow."

Finau gave him a look that suggested, *And?*

"If someone must deal with him," Tapoto said, "if someone must send him to the afterlife, well, that person might as well be me."

Finau looked around, disbelief on his face. "So you'd simply dispatch 'Aho, is that it? Then live out your days on 'Ata, grilling pigeon breast?"

"I didn't say it'd be easy," Tapoto said. "When the whale revealed itself to me, it told me I had a great destiny ahead. It also said there'd be sacrifice. I don't expect one without the other."

Finau stood. "You talked to a whale? And now you're going to challenge my uncle?"

"Actually, the whale talked to me," Tapoto said. "And I can't guarantee it wasn't a dream."

"My uncle, who's done battle with men, dogs, ghosts, and islands of vengeful women?" Finau asked. "My uncle, who fights all the way to the afterlife and back again?"

"If measures must be taken," Tapoto said, "I volunteer to be the man to take them."

Finau approached Tapoto, who, uncertain, cast his eyes among his fellow islanders. Then, with a stiff jab, Finau bopped Tapoto hard on the nose. Stunned, Tapoto lifted his hands and leaned his head back, ready for a gush of blood he seemed sure would come. That's when Finau punched him in the gut, crumpling Tapoto and bringing him to his knees.

"Got any other ideas?" Finau asked.

Papa Toki was quick to his feet. "You don't come to our island and strike one of us," he said.

Finau stormed his way. "You wouldn't be so brave if you had both your arms."

"And why's that?" Papa Toki asked.

Finau said, "You're not the first man to make boasts he knows he won't have to back up."

Papa Toki said, "I'm afraid I must invite you to duel."

"As you like," Finau said.

"Hold on," the Wayfinder said to his brother. "You can't fight this man. He's missing a . . ." Here, he pointed to his own arm.

"He's the one who aims to fight me," Finau said.

The Wayfinder turned my way. "Don't you people abhor conflict? Aren't you nonviolent?"

Old Tiri's eyes were directed into the mist. "If men willingly partake," she said, "and it's mutual, can it be considered violence?"

*　*

*

Some blood did issue from Tapoto's nostrils. The red could be seen on the back of his hand when he dabbed his upper lip. Tapoto's real injury, the one to his spirit, was visible everywhere—in his uncertain eyes, in his slumped shoulders, in the unsteady way he rose to his feet.

Once upright, he smiled, assured us he was fine, and then removed himself from the firelight.

I followed him down a path that led to the beach. "Slow down," I called after him. "Let's talk."

He didn't look back.

"Finau's not worth getting upset over," I said.

"I wasn't prepared," was all Tapoto would say.

At first I thought Tapoto was talking about the punch, but when we got to the beach, when we stood in the faint, misty glow of the moon, I understood he was talking about everything.

"The whale was right about me," Tapoto said. "In one glance, it saw my weakness."

I stood before him, placed a hand on his arm. "All I see are strengths."

"I'm unproven," he lamented.

"You sailed to an unknown island," I said. "Twice. There, you rescued a girl who otherwise would've died. That's a hero's work."

"I got drubbed by a teen from Tonga."

"You were caught off guard," I said. "He took advantage of your decent nature."

"I'm fat."

I shifted my hand to his torso. He flinched, but I didn't let go.

"You're big and powerful," I said. "Besides, who can control what they look like? Nobody."

"It's true what they said about me."

"What's true?"

Tapoto's lower lip started to quiver. When he clenched his mouth to stop it, his chin shook. "I had a secret stash of sweet potatoes," he said. "On the other side of the island. While other people went hungry, I would sneak over there to stuff my face."

"That's who you used to be," I told him. "You're not like that anymore, I know you're not."

Tapoto shook his head. "People like you, Kōrero, you're everything that's best about us. Me? I'm what's wrong."

I wiped a tear from his cheek. "You can't believe that."

He pulled away and took up one of his practice spears. "Whales don't lie," he said, and started twirling the spear around his body in flourishes that led to stiff thrusts.

I backed up, so as not to get accidentally whacked. "Do dream whales lie?"

"If the whale was a dream," he said, "then it was just me telling myself the truths I needed to hear."

I found the Tongan brothers down the beach. The Wayfinder was sitting in the sand, making one of his stupid star charts. And Finau was at the water's edge, hanging something to dry from their waka's bowline. I moved at him with purpose. Only at the last moment, when he turned, did I see he was naked. I shoved him with both hands. Knocked off balance, Finau tripped over the anchor rope and went down in the sand. "You know what you two are?" I asked them. "You're scared. You act tough, but you're hiding out on our island. The greatness of Tonga is your favorite topic, yet a single man keeps you from your home. You say you're looking for some life-granting island, yet you don't seem to search."

Finau looked up from where he'd fallen.

"My people ate bark tonight," I said. "Did you see any of us complain or run away or haul off and punch someone? No. That's because us 'nonviolent' people are tougher than you'll ever be."

I was breathing hard when I reclined on the beach between my parents. They said nothing. A dark mist hung above us, elusive and undefined. If a cloud could take on the texture of pumice, that's what the sky looked like. In the distance, we could hear Tapoto doing his practice fighting in the dark. He grunted when he thrust the spear, he shouted, *Kua mate mai i mua*, to stir his blood. He slapped his arms and thighs.

Our little family didn't review our day, we didn't talk about hunger, we didn't speculate on the hidden motivations of our guests. I wasn't asked about my trip to the island. I volunteered nothing about the little girl or the desolation we'd seen. My mother didn't say she was ready to face her fate. My father didn't say that meeting our fate was nothing to fear, as long as we met our fates together, the three of us.

Of all the things my mind could chew upon, I pondered the notion of a life-giving fan. Could it really reanimate the dead? What about a parrot after Hā Mutu twisted its neck? Could a waft from this fan cause the bird to rise and spread its wings? What of the washed-up fish that appeared like rare gifts upon our shores? Could one be convinced to shine again, to clear its eyes, flip into the water, and swim away? Could a waft of this fan invoke flowers to blossom, trees to fruit? Could such a fan make a woman bustle inside with life? What if it wafted across a depleted island? Could a murmur of this fan make all that was gone suddenly burgeon?

"Kua mate mai i mua," Tapoto shouted in the distance. He grunted, he clapped, he slapped his thighs. Over and over, he called, "Ehara i te taru te i ora."

I thought about those words. *There was death in the past. There was death in the past. Life is no light matter.*

My mother groaned. "Is he going to do that all night?"

My father rolled over. To little avail, he covered his ears.

Out loud, to no one, I said, "I can confirm, as Hine suspected, that their asses are indeed inked."

In the morning, I woke to the sound of Tapoto chanting, slapping his arms, and thrusting his spear at the dawning sun. So it hadn't been a dream. He really had battled all night: Against whom? His past self, his current one? Shielding my eyes, I saw him down the beach, lashing himself with his training drills. It was almost too much to witness. When I rose to go to him, my mother stopped me. "He'll come when he's ready."

There was good news, however: a dead toroa, the largest seabird, had washed ashore. The oily smell of its rotting guts was stomach-turning, but its carcass was covered in crabs. Quickly, we gathered these, as they'd wonderfully flavor a seaweed broth that would serve as our island's breakfast.

After our morning chores, when we were savoring that pale green broth, the Tongans appeared. Finau moved to speak but paused. He looked to the Wayfinder, who sternly nodded. "I'm sorry I struck one of you," Finau said. "We're guests on this island, and it could be argued that we've behaved poorly."

Papa Toki finished the last of his portion. "If that's an apology, it should be directed at Tapoto."

"No, I owe everyone an apology," Finau said. "I don't have an excuse for my actions. I can only say that I grew up with someone who used poetry to help me gain perspective and keep me from acting rashly. Without Punake, I haven't been myself."

People slurped their broth. Many folks were over the novelty of our guests.

"It's good that you apologize," Papa Toki said. He stood and began stretching, bending side to side. "But our business is separate from your issue with Tapoto. I've been wanting to teach you a lesson since you first arrived demanding chicken and pork."

"My brother apologizes for that, too," the Wayfinder said. "He actually has no wish to fight. We've talked, and he withdraws his consent to duel. He forfeits, or however it works."

"You've also never shut up about the greatness of your island," Papa Toki added. He leaped a couple of times, raising his knees high. "Tonga this and Tonga that. Your men were more dangerous, your women more beautiful, every meal a feast. All while you refused to even sit with us."

"We've offended you," the Wayfinder said. "For that, we're sorry. As the challenged party, we exercise our right to select the time of the combat."

"Yes," Finau said. "Let's agree to fight ten years hence."

"If sooner is better, then now is best," Tiri said. "The whole point of dueling is to settle conflicts and return to harmony."

"Yes, let's get it over with," my mother said.

The Wayfinder said, "Does my brother not reserve the right to select his favored weapon?"

"Feathers," Finau said, "I select the flight feathers of a parrot."

Amused, Tiri asked, "Grown men battling with feathers? What would a duel of that nature settle?"

Papa Toki said, "You're not getting off easy."

"Long spears are customary," Tiri said. "The terms of a duel are invariable."

"Spears?" the Wayfinder asked.

"I'll fetch them," Hā Mutu said.

Papa Toki called after Hā Mutu. "Make sure their points are good and sharp."

"You idiot," the Wayfinder told Finau. "How'd you get yourself into this? Am I to lose you now, to a one-armed practitioner of nonviolence?"

Though Finau seemed not too keen on dueling, he scoffed at the notion he'd lose. "The man's disabled."

My father shook his head at these proceedings. "You can't fight this kid," he told Papa Toki. "They're guests on our island, they don't know our ways."

"What kind of guest strikes a host?" Papa Toki asked. "Offenses, that's all these two have to offer, and I'm tired of it."

"They showed us the way to our sister island," my father said. "They took us there."

Papa Toki said, "Only because they thought it might help them find *their* island. And the price? Our greenstone clubs. Crafted by our ancestors. Clubs that are our taonga, our heritage."

My father turned to the Wayfinder. "I tried," he said. "You should know Papa Toki's undefeated."

"*Undefeated?*" the Wayfinder asked. "How often do you people duel?"

My father didn't answer. A circle of spectators formed. Papa Toki began running in place. "Never hurts to get the blood pumping," he told Finau.

"Hold on," the Wayfinder said. "Let's discuss this. There must be another way."

"Look who wants to talk about things," my mother said.

The Wayfinder turned my way, appealing to me with his eyes.

I said, "It'll be over quickly."

Papa Toki cracked his back, leaning one way and then the other. He swung his left arm in several large circles. Then the stub of his right rotated as well. The removal of this arm was one of my earliest memories. Papa Toki had scraped his palm on the reef, and within days, spidery lines began spreading up his arm. I was just a girl, but I remember Tiri shaking her head at the sight of those black tendrils. She still had her vision then. I didn't want to watch the amputation, but my mother said a woman needed to know how to take a limb, so Hine and I crouched nearby as several men held down Papa Toki. Tapoto sat on his chest, hindering his breathing. *I've accepted my fate*, Papa Toki said. *Restraint is unnecessary.*

Tiri looked at me and Hine. *Once you expose the bone*, Tiri said, *even strong men are not themselves.* This proved true. Papa Toki feverishly writhed, calling out from start to finish. So how was it I could remember the subtle sounds, like the crackling of rope as the tourniquet was tightened? Tiri used a sharp mussel shell to resolve the flesh. Once the sleeves of tissue were pulled back, the wet, shiny bone was revealed. *The bone mustn't be broken*, Tiri impressed upon us. *It has to be sawed.* With a jagged chunk of obsidian, Tiri demonstrated. The blade's serrations at first knocked along the bone. But as the teeth began to sink, the sound softened. Sawing into the pulpy marrow, the blade lowered its voice and began to hum, like an old man absently sharing a tune as he went about his work.

It's true there were things Papa Toki couldn't do, like paddling or drawing a rope, which required hand-over-hand pulling. Still, he lived a fairly normal life. He could even wield a spear by anchoring the butt in his armpit and guiding its tip with his lone hand. This he did now, fluidly whipping the tip to excite the assembling islanders.

When Finau was handed his spear, he stared in confusion at the long and flexible shaft.

The Wayfinder grabbed it. He bent it nearly into a hoop. "What manner of weapon is this?"

"It's a pigeon-hunting spear," I said. "It must be pliant to weave through branches."

He looked at me in disbelief. "Why, you'd have to strike someone a dozen times to truly hurt them."

I cocked my head. Why was he being so strange? "*Yeah*," I said.

"Doesn't that strike you as particularly cruel?" the Wayfinder asked me before snapping the spear in two and handing his brother the pointed half. Finau accepted with fear and uncertainty.

"Don't you think that's a little dangerous?" I asked the Wayfinder.

"How else is he to strike a meaningful blow?"

"But the point," I said, "is to—"

"We commence," Tiri announced.

Papa Toki backpedaled a circle around Finau, all the while twirling his spear in the air. This move generated a whistling sound that roused many hoots from the assembled spectators. Since our officiator Tiri lacked sight, Arawiwi provided commentary. She was a pragmatic person to whom nonsense was unknown.

"Papa Toki is light on his feet," Arawiwi said. "He feints, he taunts. The Tongan teen looks hesitant. He moves backward."

"Can you knock that off?" the Wayfinder asked her. "This is serious."

"Darting forward," Arawiwi said, "Papa Toki slashes the air near the Tongan's face. Papa Toki dances away, wagging his behind."

Tiri laughed with delight at this report.

"Do the pigeon," several people yelled to Papa Toki.

Papa Toki crouched somewhat, bobbed his head, and strutted in a circle while flapping his lone, spear-wielding arm. This brought cheers of approval.

"Get him," the Wayfinder told his brother.

"The Tongan advances, spear high," Arawiwi said, "only to be halted by the flash of Papa Toki's tip."

Papa Toki executed a smooth somersault to his right, coming out of the maneuver with his spear tip aimed directly at Finau. Then he fell to his left, only to spring quickly up, spear at the ready.

"The Tongan's face expresses bafflement," Arawiwi declared.

Someone called, "Do the pigeon again!"

"Come, now," my mother said. "Just finish it."

"She's right," Hā Mutu said. "Dispense with the merriment."

Papa Toki allowed himself a final ass-wag before relinquishing his smile and crouching to study his opponent. Fluidly, he dove forward into a roll—exiting this tuck, he sprawled on the ground, and from below, struck at Finau's torso. The move left Papa Toki flat on his back, smiling.

"He missed," the Wayfinder said. "Strike, now!"

Finau choked up on his shortened spear. With both hands he lifted it high, his eyes on the sternum of the man beneath him.

"No!" I shouted.

All at once, people called Finau's name, imploring him to stop.

Finau halted, spear high, murder on his face.

"What're you doing?" I asked. "The duel's over!"

Finau hadn't loosened his grip on the spear. "What?" he asked.

I pointed at his side. There, on his lowest rib, was a small wound, marked by a smidge of blood.

"The first drop," I said. "The duel concludes when the first drop of blood appears."

"They're not fighting to the death?" the Wayfinder asked.

"To the death? Are you crazy?" I asked. "What would be settled if people went around killing each other?"

"It's not to the death," the Wayfinder told his brother.

"*It's not to the death*," Finau muttered, lowering his spear.

Reaching for Finau's spear, Hā Mutu said, "Hand that thing over."

My mother asked, "You thought we were going to kill your brother?"

My father said, "They thought we were going to kill him."

My mother clucked her tongue. "These Tongans," she declared.

Papa Toki rose, astonishment on his face. "He was going to kill me," he said, not without some thrill. He spread his lone arm to collect the adulation of his fellow islanders. "I defeated a Tongan in a battle to the death!" He approached Finau, who seemed more uncertain than ever. "You were going to kill me," Papa Toki said. "But you didn't get the chance." This last part was nearly a song, sung into Finau's face.

"Step away from the Tongan," a new voice called out. It was Tapoto. His body was flushed red, his thighs, biceps, and chest bruised from self-inflicted slaps. Tapoto advanced, covered with sweat, until there was no distance between him and Finau. "Strike me now," Tapoto demanded.

Finau lifted his hands in appeasement. He took a step back.

"You wanna hit me again?" Tapoto demanded. He took a step forward. "Go ahead, give it a try, punch me anywhere."

Again, Finau sought to widen the gap between the two, but Tapoto closed the distance, bumping him with his great torso. "Strike me now!" he called before shoving the young Tongan with both hands, a move that left red marks on Finau's chest.

The Wayfinder stepped in. "Hold on," he said. "Finau has an apology to offer, we both do."

"Save your sorries," Tapoto told Finau. "I'm actually grateful you punched me. It gifted me with some much-needed clarity." He turned to the Wayfinder. "Let me tell you how things are going to work," Tapoto told him. "She!" he said, pointing at me. "Is going to kill the old Tongan woman."

People turned to look at me. They looked at me like I was an old-woman killer.

I thought, *Or seek her blessing.*

"And I!" Tapoto said. "I'm going to slay your troublesome fellow."

There was a wild look on Tapoto's face—he looked ready to murder trees and rocks and posts, anything.

"And then you," Tapoto said. "You're going to give us the island called 'Ata."

TWENTY-SIX

THE GARB OF NATURE

The Tuʻitonga's servants garbed him in a magnificent kilt. Though crafted quickly from gleaned materials, the kilt's green blades fell in double rows, suspended by a belt thick enough to support his girth.

Thus the king, in a superior mood, waited in the clearing for his guests to return from ʻAta's dense forest. Many of their costumes demonstrated true skill in anga fakatonga, the Tongan way. Then there were the rest. Who could say which outfit was most inept, incomplete, or ridiculous? They certainly afforded many "revealings" and some outright flashings of tender parts. Yes, this game of outfitting provided the Tuʻitonga with entertainment. But much information was also gained. He could see who in his company possessed practical capabilities—these tended to be chiefs from outer islands, men who were leaders, yes, but farmers and fishermen still. The Tuʻitonga could see who among his people had the gift of ingenuity, like the young chief of village Malapo, who'd built into his kilt a bamboo scabbard for his knife. The overly ambitious became likewise obvious; the chief of village Teʻekiu attempted a magnificent kilt, but, finding himself out of time, returned with an ass cheek visible. Also revealed were those who gave not a piss for the Tuʻitonga's edicts; a chief from the warrior island of ʻEua returned wearing but a string around his waist and a single leaf flapping before his ule. "This was the first attire," he said. The Tuʻitonga could make no objection to this truth.

Most entertaining were matāpule who'd not used their hands in years.

One, having failed at making an outfit, returned wearing nothing but a banana leaf. Another appeared in a serviceable kilt, yet the fool had fashioned it from hongohongo nettle. Already his groin was beginning to blister. Laughter erupted from the servants, for on 'Ata, observations of rank were suspended, and the lowly could make sport of their betters. On 'Ata, the lowly and the noble took their meals together and slept without division, the king's mat beside the load bearer's. The Tu'itonga found this practice of mixing the classes immensely rewarding. So he made himself available to those who were eternally, generationally lowborn.

Beneath a toa tree, he positioned himself between the Hau priest and Matāpule Mu'a. The Hau priest fielded spiritual inquiries. Matāpule Mu'a settled disputes. And the Tu'itonga heard complaints resolvable only by his singular power as king.

The servants knew this was a rare opportunity, so they formed three consultation lines. A female servant approached the Tu'itonga. A dispute on Niue resulted in her being sold to Tonga, where she now had a child. "I'll gladly live out my days in the service of Tonga," she said. "But what cause has my son to be indentured, except by entering the world? Please, use your great power to send him to my family on Niue."

The Tu'itonga exposited on the power of love, suggesting that separating a mother from a child was the greater harm. Then he gave to her the most valuable gift of all—good advice. "I offer an old proverb," he said. "Tākanga, 'enau fohe," which suggested that rowers must learn to move their oars in unison.

Another servant approached. The man said, "It brings me much joy to be a food-gatherer and fire-tender in service of Tonga, but—"

The king cut him off. He had just the proverb for this situation. It went, *Ala 'i sia, ala 'i kolonga*, its meaning being that a person good at finding food is also good at preparing it.

Having received his gift, the man did not, however, depart. "I'm happy to serve," he said. "But by chance I encountered some servants from Ha'amoa. They were dressed in a manner that might protect them from the elements and the flames associated with fire-tending. They had proper sleeping mats and kali pillows and—"

"Pillows? That's what you're after?" The Tu'itonga shook his head. "Do you see a pillow under my head? Yet I'm at my labors, serving Tonga without complaint. I'm afraid I must rescind the previous proverb and replace it with this one: *Pelepele pea mele*," a rebuke that meant a spoiled child humiliates all.

The Tuʻitonga was surprised to see Lolohea in line. "Here to learn how it's done, my boy? Soon you'll be sitting here, serving those who serve you."

"Father, I've been given to believe your brother is assaulting women."

The Tuʻitonga flattened his gaze.

"How've you known and not told me?" Lolohea asked.

"How have you not known? Maybe if you spent less time brooding or jumping off cliffs."

Lolohea moved to defend himself, but the Tuʻitonga lifted a hand.

"Please, Lolo, it'll be handled. But this isn't the time to discuss it. On ʻAta, we forget our concerns."

"Handled when and how? Do you intend to feast with ʻAho and sing with him by the fire?"

The Tuʻitonga's tone sharpened. "I gave my best friend to this cause. And I'm prepared to give more. What've you sacrificed?"

Lolohea didn't respond.

The Tuʻitonga wasn't finished. "You're still thinking like a subject, and not a king. You wonder, *When will this problem get solved?* Soon, my boy, every problem in Tonga will be your problem, and—" Some unknown pain made the Tuʻitonga wince. He felt his skin prickle, going suddenly from hot to cold.

"Father, are you all right?"

The Tuʻitonga clenched his teeth and closed his eyes. Before long, the pain subsided, leaving only beads of sweat and a buzz in his ears. "Your uncle ʻAho will do no harm here, for this is a sacred island. That's why we're on ʻAta, to purchase some time. And, son, you must remember that every man is plural inside. Your uncle is more than his worst attributes. He was once a thoughtful young man like yourself. That part still resides in him."

"Not true," Lolohea said. "When what commends you is assault and murder, you forfeit all else."

"You'll see. Sooner than you think, you'll see." The Tuʻitonga looked into his son's eyes, which were hot. He remembered being this age, single-minded, full of passion. "Leave it to your father to clear the stones from your path."

"There are stones other than the family rapist?"

"Do you truly wish to know? You never ask, and I've erred on the side of sheltering you. I'm happy to list the things that wrong-foot us. But by naming them, I put them on your shoulders. You know the old saying, 'Depart early for the mountain, and bear the fewest burdens.' I may have set you on your journey late. But I've encumbered you with nothing."

Lolohea left. If his son could stay resolute just a little longer, the Tuʻitonga thought, all would work out.

An old servant came forward and humbly posed a question to the king: "Why is it that some men are born into nobility, while the destiny of others is to toil in their shadows? I ask on the occasion of this trip. The great men around me have gone without their fine cloaks and rare feathers. I'm dressed as always, in leaves and grass. Equally garbed by nature, it appears I can't tell the difference between a great man and a lesser one."

"This is an important question," the Tuʻitonga said. "And it has an even more important answer."

But just as he was about to tutor this innocent fellow on the topic of inherent majesty, the Tuʻitonga suddenly realized the sun was falling, and the time for the next activity was at hand.

"We must continue this conversation on our next visit to 'Ata," the Tuʻitonga said, and then asked the old man to help him to his feet.

A WORD ON THE DESIGNATION *HAU*

The term *Hau* describes a person who's been ennobled by merit, rather than lineage. No man can change his rank, which is fixed at birth. A person can, however, attain status. This creates a path for exceptional people to rise. The Tuʻilifuka was a hau chief, earning the title not by bloodlines, but by blood spilled on enemy beaches. And when a man's divinations proved true, people turned to him as a hau priest.

Navigators had little use for priests. Could they predict storms or changing currents? Still, the Wayfinder set aside his skepticism to consult the Hau priest about Havea's fate. There was nothing "priestly" about the man. He looked and spoke normally. "Ah, the one who sailed to Fisi," the Hau priest said. "Your mother had me enchant a horn for your journey."

"I gave that enchanted horn to my friend Havea," the Wayfinder said. "Have you heard its call? Do you know Havea's fate?"

"I've heard no emergency call. As for the man's fate, I never even met him."

The Wayfinder had an idea. He removed Havea's fishhook necklace and handed it to the Hau priest. "Can you tell me of the man who owns this?"

The Hau priest took the pendant. Gazing into the middle distance, he said, "This item belongs to a great navigator, one who's spent his life at sea. I can assure you he is very much alive."

This came as a great relief to the Wayfinder. "Has he completed his epic journey?"

"His journey will be heralded as one of the greatest of our people."

"When will he make his return?"

The question seemed to confuse the Hau priest. "He's yet to even embark."

"How's that possible? When I last saw Havea, he was making departure plans."

The priest closed his eyes and concentrated. "Not only has he not departed, it seems he has no idea that he will depart. And before his epic journey even begins, he'll pilot a ghost vaka."

Stupid priests, the Wayfinder thought. *It's all ghosts and spirits with them.* That's how much he missed his old master, that he was willing to hear the prognostications of a charlatan.

"Give me back Havea's necklace," the Wayfinder said.

"Of course," the Hau priest said. "But that's not Havea's necklace."

"It's not?"

"The necklace belongs to you."

The Wayfinder couldn't quite make sense of the Hau priest's words, and he wondered if the man could be believed. Thinking of a little test, he pulled from his waistband the tooth he'd been carrying around. "This tooth was placed in my hands by a nomad, and I've often wondered why he gave it to me."

The Wayfinder dropped the tooth into the priest's hand. Immediately, however, the Hau priest returned it. "I want nothing to do with this. That tooth belonged to a man whose principal occupations are violation and bloodshed."

"Why would a nomad give me such a thing? Whose tooth is it?"

"Here's what I can say," the Hau priest said. "The tooth belonged to a man who's soon to die, but will have no burial. Yet he will continue to live, even after he goes to his grave."

All around, heads began turning. The Tu'itonga was being helped to his feet by an old servant.

The Wayfinder caught up with his father, who greeted him warmly. "If it isn't the young Wayfinder, who led the way to 'Ata. Many people slept soundly because you kept the vigil."

They walked toward the cliffs. "Father, I want to speak of Fisi."

"It's good that you saw our enemies for yourself. They're fierce, I'll give them that. If only they'd come to their senses."

The Wayfinder said, "I'd been under the impression our raids were about collecting tributes. But that's not the case. Father, we don't take a portion—instead, entire islands fall to our torches. Where villages once stood, only smudges remain."

"In war, all is forfeit. They, not us, insist on continuing the fight. Ha'amoa yielded, and now we're amicable friends. You see, nations make choices. And then war makes its own demands. War is not something you do—once it starts, it's something you bow down before."

"It's our appetites, not the war, we bow down to."

It was clear his father had tired of the conversation.

"Father, how we're treating the Fisians, it's not the Tongan way."

"Not the Tongan way?" his father asked. "Perhaps you hold a narrow view of your people. I welcome you to the other way of us."

"It's not your way, either. It's not how you taught me to treat people, at least, on the occasions you were around to advise me."

The Tu'itonga snorted. "I was often otherwise occupied, I grant you that. But you didn't lack fatherly guidance, as I did at your age. I gifted you with a supplemental father. Yet, I'm confused. Were you mentored by the great Havea, a fearless defender of Tonga? Or was there some mix-up and you instead took tutelage from a castrated poet?"

The Wayfinder didn't wilt. "You said it was important to get a look at the enemy. If you saw with your own eyes what was happening, you'd let them keep their gravestones."

"You miss completely the cost of war. When people pay in graves, what matter the stones?"

The Tu'itonga's guests assembled on 'Ata's southwestern promontory, the cliffs sooted orange by la'ā's decline. Before them, the limitless sea, where rolling swells extended to the horizon. Backlit by the setting sun, waves rose from ruddy troughs, relinquishing the sea long enough to ignite with hammered, sky-mirrored light.

The Wayfinder sat among his family, a sweet rarity. It was the hour when the seabirds returned, a sight both commonplace and spectacular, something that happened daily across the ocean yet was hardly ever observed.

By the thousands, brown boobies began arriving, only to disappear into the cliffs' tiniest crevices. These birds hunted by turning great circles above packs of driving tuna, taking baitfish from the air as they leaped to escape the predators below. A constellation of long-tailed tropic birds returned next, their white feathers lost against a draining sky. These birds straight-skimmed the water, ever calm, never veering, until the moment they dipped their beaks. Finally came the shearwaters, who swam down to their prey, using their wings as fins. They dived deeper than one could see, moving beneath the surface as bats moved, fluttering and turning, the water browning with their broadened wings. After a day apart at sea, shearwater mates affirmed their bonds with midair calls before retreating to shared nests.

The Tu'itonga, contemplative, stepped into the tempered light. Before him, columns of basalt glowed pink and flashing wings blotted the sea. "There's no land south of here," he said. "We're positioned at the terminus of the world. Except for the moment our souls depart our bodies, this is our only vista upon a world without time, without conclusion, and beyond intervention. This little island presides over the sea's indifferent industry, the way frigate birds coldly magistrate a sky without order.

"I often consider our ancestors' noble attributes. Did what was best in them make it down to us? Or did some of their defining qualities get dropped in the ongoing handoff of human lineage? Can we know what attributes never reached us? And which of *our* noble qualities will get lost on the journey through the generations, as an important object on a sea voyage, through a single careless gesture, is fumbled irretrievably into the sea?"

The Tu'itonga regarded his people. He cut quite a silhouette, the sea stretching forever behind him. "But we must remember that future Tongans will see us as the ancients. And they'll inherit from us only what we're careful to hand down." Before everyone, regret in his voice, he said, "I should've been a better father. To be king is to be the frigate bird, who keeps the highest watch. Facing the wind, he soars, his mission to maintain rank and status and order, yet he must fly alone." The king now looked at Finau. "I had to make sacrifices," he told his youngest son. "You must believe that. For years, I showed you my back. I own it. You must understand that life's like a story, and like a story, there's but a single path through it. This path is marked by the sacrifices you make, the kind that can't be unmade. A man is his sacrifices. In the end, he's made of nothing else."

The Wayfinder heard in his father's words a belief that he'd never see 'Ata again. It didn't hurt that he'd been left out of his father's reflections. The Wayfinder was thinking of Havea, anyway, the man who'd taught him to regard birds leaving the sea, not ones reaching shore, for the former could show you the direction of land. Their arrival, while inspiring, was only decorative, as arriving birds couldn't help you find your way.

The Wayfinder took leave of his people, following a path through the trees least likely to engender human contact. The far side of the island was in shadow, the trail off the plateau slick and dangerous. It was foolhardy to descend in the near-dark, and more than once he began sliding out of control. There were slick boulders to contend with and a crashing surf, but before long he was swimming through black water, and at last he was flat on the deck of his vaka, the familiar motion of the sea beneath him. He gazed upward. It brought him some solace to know this sky was also above Havea.

Accepting the fact that he'd never see Havea again was its own kind of journey, and he didn't know where he was in the voyage. There weren't stars for that kind of thing.

That evening, after a fire was built up, the Tuʻitonga tossed the meteor into the blaze.

The ensuing feast was taken uncooked, with guests seated in a large circle around the flames. Fruit was shared. So was raw fish in coconut milk. A vaka had been sent to the Teleki Reefs to retrieve mussels and limpets, which were eaten on the shell. The captain of this mission returned with unusual news: a ghost vaka, fully functional, was found drifting inside Teleki's southern atoll.

Kava was taken, and many stories of ghost ships were told, for even children gleaning the shores of Lifuka had encountered Fisian canoes that intended to make war upon the Tongans but had first lost battles with the sea.

There was no group dancing or choral singing. People sang solo or in pairs, each voice as plaintive as a longing for a home island. The Tuʻitonga sang the first line of a famous song about twin sisters from Fisi who swam to Haʻamoa with a basket full of inking tools. He crooned in the Haʻamoan language, his voice low and forlorn, "O le mafuaaga lenei ua iloa."

ʻAho volunteered the next line, "O le taaga, o le tatau i Samoa."

His singing voice was surprisingly high and childlike, with the lisp of missing teeth.

The brothers sang the next line together, "O le malaga a teine toʻalua."

People found this duet between the king and his unsavory brother most unnerving.

ʻAho sang the next line of the song, "Na feausi mai Fiji le vasa loloa."

After the final refrain, girls began dancing individually. Each, when she was finished, nominated the next. It was clear Moon Appearing was no favorite. When ʻAho rose to go relieve himself, a ripple of fear moved through the circle. When he returned, people were no less at ease.

At last, the Tuʻitonga ordered the meteor removed for examination.

Levered from the coals, the heavenly object glowed the pale yellow of the sun, white sparks crackling from its surface. No one need lend voice to the obvious: this was the meteor's true state.

After more kava, Lolohea cleared his throat. "I have a question for the Tuʻitonga."

"I make myself available for all inquiries," the king said.

Lolohea said, "You've described the ancient ones on ʻAta. But where'd they go?"

"This lamentable story is rarely told," the Tuʻitonga said. "Many generations ago, there was a Tuʻitonga who decreed his firstborn son would wed a chief's daughter in Lifuka, to help maintain inter-island peace. But the prince loved another girl. To evade the Tuʻitonga, the two young lovers escaped here. The people of ʻAta were not happy. Afraid of the wrath of the Tuʻitonga, they tried to push this couple away. The lovers retreated into a cave, not far from where we sit, and they wouldn't come out. So the people of ʻAta lit a fire at the mouth of the cave, hoping to smoke them out. Instead, the lovers were suffocated to death."

Lolohea asked, "But what happened to the people?"

"People can't go around snuffing out princes," the Tuʻitonga said.

Now Finau was curious. "But where'd they go?"

The Tuʻitonga said, "They went where people go when they can no longer be."

A somberness settled like fog.

"Let's have some levity." The Tuʻitonga smiled. "How about a poem from Punake?"

"I favor more dancing," ʻAho said. "I'd like to see that one move." He pointed at Moon Appearing.

She reluctantly rose, brought her knees together, and clasped her hands. With a teki of her head, she executed the first steps of the tauʻolunga.

"No, no," ʻAho said, stopping her. "I'm told she has a secret dance."

"Is this true?" the Tuʻitonga asked Moon Appearing. "Do you know a secret dance?"

Moon Appearing made no response.

"She knows the dance," ʻAho said.

"What do you call this dance?" the Tuʻitonga asked.

"It doesn't have a name," Moon Appearing said. "It's not even a proper dance. It's just the story of Lolongo, put in motion."

"Ah, a story dance," the Tuʻitonga said. "Nothing could be more delightful."

Moon Appearing, hesitant, displayed the tender insides of her arms. She leaned one way, then the other.

Lolohea knew these moves weren't the dance itself, but the before of it.

From the glowing coals, an umber color surged and softened across Moon Appearing, tracing the edge of her jaw, lending depth to the wells of her collarbones. The light didn't reach the trees, so there was a nothingness beyond her, like she stood before a forest that had never been, or perhaps was long gone.

"Lolongo was sent to the island of Pulotu," Moon Appearing said. The sweep of her foot suggested a shoreline and a space her movements would flow within. "She didn't wish to go, but she had no choice." The motion of her wrists suggested they were bound, while her countering hips evoked the pull of the afterlife. "All around Lolongo were nobles who'd met their fates. Alive in a world of death, her only solace was anointing them with lolo oil from the underworld's lone hea tree." When Moon Appearing applied a drop of oil to a spirit's forehead, Lolohea could practically feel her touch. "Her father, seeking a balm to her sorrow, slayed a wonderful young man for her. Lolongo was happy, but there was a problem—she alone lived in the land of the dead, and her lover's body was dead in the land of the living." She leaned back, turning, reaching for an unseen partner, and Lolohea could feel there were figures she danced among that were visible only to her. "There was only one way to get off that island. There was only one way to get what she wanted. She had to act."

"Yes," ʻAho called. He made a loud whistle through the void in his teeth. Pōhiva shushed him. "Let the girl dance."

"What?" ʻAho asked. "The dance is just getting good. This is the part where the girl steals the Fan."

ʻAho brought his hands together, clapping loud, each clap producing a wince from Moon Appearing.

"Pōhiva's right," the Tuʻitonga said. "Enough with your rough behavior."

ʻAho focused on Moon Appearing. He stood and began clapping louder.

"I'm afraid I must insist," the Tuʻitonga said. He struggled to his feet. "This is a sacred island."

ʻAho said, "If Fisian women can dance in bondage after their husbands have been slain, then this fledgling can be encouraged to move her limbs a little."

The Tuʻitonga lifted a finger, preparing to issue his brother a corrective.

Moon Appearing used the distraction to run for the trees.

"You ruined it," the Tuʻitonga snapped at his brother. "Now we've lost our entertainment."

Lolohea's instinct was to run after her. He forced himself to not act, lest his feelings be revealed. He'd have to wait for the next distraction.

A bitter look crossed ʻAho's face. He seemed ready to escalate his grievances.

Matāpule Muʻa intervened. "The moon is about to dawn," he announced.

The Tuʻitonga stared long at his brother before turning to his guests. "Yes, yes, come, come," he told them. "You've never seen a moonrise until you've beheld it from the cliffs of ʻAta, for here, you're able to look down upon a heavenly body."

Before the king could decamp, there was a commotion.

Kōkī, wings flapping, dropped from above and landed in their midst. There was something in his beak. He walked toward the Tuʻitonga. His back to the fire, Kōkī spread his wings and dropped a parrot skull, very old, drained of color, eye sockets cracked. Kōkī began pacing back and forth, glaring at the Tuʻitonga. When Kōkī glared, he hung his head low, almost upside down, and stared upward with a single eye. "Island once have parrot. What happen to Kōkī's kind?"

The king, amused, said, "My dear bird, I'm sorry you've lost your feathered companions. But these parrots were killed by the ancient ones. I'm afraid you must take the issue up with them."

Kōkī pointed a wing at the king. "Not them. You."

The Tuʻitonga looked to the faces of others to confirm the cheek of this bird!

Kōkī said, "They were people. You are people. You are them!"

Here Kōkī screeched, loud with outrage and disgust and lament, everything but grief—for, how can one grieve what is lost if it was never known?

The Tuʻitonga lifted a banana from a feasting bowl.

Kōkī shifted, studying it with one eye, then the other.

"I'm sorry for your loss," the Tuʻitonga said, peeling the banana.

Kōkī took a cautious step forward.

"Don't do it," Finau said.

The Tuʻitonga extended a section.

Punake said, "Kōkī, think of your freedom."

"Tuʻitonga friend with Kōkī," the Tuʻitonga said.

Kōkī cocked his head, blinking, looking from the banana to the king and back again.

The Tuʻitonga said, "Tuʻitonga sorry Kōkī friends extinct."

"Fly away!" Finau said.

When Kōkī took the banana, the Tuʻitonga grabbed him by the neck. Lifting the parrot with delight, he said, "I finally get to kill this bird." But then the Tuʻitonga hollered, Kōkī flew away, and the king clasped his wound. Everyone could see the Tuʻitonga grab the webbing between his thumb and forefinger. And no one could miss the red of royal blood.

Lolohea found Moon Appearing not on a moonlit cliff or at a secret cistern, but sitting on a log, just off a common path. He had no torch, so it was hard to see her face. She laughed a bitter laugh of sarcasm or disbelief, saying, "My father dealt young men into war so I could be here."

Lolohea thought, *They'd have been sent anyway*, but held his tongue.

"I can end the war," he said. "When I'm Tuʻitonga, I'll put a stop to it."

"When the young men of Hunga return from the fighting, won't they have changed, won't they be like *him*?"

He wished there was light enough to see her eyes. "Some of them, maybe," Lolohea said. "But Havea's been to war. So's my father. It need not spoil a man."

These two examples were easily rebutted. That they weren't suggested she wasn't interested in his answers. "What're we supposed to do?" she asked. "Just wait for it to happen, just wait our turns?"

"My father says there's a plan in place to handle him."

"By singing duets in the firelight?"

"I'll handle him, if it comes to that."

Moon Appearing didn't laugh at this notion, but it was something close to that.

"You said you had to pass tests," she said. "That's what I feel like, like I'm being tested."

"Sometimes a test asks nothing of you but to stay strong and keep going."

Moon Appearing took a deep breath. "People said this island was special, that it had been enchanted. But really, it's just been emptied, the people swept away."

Lolohea visualized the servants who swept footprints from the paths taken by the king.

"What're our problems?" she asked. "When entire islands cease to be?"

He put his arm around her. She accepted this and leaned her head against him.

"Yeah," he said. "What're our problems?"

The Tuʻitonga was being shaken awake. When he opened his eyes, he saw his eldest son.

"Something has to be done," Lolohea said.

It was dark. Moonlight fell through ʻovava trees. The king grasped that he was not at home, but on ʻAta.

"Lolo? What is it? Done about what?"

"Your brother. He has to be stopped."

The king was still emerging from a dream in which he hovered above a dark sea. Below, in moonlight, waves were completing their world-rounding journey. After opening their abalone-blue veins, they fell froth-white, surrendering the freight of their strife.

Lolohea said, "I'm prepared to do it."

"Do what?"

"Stop ʻAho."

This awakened the king. He extended a hand so Lolohea could help him up.

His son's eyes were flashing and uncertain yet determined. He liked how his son was formulating action, taking charge. This was a step forward, it was something a father could build upon. First, though, he had to get such a dangerous notion out the boy's head. "Son, I have much faith in you. But your uncle's a formidable figure. No single person can beat him."

"I'm younger," Lolohea said. "And stronger."

"True, true. But war's given 'Aho skills we wholly lack."

"He's weakened. His wound festers."

"Son, we're the only people in the world who can't kill him. If we do, we'll forfeit our souls. Instead, we must outsmart him."

"What if I kill him in self-defense?" Lolohea asked. "Is there an exception for that?"

"This is something you can never attempt. Promise me."

Lolohea looked to 'Aho's sleeping mat, as if to take the man's measure before vowing either way. That's when Lolohea said, "He's gone."

Among a meadow of sleeping servants and snoring nobles, there was indeed an empty mat.

"Even here," the Tu'itonga said. "Even on this sacred island, he resumes his ugly deeds."

Lolohea pointed into the trees. "There."

Surveying the heart of the forest, the Tu'itonga saw the flicker of a torch.

So the father and the son entered the woods. "Remember, no conflict," the Tu'itonga said, though the idea of coming upon 'Aho and his victim enraged the king, sickened him.

Wending through the trees, however, the orange torchlight growing brighter, they discovered 'Aho alone. In his hand was a human scapula, and with this he was digging. 'Aho looked up, warm smile crossing his face. "My brother," he hailed. "You've come to join me."

"What're you up to?" the Tu'itonga asked.

'Aho was crouched, lifting a delicate ulna from the soil. "Have you forgotten? Don't you remember our business here, many years ago?"

Then it struck the Tu'itonga. He dropped to his knees, placed his hands in the dirt, and took up a human rib. Studying it in the light, he shook his head, not in sadness, exactly, but in acknowledgment.

"Whose bones are these?" Lolohea asked.

The Tuʻitonga waved his son close, presenting the rib. "See these cut marks?" he asked. "I made them." Then the Tuʻitonga held his brother's gaze. Though they said no words, it was clear the past had become present again, that of a long-ago night when they'd teamed up to save each other.

"These are the bones of our uncle," ʻAho said.

"The one who tried to kill you?" Lolohea asked.

The Tuʻitonga said, "The very one."

"I thought he was fed to a shark," Lolohea said. "I heard you two defeated him, removed his soul, and in the moments before his death, he was eaten."

ʻAho smiled. "Sharks are messy eaters. These are the leftovers."

The Tuʻitonga uncovered another bone. "By his attempt to kill us, his own blood relatives, he abandoned any hope for the afterlife, so he couldn't be placed in the family tomb."

"So we buried him here," ʻAho said. "It's not the gateway to the afterlife, but it's sacred soil."

"Why bury him at all?" Lolohea asked. "Why not leave him for the crabs?"

The Tuʻitonga, surprised, looked into his son's eyes. "He was our uncle."

"The man taught me to fish," ʻAho said.

The Tuʻitonga said, "He shared old stories with me."

Lolohea tried to absorb this. "Why, then, do you disinter him?"

The Tuʻitonga turned to hear ʻAho's response.

Raking the soil, ʻAho said, "I think he's restless. I'm trying to give him some comfort."

Lolohea said, "But he tried to murder you."

ʻAho laughed. "I admit that the idea of someone trying to kill me was quite novel at the time, but it's no longer something I'd hold against a person."

"I used to blame him, too," the Tuʻitonga said. "But the more I thought about it, the more I understood that his entire life was a path that led to an ugly act. He simply followed along."

ʻAho came across the skull and levered it from the dirt. "There aren't but a dozen bones of him. When we find the jaw, he'll be complete as we can make him."

The Tuʻitonga handed a bone to his son. "We'll clean these off, say a few words, and then lay him down again." To his brother he said, "I see the wound on your leg doesn't heal."

"This? This isn't my real wound," ʻAho said. "I have a different injury, a deeper one."

"Let's get you some help," the Tuʻitonga said. "I'll summon the priests."

"It's not that kind of wound," ʻAho said. "If you'd been to war, you'd understand."

The Tuʻitonga was astonished. "My brother, we fought side by side suppressing rebellious chiefs. We bested the king of Tokelau, we—"

"You fought with honor," ʻAho said. "No one argues that. But you were fighting for Tongan land and lives. Therein lies nobility. I'm speaking of war, which you've never known. War is when you destroy people you don't know for reasons you don't understand, so that their lives become nothing, their deaths mean nothing, and you yourself, in time, become an unknown thing. We attack Fisi, and they defend. Theirs is the noble cause. A noble fight can actually heal wounds, it can set the broken bones of your spirit. But there's a wound that comes to the war-maker, one that lacks a source or a description and therefore a remedy."

Lolohea had no way of understanding war or the meaning of the words being spoken. All he heard was an attempt to chasten his father, to impugn his father's fortitude and ferocity, and Lolohea visibly bristled at this.

"Father," Lolohea casually said. "Have you heard there's a rapist at work on Tongatapu?"

ʻAho, scraping the soil with a shoulder blade, didn't look up.

The Tuʻitonga gave his son a grave look. Yet he spoke with calm. "That's what I've heard."

"What should be done about it?" Lolohea asked his father.

"First, the attacks must be stopped," the Tuʻitonga said. "These are honorable young women who lend Tonga its shine. When these girls are hurt, we're all hurt. And believe me, they're not hurt for a day or a season, but for lives entire. What of their families, their communities? Halting the attacks, that's all that matters."

"Wise words," Lolohea said. Then, of his uncle, he asked, "Supposing the attacker is caught, what should his penalty be?"

'Aho, using the shoulder blade, scooped soil. "First, we might consider the nature of this man. He hurts as if hurt is all he has to offer. Second, when it comes to hurting people, we should make a distinction. Some do it up close, close as you are to me. I'm one of those people." 'Aho focused only on the digging, which, stroke by stroke, deepened the small grave. "Others, through the use of proxies, administer pain remotely. An example of someone like that might be your father. As he teaches you to rule, Lolohea, know that he inherently teaches you to harm from afar, to deliver suffering by the hand of another, the kind of person you'd later rather not have around, this reminder of distant misery, so that people speak only of getting rid of him. So what kind of Tu'itonga will you be? The kind who farms out the pain, or one who'll grant audience to the suffering he causes?"

The Tu'itonga snorted. "And what of the lessons you teach your son, my fine brother?"

A calm smile crossed 'Aho's face, one that in the orange, inconstant light was truly frightening. "I confess I came late to my thinking on this matter, perhaps too late. Above all, I've endeavored to unteach what my son has learned through his proximity to war. I confess I lack the skills to undo what's been done. And who's to blame but me? I don't blame the war for making me a bad father. I don't condemn my brother, who sent me to war. In the end, I stand alone. My son pays for my shortcomings. My wife paid as well." Here, 'Aho placed his attention solely on his brother. "I freely admit my faults and mistakes. I'm happy to make further confessions, if that's what you desire, but I'm also happy to hear yours." There was a moment of silence. "Do you, my brother, wish to unburden yourself of any offenses? Have you unsavory deeds you wish to give voice to?" When the Tu'itonga was silent, when nothing passed between him and his brother but smoke from the torch, 'Aho said, "Then we understand each other."

Something unspoken had been agreed upon. Now there'd be only one solution to the problem of 'Aho. Lolohea, looking at his uncle, had the feeling of missing someone who was right in front of him. He never considered that his father might be the one who vacated life.

A warm tone, however, returned to 'Aho's voice, for that was his way, to change his emotions the way one swaps a topknot feather. He said to the Tuʻitonga, "I saw that you brought the bones of your friend."

"Yes, the tall man from Nuku Hiva," the Tuʻitonga said. "But from which island did he come? Which village was his? Even his true name is something I never learned. I could only think to bring him here."

"Bones matter," ʻAho said. "If you don't honor them, no one finds rest. How about we open the soil, say some words, and then lay your friend down together, the one you called Six Fists?"

TWENTY-SEVEN

THE TELEKI REEFS

'Ata's canopy, trapping woodsmoke, tempered the morning light. Pōhiva woke to this amber glow. Right away, she noticed the tether around her wrist led to ... nothing. She sat up to discover a trio of female attendants preparing the Fisian boy for his day—one tamed Vula's hair, while another wiped his face. The third, with her teeth, nipped his fingernails.

One attendant observed, "The boy's hair has recently been cut. A mother out there loves him."

Another looked in the boy's mouth. "How could a mother let her son be taken on a raid?"

A third attendant perused the boy. "There are no marks or scars on him. I think his mother kept him close." Wistfully, she added, "I remember when my first child was born. I inspected each little bit of her. I wasn't looking for defects, just fixing her in my mind—the dimples at her tiny knuckles, the rolls of fat on her arms, the swirl of her earlobes."

"Oh, that newborn smell," another said.

Pōhiva took the Fisian boy back from these women. "Where's my husband?" she demanded. When one pointed to the cliffs, Pōhiva told them, "Don't touch this child again."

She found the Tuʻitonga where he'd delivered his speech the night before: sitting on a stone near the cliff's edge. Before him, birds departed in great numbers, and the long shadow of the island stretched upon the sea. She sat beside him.

The boy pointed at the water. "Wasawasa," he said.

Pōhiva wasn't sure if he was saying *wave* or *ocean*. "Wasawasa," she repeated.

Then the boy pointed toward the horizon. "Vunilagi."

Was he indicating the sky or the clouds? Something about his home? It didn't matter. Pōhiva said, "Vunilagi."

"Weren't you trying to teach him *our* language?" her husband asked.

"I'm connecting with him."

"Pōhiva, I love that you adopted him. That's the kind of person you are, but don't you think we should return him? He deserves proper rearing, and you and I only have so many sunrises left."

Before them, great numbers of birds began dropping from the cliff faces, making tremendous dives, only to flatten their flight with the surface of the sea.

"Manumanu," the boy said.

"Look," Pōhiva told her husband. "Our peoples share a similar word for *bird*."

Pōhiva repeated the Fisian, "Manumanu." Then she shared the Tongan equivalent, "Manupuna."

"When we're gone," the Tuʻitonga said, "the matāpule will kill him. They hate loose ends."

Pōhiva looked at her husband. "He's the age of Finau when Finau was taken from me."

Guilt lowered the Tuʻitonga's eyes.

The tropic birds, now stirring, did not immediately surrender themselves to the sea. Instead, they rose on updrafts to warm their wings before venturing.

The Tuʻitonga turned wistful. "It was always the birds finding home that held the allure. But today, the departure speaks to me. Embarking into the unknown—that's the bigger feat." He met her eyes. "My journey didn't begin until I met you. You gave us our greatest gifts. I'll never forget the moment Lolohea was handed to me."

The boy was certainly handed to him by a stranger, she thought. When Lolo was born, he was whisked away by attendants, who cleaned him, wrapped him, nursed him, so that when he was returned, his lips shone with the milk of another woman. That would become the pattern: servant women removing her boys so they could be attended to, adorned, tutored. Later in the day, her boys would be *presented* to her. She'd been a Fefine Girl—trained to follow the rules. If only someone'd told her she could simply banish those who came between her and her sons. Her husband had spoken truth last night, right here on these cliffs, and it felt directed at her: there was but one path through life, and no step could be retraced. She caressed the shoulder of the Fisian boy. The journey wasn't completely over. For some things, there was still time. "The birds have much work to do before they rest, and so do we."

"One thing's first," he said.

Pōhiva wondered what action that would be. She'd been after him to name a new security chief. They needed to move against 'Aho. The Tamahā had to be contained.

Her husband approached the cliff's edge. He lifted his kilt and loosed a long stream of urine into the chasm below. "Ah, it'll be a good day now," he said, turning to business. "We'll use the appearance of this 'ghost vaka' as an excuse to visit the Teleki Reefs, which Lolohea will swim, and when he passes that test, we'll send him directly to fill a Tongan Hull. Meanwhile, we return to Tongatapu. I'll get rid of 'Aho, and you, my dear, must select the Fefine Girl to be featured in the Final Test. Once you have your candidate, start the rumors that she and Lolohea are secretly smitten."

Pōhiva loved it when he assumed command. Yes, her big-bellied man still had some life in him.

"Come, then," she said. "To our labors."

The shearwaters, who'd reunited the night before with calls of affirmation, parted in silence.

Most of the flotilla's vaka—the servants, the Fefine Girls—were sent home to Tongatapu, which was no navigational feat: such a large island was easy to bump into, and the soaring cliffs of 'Eua were visible over vast distances. Only three canoes sailed for the Teleki Reefs, which was a difficult passage: landfall had to be made where there was no land, for the sunken atolls never broke the surface. This meant sailing toward a patch of water that looked no different than all the water of the world. The Wayfinder had never fretted over difficult passages because Havea'd been in charge, and Havea never conveyed a single uncertainty about navigation. So fear and doubt were new to the Wayfinder, feelings amplified because his decisions affected not just him, but the fates of many. There was a force that compelled everything, all the time, to the bottom of the sea, and the weight of the faith people placed in him was his heaviest cargo.

The Wayfinder departed 'Ata midday, wind at his back. His vaka was smaller, faster, so he could maneuver among the larger double-hulls. He was surprised that no one wished to sail with him—watching Havea read the water and interpret clouds had been an endless fascination to the Wayfinder, but it seemed he was alone in that. He'd become a servant, something Havea had been trying to tell him all along. Two barges followed, one royal, one bearing matāpule and priests. When the wind was right, he'd hear singing, a roar of laughter, or a clap of applause. On his head, he wore a banana leaf, which formed a long, green brim. Still, the light off the waves made his vision sparkle as he led his people toward a destination that wasn't even there.

That night, the Tuʻitonga went to Lolohea, reclined on the vaka's deck. Together, they regarded the constellations, intermittent through mid-level clouds. Looking over, he saw the shine of his son's eyes, open to the stars. "I heard you followed a girl into the woods last night."

"You told me that if I ever liked a girl, I shouldn't say her name."

"That's right," the Tuʻitonga said. "I bet she's lovely."

"She is. She's nothing like the others."

"You know we're not going to the reefs to gawk at a ghost vaka."

"Since one of my tests is to circle the reefs, it's pretty clear I'll spend the morning fighting waves."

"It's just a swim. When you're done, we'll send you to fill a Tongan Hull."

Lolohea absorbed this. "All right."

"And when you get back, the final task will be waiting. We'll get it over with, and you'll never be tested again."

Lolohea sort of nodded.

"I'm going to tell you several things. They're practical things, so I want you to listen."

Lolohea looked toward his father.

"First, it's not the enemy club that you have to look out for, but the treacherous tale. This is also to your advantage. If you get people to believe the right story, they'll defeat themselves."

"I don't know any stories like that."

"Nobody does," the Tuʻitonga said. "That's why people will succumb to the one you invent."

A troubled look crossed Lolohea's face.

"Second, when making landfall on small islands, present yourself boldly. Be dismissive, be demanding. You must become, upon your arrival, the most important person on the island. Trust me, they'll vie to accommodate you."

Lolohea looked skeptical, but he nodded.

"Third, you must start giving commands. You have a good heart and fear diminishing others. I admire that in you. But you must understand: People are nervous around powerful figures. They're afraid of making mistakes. Orders indicate the domain of your favor. By following them, people are given safe passages through consequential matters. You help them by telling them exactly what you expect."

His son seemed to contemplate this.

"Fourth, on the mission you'll undertake, it'll be necessary to lie. Mendacity does not come naturally to you. So I'll tell you the secret to lying: it's telling the truth."

The Tuʻitonga let that one sink in.

"Finally, I must address the topic of sacrifice."

Lolohea groaned. "Sacrifice, sacrifice."

"After this, I'll never speak of it again. Just understand that sacrifice gives meaning to life. It isn't another word for suffering or loss. Most people live with little sense of purpose, and they die with less. But when we sacrifice, we give value to what we believe in. The pain of your ink made the ink meaningful, yes?"

Lolohea nodded.

"And sacrifice can reveal our inner selves. Was this not true on 'Ata, when you gave up speech?"

"I was changed by it," Lolohea admitted.

"Now, we mostly sacrifice for our own aims. But there's another kind: when you invite others to sacrifice for a greater good. You can't think of this as lessening their lives; instead, it gifts them with a higher charge. You honor them with a purpose that transcends the self. For aren't the truest sacrifices not on one's own behalf but on that of others?"

Lolohea shifted his eyes to the sky above. He said nothing.

The Tu'itonga knew he'd placed the heaviest stone yet upon his son. It was the kind of stone that could only be removed when a person lifted it off himself and set it down upon someone else.

That night, the Tu'itonga slept with the coconut containing Six Fists's soul. He dreamed he was walking down a beach. Soft waves crossed his feet before retreating. The water was bubbly and sparkling, yes, but lacking substance, leaving his toes dry after each beach break. Ahead was Six Fists, gazing horizonward.

"I've missed you, old friend," the Tu'itonga called.

"I need your help," Six Fists said. "I've found myself stranded on a most unusual island."

There were no marks upon his neck from the dog attack, no scars where his body'd been opened by an oyster shell. Only a lost look upon his face. "I wish you were around for one more mission," the Tu'itonga said. "To escort my sons on a journey and ensure their safety."

"For you, old friend—anything."

"The feeling's mutual," the Tu'itonga said. "Alas, true to my word, I've set you free."

"I'm free? Why am I not at home? I can practically hear my children shouting, Tekao! They must be grown. Might they even be married?"

"*Tekao?*" the Tu'itonga asked. "What's that?"

"Why, I'm Tekao," Six Fists said. "Don't you know me? Here, I'll show you my children's baby teeth. I also carry a lock of my wife's hair and a sprinkle of sand from Nuku Hiva." Six Fists ran his thumb along the belt of his vala kilt, but whatever he was searching for was missing.

"Six Fists, I need your advice."

"I told you—I'm *Tekao*."

The Tuʻitonga nodded. "Tekao, my friend. I'm on the cusp of sending Lolohea on a perilous mission. My middle son will navigate. My question is this: Should I send Finau as well? He has a ferocity that might prove decisive, should trouble occur."

"Would I even recognize my children?" Tekao wondered. "Might I have grandchildren, to whom I'm nothing more than a name in a genealogy chant?"

"Pōhiva says I shouldn't send all three sons, that I should keep the youngest in reserve, lest a catastrophe befall them. Yet, what if Finau is the one who might save my other sons?"

Tekao said, "I was fishing the day your agents abducted me—"

"They were no agents of mine," the Tuʻitonga interrupted. "I received you as a gift."

"I wonder how life would've been different if my son had been fishing with me. Yes, he would've become a slave as well—"

"You were never indentured!" the Tuʻitonga insisted. "You were instead a trusted friend."

"Were my son a fellow captive, at least I could've been there for him. He'd know me. I could've told him my stories, breathed his breath, seen him grow to resemble me. At night we'd have gone to sleep with our eyes upon the same stars. Would that have been worth his liberty?"

The Tuʻitonga said, "It's true that a son would gladly enter bondage to be with his father. Yet there's no situation in which a father could do that to his son, willingly endanger him."

The Tuʻitonga realized he'd found the answer to his question. He felt a great sense of relief, and for him, the visit was over. Still, he asked his old friend, "Are you happy here?"

"I suppose I want for nothing," Tekao said. "But this is a curious place. At night, the stars don't advance. There are waves but no tides. Have you noticed the lack of birds?"

The Tuʻitonga closed his eyes, focused. Then frigate birds appeared, hovering high above them.

"Say," Tekao said. "Can I show you something perplexing?" He took the Tuʻitonga's hand and brought it to his biceps. "Squeeze here. Do you feel any bone? I can't seem to locate my bones."

"I'm sure your bones are in a special place, laid down by people who revered you."

Tekao said, "You once told me that life was nothing but the sacrifices we make. I didn't subscribe to your way of thinking, not at first. Over the years, however, your philosophy tutored me in full."

"The things we do for others. They never end. In that, you and I are the same."

"Do you lack for bones as well?" Tekao asked.

"Is there anything I can do to make you comfortable?"

"I wish I had my spear. At night I dream of dogs, and I find myself defenseless."

"I've been told that most dogs are friendly and loving, that vicious dogs are the exception."

Tekao looked unconvinced.

The king made a dog pup appear at their feet. Padding around them, it left small prints in the sand. He bent to pick it up. It was not much larger than his palm—warm to the touch, white in color, with rolls of extra skin. He handed it to Tekao, who regarded it warily before smelling its newborn smell and rubbing a floppy ear, soft as the fontanels of their sons after birth.

Punake woke at dawn, arm around Finau. Bow-spray misted the vaka's deck. The first rays of sun shone pink through his eyelids. Until Finau stirred, Punake wouldn't, either. He was trying come up with a damned entertaining poem, one with thrills and laughs and flourishes. He had to compose it fast, as the Tuʻitonga had lost nearly all interest in poetry. But where were the words?

Pōhiva was awake, repeating vocabulary to the Fisian boy. "Vaka-vakamuʻa," Punake heard her say. *The lead vaka.* He could visualize her pointing to the Wayfinder ahead. "Vaka-tapu," she told Vula, patting their own deck. *The chief's vaka.* When she said, "Vaka-loa," *Ghost ship,* Punake knew they'd arrived at the Teleki Reefs. Still, Punake didn't stir, for what came next was the beauty of the Fisian boy repeating Tongan words, the sounds new-born in his mouth. On 'Ata, to express the concept of sap, the boy combined the words for tree and blood: 'akautoto. Come nightfall, the boy announced lā'amate, sundeath. Giving voice to the world, trying to say a great deal with simple words—that *was* poetry. "Hakau," Pōhiva said. "Hakau," the boy said. *Reef.* Call-and-response, rhythm and repetition. Poetry itself. On the vaka, arm around Finau, it was clear to Punake that the first verse must have been the original naming of the world. But who taught us our words? Where was the story of the gods giving us our talk? Did they place the words in our mouths or our minds? Or did the gods, patient, speak the words, one by one, while we, new in our skins, repeated them?

He heard someone speak to Pōhiva. It was the Hau priest.

"I've heard the call of the charmed kele'a shell," he said. "The old navigator must be in trouble."

Pōhiva said, "Tell no one this, understand? I can't have my son endangered by Havea's problems."

Punake imagined an old man sailing to the afterlife to reanimate a loved one. Only in the worst circumstance would he sound a call of distress. Then, to have it ignored...

If Punake composed a poem about first words, it would catalog a world before this one, before servitude and hunger and war. Before calls for help went unanswered. Words like *conscription* and *castration* couldn't have been included in the original language. No god would deliver such concepts to a people he loved enough to create.

Finau woke, stretched, and jumped to his feet. The boy wasn't one to linger on his sleeping mat, pondering life. Punake rose as well. When he went to roll up their mat, he paused: sea-spray had wet the mat, except where they'd been sleeping, leaving an outline of their embrace. Some part of him wanted to save this rough portrait of their lives, but like all true things, it was soon to dissipate. Despite how much he fantasized about liberation from Finau, in moments like this, he knew he'd miss the boy.

When the booming surf made it hard to hear, they dropped sail. Before them, a sunken atoll encircled a vast lagoon. ʻAho requested that his son Mateaki have the honor of accompanying Lolohea on the swim. The Tuʻitonga assented to this. Punake wondered why, why would the king allow a competitor to position himself against his own son? The only answer could be this: the Tuʻitonga had already made plans against such a possibility.

Matāpule Muʻa described the royal test, its history and rules. Lolohea and Mateaki ate and drank as much as they could. Then they dove into the water. Punake watched them begin to stroke. It was dangerous to swim too close to the reef break, but no person would want to contend with the raw power of unbroken swells. Punake watched their arms turn, the splash of their powerful kicks. On his home island of Haʻano, Punake had once been able to swim like this. He'd once climbed coconut trees. But after many soft years on Tongatapu, he shuddered at the thought of even working up the friction to start a fire.

The Wayfinder entered a break in the reef, delivering them into a vast lagoon of calm seawater, the surface lightly riffled by the wind. Below, each coral head and sea fan was visible. The dark wings of rays moved like the shadows of clouds. All this serenity was ringed by a wall of thrashing white. It transported Punake to his youth, when a cyclone struck Haʻano. He'd been terrified, but his fahu aunt, when the eye passed over them, took him out into the stillness. She told him, "This is the fale lōngonoa, the serene place at the center of the storm. In life, you must learn to find your own fale lōngonoa."

Punake always found refuge in verse. A poem was the strongest shelter he knew.

The ghost vaka, when they reached it, had swept lines and a high bow, yet the only thing Punake saw were human bones and dog skulls, strewn through the hull and across the deck. Aside from death, there were no signs of life—no stray garments, possessions, provisions, or artifacts. There was only this: the hull and thwarts were crusted with bird shit, likely that of petrels, who scavenged the sea. They'd stripped all this flesh, and before leaving, painted the vaka white with it.

The Tuʻitonga and ʻAho boarded first, followed by the Wayfinder, Finau, and Punake.

The Fisian boy was held back by Pōhiva, yet he cast his verdict on what he saw: "Laʻāpeau, kulimate."

Sunwave, the boy had said. *Dogdeath.*

Finau came to stand amid the bleached bones. The image triggered something in Punake—it was like the memory of something that'd yet to happen.

The Wayfinder studied the rigging, the stays, the lashings. "The vaka's new, in pristine condition."

ʻAho took up a dog skull and surveyed the scene. "Either the men brought along dogs with the intent to do harm, or the men were set adrift with dogs so harm would be done to them."

The Tuʻitonga lifted a human skull that had been grooved by dog's teeth. "You think this was some kind of punishment?" he asked ʻAho. "The Fisian version of the Old Canoe?"

"What's the alternative?" ʻAho asked. "This isn't a raiding party blown off course. Where are the weapons?"

"Where are the water vessels?" the Wayfinder asked. "Where's the steering oar? Where are the paddles and bailers?"

The Tuʻitonga offered the human skull to Punake. "Perhaps a poet can help solve this mystery."

Punake warily accepted the skull. Sport was likely being made of him. "These grooves," Punake said, "show where a dog's teeth got purchase. They point in all directions. I'd say these are not the cause of death, but evidence of scavenging."

The Tuʻitonga clearly hadn't expected a serious response. A smile appeared on his face. Was it recognition, a flash of admiration? "You say this vessel is seaworthy?" he asked his middle son.

"It's finer than any vaka we can make," the Wayfinder said. "It'd take four to crew it."

"Begin provisioning it," the Tuʻitonga said. "When Lolohea returns, he'll depart to fill a Tongan Hull."

'Aho said, "My son requests the honor of aiding the prince in his mission."

The Tuʻitonga offered a delicious smile of assent.

Punake considered the skull in his hand. A man's mind once resided here. Had the man taken his life, so as not to succumb to the sun, thirst, or dogs? Wasn't that the ultimate gesture? Did it not inscribe final commentary upon a world gone deaf to beauty and justice? Would it be so bad to lend your voice to a great tabernacle of refusal? He imagined all those before him who declined to ratify a system that allowed its own to be conscripted, set adrift, remanded to dogs. Or children.

"And I've decided that my youngest son will not join," the Tuʻitonga said.

"Father," Finau said. "I'm not missing this adventure!"

The Tuʻitonga lifted a hand, curtailing his protest.

A stroke of luck, Punake thought. Where Finau went, he went, for his prime mandate was to look after the boy. Punake had begun following Finau off the vaka, when the Tuʻitonga stopped him. "Get to work preparing this canoe, Punake. Start by getting rid of all this bird shit."

Punake picked up a shoulder blade. He began chipping the vaka's white coating. If he could avoid the manifest of a kidnapping mission, bird-shit duty would be a small price to pay. The irony that he might perish on Fisian shores, after all he'd endured, it was too much to bear. And that he'd die now—when Finau was nearly a man, when Punake was soon to be freed—it was unthinkable. Now, just as new possibilities started to seem imaginable. On ʻAta, Punake had stood face-to-face with a Fefine Girl, the two of them naked. He'd been gathering sī leaves. When he parted some brush, there she was, the totality of her. The girl paused, her own materials in hand. She didn't act as if an offense were being done to her. Perhaps if she'd considered him a true man, she'd have shrieked, covered herself, or fled. But it was only Punake, poor Punake. She regarded him closely, herself fully exposed, and he knew it had only to do with her being seen, with her having a chance, perhaps her only safe chance, to see how she was regarded by man, for the next man to see her this way would have dominion over her.

She, too, regarded him. Her face registered no repulsion. She did not recoil. In fact, there seemed some small pleasure in safely seeing a man in his true form. Perhaps he could never be a lover or a father or even a māna'ia. But could he not make a wonderful hoa to someone—a partner, a life mate, a counterpart, a companion? Was there not a widow or a barren woman who'd seek comfort in a man like Punake? Was there no possible path toward love for a well-intentioned and thoroughly harmless poet?

The Wayfinder began provisioning the ghost vaka with vessels of water and coils of rope.

The sun was hot on Punake's back. He decided to chip bird shit from the shade of the sail. Repositioning himself, he tossed a bunch of bones into the sea.

'Aho took note. "When we dishonor human remains, we dishonor ourselves."

"These bones shall be returned to Fisian soil," the Tu'itonga declared.

Pōhiva said, "Surely this poses an unnecessary risk."

"Quite the opposite," the Tu'itonga announced. "This gesture will ensure the venture's good fortune."

Punake was on his knees, chipping bird guano. He could feel the Tu'itonga studying him. A white dust lifted that he couldn't help but inhale, making him cough.

"Have I heard it said," the Tu'itonga asked Punake, "that you believe you're less than free?"

Punake knew he must proceed with caution. "I can't account for what others say, but I assure you it's my duty—no, my *privilege*—to serve as Finau's surrogate father."

"You mean *supplemental* father," the Tu'itonga corrected. "So if I were to relieve you of this duty, you'd choose to remain by my son's side because tutoring him is your *privilege*?"

"Technically," Punake said, "you're the one I serve. It's your pleasure I wish to fulfill."

"Yes," the Tu'itonga said. "Still, are you certain you don't yearn for more liberty?"

Punake hesitated. "If a Tongan has more to offer, only the selfish could refuse to be of service."

"Well put, Punake," the Tu'itonga said. "Your humble nature is a model to all."

"Leave the poor poet alone," Pōhiva said.

"Don't taunt him," Finau said. "He doesn't deserve it."

"I'm your true father," the Tuʻitonga told Finau. "Have you forgotten what it's like to turn to me?"

Finau, eyes wide, looked to his father.

"What say we let the poet go about his business," the king asked his youngest son, "while you and I spend our time together? What if I became your primary father again?"

Punake dropped his bird-shit scraper. *Freedom. Was freedom at hand?*

To Punake, the Tuʻitonga said, "This mission to fill a Tongan Hull needs a final crew member. Do you volunteer?"

It took Punake a moment to even understand the request. Had he heard the king right, was he not on the cusp of liberation? "Just to be clear," Punake asked, "the mission's goal is to—"

"Return with twelve souls," the Tuʻitonga said.

"While happy to help," Punake said, "I assure you I was born neither to sail, nor to get the best of an adversary. I've never even seen a foreign shore."

The Tuʻitonga smiled. "Have you not boasted of poetry's power to traverse any ocean, language, time, or culture?"

"These oceans I spoke of," Punake said, "were metaphorical."

"Come, now, Punake," the Tuʻitonga said. "You sell yourself too cheap. Have you not claimed that your voice has the power to captivate? This is a mission to take captives."

What could Punake offer to counter this?

The Tuʻitonga asked, "Did you not also claim your performances hold entire islands in your thrall?"

Here, Punake joined the tabernacle of the silent.

"It's decided, then?" the Tuʻitonga asked. "Excellent."

So as not to be seen openly weeping, Punake returned to chipping guano. What was happening to him, it wasn't possible, was it? Through tears, he chipped and chipped. A small cloud of baitfish rose to inspect the falling material. The fingerlings seemed uncertain as to whether this was food or not. They took it in their mouths, spit it out, tested it again.

Suddenly several shearwaters appeared and attacked the water. They dove down, brown wings slashing, starting a mad scramble to snag the little fish. Punake looked up to behold a sky now teeming with birds. Soon they were skimming and dipping and diving before leaning their heads back to swallow their prizes. There was a poem in this for sure, Punake thought: there'd be the image of little fish warming themselves in calm water, not knowing their deaths had already begun, had been under way since the birds departed 'Ata at dawn. Only conclusion remained. Until then, all was bliss. For those whose fates were sealed, there was no way to know the remainder of their world could be measured in wingbeats.

Shearwaters surfaced with their catches. As they took wing, however, the poem dissipated. To the fish in the birds' beaks, the experience wasn't one of lovely verse. And there was no poetry to being swallowed alive. Outside of poems, it seemed, death was just death.

When Lolohea returned, his arms bore the marks of jellyfish, and his legs were reef-rashed.

The Tu'itonga pulled the wet hair from his son's eyes. "My boy, full of life."

"It was more than *just a swim*," Lolohea said.

The father nodded, *I know*.

"You never had to take these tests," Lolohea said. It was an accusation.

"True. And I'm sure I wouldn't have fared as well as you. My version of this swim happened in Ha'amoa, when we attacked Savai'i. I was your age and had little business leading men. Yet it was my duty. For stealth, I decided we'd swim the last leg. It was night, and I misjudged the current. Several men, because of me, didn't make it ashore."

"So my artificial achievements pale even to your real-life failures?"

It was good that Lolo was getting this out. The Tu'itonga said, "I was quite the vale young man—rash, blind to consequences, always overestimating my abilities. While you're the model of poto behavior—prudent, measured, calm in the face of adversity."

"I've known no adversity," Lolohea said. "Except what you've created for me."

"Adversities you've risen to. When you begin commanding men, they'll know you've made your sacrifices. That your challenges have been constructed doesn't mean you haven't met them. A man pretends to be king. He pretends and pretends, and then, one day, kingly is what he is."

The Tuʻitonga fashioned his son's hair into a topknot, then pinned it with a feather.

"You'll begin ruling on the day of your return," the Tuʻitonga said. "At that point, if you still deem them onerous, you can abolish these tests for future generations."

"Really?"

"You'll be king. Kings can do anything."

It was more complicated, of course—the matāpule would harry him without end if he proposed such a thing. But the goal was to get Lolohea through the next test. To achieve that, his son needed to absorb certain realities in stages.

Lolohea said, "You must admit it's wrong to kidnap people just to demonstrate an ability to do so."

"The day you return," the Tuʻitonga said, "you can have them freed."

As for the people soon to abducted, the idea of returning them was also impossible. The Tuʻi of Foa had been troublesome lately, and to placate him, the Tuʻitonga had already gifted him the people Lolohea was to kidnap—they'd serve as workers in the obsidian mine on the volcanic island of Kao. There'd be no way to renege on this deal without destabilizing the Haʻapai islands and, of course, paying an expensive penalty, a fat plantation, perhaps, setting off a new wave of rivalries.

"I suppose that makes it only an exercise," Lolohea mused, "with no real consequences."

The Tuʻitonga embraced his son. The young man's skin was pimpled and cold, an aftereffect of the jellyfish. By holding him, he gave the boy his warmth. At last, they separated, but he didn't release his grip. "To become the Tuʻitonga, you must act as the Tuʻitonga. Your brother and cousin on this trip are your subjects, your crew, your means, and your ends. Make them swear to obey you. Never let them question your will. Be prepared for a challenge from your cousin."

"What've I not prepared for?"

The Tuʻitonga smiled. "Yes, your life has been a project. Rest assured, however: You have only your part to do. Your mother has a role in ensuring your success, and I have mine. When you return, all obstacles to your future will have been removed, including your uncle. The path will have been swept of everything, including my own footprints."

Final supplies were being lashed to the vaka. Farewells were being made. On people's faces were both the thrill and dread of the unknown.

When had the king last tightened a line or held a course? Could he recall the crackle of rope under tension or the feel of a seasoned oar? Did he remember what these boys must be feeling, the sense there was nothing beyond the farthest visible wave, that the arc of the sun was the entirety of the considerable world, that night would be dealt with only when it suddenly and surprisingly arrived? At what age had he started to think of tomorrow while it was yet today? Whence came the time when the future could be seen, the entirety of it, as if the days ahead were a story that had already been told? And at what age did the future become something that wasn't just singular and known, it was something that must, at all costs, come to pass?

TWENTY-EIGHT

KŌRERO:
UNTOLD STORIES

After Finau's duel with Papa Toki, a misty rain enveloped our island. The droplets were so light they didn't fall. Through this, we foraged. Some people walked the shoreline, looking for driftwood. Others turned soil, searching for subterranean morsels. We knew every flower that could be eaten, every tendril, shoot, bud, and root.

We waded through wet ferns, my mother, father, and I. We moved up the tree line, our foraging baskets optimistically large. In the branches above, wild parrots shuffled their feathers to shed water. Kōkī's knowledge of human trickery now protected them from our snares.

To seriously forage, you had to climb trees. Up high, you could see tidbits people'd missed on previous passes: snails and pupae and hives and nests. From a branch, I saw the Tongan brothers in the distance. They were foraging, too. I wondered why they'd joined us in such menial tasks. Then the answer struck me: they were hungry.

As I walked the cone ridge, wisps of cloud raced up the rock face before dropping into the cupped hands of the volcano's bowl. Here was where the Tongan brothers caught up to us. Our foraging baskets were far from full, but theirs were completely empty. They'd obviously been talking about us, because right away the Wayfinder asked, "Can he really do it? Is Tapoto capable of killing a man?"

My father, caught off guard, didn't quite answer.

To the Tongans, this was the wrong response.

My mother indicated their empty baskets. "Are you capable of surviving without us?"

Impatient, Finau said, "Can Tapoto murder or not? Our uncle can't be half killed, he can't be *almost* killed."

I said, "Tapoto has lifted his people onto his back. When you do that, you don't set them down again." I didn't really know this until I said the words. It was like telling a secret you didn't know you knew.

My mother asked the Tongan brothers, "Is this 'Ata all you claim? Will it really support us?"

"It's a place of pure poetry," Finau said.

"We can't eat poems," my mother said.

"Manage 'Ata's resources," the Wayfinder said, "and 'Ata will last forever."

"Will it truly be ours?" I asked.

"This island's the property of the king," Finau said. "As long as my brother rules, 'Ata will be yours. Beyond that, there are no guarantees."

At the mention of becoming king, the Wayfinder's face faltered. He looked around, at the diffused sky, at the wet foliage, at the dark, imposing ridge above us.

"What is it?" I asked.

"Just remembering something," the Wayfinder said. "A day like this, mists, ferns, a girl with wet hair stuck to her face. No girl wouldn't brush wet hair from her eyes, not if she were alive to do it."

I visualized this place called Tonga, with its wet ferns and dead girls. "Moon Appearing?" I asked.

"Come on," Finau said, leading his brother away. "Let's focus on food."

At that, we parted ways, my family heading into thickets of young trees. We didn't speak. We walked, listening, observing, trying to detect anything that might sustain us. I caught myself wiping wet hair from my vision. It was a simple act, one I'd done countless times, but now I realized you had to be alive to do it.

We came across a patch of trees where the bark had been stripped. The sight made my heart clench. I said, "Someone has snuck out here to eat bark."

My parents glanced at one another.

When I turned, I saw more trunks had been stripped. Tears came to my eyes. I don't know why I was so fragile. "Look," I said. "It must be more than one person, there must be others who're starving."

My mother put a hand on my shoulder. "It's a terrible sight," she said. "We'll figure it out. We'll discover who's so hungry, and together we'll help them out."

* * *

Can a meal be both too much and not enough? After dinner, we sat by the fire, none of us in a mood to talk. Rising smoke conducted the mist—sucked into the glow, it churned above in throbs of red.

Ihi's dog refused our food. It lay on its side, stomach growling. When, all of a sudden, it rose up, Ihi looked alarmed. The girl and the dog studied the trees, listening. "They might be coming," Ihi said.

Hine placed a hand on the girl's shoulder. "Who?"

"The people on the other side of the island," Ihi said.

"There's no one else," my mother said. "It's only us."

"What about raids?" Ihi asked.

Hine hugged the girl, who stiffly accepted the embrace. "There are no raids," Hine said. "Nobody hurts anybody on this island."

The idea of conflict was something we were unused to. We, too, stared into the darkness as we felt a new feeling, or perhaps an ancient one: that in the dark, people were conspiring to do us harm. Of course it wasn't real, there was no one out there—so why did the feeling come so easily, so strong?

Tapoto, not without a hint of suspicion, asked of Finau, "Earlier, you claimed your brother was killed by a meteor. Did a piece of the sky really take his life?"

"It's true," Finau said. "Though small, the meteor was heavy, and—"

The Wayfinder stopped him. "Did our brother have to die, and what caused his death? I've been contemplating this question. It's not the means—yes, a meteor was involved—but the reason, what's the reason he was taken? It's only here, on this island, that I think I've found an answer."

His voice was drained of emotion, the way, after much sadness, a person can sound detached and philosophical. I regretted the tone I often took with him. Accusing. Combative. "What's the answer?" I asked.

The Wayfinder said, "What killed Lolohea, I think, is this: When the time came for him to disobey, he instead complied. He was being tested. The test asked him to do the unthinkable. The true nature of the test, I've come to believe, was to see if he could resist authority, to say no to his father, to break with the past. Yet, after complying so often, Lolohea no longer knew how to say no."

"Was leaving Tonga your way of saying no?" my mother asked.

"I was being selfish," the Wayfinder said. "I couldn't believe my brother was gone. Word had reached us that Havea'd revived his dead wife, and arrogantly I thought I could revive someone, too."

Tiri asked, "Did anyone see this resurrected woman?"

Finau said, "She made landfall on an outer island."

We were quiet, each of us perhaps imagining a once-dead woman commanding a waka.

Taking our silence for distrust, Finau said, "The report came directly from the island's chief." He studied us for a response. "The chief of Nomuka is an honorable man." Here, Finau narrowed his eyes. "You often give us this wary gaze, as if you're trying to determine whether we're deceiving you. Well, I have a question for you. What if we were? What would you do then?"

No one dared field this question. Which was its own kind of answer.

"Tomorrow," the Wayfinder said, "we'll take you to Tonga." He turned to Tapoto. "But make no mistake. Our uncle's heart must stop beating. His breath must wholly expire. Can you do that?"

Tiri answered for Tapoto. She looked into the crimson mist, seeming to behold every aspect of it. "Some things aren't spoken of," she said. "Certain stories aren't told."

Exasperated, the Wayfinder said, "The question is simple. Is Tapoto capable of—"

My father lifted a hand. "Wait, listen."

Tiri said, "When I was young, my father husked coconuts with a pointed pole. I thought nothing of it until one day I fetched the pole for him. The wood was heavy. It was engraved with a pattern I didn't recognize. I'd never seen a spear, but the old stories were filled with them. I asked my father if his husking pole wasn't actually a weapon. *We're a people who've turned our backs on violence*, he responded. *What use would we have for spears?* I accepted this. The pole, however, soon disappeared.

"I asked my grandfather about the spear. He said, *Child, I imagine you've heard scraps of a certain story, have you not?* If I suggested I hadn't heard this story, he'd never tell me. So I nodded. *Put your mind at ease*, he said. *Think of the ways this tale cannot be true. How could we, we who were tired and hungry and storm-battered, murder people on the beach, on the day we first set foot on this island? It's simply not possible. So don't dwell on long-ago things that never happened.*

"The next season, when we kids were clearing new ground for planting, Grandpa Toki came to us and indicated some soil. *Do not disturb this earth*, he said. When asked why, he said the soil was busy. *Busy?* we asked. *This ground*, he said, *is occupied with another task and mustn't be distracted.* How could dirt be distracted? Instead of responding, Grandpa Toki said a prayer."

Animated, Papa Toki called out, "That was him. Father was always praying for the dead."

Tiri continued, "I went to my great-aunt, who could be counted upon for straight talk. I told her I knew a certain story, one that took place long ago, one that started on our beach and concluded in the fields. Accusingly, she asked, *You think you know this story?* I could tell I was supposed to say no, but I nodded. *Could you comprehend a poem by hearing its last line? Or know a man by the final words he utters? Unless the answer's yes, don't go around saying you know the nature of night because you got a glimpse of the moon.*"

Observing Tiri's wide, indiscriminate eyes, I realized the only thing she was blind to was the now. The past and all the stories that constituted it were clear and vivid in her sight. "I went to my grandmother. Were there people on this island before us? I asked breathlessly. Did we fight them on the beach and bury them on the lower plains? Without looking up from her weaving, she asked, *Where do you get such foolish notions?* There was no greater confirmation than my grandmother's denials.

"At last, I went to my mother. I told her I knew our primordial story—how there were people here before us, how we fought them on the beach, how we buried them in the fields. My mother said, *Sounds like you already know the story.* Not the details, I said, not the how or the why. *My mother studied me. People don't just adopt peaceful ways,* she said. *Only violence can truly teach nonviolence."*

At this, Hine stood. Taking Ihi's hand, she led the girl away from this narrative.

Tiri paused, should others wish to depart. Instead, we narrowed the circle. "My mother told me they spoke a different language, these previous residents. *If you chose to understand, you could make out their words; otherwise, you didn't have to hear their welcomes, their entreaties, their pleas, their curses and final words. Yes, a clash at the beach led to initial deaths. Understand that we'd nearly died in a storm, we were scared, we were ravenous, we were wild with liberation. We didn't set about to depopulate the island. But we knew all too well that a cycle of retribution had started, that if these people were allowed to live, they'd return the favor of murder.* You've already surmised the skirmishes, the ambushes, the fighting in the fields. What matters is this: when they'd finally been subdued, they were invited to dig their own graves. They interred one another. This continued to the last man. He, too, opened the soil and sought, scoop by scoop, his own resting place. Alas, he climbed inside, and as instructed, began pulling soil in after him—atop his feet and legs and waist—until, when it became no longer possible, our people helped him complete his task."

"Hold on," Tapoto said. "Are you suggesting people were buried alive?"

"This must be taken back," Papa Toki said. "There's no way we'd engage in such behavior."

"Is this method not bloodless and painless?" Tiri asked. "Is drowning in soil not as fast and certain as in water?"

"I don't believe it," my father said. "This is beyond us."

"Believe as you like," Tiri said. "My mother's mother was there. She'd been among those who'd chosen to understand these strangers' words, the last of which, from the last of their kind, she committed to memory:

Ko e ngāahi peaua 'oku tahifo ma'u pē,	*Where waves ever crest,*
hoku laumālie oku i 'api.	*that's where my soul resides.*

We recognized the lines from a poem Finau had uttered.

There wasn't a sound. People'd stopped breathing.

In disbelief, Finau gazed into the mist, looking like a blind man himself. Was he outraged, confused?

The Wayfinder stood. He looked ready to question, to condemn, to deny. But there was nothing to say, because the truth was before us, as was the answer to his question: We could kill Tongans. We'd done it before.

* * *

That night, our little family reclined on the beach. I don't remember the sky or the clouds. I couldn't tell you the state of the sea. In my mind, I kept seeing men climbing into graves they'd been forced to dig. I saw it from above, like I was one of the killers. By killers, I mean ancestors. Tiri was fond of saying that in bad stories, missing things were a kind of proof. Absence as evidence. Missing from the tale she'd reassembled were children. Absent were the old and unable. If we'd killed everyone, there must've been kids, there must've been the feeble and the blind. One by one, they uttered their final words. Under the weight of gathering soil, one uttered a poem. Others, curses.

"A curse," I said aloud. "Could that be what's happened to us? Is that why we're hungry, because we fertilized our fields with death?"

My father said, "We're hungry because we've been poor stewards of this place. That, and there's too many of us."

I said, "Maybe a curse is why we're trapped here. We wanted this place so bad we killed for it, and now we're stuck here forever."

"We're stuck on this island," my father said, "because we forgot how to navigate. Or perhaps, being subjugated, we were never taught."

My mother wondered aloud, "What if the arrival of these Tongan boys is the completion of a curse? Or what if it's the beginning of one? What if a curse is leading us to Tonga, where the repayment of a generations-old debt awaits?"

My mother didn't talk like this!

"What if . . ." I said, then stopped. I looked up to see Finau, standing over us in the dark.

When I gasped, so did my parents. We nearly jumped.

Finau wore only a loincloth. "I can't go home like this." He indicated his legs, one inked and one not.

My mother studied the belt of ink about his midsection and the patterns descending his right leg. "The artist who began your ink should be the one to finish it," she said.

"I'll never see him again," Finau said.

"Moko's sacred," my mother said. "I can't just mimic another pattern. How the needles adorn you—it's about who you are, it's about how the ink flows through me."

"It's acceptable if my legs don't match," Finau said. "As long as one isn't bare."

"Ink isn't meant to cover up skin," my mother said. "Ink announces the real you. It speaks of attributes we don't have words for."

"I can't go back like this!"

I knew what my father was thinking: if Finau didn't go to Tonga, neither did we.

I said, "The koru pattern is about new beginnings."

My mother looked up to Finau. "Could you have one leg marked by shark's teeth, while the other was adorned with unfolding ferns?"

Finau asked, "Are new beginnings really possible?"

My mother didn't ponder that. She simply told me, "Light the candlenut lamps."

Inside our whare, Finau loosened his topknot and released his hair. Free, it curled about his shoulders. His tight muscles were prominent in the soot-orange light. I showed him the mat. When he reclined, the curve of his ribs framed the hollow of his stomach. He'd lost much weight since he'd been here, making him look less like a foreigner and more like one of us.

His collarbone was inked with the stars that formed Matariki.

"This is an important constellation to us," I said. "Its rise signals the new year."

"My father and I got this inked together," Finau said. "Mataliki was supposed to protect us, keep us from losing our way. Right after that, my father died, and I ended up here."

My mother often asked her subjects questions, to put them at ease, to distract them from pain. Questions meant to evoke pleasant, reassuring responses. Instead, she asked Finau, "What made your uncle into such a menace?"

Finau thought about it. "I don't remember him another way."

I said, "Didn't you tell me that your father sent him to war?"

"Is that what'll happen to you," my mother asked, "if your brother becomes king?"

I didn't think Finau would answer, but he spoke. "Actually, I think my uncle wanted to go. He was good at war. War made him feel alive. Other ways of living, that's what eluded him."

My mother gave her needles a final sharpening.

"I've never seen anything like tonight," Finau said. "Where people talk about bad things that happened and who did them."

My mother asked, "What if saying things is the only path to healing?" She tested the ink by sinking needles into her own skin. Satisfied, she began.

Finau silently absorbed the first strikes. "I know I owe you a gift. I'm ashamed I have nothing to offer."

"Words are acceptable," my mother said.

Finau began reciting a poem called "Matangi," which evoked a longing for favorable winds. I was always struggling to understand the Tongans' language. I didn't want to miss anything they said. But Tiri's story gave me permission to let the words wash over me.

When the poem was over, Finau asked, "Is it strange that I like the pain? It's not that I *like* it. It just does something."

My mother didn't answer. She was focusing on his skin, trying to see the pattern emerge.

She inked people's faces by having them recline their heads into her lap. Now she invited Finau to extend his bare leg across hers. He hesitated.

"My mother was a woman of exceptional rank," Finau said. "It was tapu to touch her."

"You couldn't touch your own mother?" I asked.

"There wasn't any need," Finau said. "My requirements were met by attendants."

Finau recited a poem about the wind, and now a breeze kicked up. The walls around us shimmied with it, and with stronger buffets, the panels moaned.

"When the old woman was telling that story . . ." Finau said, his voice trailing off. He stared into the nothing of our roof thatching. "I participated in a mass drowning," he suddenly said. "People being drowned one at a time, I mean. But many in a row. It happened in a way that no particular member of our party seemed responsible. So when they were going down—the drowning people, that is—I didn't have the sense they were addressing me with their last words. At the time, I wasn't quite able to hear them. But since then, their words have come clearer and clearer. Now, when I recall the day, it seems like I was the only person there, like the dying were speaking directly to me. As the old woman told her story tonight, that's all I could think about."

My mother's response to this confession was an unfolding fern.

New beginnings, I thought.

When the needles sank, Finau closed his eyes.

※

In the morning, I came across my father and the Wayfinder on the beach. They were staring at the Wayfinder's waka. I studied it, too, trying to figure out what was drawing their attention. "Twenty's the limit," the Wayfinder said. "There's no way around it."

"It's got to hold more," my father said. "If we don't get enough people off the island, the folks left behind won't have enough food to survive on."

"That's me and my brother, plus eighteen of you," the Wayfinder said.

"What about twenty-five people?" my father asked. "Or even twenty-four?"

"It's not a migrating vaka," the Wayfinder said. "It's built for a single family of nomads. When we escaped Tonga, we were lucky to get it, we owe those nomads our lives. The point is: any more than twenty passengers, and we'll start taking on water."

"We have plenty of bailers," my father said. "We can bail nonstop, if we have to."

To this suggestion, the Wayfinder made no response.

My father moved down the beach to where *The Red Cloak* sat forlorn at the waterline, one hull completely submerged. "What if we could replace this hull?"

"You'd have to replace them both," the Wayfinder said. He waded beside the still-floating hull to point out a crack running the length of its bottom. "The wood dried out over time. It's ready to split. We don't know how much stress it could take, perhaps none at all."

"You made passage with it," my father countered.

"A short trip, across calm water," the Wayfinder said. "Trust me, this hull is just seaworthy enough to sink very far from land."

"What if we carved new hulls?" my father asked.

"Carved them from what?"

We soon found ourselves high on the slope of our peak, standing before the last great tree on our island. We had many smaller trees, but our predecessors had cut down the giants—all except this one, too remote to bother with. Looking at its great trunk, you could visualize the hulls, standing on end, hidden inside. We'd brought with us the greenstone adze and ax, carefully resharpened, though they seemed hopelessly outmatched by the tree's enormous size.

"What you're proposing," the Wayfinder said, "would take a season of labor."

My father studied the tree's height, its width, how it might fall, where the hulls would be hollowed, the routes to then drag them down to the sea. He seemed to conclude that it would indeed take a very long time.

"If we cut it down," I asked, "how'd anyone else get off the island?"

My father scanned the ridge, studying other trees, gauging their ages and maturity. He was making an epic decision: whether to make a safe craft for our departing party, thus robbing the people left behind of options, or to risk an unsafe crossing himself, one that might endanger not unmet, future people, but the people around him, his own wife and daughter.

"Everything that went wrong on this island," he said, "can be traced to people not making sacrifices for the future." He sank the ax into the bark. He did the same with the adze. Affixing the tools to the tree they'd eventually cut down meant the next generation wouldn't have to dig up graves to save themselves—the tools to craft a waka would patiently wait, right where they'd be needed.

The Wayfinder weakly nodded, as if to say he respected our decision but would be sad to see us drown. Then he turned to regard the sea. The view up here was unmatched: sunny patches highlighted parcels of water, while the remaining seascape was darkened by clouded-over skies. I tried to imagine what he was going through. By convincing himself he could bring Lolohea back to life, he never had to deal with his brother's death. By fleeing Tonga, he never reckoned with what had gone wrong. Now the time had come. My father might've been thinking the same thing, since he placed a hand on the Wayfinder's shoulder. "You're not alone, son," he said. "We're here."

My father glanced at me like I should also comfort the Wayfinder. But what did I know of loss, except in a secondhand way? Besides being descended from slavery and being stranded on a remote island, besides my ancestors' murderous inclinations, the Great Wave, the extinctions, and the hunger we were facing, I was a perfectly innocent girl. Still, I placed a hand on the Wayfinder's shoulder.

"You're probably a little nervous," the Wayfinder said. "I know I once told you that to become the king of Tonga, a person had to fill a vaka with captives."

I *hadn't* been nervous. I glanced at my father, who returned a troubled look.

"I want to reassure you," the Wayfinder said, eyes on the horizon. "There already was a kidnapping, and I played my role. It's an ugly thing to admit. So, bringing your people to safety, that's a way of making amends."

My father adopted a chipper tone. "How about this solution? What if we remove *The Red Cloak*'s rotten hull and replace it with an outrigger? Instead of twenty people, it'll carry a dozen. That'll put less stress on the remaining hull. By using two waka, we can get thirty folks off this island. That'll cut our population nearly in half, and the people left behind will at least have some hope."

"Did you hear nothing I said?" the Wayfinder asked. He glanced at us both, disbelief on his face. "That cracked hull will drown anyone reckless enough to trust it. I can't tell if you're a brave people or fools who lack any fear of death."

My stomach growled. *When you're hungry,* it was saying, *what's the difference?*

* *
 *

Things began moving quickly. Arawiwi, leading a team of carpenters, went to work refashioning *The Red Cloak,* replacing the rotten hull with a sleek outrigger and winnowing the deck to lighten the load. The steering oar was trimmed and repositioned. The sail given a sharper outline. All day, my father and the Wayfinder re-fit the cleats, stays, leads, and lines.

Tiri commanded a group of botanical hunters to gather the seeds, cuttings, and saplings she'd need to work her medicine in distant lands. She wrapped the root balls of live specimens—barbed piripiri and flowering pia—in woven flax. You might think it impossible, a blind woman gathering plants, but she knew the smell of tamanu oil, could feel the hairy leaves of puaikao, understood that kōki'i grew along the shady bases of low-lying trees.

Tapoto was in charge of provisioning. Calabashes were filled, rope was coiled, mats were woven. It was only when Tapoto's spears were stowed that I remembered the trip's true mission. Tapoto also lashed a conch shell to each mast, a reminder that, though we'd depart together, there was no guarantee we'd arrive together or even at all.

My mother continued her work on Finau's ink. We were shaded by mangroves, at the edge of the beach. We weren't racing to finish his moko—that would take many sessions. It was more like, amid the chaos, we found comfort in routine. My mother worked her needles. I wiped blood and ink. All the while, Finau described things he missed about Tongatapu: the winds, the beaches, the outline of 'Eua at dawn. "Wait till you taste our mangoes," he said. "Wait till you eat one while floating in a bathing pond."

What would I remember of our little island? Was it possible to know what you'd miss before you'd left? Could I know that for the rest of my life, when I closed my eyes, this cove was what I'd see?

Hine and Ihi set about making necklaces for the people who'd depart. Each was adorned with a pendant of our sand—just a pinch—folded inside a leaf. When the girl had completed a few, she took the time to hang one around my neck and another around my mother's. "Doesn't Hine get one?" I asked Ihi. She shook her head.

"You sure you're not coming?" I asked Hine.

Ihi answered. "She's staying with me until my mother comes."

That silenced the protests I had ready. I'd wanted to tell Hine that she was a guardian now, that she had to do what was best for Ihi, even if that included seeking a better life on a new island. But I also knew that friends ranked less than guardians, so my concerns were now lesser and admittedly selfish: I just wanted Hine in my life, to sing with, to share with, to lean on when things went wrong.

"Will you make sure Hā Mutu doesn't return to parrot-hunting?" I asked Hine.

"Will you make sure Tapoto doesn't do anything stupid?" she asked.

"Like fighting dangerous men on faraway islands?"

She smiled.

"You won't change your mind?" I asked.

"You'll be okay without me."

I wasn't sure I could say the same.

Hine said, "I guess I'll never know if Tapoto killed the dangerous fellow."

"Don't worry," I said. "He did."

"Focus," my mother said. I wiped ink and blood from Finau's leg.

"And the sunsets," Finau said. "The sunsets when Kao is erupting to the west, they're as lovely and magical as..." He strained for the right metaphor. "As the beauty of childbirth."

My mother rolled her eyes.

Hine and I tried not to laugh.

This time, the Tongans didn't dictate who'd go. Neither did we engage in endless discussion. Instead, Ihi wandered about, offering necklaces. Those who adorned themselves would depart. It was that simple. Papa Toki refused a necklace. When he tried to hang them on his sons, telling them he wished them better lives, they also refused, saying family mattered most. Hā Mutu was carving a piece of wood when Ihi presented him with a necklace. He, too, refused.

Finau was shocked to see Tiri wearing a necklace. "You're bringing an old, blind woman on a voyage to battle my uncle?"

The trip was about much more than that, but I nodded, *Yes*.

Tiri and I took Hine to a small clearing. Like it or not, Hine would become our Rangatira Kaikōrero, our storytelling captain, and we didn't have long to press all our important narratives into her. Tiri told the story of Tāne-nui-a-rangi and the story of Hine-nui-te-pō, who brought moko from the underworld. Ihi studied me as I began the epic narrative Tānerore, the Summer Maiden.

Hine threw up her hands. "They're all blurring together," she said. "I can't keep them straight."

"That's good," Tiri said. "There's only one story, the story of our people. It can come in scraps."

Tiri next recited the romance of Hinemoa and Tūtānekai.

Ihi, uninterested in a love story, said, "Tell the one about Irawaru turning into a dog."

"Why're you doing this?" Hine asked. "I'm a horrible storyteller. I'm bad with details. I mix stuff up."

Ihi, I could tell, was absorbing everything.

When Tiri started the story of Rātā's Canoe, Ihi interrupted to discuss an aspect she'd heard differently.

Hine turned to me. "Who cares about old-timey stories from faraway places? Remember when Tapoto lit the canoe house on fire?"

"Yeah, it was the middle of the night," I said. "He was trying to secretly bake a sweet potato."

Hine laughed. "Out where he thought no one would smell it cooking."

"So he brought his torch indoors."

"And when he bent over, the flame . . ." Hine paused.

"What?" I asked.

Her eyes got wet. "I'm never going to see Tapoto again, am I?"

I didn't answer. I just started telling funny stories from when Hine and I were kids. Like the ones about the exploding coconut and the diarrhea outbreak. We could make each other laugh just by mentioning a single detail, like *fish lips* or *infected toe*.

As night fell, I noticed Ihi had begun telling Tiri a story. I wanted to hear it, but a conch shell trumpet blew. A certain constellation had begun to rise. People walked past us, headed toward shore. Suddenly I was hugging Hine, and my eyes were wet. We, too, started walking to the beach, each with a hand on Tiri to steady her. I noticed Tiri wore in her hair a feather from the extinct huia bird. It was her only possession.

Finau was calling for his parrot, Kōkī. I began calling for Aroha.

Hā Mutu intercepted me. He handed me a piece of wood. It was carved in the shape of his face, with all his moko lines reproduced. It was a death mask, fashioned while still alive. "To remember me," Hā Mutu said. "You wouldn't think it, but faces fade." He and I had crouched in the predawn forest a thousand times. His face was often never more than a shadow, and what we shared most of all was silence, as if we'd been preparing all that time for this parting. We closed our eyes, and, without words, shared the breath of life.

The Red Cloak had been turned to face the waves. My mother was already on board. She held her feather box and inking tools, nothing more. A hand reached out to pull me aboard. Instead, I turned to Hine, my friend, my sister, the person dearest to me. We threw our arms around one another. I'd never held anyone so tightly. Her hot tears landed on my shoulder. My own tears fell through clenched eyes. I had countless things to say to her, but making earnest exchanges, that wasn't Hine's way.

"Don't forget the crab dance," she told me.

"Don't forget *stinky poi balls*," I said, laughing through tears.

"*Ghost fingers*."

"*Papa burps*."

"If anybody asks what the ocean looks like," she said, "tell them it's blue."

"You'll be a great mom," I told her.

"Keep your eye out for dogs," she reminded me. "I still don't trust them."

"Don't forget who your best friend is."

"Don't forget yours."

Someone pulled us apart. Our waka was being pushed off the sand. I had to scramble up the stern.

Kōkī and his flock flew in, landing in the mangroves. "Kōkī no Tonga,"

Kōkī declared. He spread his wings. "Tonga murder. Tonga war. Tonga extinction."

The people left behind shouldered us into the surf. I glanced toward the open sea—the Wayfinder's canoe was ahead of us, already raising sail. When I looked back, there were figures, waist-deep in the water, watching us depart. On shore were those holding torches, flames warping their features. They started waving, hands yellow in the light. It looked like they were instead beckoning, like they'd changed their minds and wanted us back. Beckoning me home, that's how I'd remember them, these people I'd never see again.

TWENTY-NINE

THE SEA, THE SOLE MAP OF ITSELF

It was about this time that Havea's wife Vaivao returned. Vaivao no longer took the form of a sack of bones, for she'd been reanimated. Alone, she made landfall on the Tongan island of Nomuka. White-lipped and sun-beaten, she piloted a vaka tinged purple-red, as if her umbilical journey back from the afterlife had taken her through the velvet walls of a great womb. She had no provisions or cargo, except, hanging from the mast, a fishing net of human bones. She turned to these and spoke a private word, for the bones must've been her only companions upon the sea. Then she waded ashore, declaring, "I come from the land of lalo fonua, the land of darkness, the land of below."

As light off waves can stun, so she seemed stunned, seeming to see and not see those around her. "What land is this?" she asked.

A woman who'd been mending nets said, "You've reached Nomuka."

"But what land is it?" Havea's wife asked. "Is this the land of flesh and blood?"

Average Nomukans going about their day stopped to listen.

Receiving no answer, she moved toward a boy and—causing some panic—seized him. Placing a hand upon his heart, she felt its beat. "You're alive," she announced. "You're a perfect, living boy. I've no idea where my boys are. I can only guess if their blood yet pumps." Then, as if gripped by a sudden idea, she placed a hand to her own heart. "When did death become life for me? When did the two trade places?"

The boy's mother pulled him to safety. "Who are you?" she asked Vaivao. "What do you seek?"

"I seek my husband, the navigator Havea. Has he made landfall here? Two young men would've been with him."

The net-mending woman rose from the sand. "You're the wife of Havea? All of Tonga discusses how he voyaged to save you."

"Yes," Vaivao said. "He made it to Pulotu. He restored me. But on the journey back I lost track of him." She turned to the purple-red vessel. "Here's his vaka, but where's my husband, where're my boys?"

The villagers gazed at the bones hanging from the vaka's mast.

An old woman asked, "You've seen the afterlife? Tell me, are reunions made, are bodies restored?"

"You ask of the afterlife? You might as well ask of the beforelife. There, waves crash before they rise, yet are ever cresting. Trembling at their peaks, they flash with light. That's the afterlife, the place where waves ever crest."

At this cryptic response, several Nomukans exchanged glances.

"I'm near the end," the old woman said. "Can you tell me what awaits?"

"*What awaits?*" Vaivao said. "I forget that you live in the now. It's coming back to me how life was divided into moments. *What awaits?* Yes, that was the only question when I was alive."

"Are you not living?"

"I can only say I was mortal, and then I was eternal. And now I'm something else. My heart beats, I stand on solid ground, yet when I regard the sea, the wave and the trough are one. The turn of the firmament has been made observable. Audible is the breath that blows the wind. All always was, and what will be visibly is." Vaivao pointed at the boy. "His three daughters are already born, and his death has already taken place. In Pulotu, we hear the clacking of black stones at your funerals. Do you hear us snap branches from the uhi tree and fill our dippers from the river of life?"

A fisherman was sitting beneath a tree. "But you're no longer in Pulotu," he said. "This is Nomuka."

Havea's wife gazed upon her surroundings, causing Nomukans to survey their own island with her, trying to see as she did—a reality where niu trees were both just-sprouting and also fallen, where stars had finally dimmed yet also awaited their initial ignition.

The net mender asked, "Whose bones made the journey with you?"

Vaivao turned to look at them, swinging from the mast. She seemed unable to answer.

"When did you come into possession of them?" the net mender asked.

Angrily, Vaivao said, "*When* no longer troubles me. *When* only applies to people like you, but I'll oblige you with some *when*. You," she said to the net mender, "shall make your arrival in Pulotu when your second grandchild gets her first tooth. You shall see the purple light," she said to the old woman, "before the solstice arrives. And you," she told the fisherman, "will step on a poisonous u'ui shell on the reef called Hakaufisi."

The Tu'i of Nomuka arrived with his matāpule. "What's this commotion?" he asked Vaivao.

"You," she told him, "will die in a Fisian raid."

"You mustn't speak like this," the Tu'inomuka said. He commanded some men to restrain her. When they took hold of her arms, they found her limbs loose, as if her bones hadn't knitted.

"I've seen more," Vaivao called. "On Pulotu, where duels are eternal, preparations are made for the Tu'itonga himself. His enemies gather to confront him. And they won't wait long. The Tu'itonga will die when the rains arrive."

"Fe'unga," the Tu'inomuka shouted. He ordered a stick tied in her mouth. Then the great navigator's wife was forced back onto her vaka and pushed out to sea.

The Nomukans stood at the tide line to watch her go.

The fisherman shook his head. "Imagine it," he said. "She, alone in the afterlife, is separated from her earthly family. Yet after Havea's epic voyage to reunite, they simply exchange places."

The boy asked the fisherman, "Will you continue to fish the Hakaufisi Reef?"

They watched a purple-red sail luff and then tighten as it caught the reefward breeze.

The fisherman didn't answer.

"Vaivao's family traded in funeral stones," the net mender said. "They overcharged everyone."

None could argue this point, for Nomuka had to import its funeral stones like all the rest.

"Where'll she go?" the boy asked.

"She'll go where she's already arrived," the old woman said. "And I'll soon embark upon ever-cresting waves."

Gathering his matāpule, the Tuʻinomuka commanded them, "Send word to Tongatapu that the wife of Havea has paid us a visit. Make no mention of her dark prognostications, especially concerning the king. Do not mention the fate of Havea. Relay only that the woman exists, that she came and that she went."

With the Tuʻitonga and his entourage at the Teleki Reefs, Tongatapu was unusually at ease, as if a great exhale had taken place. Without royal matāpule to moderate public behavior, people actually ate the food they grew and bathed in pools reserved for their betters. Without chiefs to admonish them, villagers sat chatting along the paths, catching up with friends.

The Tamahā took the opportunity to glean. She enlisted some aimless, troublemaking boys who seemed to sense that she, too, would break some rules. Right away, she dispatched two boys to steal the eggs of a rare and recently arrived pair of mangrove herons. These eggs she'd incubate by hand since these birds, much persecuted, likely wouldn't survive. Their crimes? Their leg bones made the most delicate flutes. Their wing bones were perfect for inking needles. Finally, they produced the most ineffably rich yolks a king ever tasted.

She brought the other boys to the royal compound. From the king's middens, she had them pile two skids with oyster shells—when crushed, this was second only to bone meal as fertilizer. She helped herself to mounds of kava cud, which, when dried, fueled her kiln.

The Tamahā wandered the royal compound. Atop the langi tomb still sat a greenstone club and the bones of ʻAho's wife. After the Tuʻitonga's death, this was where his matāpule and security men would die. It was where Pōhiva's priests and waiting girls would die, and it was where Pōhiva herself would kneel and allow a kafa rope around her neck. This was where, as the rope crackled taut, she'd review her life, her good fortune, and her lifelong ratification of the system now strangling her.

Inside the Fefine Girls' fale, there was nothing but a vessel of drinking water, a few candlenut lamps, and rows of empty sleeping mats. The air smelled of turmeric, sandalwood, and youth. She lifted a mat. Beneath it was nothing—not a hidden pouch or a secreted feather or a scrap of tapa cloth inked by a mother. These girls lacked even a single possession. They'd have nothing in this world until their husbands took it upon themselves to give it to them.

She entered the royal fale, starting with the room where the Tuʻitonga's security team slept. The Tuʻitonga's new security chief had yet to be named—whoever claimed this honor would serve the king in his remaining days, and, after being put to death, continue serving in the next life.

In an antechamber, she found the royal cloak, made from the feathers of a thousand birds. The Tuʻitonga rarely wore it—out of humility, he claimed. The truth was he'd grown quite heavy, and the garment no longer properly draped upon him, giving the impression it was made for another man.

At last came the royal chamber, where dozens of sleeping mats were piled high to form a grand bed. These mats had been taken by the hand of the king, each from the sleeping chamber of an "enemy," and they sheafed high like so many trophies to the king's former prowess. It was a monument also to comfort. How to reconcile the man he once was with the one he'd become?

On the top mat were traces of ink and blood and dribbles of urine. This she bent to sniff, the piss smelling too, too sweet—failing kidneys. The Tuʻitonga wouldn't die in any heroic manner, but here, his skin taut from fluid retention, his feet cold, his eyesight failing, and no herbal drink would save him.

The Fefine Girls soon returned. They'd been at sea and sleeping in the open, so the Tamahā did not restart their lessons. Instead, they sank soot-faced, wind-burned, and insect-bitten into the royal bathing pool. The Tamahā reclined in the sand, observing them. Was one only pretending to feel cleansed and relaxed? Had one among them felt the jellyfish sting?

She studied Moon Appearing, chest-deep in the cleansing waters. The girl located herself among the other girls, laughing when the others laughed, nodding when one shared a lament. Was this not how a girl might camouflage her pain? The Tamahā liked to think she'd know when a girl'd been hurt, but when she herself had been hurt, long ago, no one had had an inkling.

Kōkī landed in the sand beside the Tamahā. "Kōkī so alone," Kōkī said. "Kōkī need some love."

"I heard you attacked the king," the Tamahā said.

"Yes, Kōkī bad," Kōkī said. "But Kōkī only self-defend."

"You can dispense with the 'bad bird' act. You have at your command all of Tongan poetry."

"Those are people words. Where the poetry birds were made to speak? Where the sounds, where the beak, where Kōkī discover parrot speech?" Kōkī's wings drooped. "No matter. Tu'itonga mad. Tu'itonga kill."

The thought that, without another, a kind couldn't truly be known ... it made the Tamahā unexpectedly sad, for she herself was a variety of one. "Perhaps your speech is somewhere inside you."

Kōkī cocked his head, pinwheeled an eye. He raised his beak, looking uncertain yet hopeful. Out came an extended squawk. Disappointed, Kōkī said, "*Nea, nea.* Kōkī not some stupid bird who chirp and screech. If only there was another of Kōkī's kind. Why people save but one of me?"

"If there was another of your variety," she said, "if I thought I could bring your kind back, I might risk the king's wrath to protect you."

"Nice woman save Kōkī?" Kōkī asked.

The Tamahā shook her head.

"But Kōkī danger! Kōkī go extinct."

"Welcome to the human world."

"The human world," Kōkī said, spreading a wing, mockingly showcasing its delights: fruit trees lacking fruit, fields voided of trees, smoke from countless fires. "Human woman listen Kōkī. Don't let king get Kōkī's feathers. Don't let Kōkī adorn the Tu'itonga's hair."

The Tamahā regarded the crestfallen parrot.

"Kōkī gift you Kōkī's feathers," Kōkī said. "When Kōkī die, Kōkī give you his plumes."

"If you can get them to me."

Kōkī gazed at the Fefine Girls, as if he shared something with them. Then he spoke:

Fuifui fa Kōkī 'i Tonga,	Flock of parrots in Tonga,
ngangana 'e he kakai.	felled by the many.
Fuhi fa fulufulu 'i fatafata,	Patch of breast feathers,
toli 'e he Mu'a.	plucked by the one.

"What old poem is that from?" the Tamahā asked.

"Kōkī the one who say those lines," Kōkī said. "Only Kōkī spoke them."

Four young men sailed north, theirs the only sail to be seen. The weather was starting its seasonal turn—light rain in the afternoon, and once even at dawn. Whales with calves had begun departing Vava'u, their night calls appearing to come from all quarters, often seemingly voiced by the outrigger itself.

Evenings came imperceptibly at first, and then the cloak was lowered. Night near the Koro Sea: purple froth, rope creak, the sail endlessly communicating its complaints. Behind them, a hull-shaped void in the waves. The Wayfinder worked the sheet in the large Fisian canoe, while the others took turns at the steering oar. Lolohea was good at holding a line—he understood how to greet a wave head-on, how to face them at angles, and, tonight, how to be overtaken in the troughs.

Punake'd been annoying the Wayfinder since the moment they'd left, constantly proposing cheats and evasions to the mission they were on. No one wanted to kidnap people, no one wanted to abduct innocents off beaches. Punake's impossible work-arounds only called attention to this.

Mateaki crafted a flute from the slim fore-bone of a human arm. The holes he worked by feel in the dark. At various stations in the night, dry notes sounded as Mateaki shaped and tuned his little instrument.

Punake sat up. "What if we hire people? All we have to do is return with a dozen, right? The test says nothing of how it's done. In fact, a prince is supposed to use his ingenuity. What say we go to some friendly shores, like Haʻamoa, and make a deal? We hire them to—"

"Hire them with what?" Lolohea asked.

"With a future payment," Punake said. "We ask people to make a brief journey with us. In pretend bondage. When Lolohea's king, he'll free them and handsomely reward them."

"What person would agree to that?" Lolohea asked.

Mateaki played an arid note on his flute. "The whole point is that we don't ask permission."

"First we get rid of these bones," Lolohea said.

It was clear he was using this task to buy himself some time.

The Wayfinder said, "I'm holding a general course, but soon we'll need an actual destination."

"Why don't you pick an island?" Lolohea asked. "You're the one who's been here before."

The Wayfinder thought of how he'd crossed this water to free a captive, not abduct one, how Havea had always taught him to protect people. The Wayfinder was doing the opposite. The only person who had it worse was Lolohea himself, who, if successful, would direct such activities for the rest of his life.

"I've got it," Punake called out. "We sail to the island of Kao, where men slave in obsidian mines. They'd be happy to join us. We'd be giving them a holiday from servitude. They'd eat well, breathe clean air, and, after a brief excursion to Tongatapu, return refreshed to their toils."

Punake received only this response: Mateaki, having decided the flute was tuned to his liking, began to play, the notes feathery and pale, more breath than sound, yet all the more human and haunting. The Wayfinder expected a song to emerge, yet none did. It was like a child's composition, notes dry and pitchless, offered without regard to pattern or melody. Yet after a while there was something hypnotic about it, the way wind clacking bamboo poles created rhythms that echoed inside you. Lolohea was clearly unnerved by the sounds, and Punake, who organized all his thoughts into the cadence and rhyme of poetry, looked ready to go mad. But the Wayfinder found such seemingly random notes familiar, soothing even. Each wave, in its way, was similar to every other wave, yet no two were alike. No wave was the same as any other wave that'd ever been, and each wave was not even like itself, from moment to moment. And so with Mateaki's playing. It was reminiscent of flute music but was in no relation to any fingering or melody that'd ever been heard. Yet the notes weren't random: they were arranged by the mind of a boy raised in a dangerous land by a dangerous father, so this was the melody of a world where at any moment, anyone could be lost and anything could happen and often did.

That night, the Tamahā reclined upon her floating bed. Against her chest, she clutched three heron's eggs. She lit no lamp, leaving the moon to decide what could be seen. Wind, moving through her fale, rocked the bed on its woven cables, and she lay there making no effort to shield herself from mosquitoes. Above, between the fale's lodge poles, where other people stored their wedding mats, was nothing, just black air.

Her bed swayed. The rope creaked. On its peg, her Fan trembled with the breeze. Inside the wind, she sensed an animating force. The animals felt it, too. Outside, fish, restless, splashed from tier to tier. The malau birds, visible through the door, huddled together, their dark backs forming one back. The feeling she felt was the feeling of change.

She pondered the royal chamber. After the Tuʻitonga was gone, what would be done with his sleeping mats? Who'd preserve a previous king's trophies? They'd be dragged to the middens or simply burned—taking flame would be ancient weaves imbued with blessings for the newlyweds who'd soon lie in union on their marriage nights, couples who'd further the mats' patterns with their blood and semen and sweat and hope.

Who would one day sleep in her floating bed? the Tamahā wondered. When she was gone, the bed would likely be broken up, the slats used to build hog pens. What would happen to her compound, her tapu being the only thing protecting it? The malau—fat, flightless, clearly put on these islands before the invention of people—would be eaten in a day. The freshwater fish—secreted here from a remote volcanic lake—would supply but a single feast. Her medicinal herbs—some gone from the earth and continuing only by her germinations—would be tilled to grow more kava. Preservation of the herons was unlikely. Even if the eggs hatched, they were fragile creatures. The bird had developed a little trick to survive: it would pluck one of its own feathers, and, jigging it at the water's surface, strike at the fish who surfaced to investigate. A fisher who used its own body as bait. How could such a bird come to be? How could it hope to continue, this bird that consumed itself in order to keep consuming? How could Tonga hope to persevere? It couldn't. Yes, there'd be another Tonga, and another after that. But they wouldn't be this one. The little parrot had reached a conclusion. It had made a plan. And now the Tamahā must face the future, too. Who would she gift her feathers to? To whom would she pass her Fan?

In the morning, the Tamahā's rafters were no longer empty. When she woke, she discovered a mangrove heron perched on a lodge pole, staring down at the eggs in the Tamahā's hands. The bird showed neither anxiety nor agitation, just puzzlement over how her eggs had come to be thusly situated. The heron, in short hops, followed the Tamahā outside, where its mate was perched at the edge of the fishpond, the fish having sunk into the dark recesses. She set the eggs in the soil beside the pond, and right away the mother heron rolled them under a shrub and began pulling reeds to nest them.

Yes, some fish would be lost to these newcomers, but sacrifices must be made.

The Fefine Girls, sullen, arrived later in the morning. The Tamahā gave them no lectures or lessons. Instead, she put them on their hands and knees before the stones they'd use to crush oyster shells. The Tamahā, arms crossed, walked among them as they worked. It was maddening that she couldn't determine which girls had felt the jellyfish sting. She could help such a girl, if only she could identify her.

Before long, Pōhiva came visiting. Passing through the gates, she appeared astonished by the trees, dripping with fruit, the flightless birds, the fishponds, the immense living wall. "Why, it's like this is the island, and the rest of Tongatapu is the sea." Before the Tamahā could respond, Pōhiva asked, "Are those mangrove herons? I thought they were no more."

"It seems a few remain," the Tamahā said.

Marveling, Pōhiva asked, "Have you ever tasted oysters cooked in heron yolk?"

"What brings you here?" the Tamahā asked.

"I bear a gift," Pōhiva said, for she did have a basket in hand. "Candlenuts from 'Ata. Many believe they have the power to illuminate spirits. How come you never join us on 'Ata? You're always welcome."

The Tamahā would never put herself at the mercy of the Tu'itonga's hospitality. Still, she answered honestly. "There are many struggles in this world, and females face them double. To do that, women must look forward. The trips to 'Ata, as they are recalled to me, are about men turning to the past."

"But the past is where we locate our nobility," Pōhiva said. "Who'd we be without that?"

"We'd be like everyone else."

"Exactly," Pōhiva said. Then she turned her attention to the Fefine Girls, kneeling before their stones. "Your methods are unconventional. But you do have a gift for teaching these girls obedience. What could better prepare them for their futures?"

"It's resilience I teach. That leads to perseverance. From there, independence is but a step away."

"Describe it as you will. They've certainly learned to obey. The future husbands of Tonga thank you."

The smile they exchanged was popoto mo manu fekai, as they say.

"You've come at snack time," the Tamahā said. She produced a basket of nonu fruit, dark seeds spilling from milky flesh. The girls recoiled from the rancid-smelling fruit as each received a piece.

"What's this?" Pōhiva asked. "Even animals avoid nonu."

The Tamahā took a bite. "Though distasteful, it's quite edible. We can't forget our famine foods. And I assure you, hungry people consume nonu on this island every day. You just don't see them."

"If this is so, it's sad to learn," Pōhiva said. "I'll ask my husband to address the topic of hunger."

The Tamahā spit seeds and looked to Kakala, who closed her eyes, took a bite, and silently chewed. Highborn Heilala, however, only pantomimed eating. Moon Appearing partook of the fruit. She said, "On Hunga, everyone knows the taste of nonu."

"Hunga?" Pōhiva asked, suddenly interested. "Such a remote island." Pōhiva turned to the Tamahā. "Tell me this one's name."

The Tamahā had no idea what Pōhiva was doing here, but she was not surrendering Moon Appearing's name. Instead, she offered Pōhiva a bite of nonu, saying, "Nothing would inspire the girls more than a ratifying taste from their queen."

At the smell of the fruit, Pōhiva crumpled her face.

"It's not so bad," one girl told Pōhiva. "You get used to it."

"And who are you?" Pōhiva asked her. "I can tell by your speech you're from Tonga's northernmost islands, yes?"

Embarrassed to have her ruralness pointed out, she looked down. "I'm Sun Shower."

"Sun Shower," Pōhiva said. "Sun Shower, Sun Shower. Such an unforgettable name."

The Tamahā leveled her eyes on the queen. "To what honor do we owe your visit, again?"

"Why, I just wanted to drop off these candlenuts. Say the word and I'll send a chef to whip up those oysters I told you about. It's obvious you treasure oyster shells—wait till you taste what comes inside."

The malevolence of nature occasioned much verse. The sky and the sea were known to collude. Men were targeted with lightning. Waves rose, shouldering sailors into the sea, where it was their turn to be paddled. So, on Punake's first open-ocean voyage, his eyes scanned the horizon, searching for the dark forces poetry had promised. When the cameo of an island appeared through morning mist, it was Punake who spotted it.

Lolohea shielded his eyes to study this patch of land. "Looks pretty small."

"At the first sighting of Fisi," Mateaki said, "men paint their faces."

"Which poem is that from?" Punake asked.

Mateaki laughed and shook his head.

Punake returned his attention to the island. What had he been expecting? In poems, Fisi's Lau Islands were formidable, with tall fires and warriors in constant states of agitation. The names of some Fisian islands had found a permanent home in Tongan verse. There was Lakemba, with its great fortress. And Moce, where men never bothered to remove their battle turbans.

Punake looked to the Wayfinder. "Which island is this?"

The Wayfinder shrugged.

"You don't know?" Feeling panicked, he turned to Mateaki. "You've been to Fisi many times, yes?"

"As a passenger," Mateaki said.

Punake let that sink in: they didn't know where they were.

They sailed around to the island's lee, where the shore break was lighter. This allowed them a good look at this nameless place—endless coconut trees, a thin strip of beach.

"I don't see any orchards," Lolohea said, "so it's likely uninhabited."

Punake said, "No one lives on coconuts alone."

"What great poem is that from?" Mateaki asked.

Punake had thought it a fair observation, but Lolohea, eyes fixed on the island, laughed.

Who was Punake to the prince, to any of them? He'd never wanted to be anybody's surrogate father, but there'd been no choice, and over the years he'd grown comfortable in the role. Sentries bowed at his approach, servants lowered their eyes. As long as Finau was protected and tutored, Punake was free to gaze at Fefine Girls, swill gossip, indulge at feasts. But who was he without Finau? A deckhand, a warrior, a slave? He suddenly considered this possibility: that of the twelve souls Lolohea needed to conscript, he himself, by setting foot upon this vaka, had unwittingly made himself the first.

"I see no structures," Lolohea said. "No woodsmoke, no fishing boats. We'll dump the bones here. Mateaki, you'll make the swim. When you make it ashore, just drop the bones and go."

It occurred to Punake: This might be the only nonviolent excursion.

Perhaps this was his chance to safely garner some kind of credit against the dangers to come. "This mission's mine," Punake declared. Then he leaped into action, unfurling some spare sail. With great haste, he began bundling the bones. These weren't parts of people, he thought, just stuff, things to be gotten rid of.

"I can land on the beach," the Wayfinder said.

"No," Lolohea said. "We keep our distance."

With the bundle of bones, Punake lowered himself over the side. The panic didn't hit until he felt salt in his eyes. As the bundle filled with water, it lumbered like a swamped canoe. Soon Punake was struggling to keep the bones from sinking, and could see nothing but sky when he snatched breaths.

From the deck, Lolohea saw what Punake could not from the waves below: on the beach, a few children had appeared. "Mateaki," Lolohea said. "You better go with him."

Mateaki cinched his loincloth before diving toward the struggling poet.

The Wayfinder joined Lolohea in watching them go.

"What's got into Punake?" Lolohea asked. "He's never volunteered for anything."

"Why'd our father insist on our bringing him?" the Wayfinder asked.

Lolohea had no idea. To toughen the poet, to test him, to punish him for something?

Lolohea pointed at the children. There were several now. "Can you be ready to raise anchor?"

"I'm ready right now." Then he said, "You originally asked Mateaki to do this alone."

"Yeah?" Lolohea asked.

"Would that've been our chance to leave him?"

Lolohea asked, "Would you have done it, sailed away?"

"Why's he even with us, why's he being allowed to pass the tests that could make him king?"

"It's part of a bigger plan," Lolohea said.

"What plan?"

"The one to get rid of his father," Lolohea said. "I expect that's happening as we speak." He watched Mateaki and Punake battle the crests into shallow water. Despite all his cousin had been through—getting dragged to war as a kid, losing his mother, being bound to a dangerous father—Lolohea had never felt sympathy for him. He wasn't sure he felt it now, but talk of abandonment made him feel something. "We do need him," Lolohea added. "There are only four of us—to kidnap a dozen people."

The Wayfinder said, "Imagine if Fisians came to our shores to dump the bones of Tongans."

In the distance, Punake and Mateaki at last emerged from the waves, the children now circling them.

"What're those kids doing?" Lolohea asked.

"You'd think they'd run away," the Wayfinder said. "Don't they see our Tongan ink?"

Lolohea strained to peer through the mist of beach break. The kids somehow looked bigger now that they were in motion. "Maybe they aren't exactly children," he said. "Let's get closer."

While Lolohea paddled hard to turn the bow, the Wayfinder raised anchor and tightened the sheet. Punake and Mateaki, visible only on the crests, had begun the swim back. A third person, right at their heels, seemed to be pursuing them.

Mateaki yelled something. Lolohea couldn't make it out.

Punake lifted his head, but instead of calling, he scrambled for breath.

There was much thrashing in the water as they finally drew close.

"I got one!" Mateaki managed to shout.

From the outrigger, ready to help them aboard, Lolohea could see they each pulled an arm belonging to a person whose features weren't visible because his face was in the water. At last, they splashed their way home. Punake needed help onto the deck. Mateaki hoisted himself—his bloody face now visible. The wound wasn't from knuckles but fingernails.

"I got one," Mateaki said.

The Fisian, face down in the water, began to sink.

Lolohea hauled him aboard. "He isn't breathing."

Punake turned to Mateaki. "He's just a kid."

Mateaki said, "He was old enough to attack us."

"I don't want a dead man on board," the Wayfinder said. "We just got rid of our dead men."

"He counts," Mateaki said. "He was alive when I kidnapped him."

The Fisian boy's eyes were open, staring at the sky.

"It doesn't matter if he attacked us," Punake said. "He's a kid."

"How'd you expect him to breathe?" Lolohea asked. "How could he keep his head above water if you were towing him by his arms?"

"That's one down," Mateaki said. "The next ones will be easier."

Lolohea regarded the boy, who was younger even than Finau. In fact, Lolohea remembered exactly what Finau was like at this age—composing his first lines of verse, so proud of his own poems, *his*, not the ones Punake had him memorize. The sight made Lolohea miss his brother desperately.

The Tufuga tapped ink into Finau's flank. They were again beneath the tuitui tree. The boy kept asking, *What motif do you ink now?* and *How does the pattern progress?* Though Finau wanted wholly original ink, the safest bet was to give him the usual motifs.

Since the ink was progressing on both his subjects, the Tufuga started to believe he might see home again. The notion that he'd survive this trip allowed him, for the first time, to see the beauty in this island: the white skins of kilns glowing in the predawn light, spinner dolphins leaping in the green lagoon. What would he say of this place upon his return to Samoa? Would he relate tales of men killed by dogs, men flayed alive, men gutted while yet breathing, men drowned by the canoeful?

Pōhiva came by. She said, "The girl has been selected."

"What girl?" Finau asked.

"It's done, then," the Tuʻitonga told his wife.

"What's done?" Finau asked.

"We should start the rumors," the Tuʻitonga said.

"What rumors are you talking about?" Finau asked.

Pōhiva studied the blood leaking from her son. The Tufuga nervously wiped it away. He pivoted to the Tuʻitonga, also face down in the shade. The king was bloated, his tissue taut. He looked to be wearing a cloak of fluid beneath his skin. The Tufuga took a breath, dipped his needles, and began crosshatching the Tuʻitonga's inner thigh, a sensitive region. "This gives you no discomfort?" the Tufuga asked him.

"None," the Tuʻitonga said, head sideways on folded arms.

Rather than blood, a clear fluid welled from the site.

"What about this?" the Tufuga asked, but instead of sinking his needles into the king's skin, he merely tapped his inking sticks in the air.

"Of course I feel it," the king said. "But it doesn't hurt. I've befriended pain, I've tamed it."

Concern crossed Pōhiva's face. "The plan moves forward," she told her husband. "Regardless of how many days remain, we'll secure our boys' futures."

Finau asked, "How many days remain until what?"

"Are you surprised to learn a life can be measured in days?" the Tuʻitonga asked Finau. "Whether you realize it or not, all lives are counted that way. And you wonder what we're planning? We've planned for everything, son, since before you were born, because unless you make the future, the future makes you."

The royal entourage arrived to give the king his morning briefing. They took no notice of the Tufuga. There were the usual reports of shortages, disputes, and infractions. Another island had fallen in Fisi.

"I gave no order to take an additional island," the Tuʻitonga said.

"We were attacked," the war captain said. "There was a counterattack. The offending island was subdued."

The Tuʻitonga looked up, visibly suspicious. Still, he nodded.

A matāpule announced there'd been an insurrection in Haʻamoa.

"*An insurrection?*" the Tuʻitonga asked. "Are they not our peaceable friends?"

"With them, it's always one trouble or another," the matāpule said. "Usually their antics are not worth reporting. But some quelling will be necessary."

The Tuʻitonga waved his hand. "Very well, then. Quell away."

So this was how it happened, the Tufuga thought. This was how a district in Samoa got decimated. And the Tuʻitonga hadn't even bothered to ask after the offense or the figures involved.

Matāpule Muʻa stepped forward. After a cautious pause, he said, "The Tuʻitonga has authorized his brother to lay his wife's bones to rest."

"Yes," the Tuʻitonga said. "But his satisfaction can wait a little longer."

"I point out that your brother has promised to depart afterward," Matāpule Muʻa said. "Tongatapu will be much relieved."

"Those bones hold our only sway over him," the Tuʻitonga said.

"We don't know how he'll react to further postponement," Matāpule Muʻa said. "Were he to attack another girl, her fate would rest on your shoulders."

"Everyone's fate rests on my shoulders!" the Tuʻitonga snapped. "He thinks I feel no pain. He thinks I know nothing of suffering. When in fact I bear the burdens of an entire people."

Matāpule Muʻa skipped to the good news: "Your new security chief has been selected!"

A short servant delivered Six Fists's great spear. The Tuʻitonga looked around for the man who'd claim it. "Well, let's see this security man."

"He stands before you," Matāpule Muʻa said.

"The little fellow?" the Tuʻitonga asked.

"Don't let appearances deceive," Matāpule Muʻa said. "The military chiefs swear they haven't seen his equal. He's not large, it's true, but he's quick as lightning and a terror at hand-to-hand."

The Tuʻitonga studied the compact fellow. His arms, though short, were heavily veined. His calves were nothing but knots. "What's his name?" he cautiously asked.

"That's the best part," Matāpule Muʻa said. "Because of his fighting prowess, his fellow warriors call him Seven Fists."

A pained look crossed the Tuʻitonga's face.

"I assure you," Matāpule Muʻa said. "The moniker is one he's earned. It's born from the admiration of all the Tongan warriors he's bested."

"Does he harbor any fear of dogs?" the Tuʻitonga asked.

Seven Fists spoke: "I'm trained in canine combat."

"I have a difficult task in mind for you," the Tuʻitonga told him.

"Name it," the compact man said.

"Soon enough," the Tuʻitonga told him. He waved them away before rolling, with great difficulty, onto his back. "I do not forget you, old friend," he said to the sky. To the Tufuga, he said, "Six Fists's skin was much adorned, but one bit of ink meant more than the rest. At his collarbone was the constellation Mataliki, which he believed kept him from losing his way. Can you ink that on me?"

Finau also rolled to his back. "If my father gets Mataliki, I get Mataliki."

The Tuʻitonga offered his son the kind of benevolent smile that made the Samoan miss his own family. It made him miss his wife and his garden and the feeling of a pole against his back while a breeze crossed his legs in his village's faletele longhouse. The Tufuga located the needle he'd use to ink the seven stars that formed the "Little Eyes of the North."

"We mustn't lose our way," the king told his son. "We do what we must, but we can't lose ourselves."

"I won't let that happen," Finau said.

"I'm sorry I took Punake from you," the Tuʻitonga said. "I know you had tender feelings for him."

"Did you really do it so you could be more of a father to me?"

The Tuʻitonga nodded.

Finau said, "Well, I suppose Punake will be okay. What harm could come to a man who wields the power of the Tongan language, the mightiest weapon of all?"

THIRTY

THE PEACE-LOVING ISLAND OF ROTUMA

THE STORY OF KANIVA

On the peace-loving island of Rotuma, there lived a lonely young woman named Kaniva. She was the island's kau fangota, its "gleaner of the sea," and her duty was to walk the tidal flats before dawn, harvesting shellfish, baby eels, and limu in the faintest light. Long after the moon had set and well before the morning fires were lit, she'd traverse the island's placid, knee-deep bay, gazing at the stars and reaping the sea's bounty.

So Kaniva was the first on Rotuma to spot the comet. All were soon fascinated by this new celestial guest, but none as much as she. Each morning, basket in hand, she stood perfectly still and stared upward, regarding the comet. Its heavenly wake was exactly like an earthly vaka's wake, twin white crests trailing behind. This told her the comet was but a different kind of canoe in a different kind of sea. Does having a comet for a friend give a girl comfort or make her more alone?

Being from such an isolated island, how was Kaniva to experience something new? She yearned to see sunlight filtered through a different canopy and hear an unfamiliar surf. Mostly, she wanted to meet someone new, for she'd always known the people on her island and always would. How she longed to encounter an unknown human! Meeting him would be like engaging a living mystery. Slowly, she'd unravel him, discover him. He wouldn't always have been, like the other boys. He'd have different things to say, and it'd take years of sharing and conversation to know his *before*. And this boy, if she fancied him, would be the boy of her choosing, rather than one selected by Rotuma's elders. But how to meet him? If only one could travel as the comet traveled and see what the comet saw. If only the comet weren't so out of reach.

But was it out of reach? Looking down at the still and shallow water, Kaniva saw the sky perfectly mirrored. The comet was actually at her feet. To touch it, she needn't rise into the inaccessible heavens. Instead, she need only touch the sea's thin surface. And all she had to do to catch a ride was lower herself and climb aboard. One night, alone on a perfectly still tidal flat, she did just that, she climbed aboard the comet's reflection and away she went.

The comet disappeared southward into that milky band of stars, and Kaniva disappeared with it. Now, when people look to the heavens, they can see her glowing hair across the sky, flowing behind her cosmic vaka. The proof of this tale is irrefutable: Come sunrise, Kaniva's basket was found floating alone. The girl was nowhere to be seen.

During the moon's initial rise, it exerts maximum glow, a light bright enough to tell fortunes by. Inside the Fefine Girls' fale, the moon extended long and pure through the open doorway, illuminating a swath inside, including Moon Appearing's feet upon her sleeping mat.

Many young ladies remained awake, reviewing the day and gossiping with friends on nearby mats. Several lamps were lit. These were simple bowls holding candlenuts that had been broken open to expose the oily meat inside. The light from these tender flames wasn't enough to reach the roof or the walls but was ideal for illuminating the face of a confidante.

Ever since Moon Appearing had eaten the nonu fruit, the other girls disdained her. Sun Shower, however, treated her like a sister. Sun Shower, anxious about marriage, talked instead about available boys. Her family, poor as they were, wanted to make the most of their daughter becoming a Fefine Girl. They'd hired a Tongatapu matāpule to secure a favorable match. Soon there'd be no mistaking what she was worth, based on what a southern chief would pay. All the more reason she mused about the handsome young men she fancied, avoiding the topic of the big-bellied chief who'd actually acquire her.

"If only we could meet boys with strong hands," Sun Shower said. "Then we'd know what it meant to be held. When we danced, it would be for him alone."

"You won't meet him on Tongatapu," Moon Appearing said. "The boys here idle their days. They debate the shapes of clouds and dwell at the kava bowl."

"Is there no young man you fancy?" Sun Shower asked coyly.

"Lolohea's not so bad," Moon Appearing said.

"You mean the one whose chest your fingers ran down?"

"Before he dove from a cliff in the dark!"

They both laughed.

Moon Appearing thought of 'Ata, of the way wind blew down dark paths, lifting leaves, as if returning them to the trees, as if time had been reversed. She thought of Lolohea, the green of his improvised kilt, the way he ladled water upon her feet. The cords in his neck, his soft lips.

"Seriously, though," Sun Shower whispered. "Would a girl want a Tongatapu boy? On Tafahi, we don't need to invent tests. Who'd concoct a challenge like diving for a necklace? Are there not cyclones enough? Or foreign attacks? Try hunger, try that test."

"It could just be the island," Moon Appearing said. "Maybe on different islands people are different."

She thought of 'Ata, of Lolohea's feet against a dark stone, of Lolohea's face contoured by flame-light, the constellations behind him bracketed by the boughs of a toa tree.

"Or what if the same person was different on different islands?" Moon Appearing mused. "What if on one island, a boy acted imperious, while on another, he made you laugh and washed your ankles?"

Did she really mention ankle-washing aloud? She braced herself for the teasing she was likely to get. But Sun Shower was silent.

The candlenut flame was burning low. Moon Appearing held it toward Sun Shower's mat, discovering the girl was fast asleep. All the better, she supposed. The other girls had hushed, too, their lamps extinguished, and when Moon Appearing lifted her small flame, she saw every girl had nodded off, the lot of them falling into uniform slumber.

Then Moon Appearing saw the long bolt of moonlight falling into the fale was interrupted by a man. He stood in the doorway, a silhouette. His body was almost limp, hip to one side, both his hands holding the beam above the entrance, lazily supporting his weight. He made no move to enter or leave—having established himself, he seemed at his leisure.

She thought to call out, to ask who it was or what he wanted. But she knew. Hands shaking, she lifted the lamp in the hopes that she might see his face, but this only served to illuminate hers.

Around her, the other girls were the very portraits of deep, contented sleep.

The man stretched, as if he'd just awakened and was preparing for his daily labors. When his lips parted, she could hear a faint whistle in his breathing. "This isn't my doing," he said. "It's the king that does this to you." Then he came her way.

Come nightfall, Punake chose not to share the deck with Mateaki, Lolohea, and the Wayfinder. Instead, he climbed inside the hull. It was colder here. Bow spray misted him. But he could imagine he was alone. His view was of the thwarts above and the stars beyond. Aspects of the boy they'd attacked kept flashing in Punake's mind. Mateaki wouldn't quit playing that maddening flute, so these images were accompanied by barren, wayward notes. The boy'd been wiry and strong. When they seized him, he resisted, his tendons flaring as he fought. That's what Punake kept seeing, straining ligaments, in his neck and elbow and wrists, like something inside the boy was trying to escape, like he was trying leave his captors with nothing but a body, which was essentially what happened.

Eventually, the flute went silent. Punake could now hear the vaka's song: the intermittent kiss of the outrigger on the surface, the thump of the bow dropping into troughs, a rustling sail like the sweep of casuarina limbs. Still, the poet couldn't sleep. Images kept visiting him. The thrash of the boy in the waves. The color of his skin against the deck. Punake thought of how, when the Tu'i of Tonga wanted to kidnap you, he didn't seize you off a beach, he simply named you "Royal Poet." That was the way to take a captive—invite him to kidnap himself.

It occurred to Punake that Mateaki had carved his flute from one of the Fisian bones they'd sworn to return. Anyone familiar with epic poems understood they hinged on fateful decisions, as when a hero takes a bite of Hikule'o's sweet potato or when a villager withholds one of Tangaloa's sacred fish. The consequences were as fatal as they were legendary.

Deep in the night, someone rose and crossed the deck. Instead of piss hitting water, Punake heard a grunt, followed by a splash in the sea.

In the morning, no one spoke of the Fisian boy's absent body. Tropic birds worked the waves—somewhere beyond their view was land. A dry wind whitened the salt on their skin. They landed a bonito and savored the pale sunset of its flesh.

That afternoon, an island came into view. It was substantial, with an ancient volcanic cone on the windward side, its partly collapsed rim allowing the green of its bowl to spill into the remainder of the island. It took until nightfall to finally approach. A spark of light shone on a distant beach.

So by starlight they aimed for that orange beacon. Soon they could see dugout canoes along a beach, and then forms moving against the glow of a fire. They heard calls and hoots and what must've been laughter. A figure rose and crossed the sand toward the trees.

"He's taking a piss," Lolohea told Punake. "They must be drinking kava. We're the last thing they'll be expecting. You and Mateaki identify the weakest one. Subdue him when he goes to the latrine."

"Mateaki?" Punake said. "I'm not doing anything with him."

There was a silence. No one protested this declaration. No one else volunteered to go with him.

"Bring him back in one of those dugouts," the Wayfinder suggested.

"And tie a stick in his mouth so he doesn't alert the others," Lolohea said.

"Best to just knock him senseless," Mateaki offered.

The Wayfinder handed Punake some rope.

Lolohea clapped him once on the shoulder.

So that was it—they were really going to let him do this?

Punake snatched Mateaki's flute from his waistband.

"You'll thank me," Punake said. "This flute will curse us."

Looks of concern crossed his mates' faces.

"We're already cursed," Punake added. He dropped his kilt and cinched his loincloth. He slipped the coils of rope around his arm and neck. Taking a few deep breaths, he lowered himself into the water. To bolster his confidence, he uttered lines of verse:

Efiafi naʻe haʻu ha tangata,	*In the evening came a man,*
ene haʻu ki he feituʻu tau tangata.	*came him to the fighting place of men.*

Then Punake placed the flute in his teeth and started swimming.

Punake made it ashore near an outcropping of trees. He began searching for some kind of club to take down a Fisian warrior. On his hands and knees, he began feeling through the underbrush for a proper length of wood. His nose told him he was crawling through the men's pissing ground. He kept glancing toward the warriors at the fire. Punake couldn't make out their words, but they wore their hair in topknots, like Tongans, and with regularity they all leaned back to laugh, just as any Tongan might laugh. This made what had to be done all the harder. Then he realized one of the warriors was walking his way. Punake had hoped to study the men to determine the easiest target and wait until he was sleepy, belly full of kava, walking heavy-legged to take his last piss of the night. But there was no time. Punake's hand landed on the perfect-sized club, but it turned out to be a root, connected to the ground! He quickly felt out another stick—it didn't seem too formidable, but it would have to do. Suddenly the man, backlit by firelight, was standing but two steps away. When Punake heard the urine start to flow, a poem came to mind, one about the great Tongan hero Munimatamahae, "Muni of the Torn Eye." Punake didn't recall how Muni, as a baby, still in the placenta, was cast into the sea. Punake didn't recall how a seabird pecked out Muni's eye, or how, after rescue, Muni grew to be an angry boy, beating the other boys in the village. Or how Muni became a brutal man who pounded the earth with a giant kava bush, or even how Muni became famous for throwing men so high, they crushed themselves upon landing. Punake recalled how, when the villagers came to kill the dangerous Muni, his surrogate mother, a peaceful woman who'd found a baby in the waves, who abhorred violence, who only wished to teach an adopted boy poetry and song, was forced herself to take up the club and begin to strike.

Punake himself would have to strike before the stream of urine ended. Crouched low, he issued forth a blood-slaking scream. This sent the flute, which he'd forgotten was still clenched in his teeth, flying from his mouth. And when Punake leaped up, raising his arms high, wet coils of rope around his torso and neck tightened, bending his head at a funny angle. In this position, he struck at the figure in the dark.

When Punake woke by the fire, the ocean had relocated itself inside his head. He heard words, but words the way they're warped beneath the water's surface. Worst of all, Mateaki's flute was playing in his head.

When he sat up, he saw seven warriors sitting around a fire. Or maybe it was eight. The eye that was able to open didn't quite focus. His face felt twice its size.

"Look," one of the warriors said. "Puko's attacker is awake."

"Or maybe it's Puko's lover," another warrior said. "We don't know what happened in those trees!"

Puko defended himself. "I swear, I was taking a piss, and this . . . this *fellow* hit me with a stick."

Punake understood the words they were speaking. He saw the ink on their skin. "You're Tongan!"

This produced a volley of laughter.

"Do you normally perform latrine attacks on other peoples?" one asked.

"I just . . ." Punake said. "I thought you were a Fisian warrior. This is Fisi, isn't it?"

They laughed again—was everything funny to them?

An older warrior spoke. His gray hair hung loose. "If Fisi's what you're looking for, Fisi is what you've found. And if you'd landed on the other side of the island, you'd have met your Fisian warrior."

Punake again noticed the sound of that flute—it'd probably been playing all along. He lumbered his eye among the men until he located the player. "I wouldn't mess with that flute, if I were you," Punake cautioned. "It's cursed."

From the bone-white flute, the warrior produced a haunting little melody. "It likely is," he said.

"Trust me," Punake said. "You don't want to know where that flute came from."

"Having made the flute myself," the warrior countered, "having battled the man it came from, I feel pretty sure I know its origin. The truest flute, one that carries the tunes of life and death, can only come from an arm that was raised against you."

Another warrior produced a bone flute and played some hollow notes. "That's the proper sound. Show me a Tongan warrior who hasn't made a flute from a Fisian he killed."

Punake's contemplation of this news must've shown on his face.

One warrior asked, "Do you not know of this practice?"

Another asked, "Are you not a warrior of some kind?"

Punake heard the phrase "of some kind" as a comment on his soft midsection and his embarrassingly meager calves. He didn't respond.

The warrior pressed further. "You seem unaware of this custom, yet you were carrying your own bone flute." He pointed at the sand beside Punake—here was Mateaki's flute. "Have you not taken a Fisian life and learned the tune of war?"

"Well," Punake said, "the flute *is* made from the bone of a Fisian." But now that he thought about it, he had no real way of knowing. "At least I think he was Fisian."

Here the true laughter came.

The gray-haired warrior addressed Punake in a newly serious tone. "Who's the war captain who trained you, and on what islands have you seen fighting?"

Punake shook his head.

The gray-haired warrior asked, "If you're not a fellow warrior attacking one of us in mistake of the enemy, who exactly are you, and what're you doing here?"

Punake hesitated. "I'm Tongatapu's royal poet."

There was no laughter. The warriors studied him without expression.

"I travel with the prince of Tonga," Punake offered.

The older warrior pulled back his gray-streaked hair and fastened it, the better to gaze upon Punake. It was then that Punake saw that inked on the man's shoulder was a jellyfish that could only have come from one source. Had this man come into combat with 'Aho? If so, how had he lived? Had 'Aho killed this man, yet by some force he was revived? Had 'Aho marked him, mistakenly thinking him dead? Had something uglier happened?

The older warrior said, "You claim you're a poet, and you claim you travel with the prince. But this doesn't help me understand why you ambushed one of my men in the dark."

"It's a long story," Punake said. "A sad and strange and tragic one, and I have to laugh when I think about it, though there's nothing funny about it, nothing funny at all."

"Pass the poet some kava," the older warrior said. "We have time for a tale."

The vaka tugged at the anchor line. At the bow was Lolohea, flanked by the Wayfinder and Mateaki, the three of them studying a distant bit of firelight.

Rather than contemplate what might be happening to Punake at the hands of Fisian warriors, Lolohea's mind took him to 'Ata, to Moon Appearing. Her ankles in his hands, the warmth of her cheek against his shoulder. The way she'd illustrated her fears upon his palm.

"That poet's been gone a long time," the Wayfinder said.

Lolohea's mind returned to facts: That Punake wasn't capable of kidnapping a chicken, let alone a Fisian warrior. That Lolohea'd been a fool to let him go alone. That the innocent, annoying, and lovable poet was likely dead. Finau would never forgive him. Why had Lolohea listened to his father, with all his talk of commanding people and soliciting sacrifice?

"Those Fisians will only be more dangerous in the daylight," Mateaki said. "We need to rescue him."

Lolohea shook his head. "We can't risk losing anyone else."

"So, what, we do nothing?" Mateaki asked.

Lolohea said, "Maybe Punake can talk his way out of things."

"In a language he doesn't speak?" Mateaki asked.

The Wayfinder said, "Mateaki's right."

"What if it was your brother on that beach?" Mateaki asked.

The answer to this question was too ugly for Lolohea to say: he'd do anything to save his brothers—as for Mateaki and Punake, it was a little less than anything.

"Warriors don't leave warriors behind," Mateaki said.

"We're not warriors," Lolohea countered.

"Obviously," Mateaki said.

The more they talked about Punake, the more Lolohea could hear Punake's voice, the way his voice rose when he was telling a story, the overly dramatic way he said the simplest things. Lolohea could even make out the words Punake was saying. "Then the Tuʻitonga wiped the grease from his face and shouted, *Feʻunga!*"

Materializing from the darkness was a dugout. In it were four figures, one of whom was gesturing large and feigning voices for the characters in the story he was telling. By the time Lolohea understood it was truly Punake, Punake had paused his tale. Turning, he seemed chagrined to see his mates.

Climbing aboard, Punake looked terrible, face swollen and discolored. A gray-haired warrior escorted him. "Lost a poet?" he asked.

With great relief, Lolohea said, "You're Tongan."

"I guess that means he's yours," the older warrior said. "He attacked my man Puko."

Lolohea smiled. He knew it looked bad, but he couldn't help his grin. *Punake had sailed to Fisi and somehow stumbled into the safety of Tongans.* "Sorry about the misunderstanding."

Now the warrior grinned. "Puko managed to survive."

"What about me?" Punake asked. "Did you see what happened to me?"

"Your friend's an amusing fellow," the warrior added. "You might want to keep better track of him."

The Wayfinder interrupted. "Can you tell us what island this is—Lakemba, Tuvuca?"

The warrior's eyes dropped to the fishhook around the Wayfinder's neck. Then he cast a skeptical gaze upon them all. Instead of answering, he asked Lolohea, "Am I meeting the prince of Tonga?"

Lolohea tipped his head.

"The poet told us many stories, yet he never got around to explaining what you were doing out here."

"Just being of service to Tonga," Lolohea said.

The warrior contemplated this vague answer. "One of my comrades says the prince of Tonga recently released a Fisian captive on the island of Matuku."

"That was someone else," Lolohea said.

"I appreciate the correction," the warrior said. "Out here, good information is hard to come by. We've also heard the Tuʻitonga has died, that no one's in charge of the war."

"I assure you my father's very much alive," Lolohea said.

"Wonderful news," the warrior said. "Please relay an invitation for him to visit his war—we'd be honored to give him a tour."

Curtly, Lolohea said, "You're too generous."

"And if I might deliver a message to you," he told Lolohea. "It would be a reminder that a Tongan does his own fighting. He doesn't send an entertainer in his stead." The warrior let that sink in. "And be careful in these waters. You didn't exactly land on the peace-loving island of Rotuma."

Mateaki, taking offense at the senior warrior's tone, said, "You've got a jellyfish inked on your shoulder. Might you share how you came by it?"

The older man measured the younger. "This mark was given to me by the lowliest of Tongans."

Mateaki said, "Don't you mean the fiercest?"

"So you're familiar with the man I speak of," the warrior said. "I'll grant you his ferocity. But that's what affords him the luxury of being low. The man we speak of indulges in behavior so base I count him not among the Tongan people. In fact, after he murdered his own wife, his men refused to serve under him, and he was forced to retreat home."

This was clearly not the response Mateaki had been expecting.

"We must take our leave," the warrior told Lolohea. "Dawn is when the war awakens." To the Wayfinder, he said, "This is the island of Cikobia." To all of them, he said, "We Tongans must ever retain our honor. Lose that, and we lose everything."

Lolohea watched them paddle away. He experienced the same feeling he'd had when he stepped off the Old Canoe and watched it go down. That task had been awful, but when it was over, he got to go home. Not these warriors.

"What's our destination?" the Wayfinder asked. "Now that I know this island, I know them all."

"It's time to do what we must," Lolohea said. "Head for the peace-loving island of Rotuma."

It was said the Fisians used dogs to secure their islands. These four-legged creatures supposedly raised much fuss if foreigners set foot upon their shores. The Tamahā didn't discredit this notion, but in her opinion, there could be no better sentry than a bird. This very morning, in the misty light of dawn, the Tamahā was preparing the Fefine Girls' workstations when her malau birds began calling in alarm. Standing at the front gate was a lone figure. Assuming it was a man, since the gate was the limit of their liberty, the Tamahā went to shoo him. Nearing, she saw was it was Moon Appearing.

"Child," the Tamahā called out.

The girl didn't move. She was holding her arm, as if it'd been injured.

"Why're you so early?" the Tamahā asked. "There's nothing for you here but work."

"You told me to come," Moon Appearing said.

The Tamahā searched her memory.

"You said if something happened, I should come to you."

"*Did* something happen?"

Moon Appearing didn't respond. Though she was dressed as usual in a modest wrap, her hair was a mess. Glancing up, she revealed puffy eyes. When the Tamahā neared, Moon Appearing leaned toward her, expectant, like she was hoping for a hug.

The Tamahā took a step back. "I am no one's mother."

"They pretended to be asleep," Moon Appearing said.

"Who pretended?"

"He did it right in front of them. They closed their eyes."

The Tamahā inspected the young woman's body, noting the points where a man would pin a shoulder, a wrist, a neck. There were no visible bruises. "Something did happen, yes?"

Moon Appearing's eyes welled. She looked up, to keep the tears from falling.

The Tamahā moved closer. The young woman looked ready to fall into the older woman's protective embrace, where her hair might be stroked. Instead, the Tamahā sniffed her. About the girl was the faint scent of burning hair. "This happened inside the royal compound?"

When Moon Appearing nodded, the tears spilled.

The Tamahā stepped outside her compound. She stared into the mist, scanning the field of ferns surrounding her entrance. She wasn't looking for anything—she was just perceiving.

"Step inside," she told Moon Appearing. "Wait for me."

By taking that simple step, the girl was beyond the grasp of men.

The Tamahā advanced to her subordinates' quarters. By making a sudden move at a sow, she awakened them with a volley of panicked pig squeals. Out came her matāpule and security men, their kilts barely thrown on. When they saw it was the Tamahā, they lowered themselves to the ground. "Go to the royal compound," she commanded them. "Tell the Fefine Girls we won't meet today. Or tomorrow. Then post yourselves at their fale. If a man attempts to enter, notify me."

"*A man?*" a matāpule asked.

"You know the man I speak of. And don't tangle with him. I can't afford to lose more of you."

The security man asked, "What if the girls leave the fale?"

"Are you stupid?" she asked. "Follow them. If he approaches, report it. Do not engage him, understand?"

The men nodded.

The Tamahā rejoined Moon Appearing, escorting her inside.

"I was talking to Sun Shower about home islands," Moon Appearing volunteered.

"Did he mark you?"

Moon Appearing turned, the perfect face of confused innocence.

"Have you looked?"

"I did no different than the other girls," Moon Appearing said. "You must believe me."

"There's no reason to look."

"I blew out the lamp. I placed my head on the mat. I closed my eyes. But it was too late."

"Come," the Tamahā said. "Let's tend to you. I know a thing or two. I ask only this: We never speak of it. Words give it power, they bring it back, they'll hurt you all over again."

Inside the fale, she laid the girl on the suspended bed and sat beside her as morning advanced. The young woman couldn't sleep—she'd begin drifting off, then her breathing would increase, her eyes would snap open, and she'd find herself calling out. It was very possible that after this, Moon Appearing's sleep would never be the same. The Tamahā did feel for the girl, she had the urge to hold the young woman's hand, but such precedents of affection could never be set. Instead, rocking the floating bed, she'd say, "Hush."

When at last her guest had found some slumber, the Tamahā began heating water. She gathered botanicals to infuse a broth—volovalo leaves for inflammation and lautolu ʻuta vine to calm bad spirits. All through the gathering and crushing of herbs, the little flock of flightless birds followed her. They seemed genuinely curious about this woman who cared for them. It was an irony that most of the humans she cared for weren't a vulnerable or endangered breed, but the elite girls of Tonga, the ones you'd think were least likely to be in need. But need they did, whether they knew it or not. And in the end, whether from a wealthy family or a remote island, a girl was a girl was a girl.

At some point in her herb harvesting, the Tamahā stood straight, to stretch her back. She stared into the branches of a toa tree, its limbs strung with slumbering peka bats. It was like she'd seen this all before, like what hung from the toa limbs was actually the past, ready to fall black and flapping your way. She understood Moon Appearing's urge to give speech to what had happened, to vocalize the details—the other girls, the lamp, the whispers. Though Moon Appearing hadn't shared the potent aspects. No one did, they couldn't be uttered. Like the way a man breathed his breath on you, and you had no choice but to inhale it, to take it inside you and absorb it. How sweat dripped from his nose, into your eyes, stinging them, and you're unable to wipe it away. Sweat dripping into your mouth, where you're forced to taste the excreted salt of him.

She took a breath, cleared her mind, and then got back to work. Work was the first cure.

She harvested a fish, using only concentration and a bare hand, though a heron, watching close, helped school them. She used to think the fish she caught was meant to be caught, like it was at fault for carelessly swimming about or innocently taking the sun at the surface where it was easily seized, while the wary, elusive ones survived below. She once felt that using a net would make her catch what she considered the "wrong fish," the one that'd developed the smarts to exist in a small and dangerous world. But the longer she was at her ponds, the more she understood that the same fish was by turns wary in one moment and exposed in the next, its behavior having more to do with being in the sunny pool by morning and leaping into the shaded pool midday. No, what the harvested fish had in common were only unforeseen developments, like the arrival of a heron or the caprice of a hand that entered their little world and stole them away.

The Tamahā, bowl of medicinal fish broth in her hands, returned to find Moon Appearing not only awake but standing. Her gaze was directed at the Life-Affecting Fan on its peg.

"Does the Fan's power exist inside the Fan?" she asked. "Or does it reside in you?"

The Tamahā didn't answer. "Sit. The broth's hot. Sip carefully."

The girl was contemplating revenge, which was good. What could be more therapeutic?

Moon Appearing accepted the bowl, though she took no notice of what she consumed. "If I acted now, I think I could do it."

"Drink your broth."

"But if I waited, if I waited even a single day, I'd lose my nerve."

"Hush, child. Take nourishment."

Moon Appearing obeyed, though it was clear her mind was elsewhere, everywhere. She spoke suddenly. "You said *we*. Earlier, you said, *We never speak of it*. You said *you—they hurt* you *all over again*."

The older woman flattened her mouth into an unreadable smile.

"Did it happen to you?" Moon Appearing asked.

The Tamahā said nothing.

"How could it happen to you? You're the most powerful woman I know. If you're not safe, no woman is." Moon Appearing set aside the still-brimming bowl. "I don't want to be the girl in that story."

"What girl? Which story?"

"The one who married herself to a grave. Who spent her life alone on a hill, in a garden of her own confinement."

In a garden of her own confinement, the Tamahā thought.

"He lifted his hand," Moon Appearing said. "He wanted to show me the ink that would—"

"No words," the Tamahā said sternly. "I told you. No words, or you leave."

"How can I face those girls? There's no way I can do it."

"Believe me, their only concern is for themselves."

Moon Appearing covered her eyes. "How'll I survive their gaze?"

"Don't talk like a fool," the Tamahā said. "Have you no notion of the strength inside you? You're stronger than all of them, believe me. You're here, aren't you?" The Tamahā gave that a moment to sink in. "You won't have to worry about them, though. I'm not letting you return to that place. Here is where you'll stay. I know how to get the pain out of you. Over the coming days, I'll show you, I'll take care of it. And if we find there's a baby, I'll take care of that, too."

Moon Appearing's face flashed with fear. "But what about—"

"Don't say his name."

Moon Appearing exhaled. Her eyes traveled to the Fan on the wall.

The Tamahā took up the bowl and sipped the broth—she could let nothing go to waste. She said, "As for the man with ink on his hand, you must wipe him from your mind. Forget him completely, because you'll never see him again. That you leave to me."

It was dark when they arrived at Rotuma. First came the muted crash of reef-break. Shifts in the wind brought the scent of woodsmoke. At last, their eyes began to detect certain whites—the froth of broken waves, the glowing expanses of sand, the beards of palm.

The lagoon shallowed into a tidal flat, the water so still it reflected the firmament. In this placid expanse stood a person, appearing to inhabit the milky spill of the sky's reflection.

"She's beautiful," Mateaki said.

"Beautiful?" the Wayfinder asked. "From here, you can't even tell if it's a woman."

"I can tell," Mateaki said. "She's lovely."

Punake had spent much time gazing at women from afar. He turned his head slightly, the better to direct his right eye forward, for, though the swelling had gone down, his left eye had only begun to open. "She's holding a basket," he added.

"That girl," Lolohea said, "is the first step in our plan."

In this stillness, in this *before*, they took a moment to regard her.

Lolohea turned to his brother. "We'll need a second vaka," he said, pointing to a row of beached fishing canoes. "Find the most seaworthy one and slowly sail it toward the girl. She'll recognize a Rotuman vaka and think nothing of a fisherman getting an early start."

To Punake and Mateaki, Lolohea said, "You two swim toward either side of the lagoon and approach her from behind. Wait till the Wayfinder takes her attention. Then come for her."

Lolohea took a moment to study the girl. After many days on the water, absorbing the sun off the waves, his eyes were uncertain. Still, he could see well enough to know that one moment the figure was peering into the dark water, while the next found her gazing upward. So she appeared not to notice the distant outline of a Fisian war canoe. Though a plan featuring her was already in motion, she appeared to have no inkling of what was in store. This was a state Lolohea knew well.

When his mates were in the water and about to swim away, Lolohea had final messages:

To the Wayfinder, he said, "It's okay if she calls out. In fact, the more fuss, the better."

To Punake, he said, "Make sure she leaves that basket behind."

To Mateaki, he said, "Whatever you do, don't drown this one."

When the inking needles fell, the Tuʻitonga felt the pain as merely an echo of pain. He was even able to doze while taking his ink. So he'd brought one of his coconuts to the Tufuga's tree. When he and Finau were on their backs, they gazed upward at an ever-shifting skein of blue, filtered through candlenut leaves. When they took their ink belly down, the Tuʻitonga closed his eyes and communed with the coconut's dark interior. There, he began walking a beach where the waves weren't wet. It didn't seem so bad, this lovely little world. He encountered the Fisian chief, who threw a stick down the beach. It was retrieved by a puppy. "What you've heard is true," the Fisian chief said. "Dogs are born sweet-tempered. It's men who make them otherwise."

The Tuʻitonga offered no pleasantries. "To get what you wanted, you paid the steepest price. You lost your son, your family, your life. You came away with nothing."

The Fisian chief wrested the stick from the puppy. "I also lost my afterlife."

Yes, the man would spend eternity here, alone. But what was done couldn't be undone.

The Fisian chief rubbed the puppy's ears. "You're wondering about the price you'll pay, is that it? You must know the cost of making your son king will be the highest. But you needn't worry about the price, as you paid it long ago."

"What price did I pay?" the Tuʻitonga asked.

The Fisian chief looked at him, his eyes warm and benevolent. "Have you let yourself forget?"

"Father," Finau said.

The Tuʻitonga opened his eyes.

"Father, you were sleeping. We have a visitor."

Before them appeared the Tamahā. "I hear that tonight your brother will lay his wife to rest."

"Yes," the Tuʻitonga said. "And then he'll finally take his leave."

"Is that what you believe, that *he's* the one who's about to disappear?"

"I'm afraid I don't follow," the Tuʻitonga said.

"Concerning his wife's interment," she said, "does your brother desire an island-wide funeral service? Or does he wish something private, under the cloak of darkness?"

The Tuʻitonga, uncertain, said, "He requests a simple ceremony. Yes, it's to be at night."

"A simple ceremony—at night, with few witnesses?"

The Tuʻitonga had no response.

She asked, "What prevents you two from simply ambushing one another?"

The Tuʻitonga was taken aback. "Why, he's my brother, we're family."

"Of course, of course. And?"

"When family kills family, blood feuds are started. Revenge slayings cascade."

The Tamahā nodded. "Yes, yes, and . . ."

"If my brother were ambushed by me, I'd abdicate my afterlife. And unless his bones went into the family vault, his afterlife would also be taken. The opposite's true, as well. It's how the gods ensured harmony among us nobles."

The Tamahā nodded. "It appears to be a predicament. But is it? What if one brother placed another brother inside the crypt and then closed it?"

With a look of horror, the Tuʻitonga asked, "Alive?"

"Who then would be the killer?"

The Tuʻitonga tried to imagine such a darkness. Sealed off from sound. Airless. A person thirsty and suffocating, waist-deep in bones, coated in the meal of the dead. Worst was the time that would transpire, time to think, to hope, to despair, to succumb.

"Can't you see," the Tamahā asked, "that this has been his plan for you all along?"

The notion was truly shocking to the Tuʻitonga. "But, how can you claim to know this?"

"How can you claim not to have known it?"

The Tuʻitonga lifted his eyes to the shifting patterns of leaves against the sky.

"From the beginning," she said, "he arrives with bones he claims are his wife's. Notice how quiet his boy is on the topic, a boy who as we speak completes his training to be king. Then your brother rapes and maims until you relent and give him what he wants. If the tomb is opened, he gets everything—you disappear, but retain your afterlife, for your bones are already deposited. He and his son are in line to take command, without risking their souls, because you'll die slowly, of natural causes. And if you vanish, if there's no proof of your death, he'll take your place, he'll take your wife, he'll adopt your sons, he'll take his slumber each night upon your sleeping mats."

The Tuʻitonga visualized each of these things.

"But you have the upper hand," the Tamahā said. "He has no friends. He can muster no manpower to open the crypt. He needs you to do it for him. Shouldn't you be the one who decides which of you goes inside?"

THIRTY-ONE

KŌRERO:
IN THE HIGH WATER

Morning on the open sea. Aprons of rain over side-lit water. Scent of far-off lightning.

I stood and rubbed my arms. Light-headed, I had to brace myself. The wind was picking up. The outrigger, used to plunging through swells, now skimmed the surface, lifting so that only a trail of spittle touched the sea. My father told Tapoto to move above the outrigger, so his weight would counterbalance the wind. "She awakens," Tapoto said as he stepped around me. I realized the men had been up all night. Or maybe everyone had. My mother was sharpening fishhooks. Tiri was up front, feeling the slow rise and dull flop of our bow overtaking north-facing waves. "Kōrero, is that you?" she asked. "Tell me what the sea looks like."

You know that stage of hunger where your stomach hurts? It passes, of course, soon to be replaced by a shrunken feeling. Still, it hurt when I crouched behind Tiri. "Ahead the horizon is clear and flat," I said. "To each side are squalls. They lean forward like they're trudging up hills. You know the kind of clouds. Soon they will stall, unload, and, going belly down, flatten the sea."

"Yes," Tiri said. "I can see them."

I said, "I miss how Hine would describe the ocean, saying things like, *Looks the same as yesterday.*"

Tiri smiled. "*Watery*, she'd call it. Or *very wet*."

I could perfectly hear Hine's voice. I remembered Hā Mutu saying faces faded from memory. I knew I'd just seen Hine, but was it possible to forget what she looked like? It wasn't possible, was it? I said, "We forgot to tell her the story of Rongo."

"I was just thinking of all the stories we neglected to share," Tiri said. "Like the story of Taranga's premature baby, how Taranga wrapped the infant in seaweed and let the ocean incubate him."

"Or the tale of Kōpūwai's two-headed dogs."

"How could we forget the tale of Ahi-a-Mahuika?"

"I love that one," I said. "I love the moment Mahuika's flaming fingernails are stolen."

"So many stories, lost," Tiri said.

"Maybe missing stories make room for new ones."

"Is there such a thing as a new story?" Tiri asked.

I tried to imagine the teller of a new story. In my mind it wasn't someone I'd recognize.

Tiri asked if I could see the other waka.

Far ahead, the Wayfinder's sail. "It's out there, pointing the way."

"Last night," Tiri said, "we exchanged bellows of the conch shell. That was quite reassuring, hearing exactly where they were."

"Tiri," I said. "Before we left, you pulled Hine aside. What'd you tell her?"

She thought about this. "Remember the other night, when I told that story? The one about the deaths of our island's former inhabitants? It felt good to let that secret go. So I told Hine something she needed to hear, something I'd been holding on to."

"A secret?"

Tiri turned in my direction. It was eerie when she did that, looked at me without seeing me. "I told her who her father was."

"You've known, all this time? Well, who is it?"

"Bearing a secret is like swallowing a stone. You carry it in your gut."

I waited for her to tell me.

"Is that what you want?" she asked.

"No," I said. "But yes, of course."

"Hine's father is Tapoto's father."

"Tapoto's father?" I repeated.

"You remember him as a man who drowned," Tiri said. "But he had a life."

"Hine and Tapoto are siblings?"

"Half," Tiri said.

I turned to look at Tapoto, who was fishing from the outrigger. "Why can't I catch a fish?" he called out in frustration. "I can see the stupid things jumping."

I studied him for signs of Hine: In the lines across his forehead. In the roundness of his eyes.

"If they're jumping," my father told him, "a predator's working the water. No fish will take a lure while swimming for its life."

"You'd know that," my mother told Tapoto, "if you'd ever helped with the fishing."

Tapoto scrunched his face in a kind of pout. *That* was exactly Hine. How was it I had never noticed before?

The Mānunu family shared our waka. As did the Kohimu brothers, who were older. They sat in back, like uncles, taking turns at the steering oar. "The fish might not be jumping," one of them said. "They might be flying fish."

"The maroro fish," my mother said. I imagined her inking an interlocking pattern of their slim, winged bodies, their dark backs and white bellies.

Finau said, "In Tongan, we call this fish mālolo. There's an old poem that mentions them:

Hangē ha fanga kakā āutō hifo mei	Like parrots alighting from
he ʻulu ʻakau nonu,	nonu trees,
ha takanga mālolo kuo nau mapuna.	a flock of mālolo takes flight.

Moments later, several flying fish rose from the water, the tips of their winglike fins tapping the surface as they raced past. Then came dozens. Then there were countless flying fish, the insect buzz of their collective flutter. They flew into our hull, our rigging, our deck, into us. We batted them down and soon were eating their pale pink flesh, seasoned only by the brine of their orange egg sacks.

Tapoto passed me a nearly translucent fillet. I forced myself to chew, not just swallow, that's how hungry I was. Soon I could feel the flesh restoring me, spreading through my body. Tapoto smiled at me. I smiled back, wondering how I could ever tell him that his sister had been left behind. Worse, how could I not?

*　*
*

All day, my mother gave Finau his ink. She learned to tap her needles to the rhythm of the swells, and after a while the motif on Finau's leg began to change: the unfurl of fern stems became the curl of wave crests. At first I don't think we realized it was even happening—the pattern simply turned from terrestrial to oceanic. Still, there was a symmetry between land and sea, with one leg evoking spear points and shark's teeth, while the other depicted bracken and wave-faces.

"The pattern evolves," my mother informed Finau.

He lay on his side, eyes focused on the pain. He nodded.

There's something trancelike about giving ink. In the flow and rhythm, it's hard to remember individual moments, but in the afternoon was a shower, the raindrops mixing blood and ink into a tincture I'd only seen once before, when my father dressed a still-squirming octopus in ankle-deep water. The clear, the black, the red—elemental, ephemeral, yet, in my mother's hands, forever.

Toward sunset, we had visitors. Heavy westward clouds blotted the sun, but around the edges, the gray glowed maroon and purple-brown. We heard the screeching and squawking of our guests before we saw them. Then a voice called *"Nea, nea!"* across the water.

Finau rose from the deck. "Kōkī," he called to the arriving flock. "You changed your mind!"

But this didn't seem a social visit. Soon a dozen parrots had come to rest upon our upper spar. Kōkī, larger, colors bolder, addressed us: "Tonga remove soul, Tonga bury alive, Tonga use dog to kill!"

Horror on my face, I turned to Finau.

Reluctantly, he said, "Remember how there were some drownings? There were other incidents, too."

"Tamahā banish Kōkī. Tuʻitonga try to kill Kōkī!" Looking defeated, Kōkī hung his head. "But Tonga banana. Kōkī not live without banana."

In the fading light, my mother and I leaned over the washboards to scrub the ink from our hands. There were few places on a crowded waka to get a private moment. She asked me, "How long would it take those parrots to fly to us?"

"Why?" I asked.

"This morning," she said, "Finau recited poetry about flying fish, and suddenly there were flying fish."

"I think the flying fish were seen first," I said. "That's what made him think of the poem."

"Maybe," my mother said. "But also in that poem, some parrots took flight, and now here they are."

"What're you suggesting?" I asked.

"I don't know," she said.

I remembered Finau reciting a poem about the wind, one called "Matangi," just before it became windy. Or had the wind, just kicking up, occasioned the poem?

Finau tried to talk to Kōkī, but Kōkī wouldn't respond. Instead, the parrots huddled on the spar above us, resting their wings. Dejected, leg still weeping blood, Finau leaned against the hull. "I remember when Kōkī couldn't even fly. He couldn't make it to the top of a tree without huffing for breath."

"A parrot that can't fly?" I asked. "How's that possible?"

Finau said, "I hand-raised him, carried him everywhere."

"Surely he must have flown sometimes," I said.

Finau shook his head. "I kept him tethered."

My mother was listening. "I can see how you'd become close to your bird," she said. Unspoken was the fact that Finau hadn't been allowed to touch his own mother, that he'd been given a supplemental father.

"He's his own bird now," Finau lamented. "I must accept that."

I glanced at my mother. "Does that make you think of poems about parrots?" I asked Finau.

"Not really," he said.

"I mean, when you quote a poem," I said, "how do you know which poem to reference?"

"It's just, whatever makes me think of something," he said.

My mother extended a hand to indicate the world around us. "Now, for instance. Might you think of a poem about being far from land?"

"It's not that simple," Finau said.

"Let's say you catch an octopus," my mother said, "or perhaps you see a whale."

Finau said, "Yeah, but in the old poems, there are angry whales, vengeful whales, whales who make whirlpools, swim to the heavens, even set foot upon the earth."

I asked, "What about an average whale?"

Finau didn't hesitate. He said:

I he ongona e hiva fakaʻānaua a e tofuaʻa,	*Hearing the whale's forlorn song,*
naʻe hiva e Maui a e taha mei hono ʻapi.	*Maui sang one from his home.*
ʻO moʻusioa ki he kanoʻi mata lahi fakalilifu,	*Staring into its monstrous eye,*
naʻe taku e Maui hono ʻoʻonā kanoʻi mata.	*Maui regarded his own.*

I said, "I love how Maui meets the whale in its own realm."

"And how Maui meets himself," my mother said.

"Yeah," Finau said. "The poem's *of* whales, not *about* whales. It's about an essence, not a thing. Punake taught me that."

Come dark, my father lit a brazier, and we grilled the maroro remains, as these were filled with nutrients. The only conversation was between the bow and the waves as we crunched down on crispy maroro heads and salty spines. When I curled up to sleep, a parrot descended to nestle with me. It was Aroha, and she repeated the words I'd once taught her: *Men, peace*. When I lay my head upon the deck, I heard strange sounds resonating through the outrigger. Moans, low and plaintive. Long, drawn-out calls in the dark. I wasn't used to sleeping on the water, so I was slow to recognize a whale song.

The call-and-response of conch shells marked the progression of night. I welcomed these trumpets—it meant my father and Finau were at the helm, it meant the Wayfinder was out there, leading the way. Deep in the night, however, an event happened that would change everything. At the time, I thought we'd been struck by lightning, such was the sound that woke me. There was a great cracking sound—like the waka had split in two. The sound sent the parrots skyward, it jolted us to our feet. We called each other's names, but that wasn't enough, we had to touch one another, to confirm we were all okay. Then it became quiet, except for the sound of our breathing. By starlight, we took stock, but of what—what had happened?

My father'd been awake. "Two swells stacked," he said. "They lifted us, dropping us into a trough."

"We landed like a felled tree," Finau said, "smacking flat against the water."

"That's when it happened," my father said, "that sound."

Everything seemed fine. The deck was dry, the sail full. But that cracking sound, it was like nothing we'd heard before. Tapoto set about lighting a fire to spark a torch. The distress call was sounded—three blasts of the conch shell. In the dark, my father ran his hands along the outrigger limbs, feeling for a pole that might have snapped. Finau leaned over the passing sea to inspect the length of the float. They crawled through the hull, feeling for damage, feeling for water. When the torch was lit, we looked up to the mast and spars, all intact. Finau nearly lit the waka on fire crawling under the thwarts to inspect every bit of the crack that traversed our hull. Nothing seemed damaged.

When the Wayfinder arrived, he held his own torch. He hesitated to come aboard, choosing instead to study us a moment, as if what'd happened was recorded in our faces. His torch illuminated those behind him; the others of our people wore expressions of wariness and relief, relief that they were on the sounder craft, that they had the Wayfinder to protect them, for one thing seemed certain: no harm would come to him or his passengers.

On the day we first met, the Wayfinder had stepped to me. This he did again, setting foot on *The Red Cloak*. The flame-light made amber of his eyes, and as I told him what had happened, I felt I was somehow revealing myself, that I was laying my life bare. As he listened, I began to doubt what I was even saying—had there really been a cracking sound, had I imagined it? By torchlight, he studied the waka, the whole of it, rather than its particulars, like how it sat in the water, how it rolled with the swells, the complaints it seemed to make. Contemplating, contemplating, he was like Maui, looking beyond something's attributes in an attempt to know its essence.

Over the next days, we finished Finau's tā moko. Did I mention Finau was naked during these inking sessions? My mother positioned a scrap of tapa cloth to preserve the young man's modesty, but his ure was prone to flop with the motion of the deck, and his hairy raho kept swinging into view. Nearing completion, the waves my mother inked grew frothy with the chaos of shore break. A ring of driftwood around Finau's leg completed the pattern: here, the sea and shore made their peace. My mother'd never inked beyond the human face. She'd never departed from known motifs. She'd never spent so long on a single work.

Finau, when we sought his final approval, was asleep.

These inking sessions had been a welcome distraction from the behavior of our waka, whose lashings were crackling with strain. At some point, the hull had begun to flex. Each time the bow lifted, the center of the waka yawned so that light shone through the joints of once-snug thwarts. And when the bow fronted a stiff wave, instead of making a satisfying thump, the waka seemed to go *oof*.

The Wayfinder had taken to sailing astride us, close enough that a calabash of water, with a proper throw, could be tossed between decks. His own waka rode perilously low, and his figure was visible through sprays of bailed water. He'd call for my father to touch a certain stay line and report how taut it was. He shouted for my father to put his ear to the mast and report what he heard. Was the bow pulling one way or the other? Were vibrations felt through the steering oar?

My mother called to the Wayfinder, "Are we past halfway?"

The Wayfinder didn't respond. He knew the meaning of the question: We were wondering whether it was too late to turn back. In the stern, I marked the vastness of the sea. Purposeless, without feature, the roaming waters were punctuated by nothing but petrels and frigate birds and the rolling hillocks of the deep. How was it that we'd left our beautiful little island, so solid, so steady? How rare an island it was. How impossible to ever find again.

Though *The Red Cloak* was still under sail, though its deck was dry, something was very wrong. Everything complained. *Oof* went the bow. *Creak* went the hull, and as we lofted a swell, a dull *groan* followed. The Wayfinder reefed his sail to match our slowing pace. At last, he saw something that made him shake his head. "We need to reduce your load," he called to my father. "Send Tapoto over." To compensate for Tapoto's weight, the Wayfinder cut the lines to his anchor stones and pushed them into the sea.

Our crafts were maneuvered close, hulls heaving and falling in perilous proximity. Tapoto came to stand on the outer edge of our hull, toes curling overboard. He stared at the Wayfinder's waka, plunging before him. To time the leap, he'd have to jump where the other waka wasn't, trusting it would surge up to receive him. One slip, one mistake, and he'd get caught between the pitching hulls, or, worse, drop into the sea. I remembered how he'd been unable to hoist himself aboard a stationary waka in a peaceful cove. People in the Wayfinder's waka were bailing. They looked at Tapoto the way you'd regard a sick person whose fever might be spreading. They looked at me like that, too.

Tapoto leaped, a surprisingly powerful jump, but, landing, his foot slipped, and he took an awkward spill, tumbling into the hull. The Wayfinder's waka then climbed a hill of water and slid away before floating back. At last, Tapoto rose from the thwarts. Unsteady, a red mark on his forehead, he looked back at me with concern. Or perhaps it was guilt. Yes, he looked guilty for making it off our waka. Seeing that look, I finally understood: *The Red Cloak* was going to sink.

That afternoon, a squall advanced. The cool smell of rain blew in. It carried the unmistakable scent of land: of wet fronds bent by the wind, of storm tides that exposed the reef and littered the beach with broken stalks of coral. Was it possible this weather had passed over our island? I could almost see the rain lensing our cove, hear it pattering the mangroves.

Through the ensuing shower, the Wayfinder sat on his deck, shielding his eyes as he contemplated our canoe. Whatever he saw was undetectable to me. I'd noticed our waka had slowed. And each time the bow came off a swell, it floated to the side. Then there was the mast. Each gust elicited groans from below.

After the squall, the light didn't recover. Darkness was falling. The Wayfinder made an announcement. "Let's get the women off," he said. He looked at me as he said this. Then he began dismantling the little hut on his deck and tossing it into the sea. He discarded a set of poles meant to right the vessel in case of capsize. He ditched his sea anchor, his landing lines, and the spare steering oar.

Yet my mother, knowing my father wouldn't leave, said, "I remain."

Tiri said, "Neither do I depart."

"I also stay," I said, though it was kind of my mouth that said it, rather than me.

"No," my mother said. "You're going. That's final."

We didn't get a chance to debate the topic. The Mānunu family was happy to oblige. They scrambled to the other waka and were gone.

That night, the Kohimu brothers helped my father and Finau attach extra stays to the mast, which had been determined to be the problem. The mast was anchored to the hull by a cleat that straddled the crack traversing the bottom of the hull. Lateral winds pried the wood one way and another, opening the split to the sea below.

While the men conferred—there was lots of conferring—I sat on deck between Mother and Tiri.

"Describe the night for me," Tiri said.

The sky was after-storm-clear. Between us and the stars, there seemed to be nothing, but of course we were separated by the entirety of the heavens. "I know we're going down," I said.

"Don't be disrespectful," my mother said. "Tiri's made a request of you."

I said, "I fear that when the time comes, Father won't leave. I fear he'll blame himself, that he'll punish himself by staying behind."

My mother said, "Just tell Tiri whether there are clouds or not."

"And you," I said. "I'm worried you'll stay by his side."

Tiri said, "Every decision a parent makes is for the good of the child, even if it seems otherwise."

My mother glared at me.

"Fine," I said. "The sky's clear. The night's dark. The stars are very bright."

"I've always wondered," my mother said to Tiri, as if making after-dinner conversation, "can you see the stars in your mind? How do you keep them in the right places?"

"I simply use my memory," Tiri said. "Even if I lose something, in my memory, it's forever."

That wasn't true. Memories faded. "You two are scaring me," I said. "Don't you know we're sinking?"

My mother turned to me. It was dark, but I could see the wet shine of her eyes. "We're descended from Kupe, the great Māori navigator," she said. "He survived a sinking. He also survived a battle with a great octopus."

Tiri said, "Let's relate the story of Kupe and the Octopus . . ."

The men were lowering our sail. The Wayfinder boarded us and joined a discussion about whether the mast, too, should come down. To settle this point, my father and the Wayfinder stepped into the hull to inspect something. There was splashing. So water was coming in.

"To be clear," the Wayfinder said, "I've got a duty to the passengers I already have. I can take no more."

No counterargument was offered. "Could *The Red Cloak* be towed?" my father asked.

Finau asked, "What if we turned *The Red Cloak*'s outrigger into a small canoe? Couldn't that hold a few people?"

Even I knew these ideas wouldn't work. Here's how dire our situation was: no one bothered to bail.

I can't exactly remember where the night went. The sun went down, and then there was a morning glow. First light allowed me to see our mast and sail floating lifeless beside us. It allowed me to see my father, lost and uncertain. His hopes and plans and labors had come to nothing. I saw Tiri had taken up her satchel of botanicals, lest salt water contaminate their roots.

The first laps of water were coming through the decking.

The Wayfinder glanced at his brother with a look that said, *It's time*.

Finau shook his head. "We're not giving up. We're not leaving anybody behind."

My father fixed his eyes on the Wayfinder. "You must find room for Kōrero."

Several aboard the Wayfinder's waka called for Tiri to join, for she knew the ways of medicine and was responsible for the health of all.

"You must go," my mother told me. "If they can find a place for you, you must take it."

"I won't go without you," I said. "You've said countless times we're meant to be together."

"You're not thinking," my mother said. "You're not imagining being alone in the ocean. Picture them sailing away."

"Worse would be me sailing away."

"Kōrero," my father said, "you don't know what you're saying."

I asked, "How many times have you said *we go together*? I can't count the times you said you'd join me in the sea."

"That's *us*," my mother said. "That's us joining *you* if *you* were lost. It doesn't work the other way."

"You're going," my father said sternly. "That's all there is to it."

My mother reached out to me. I knew she wanted to share the breath of life.

"No, we don't separate. I won't be without you."

My father said, "*Kōrero*."

Finau turned to his brother. "You don't want to leave her, I know you don't."

The Wayfinder looked not at my parents, or the Kohimu brothers, or an old blind woman, or me. He turned toward the people on his waka. "I'm responsible for them," he told Finau. "Those are my passengers."

"You can't leave her," Finau said. "You'll regret it."

My mother turned to the Wayfinder. There was a look in her eyes I'd never seen. "I implore you," she said. "I beseech you. Take her."

The Wayfinder looked about, as if trying to find the person to blame for this mess. He grabbed his brother, and, returning to their waka, they hauled out their spare sail. The bulk of this, with great effort, they heaved to the edge of the deck. "This is the weight of two people," he said. "There's nothing else to abandon."

This they rolled into the sea. No one spoke, but a great unease could be registered from those who doubted the wisdom of this move. Still, people began calling for me and Tiri to join them.

My father turned to me. "This is my doing," he said. "I made the wrong decision. I've no regrets, yet neither can I ask others to pay. But if you survive, I survive. I'll live on through you."

Mother took hold of her husband's arm. "By saving yourself," she told me, "you save the both of us."

I looked to Tiri. "I've lived my life," she said. "Let another be saved."

Who would I be without them? A stranger, an unknown person.

"I don't depart," I said. "I remain."

With that, the Kohimu brothers, though they were older than my father, scrambled to safety.

"You *remain*?" my mother asked. She burst into tears. "The waka is down, there's nothing left to remain on. How can you not choose life? How have we taught you so wrong? How have we failed so miserably?"

My father put a hand of support on her shoulder, and she closed her eyes.

As our waka lowered to water level, the Wayfinder's canoe loomed ever larger. Above, I saw Tapoto step forward to the Tongan brothers. I couldn't hear what Tapoto said to them, but Finau answered in the negative. "You can't stay behind," Finau said. "You've got a job to do, you've got a man to kill. Taking care of our uncle is the whole point."

"Let him go," the Wayfinder told Finau. "First we survive. Then we'll deal with our uncle."

With that, Tapoto lowered himself to our waka. With his weight, the deck finally went under, hovering ankle-deep below the surface. "The problem with our people," Tapoto said, "is that everybody gets a damned say in everything, and nobody can be overruled. Well, not today." He lifted Tiri and passed her up to her fellow islanders. Then he turned to me. "We decide what's good for you," he said. Then I was up in the air, over his shoulder. Quickly, my mother handed me her inking tools and my father passed me his binder of fishing lures. Then I was being handed over and hauled up.

Tapoto looked up to me, safe on a dry deck. "You said I lifted my people onto my shoulders. Today, I live up to it. Now get out of here."

I was next to Finau. He asked his brother, "How can we just sail away from them?"

The Wayfinder had yet to tell me about kidnapping Rotumans, abandoning Punake, or casting his cousin into the open sea, so I didn't know how to take his next words. "The way you sail from people," he told Finau, "is the way you leave your master, it's the way you leave your parents and Tonga and everything you know. You raise your sail, you take a line against the wind, and you go."

* +
*   +

The sun crested the horizon, orange daggers of dawn. Lifting swells lapped our washboards, and the mist of bailed water was chilly and mineral. I rushed to the Wayfinder—the sail had snapped taut, the waka was in motion—and begged him, "There's got to be a way. It's only three more people."

He looked into my eyes, and I could tell he was assessing whether I understood that his waka was beyond overloaded, that a line had to be drawn.

I appealed to his self-interest, to his stupid mission. "We can't leave people behind. How'll we defeat your uncle if we first defeat ourselves?"

I knew the Wayfinder'd fled Tonga with only his life and his brother's, so there was sympathy in his eyes. His expression suggested that with time things got better, that there were futures I couldn't imagine from here. Not without some feeling, he said, "They made their choices."

"Their waka was sinking," I said. "Where's the choice in that?"

"Their choices were made long before."

"They're my parents!"

"I tried to save them," the Wayfinder said. "They refused. What more can I do?"

"Just save them," I said.

I looked back to the receding *Red Cloak*. My mother and father and Tapoto were regarding me. No one called out or lifted a hand. Where was the gesture? Where were the words? A swell came, but rather than lifting *The Red Cloak*, it rushed over the submerged craft, knocking my mother off balance. I gasped.

The Wayfinder looked into my eyes. "The one whom fate spares," he said, "must also spare himself."

"What?" I asked. "What's that even mean?"

"It means that surviving's only half of it."

"Half of what?"

"Learning to live again, that doesn't come easy, if it comes at all. On that, my master was clear."

Someone spoke to me. "Their sacrifices won't be forgotten." I turned to see who'd uttered this, but I didn't recognize these people. They were strangers, all of them. Someone else said, "Songs will be sung about your folks."

"This feels like a test," I told the Wayfinder. "One that's pointless and absurd, like the ones you said your brother had to face."

The Wayfinder studied me, his concern visible.

"Didn't you say that's what killed Lolohea?" I asked. "Complying with a test when he should've refused?"

The Wayfinder winced at the mention of his brother's name. "Yes, but it was complicated."

I looked southward—my breath clutching when I saw *The Red Cloak* had fallen from view. I scanned the water behind us, but the waka was gone. Then a swell lofted it, as upon the palm of a great hand, before setting it down behind a berm of shimmering, dawn-lit water. It wasn't possible, what I was seeing, it couldn't be comprehended.

The Wayfinder placed a hand on my shoulder. I shrugged it off.

"Doing as he was told," I said. "You told me that's what cost Lolohea everything."

Only in that moment did I realize I was holding things. Arawiwi looked baffled when I handed her Hā Mutu's death mask, my mother's feather box, her inking tools, my father's binder of hooks and lures. I didn't even take deep breaths. I forgot to note our wake and the wind. When *The Red Cloak* flashed once more into view, likely for the last time, I dived.

The ocean is one thing when you're atop it, but when it's on top of you, every swell's a mountain, each trough a valley in long shadow. You lose the horizon, the direction you're headed, where you were coming from. And the ocean is reduced to single swells—the one, at that moment, you're swimming through. I gulped water. I felt a jellyfish sting. *Mother, Father*, I thought as I stroked. *Tapoto*, as I kicked my feet.

I would've swum right past *The Red Cloak* were it not for the shouts of my parents, and it was unreal to be pulled into the safety of a waka yet not leave the sea. My mother clutched me like no thing has been clutched. "No," she whispered as she kissed my hair and held me tight. "No, no, no, no, no."

"I'm sorry," I said. I didn't know what my sorry was for, just everything.

My father wasn't used to feeling emotion. On his face was joy and relief, but that didn't erase the helplessness he'd been feeling. Visible, too, was regret and self-blame but most of all, fear, fear that I'd left the safety of his influence, that I'd be subject to the vagaries of life without his guidance and protection. "I was stupid," he said. "We stay together. A sacrifice is no sacrifice if it comes between us. The moment you were gone," he said, his voice quavering, "I regretted everything."

I heard Tapoto. He was either laughing or crying. I couldn't see him, because my mother had pulled my face to her chest. You know how you can laugh with tears streaming down your face? Or cry while chuckling at the absurdity of something?

My cheek was against my mother's skin. I closed my eyes and let myself sob. The immensity of the sea was still about me. Empty water, that's what I saw with my eyes shut—the empty water I'd beheld when I looked for my parents and saw nothing. That anyone would sacrifice their lives for anybody, especially for me, a girl from an island people couldn't find if they tried—that made me cry hardest of all.

"Deep breaths," my mother said, holding me. "Just breathe."

Sitting there, breathing, I wasn't on the submerged deck of a sunken canoe in the middle of the sea. I was with my family, and despite everything, I felt safe.

A hull, splashing and thumping. I looked up. It was the Wayfinder, who'd circled around. His passengers gazed down at our sad tableau. Tiri spoke. From my seat of salt water, she seemed atop a mountain.

"I reclaim them," she said, pulling the huia feather from her hair. "To do so, I lighten our load."

"Wait," someone said. "The huia bird's extinct."

"It's from the old world," another person said. "From Aotearoa."

Tiri released the feather, letting the wind carry it over the water.

Then she removed her necklace, which contained a pinch of sand from our beach. It couldn't have equaled the weight of a beetle. This she released. We all subscribed to the belief that "land finds land," that without this sand, she was resigned to never reach home again. Then she unshouldered her satchel of botanicals. Before folks could protest, these, too, were remanded to the sea. "There'll be new medicines where we're going," she said. "I trust the Tongans to share what they know."

We looked to Finau and the Wayfinder, whose faces betrayed nothing.

Tiri turned to Arawiwi. How Tiri knew Arawiwi was holding the objects I'd handed her, I can't say. Arawiwi obliged. Into the water went my father's fishing lures. "How'll we eat?" a Kohimu brother asked. My father pointed at his head. "Fishing's up here," he said, and when my mother's inking tools were cast into the water, Mama Mānunu said, "But our children will need their moko."

My mother nodded in a way that said, *Not to worry*.

Arawiwi then sacrificed her own necklace and her set of chisel blades. At last, she surrendered Hā Mutu's death mask, which floated face up like the visage of a drowned man.

Others began relinquishing their prized possessions—feather boxes, family carvings, birth beads, porpoise teeth, combs of bone. In went greenstone earrings, poi balls, family cloaks. Tapoto climbed aboard the Wayfinder's waka, and, taking up his load of spears, released them to the deep. Finau, observing this, retrieved his bundle of greenstone war clubs. Even my father, whose weight was being made in personal treasure, was given pause by this. "That greenstone is our taonga, our cultural inheritance," he said. "If we abandon this, will we not become a different people? If we drop into the sea *everything*, will we still be us?"

"We have our stories," Tiri said.

"Yes, but," someone said, "we've lost our land—twice lost it—and now we're without possessions. We're separated from the graves of our ancestors. We find ourselves at the mercy of others. We don't even have food. If we release our greatest treasure, if we lose our greenstone, who'll we become?"

"What is a people," Tiri asked, "but the people themselves? Here we are. We endure."

Finau released the stone clubs from the heavy sack. One by one, they smacked the water.

"If we perish," Tiri said, "we perish knowing every sacrifice was made."

My mother and father were helped aboard. I took the hand that reached for me.

Did our discarded objects equal the weight of one person? Two? Or did they bear the weight of us all?

The Wayfinder removed the necklace holding his bird-bone whistle. "This is the source of my power, but I relinquish it." He cast it into the sea. He then removed his own fishhook necklace. "For ten years I wanted nothing but this pendant," he said. "Yet it's just an adornment. I see that now."

"You can't discard it," I said. "It marks you as a navigator. It brings safe passage over water."

He shook his head. "It's a sign of my foolishness, of my pride. What I really wanted were the things your people have."

"You once told me we possess nothing of value," I said.

"I was wrong," he said, and released his necklace into the sea.

He still wore my green fishhook pendant. "What about that?" I asked.

"It's not mine to discard," he said. "Yet no one else can possess it."

Finau tilted back his head. He closed his eyes. It was the posture you'd take to feel the rain on your face. "I know what we have to do," he told the Wayfinder. The brothers then dragged from the hull the remains of three people. Finau spoke to Six Fists's bones. "I'm sorry for all that happened to you," he said. "I'm sorry you were made a slave, that you were torn by dogs, that you never made it home. I'm sorry we dug you up. I promise to make things better in your honor." Finau then offered the following lines:

Ko manupuna fuiva ʻoku fusi	*The fuiva bird plucks*
ha fulufulu ʻo ha kaumeʻa mate	*a dead mate's plumes*
ke faʻuʻaki e pupunga hona fua.	*to feather a nest for their egg.*

The Wayfinder placed his hand on Moon Appearing's bones. "You claimed to be a nothing-special girl from a no-place island," he said. "That my brother loved you meant he knew better. It meant you were what was best of Tonga."

When they turned to their brother's bones, Finau began to weep. "How many times was I secretly grateful you were born first, that your unhappy fate spared mine? Now I'd give anything to trade places."

The Wayfinder regarded Lolohea's bones. "You're gone," he said. "You're really gone."

At last, they opened the bundles, spilling the bones. The bones plipped and plopped into the sea, mingling as they made their way down. When they were gone, a dust of white meal coated the water, sparing the Wayfinder his reflection.

THIRTY-TWO

DUTY AND SACRIFICE

Once Kaniva was abducted, they sailed offshore until Rotuma was nearly lost on the horizon. After lashing their canoes, they set a sea anchor and took turns watching her, for she was badly shaken, and they worried she'd try to swim for home.

Lolohea said, "We'll give them a day to get worked up over her disappearance. Then we'll go ashore and talk to them."

"Talk to them?" the Wayfinder asked.

"We'll have to tell them a story that makes sense of things," Lolohea said. "One that offers an explanation of why their daughter is gone."

"And what story might this be?" the Wayfinder asked.

"I'm working on it," Lolohea said. He turned to Punake. "You're good with words. I'll need your help."

Punake hesitated.

"We'll use words, not fists," Lolohea assured him. "I've no intention of fighting an entire island."

"I warn you, I'm not much for lying," Punake said. "Poets are dedicated to truth."

Lolohea felt the absurdity, the impossibility, of what he was faced with. He wanted to laugh. "Maybe that's what we should do, just land on their beach and tell them the truth."

That night, they gave Kaniva fruit and water before tying a long rope to her vaka and letting it drift to the end of the tether. She'd found her voice at some point and had begun making promises that her father, a priest, wouldn't rest until she was returned, that the young men on her island would do anything to get her back. Lolohea was counting on these to be true. Still, it was difficult to hear her laments. Plus, Mateaki's fixation with her only increased. He kept offering to comfort her, saying things like, "I know what she's feeling." He seemed to forget the way she'd stared at the scabbed-over scratches on his face. It was clear she'd seen those marks as the record of a previous woman's struggle, perhaps even as a warning, sent from one woman to another, via Mateaki's skin.

Four young men ate the shellfish from Kaniva's basket. The moon had yet to rise, so candlenuts were lit in spent oysters. "We've certainly riled up the Rotumans," Lolohea said. "Now we must give them a narrative. Tomorrow we'll become the hunters of a kidnapper."

"And who's this villain?" Punake asked.

"We'll invent someone," Lolohea said. "What matters is that we're after a man known to hurt women, a man believed to be in the area, and the Rotumans, having just lost a daughter, will want to join our mission to capture him and recover her."

"We'll have to describe this villain," the Wayfinder cautioned. "He'll need a name."

"Yes, but most important is our posture," Lolohea said. "What matters is that we're convincing."

Mateaki was on his back, looking at the sky. "What'll happen to the men who fall for the story?"

"Nothing," Lolohea said. "I'll eventually free them."

"The gossip Kōkī told me," Punake said, "is the men'll be sold into the obsidian mine on Kao."

They took a moment to absorb that notion.

"This is all an exercise," Lolohea said. "When I'm king, I'll make everything right."

The Wayfinder caught Lolohea's eye. He glanced at Mateaki and then tossed his head to suggest they might want some privacy from their cousin.

"I suppose it's time to check on the young woman," Lolohea declared.

"I'll do it," Mateaki volunteered, and began hauling in the rope. Kaniva's vaka appeared from the darkness. When Mateaki climbed aboard, he pushed off so that he and the girl removed themselves from view.

"We mustn't underestimate rural people," the Wayfinder said. "They're clever and resourceful. There must be agreement on who the culprit is. What if the Rotumans question us separately?"

"What do you propose?" Punake asked.

The Wayfinder said, "Last night, you suggested telling them the truth."

"I was joking," Lolohea said.

"We know a man who has kidnapped women," the Wayfinder said. "A man who's assaulted them, and, at least concerning his wife, killed them. The story's a good match. A person central to the royal family has been disrupting stability, disgracing the family, causing harm. So the king's son is sent to bring him to justice. These people will never have heard of 'Aho, so we'll be at liberty to describe his missing teeth, his dog-bite scars, the black jellyfish on his hand. In describing him, we'd all be describing the same person, and doing so truthfully. Any inconsistency could be ascribed to withholding in order to protect the family name. In fact, the more reluctant you are to divulge ugly truths about a family member, the more genuine you'll sound."

"But what of Mateaki?" Punake asked. "We couldn't describe his father like that in front of him."

"That's the drawback," the Wayfinder said. "Our cousin could take no part."

Punake reclined on the deck. Above, the sail luffed in the wind. He said:

Kauvaka 'Eua, kuo mafasia he mofi, fakahifo e hono kaungā folau tahi o li'ekina tokotaha si'ene heka pōpao.	*'Eua sailor, unseated by fever, was relegated by his mates to ride the outrigger alone.*

Lolohea looked to Punake. "So it'd be just you and me?"

Before Punake could respond, the girl on the vaka cried out.

"Mateaki?" Lolohea called into the darkness. There was no response.

All that was visible was the tether going taut and slack with the tug of the waves.

Come dawn, the Wayfinder was the first to wake. He checked their drift. The clouds foretold afternoon rain. The girl at the end of the tether wasn't visible—she must have wrapped herself in the lowered sail. With everyone sleeping, the vaka was quiet. He thought of Havea, of the silence they shared, of days that flowed without speech. But, Havea. It was time to accept that the man didn't return from his final landfall. The Wayfinder was sure he could've helped Havea make it back, and the hardest part to stomach was the idea that when his master needed him most, he wasn't there.

The Wayfinder woke his older brother. "I'm coming with," he whispered.

Lolohea blinked his eyes. "What happened to, *The navigator only sets the course?*"

"That's for passengers. You're my brother."

"But if you land with us," Lolohea said, "who'd sail the vaka with Kaniva?"

"One problem at a time," the Wayfinder said. "Isn't that what Father tells us? Besides, you'll need me. Otherwise, how'll you explain finding Rotuma without a navigator?"

"Mateaki's no sailor," Lolohea whispered.

"All the better that I helm the chase boat. I can make sure we don't overtake him."

"What about the girl? Alone with our cousin?"

The Wayfinder glanced toward the fishing canoe. "Yeah, there's that."

That night, the Tuʻitonga told his wife what the Tamahā had said, that ʻAho planned to inter him alive.

Pōhiva paced the royal fale. "Obviously, she tells you this in the hopes you'll do the same to him. But why? The Tamahā has made much profit by pitting you two against one another. Something must've changed. There must be a development we can't see, something that's made her conclude being rid of ʻAho is her best option."

The Tuʻitonga leaned against a lodge pole. "Perhaps she's decided he can't be controlled."

"She's managed him thus far," Pōhiva said. "Why not wait to see if he leaves the island, as he's promised to do after tonight? What can't wait a day?"

The pole felt good against his back. He'd had no massages since he'd begun taking the ink. Though they were speaking about burying his brother alive, he couldn't really let himself comprehend it. When he thought of the night ahead, he saw it in parts he couldn't put together: his brother, moonlight, a gathering, a tomb exhaling the breath of their ancestors.

"Perhaps," he mused, "knowing I'm not long for this world, she wishes me to finish him before I go, and thus she's rid of us both."

"No, the Tamahā's most secure when there's a king strong enough to control the other chiefs but distracted enough to leave her to her own devices. She'd do much to keep you in power."

The Tuʻitonga scratched his back against the pole. It was very satisfying, but his body felt muted and far away, the way one perceives the world through waterlogged ears. "Remember that girl? The one the Tamahā planned to pass the Fan to? When we got rid of her, that was a turning point, that was a sting the Tamahā hasn't forgotten."

"The Tamahā does what she has to do," Pōhiva said. "So do we."

"So we do it, then, we send my brother to the afterlife?"

Pōhiva said, "Whether ʻAho leaves tomorrow or enters the tomb tonight, the outcome's the same, except that with the latter, we can be sure he never returns to threaten Lolohea's rule."

The more the Tuʻitonga scratched his back against the pole, the less it seemed to satisfy him.

"It'll be no easy evening," he said.

"When the time comes, you'll, what, just push him in? Do you subdue him first?"

"Like I've done such a thing."

"Deceit is always easiest," she said.

Some look on his face made Pōhiva near him and embrace him. Inside her grasp, he thought not of what was ahead—the darkness, the struggle, the lid sealing shut—but instead of when he and his brother were young. To distract 'Aho from the ache of their absent father, the Tu'itonga taught 'Aho how to tame peka bats with slices of fruit. 'Aho was good at waiting in the dark for the delicate creatures to appear. He was tender with them. Despite their sharp claws, he'd let them hang from his wrist so he could regard their expressive faces.

When Pōhiva released him, her hands came away blood-speckled.

His feet and hands had taken their turns at numbness—he'd gotten used to that. But how could a person come to lack feeling all over?

Pōhiva gave him a look that said, *It's time.*

Outside, Matāpule Mu'a and Seven Fists stood in the moonlight. The Tu'itonga asked Matāpule Mu'a, "Have you recruited the hundreds of men necessary to open the vault?"

Matāpule Mu'a said, "Hundreds of men are needed to *fully* open the vault. We intend to just crack it a bit. For that, we'll need but twenty men."

A bit, meaning the width of a man. "Promise me," the Tu'itonga said, "that when my time comes you'll deploy the full two hundred men, yes?"

"Why not three hundred?" Matāpule Mu'a responded.

Rare that a matāpule could make him smile. The Tu'itonga turned to his new security chief, asking, "Is it true you fought alongside my brother in the Fisian war?"

Seven Fists nodded. "Is it true he's been attacking women?"

"Sadly."

"I've seen this before," Seven Fists said, "men who love combat so much they bring it home. Such men have been seduced by battle, the way it heightens all: at the edge of death, everything's possible, everything's yours, and what you knew before, who you were before, it falls away, like cliffs into the sea." Seven Fists paused to regard the Tu'itonga, to make sure he was understood. "So if you ask about my loyalties, I need only tell you this: I'm a father and a warrior, so I know twofold why some men should never return."

The Tu'itonga lamented that there wasn't enough time left to get to know Seven Fists.

"Tonight, when the moment arrives," the Tu'itonga said, "you'll be ready?"

Though Seven Fists was a small man, there was a hard, angular cut to his jaw. "I await the command."

Matāpule Muʻa asked, "Shall I send a runner to Heketā to fetch your brother?"

"I'll escort him myself," the Tuʻitonga said.

"It's a long walk," Matāpule Muʻa said.

"If the walk were any shorter, I should not be able to make it."

When the morning shadows had shortened, Lolohea stepped onto the fishing vaka to give Mateaki the plan. Lolohea's weight unsteadied the small canoe, a coastal craft not built for open-ocean swells. Mateaki looked less than crestfallen to learn he'd be sailing on alone with Kaniva. "When you next see our canoe," Lolohea told him, "head south. Use all the sail you've got."

"I know we were raised apart," Mateaki said. "I know our fathers have their differences. But I want to say, especially if something goes wrong, that these last days, they've been my best days since my mother—"

Lolohea lifted a hand. "There's no need. We'll see each other soon enough, so let's save the goodbyes."

"It's not a goodbye. It's just that I never had a brother, and on this trip, I've come to see you guys as—"

"The feeling's mutual," Lolohea said. He had no idea where his cousin was going with this talk, but it wasn't anyplace good. "There's one more thing. The girl."

"Yes, her," Mateaki said, brightening.

The Tongan and Rotuman languages were close enough that the young woman understood she was being left at the mercy of Mateaki. "My father's a powerful priest," she said. "Just let me go. Spare yourself any consequences."

"You'll be freed," Lolohea told her. "I swear I do no more than I must." Lolohea turned to Mateaki. "It's important that she's released in good condition." Lolohea wanted to phrase things so the girl couldn't comprehend. *Toho* was the Tongan word for dragging a canoe through sand, which the canoe was not wont to do. Force was required to make it comply. So *tohotoho* had become a term for rape. "Promise me you won't drag the canoe."

Mateaki looked offended. "I'd never do that. I have feelings for her."

Lolohea glanced at the girl, who was trying to follow their words. "Feelings?"

"Warm ones."

"Why'd the girl call out last night? Did you take your advantage?"

"My *advantage*?" Mateaki looked wounded. "Have you never cared about someone? When you care about someone, it could never be like that."

"We're on a mission. Your *feelings* can wait."

"She and I didn't meet under ideal circumstances," Mateaki said. "And we've yet to get to know each other. But what if she wants to be with me? What if, when she's freed, she chooses to stay?"

Lolohea loosened the landing line and pushed the canoes apart. "She's not your girlfriend, so don't drop your guard." The farther the canoes drifted, the more Mateaki and Kaniva diminished. Or was the ocean reasserting its immensity? What was love or death when measured against the sea?

When Lolohea set foot on the sands of Rotuma, he had to steady himself. He hadn't touched solid ground since 'Ata. People who'd seen their approaching sail had gathered at the beach and now stood watching.

The Wayfinder tossed a landing line to a man who asked, "Where're you from?"

Before the Wayfinder could answer, Lolohea said, "Ignore them."

When Punake's feet touched the beach, he inhaled deep, wowed by the island's loveliness: its verdant peaks, sticky with clouds, and a dark, dramatic isthmus, rising from the island's fala of green. Green! How long since he'd seen this vibrant color? Punake smiled at several of Rotuma's lovely ladies— each the more beautiful because she'd not been abducted in the night. He looked to the coastline, hearing some rhythm in the surf, and his eyes were following a colorful flock of birds, when Lolohea slapped him in the face. Punake recoiled, holding a cheek still discolored from his beating in Fisi.

"We're hunting a dangerous man," Lolohea told him. "Not sightseeing."

Punake, looking stunned and uncertain, nodded.

Several armed warriors appeared. One stood before the rest. "Who are you?"

"You level a spear at me?" Lolohea responded. "Is this not the peace-loving island of Rotuma?"

"In what other way is peace maintained?" the young warrior responded.

Lolohea asked, "Have you tried hospitality?"

The warrior was inked with turtles and flying fish. "A Tongan tutors me on courtesy?" he asked. "Just tell us what you did with her."

A man came running. He was middle-aged, with bright eyes and a patch of hair on his chin. "Raho," he said to the warrior. "Lower your weapon." He turned to Lolohea. "Welcome, welcome. I'm Rotuma's Mua priest. Please, tell us you've brought news of Kaniva. I've been praying for answers, and here you are!"

"We're here on another matter," Lolohea said.

The priest looked confused. "What matter could that be?"

"It's to be discussed with your chief," Lolohea said.

"Kaniva didn't just vanish," Raho said. "Something happened to her."

"Raho, is it?" Lolohea asked. "As you can plainly see, our vaka bears no other passengers."

"Don't tell me what's plain," Raho said. "Tongans are the menace of the seas. You won't stop until you've taken everything."

"Raho!" the priest shouted. "We found accord with the Samoans. We achieved peace with the Fijians. Treat these Tongans as guests."

Spear raised, Raho rushed toward Lolohea, to see if he'd flinch. Lolohea mustered the will to remain placid. This calm demeanor seemed to enrage Raho all the more. In frustration, he whacked his spear against the vaka's bow.

Punake calmed this tense moment with a couplet:

Ko langi naʻe hoko ai e fetāʻaki sīlogo—	*The sky was the scene of a silent duel—*
ha katafa fepaki mo e matangi.	*a frigate bird against the wind.*

"Don't worry about Raho," the priest said. "He's like that. We'll take you to our Sau chief."

They began walking a coastal path toward the chief's residence—along the way, the priest would give Lolohea no peace. With every pace, the priest became more animated; soon tears rolled down his cheeks. "My prayers are what brought you," he said. "When we lost Kaniva's mother, it had a terrible impact on Kaniva, it shook her faith, it made her stop believing in the rightness of the world. But your presence is proof that there's an order to things. I foresaw that someone would arrive to help. I couldn't have imagined it would be Tongans in a Fijian canoe, but—"

"Fe'unga," Lolohea snapped. "Can't you see I have no interest in a misplaced girl? And I'm summoned nowhere by the tears of a priest. A matter of grave consequence brings me to this nowhere-facing nothing of an island."

"I beg forgiveness," the Mua priest said. "Of course no one wants to hear a lamenting father sing his daughter's praises. Since I lost my wife, I go on too much. If only you'd met Kaniva, you'd understand why I speak of her so, you'd agree she was the kind of daughter to make a father proud, one who . . ." As the priest continued in this manner, Lolohea repeated in his mind that the girl'd be released, that as long as she went free, all the distress caused by this subterfuge would be undone.

When the priest's eyes misted again, Lolohea unloaded him onto his brother, saying a navigator might have insights into a missing girl. But no sooner was Lolohea free than Punake sought his confidence. Lolohea preempted him. "I hope you understand why I had to strike you."

"I confess it stung," Punake said. "Especially by your hand."

"Don't poets remind us that words hurt worse than strikes?"

"I see you turn to metaphorical speech," Punake said, "when the pain is mine."

The Sau chief, identified by his apron of red feathers, held meetings on the island's isthmus, where breezes kept mosquitoes at bay. At his side was a woman with white hair. When Raho and the priest knelt first to her, Lolohea understood she was the island's ranking aunt. O'honi, they called her.

"We're in pursuit of a fugitive," Lolohea told her. "We've been chasing him since he fled Tongatapu."

"What's this man done?" the Sau chief asked.

"His offense is a private matter," Lolohea said.

This response was greeted with a silence that allowed Lolohea to wonder why he was here, why he was lying, why he'd left an innocent girl on a canoe with his cousin, why he'd left Moon Appearing in Tonga with his uncle. To regain his focus, he thought of the sea, seen as he fell from a cliff toward the water, the way time slowed in that moment, the chaos and brutality of the waves seeming to dissipate, to still, and, once he was underwater, to cease.

The Wayfinder rescued the moment. "What hasn't this fugitive done? He's assaulted, abducted, maimed, and murdered. The last we saw of him, his bow was pointed in this direction."

The Sau chief said, "No unfamiliar sails have crossed our horizon."

Lolohea said, "We've been close enough to touch this fugitive. It's only by the treachery of rural islanders that he's eluded us."

Raho indicated Punake's discolored face. "It seems this fugitive has touched you, too."

"This fugitive, as you call him," the Sau chief asked Punake, "he got the best of you?"

"We were caught off guard," the Wayfinder said.

Lolohea admitted, "He's a formidable figure."

Punake spoke for himself. "The fugitive may have gotten the best of me, but I assure you he's missing a couple of teeth."

The Oʻhoni aunt asked, "Why would rural islanders, known to be humble and dutiful, seek to protect a criminal?"

Lolohea tried to regroup, to summon the attitude his father had called for. "*Humble and dutiful?*" he asked. "Why, I assure you rural people are quite the opposite. They are self-interested and defiant by nature."

"The arrogance of Tongans!" Raho exclaimed.

The Sau chief did not address the insult. "You ask us to take your word for many things. Can you offer any evidence that the man you seek even exists?"

"Oh, he exists." Lolohea conjured the menacing specter of his uncle. "He has dog-bite scars about his limbs and holds the power to strike his mark upon you. By daylight, male combatants fall before him. At night, he takes, without discrimination, his female victims."

"You think we'd harbor such a man?" the Sau chief asked.

"He's quite forceful," Lolohea said. "Many have found themselves abetting him, including Tongans."

"Formidable and forceful," the Oʻhoni aunt said. "That's how you describe him, yet you seek to apprehend him with the help of but two compatriots?" Her eyes glanced from the soft figure of Punake to the Wayfinder, who was clearly no warrior.

"I'm the one who must stop him," Lolohea said. He remembered how Moon Appearing had spoken of ʻAho on ʻAta, how at the thought of him, her breathing sharpened and her eyes didn't know where to land. "No one else has been able to end the menace of him."

"And why do you believe you'll succeed where others have not?" the Sau chief asked.

"I aim to rise to the occasion," Lolohea said.

"I assure you," the Sau chief said, "no foreigners enjoy safe haven on this island. You're free to look around. But understand that we're occupied by the search for a beloved daughter."

"We'll be on our way, then," Lolohea said. "However, should this fugitive seek refuge after we depart, your hospitality would come with consequences."

"And what would those be?" Raho asked.

"For sheltering an enemy of Tonga, after a personal warning not to?" Lolohea mused. "Depopulation."

Incredulous, Raho asked, "Depopulate Rotuma? Give it a try, if you think it's so easy. In fact, I'll oblige you right now."

The Wayfinder asked, "Do you doubt the number of islands Tonga depopulates?"

"Tonga even empties its own islands," Lolohea said.

"This is quite a threat you make against us," the Sau chief said.

"I only offer the past as oracle against the future," Lolohea said.

"Be on your way, then," the Oʻhoni aunt said. "And make no further threats, especially as you offer only a story and some colorful description."

"Would you rather I submit the blood of the fugitive's victims?" Lolohea asked her.

The Oʻhoni aunt gave no response. Loose strands of her white hair entertained the wind, lending her a conveyance of placid indifference.

"We have evidence of the man we seek," the Wayfinder said. From his waistband, he withdrew 'Aho's lost tooth. "If your priest is up to the task of interpreting it."

With his daughter missing, the Mua priest hesitated before taking possession of an item that reputedly belonged to a man who hurt women. But he accepted the tooth and closed his eyes. "This belonged to a royal. I hear the snap of dog teeth. I see the light fade in the eyes of many. I see sharks following war canoes as bloody water is bailed into the sea." The priest set the tooth aside. "The man is a warrior, one who knows death."

Concerned, the Sau chief focused on Lolohea. "Why wouldn't the Tu'i of Tonga send an armada to remand this dangerous man?"

Lolohea said, "It's a family matter. We prefer to deal with it internally. My mates here, they're family."

"So this fugitive," the Sau chief asked, "he's related to you?"

Reluctantly, Lolohea nodded. "We share blood. The fugitive is the brother of the Tu'i of Tonga, and I'm the king's first son."

The Sau chief was astonished. "Why would the Tu'itonga risk his own son?"

"The king hasn't sent me," Lolohea said. "The reason I'm here . . . it's personal."

"What's this man done to you?" the O'honi aunt asked.

"Not me. Someone close to me," Lolohea said. "He harmed her. I fear he's harmed her forever."

The Sau chief asked, "Your uncle has ravished the woman you love?"

In order to believe his own words, Lolohea had to make his worst fears real, he had to put 'Aho and Moon Appearing together in his mind and imagine the wound to Moon Appearing's spirit that would result from an assault upon her. "My uncle, he has . . ." Lolohea paused. "And Moon Appearing, she . . ."

Lolohea could say no more, but these words were enough to conjure the sweetest and the most troublesome figures in his life and put them in proximity. He'd just told a one-line story, one whose entire plot was but two names, yet he might as well have taken the hands of 'Aho and Moon Appearing and interlocked them. *Now inevitable*, Lolohea thought. *Now irretrievable.* For Lolohea had lived long enough to know that, while a story is molded from the clay of invention, a single telling can fire it in the kiln of real life, resulting not in a fabrication, but a reality hard enough, sharp enough, to draw blood.

The Sau chief said, almost dismissively, "So your uncle's taken a fancy to your girl. It's an old story."

"There's more," Lolohea said. "Your priest abandons his reading too soon."

"Yes," Raho said. "We must know if the tooth has anything to say about Kaniva."

Reluctantly, the priest took up the tooth again. "I hear a man lisp his dark intentions. A woman struggles, she resists. A woman is—" The priest dropped the tooth once more. "I can summon no more appetite for this."

"You must see this through," the Sau chief said.

"You must," said the Oʻhoni aunt.

The priest consented. He took a breath and continued. "Black jellyfish unfurl before me. I see a tentacled hand. I smell burned hair. I see his victims, male and female, living and dead." The priest's eyes snapped open. He was shaking. "If Kaniva's in this man's grip, I fear she's lost, forever lost."

The Sau chief took an inward gaze. "What makes such a man?"

"She must be rescued," Raho said, and by his faltering voice, it was clear her fate was a personal matter for him, too.

The Oʻhoni aunt turned to Lolohea. "Raho's right," she said. "The girl must be rescued. We're a small island. Our population is carefully controlled. So our young people, they're everything. Losing even a single daughter, it's not something we can afford."

"But as you say, the fugitive's not here," Lolohea countered.

"But the hand of this fugitive must be at work," the Sau chief said. "The coincidence is too much: You saw him head this way. Kaniva goes missing. Then one of our vaka disappears."

"A vaka?" Lolohea asked. "You mentioned nothing about a missing canoe."

"Yesterday we noticed it gone," the Sau chief said. "But compared to Kaniva, a canoe is nothing."

The Wayfinder added to the unfolding fiction. "We saw an unfamiliar sail headed south as we arrived but thought nothing of it."

Lolohea asked, "Were any of your people headed south?"

When the Sau chief shook his head, the Wayfinder said, "He's doubling back on us."

Punake said, "He must have scuttled his own canoe, knowing we'd recognize it."

"He's eluded us again," Lolohea said, then turned to the Sau chief. "Can we trouble you for some provisions?" The man had barely time to answer before Lolohea said, "Have them sent to the beach, with great haste, for we depart immediately." When Lolohea stood and turned for the shore, his mates stood with him.

"Wait," Raho said. "What about Kaniva? Your uncle must've taken her, too."

Lolohea's face was wild with the need to return to Tonga, for this escapade had made Moon Appearing's danger newly urgent to him, and what he must do to save her had never been clearer. "You have my word that I'll make him pay for this abduction."

"But Raho's asking about our girl," the Sau chief said. "What about our daughter?"

The Tuʻitonga had assured Lolohea that the problem of ʻAho would be dealt with, but Lolohea had to cross the ocean to realize only he himself could truly do it. "I won't let the moon disappear," he declared.

To the confused Rotumans, the Wayfinder said, "He means we won't sleep. And if we find your daughter, we'll send her back on the first canoe we encounter heading north."

"We have few visitors," the Sau chief said. "It would be a rare canoe that—"

"What if the fugitive eludes you again?" the priest interrupted, his voice unsteady.

"What if you're too late?" the Oʻhoni aunt asked.

"If we're too late?" Punake responded. "We'll make sure her bones find their way home."

The Mua priest nearly collapsed.

"We'll save Kaniva," Raho said. "You have your mission, and we have ours. Let us sail by your side."

The Wayfinder shook his head. "Our vaka's the fastest on the water. You could never keep up."

Raho stood, his spear upright before him. "You could use the help. You said yourself the fugitive is formidable. We could join you. Your vaka's quite large. Together we could administer justice."

Lolohea looked at the Wayfinder and then at Punake. For a moment it seemed none of them breathed. "Sorry," Lolohea said. "This is a family problem."

"Tongans and Rotumans should join forces," the Sau chief said. "Working together is our way."

Punake said, "We have extra room."

"I've seen your vaka," Raho said. "It's capable of holding another dozen at least. Our warriors are quite fierce. When you're neighbors with Fiji, Samoa, and Tonga, you have to be."

"Ten, at most," the Wayfinder said. "We could take no more."

"You get ahead of yourselves," Lolohea said. "I don't know if this man has your daughter. I don't even know if we head in the right direction. All we have to go on is a single sail headed south."

Raho faced Lolohea. "We know there's a girl you love. And the portrait of your uncle has come clear. It must be difficult, knowing he hurt her. But there's still time to help Kaniva. You can save her from that fate."

The nature of what was real, what was story, and what was fantasy, they were getting hard to separate in Lolohea's mind. The Wayfinder and Punake regarded him with concern.

The Sau chief stood. "What happened to the girl you love, it can be survived, it can be overcome—but only if you accept help. If you try to face such things alone, they'll destroy you."

The priest advanced, taking up Lolohea's hand. Eyes closed, he gripped Lolohea's palm. Lolohea imagined the man perusing his life. What of him would be visible to a stranger—that he was filled with doubts, that he didn't have his father's ability to lead? That he himself was the villain of this tale?

"You're a good young man," the priest said. "I can tell you're good. You wouldn't let a girl get hurt, not if you could stop it. I know that about you."

Lolohea looked into the eyes of the priest. They were red and wet and sad, but worst of all, they glistened with hope. Lolohea tried to say some affirming words, but they wouldn't come.

At the beach, Raho selected his compatriots, nine of them, and much was made of who'd go and who wouldn't. The chosen men tried to pack the hull with every possible store and supply, including a pair of hogs, but the Wayfinder allowed only the basics: bananas, dried fish, and water.

A Rotuman made his way to the vaka with a bundle of spears.

"No weapons," Lolohea said.

"Aren't we facing a dangerous man?" Raho asked.

"Do you see us bearing weapons?" Lolohea asked. "My uncle may be a dark figure, but he's still family. We don't hunt him like a pig on a wild island."

There were thirteen of them, so the vaka was easily turned to face the sea.

The Oʻhoni aunt arrived at the beach. She watched as the last items were stowed and farewells were made. She waded into the surf to study the vaka by running her hand along its dark wood. She seemed to see something in the adze marks faceting the curve of the hull. Was she wondering about its origin, its seaworthiness, its history? Circling the craft, she inspected the section of decking where they'd stowed the body of the boy they'd kidnapped, though there could be no remnant of this event, could there? She reached over the hull for something. What she retrieved wasn't visible at first. Then Lolohea saw it: Mateaki's flute of human bone. This she studied in silence before replacing it.

When she exited the water, Raho's warriors were performing their last task: each took up a sprinkle of sand, folded it inside a leaf, and then tucked it in his waistband.

"We do not go," the Oʻhoni aunt said.

Raho countered, "But—"

She lifted a hand. "The reason we do not go is the same reason we first decided to go—because our young people are irreplaceable."

The Sau chief said, "But we embark in the spirit of cooperation, one that might unite our peoples."

"I understand," she said. "But if these young men don't make it back, we lose a generation."

"The matter's been settled," Lolohea countered. "We're taking up the landing lines."

"I thought you were averse to hosting a Rotuman crew," the Oʻhoni aunt said.

"I heard the wisdom of your chief," Lolohea said. "And the priest's love for his daughter swayed me."

"So it was *you* who were swayed?" she asked.

Lolohea said, "And upon consideration, I saw the value of your aid."

"You see our value, you say," she said. "Yet you haven't guaranteed the safe return of these warriors who've pledged to fight with you."

"I assumed that was a given," Lolohea said. "Isn't this mission about a safe return?"

"Nothing in this world's a given," the Oʻhoni aunt said. "For us it's about Kaniva. For you, I'm not so sure. After our young men have been of service, what's to stop you from stranding them on a distant island?"

Lolohea said, "Now it's you who make outrageous accusations."

The priest dropped to his knees. "Do not take hope from me," he implored.

The Oʻhoni aunt addressed him without sympathy. "You've had your children, and your wife is gone. If you wish to join these Tongans, feel free. But we can't jeopardize so many young men."

When Raho took a knee, so did the men behind him. "We're the young men you speak of. If we don't fight for what we believe, then who are we and what's left to preserve?"

Silence fell when the Sau chief went to his knees, his apron of red feathers darkened by wet sand. "We've made peace with the Samoans. We formed an alliance with the Fijians. This is our chance to build goodwill with the Tongans. That's what'll safeguard our next generation."

Lolohea said, "I see now that the issue is trust. I personally guarantee the safe return of these young warriors. And I offer collateral as well."

Surrounded by men on their knees, the Oʻhoni aunt asked, "Collateral?"

"Yes," Lolohea said. "Now that we have a team of warriors to help subdue the fugitive, I can spare a man to stay behind. That'll guarantee our return."

"Which man, and who is he to you?" the Oʻhoni aunt asked.

"Punake here is a very fine fellow," Lolohea said. "He's the supplemental father to my youngest brother. As such, he's a valuable family member."

"What's a supplemental father?" the priest asked. "Have you lost your true one?"

"No, no," Lolohea said. "My father's a busy man, so he appointed a surrogate."

The Sau chief cocked his head. "How could a father be too busy to raise his son?"

The Wayfinder regarded Lolohea with the same question in his eyes.

"I can only say that my father wished to double his efforts by appointing a substitute."

"Or triple them," the Wayfinder said.

"Are we agreed?" Lolohea asked. "Time is of the essence, for we depart."

It was clear the Oʻhoni aunt disapproved of this course of action, but she surveyed the will of the men around her and bowed to their desires, the look on her face suggesting that wisdom cannot be put into the heads of men—they must bang understanding into their skulls themselves.

The men rose and pressed their shoulders against the hull, waiting for the next surge to lift the vaka. Lolohea took the opportunity to clap Punake on the shoulder. "You're very loyal, my friend. Your sacrifice will be rewarded, trust me. We'll be back sooner than you think."

"*Friend?*" Punake asked. "I thought I was *family*."

Behind Lolohea came the break of a wave and the communal grunt of synchronized pushing.

"Of course you're family," Lolohea said. "And family's forever."

The insincerity of this line was something even Lolohea heard.

"You know those tests your father has you taking?" Punake asked. "They're working."

"Please, harbor no reservations about your fate," Lolohea added. "We stick to the plan. When I'm Tuʻitonga and I free these men, I'll get you back, I promise."

"Who am I to you?" Punake asked. "Am I like a distant cousin, a helper, a servant, less?"

"To make it through this, you'll need to stay focused," Lolohea said.

"There'll be time for a healthy chat later. Trust me, we'll soon be drinking kava and reminiscing."

"Your father isn't long for this world," Punake said, offering no laments or condolences. "He's the one who made me the royal poet. Who'll I be when you're Tuʻitonga? Will I hold any place at all?"

"Punake, you hold the admiration of all. You're the royal poet, and you'll continue to be, no matter where you are, no matter what comes to pass."

Punake nodded, not with affirmation but with the acknowledgment of a truth. "That's what your father would've told me."

But Lolohea barely heard these words. The vaka's sail now billowed, and he'd have to run through the surf to catch up, lest he be left behind.

Torch in hand, the Tuʻitonga left the royal compound to fetch his brother. The Tonga he encountered matched his mood. Flowers had folded closed for the night. Ropes of smoke pulsed black from the flame before him. And by this proximal light, the sky didn't seem to exist, trees consisted only of trunks. He felt as if he'd been journeying to his brother a very long time, though his footfalls suggested he'd barely begun. And the torch—the torch made him feel like a vigilante, moving at night toward a justice of his own construction.

So he dropped the flame and began orienting by moonlight. This was how he and his brother had moved when they were young—without escorts, entourages, security men, or matāpule. Just boys under a Tongan moon. Soon his senses came alive. He heard the beating of beetles in slow flight, the rustle of piglets in the underbrush. He reminded himself it was a beginning he was headed toward, not an end. Lolohea's ascension was ahead, not a series of burials, starting with his brother's. Still, the prospect of death conjured the sublime—zithers of wind through toa needles, cool Tongan soil between one's toes, high white clouds percussed into ribbons by some heavenly beat. He wondered if, in the afterlife, the sky was visible.

Following a bend in the path, the Tuʻitonga came upon a downed tree. A figure was sitting upon it, one leg crossed over the other. It was ʻAho.

"Do I find my brother?" the Tuʻitonga asked. "I was headed your way."

"I was making my way to you," 'Aho said.

The Tuʻitonga sat beside him. Even by the subdued light, the wound on 'Aho's leg had visibly worsened. Dark veins surrounded an open lip of flesh.

"Nights like this bring back memories," the Tuʻitonga said. "How often did we roam these paths?"

'Aho shrugged.

"You must have some fond recollections. We climbed these trees, we swam these waters."

"If you think you can remember your innocence, you can't. Innocence is an idea."

"It's a time," the Tuʻitonga said. "Why not remember back to before our troubles began?"

"Between me and those days, a mountain has sprung up. I do not make the climb."

"Nonsense. Don't you remember feeding peka bats by hand?"

'Aho said nothing.

"How about that little ground dove we tried to snare?" the Tuʻitonga asked. "Each morning, we'd hear it coo, and we'd say to ourselves, *We should like to catch one of those before they're gone.*"

'Aho smiled at that. "How many snares did we set?"

"The trees were nothing but traps."

"Yes, we set trip wires everywhere, enough that we kept ensnaring ourselves."

"Alas, we never caught that dove. And now they're gone," the Tuʻitonga said. "Is it your wound, is that why I find you here in the dark?"

'Aho shook his head.

"Do you have second thoughts about laying your wife to rest?"

"I did imagine it going differently," 'Aho said. "The way I'd pictured it, my son was by my side, and I was able to say some words to help him understand why she was gone."

"Nothing has to be tonight. We can postpone this whole affair and take it up when our boys return."

"You won't delay my satisfaction again. The least I can do is make sure my wife makes it to the afterlife. When my time comes, I'll have eternity to make up for what happened to her."

"What did happen to her?" the Tuʻitonga asked. "Was it some kind of accident?"

"I know what you're really asking. I'd like to think you were the one person who didn't press me."

"As far as I know, I'm the only person who has asked."

ʻAho took a sudden interest in his wound, using his thumbs to express fluid from it. "If I had to say what happened to her, I'd say she just... became ensnared."

"The snare in your metaphor, were you the one who set it?"

"Sometimes I feel like I am the snare," ʻAho said. "Only when the device is triggered does it get any rest. Only after I'm set off do I feel normal again. But within a few days, I discover the trigger has been reset." ʻAho looked to the moon. "Sometimes I think war is the only place that's safe for me."

"But your son."

"Yes, my son," ʻAho lamented. "I thought coming here would restore something in him."

The Tuʻitonga understood now why ʻAho had made that crazy proposal of living in Fisi.

"We just need to find the proper place for you," the Tuʻitonga said.

"And what place is that?"

The Tuʻitonga thought of distant islands, ones where he had influence. If ʻAho went to Haʻamoa, only to begin attacking young women... He didn't finish the thought. His mind perused the archipelagos of Haʻapai and Vavaʻu. He considered Tokelau and Niue and ʻUvea. "What about ʻAta? I could give you its exclusive use."

"Your personal island?"

"I could make it tapu for all but the two of you."

"Just the two of us," ʻAho said. He said this with a sense of possibility, but then went quiet. "You don't know how much I miss her. I need her now more than ever. My son, I'm all he has, he has no one in the world except me. But..."

"But what?"

"What if I'm all he has?" ʻAho asked. "And what if I'm also the worst thing that ever happened to him?" Tears threatened to tumble down ʻAho's cheeks, and he stifled his breathing.

"Such a thought isn't possible. You mustn't even think it. Your son loves you as much as a son ever could. These dark notions, they come from the loss of your wife, from her impending burial. The first thing you said on this island was that it'd be difficult to face the royal tomb, and tonight that's what we do. So these ugly thoughts, that's where they coming from."

"He'd be better off if I was gone. I've imparted everything I have to give, and now I'm just a liability."

"Nonsense," the Tuʻitonga said. "Your son needs you."

ʻAho turned to his brother, anger flashing in his eyes. "You made me climb the mountain. You made me think such thoughts."

The Tuʻitonga stared at his brother. The sensitive man with boyish hope in his eyes was gone. Before him was a warrior marked by dog-tooth scars.

ʻAho wiped his eyes. "I told you," he said, voice trembling with violence. "I do not make the climb."

It was then that a memory came to the Tuʻitonga. Perhaps a year after they'd tried to snare the ground dove, the Tuʻitonga came across a snare they'd placed but had forgotten. The bait was long gone, but the trigger was still set. The sapling was bent all the way to the ground, held in place by a cord. For a year the little tree had survived under that strain. The Tuʻitonga tripped the snare, expecting the sapling to snap upright, but it didn't move. Over time, it had grown that way. Under that strain, it'd taken its permanent shape.

"Come," the Tuʻitonga said. "Let's open the tomb. That'll help you find peace."

The Tuʻitonga, used to others helping him up, mustered the strength to rise and extend his grip to this man with a wound that wouldn't heal. Standing, the two men sheathed their emotions.

"As soon as my son returns," ʻAho said, "we'll be on our way."

"Where'll you go?"

With a tilt of his head, ʻAho dismissed the topic. "Will you miss me when I'm gone?"

The Tuʻitonga felt a surge in his eyes. "I miss you already."

ʻAho said, "Yet I recall something you told me after my arrival: when you're gone, Tonga continues being Tonga without you."

THIRTY-THREE

SALTED SLEEP

With the weight of eight extra men, the vaka's bow now broke the waves, rather than cresting them. This sent back lashes of spray. The Rotumans were young, none of them married. They seemed not to mind being cramped in a hull, sopped with seawater, and sickened by swells.

Heading south meant facing the prevailing winds, which they took at angles—a natural search pattern. The Rotumans scanned the horizon for sails, each vying to be the first to spot their quarry.

"What's this monster's name?" Raho asked Lolohea. "Your uncle, I mean?"

"Let's not honor him with a name," Lolohea responded.

"I suppose you're right," Raho said. "When you commit certain acts, you should lose your name."

One of Raho's men asked permission to be first to board the fugitive's vaka, and immediately another asked to strike the first blow. This led to a debate about who would follow, and in what order. Each wanted a stake in the matter, so they agreed on who would first lay hands on the fugitive, who would knock him from his feet, and so on, down to the man who'd tie the stick in his mouth. It was pointed out that Raho had given himself no role in the fight.

"I'll be tending to the needs of Kaniva," he said.

This brought knowing smiles from his men.

In the late afternoon, a lowering sun cast long shadows. Wave troughs darkened, and when swells rose, they were smudged carbon-orange. It made Lolohea recall a night when Punake recited a poem by the light of bonfires, one about lean pigs and extinct birds. Lolohea couldn't remember how it went, but the lines were about missing things. As flames illuminated the poet, one couldn't help but consider all that'd been taken from him—his freedom, his manliness, his dignity. And now his very self.

The setting sun dipped below the clouds, extending a sideways light to the horizon. That's when they spotted a tiny sail. Raho studied the distant sight. "Kaniva," he said. "Never was a girl so full of life. She organized every ceremony. She loved weddings. Who could harm such a girl?"

"We'll get her back," a warrior reassured him. "We'll have her home for dinner tomorrow."

"Not that soon," Lolohea cautioned.

"The next evening, then," another added.

The Wayfinder ended such speculation. "The pursuit has only begun."

It was Mateaki whom the Wayfinder thought about. He was no fan of his strange cousin, but it was hard not to feel for someone under pursuit. While the Wayfinder didn't count himself among the hunters, he'd done more than simply set the course, as Havea had taught.

But wasn't this the kind of sailing that'd formed Havea? The man had spent many seasons helming Tongan armadas of war. The Wayfinder had once imagined these flotillas as frigate birds might see them—a fleet of sails, glimpsed from a great height, catching wind to Fisi. He hadn't imagined the return voyage, with the suffering wounded. It was the Rotuman priest who'd reported reddened water being bailed into the sea. And, of course, the sharks awaiting their souvenirs of a Tongan holiday. Perhaps Havea kept his eyes on the horizon to avoid seeing the suffering around him. Perhaps his philosophy that "the navigator only steers the course" was a remedy for the wound one suffers from being a party to the misery of others.

In the final light, they soaked salted fish and ate the tepid flesh as soon as it softened. The vaka they sought disappeared with darkness. Eventually, the moon rose to reveal they'd closed much distance. That moon, its light: black waves glimmering as midnight lagoons glimmer with iridescent shrimp. Against this wave-shine, a distant sail seemed to hail them as it pitched.

"We're going fara!" one of the Rotumans shouted, and the rest whooped.

"What's fara?" the Wayfinder asked.

"It's when we go visiting and make good times," another warrior said.

The Rotumans began singing and clowning one another with splashes of water, and coconut shells bounced off unsuspecting heads. They sang until their voices surrendered, and when they slept, they used each other as pillows.

This shared familiarity was something the Wayfinder marveled at. Of course, the Rotumans had been raised together in longhouses, rather than individual fale, as was the Tongan way. The Wayfinder hadn't even had a roof, spending his youth sleeping on an open deck. And human contact with Havea? Maybe they had occasion to touch when handing off a rope. Of contact with his own father? A clap on the shoulder, perhaps.

Once they were soundly asleep, the Wayfinder made his way—carefully stepping between limbs—to the stern. There, he lowered the anchor stone into the water. Hanging by a rope, it would create drag, slowing them.

In the morning, the Rotumans were frustrated to discover they'd nearly lost sight of the fugitive's sail.

"I thought this vaka was fast," Raho said. "It can't even keep up with a fishing canoe."

"It was fast," the Wayfinder said. "Before you added eight men as cargo."

Lolohea turned to Raho. "Did you think this would be easy?"

Raho's men looked to him for a response. He said nothing.

As the day wore on, several Rotumans availed themselves of the need to shit in the sea. Perhaps afraid of falling into the water, they did not extend far enough over the side, and to the man, they streaked the outer hull with their waste. The offense did not abate as the day progressed, for the foul material was alternately warmed by the sun and licked by the waves.

Then they started singing again—endless, endless songs. When it seemed things couldn't get worse, one found Mateaki's flute and proved it capable of bouncy melodies.

The next day, the drinking water began tasting of the pigskin that contained it. The afternoon smelled of rain that never fell. Mateaki, perhaps confused, began sailing easterly, though no one seemed to notice this change in course. Toward sunset, Raho, pissing off the side, observed the rope dangling in the water. He began hauling it in, with more and more alarm. When he at last landed the anchor stone, he turned to the Wayfinder, his confusion becoming suspicion. "Have we been towing this the entire time?"

Lolohea intervened. "You stupid Rotumans!" he shouted. "Are you capable of nothing? When we left, we called for the anchor to be taken up. We must've dragged it off the beach with our launch. We must've been dragging it the whole way. All owing to you idiots!"

Raho asked, "How could we have made it across our reef while dragging an anchor?"

"What do I know of your stupid reef?" Lolohea asked.

For the first time, Raho seemed to undertake a mental study of this mission he'd joined. Suddenly it wasn't the Tongan on the other vaka he was contemplating, but the Tongans on this one.

The Wayfinder now tried to create drag with the sheet and the steering oar, but every glance brought the other vaka closer, so that when darkness fell, the two canoes were tracing opposing paths as they cut back and forth across the wind. With dawn came no songs, just the creak of lashings as they took the swells side-on. The wind stilled as the day wore on, the sail occasionally at full rest. The other vaka was almost close enough to make out figures, but the dying wind would bring them no nearer.

The mood soured more when a Rotuman warrior discovered, lodged firmly under a thwart, a human rib. It was passed hand-to-hand to Raho, who held it up.

"What's the meaning of this?" Raho asked.

"We told you it was a Fisian vaka," Lolohea said. "Who knows what their warriors might've been up to? Look at how bleached the bone is—it's probably been here many seasons."

"How come you didn't want us to bring any weapons?"

"If you fight with us, you fight the Tongan way, with honor."

Raho said, "No honor is lost by taking your advantage on the field of combat. Even a 'peace-loving' Rotuman knows that."

Lolohea took the bone, looked it over. "See here," he said. "These marks are from dog teeth. Would you consider the use of dogs an honorable advantage?"

Raho was silent.

"So your way is different than the Fisian way," Lolohea said, "as ours is from yours. Don't mistake us for the enemy. We're the ones helping you save your missing girl."

"Helping us?" Raho asked. "Is that what you call what you're doing?"

After sunset, the wind died completely, and as night wore on, the sea calmed. The moon at its zenith illuminated this tableau: an ocean as still as an inland lake, their vaka a weave of sleeping men, while across a stretch of water rested another vaka, close enough to see two figures at their slumber.

The Wayfinder patted Lolohea's cheek. "The wind has died," he whispered. "It'll soon reverse."

Lolohea, waking, took in the unbelievable sight: the ocean at rest, the sought-after canoe before them. He whispered back, "Isn't that good? Won't a shift in the wind get us home faster?"

The Wayfinder shook his head. "It likely means a storm's pushing in."

"A bad one?"

"There's no way to know." The Wayfinder slipped over the side, lowering himself into the water. "This is my chance to get to the other vaka. Mateaki's been awake for two days, and he certainly has no idea where he's going."

"Who'll navigate this canoe?"

"Just follow me. I'll make sure the fishing canoe doesn't get caught, which is what'll happen if I'm not on it."

"What'll I say when it's discovered you're gone?" Lolohea asked.

"You're the one who would be king. You'll think of something."

With that, the Wayfinder started swimming.

When the Tuʻitonga returned with ʻAho to the royal compound, he saw no sentries, no security men. There wasn't even a Fefine Girl to greet them. When did an evening last progress without kava or songs or lovely bodies in motion? Where even were the cooks? Devouring their late-night scraps?

In the royal garden, they found Finau holding a banana and calling for Kōkī.

"Trying to lure that parrot back?" the Tuʻitonga asked. "I told you boys not to free your birds."

"I miss Kōkī," Finau said. "I miss my brothers, I miss Punake. Mother's at the night bath with the Fefine Girls, so I have no one."

ʻAho said, "It's your father the parrot avoids, not you."

"You're not really mad at Kōkī, are you?" Finau asked his father. "He's just a bird, and you're the most powerful man in the world."

The Tuʻitonga looked into his son's eyes. Was Finau distracting himself with the parrot? Had he forgotten what would happen tonight? The Tuʻitonga placed a comforting hand on Finau's shoulder as they approached the royal tomb, atop which resided the basket of bones and the greenstone club. Here, too, were the missing sentries and security men, perhaps two dozen in total. By torchlight, they discussed how the tomb's opening would be engineered.

When ʻAho first returned, he'd said, *I'm not ready to face the grave.* The Tuʻitonga had dismissed this concern. Did the king not take his kava every night atop the grave, a place from which to regard dancing girls, comets, and the boys who swept their footprints from existence? Only now was he *facing* it, this device that removed the forever from your flesh.

Seven Fists and Matāpule Muʻa joined the Tuʻitonga.

"The tomb will be opened shortly," Seven Fists said.

ʻAho seemed dismayed by what he saw. "Where are the scores of laborers? Where are the ropes from which the stone will be suspended?"

With a tone of warm diplomacy, Matāpule Muʻa said, "We don't aim to raise the lid entirely. Instead, we hope to lift one end."

"So, what, then?" ʻAho asked. "Will my wife's remains be pitched through the gap like chicken bones into a midden? Did you not even summon a priest to pray for her troubled soul?"

"The time for priests is past," the Tuʻitonga said. "Tonight, we put *your* troubled soul at ease."

The men formed two stacks of wooden blocks. Atop these fulcrums were positioned a pair of long poles cut from the strong limbs of a toa tree. The ends of these poles were extended under the lip of the tomb's slab. A dozen men took hold of each pole, leveraging their full weight. ʻAho himself pitched in, and finally, the Tuʻi of Tonga resigned himself to lending his great gravity.

The moment the lid began to rise was not entirely detectable, except for this: the grave offered an exhalation. It could be felt, the musty breath of the afterlife. As the tomb opened wider, it seemed to then inhale the warm, fecund air of living Tonga. No one knew what it meant to exchange breath with a grave.

When the slab could be raised no higher, Seven Fists and Finau scrambled to place two pre-cut bamboo staves under the lid to prop it open. As the men released their grip on the poles, they eyed these sections of bamboo with great wariness, but each held.

Now the Tuʻitonga was forced to confront what they were about to do. Soon his brother would be strong-armed through the small opening before them. The king could already see his brother clinging to the world of the living. Hands would have to be stomped in order to drop him into the bones below. This image—of his brother's fingers under the sharp heels of his men—changed the king's disposition. In fact, the king and his brother managed to swap dispositions, ʻAho turning wistful as the moment of his wife's farewell approached, and the Tuʻitonga now becoming the aggrieved one, aggrieved at what was being taken from him, at what he was being forced to take from himself, and at the seediness of how it would happen. "What kind of royal burial is this?" he asked Matāpule Muʻa. "Where a king must hang from a pole?"

Matāpule Muʻa looked suddenly worried.

"It's no concern," ʻAho said, looking into the dark void. "All that matters is that my wife finds peace."

"And look at that meager opening," the Tuʻitonga barked. "Is it befitting a royal to squeeze through such a puny gap?"

"I take no issue," ʻAho said. "And your matāpule was right. My wife's not of royal blood. She was a common girl, one I married for love, so she can't be offended by the manner of her burial."

Seven Fists, new to the royal entourage, was caught off guard by the king's sudden displeasure. "If the king prefers," he said, "we could—"

"If the king prefers, what?" the Tuʻitonga asked. "We behold the threshold of eternity. Yet a thief, hoping by stealth to plunder, could make no smaller opening."

"If I might suggest—" Matāpule Muʻa said.

The Tuʻitonga wheeled upon him: "Do you suggest entering the grave yourself to ensure a human can make a dignified passage?"

Finau, in a voice of concern, said, "Father."

Matāpule Muʻa must've believed the Tuʻitonga would snap at his son, for he dared contradict the king. "The opening is plainly large enough."

The Tuʻitonga's eyes went wide.

"Feʻunga," ʻAho said. "Decorum, please."

"Enough?" the Tuʻitonga asked ʻAho. "You say *enough*, to me?"

ʻAho said, "I only wish a moment to say farewell, and then my work is done."

Now the king turned his anger toward the person who'd caused this fiasco, who'd filled the island with strife and in the end was the one person who'd truly determined that the king's brother must die: ʻAho himself. "Will your work be done?" the Tuʻitonga asked him. "Or do you have more rapes and murders to perform?"

Was it shock on ʻAho's face? Or disbelief that he could be confronted in such manner?

He asked, "You say such things in the presence of my wife, at the moment of her burial?"

"Speaking of murder," the Tuʻitonga said.

ʻAho's mouth opened, but no words came out.

"But tonight's not about punishing your past crimes," the Tuʻitonga said. "Only preventing future ones."

ʻAho scanned the faces of those assembled, trying to make sense of what was unfolding.

"While you ply yourself with designs against me," the Tuʻitonga said, "I instead offer you a gift, the gift of reunion. Isn't that what you truly want, to be reunited with your wife?"

ʻAho asked, "Is this about your bizarre suspicion that these bones are not my wife's?"

"I invite you to enter the grave first," the Tuʻitonga said. "That way we can hand your wife's bones down to you, and you can place them with the utmost regard."

"And trod upon the remains of our ancestors?" ʻAho asked, incredulous.

"I'm afraid I must insist," the Tuʻitonga said. "Tonight, you reunite."

They watched something dawn on ʻAho's face.

"Is this not what you had planned for me?" the Tuʻitonga asked.

The boy that ʻAho used to be, that vulnerable young man, showed himself. His brow furrowed in confusion, and his shoulders, for a moment, softened. "Planned?" he asked. "For you?"

The Tuʻitonga said, "Your actions, not mine, bring us to this moment."

"What're you suggesting?" ʻAho asked. "You'd have me go to my grave? Your own brother?"

The Tuʻitonga didn't respond.

"Well, I don't go willingly," ʻAho announced. "Someone'll have to put me there." The fire returned to his eyes. "And I nominate you," he said, pointing at the Tuʻitonga. "Then we'll see which of us makes reunion and which does not. If my brother wants me in there, he should risk his own untimely entrance."

Seven Fists said, "I'm afraid that's impossible."

"Yes, impossible," Matāpule Muʻa echoed. "The width of the grave's opening has been engineered to prohibit persons above a certain size." He indicated the king's big belly.

The Tuʻitonga inwardly took back every ill thing he'd said against matāpule.

"This is outrageous," 'Aho said. "My own *brother*. How long has treachery been in your mind?"

The Tu'itonga said, "I invite you to see the good in this. I've spared you from your own dark stratagem against me. And I offer a homecoming with the woman you love. After a life of bloodshed and mayhem, you'll exit this world of natural causes on the island of your birth."

"*Natural?*" 'Aho asked. "Do you mean expiring in darkness for want of breath? Or will it be thirst?"

"It's what you had planned for me."

'Aho scrutinized his older brother. "And you suppose my plan was to place you alive in this tomb, in front of all your men and your security detail?"

"You did arrive with the Tu'ilifuka," the Tu'itonga said. "He had the fight of ten men."

"I see your delusion is complete." 'Aho surveyed the men around him. "Which of you will be the first to attempt it?" When none stepped forward, his gaze returned to his brother. "Shouldn't it be you?"

"I don't fashion myself as your adversary," the king said.

'Aho laughed, as if now he'd heard it all. "You understand that even if you manage to get me into this grave, I'll outlive you. Look at your yellowed eyes and bloated skin. Look at the weight you carry. I face darkness, hunger, and want of air, yet it's you who'll welcome me to the afterlife."

"I'll fight you for all of eternity if it'll halt your unsavory deeds."

'Aho said, "If you're against ugly deeds, you should end your war."

The Tu'itonga had no response.

'Aho said, "Let's at least exchange the breath of life."

"Don't do it, Father," Finau said. "Don't go near him."

"I've made my farewell," the Tu'itonga told his little brother.

"So be it," 'Aho said. He turned to the men before him. "Who'll be the first to rush me?"

The moment that followed contained all the possible ways to be a man: eyes aflash, muscles twitching, some warriors took sincere steps forward, only to be halted by their wiser mates. Others took false, showy steps, even as some retreated into the shadows. In the end, none made hazard to do anything at all.

"If this fat king won't do it," 'Aho asked, "who will?"

No one moved.

'Aho asked, "Who'll defend the honor of a coward who claims—"

At the word *coward*, Finau raced forward. Lowering a shoulder, he caught 'Aho full speed in the gut.

'Aho attempted to brace himself with his weakened leg, yet the impact sent him tumbling back. Finau encouraged the tumble by throwing his weight so that 'Aho's lower half was lofted into the tomb's open maw. Instead of halting his progress into the grave, which he easily could've done by gripping the stone, 'Aho chose instead to grab Finau's leg and let his momentum drag the young man inside with him. Sliding backward into the darkness, Finau clutched the bamboo stave, but when 'Aho's full weight jerked Finau back, the bamboo pole tore loose, and in he went.

"Finau!" the Tuʻitonga shouted.

"*Nea, nea!*" called Kōkī, for he was in a branch above them, watching all.

The other bamboo stave splintered under the stone's full weight. Then the tomb slammed shut, the impact sending a concussion through the dirt and slapping a layer of dust into the air.

The Tuʻitonga rushed forward and placed his hands upon the stone. All he could see was the fear on his son's face as he slipped inside. Around him, men scrambled to re-stack blocks and reset poles. Still, the king felt desperately alone. He lowered his ear to the stone, hoping to detect a sign of life. This was what he heard: every sharp word he'd uttered to his boy and every time he'd shown his son his back—this sound, the sound of him turning his attention to something other than his son, was deafening. The Tuʻitonga heard the crunch of leaves under Finau's footfalls as the boy wandered Tongatapu's paths alone. He heard his son talking to a bird the way one would talk to a close friend. He heard his son reciting old poetry to trees, to clouds, to the air itself.

People were shouting at the king. When he looked up, his men were straining at the poles. The Tuʻitonga, still shaking inside, moved to the end of a pole to help loft the great lid, which was then propped open with a lone bamboo stave balanced in the middle.

A hand became visible. In a moment, Finau, dazed and dusted with bone powder, was pulled into the land of the living. "My boy," the Tuʻitonga said, embracing his son. "I have you back."

Matāpule Muʻa asked, "How'd you survive, did you two grapple?"

"In the dark, I landed atop him," Finau said. "My hands found his throat."

"Does he live?" the king asked.

"I could feel the pulse in his neck as I squeezed."

Matāpule Muʻa said, "It seems his hands found your neck as well."

"What?" Finau asked.

It was then that the Tuʻitonga noticed what his matāpule had: a jellyfish burned into Finau's throat, the inky tendrils extending around his neck.

From above, Kōkī made a crazed call, and it was not human talk. The parrot had summoned something from its ancient self, some remembered manner of bird-speak, a sound that encapsulated thrill and relief and dread and danger, as well as some feather-raising feeling no human, and certainly no tame bird, ever had felt.

"Kōkī," Finau called. "You came back!"

Kōkī called, "Finau die, Finau live, Kōkī scare, Kōkī joy!"

Finau called for Kōkī, but the Tuʻitonga shouted, "Kill that bird!"

With that, Kōkī escaped into the Tongan night.

A moan emerged from the open tomb.

The Tuʻitonga took up the basket of bones. "We should finish this."

Matāpule Muʻa lifted a finger. "If our plan is that ʻAho should seem to disappear, then perhaps all should remain as it was."

A look of horror appeared on Seven Fists's face. "You mean, deny ʻAho the thing he wanted most?"

Matāpule Muʻa tipped his head to the side.

Seven Fists said, "So his fate is to be both interred alive and without his wife for all eternity?"

"The matāpule's right," the Tuʻitonga said. "The presence of bones suggests a missing person, while their absence speaks to foul play."

"For no Tongan could possibly imagine," Matāpule Muʻa went on, "that a man could be sent to his grave, yet the remains of his wife be held back."

"Yes," Seven Fists said. "It's... unthinkable."

A muffled call for help rose from the grave.

"It's agreed, then," the Tuʻitonga said. "We return the bones to their former state." Here, he tossed the greenstone club into the grave. "I'll be glad to see this accursed weapon gone."

Then he kicked the bamboo stave. After the slab crashed down, he placed the bones of a common girl, one known for the loveliness of her tapa cloth, back where they'd resided since the day of Six Fists's death.

THE STORY OF SUN SHOWER AND THE JELLYFISH

Sun Shower was from Tafahi, the northernmost island of Tonga. Remote and easily forgotten, this tiny island felt closer to other nations like Ha'amoa and 'Uvea. In this dangerous neighborhood, a girl had to speak many languages and think on her feet. When foreign warriors wanted to burnish their reputations by bloodying up their war clubs, it was to Tafahi they went.

Relatively defenseless, and with an older population, Sun Shower's people had to be crafty regarding these marauders. Given enough warning, her people would take to the sea, hoping the invaders would arrive and, finding the place deserted, burn a few things and leave. As a girl, sleeping upon fishing boats, she had unparalleled views of the flames.

Given no warning, Tafahi's residents resorted to a defense of 'ofo'ofa-'a-kui, or "grandparents' love," which referred to the kind of fawning attention only the elderly could lavish. While the young were removed to safety, the elderly would hasten a welcome party. Nothing was worse for ambitious warriors looking to redden their kilts than being greeted by old men who complimented their physiques and grandmothers whose shaky hands offered refreshments.

Imagine these young marauders: they've sailed great distances, fantasizing all the while about the combat ahead. Their bodies are painted. They wear war turbans. Taking up their clubs, they leap from their vaka, ready to chase those who take flight, hoping for a stampede of terrified villagers, screaming and crying, flashing the backs of their skulls, which was the same as begging to be struck down.

But what if no person flees? What if, instead, greetings are called? *Mālō te ma'uli!* to 'Uvean warriors and, *Talofa lava!* to Ha'amoan invaders. *Fakalofa lahi atu!* to those ill-intentioned neighbors from Tokelau, and to Tongan bandits (yes, Tongans weren't above having sport with some of their own) it was a warm, *Mālō e tau lava!* Blossoms are pressed into spear-clutching hands. Rape-minded strangers are called *son* and *nephew*. They're asked about elderly friends on other islands, about the latest news. Old people can't help but share news of their own, about crop fungus and awful weather and their own various ailments—bad backs and knees and eyesight—not to mention the diarrhea going around.

What young man proved his bravery by striking down such people? What warrior made his name by dealing death to the old and the infirm? None, is the answer, but finding himself thus thwarted, a young warrior naturally becomes frustrated. Frustration turns to anger, and anger finds a home. Thus a grandparent or two would fall. It was the same impulse that led warriors to burn an empty village. Slaying the elderly was an ugly business, even for a warrior who hoped to be regarded as murderously indifferent. Seeing what they'd done, their appetites would slack, and their withdrawal would prove imminent.

For Sun Shower and her people, it took bravery to welcome their attackers. To keep smiling and singing as marauders struck their seniors down—that took true mettle. To not react, to not retaliate, even if futilely, required the most strength of all, and in this way, a remote people, an easily forgotten people, developed a rare kind of fortitude.

When Sun Shower was sent to Tongatapu, she found it ironic that "duty" and "sacrifice" were hallowed traits, when no one on that island would do as her great-aunties had done: hail dangerous men, and advance—bearing oil and blossoms—toward those who might kill them. And on Tongatapu, danger didn't arrive from distant islands; it walked among them with a jellyfish on his hand.

Sun Shower would encounter the Jellyfish four times.

The first came when she and Moon Appearing were talking one night. A dark shadow fell across the entrance to the Fefine Girls' fale. She gave Moon Appearing a look, to warn her, but it wasn't received, and before it was too late, Sun Shower took to the sea. Around her, other girls also set sail—slowly, they lowered their heads to their mats, closing their eyes to the proceedings before them. With your eyelids lowered, you didn't see the village burn. Hearing it, however, was worse, and nothing compared to what your imagination could conjure. So she calmed her pulse and traveled to Tafahi, to baby coconut crabs emerging from the waves, their red legs patterning the sand as they made their humble crawl, beneath the circling shadows of harriers, toward the sweet cover of sea daisies.

Their next encounter happened at the bathing pond. Morning mists, indeterminate light, the scent of damp woodsmoke. The Fefine Girls had just entered the water. Soon the elites would arrive, looking for their morning scrubs. For now, the girls had time to gossip, and *he* was their only topic. If the Jellyfish became king, one girl said, his appetite would abate, just like the current king, who'd lost his hunger for girls. Another believed only a queen could moderate a man with such tendencies. Deep down, they all suspected nothing would stop him.

Then there he was. He emerged from the surrounding trees wearing a loose kilt. He carried nothing, said nothing. His hair suggested he'd just awakened. The girls quieted as he perused them. His eyes did not land on the girls he'd already wounded. Their faces had lost something, so, to him, Heilala and Sakiki and Kakala were no longer visible.

It was about the look a girl held, the fear, the uncertainty, the growing resignation. He himself must've once worn such a look, Sun Shower believed. Deep inside, he likely still possessed it, so that it was more about recognition, about seeing his former self in the faces of others. This look would have key elements, like *bewilderment*—at finding yourself isolated, targeted, betrayed—and *imminence*—of what was about to happen, of its inevitability—and *fatedness*—that there must be a reason you were selected, that it was somehow ordained, and was somehow—it must be, yes?—your fault.

Sun Shower knew she had to separate herself from the girls around her. She summoned the strength of her aunties and emerged from the water. With a welcoming look, she moved toward the threat. "What's your pleasure?" she asked him. "A body scrub or a massage?"

He looked pleasantly surprised to be thus engaged.

"I confess," he said, glancing at the other girls, "that choosing is always the hardest part."

"You don't have to choose," she told him. "While these girls begin your scrub, I'll fetch the oil for your massage."

He turned his attention to Sun Shower, studying her, and she understood she'd now been seen.

He said, "There's a woman near Heketā who's said to produce the finest oil. My friend the Tuʻilifuka visited her on the day he died."

"He would know what things were most pleasing," she said.

He searched her expression—for irony, sarcasm, for some inference?

"I'll go there directly," she said. She began down the path. Feeling his gaze, she was careful not to hasten. She imagined the other girls behind her, the looks on their faces as she took her safety at their expense.

If evasion or engagement ever failed, Sun Shower's mother once told her, a last tactic might preserve her: marking herself to appear like other victims. *If we ever fail to appease Tafahi's marauders,* she said, *take up the blood of the fallen and apply it about your face and neck. Then assume your place on the ground, positioning your limbs among the freshly strewn.*

With this advice in mind, Sun Shower prepared for her next encounter with the Jellyfish.

When it happened, it was an unexpected meeting, the two of them converging onto the same path. Others were in the lane. Workers were in the fields. He seemed indifferent to this exposure, calling to her the moment he saw her. "You," he said, a spark of recognition in his eyes. "The oil girl."

She thought, *Could it happen here, in full light, within view of spectators?*

"Oil girl?" she asked. "Perhaps you mistake me for another."

"No," he said. "I'm certain of it. Did you not recently promise to fetch me oil?"

She said, "Perhaps you call upon too many young ladies, if you begin to confuse them."

He looked disappointed, almost wounded. "I remember you because of your lovely smile, and because of, I don't know. I waited for your return."

"I'm sorry," Sun Shower said. "I'm on an errand for the queen. Pōhiva will be quite cross if I'm delayed. If she comes to anger, so will the Tuʻitonga."

"Do you not remember offering me oil? The pond was misted over. You alone emerged from the water."

"I must go," she said, taking a step back.

He advanced a step. "Even if you claim you didn't come to me, and I know you did, do you say you weren't there? All the Fefine Girls were there."

"Moon Appearing wasn't there."

"Which one's she?" he asked.

"Something happened to her. After, she never returned."

"So you admit you were there," he said, intrigued. He smiled some, revealing the well of his front teeth. "Yet you don't admit to coming to me?"

"Do *you* claim no memory of coming to *me*?" she asked, with some bite to her words. "Why do you come at me again, when other girls remain untouched?"

He looked confused. "What's this you say?"

"Have you attacked every possible girl on this island, that now you must start over?"

"I've had no relations with you," he said. "Of that I'm certain."

Having been on the mat next to Moon Appearing, Sun Shower knew the things he'd said to her. "Do you not remember telling me that you'd *give me some hurt*, that we'd then *share hurt in common*?"

Confronted with his own words, he paused.

"You said you were *going to tell me a story*, one that would make me kin to you," Sun Shower told him. "You said, *something was about to happen and nothing was to be done about it.*"

Though he clearly recognized these words, his eyes narrowed in suspicion.

Sun Shower said, "You said that, after, *we'd no longer be strangers in this world*. Yet, it seems, we are. I'm happy to keep it that way."

She turned to go, but he took her by the upper arm, hard enough to turn her.

"What sort of scheme do you undertake?" he asked.

"Do you deny it?"

"I forsake none of my actions," he said. "That doesn't mean I've done you any harm."

"Must I prove it to you? Do you make me demonstrate it?"

"Demonstrate what?"

She placed a hand on her hip and fingered the twist of fabric that held up her garment.

When he saw what she aimed to do, he released her and took a step back.

Sun Shower summoned the courage to betray her modesty in a way rivaled only by a visit she paid to the Tufuga from Haʻamoa. She'd made her appeal in the Haʻamoan tongue. He seemed to already understand the matter. He knew how the jellyfish should look and where it would go. "I've never applied ink in such a manner," he said as he prepared his tools. "But I'm a grandfather. I have granddaughters."

While he worked, she spoke to him. Perhaps it was to mitigate the pain, or perhaps to distract herself from the wrong she did her own body. She told him of the island she was from. She described the burning of their dwellings, as seen from the sea. She listed the people she loved and missed, alive and dead. She described the plight of her people, to be preyed upon by those who were stronger. She described how they came, the looks in their eyes, the delight they took. She asked the Tufuga if, when he was young in Haʻamoa, he'd known such men, if he'd seen others departing on such adventures, if he understood why they took such pleasure from their deeds. He was leaned over her pubis, tapping his ink. He made no response.

"Were you one of those young men?" she asked.

Shame and regret flashed on his face. "I'm wiser now," he said. "But wisdom is wasted on the old."

Now, in the lane, when Sun Shower let the tapa cloth fall to the dirt, she stood bare before ʻAho.

His eyes fell to the mark. He shook his head, but his face recognized the truth of what he saw.

"Do you not smile to look upon your work?" she asked.

Confused, bewildered, he backed away, and there, there, she saw the look of innocence he'd once held, the look he'd dedicated his life to erasing from others.

He turned and made his departure.

Sun Shower would have a final encounter with this man, and it wouldn't be a close call or a near miss. There'd be no evading him. There'd be a deadly struggle. But this time, it would be she who sought him out, and she wouldn't be alone.

A WORD ON NOMADS

Do nomads actually exist? Are they more than metaphors in poems or refrains from forlorn love songs? Can people live entire lives without so much as a splotch of dirt to plop their sleepy heads upon? What does one fight for when one lacks a home? What is it one remembers when one doesn't come from somewhere?

No doubt terrestrial folk ponder such questions. Leaning on a planting stick, season after season, haven't you caught yourself regarding the sea, wondering if another life was possible? Haven't you glimpsed, out beyond the reefs, unknown sails advancing in the moonlight? Or caught the scent of grilling fish wafting from inaccessible coves? Could a person truly live free, governed only by the wind and the currents, which favor no man over another?

Having never been pushed into the sea, it's hard for the Tongan to imagine an unanchored life. Our language doesn't even have a term for "nomad." The best we can say is, *taha 'o e fa'ahinga 'oku nofo fano holo ma'u ai pē*, or "one who dwells ever at large." Interestingly, an old Tongan term for death, *mohe 'uta*, "to sleep on solid ground," raises the question of whether we once dwelled upon the seas. Some might dismiss nomadism as a fanciful notion, a mirage. But what if it's a memory? Or a premonition?

What might a nomadic life look like? Consider Vaha-loa. Cradled by wave troughs and weaned on limu, this maritime vagabond had, before his first whisker, felled a man with a Tahitian sling, shared breath with a volcano in Vanuatu, and seen the seas luminesce against submerged reefs. His father taught him the arts of barter and ransom. His mother, stealth and evasion. And he had a third parent: the vastness of the sea, whose tutelage remediated all other lessons but one: a human's lowly place in the oceanic scheme.

The nomad's only relative is the navigator. This figure was perhaps saddest of all, for navigators had the ability to live free, yet maintained an unaccountable allegiance to the soil. Could an island move from the path of a typhoon? Could an island avoid an invasion, a plague, or the rise of a tyrant? Had Havea not apprenticed himself to earthly ways, no war would've found him, no king could've conscripted him, no force could've taken his family. Instead of setting permanent sail, Havea hauled tombstones from island to island. He delivered warriors to the beaches where they'd become manure. He buried his boys' umbilical cords beneath his king's feet.

It's been said that nomads are bandits and scavengers, that they glean war corpses and strip sleeping villages of their goods. That they steer women and traffic in tapu items. All accusations, mind you, leveled by land dwellers, people who lived among pigs and graves and yesterday's shits. Islands were home to distasteful institutions like marriage, chastity, and obedience, not to mention "duty" and "sacrifice." And land dwellers willingly agented themselves on behalf of their superiors. Accuse the nomad of mischief, but at least his actions were to his own benefit. And nomads were free of a malaise that plagued land dwellers: a collective amnesia, a forgetting so bad that they forget what they'd forgotten: namely, that they were once fearless, that they were once free, that long ago they'd held the world entire—not just a patch of sand—in unblinking regard.

Here are some things only nomads remembered:

That the wind was the only path, the sea the sole map of itself.

That only by losing everything could people see what they couldn't afford to lose.

That no temple or tower or tomb was needed to mark a life freely lived.

That there'd been a time before islands, when all was water. That a day would come when the islands slipped back beneath the waves, taking all the drowsy dirt-dwellers with them.

And only nomads, with their endless survey of the sea, knew the true state of the islands, which were becoming, one by one—through war and profit and depletion—denuded, so that everyone, before long, would get to try their hand at nomadism.

THIRTY-FOUR

KŌRERO:
THE FREEST PEOPLE

We sank again two days later. A wayward swell flooded one hull, and, listing, the other soon swamped. The Wayfinder remained calm. He ordered us into the sea, where we began bailing from the outside. Having sunk once before, we weren't too concerned. In fact, having lost everything, our people were surprisingly unafraid. "There's no better feeling," Tiri said, "than knowing the worst has already happened."

After bailing, I rested in the water, one arm holding the steering oar, the other clinging to Tiri. If I let go of her, even for a moment, I worried she'd disappear beneath the waves. She asked me what I saw. I described rays of light penetrating the water, a little community of fish that'd adopted our hulls, the way parrots sunned their backs from the upper spar.

"Do you recommend sinking in the day over the night?" she asked.

I thought on this. "Day is definitely better," I said. "But if it's your first sinking, darkness might be the way to go."

That night, the skies clouded over, slouching with rain that wouldn't fall. The moon, the stars, obscured. I sat near the Wayfinder, watching him make subtle decisions regarding sail, steering, and course, though it seemed he had nothing to orient him. When I remarked on this, he said, "People think navigators know everything. Often, it's about moving forward despite not knowing."

"Do you think people are like that?" I asked. When he gave me a strange look, I said, "I mean, you can't really know what's in another person's heart."

"People make themselves plain enough," he said.

"*Do* people make themselves plain?"

"My old master Havea always said, *The ocean will show you everything you need to know to navigate it.* People are no different. The question is whether you're able to see it."

"So, what's a truth about you that I'm not able to see?"

He thought on this. "Havea gave all the signs that he didn't want to be my supplemental father. I was oblivious to them. Then I saw him with his real sons."

I felt sad for him. Still, I said, "You didn't answer my question."

"Didn't I? A truth about me is that I can be oblivious, but then comes a moment when I see what's right in front of me." The way he looked at me, it made me look away.

Bailing was thankfully distracting. It kept you from thinking about the past and the future and being hungry all the time. In shifts, we lowered ourselves into the hulls. From below, each approaching swell loomed, seeming certain to swamp us. Like rolling mountains they came, drawing us up their slopes. The waka would sluggishly rise—our stomachs in tow—before the swell swept under us, leaving the wave cap to break over the washboards and pour inside.

Mornings, when the sea was side-lit and glowing, the swells looked especially terrifying. You couldn't help but give attributes to them, names even. One wave slapped our faces with spray. Tiri, who couldn't even see the wave, named it "Man Sneeze." An awe-inspiring swell that dissipated into nothing was named "Wedding Night" by Arawiwi. Kōkī took his turn. Right as a wave was swamping us, Kōkī screeched, "Salted Sleep!" We shook our heads as we went into the water. Never had we heard so ominous a term.

Nights, the Wayfinder and I would stay up, talking. We'd recline on the deck, regarding the stars until they fixed themselves in our eyes. It felt like just the two of us, though exhausted people were strewn everywhere, arms and legs thrown over one another. Finau was often up with us, too, composing poetry, and Tapoto, eager to start a new life in Tonga, seemed immune to sleep. He'd muse aloud over what he might become in a place where he wasn't known as a layabout. "Maybe in Tonga," he said, "no one'll look at me and think I'm a sweet potato thief."

The Wayfinder said, "I'm afraid we have our share of sweet potato thieves."

I said, "You told us food was plentiful in Tonga."

"It is," the Wayfinder said. "But farmers must give their crops to the matāpule."

"Who take their cut," Finau said.

"The matāpule present the rest to the king," the Wayfinder said.

"He takes his share," Finau said.

"The king gifts the remainder to his chiefs," the Wayfinder said, "who give what's left to the sub-chiefs."

"They take theirs," Finau said.

"Alas, leftovers, if any, go back to the farmers," the Wayfinder said.

Tapoto didn't seem concerned about hungry farmers. He asked, "Are there men my size in Tonga? I mean, might I be seen as normal there?"

Finau said, "You're bigger than our uncle 'Aho. That's all that matters."

Tapoto went quiet. I knew what he was contemplating. The comment also started me thinking about the person I had to face. "This Tamahā woman," I said. "What's she like?"

"She's older and thin," the Wayfinder said.

"Much like the blind woman you travel with," Finau added. "She'll be easy to kill."

There was a quiet, or at least something went quiet in me. In my mind, it was now Tiri I saw when I thought of the woman I'd have to confront. I wasn't planning on killing anyone. I mean, I had no plan. But the woman I was supposed to kill, the one I didn't intend to kill, but had no plan for not killing—she'd become Tiri.

"Don't worry about the Tamahā or what she's like," Finau said. "Does the frigate bird think of the fish it eats or the bird it steals from? No, it does what it has to do." He leaned back to regard the starscape above, vast and dark. Lines came to him from an old poem:

Mohe 'i he kapakau,	*Asleep on the wing,*
fanga tavake 'i he po'uli:	*frigate birds at night:*
'uli'uli fa'aki he 'uli'uli, nau	*black against black, they*
to'i māama fakalangi.	*blot celestial light.*

"That's how you handle it—remain above, blot it out. Later, it'll be like it never happened."

Tapoto spoke. "But this woman, what about her all-powerful fan?"

The Wayfinder said, "She hardly ever uses it."

Finau said nothing.

"If a girl got her hands on this fan," I asked, "what could she do with it?"

"Anything she wanted," the Wayfinder said.

"*Anything*," I repeated. At that point, I was still imagining myself using the fan to do acts of kindness, rather than brutal, unrevokable deeds.

From somewhere on the dark waka, a voice asked, "Could it heal a bad hip?"

Only one person had such an affliction: Mama Mānunu.

"What about ngoikore?" a female voice asked from the dark, using a subtle term for male impotence.

I heard my father's voice. "Can't you see they're having a private conversation?" he admonished them.

There was a pause. Then a voice asked, "Could that fan be used to alleviate a guilty conscience?" This voice was my mother's.

When it looked like the others had gone to sleep, I whispered to my mother, "What'd you mean by that guilty conscience remark?"

"Aren't you troubled by the duty you've agreed to perform?"

"Troubled?" I asked. "It's all I can think about."

"You can't kill an old woman."

"I have no intentions of killing an old woman."

"They think you're going to kill an old woman," she said. "What family solves its problems by killing relatives?"

"I don't think the Tongan brothers are really killers," I said. "Look at the sacrifices they've made for us. They took us to the other island, they've brought us on this voyage. At their own peril, they rescued us."

My mother said, "We must take them at their word. They've told us about kidnappings, dog attacks, forced drownings. Don't let the Wayfinder's charm blind you."

I paused. "Do you think he's charming?"

"Has he not charmed you?"

"What d'you propose, breaking our deal? When they've fulfilled their part of the bargain?"

"We haven't made it to Tonga yet," my mother said. "We've been given no island. And I'm not letting you kill a strange woman. I'll do it myself first. By that I mean, no one's doing it."

"No one was ever going to do it."

It was too dark to read my mother's expression. She reassuringly patted my hand.

"Still, I fear death is ahead," she said. "And our people, we don't know anything about unnatural death."

We heard Tapoto's snoring above the rest.

I said, "I'm afraid Tapoto actually intends to fight this dangerous fellow."

Deeper into the night, from far away, came the bellow of a conch shell. We sat up—others rousing around us—and stared into the dark. There came another distant call. And then another. Four, five, six more calls.

"A flotilla," the Wayfinder said. "Keeping track of its vaka."

Our conch shell trumpet hung from the mast. Somehow it had been overlooked in the purge.

Tapoto grabbed it, took a big breath to blow.

"Wait," my father said. "We don't know who they are."

"Yeah, hold off," Finau said. "Those could be Tongans out there."

"Finau's right," the Wayfinder said. "We don't want to risk encountering Tongans."

"But aren't you two Tongan?" my mother asked. "Aren't Tongans your people?"

My father said, "Won't you boys be welcomed back? That's what we've been assuming."

"I'm not sure which Tonga we return to," the Wayfinder said.

"Any Tonga will do," Tapoto said. "We're without food. We're drinking rainwater. I can't count the times we've swamped." He lifted the conch shell and sounded it long.

It was our last night at sea, though we had no way of knowing that.

There was a silence. Then, one by one, six distant trumpets sounded. Tapoto blew the conch again. Far in the distance a torch was sparked. We didn't have a torch to respond with—even if we did, we had no means of sparking it. Instead, we began sailing toward the light.

* * *

The torch we sailed toward was more distant than it appeared. At times, it even seemed to recede. First light revealed mist across the water. Through it, we heard the calls of a bird I didn't recognize, and eerie grunts and squeals. "Pigs," Finau said when he saw our faces.

At last, several waka became visible through the gloom, vacated outlines against a vacating sea. A frigate bird—wings bent, tail split—was carved down each canoe's side. It was the same insignia on our hull. My mother gave me a look, her eyebrows asking, *Didn't Finau just recite poetry about frigate birds?*

Entering a loose collection of nomads' canoes, I smelled cooking fires, heard the whimpers of curious dogs. The nomads wore their hair loose. Their skin was salt-shined. One woman stopped plucking a bird to watch us paddle by. I waved at her. Impassive, she followed us with her eyes, a sheen of down on the water around her. All I'd been thinking about, day after day, was getting to our destination. But what if we never arrived? If we remained forever upon the water, was this who we'd become?

A woman called Finau's name. As we paddled past her waka, she leaped aboard, everyone making room. She was tall, broad-shouldered, and had the curves of two women. "Finau," she said, embracing him, pulling his face into her bosom, for she was an entire head taller. "You're alive." She closed her eyes, saying, "First we heard you'd been entombed. Then they said you'd gone to the afterlife."

One thing seemed clear to me—Finau didn't quite know who she was.

"How many times did I dance for you?" she asked, holding him close. "How many times did I sing while you took your ink?" She separated, to get a look at him, and when she saw the black jellyfish on his neck, she said, "Oh no. He got you."

"Nobody got me," Finau said. "When we fought, 'Aho's the one who nearly died."

She shuddered at the thought. "Tell me you've returned to finish him off."

"It won't be me," Finau said. "We've brought a special man for the job."

She let her eyes peruse the rest of us. "Who are these people?"

Instead of answering, my mother introduced herself. It turned out the girl's name was Sun Shower.

"Are you a Fefine Girl?" I asked her.

She released a laugh. "Do I look like a cherished daughter of Tonga?"

I didn't know what to say to that. She was the most powerful and voluptuous woman I'd ever seen.

"Did the other girls get away?" Finau asked.

She shook her head. "They're in a terrible state. Your uncle only gets worse. He's banished all matāpule. So no rules are enforced, no order is upheld. And the Tamahā, her compound's been ransacked, everything smashed or stolen."

The Wayfinder looked astonished. "But her compound is sacred."

"Is the Tamahā not a thorn in Tonga's side?" my mother asked, throwing the Wayfinder a stern look. "I heard she was a menace who needed to be dealt with."

"Who'd say such a thing?" Sun Shower asked, still trying to understand who we were.

I asked, "Did you know Moon Appearing?"

Sun Shower didn't answer me. She turned instead to Finau. "Did you hear Moon Appearing's bones were stolen? What kind of person takes a dead girl's bones?"

The color drained from Finau's face.

"Who'll tell Moon Appearing's parents?" Sun Shower wondered. "Who'll break the news that she's gone, without any remains to lay to rest?"

"We're here to put things right," the Wayfinder assured her.

"Meaning your uncle?" Sun Shower asked. "Much as I want him gone, you can't fight him. Everyone who challenges him dies. If only you could banish him or send him to some godforsaken island like 'Ata."

My mother's eyes widened. "Is 'Ata not a lovely and fertile island?"

"If you like sheer cliffs and bird shit!" Sun Shower said. She turned to the Wayfinder. "You're the king," she implored him. "Use your power to expel him."

"Me? King?" the Wayfinder asked. "I spent my life at sea. I don't know anything about—"

"Your father was king," Sun Shower said. "And then your brother, and now you are."

Tapoto spoke. "Power isn't heritable. It's a gift, given by people who trust you and believe in you."

Sun Shower studied our faces to see if we agreed with such an audacious claim. She asked the Wayfinder, "Is he the *special man*?"

Tapoto answered for himself. "Handling this dangerous fellow has been entrusted to me. I'm not afraid of him. In fact, I've crossed an ocean to kill him."

Sun Shower neared Tapoto, looked into his eyes, this woman who was Tapoto's physical equal.

"I've conversed with the whale," Tapoto told her. "I've visited a ghost island, boarded a sinking ship, and fought a duel with the night itself."

"Still," Sun Shower asked, "you haven't actually met the man we speak of, have you?"

"Met him?" Tapoto asked. "Maybe not, but I've felled him a thousand times."

Sun Shower studied Tapoto's large, calm eyes, the broad planes of his cheeks, the inked lines radiating across his forehead. "At night, we hear no singing from Tongatapu," she said. "And no one has danced since 'Aho took power." She removed her necklace of white flowers, and when Tapoto lowered his head, she garlanded him. "I believe you're the one to bring them back."

With that blessing, she'd somehow joined our cause. If she had possessions, she didn't retrieve them. I wondered what would make a girl take up with nomads. And was there a price for leaving them?

Through the gloom, we could hear the screeches of parrots trapped in cages. I admit to having once tethered Aroha, but I never caged her, never. From the upper spar, Kōkī called down to us, "Change course, steer away!" With a wing, he pointed to the various animals in their pens and hutches. "Parrot not safe, parrot capture!"

"It's all right, Kōkī," the Wayfinder said. "These are nomads—they're not like that. Nomads are the freest people of all."

"If one bird not free," Kōkī said, "you not free."

"We love parrots," Sun Shower said. "Nobody wants to eat them."

"Yes," Finau said. "Everybody loves parrots."

Kōkī cocked his head, entertaining this notion.

"We only eat them because we must," Sun Shower said.

With a clatter of wings, Kōkī and his flock departed in the direction of what must've been Tonga.

We paddled to the lead vaka, where the Wayfinder saw someone he recognized. "Vaha-loa," he called.

A man turned our way. "The Second Son?" he asked. He waved, though his arm lowered as he saw how many of us packed the deck of his former waka. The Wayfinder had told me about this nomad, how when they were fleeing the chaos in Tonga, he'd helped outfit their journey to resurrect Havea. "What have we here?" Vaha-loa asked.

"Some folks in need of safe passage," the Wayfinder responded.

Vaha-loa's bemused expression suggested *safe* wasn't the word he'd use. "Since when does the Second Son help others?" he asked.

The Wayfinder said, "Havea always taught me to assist those in need."

"The same way he taught you to be friendly and generous?" Vaha-loa asked. "Were you not known to appropriate the catches of fishermen? Or to have your father's warriors clear islands you wished to visit?"

Looking wounded, the Wayfinder asked, "Havea told you those things?"

"This young man risked everything to help us," my father told this nomad person.

"An act of charity?" the nomad asked. "Or did he ask a price?"

My mother, never a defender of the Wayfinder, asked, "Does he look like he's made himself wealthy?"

Vaha-loa appraised the Wayfinder, possessionless and all but naked. "You have lost weight," Vaha-loa acknowledged. "And where's the necklace Havea initiated you with?"

"I no longer wear it," the Wayfinder said.

"What?" Vaha-loa asked. "You coveted that pendant."

"Don't pester him," Sun Shower said. "He's returned to save Tonga."

A grunt was Vaha-loa's sole comment on the worthiness of that cause.

"I'm no longer the person you remember," the Wayfinder said.

"No longer the person who took a whistle from my daughter?" Vaha-loa asked. "Did you ever make use of it?"

"I did," the Wayfinder said.

"And?"

"When a storm blew us off course," the Wayfinder said, "the whistle summoned a frigate bird to show us the way."

"You don't sound too impressed," the nomad said.

"I am. But I've learned it's sometimes all right to be lost," the Wayfinder said, glancing at me. "When you're lost, you never know what you'll find."

"That's the first wise thing I've heard you say," Vaha-loa said. He invited us aboard. His waka was quite a step up, so low was ours in the water. Together, we surveyed the nomad's deck, packed with bundles and baskets and things hanging in nets. Sacks of fruit were strung from the spars, and creatures peered from coops.

The nomad regarded the ink on the faces of my mother, myself, and Tapoto. "Son, are these people from Aotearoa?" he asked the Wayfinder. "Is that where you've been?"

The Wayfinder shook his head. "We came across them in the southern waters."

"The southern waters?" Vaha-loa asked. "No one's ever returned from the south."

"Havea's wife made it back alive," the Wayfinder said.

"Depends on how you define *alive*."

"Have you heard anything from my old master?" the Wayfinder asked.

"I don't expect we will."

"For a while, at least, they were together," the Wayfinder said. "Havea, his wife, and their boys."

Vaha-loa shook his head. "Says the man who kept them apart."

"That's not fair," Finau said. "That was our father's doing."

The Wayfinder lifted a hand. "No, it's fair. I wish it weren't so."

"You *wish it weren't so*?" Vaha-loa asked. "Did you ever press for Havea's freedom?"

The Wayfinder was silent.

"You don't overrule the king," Finau said. "Supplemental fathers were his idea. We had no say."

"*We?*" Vaha-loa asked. "So there's another man out there who's lost his freedom?"

Now Finau went quiet.

The nomad let the silence linger before adding, "Every man is free, whether he knows it or not. Havea could've left anytime he wanted."

"But he didn't," the Wayfinder said, consoling himself.

"That's right," the nomad lamented. "He didn't."

The nomad studied the Wayfinder. "You say you intend to save Tonga? Won't your uncle have a say in the matter?"

"I wouldn't use the word *save*," the Wayfinder said. "But that's the idea."

"You're going to take him on?" Vaha-loa asked.

"Not me, personally," the Wayfinder said. "We've got someone in mind for the task."

The nomad found this immediately funny. "You're getting someone else to do it?" He surveyed us: my mom and dad, blind Tiri, the older Kohimu brothers, Mama Mānunu with her bad hip, big-bellied Tapoto. I was only glad that one-armed Papa Toki wasn't with us. "Please," the nomad said, smiling. "Whatever you do, don't tell me which one gets the honor."

A moment ago, I was sure Tapoto would be triumphant. Now I couldn't shake the image of him doubled over from a punch to the tummy.

Finau crossed the deck to place his hand upon a birdcage. Only when he knelt to admire its handiwork did I understand he was inspecting the pen, rather than the birds inside. "Lolohea made this," Finau said. "He was always one to craft his own cages."

Inside were two large birds. "Are those chickens?" I asked.

"These rare creatures," Vaha-loa said, "are malau."

Finau said, "The only person who raises malau is the Tamahā."

"Used to raise them," Sun Shower corrected. "People ransacked her estate, destroying her fishponds, uprooting her crops, stealing everything."

"How, then," my mother asked Vaha-loa, "did you come by these birds?"

"I bartered them off someone escaping Tonga," Vaha-loa said. "I'm told they're the last ones in existence."

"But the Tamahā has an all-powerful Fan," Finau said. "How could she let herself be overrun?"

Sun Shower asked, "Is the Tamahā to flay the poor and oppressed? Tonga's not as you recall. 'Aho delivers harsh verdicts. People are brought low."

I looked inside the cage. The birds were dark, patterned brown and gray. One called, and then the other.

"These birds belonged to the woman with the fan?" I asked. "Who's now lost everything?" I turned to my mother. "Maybe we could use them to help the Tamahā see our good intentions?"

My mother asked the nomad, "Can we make a trade for these birds?"

Vaha-loa couldn't help but smile, for it was obvious my people possessed nothing. Even our waka was his. "Sorry," he said.

"Credit us these two birds," I said, "and later, we'll return four."

Vaha-loa shook his head.

"Eight?" I asked.

"For these birds," Vaha-loa said, "I'd require something equally singular."

"You really need these birds?" the Wayfinder asked me.

"I think so," I said.

The navigator turned to the nomad. "Name the island of your choice," the Wayfinder said.

Vaha-loa found this most humorous. "Says the man without any islands at all? Besides, what would you propose a nomad do with land?"

"The Teleki Reefs," the Wayfinder said.

The nomad contemplated this.

"The reefs lack land, in keeping with your way," the Wayfinder said. "Yet there's safe harbor, wrecks to salvage, a bounty of delicacies to harvest. An eternal, landless refuge of your own."

"To make good on your payment," Vaha-loa said to the Tongan brothers, "you'd have to take back Tonga. Take it back from your uncle. Something no one seems able to do. And there won't be anyone to protect you. Not your parents, not Lolohea. No matāpule, no security men."

My mother responded, "How many navigators have returned from the southern waters?"

Vaha-loa leaned against a stay line. "Did you really behold the southern seas?"

The Wayfinder nodded.

"Tongatapu's not far from here," Vaha-loa told him. "You know what awaits. Conflict, grudges, graves. Havea told me you dreamed of seeing the world. We travel to Tahiti for turmeric, Vanuatu for sandalwood, Haʻamoa for the reddest feathers. We could use a good navigator. The wind could be your only master, the sea your everlasting servant. We adhere to no one's mandates. We obey no tapu. You call yourself a navigator, but have you truly lived the oceangoing life?"

The Wayfinder looked at neither the sky, nor the sea. Instead, he turned to us. "Havea taught me that a navigator doesn't voyage for himself. We raise the sail for those in need. They set the destination. We simply tighten the sheet."

"Havea taught you well," Vaha-loa said. "But have you considered that his were the lessons of an imprisoned man? Had he been free, he might have taught you to preserve your liberty, rather than serve others."

The Wayfinder said, "Had Havea been free, only his students would be different: his real sons exchanged for an assigned one."

Vaha-loa nodded. "Still, Havea's lessons won't serve you on land. To take charge of Tonga, you'll have to set the course, you'll have to make the way. By force. You ready for that?"

The Wayfinder looked north, in the direction of Tonga. He didn't answer.

"Go ahead, take the birds," Vaha-loa said. "I prefer chicken, anyway."

"You've been eating them?" I asked.

"And keep your precious reefs," Vaha-loa added. "We visit them anytime we like."

THIRTY-FIVE

SOLILOQUIES

Leaving Lolohea, the Wayfinder began swimming through open water. The wind had died away. Normally, wind sounded off everything—the drone of taut ropes, the dry whistle of eddies through the hull, a filling sail's crackle and clap. Now the only sound upon the entirety of the sea was water through his hands.

When he'd put some distance between himself and the Fisian vaka, he rolled to his back. The stars, starkly layered, extended in celestial sprawl. The Ten Heavens of Tonga rarely announced themselves so fully. Even so proclaimed, the movement of the stars couldn't be detected. So it was with the comet, making its slow southward progression. So it was with people. He couldn't see his brother turning into the next Tuʻi of Tonga, yet Lolohea was no longer the young man who doted on his birds. His father's declining health wasn't something you could see, yet every encounter found him lessened. And what of the Wayfinder himself, what was he becoming without his knowing? It seemed a stupid question beneath these teeming vaults. What were the concerns of a single person, backstroking in the middle of the sea?

When he reached the fishing canoe, it sat low in the water, making it easy to hoist himself aboard. Water sloshed in the hull—Mateaki hadn't been bailing, it seemed. The deck was also loose under his feet—the vaka's lashings had fatigued. He checked the sail, the rigging, and the stays before turning to the passengers.

Mateaki slept face up, snoring lightly.

The girl lay across the deck, her back to them.

The Wayfinder shook Mateaki, who woke with a start. "Cousin, you came," he said.

"A storm's coming," the Wayfinder said. "We need to put some distance between us and the Rotumans."

Mateaki turned. There, quiet upon the water, was the Fisian vaka. "I'd like to meet them. Is there such a thing as a 'peace-loving' people?"

"Those Rotumans believe they're chasing a bad fellow. We told them a story about a bad person, and that person's you. So we can't let them catch you."

A look of mild betrayal shone on Mateaki's face.

"We had to tell them something," the Wayfinder said.

"I suppose you only said what came naturally."

"Hopefully, the Rotumans will never lay eyes on you. So let's paddle, yes?" The Wayfinder looked around. "Where's your bailer?"

"She threw it at me."

"She threw it at you?"

"She missed, but it went overboard," Mateaki said.

They took up oars, dipping them in unison, Mateaki in the bow and the Wayfinder behind.

"You didn't happen to bring any water, did you?" Mateaki asked. "I'm quite thirsty."

"She throw that at you, too?"

"You laugh, but she's not to be underestimated. We had quite a fight, more than one, actually." Mateaki sunk his paddle into unruffled water. "She said some very hurtful things. Don't be deceived by her beauty. The stuff that came out of her mouth, it was difficult to hear."

"We'll soon have bigger worries than hurtful words."

"I told your brother this. So I suppose I can tell you. I have feelings for her. Well, I had feelings. I think I was kind of in love with her."

The Wayfinder didn't know what to say. He glanced at the girl on the deck.

"I admit I had hopes," Mateaki went on. "I thought things might work differently between us. You'll see tomorrow how impossible that idea's become. I suppose I've accepted the fact that there's no future between us." Mateaki looked upon the water. "Remember when we first saw her? We'd sailed so far, and there she was, standing in a river of stars. That's what I'm going to remember, not the terrible things she said. Just like if a storm comes, it's this perfect night I'll look back on."

It was true, the reflected constellations extended to the horizon, where the stars below and the stars above stitched together.

"No matter what happens," Mateaki said, "remember us this way—you and me paddling through stars."

"We'll make it," the Wayfinder said. "We'll recall this all from a safe place."

"We were safe before our fathers sent us out here. We can't forget that everything we're doing, it's really about them."

Through still water, the vaka advanced. With each dip of a paddle, existence itself seemed to ripple.

"Did you enjoy it?" Mateaki asked. "Telling the Rotumans a story in which I was the villain? It was probably easy, since you knew it by heart, this tale that your father is good, and that me and my father are bad."

"I understand you probably have your side to things."

"My father and I," Mateaki said, "we don't have a 'side.' I don't believe any of the stories they say about us. I actually don't place my faith in stories at all."

"How could you not believe in stories?"

"A story's a fragile thing, made of words. And what use are they?"

"Stories endure for generations," the Wayfinder said. "And what use are words? You must be joking. What've we got but words?"

"Words are all you have if you haven't lived something. And if you've lived it, words are beside the point." Mateaki extended his hand to display the mirrored surface of the sea. "Could words do justice to this?"

"Not having the right words is no reason not to speak. And stories, sometimes that's all you have." They were all he had of Havea.

"I hear the stories that get repeated around the fire in Tongatapu. They take the premise that war is bad, that the warrior is lessened by war. Yet these stories affirm the need for war. And a person who lessens himself for the greater need, he becomes ennobled, yes? So a good person goes to war, where he does bad things, yet he emerges wiser, exalted, worthy of reverence."

"I suppose that rings true."

"Then none of my stories would make sense to you. We wouldn't even agree on the meanings of words."

"Words like *murder* and *rape*?"

Right away, the Wayfinder regretted these words, which stung even to say.

Mateaki, however, didn't take umbrage. "Yeah, words like those."

"I think it's not the tales themselves but rather their content you dislike. I'd hate stories, too, if my father went around salting people's sleep."

Mateaki said, "I didn't expect a kid from Tongatapu to understand, one born to all life's benefits."

"Life's benefits? I grew up on a canoe like this one, far from my family, with nothing but the elements to support me."

Mateaki turned to his cousin, smiling. "There you go," he said. "Believing a story."

Before long, the day dawned, rinsed and clear. Night lingered to the west in the form of mountained-up clouds—their dark essence only understood when lit from within by lightning. First came the smell of rain. A gust snapped the sail taut. With another, the sea's surface shuddered white. The Wayfinder studied the sky. He breathed deep the staticky air. It was how the original day must've felt, when wind and clouds and waves were first introduced.

"It's happening," the Wayfinder said. "Let's rouse the girl and get to work. I'll need you on the steering oar. We'll have her lashing while I work the sail."

Mateaki didn't move.

"Also," the Wayfinder said, "let's strip the anchor and landing lines—we'll need the rope."

Looking behind, the Wayfinder saw the Fisian vaka's sail was full.

"I don't think we can count on the girl to do her share," Mateaki said.

There was enough light to read the expression on his cousin's face: a weak smile betrayed a mix of uncertainty and childlike hope. Rain began to tap their shoulders, the kind of fat, intermittent drops that fall from wet trees. A realization came to the Wayfinder, the type where you don't need to understand something to know it. He placed his hand upon the Rotuman girl: her skin, wet from rain, was without warmth. "What'd you do to her?"

Mateaki shook his head. "None of this is our doing."

The Wayfinder rolled her, bruising around her neck now visible. "She's dead, isn't she? You killed her."

Mateaki said, "You must understand I didn't want to."

"She has family. People care about her."

"You don't know anything about her," Mateaki said.

The sail snapped full. The vaka rocked, and Mateaki sought his balance.

"Did you rape her?" the Wayfinder asked.

"How can you ask me that?"

The Wayfinder stood to face Mateaki. "Did you?"

"It's not like that. When you care about someone, it could never be like that."

"What does your father call it? I'd think you two would share the same term."

The Wayfinder prepared to be struck for saying that.

"Actually," Mateaki said, "it's you and my father who share something in common. When my father became inconvenient to your father's aims, he was sent to fight the Fisian wars. And when you became inconvenient to your father's plans for Lolohea, you were relegated to the waves."

"I'm nothing like either of you."

The surface of the water flashed with lightning.

"Really? I've seen you kill at your father's command," Mateaki said. "You drowned men, one by one. You drowned women, I witnessed it."

"That wasn't me. I'm not a person who'd do that. I only steered the course."

A smile crossed Mateaki's face, one that sent a shiver through the Wayfinder.

"Don't you see how this'll go?" Mateaki asked. "When your father became Tuʻitonga, his brother became a liability. When your brother becomes king, so will you."

"You don't know what you're talking about."

"You know your father. Can you imagine that he doesn't already have a plan for you?"

"This is some great treachery you trade in."

Mateaki pointed at the vaka behind them. "Those fools think they sail to rescue a girl. They can be forgiven for their ignorance, as they're strangers to the Tongan way. But you? You think you sail home to deliver Lolohea to his coronation, but you head back to face what was my father's fate: being banished, by his own brother."

The Wayfinder pushed Mateaki, who looked quite surprised to find himself stumbling backward into the sea. The Wayfinder hadn't meant to do it, the push just happened, but the sight of Mateaki swimming for the canoe made the Wayfinder tighten the sheet, causing the little vaka to pull away. The outrigger lifted, rolling Kaniva across the deck to stop at his feet. Her lifeless ribs flexed unnaturally across the arch of his foot. Only in this moment did the Wayfinder understand what had happened: Mateaki had passed the Final Test. He'd taken the life of someone he professed to care about and now was eligible to become king.

At dawn, the Tamahā brought broth to the sleeping Moon Appearing. The girl had slumbered too deep and too long. "Come, child," the Tamahā said. "This morning we make progress." The Tamahā had said this yesterday and the day before. Each time, she'd given the girl a choice: Begin the journey of her recovery. Or labor. Labor, at least, was a kind of medicine.

Moon Appearing rolled to her side. Eyes closed, she scratched at mosquito bites.

"Arise, child," the Tamahā said. "You must move your body."

"I can haul no more water," Moon Appearing said. "I can't lift another rock."

The Tamahā shook the bed until Moon Appearing rose. Her hair was tangled, her face dotted with pimples. "I want to bathe," she said.

"There's no point in bathing. You'll be sweating soon enough. Unless this is the morning you choose dance over work."

They stepped outside into a pale morning light, the color cast by coals in their final white.

"Do we dance?" the Tamahā asked. "Or do we work?"

Moon Appearing shook her head. "I can't dance."

"Our space is secluded," the Tamahā said. "Here, you'd dance only for yourself."

"Dancing is what happy people do. Do I look happy?"

"Where do you girls learn such nonsense? If happiness were the key to dancing, only fat men and idiots would do it."

"Don't you understand?" Moon Appearing asked. "I don't feel like dancing."

The Tamahā crossed her arms.

"Do you never relent?" Moon Appearing asked. "Can't you leave me alone?"

"If I provide the dancing partner, will you dance?"

"I'm going back to sleep," Moon Appearing said, then lay on the ground beneath an 'ovava tree. She didn't curl like a child, but reclined like a corpse displayed for viewing.

The Tamahā fetched the Life-Affecting Fan, whose name, Ī Taumo'ui, could mean both "Fan That Strikes at You" and "Fan That Fills You with Being." She offered it to Moon Appearing.

"Can it fix what happened to me?" Moon Appearing asked.

The Tamahā shook her head. "Only you have that power. But it makes a good dance partner."

Moon Appearing accepted this object she'd long contemplated. Now that she held it, however, she only laid it across her chest and closed her eyes.

"Dance is not entertainment," the Tamahā said. "It isn't meant to be *lovely*. It doesn't exist to *please*."

Moon Appearing made no response.

"You think you can avoid dancing by sprawling on the ground?" the Tamahā asked. "When was it said a dance can't be danced lying down? Dance is your story, flowing through you. Your position doesn't matter."

Moon Appearing called out in frustration. She lifted the Fan and sent a waft through the boughs above. Not knowing the Fan's strength, she lifted the branches, shaking them violently, so that all but the strongest leaves were stripped. The rest came floating down, coating the ground the way ash from Tofua's eruption buried the island of Kao, leaving only the outlines of rocks and trees. Soon all that was visible of Moon Appearing was a girl-shaped mound of foliage.

The Tamahā waited for the girl to emerge. But she didn't move. The Tamahā had perhaps pushed her too hard. Tomorrow, she'd try again. Then a hand rose. It bore the Life-Affecting Fan. By pulling air, it caused the girl to rise, emerging from the mound like a spirit leaving the body.

Upright, Moon Appearing used the Fan, ever so lightly, to gather leaves into a pile. Circling, she re-created the girl-shaped mound of leaves. With the Fan, she sculpted the pile until she seemed to recognize the girl inside.

The girl of leaves hadn't known a man was coming for her. The girl of leaves had thought gossip and favoritism were the worst that could happen. Moon Appearing stood, backlit by the morning sun, so that her long shadow fell upon the girl of leaves, just like a shadow had fallen that night across her. Her only defense had been to extinguish the lamp inside her, and, closing her eyes, to feign sleep. Moon Appearing now beheld this girl of leaves tenderly, as one would regard a childhood friend, but there was also a farewell in this last look upon a girl she'd never see again, a girl who truly no longer existed.

Moon Appearing then circled the leaves, moving in sympathy for the other girls who'd been in the fale, the ones who hadn't screamed or fought or scratched, the ones who'd learned to pretend to sleep. With her Fan, Moon Appearing tried to usher life into these girls, to urge them to rise, to move to safety. Now that they'd learned to defend themselves with sleep, who would teach them to wake?

With the Fan's breath, she rearranged the leaves, and even the Tamahā could see they now formed Hunga, Moon Appearing's home island, with its famous lagoon. While Moon Appearing couldn't rescue the girl she used to be, she seemed determined to contact her through dance, to reach her *before*—before Tongatapu, before the Jellyfish's sting. To say what, however? That trouble lay ahead? That a man would come for her? Who'd send such a message, who'd do that to a young woman, innocent of what was to come? No, it wasn't her former self she was speaking to.

She rearranged the leaves into a map, one that gave position to every island in Tonga. Moon Appearing could now traverse the whole of Tonga and visit all its women. If she'd danced for her future self and her past self and those who'd attended her dark awakening, she now moved for the others, each woman individual enough that no single story could speak for her, yet through movement Moon Appearing could extend a hand to them all, and in exchange claim their reciprocating grasp. In life, it's easy to think there's a single moon, but eventually you realize there had been ten thousand. She moved for the girls who'd snuffed their lamps, she moved for the girls who thought loveliness would protect them, she moved for the girls who'd learned from men that hurt was what they deserved.

There was one person she hadn't danced for. Though the women were multitude, the threat had many tentacles. How do you make a man out of leaves? How do you give shape to his dark intentions? How do you make leaves pay for his deeds? She sent skyward bolts of lightning. From the earth, she commanded great tremors. With a final turn, Moon Appearing discharged the Fan toward the Tamahā's great toa tree, and, while the tree signaled no visible response, one could hear the crackle of a fire that had been struck deep in the heartwood.

When Moon Appearing returned the Fan, it was emanating light. Moon Appearing looked exhausted, though it was a different kind of fatigue. For the first time, she didn't want to be comforted.

"You can rest now, if you want," the Tamahā said.

Moon Appearing shook her head.

"Today's the first day," the Tamahā said. "That's how you should think of it."

"The first day of what," Moon Appearing said, and it wasn't a question, as if "what" were the stuff she was now living in.

They both regarded the now-scattered leaves, though the girl who'd resided in them hadn't really dispersed.

"The journey back is a long one," the Tamahā said. "But you've embarked."

"Embarked for where?" Moon Appearing lamented. In her voice was cataloged all the impossible destinations: of returning home, of facing her parents, of rejoining the Fefine Girls, of trusting again.

"Never mind the destination," the Tamahā said. "You're no longer where you were. Tomorrow will bring more progress. And after that, even more. You'll learn where you went when at last you discover where you are."

The smell of lightning hung in the air.

"It's time," the Tamahā said, "to bid farewell to the girl of leaves."

"Kuo pau ke ke 'alu," Moon Appearing said. *You must go.*

The Tamahā spoke for the leaves. "Pea ko koe e nofo." *And you remain.*

With a sweep of her Fan, the Tamahā sent the leaves tumbling down the path. "Now, shall we work?"

Moon Appearing glanced up. "What does a girl do if she has no one to help her? What's she do if she lacks an all-powerful Fan?"

The Tamahā looked beyond her compound, into a realm not in her control.

"What does she ever?" the Tamahā asked.

Thunder woke Lolohea. He opened his eyes to the first sting of driven rain. Behind him, the midnight of a tremendous storm. Ahead, a watered-down dawn. Shielding his eyes, he studied the horizon for his brother's sail, intermittently visible through screens of rain. When he'd gone to sleep, the sea couldn't have been more placid. Now swells approached from all directions, troughs merging to create great hollows soon filled by overtaking waves whose crests stacked and fanned.

The Rotumans were roused as well. There was shouting when a surge pitched the outrigger.

A call went out for the sail to be trimmed. Raho rushed to Lolohea.

"Who's sailing this thing?" Raho asked. "Where's your brother?"

Lolohea pointed in the direction of the vaka ahead. "He went there."

Horizon missing, waves rebellious, Raho didn't know where to look. "How?"

"He swam," Lolohea said.

"*He swam*, through this?"

It now seemed like a dream. Had his brother really slipped over the side and entered a sea of stars? "He knew a storm was coming, so he went to make an appeal to our uncle's sense of self-preservation. Right now he's leading us into the worst of it."

They fronted a large swell. The bow, heavy with passengers, plowed deep.

"Man in the water!" was shouted, and sure enough, Lolohea saw a figure struggling in the churn as their vaka swept past. Hands went out, a rope was missed. Finally, from the stern, Lolohea extended the steering oar—it was grabbed, and suddenly Mateaki, drenched and wild-eyed, was hauled aboard. Exhausted and coughing, he gripped the canoe with both hands.

"Who's this?" Raho asked. "It can't be the fugitive. He's young, he has his front teeth."

"I told you," Lolohea said, "this is a family matter. He's my cousin."

"The son of the rapist?" Raho turned to Mateaki, still coughing. "What've you done with Kaniva?"

Mateaki took deep breaths, his eyes surveying the men before him.

Raho turned to Lolohea. "You said nothing of another man. How many are on that vaka?"

Lolohea asked his cousin, "Is my brother also in that water?"

"That's where he deserves to be," Mateaki said. "You, too, for that matter."

Raho found this response shocking. "This is the man who just saved you."

"Saved me?" Mateaki asked. "Tongan treachery is the reason you find me in these waves."

"You don't count yourself a Tongan?" Raho asked.

"Sometimes I wonder," Mateaki said. "Do the people of Rotuma abandon one another in the sea?"

"Were any among us prone to kidnapping," Raho said, "then yes, we might."

Mateaki eyed Raho. "Says he who kidnaps himself."

Bow high, they dropped into another void, the seascape suddenly mountainous.

"Put no faith in his claims," Lolohea said. "He fancies himself my rival, he takes measures to position himself to rule Tonga. That's the source of his outlandish talk."

"Him?" Raho asked, looking at Mateaki, wet and diminished. "The king of Tonga?"

"I'm not your rival," Mateaki said. "Though someone'll have to restore Tonga to what it once was. Who'll end the war with Fisi? What about the tributes everyone must pay?"

"The Tonga in your mind," Lolohea said, "takes no measure of the real place."

"Ask Punake which Tonga he lives in," Mateaki said. "Wait, where is Punake?"

"The poet fellow?" Raho asked. "He awaits our return on Rotuma."

"Abandoning your friends," Mateaki said. "That's not one of the tests. Though, to rule as your father does, it should be."

"What does he mean, *tests*?" Raho asked.

"Nothing," Lolohea said.

"You know what a good test for a prince would be?" Mateaki asked. "How about spending a single day as a common Tongan, bowing nonstop, 'offering' your daughters to Tongatapu and 'volunteering' your sons to the war?"

"Enough of this talk," Raho said. "What about Kaniva?"

"Yes," Lolohea agreed. "The time for your opinions is over, cousin. Tell us of the girl."

Mateaki cast his eyes against the water. He said nothing.

"If you're so honorable," Lolohea said, "then let's establish a couple facts. Does your father not wantonly destroy people?"

Behind them, men worked to trim the sail, for they couldn't steer into the waves without the power of the wind, yet every gust risked tearing the rigging.

"What're the deeds of one man?" Mateaki asked. "Compared to the those of the Tuʻitonga? Your father makes mayhem the policy of a people."

"Perhaps we need specifics," Lolohea said. "Those bones your father trounces around with, are they truly your mother's?"

"For you to ask such a thing," Mateaki said, "loss must be unknown to you."

"Did he murder her?"

Even in the wind and sideways rain, Mateaki's eyes visibly reddened. "My father would never do such a thing, not on purpose. He wasn't like this before, things like that didn't used to happen."

Raho looked toward the distant vaka, where he imagined the man they discussed.

"Did the kidnapping of those Fisian girls just happen?" Lolohea asked. "Did your father's rapes of our Tongan daughters just happen?"

"You make him out to be a monster," Mateaki said. "But he's the opposite. He was the compassionate brother. That's why he was susceptible to what the war did to him. Your father, however, proves impervious."

Raho suddenly shouted, "Did you molest her or didn't you?"

Mateaki averted his eyes. "I admit she's not in the same condition as when she was found."

"Condition?" Raho couldn't believe someone would use such a term, that a simple word could be so perverted. He pulled a small knife from his waistband. The obsidian blade was rough and thick. Its jagged edge would create a wound that wouldn't close. "One thing I've never understood," Raho said, "is how my people got the reputation of being *peace-loving*."

Mateaki glanced at the blade. "You pitiful stooge. Don't you see what's really going on?"

"I see your nature quite clearly," Raho said.

"You fool," Mateaki responded. "Awaken to the treachery of your situation!"

Raho said, "You speak of treachery. I offer you a balm against deceit by showing you the blade I'll use on you."

Mateaki said, "We sailed for days to get to your gullible island. We thought to ourselves, *Where can we find the greatest fools upon the sea?* And here you are."

"You're wrong," Raho said. "I'd never set sail with the likes of you. I sail with those who'd hunt you down. And judging by the claw marks on your face, I know Kaniva went after you, too." Here, Raho paused. He lowered his blade and spoke to Lolohea. "Now that I think about it, justice had already been done to this fellow when he was cast into the sea. Shouldn't we return him there?"

"Don't you hear me?" Mateaki asked Raho. "You sail to your doom."

"It would feel good to toss him," Lolohea pointed out. "But remember: He's only the apprentice. The master lies yonder. My cousin can still be of use in securing the return of Kaniva and my brother."

Mateaki tried one last time with Raho. "You idiot. Can't you recognize your true adversary? The only question is whether Lolohea will dispatch you quickly or sell you into slavery."

"All right," Raho told Lolohea. "We'll keep him for barter. Can we at least shut him up?"

Lolohea called for a stick, but the canoe contained little in the way of stray objects.

Something was passed back, man by man. When it arrived in Lolohea's hand, he smiled at the delicious justice of it—it was Mateaki's flute. He could already see it jammed in Mateaki's mouth and fixed by lashes tied around the back of his head. "Open," Lolohea commanded.

Reluctantly, Mateaki lowered his jaw.

Lolohea jammed the flute, molar-deep, into Mateaki's mouth.

Before the flute was cinched in place, Mateaki managed to utter the word "water."

"What's that he said?" Raho asked.

"Who could know?" Lolohea answered.

Lolohea made his way to the bow. Sheltering his eyes from the rain, he tried to catch a glimpse of his brother's vaka. Shifting winds made itinerants of waves, and there was no ready course through their random migrations. Though he'd put some distance between himself and his cousin, it was not so easy to shed himself of the words that'd been spoken. Words that had once felt solid and secure had somehow slipped their meanings. Words like *family*, *duty*, *loyalty*, and *sacrifice* seemed newly open to interpretation. And if he wasn't sure about these terms, how could he know what the word *Tonga* meant? Lolohea studied the water. The sea was rising still, the waves shouldering one another for position, some stacking up while others plunged, the way drowning men rise by pushing others under.

Kōkī, after witnessing a human entombed alive, slept alone in a tree. He didn't really sleep. The bark was rough. Dirty insects kept touching him. Kōkī shivered and shivered, though it wasn't cold. The only thing that gave him comfort was imagining a nest formed from cupped human hands.

When the night felt darkest, and things seemed their worst, Kōkī plucked a lone feather. It stung, yes, but felt good in a way he couldn't express.

Come dawn, Kōkī saw humans with nets moving along the eastern paths. Peeling bananas, they kept calling, "*Nea, nea.*" Kōkī knew they were hunting him. The men set scary traps, suspending rocks above bananas used as bait. The smell of those bananas!

What even were people? Kōkī had never really asked that question. Like parrots, humans preened and gossiped. They walked on two legs. Yet they were unaccountably murderous. And had a habit of eating birds. Kōkī knew he should turn from the world of men. But with whom would he flock? He'd never interacted much with birds of other varieties, except for the ones he'd lost his virginity to. He flew to the central lagoon. Here was a kind of bird he didn't recognize. They made little nests on limbs that hung over the water. Kōkī tried to talk to these birds. The poor things were brown. At the risk of sounding too showy, he told them he was pretty good friends with humans. In fact, humans fed him by hand. Was it bragging to mention that he snuggled with humans at night on their soft sleeping mats? These birds were unimpressed.

When the sun was high, Kōkī, quite hungry, flew to one of those lovely bananas. Floating above it was a large stone. Kōkī didn't really understand how snares worked, but he knew that if you weren't careful, you could trigger a little thing, and that triggered a bigger thing. Like the way the Tu'itonga had kicked a little bamboo stick, and then a big thing happened to his brother. Kōkī inhaled the rich scent of banana. There must be an island, Kōkī thought, where the spirits of extinct parrots resided. Would it be so bad to join them? Perhaps they were awaiting the last of their kind. He wondered if, when he finally met them, he'd understand their talk. To find out, all he had to do was take a bite.

Instead, Kōkī decided to give life one more try. He flew to the Tamahā's compound. Inside, she was tending her garden. Landing on a branch beside her, he performed some moves proven to entertain humans. He bobbed his head, hung by one foot, and imitated a human laugh, "Ha-ha."

The Tamahā ignored him. There was sweat on her face and dirt on her hands.

"Kōkī pay his friend a visit," Kōkī said. "Maybe Kōkī stay?"

"Has Kōkī thought about the mistakes he's made?" the Tamahā asked.

"Kōkī do his best. Kōkī just a bird."

"What about last year, when you repeated the joke that chief told about the king's weight?"

Kōkī lowered his tail feathers, and then his wings, and then his head. He held this position before rolling a lone eye upward to measure the effect. This almost always worked with humans.

She said, "That man was sent to fight in Fisi."

"That joke was a human joke," Kōkī said. "Humans laugh when Kōkī tell it."

Something caught Kōkī's eye. He stared at a bush behind the Tamahā.

"Does this plant interest you?" The Tamahā plucked a berry from the bush. "Do you not recognize the favorite food of the red-shining parrot?"

"*Nea*," Kōkī said. "Kōkī never see this bush. Banana is Kōkī favorite food."

The Tamahā smiled. "From the beginning of time, this berry has appealed to the parrot, and the parrot has in turn spread its seeds. When the parrot disappeared, so did the bush. I keep this last one around for preservation's sake. Do you really not know it?"

Kōkī studied it with one eye, and then the other.

"I'll make you a deal," the Tamahā said. "Apologize for the girl you got banished last year, and I'll give you the first taste of your favorite berry."

"Kōkī no banish girl. Kōkī only mention her secret boyfriend."

"When a powerful man pursues an innocent girl, he's not a boyfriend. I cared about that girl. They blamed her for being promiscuous. She was never heard from again."

"Kōkī no hurt," Kōkī said. "Kōkī peace."

"I've heard you rhapsodize with total eloquence," the Tamahā said. "So enough with your *Kōkī-good, Kōkī-bad* talk."

"With you, maybe Kōkī stay?"

The Tamahā waved him away.

"Kōkī know a bit of gossip," Kōkī said. "It concerns the Tuʻitonga's brother. He disappear. Kōkī know where. Perhaps trade for permission to live with you?"

"There's a reason you've gone extinct."

Kōkī recoiled. "Kōkī not extinct!"

"Let me know when you lay an egg," the Tamahā said, and shooed him away.

Kōkī flew to the crown of a palm. He looked down at the gardens, orchards, and ponds, now out of reach. Had a bird ever felt so low? For the first time in a long time, Kōkī sensed a soliloquy coming on:

"Extinct yet still alive," he said aloud. "And what of those who came before, dead yet living on in me? Can you miss a bird you've never met? Would he find his missing flock identical to him, or were his species varied in nature and temperament as clouds before the sky's blue baize? What's lost with the disappearance of that which is already gone?"

Kōkī paced upon a palm frond, so that with the wind, he rose and fell.

"A delicate vessel, the egg," Kōkī said. "This shuttle from womb to world imposes darkness and isolation, yes. Yet when at last a tiny beak breaks free to the welcome of light and air, were a fledgling to know the human world in wait, what chick would not preserve its shell, preferring not to enter? For make no mistake, it is a human world, shaped by human hands now poised to pluck this still-wet innocent from its nest. What wing of nature crafted the human grasp, gifting it the capacity to ruffle and reassure but also to wrest and wring? Not only does the human in a single gesture both strangle and embrace, it perverts the very nature of the natural, making a menace of the simple dog, fattening the pig's life into a single lie. Even the life-giving banana—*nea*, the banana!—becomes an instrument of treachery in the human hand."

Spathe pollen lifted, set aglow by morning light. Kōkī spread a wing.

"To return to the safety of the egg, isn't that the need? To become unlaid, to regain the enveloping womb's embrace, of a mother, of a kind. What other goal in a world of one? But there is the other way. Not far off is the baited banana, whose nourishment is enough to fuel a flight to the afterlife. One nibble would pardon the levitating stone of its unnatural state. One peck, and Kōkī could find his kind. Kōkī could go back, to before a human hull first kissed a Tongan beach. To before this land had need of human name. All Kōkī had to do was indulge his need."

Kōkī felt even more lonesome and forlorn. The problem with soliloquies was there was no one around to hear them. Kōkī lowered his head. That's when he saw, in the compound below, an interesting sight:

An older woman and a younger, dancing together. In procession, they moved, turning in one another's orbit. The flowers around them bent to their movement, the trees shimmying above. How was it they commanded nature to join their pirouette? They spun one another, lowering to the ground, before rising up again. They turned together, and, *boom*, a lightning crack, bark blasting, the scent of burning sap. Kōkī realized that in their common grasp was the Life-Affecting Fan. How lovely was a fan—the closest thing humans had to wings. When the dance wound down, the Tamahā handed the Fan to the younger woman.

Kōkī flew, over ponds and graves and fields of stumps, past foot-worn paths and ovens belching steam.

He landed before the Tuʻitonga, now on his stomach, taking his ink with Finau.

Kōkī bent a wing and bowed. "My king."

A delicious smile crossed the Tuʻitonga's face. To his son, he said, "It's better if you don't see this."

Finau said, "But, Father—"

"Move along," the Tuʻitonga said before whispering something to Seven Fists, who dashed off and returned with a banana. "What's Kōkī been up to?" the Tuʻitonga asked.

"Kōkī up to many things."

The Tuʻitonga peeled the yellow fruit. "Has Kōkī been a good bird?"

"*Nea*," Kōkī said. "Kōkī bad bird. But Kōkī sorry. Kōkī good now."

"Is that so?" The Tuʻitonga popped some banana into his own mouth. "Mmm."

Kōkī took another step. "Kōkī bring the king a special gift."

"Yes," the Tuʻitonga said. "Kōkī has. The king appreciative."

"But Kōkī not tell you what it is," Kōkī said. "Is secret. Only Kōkī know it. Kōkī and the Tamahā."

"A secret?" the Tuʻitonga asked. "Regarding the Tamahā?"

"Kōkī know the girl."

"The girl?"

"Yes," Kōkī said. "The girl the Tamahā give her Fan to."

The Tuʻitonga handed Kōkī a little banana.

Kōkī took his time eating it and, as usual, dropped half in the dirt.

The Tuʻitonga said, "Tell us more about the one who inherits the Fan."

"Kōkī lonely," Kōkī said. "Kōkī miss his human friends."

The Tuʻitonga cupped his palm. When Kōkī stepped inside, the king raised him up, eye to eye.

"Do humans miss their feathered friend?" Kōkī asked.

"I think about you all the time."

"Maybe Kōkī can come home?"

The Tuʻitonga said, "Maybe tell Tuʻitonga your secret?"

Kōkī stepped onto the king's shoulder and whispered the girl's name.

"That's a good bird," the Tuʻitonga said, cupping the colorful parrot and stroking his feathers.

Kōkī said, "Ruffle, please?"

The Tuʻitonga ruffled Kōkī's feathers. "If I call my wife over, will you tell her, too?"

"Of course," Kōkī said. "But Kōkī more banana?"

The king complied. It was just the way a mother would feed you—you simply leaned your head back and received. "Please tell Kōkī—the banana is a people food?"

"Oh yes," the Tuʻitonga said. "In our first vaka, we brought the tuitui and uhi and tava and of course your favorite fruit. Before we came, this land had never seen such things."

Kōkī nodded at the rightness of this. Before people, his species had never tasted such a treat. He closed his eyes and folded his wings. It'd been so long since he'd had any comfort or sleep.

The storm's dark bands cut one after another across the sun, leaving the Wayfinder to navigate the lens of the sea from within its cataract. *Navigate* was too generous a word. A wayfinder could be anything but lost. And he was nothing but. Waves assailed him from different directions, the wind approaching from quarter after quarter. When he tried to get any kind of look at the storm, driving rain stung his eyes. But what was there to see? Then it was night.

In the dark, he let the hull swamp. Sluggish now, it was less prone to capsizing in the mountainous swells. He lashed Kaniva to the outrigger, the rope creasing her skin. He had to secure every bit of her, as her limbs were wont to trail in the water. He anchored himself with a rope about the waist. Defeated, he curled on the deck, so they faced one another. When a swell lifted under them, water rose through the bamboo slats. Lightning revealed her cloudy eyes and the way surging water filled and drained from her mouth. He recalled the sight of Mateaki falling backward into the water, of Punake diminishing as they sailed from Rotuma. These things made the Wayfinder vow never to use his abilities to do harm again. In the heart of the storm, this vow was the only thing that offered any solace, though Kaniva—her face submerging and surfacing—seemed unimpressed.

Dawn never happened. Dark clouds unseated the sun, leaving only a dim, evaporative glow. He'd lost all sense of the direction he'd come from. And there was no sign of Lolohea. He rolled to his back. Beneath the cloud cover hovered a lone frigate bird. He recited a line he'd heard Punake once utter:

| Ka puna ha lofa pea ke, vakai, | *When a frigate bird takes flight, observe,* |
| ko eni homou hala ki 'api. | *this is the path home.* |

Around his neck was Havea's fishhook necklace. There was also the whistle gifted him by the nomads. He blew it now, though the thing made no sound. Before long, the frigate bird descended until it hovered just above him, scissoring its black wings.

The Wayfinder spoke to the bird: "If only you could point to Tongatapu."

He thought himself a son of the sea. Yet the idea of land, especially the land of his birth, had never been so appealing. He let the word *fonua* fill his mind, the word rich as Tongan soil, sustaining as umbilical blood.

The bird altered its heading a little, pointing in a new direction.

"But I could never go home without my brother," the Wayfinder lamented.

The frigate bird reversed direction, feathering its tail to maintain loft.

The Wayfinder lifted his head and looked in the direction the bird was pointing. Shielding his eyes, he peered deep into the horizon. There, a lone sail. He looked to the bird. "Rotuma," he said. The bird pivoted. "Ha'amoa," he said, and watched the bird turn in the direction he now knew was north.

The Wayfinder was a direct descendent of the gods. He, too, was a child of Tangaloa. But it was Lolohea who was anointed, Lolohea who stood in the light, while he himself was but a second-born. So it never occurred to him that he might receive his power before his older brother.

There was no lightning strike. No transformation was felt, no shuddering effect. It didn't feel like he'd gained a divine ability. It was more like it'd been there, waiting for him, the way a laborer rose from slumber and took up his tool from the place where he'd left it the day before.

THIRTY-SIX

KŌRERO:
THE SAND BETWEEN YOUR TOES

Tapoto talked the nomads out of a spear. Though he intended to fight 'Aho barehanded, handling a spear brought him clarity and focus, he said. Many mornings on our beach he'd execute a routine of thrusts, leaps, and blocks. This he did now on the deck of our waka as people leaned away from the churning weapon. "Ya!" Tapoto shouted each time he deflected an enemy strike—then he grunted while delivering a whistling counterblow. The entire waka shuddered when he jumped high to simulate a death lunge.

So focused was Tapoto that he didn't notice Tongatapu's coast coming into view. For Tiri, I described the cliffs, the crashing waves, the Blowholes erupting. Mostly, though, the island was large and flat, more fields than trees. It paled compared to depictions of Aotearoa, where towering, icy ranges were said to preside over vast rivers and lakes. Stories of Aotearoa started coming to me: tales of conflict, suffering, and dislocation.

I asked Tiri, "Why do we repeat only troubling stories about Aotearoa?"

"Aotearoa?" Tiri asked. "Child, where's your mind?"

"Where are the stories of our ancestors' daily lives?" I asked. "On Aotearoa, didn't families recline under the stars? Didn't they laugh and gossip as they foraged for food?"

Tiri said, "*You* insisted on telling the Tongans our worst story, that of the Great Wave."

I winced.

Tiri asked, "Couldn't you have told them about you and Hine singing as you stripped flax? Wouldn't that have conveyed who we are?"

Who we were, I thought. And then I thought, *Hine*.

"Of this voyage," Tiri said, "you could recall a canoe going down. Loved ones at the edge of perishing. Or you could recall the welcome sight of flying fish, the reassuring call of a conch shell in the dark. Our stories will soon be yours. Yours to recount as you like."

I didn't like Tiri speaking of a time when she'd be gone.

"Now," she said. "Keep describing this Tonga place."

"Tropic birds skim the coastline," I began. I saw the Wayfinder close his eyes to listen.

I reached over and nudged him. "Shouldn't you be watching where you're going?"

He opened an eye. "I know where I am. I wanna know where you are."

Tongatapu's lagoon was murky and still, the surface dusted with pollen. We paddled beneath a limp sail. Along the shore people halted their sullen affairs to observe our passing. No one waved or called out. An arrival seemed to be of no concern.

Beside me, something unseen moved in the green-brown water. Eddies of hidden, muscular movement. Suddenly a large shark surfaced. Its mouth opened a little, like it was trying to breathe. It rolled to its side, exposing a remora fish. I looked into the remora's thin, watery eye, this creature that'd attached itself to such a dangerous host. *Welcome home*, the remora seemed to say. Then the shark slashed its tail and was gone.

We made landfall at a series of stone docks, where tied-off barges awaited unloading. There wasn't a person in sight. Finau looked around for a greeting party. "Where are the flowers and scented oils?" he asked. "There's nothing here but stupid war barges."

War barges? One was filled with carved poles. Another was loaded with black stones. What could they have to do with war?

Setting foot on Tongan soil, we found our legs barely functioned. Tapoto especially looked unsteady, moving as if his feet were dizzy. He had to lean against a niu tree. "I've never felt like this," he said.

"Take your time," the Wayfinder said. "It passes."

"I'm supposed to fight someone?" Tapoto asked. "In this state?"

"Not *fight*," Finau said with calm encouragement. "*Kill*."

"You'll get your bearings," the Wayfinder told Tapoto. "We've got all morning."

"*All morning?*" Finau asked his brother. "When 'Aho learns of our arrival, he'll rally against us. We must catch him unawares."

"Everything's woozy," Tapoto said. "Maybe I should lie down."

"That'll make it worse," the Wayfinder said. "Better to keep moving."

Tapoto didn't loosen his grip on the tree.

"I know you feel bad," Finau said. "But remember: Our uncle's leg is wounded. He can barely get around. You'll be feeling better in no time."

The Wayfinder studied the look on Tapoto's face. "I think he might vomit."

Tapoto's look was clear to me. Feeling miserable, he was thinking of home, of napping on his own mat, the world around him feeling small and known.

Sun Shower went to him, placing a hand on his back. "He needs time," she said to Finau. "You can't make him fight 'Aho, not in the state he's in."

"*He*, meaning 'Aho?" my mother asked. "What state is that?"

"Endless rage," Sun Shower said. "Aside from being buried alive and losing his wife's afterlife, his son was sold into slavery."

My mother looked at the Wayfinder, betrayal on her face. "You neglected to mention the slavery part."

"Slavery isn't the right term," the Wayfinder said. "Mateaki's at his labors, yes, though I assure you his service is temporary."

"*Labors? Service?*" my mother asked. "We know your code words."

"Freeing him will be our first order of business," the Wayfinder said.

"Second," Finau corrected. "After we free Punake."

"How many people have you enslaved?" my mother asked.

Tapoto, bent against the tree, let a ribbon of saliva run from his mouth. Perhaps he did aim to vomit. "Wouldn't separation from a son," he asked, "cause a father to fight with exceptional ferocity?"

This Tapoto asked of boys raised by substitute fathers.

"Who could possibly defeat such a wronged man?" Tapoto asked.

"*You*," Finau said.

"And you must completely kill him," the Wayfinder said.

"He must stop breathing," Finau sternly added. "We have a deal."

My mother turned to the Wayfinder. "Your part of the deal is giving us the island of 'Ata. Until that happens, we follow our own interests. And you must understand that no one's killing anyone, not Tapoto, especially not my daughter."

"We have an agreement," the Wayfinder said.

"We're a nonviolent people," my mother said. "You knew that when you solicited us. We seek consensus. We talk things through. That being said, we still intend to uphold our end of the bargain."

"You'll, what, defeat them with words?" Finau scoffed.

"My daughter doesn't kill old women," my mother repeated.

Finau kicked at the dirt. "How'd we get ourselves into this?"

"Listen to me," Tapoto said. His cheek was against the tree. He spoke slowly, with quavering determination. "I'm going to defeat him. But I fight him our way: We duel until the first drop of blood. If he's a man of honor, he'll accept. If he's—" Here, Tapoto closed his eyes and began to retch.

It pained Tiri to hear this suffering. "Back home, I'd have the plants needed to treat his nausea."

Sun Shower studied this tableau—barges of dark stone, mountains of broken oyster shells, Tapoto doubled over—her face suggesting she was second-guessing her decision to leave the nomads. "There's only one place to get the botanicals you need."

Our people followed the Tongan brothers through the royal compound. My mother and I each held one of Tiri's arms. Tapoto managed to join, moving slowly, leaning on his spear. Sun Shower acted as a guide, narrating what she saw. A patch of stained soil was the site of a man's death. A vast array of shells was the war. She pointed to some firepits. "This's where we danced nightly, but really, it's where he'd make his selections." She indicated a thatched structure. "That's where we once slept. Our own little coop."

At last, we came to a great tomb, its stone cap still propped wide from when it'd been opened to release ʻAho. Through the gap, human remains were visible. We stood back, to let the Tongan brothers pay their respects.

Sun Shower said, "When I first arrived, I danced for the Tuʻitonga. Though his throne was a tomb, you were safe when you danced for him. Anytime you were near him, you'd be free from harm."

"And when you weren't around him?" my mother asked.

Sun Shower didn't answer.

The brothers started bickering. I missed the beginning of their disagreement because I was scanning the distant trees—out there, beneath that canopy, a malign force lurked. It was a thought I'd never had on my home island.

"It's not my fault," the Wayfinder told his brother.

"You lost your secondary father!" Finau snapped. "And then you took mine."

The Wayfinder said, "I've told you, we're going to get Punake back."

"Yet we never do," Finau said. I'd never heard poetry recited in anger, but he nearly spit these lines:

Ko e havilivili iho loungutu—	*The wind across your lips—*
Ko koe eni!	*That's who you are!*
Ko e ʻoneʻone iho vahaʻa louhiʻi vaʻe—	*The sand between your toes—*
Ko ho ʻapi eni.	*This is your home.*

I didn't always understand Finau's poetry, but I knew these lines suggested that, exposed long enough to distant winds, Punake would become someone else. Soon enough, foreign sand would lodge between his toes.

Walking on, we passed empty fields and dwellings whose inhabitants, Sun Shower said, had fled to their home islands. Soon we intersected another path. It led into trees and curved out of sight.

"That's the path to the bathing ponds," Sun Shower said. "That's where he keeps the Fefine Girls, sleeping in the open, living raw." She turned to me. "Don't ever get caught on that path. If you must go there, move through the adjacent foliage. Even then, he often locates himself as a soldier does, in unexpected places."

I'd spent my youth in such trees, lying in wait for unsuspecting birds. That's what women must be to him, forest birds, too free for his taste.

Hearing the threat was near, Tapoto abandoned the spear he'd been leaning on to walk upright, fists on hips, eyes half-closed. He breathed through his nose, nostrils flaring, as he tried to muster himself.

At last, we encountered a field of ferns. Beyond it was a compound whose towering wall was formed from living trees. Imposing as the wall was, its front gates lay broken on the ground, the compound's entrance open and unguarded. Instead of approaching, Finau, the Wayfinder, and Sun Shower pulled up short, staring into the ferns.

"That's where it happened," Sun Shower said. "At first I was glad I didn't see it. But now I have so many questions."

"It was late morning," Finau said. "Rain was falling."

"The bracken rose and fell with the drops," the Wayfinder added.

"It was over quickly," Finau said.

For a while, they just looked at the field.

The Wayfinder turned to Sun Shower. "We're the ones who took Moon Appearing's bones."

Sun Shower, unsure whether to believe this, narrowed her eyes.

"We were trying to save her," he added.

"Nobody tried to save her," Sun Shower said. "Nobody did anything." She pointed at the Tamahā's compound. "Least of all, her."

It was then that we heard a sound, rough and constant. We turned to see the source of the commotion, and what we saw made us fall silent. Tiri looked blankly around, trying to better understand what she was hearing. "What is it?" she asked. "What's going on?"

"There are several beautiful women," I told her. "Together, they struggle to pull a rope, which is attached to a sled. On the sled is a dead man."

"Are you sure he's dead?" Tiri asked.

The man's body shook with the motion of the sled. One of his arms dragged in the dirt. It was bent backward, broken at the elbow. As they passed, his head lolled in our direction, dust coating his open eyes.

I was holding Tiri's arm. I squeezed her hand once to say, *Sadly, yes*.

"If they're dragging him into the Tamahā's compound," Sun Shower said, "you'll have to adjust your definition of *dead*."

＊
＊ ＊

We followed the Fefine Girls to the Tamahā's compound, though my eyes were on the dead man, the dust he kicked up, the jiggle of his agitated flesh, his wrong-bent arm.

At a set of smashed gates lying broken in the dirt, Finau said, "This is as far as we go."

I looked to the Wayfinder. "From here, no men are allowed," he said.

I could see that inside, a boy was assisting an older woman. "What about him?" I asked.

"He's not a man," Sun Shower said.

My father saw my hesitancy. "It's all right," he assured me. "We'll be right here."

Tapoto laced his fingers behind his neck, walking in slow circles to control his land sickness.

"Come," my mother said. Together, we took Tiri's arms.

Inside, we encountered the burned remnants of a dwelling and the strewn kindling of unknown structures. There were trampled gardens, broken ponds, and heavy branches, now grounded, that had been torn from fruiting trees. Who would hurt trees? Untouched was a single nonu, yellow with fruit. When had we last eaten? In a sort of trance, we migrated there, plucking at will. Free and fully available, it was food, food for the taking! Not once did I notice its horrible smell or slimy texture. As I sank my teeth into nonu flesh, my eyes rolled closed in a sustaining, restoring satisfaction.

As our party stripped the tree of its offerings—Mama Mānunu sharing with the men outside—we began taking note of the events unfolding before us. You know how when you eat, you kind of wake up and only then realize you'd been partly asleep? This "Tamahā" woman was not far away. She glanced at us a time or two, though she was focused on some business with the dead man. Who, it turned out, wasn't dead! The boy assisting her poured sips of water into the man's mouth and irrigated his eyes. The Tamahā then fanned him. All it took was a cool breeze—then the man was sitting up, talking! It took me a moment to realize this was *the Fan*, the one that moved life.

Sun Shower approached the Tamahā, and I came along.

"You're back," the Tamahā said as we neared.

"No thanks to you," Sun Shower said.

Rather unwarmly, a Fefine Girl named Kakala asked, "So where'd you run off to?"

The Fefine Girl named Heilala asked, "And how'd you hide so long?"

"I took to the waves," Sun Shower said.

"You mean the nomads?" Kakala asked.

Heilala said, "I hear they steer women."

Sun Shower didn't respond.

The dead man found his resurrected status astonishing. "When 'Aho began beating me, I was sure I'd die, but here I am, breathing and talking and"—chuckling, he marveled to himself—"laughing."

The Tamahā asked him, "What was your business with 'Aho?"

"He has us matāpule sequestered on the island of Fafā."

Impatiently, the Tamahā said, "I know that."

"Do you know what it's like to be trapped on an island of matāpule? They make rules about everything, even rules about rules. We made a delegation to plead the injustice of our treatment. I was selected as our delegation's delegate. I had to swim here! From Fafā! Do you know how far—"

"I know where Fafā is," the Tamahā said. "What was your business with 'Aho?"

"Why're we banished?" the dead matāpule wondered. "He offers no reason, no rationale, no precedent. He just pushes us aside, we who are born to serve nobles and royals!"

The Tamahā, shaking her head, raised her Fan.

Quickly, he said, "I proposed that, should he release us, we'd recognize him as Tu'itonga."

"Is 'Aho not the king?" Sun Shower asked.

"Not technically," the dead matāpule said. "There was no ceremony, no transfer of power, no kava was served. A king died and then a prince died, and then 'Aho began giving orders. But if he freed us, I explained to 'Aho, we might legitimize him."

"And his response?" the Tamahā asked.

"He said he had no desire to be king. Can you imagine that? My memory gets a little fuzzy at this point, but I recall he grabbed my arm." Only now did the matāpule seem to notice his wrong-facing limb. "Oh my," he said. "I guess I'm lucky to be alive."

"Are you alive?" the Tamahā asked.

The dead matāpule didn't know how to answer this question.

"Is he not alive?" I asked.

The Tamahā looked up from where she knelt in the dirt. "Who's she?" she asked Sun Shower. "Who are these people?"

"They arrived with the princes," Sun Shower said.

The Tamahā glanced at our people. "The Tuʻitonga's sons are back?"

"We've brought you a gift," I said.

The Tamahā returned to the matāpule. "I can give you more breath," she said. "But you'd have to help me with some things. First we must end the war."

"But you helped start the war," the matāpule said.

"All the more reason to ply for its conclusion."

"But if the war ended, the warriors would return," the matāpule said. "Then we'd have an island filled with aggrieved, ill-treated veterans. Men who were asked to do the ugliest work. Men who learned to slay before breakfast and after a long day's killing, murdered on in their dreams!"

"It would be a challenge," the Tamahā said. "But if we could reinstate order. If we could make rank and status and tapu respected again. If we restored the sanctity of women, then we could rebuild."

"Matāpule are sworn to serve the king," he said. "Who'd rule, in your scenario?" A little chuckle escaped his mouth. "You?"

"Is he grateful?" the Tamahā asked the boy crouched beside her.

The boy shook his head.

The Tamahā, with her Fan, drew forth the matāpule's breath. His head rolled to the side, and an emptiness came over him. He was gone. The

Tongan brothers wanted me to get my hands on that Fan, but I didn't like how readily it recalled the living, how, without effort or care, it snuffed the human flame. Looking around, I noticed the corpses of other men—four, five, six—sprawled in various states of decomposition. Had these men also been killed by 'Aho? Had the Tamahā interrogated them? And just left them to the elements?

The Tamahā said, "If one of them acknowledged that a woman was the source of his revival, if one, just once, thanked me, I'd let him live." Then she asked aloud of no one, "Is every male on this island worthless? Is there not one man who can help me deal with my nephew?"

"We have a man," I said.

"Who's this girl, again?" the Tamahā asked.

"You have the Fan," Sun Shower said to the Tamahā. "Use it."

"I can't draw my nephew's blood," the Tamahā said. "More importantly, that's not what the Fan's for—it's made to give life, to defend and restore it."

"What about us?" Sun Shower asked. "If the Fan isn't for defending us, what's it for? What good is the thing if it's only used to blow leaves and question the dead?"

Kakala and Heilala turned to the Tamahā, awaiting her answer.

"The killing, the violence, it has to stop," the Tamahā said.

I asked, "Did we not just witness the Fan take a life?"

The Tamahā looked at me, her expression suggesting that everything had now gone wrong with the world, that a strange girl was questioning the Tamahā of Tonga in her own compound. "You did not," she said. "My nephew took that life. I actually restored it, if but briefly."

"But we've seen you use the Fan to take life," Sun Shower said. "During Six Fists's duel, you flayed a man alive. And you did it to protect the man who preys upon us."

The Tamahā paused. She looked like she might say any number of things but, frustrated, rejected them. At last, she blurted, "I can't save everyone."

"Can't you?" Sun Shower asked. "Pick and choose, then. Save only some of us, if you will. Even if you save but one of us, we'll take that. Otherwise, pass the Fan to someone who'll use it."

"I had a candidate," the Tamahā said. "I was going to pass it. But *they* stopped us. The problem isn't us, it's *them*."

"She's gone," Sun Shower said. "Accept that Moon Appearing's gone."

"I suppose *you* want the Fan, is that it?" the Tamahā asked. She extended the Fan to Sun Shower, who regarded it warily.

"You can't give Sun Shower the Fan," Heilala protested. "She evaded 'Aho at our expense."

"When strength was needed, Sun Shower ran away," Kakala added. "She joined the nomads, who believe in nothing."

The Tamahā then directed the Fan toward Kakala and Heilala, who hesitated.

"You can't give them the Fan," Sun Shower said. "They fell limp."

There was a silence. "The problem isn't us," the Tamahā said. "It's men. Feeble, worthless, cowardly men. Where are the men of honor, where are the brave ones, where are the ones who, instead of duty, act out of devotion?"

"We have a candidate," I volunteered. "We've brought such a man."

"Who're you, again?" the Tamahā asked me.

I didn't know how to say who I was.

"And what're you doing here?"

Flustered, I tried to start at the beginning, explaining how our people had cut down too many trees and depleted our food sources. Then I realized I forgot the entire part about being from Aotearoa, which was the source of our moko tradition, so I started naming my ancestors, but I only got to Hā Mutu before thinking of the birding we did with my parrot Aroha and how we used her to lure other parrots to their deaths, though parrots were protected on our sister island, where we'd found the girl that Hine stayed behind to raise, which meant I had to explain our ban on children, which wasn't really against children, we loved children, we wanted children, it was just that things were scarce, and with too many mouths to feed it wasn't right to add more, which was why we brewed red tea, but none of this made sense without explaining the royals on *The Red Cloak* and how we came to be on our island in the first place, so I described the storm and the chants and—

The Tamahā lifted her hand. "Finally, a girl who's found her voice," she declared. She looked at Kakala. "A girl who doesn't stand mute when you ask her a question." The Tamahā regarded Heilala. "Who doesn't vapidly smile when you ask her the matter." The Tamahā glanced dismissively at the dead matāpule. "Who doesn't use words to serve himself." Then she returned her attention to me. "Did you say you brewed a red tea?" When I nodded, she asked who'd taught me this remedy.

"My mother, by way of Tiri," I said. "Tiri's the aunt of our entire island. Well, was. I mean, she still is, it's just that we're without an island, at the moment."

"*Without an island?*" The Tamahā raised an eyebrow. "*At the moment?*"

It was easier to bring the Tamahā to Tiri, who stood with our women under the nonu tree.

"Thank you for the fruit," my mother said. "Never have I had a better meal."

The Tamahā studied my mother. "You found the nonu to your liking?"

"If you only knew the things that've sustained us," my mother said.

"We have a gift," I said, and opened the cage containing the malau birds. "We're told you once had an entire flock. Perhaps this pair could restore them."

When the birds stepped into the light, pleasure flashed on the Tamahā's face, but she quickly quashed it, dismissively saying, "They're both male." She turned to Tiri. "Auntie, I hear your people brew a red tea for your young ladies to drink."

"Only when necessary," Tiri answered. "I detect the scent of kaute blossoms in the air. Which makes me think girls find occasion for such a remedy, even on so fine an island as this."

"Can you help us?" my mother asked. "A member of our party has nausea after his long journey."

"Back home," Tiri said, "I'd treat nausea with akakōare root or a karamu infusion. Are either of these cures familiar to you?"

"Regretfully, no," the Tamahā said. "I'd recommend an extract of polokai. It's a small bush with white flowers and purple berries."

"Perhaps this is the plant we call pōporo," Tiri said.

The Tamahā took us to the bush, which grew beside a series of stone ponds, all knocked down but one. The way the malau birds followed her, I could tell she'd once doted on them. At the pond, I stared into the shaded water. I asked, "And these were filled with fish—waiting to be eaten anytime you liked?"

"The project was more about preserving fish than eating them," the Tamahā said. She handed Tiri a sprig of pōporo. "Why was that one pond spared?" the Tamahā wondered aloud. "Perhaps the raiders were too tired from smashing the other ponds to smash this one. They simply took the fish. Fish, mind you, that came from the high mountain lake of Tofua. Getting them here was a near-impossible task, so the project is lost."

My mother said, "I wish our men could see these ponds, so they might be re-created on 'Ata."

At the mention of 'Ata, the Tamahā narrowed one eye.

The boy joined us. He used a hand to mime a bird pecking at the water.

Sun Shower said, "A pair of herons once called this pond home. They're no more."

Kakala said, "Unfortunately, their wing bones make fine inking tools."

"And their legs are perfect for flutes," Heilala added.

"I suspect their flavor condemned them," my mother said.

The Tamahā's eyes recognized the truth of this.

Gazing into the water, I saw tiny fish, no more than slivers, lurking in the shadows. "Won't these minnows grow into new fish?" I asked.

"Minnows, you say?" the Tamahā asked, hiding, for some reason, her delight.

Tiri chewed the sprig and approved. "What other nausea remedy would you prepare?" she asked the Tamahā. "Our man must recover enough to participate in a fight."

"*Fight?*" the Tamahā asked.

"It's more of a contest," my mother said. "Our people don't believe in violence, so though Tapoto, for that's our man's name, faces a most dangerous opponent, he aims to defeat the fellow in such a way that no life is lost."

Here, the Tamahā nearly smiled—in irony, disbelief, amusement? "This manner of combat is new to me," she confessed. "To restore your fighter, I'd make an infusion of pukovili or sipi bark, maybe adding some takafalu."

"Can you show us these plants?" Tiri asked.

The Tamahā led us through her dashed gardens—stomped turmeric stalks, trampled kumala vines, and turned seedling pots. We arrived at a sipi tree, whose gnarled trunk was strung with seedpods. The Tamahā cut away some outer bark and made white strips of the inner. "Have your warrior chew this," she said. "But it's not to be swallowed."

Tiri tested it on herself, wincing at the bitterness.

"So this man of yours, this Tapoto," the Tamahā said. "Who does he intend to fight?"

"The opponent's name is 'Aho," my mother said. "I'm told he's quite the dangerous fellow."

"I hope Tapoto's a capable rival." The Tamahā indicated the nearby bodies. "For, as you see, 'Aho dispatches men left and right."

"That's the unfortunate thing," my mother said. "Tapoto seems to have no aptitude for fighting at all."

Arawiwi said, "Any one of us could defeat him."

"Sadly, this is true," Tiri said.

"Yet you send him to his fate?" the Tamahā asked us.

"He does have one advantage," I told the Tamahā. "It's the attribute you claimed a man needed most of all. He's devoted to us."

The Tamahā studied me a moment. "You mentioned the island of 'Ata."

"That's where we'll live," I said. "After Tapoto defeats his dangerous opponent."

"But 'Ata is the personal property of the king," the Tamahā responded.

"If 'Aho is defeated," I said, "the Wayfinder will become king, and he'll give us the island."

"Ah," the Tamahā said. "Things are coming clear."

The malau birds followed us to the front gates, moving almost entirely within the Tamahā's shadow. On the way, we passed the burned structure, which was nothing more than a net of ash cast black against the soil. Here, two mats lay upon the ground. The only possessions in sight were a wooden bowl for rainwater and a ceramic pot in a cold firepit.

"That's how we slept," I told the Tamahā. "Back when we had a place to sleep."

She studied me, trying to determine, I think, if I was making a play for sympathy.

I said, "When you sleep in the open, you can talk about little things, like stuff that happened that day or what people said. But there's also the sea and the sky, which make you ask the big questions. And your parents, under the stars, remember more."

The Tamahā said, "You sound like a fortunate girl." Then she took a piece of char from the firepit.

At the front gates, we discovered the men hadn't been idle. Working together, they'd managed to reassemble the gates and hang them. The Tamahā placed her hand on the bamboo uprights. When she pushed the gate, the lashings satisfyingly creaked.

"We reused the old rope," my father said. "So its lifespan is limited."

The Tamahā offered no praise or thanks, but a twitch of appreciation was visible about her face. I was beginning to understand how to read her.

"Who'd want to ransack such a special place?" one of the Kohimu brothers wondered.

The Tamahā said, "The former king enforced a system that excluded many from the island's bounty."

"What's more exclusive than gates?" the other Kohimu brother asked.

"Or making a rule that excludes all men, which is half the population?" Papa Mānunu asked.

The Tamahā defended her practice. "I've created the island's lone haven for women."

I looked at the Fefine Girls, who, wary and uncertain, kept their mouths shut.

"And I've been safeguarding our island's most precious resources," she added.

Tapoto said, "That's what I'd tell myself when I snuck off to my sweet potato stash."

Tiri, hearing Tapoto's voice, asked, "How're you faring, my son?"

"How is it that I didn't get sick upon the waves," Tapoto wondered, "but fell queasy the moment I touched ground?"

"Come, take your medicine," Tiri told him.

He glanced at everyone, hesitant. "I think most of my problem was hunger. I'm actually feeling better since eating a little fruit."

"*A little?*" my father asked. "You ate seven pieces of nonu."

Tiri reached for Tapoto's face. Pinching his cheek, she guided the bark into his mouth.

"So you're *him*?" the Tamahā asked. She studied his size and bulk. "You remind me of someone."

Tapoto didn't know what to say.

The Tamahā said, "You're big like him and not without some humor."

Tapoto responded with a guileless smile.

"I hear you're going to fight my nephew," the Tamahā said. "You think you can beat him?"

Tapoto shrugged. "I'm going to try. I hear he's wounded."

"He is," the Tamahā said. "He's wounded here." She pointed to her chest. "And here," she said, indicating her temple. "So you intend to fight him in a way that doesn't hurt him?"

"If he agrees to our terms," Tapoto said.

"Nonviolent combat?" the Tamahā mused. "I give this strange notion my blessing." She drew a streak of soot down each of Tapoto's cheeks. Here, she turned to the Wayfinder, asking him, "And you want to become king, is that it?"

"I don't know if I *want* to," he said.

"Yet you aim to?"

"I suppose."

"What makes you think you're qualified? What makes you think you'll be a good king?"

"Nothing, nothing at all," the Wayfinder said. "But I have to try. It's the only way to terminate the war, to give these people a home, to stop our uncle. My worry is I'll be a terrible ruler. I was raised apart from others. I have little sense of royal life. My supplemental father owned nothing but a loincloth."

"Those," the Tamahā said, "are your strongest qualifications." She sooted each of his cheeks.

Then she turned to me. Though we were surrounded by many, the Tamahā looked at me like I was the only person in the world. "And you, what'll be your role in the coming proceedings?"

She didn't know my name or anything about me.

"I don't know," I said. "I've never been a part of something like this."

"Do you believe in life, or do you believe in death?"

No such inquiry had ever been put to me. I said, "Life."

"Do you register human weakness when it's before you?" the Tamahā asked. "Is frailty visible to you?"

"I think so," I said.

"Do you have sympathy for those who're ill-fated? For those born to toil? For those who've been corroded by war or those who unknowingly act as agents in cautionary tales? Do you believe we're obligated to even the lowliest among us, the least deserving, that even the worst of us are still fathers and husbands and nephews?"

This was all hypothetical to me, but I nodded.

She whispered the following to me, even though we were surrounded by people and everyone could hear: "Then I loan you this, to be used judiciously and solely for the preservation of life." She held out the Fan. It wasn't like I took possession of it—that would be unthinkable. But my hand did close around it.

The Tamahā then sooted my cheeks. "This'll keep you humble, which is important when wielding an agent of omnipotence."

Holding the Fan, I looked at my parents, at the Tongan brothers, at Tapoto. They regarded me differently, though I couldn't say how. The Wayfinder said, "It couldn't hurt to bring a matāpule."

I walked to the dead matāpule and awakened him with a breeze. It didn't take much—his eyes popped right open. "Do you know the rules of Tonga?" I asked him.

He nodded.

"Are you grateful to be restored?"

"Most certainly," he said. "Very grateful."

"Will you be loyal to me?" I asked.

"I'm afraid I'm loyal only to the king," he said.

"And who's the king?"

His eyes flitted around. He had no answer.

The Tamahā vaguely indicated the other dead men. "Extinguish him and revive another," she said.

"I swear it," the dead matāpule blurted. "I'll be loyal to none but you."

Before I fully awakened him, so he wouldn't feel the pain I twisted his arm in the proper direction.

THIRTY-SEVEN

LOOKING DOWN UPON THE MOON

Something made the Tuʻitonga open his eyes. It was before dawn, and his sleeping chamber was dark save for a single candlenut lamp. "Pōhiva," he called. When he reached for her, she was gone. Eyes adjusting, he discovered the Tamahā standing beside his pallet. "Yes?" he asked.

She ran a hand over his extremities, pressing, pinching. "Your attendants sent for me. When was the last time you made urine?"

"How do I find myself so reduced?" he asked. "Betrayed by my own body."

"Have you been urinating, or no?"

"In my imagination, I piss all the time. I want to piss, truly I do, but alas, nothing comes."

"When that urge goes away," she said, "that's the last sign."

"Last sign of what?"

She started massaging his ankles, trying to move the fluid in his tissue.

The Tuʻitonga absently flipped through the corners of the mats he reclined upon. These last few days, stuck on his stack of mats, he'd had nothing to do but think of Lolohea upon the water, think of his brother, not sixty paces from him, trapped in total dark. So he let the mats draw his attention. He'd never looked at them closely, how each one had a particular weave, a weave that spoke of the weaver, her family, her clan, her village, her island. What else was woven into those mats? he wondered.

Pain flashed in his leg. "Fe'unga. Just give me my medicine, would you? What foul brew have you cooked up? I know you take great joy in making me drink your concoctions."

"That time has passed. If things have stopped coming out, it's time to stop taking them in."

How could a person stop eating and drinking? he wondered.

"I see you flip through the mats beneath you," she said. "Do you review your life?"

"I simply admire their intricacy. It's amazing how unique each pattern can be—it's proof of how a person can live on."

"Or proof of how one doesn't," the Tamahā said. "Those mats are the last effects of emptied islands, of entire dialects fallen silent."

Above, predawn rain started to spatter against the roof. He thought, *The seasons are changing.*

The Tamahā said, "I suppose it's natural to make a final inventory of your trophies."

"I assure you, these mats were never trophies. Nor do I stack them as boasts. Upon these mats great men once took their recumbency. Men who did not go easily into the afterlife. I stacked them thusly so I could commune with their life forces. I'd hoped to absorb their strength, but now look at me."

"Have you considered that you absorbed something else from these mats?"

"Like what?"

She didn't respond.

"Do you attempt to undermine me even now?" He looked up—rain sounded against the thatching. Seeping water dripped to his chest. "Why won't my son return?"

"You mean sons."

"That's what I said," he snapped. He took a breath. "I suppose I can't blame you for taking your advantage. After my passing, I assume you'll try to install that Fisian boy as Tu'itonga and extend your power by exerting influence over him."

She gave him the pleasant look you'd offer a stranger who'd landed on your home island, one who must be afforded hospitality but also be handled with great caution. "My daily labors await. I'm sorry you never knew labor. Few things are more satisfying than tending my garden."

Several hurtful responses came to him—that, lacking friends, siblings, children, or a husband, a garden would be the next best thing. Instead, he nodded. "Perhaps I'll plant some seeds in the purple soil of Pulotu."

She waited a polite moment, then turned to go.

For some reason, he couldn't bear the thought of her leaving. "Do you think Lolo will return?"

She paused. "The boy lives to please you. Do you think your pleasure can be satisfied?"

Before she could turn again, he said, "My brother. Do you think he . . . do you think he yet lives?"

"Define *living*."

The fale seemed to darken. "I know we've been at odds," he said. "But something you once told me has proved true. You said you were the only one who could truly understand me."

"I'm the family's ranking aunt. I only do my duty." Then she withdrew.

He felt dripping water. In the past, he might've admonished someone about the state of the roof, but the drops felt divine. Why had he sent the foolish, incompetent Punake on the voyage instead of Finau, Finau who'd dive into a grave and come up smiling? Why'd they use that obviously cursed Fisian vaka? And could he himself not have gone along to tutor the boys firsthand on the ways that fates were meted?

An eddy of wind moved through the fale, extinguishing the lamp.

Only in the dark and quiet did he realize how thirsty he was. It seemed, however, that he'd already taken his last drink. He pondered whether rainwater could seep through the slab that sealed the family grave. Might that trickle be enough to extend one's life? He shifted on his pallet so that drops fell onto his tongue. In the dark, mouth open, he was certain he and his brother both sipped from the same sky.

The Tuʻitonga didn't have a mind for poetry, but something Punake once uttered came to him:

I hoʻo tangaki e fonualoto o e kainga,	*When you open up the family grave,*

o ke vakai 'atu ko e ngaahi hui pē 'o'ou.   *the bones you discover are your own.*

The Tu'itonga felt like he'd only closed his eyes when a horn signaled Lolohea's return. The king's attendants managed to hoist him up and install him in a vala kilt. Wherever they touched him, handprints remained in his flesh. "It's a special day," he told his servants. "Fetch the royal cloak."

As he was too large to properly wear the cloak, they draped it loosely about his shoulders. Still, when they stepped outside, the cloak shone brighter, more intense, than any object known. The pale morning light, muted beneath cloud cover, only amplified the yellow quills. When rain struck the cascade of feathers, beading drops formed brilliant pearls of yellow.

Seven Fists offered the king his spear as a walking stick, while supporting him on the other side. They made their way toward the landing, the Tu'itonga's swollen feet leaving prints like clubs.

"As my security chief," the Tu'itonga said, "it's your duty to join me in death. But if I spared you, if you could withstand the humiliation of being left behind, would you be a loyal servant to Lolohea?"

If Seven Fists felt any shame at the prospect of not being slain, he didn't show it.

"I'll serve Lolohea," he said. "If he'll have me."

This Seven Fists was a pretty good fellow, the Tu'itonga thought. "When Lolo becomes king, he'll need to kill a matāpule. That's the only way to put the others on notice. You'll help him with that, right?"

Seven Fists, under the weight of the king, grunted his assent.

When they made it to the landing, the Wayfinder'd already arrived and was securing his lines.

"My son!" the Tu'itonga called.

The Wayfinder, turning, was aghast. "Father—your color, your skin."

"I live," the Tu'itonga said. "You live. That's all that matters."

He wanted to clap a hand upon the boy's shoulder, but it wasn't possible.

His left hand exerted its full force upon the staff, while his right gripped Seven Fists.

"What of Lolohea?" the Tuʻitonga asked.

"His vakaʻs right behind mine."

The Tuʻitonga asked, "Were you . . . successful?"

The Wayfinder offered a reluctant nod.

The Tuʻitonga beamed. "And behold, their Tongan Hull overflows. They got so many, they had to lash the extra to another craft!"

The Wayfinder glanced at Kanivaʻs corpse, bound to his outrigger.

"And what of our poet?" the Tuʻitonga asked. "Did he drive you mad? Did he shirk his duties or perform any boneheaded antics?"

"Punake . . ." the Wayfinder said, and paused. "Well, Punake."

"Say no more," the Tuʻitonga said. "Fret not over the lost, for this is the way of things."

The Wayfinder had a question. "Havea didn't make it back, did he?"

Seven Fists said, "Rumors say his wife made landing on the island of Nomuka."

"She lives?" the Wayfinder marveled. "Havea made it to the afterlife? What's her condition? What's she say of Havea?"

"Word is only that she lives," Seven Fists said.

The Tuʻitonga studied his son. "You've changed. I can see wisdom in your eyes."

"Whoʻd want to be wise on the topics of deceit and treachery?"

"Whoʻd want to be innocent of them?"

"Father, you must tell me. Will I be sent to war? Does Lolohea intend to be rid of me?"

"Where'd you get such a notion?"

"My cousin. He said you'd plot against me."

"That treacherous little . . . You didn't listen to him, did you?"

The Wayfinder hesitated. "When you became king, did you not get rid of your brother?"

"I *got rid* of no one. Your uncle went to Fisi in the service of Tonga. He gave his all, and then some. Many a Fisian gravedigger wished ʻAho had not been half so dutiful." Now that ʻAho and his ugly ways had been erased, the king wondered if perhaps his brother's legacy shouldn't be bolstered. "In fact, I intend to name a new punake and commission an epic poem on the greatness of my lost brother."

The Fisian vaka, sail lowered, soon paddled into view. Its passengers stood in anticipation of shore.

Seven Fists volunteered, "My men are at the ready."

In awe, the Tuʻitonga asked the Wayfinder, "Where're they from?"

"The peace-loving island of Rotuma."

The Tuʻitonga shook his head at this sad and delicious irony.

Matāpule Muʻa came running. "I heard the alarm," he called. Wet hair suggested he'd been at the bathing ponds.

"You derelict," the Tuʻitonga said. "Where've you been? I'll need a new punake, right away."

"What happened to your old punake?"

The Tuʻitonga glared at him.

"Right away," Matāpule Muʻa said.

When the Fisian vaka made landfall, ten Rotumans dashed across the soil from one canoe to another, this one empty save for the young woman they'd sought, her body lacerated by rope.

"Welcome to Tonga!" the Tuʻitonga called.

Raho turned. He looked truly crazed, the way grief, anger, and confusion can splinter a person's identity. "Produce him," Raho demanded. "You must produce the fugitive."

"What fugitive is that?" the Tuʻitonga asked.

Raho shouted, "The rapist who's taken Kaniva's life. He's known by his missing front teeth."

"I know the figure you speak of," the Tuʻitonga said. "He has a habit of disappearing."

Matāpule Muʻa chuckled, "Only matched by his habit of reappearing."

The king turned on him. "What'd you say?"

Matāpule Muʻa's eyes widened. "Was ʻAho's return not the start of our troubles?"

The Tuʻitonga said, "You used the word *habit*, as if we should expect to see him again."

"Will you produce the fugitive?" Raho asked. "Or must we apprehend him ourselves?"

But the king wasn't done with his matāpule. "Am I to spend my eternity with your incompetence? Is this the kind of service I can expect in the afterlife? I swear I've half a mind to leave you behind."

"I demand you surrender him," Raho said.

The Tuʻitonga looked to the Wayfinder. "Whatever ruse you offered them, they've taken it whole."

The Wayfinder, looking dispirited, said nothing.

The Tuʻitonga spoke to Seven Fists, bent under a kingly weight. "It's time to disabuse these fellows of their fantasy. I don't want them injured—they've another destiny to fulfill."

Seven Fists whistled for his warriors. There were dozens of them, overwhelming numbers being the Tongan way. The Rotumans made some protests, but who would hear their entreaties? And only now, as the Tongans were upon them, only here, outnumbered, weaponless, and on foreign soil, did they attempt to fight.

Two souls remained on the Fisian vaka—Lolohea and his cousin Mateaki, bound at the hands, a flute fastened in his teeth. Lolohea helped his cousin onto land, where they joined the Tuʻitonga, the Wayfinder, Matāpule Muʻa, and Seven Fists.

"Father," Lolohea said. "You don't look well."

Sweat beaded the Tuʻitonga's upper lip. "On the contrary. My sons have returned. I am restored."

"And you don the royal cloak," Lolohea said. "This isn't like you."

The Tuʻitonga smiled. "Can a man not look his best on his last day as king?"

Behind them, Raho shouted, "Treachery!" as he was subdued and a stick was forced into his mouth.

"I'm proud of you, son," the Tuʻitonga said.

Lolohea said, "I take no pride in my work, but it's complete."

Mateaki's lips were red and cracked. He was quite animated, but his words couldn't be understood. He wriggled his hands to indicate they were in need of being untied.

"I didn't get rid of my brother," the Tuʻitonga told Mateaki, who could do nothing but listen. "And I don't get rid of my sons." To Seven Fists, he said, "Tell your men they missed a slave."

"But this young man," Seven Fists said, "he bears much resemblance to your nephew."

"So he does," the Tuʻitonga said.

"He wasn't part of the deal," the Wayfinder said.

"Now you defend him?" the Tuʻitonga asked. "Did he not just deceive you?"

Lolohea asked, "Won't ʻAho respond if his son is enslaved?"

"Sadly, your uncle's gone missing," the Tuʻitonga said.

Mateaki's eyes went wide. His attempts at speech, however, couldn't be interpreted.

"We have a search party looking for him," the Tuʻitonga said, "but the man seems to have vanished."

Lolohea said, "Mateaki's not a menace without his father to back him. And these Rotumans have served their need. They should be freed. No, I order them released."

The Tuʻitonga couldn't have heard a sweeter sound than his son giving commands. He signaled Lolo close, so they could speak in confidence. "Listen, I've made a deal with the Tuʻi of Foa Island. With these slaves, I buy the Tuʻifoa's loyalty in the war. If I break this deal, there'll be consequences. It'll foment a grudge that'll transfer to you upon my death."

"Father, don't talk about dying."

"Listen," the Tuʻitonga said. "Many Tongan islands hate us for our safe and comfortable lives. The only thing stopping them from warring with Tongatapu is the greater war with Fisi. Only an external enemy keeps us united. The Tamahā helped me see this."

"You really count her among your counselors?"

"You'll have to learn to exist with her. And though I've cautioned you against her, you'll find she's not without her uses. All she needs is someone to occasionally clip her wings. Today you and I will do that."

"You promised I could free those we captured," Lolohea said.

"Yes, but you have to think things through. If I break my deal with the Tuʻifoa, you'll inherit his wrath. If I die and then *you* cancel the deal, he won't know where he stands with you, he'll seek to win your favor, he'll *give* you those slaves. So we let them sail to their fates. Later, *you* command their liberty. Trust me, those Rotuman boys will appreciate freedom all the more once they've labored under the hot sun of Foa. As for your cousin, I suggest the obsidian mines in the volcanic island of Kao."

"But they're innocents," Lolohea said. "I insist they be freed."

"I take your point, but there's a problem. You're not the king."

"Then I take the Final Test now."

The Tu'itonga smiled. "The ideal girl has already been chosen."

Finau came running. "You're back, you made it!" he called before embracing his brothers, who immediately saw the black jellyfish on his throat. This marking did not escape Mateaki's notice as he was being led away—the jellyfish was placed exactly where, fighting to the death, one would throttle the neck of another.

"How'd you come by that mark?" Lolohea asked.

"Where's Punake?" Finau asked.

The Wayfinder and Lolohea glanced at one another.

Their father spoke up. "Punake got delayed."

"Delayed how?" Finau asked. "Where?"

"Just answer Lolohea," the Tu'itonga said. "All will be explained in due course."

Finau touched his neck. He described his confrontation with 'Aho, falling into the tomb, how it sealed them inside, how they began to strangle one another in the darkness. "At first, 'Aho had the upper hand. I began to lose consciousness, and as I did, my spirit voyaged to the afterlife."

The Tu'itonga studied his son with great concern. "When you went into the grave, I thought I'd lost you. I only cared about your current life. I didn't know you'd glimpsed the next one."

Finau said, "Uncle 'Aho's hands were around my throat, and mine were about his. Even in the dark, his grip made my vision sparkle. Somehow, I never released my hold on his throat."

"And?" Lolohea demanded.

"I squeezed, and he squeezed, and then I began to see, faintly, the purple twilight of the afterlife—palm trees with lavender beards swayed against a violet sky."

"Were there people?" the Tuʻitonga asked.

Finau, tears forming, looked to his father. He nodded.

The Tuʻitonga asked, "Were they there to welcome you?"

Finau shook his head. "Don't go there, Father. It's you they were waiting for. All your enemies have gathered to await your arrival."

"What happened next?" the Wayfinder asked.

"The hands around my throat went limp," Finau said. "Uncle ʻAho had gone unconscious, and I found myself in the dark again. That's when they opened the tomb."

"How close I came to losing you," the Tuʻitonga lamented.

Finau looked down, causing the tears to spill. "If you must leave us, Father, don't go there. Put your soul in a coconut. Anything. I can't stand the thought of you at the hands of your adversaries for all eternity."

"It was probably a dream," Lolohea said. "You were in the dark, having the life choked out of you."

"Then how did I get this?" Finau produced a folded leaf from his waistband. When he opened it, everyone beheld a sprinkle of Pulotu's purple sand. "I brought back a pinch of the afterlife."

The Tuʻitonga wanted to know the face of every adversary his son had seen in Pulotu. He wanted to develop a plan to his advantage. For now, though, there were more pressing matters. He took that packet of purple sand and tucked it in his waistband. "The Final Test will now commence," he told Matāpule Muʻa. "Get the girl ready. The deed shall be performed at the gates of the royal compound, where everyone can see."

"No," Lolohea said. "It's my test. It'll be just the two of us, no witnesses."

"Nonsense," the Tuʻitonga said. "We'll gather the entire island. It'll implant in them a searing collective memory of your stony nature."

Lolohea said, "It has to happen in the ferns outside the Tamahā's compound. Have the girl kneel so the fronds obscure her features."

"*Outside the Tamahā's compound?*" the Tuʻitonga mused. "That's bold. That'll send a delicious message."

"What message?" Lolohea asked.

"What message, indeed! Son, you're really starting to get this." The

Tu'itonga then saw the uncertainty in Lolo's eyes, the longing to avoid this, the worst test of all. "It'll be no pleasure, I grant that. But it'll take only a moment. You need only approach the girl, do the deed, and walk away. Don't even look back."

They heard the flapping of wings. Kōkī was descending.

"Kōkī," Finau called, and lifted a hand to receive his parrot.

But the bird came to rest upon the Tu'itonga's shoulder.

"So you move up in the world," Finau said.

Cocking his head, Kōkī asked, "Where Punake?"

"Yeah," Finau said. "Where's Punake? You said he'd be coming."

"It's complicated," Lolohea said. "We'll actually have to go get him."

"What do you mean, *go get him*?"

"All will be set right," the Tu'itonga said, making eye contact with each of his sons, that he might command their attention and speak some unifying and motivating words.

Matāpule Mu'a interrupted. "Just to confirm, I don't take the girl to the royal gates but to—"

"Fe'unga!" the Tu'itonga told the matāpule. "Your incompetence is staggering. Do you think you can enter the afterlife without me? Unless you wish to be stuck on this earth, living out your shame for the rest of your pathetic days, you'd better attune yourself to me." The Tu'itonga then turned to Kōkī. "Kōkī, you'll send the instructions instead. Go tell Pōhiva to meet us with the girl outside the Tamahā's compound."

"She must kneel in the ferns," Lolohea said. "Her face must be obscured by their fronds."

Kōkī bobbed his head, then repeated his instructions: "Pōhiva, girl, kill, Tamahā, kneel, fern, banana."

"No bananas!" Lolohea said.

Kōkī looked to the Tu'itonga. "No banana?"

"Yes, banana," the Tu'itonga said. "Much banana, but banana later."

Kōkī pinwheeled his eyes, thinking. Then he flew away.

"I'm a royal matāpule," Matāpule Mu'a said. "I can't be replaced by a bird!"

"Did you see that level of service?" the Tu'itonga asked Matāpule Mu'a. "For a banana. You steal tracts of land from me, entire islands."

The Tuʻitonga, now that he was on the topic of incompetent matāpule, felt a speech coming on. But he felt a sensation growing inside him. It came from deep within.

Finau studied his father's face. "What's going on?"

"Yes, Father," Lolohea asked. "Are you okay?"

"I think it's happening," the Tuʻitonga said.

"What's happening?" the Wayfinder asked.

"Get me to that niu tree," the Tuʻitonga commanded. "Right away!"

Pitching in, they guided him to a nearby coconut palm.

All this hope the Tuʻitonga was feeling, all this possibility, the tremendously bright future, the successful outcomes of all his designs—it was converting itself into urine, glorious, golden, hoped-for urine. This morning he'd felt so low he'd nearly given up, but now he felt the warmth of a life-affirming piss generating deep inside. When he neared the tree, he shook off his helpers and threw his arms around the trunk. When he held fast, cheek to bark, his hands were just able to clasp on the far side. His boys were alive. His rivals had been vanquished. He'd soon clip the Tamahā's wings. When he pushed, however, the warm sensation turned to pain. He pushed harder—a sharp, brutal throb followed. He spread his legs to sturdy his stance. Now he could really push. Yet to what avail? Try as he might, the Tuʻi of Tonga could produce none of the precious yellow fluid. Instead, he found himself trapped, unable to unclasp his hands without falling, unable to see or know what was happening below. It was the exact posture Punake had maintained during his castration.

The Tuʻitonga's entourage began walking toward the meadow of ferns, a journey that moved at the king's slow pace. Seven Fists's men took turns supporting him, which was awkward and laborious. But the king wouldn't allow himself be carried. His spirits were high, though. He solicited entertaining anecdotes of the voyage to Rotuma, where "an entire people'd been outsmarted by my sons." And in order to "honor" Punake's memory, the Tuʻitonga kept recalling the poet's most famous mistakes, moments of shame and colorful acts of foolishness, as when Punake attempted to seduce a Fefine Girl, or when, after a chief had taken murderous offense at a poetic portrayal, Punake begged the king to adopt him.

When Lolohea looked back, he saw they'd forgotten about Kaniva, still lashed to the outrigger. He remembered when they'd first seen her: standing amid the very firmament, reflected in the stillness of a predawn tidal flat. He wondered if he'd be able to tell any part of the story to Moon Appearing, if he could put into words that he hadn't meant to harm Kaniva, that her loss was a side effect of something he was forced to do.

When Seven Fists's men stopped for rest, the king had a private word with Lolohea. "Everything's going to plan," he said. "Just as you return, your uncle disappears. People will connect these things. In their minds, it'll be no coincidence that he falls as you rise. Might I suggest using my battle club to pass the Final Test? That would strike a note of continuity between your rule and mine."

When Lolohea assented, the king summoned a servant.

"No, I'll get it," Lolohea said. "It'll put me in mind of what I'm about to do."

To delay the unthinkable, Lolohea set out to fetch the weapon that would make it inevitable.

Inside the royal compound, Lolohea contemplated his inheritance—the servants, the gardens, the fulfillment of his every intention. These much-sought privileges asked only in return the forfeiture of his parents and all who'd served them.

The royal chamber smelled of sickness. His father's sleeping mats were hued by suffering—blood and sweat and urine. Lolohea couldn't imagine spending a night here, let alone showing it to Moon Appearing. Which made him think of ʻAta. Could Tonga be ruled remotely? Would matāpule make the voyage south to entertain his instructions? Could he and Moon Appearing pick up where they'd left off, he garlanding her with a belt of yellow blossoms? Or she, head on his shoulder, beneath the moon, sharing her concerns? And he, assuring her of the one thing he knew in the world: that he could protect her?

He came across his mother's feather box. There was a story behind every quill, and he knew them all. Rather than flipping through the feathers, he inhaled the scent entire—sandalwood, sky, his mother's hair. He had the illusion he could hear the wind these feathers had flown through.

He took up his father's meteor. This lonely piece of heaven had traversed the firmament, until what? Until it stumbled from the sky? Or was Tonga its destination, the place where it would finally breathe its fire? There was a resonance to the stone, the vibration of the oldest story. Yet who could interpret the meteor's ancient and unknown tongue?

At last, he came to his father's club. A simple device, cut from toa wood, lacking any fancy name. Yet there was a menace to the tool—it seemed to say: *I gladly convey death's aim.* When he took up the club, a catalog of fatality entered Lolohea. In flashes, he saw the face of every person the club had killed. All at once, he knew the multitudes the device had retired.

Should birds flutter down to inform a person he's inheriting a royal power? Should the god Tangaloa take a knee to offer human edification? The truth is that lightning doesn't flash. Lolohea's royal power came without him even knowing it: there was no "moment" when he realized he could hear inside the minds of others.

Outside, rain looked ready to fall. He strode past the family grave, stone darkened by earlier showers. Here was where Finau and 'Aho had grappled in darkness. Looking at the tomb, Lolohea heard the phrase *I do not climb the mountain.* It must've been one of Punake's many utterances, rolling around in his mind. Another thought leaked from the tomb: *When you're gone, Tonga continues being Tonga without you.* It gave him the shivers.

Atop the tomb sat a basket of remains. Lolohea had never really known the woman who possessed these bones, yet now they clearly asked, *What husband values a wife's soul above her life, her beating heart beneath his own devotion?*

Two Fefine Girls approached. Hair wet, they were returning from their morning bath.

Fresh rain had filled the bathing pool, so the girls smelled both of sky and earth.

"Lolo," Kakala said. "You've returned!" She thought: *He looks like he's seen a ghost.*

"And you're carrying a club," said Heilala. "We never see you with such a device." She thought, *If it's not a pigeon in his hand, it's a flower that he carries.*

The words they said mingled with the words they thought, leaving him very confused.

Lolohea asked, "Where's Moon Appearing? Is she not among you?"

Kakala and Heilala exchanged a look. *Why would he care about so rural a girl?*

Kakala said, "She's left our company."

"Recent events mark her as no longer one of us," Heilala said. "Now she lives with the Tamahā."

"Recent events?" Lolohea asked.

"Nothing worth the bother of mentioning," Kakala said. She tilted her head and offered Lolohea an alluring look. *If only he'd recline and place his head in my lap, I'd rub oil upon his chest, my long hair draping his body. Looking up, his only study would be of me.*

Lolohea blushed, and, seeing him blush, Kakala blushed as well.

A patter of rain, not enough to muddy the path. The tamped soil beneath his feet speaking of those who'd come before. Each step bringing him closer to the thing he must do. He passed sluices of taro. *Māhina Mate*, their broad leaves seemed to say. The last stage of the moon. The experience was like being on 'Ata, where your thoughts echoed back. Should he let his mind scatter? Or should he pull himself together and take charge of his faculties? Which would better lend itself to striking down an unknown girl?

Ahead was the Tamahā's compound, and, rounding a bend, he came to the meadow of ferns.

A field of extending fronds shook with taps of rain—when a drop knocked off other dangling drops, the fronds, unburdened, sprang up, only to slowly become weighed down once more. Before him, somewhere in the green, a girl was kneeling. He left the path and entered the ferns, their chilled arms wetting his midsection. Not far off, he could see his father and various others looking on from the hanging roots of an 'ovava tree. In the other direction was the Tamahā's living wall. He wondered if the Tamahā observed him from her compound. He wondered if Moon Appearing was at her side. What if Moon Appearing witnessed what he was about to do? What would she think of him? And simple as that, Moon Appearing was in his mind as he traversed the bracken. He heard her voice say, *Why didn't you listen to your aunt? She told you to never become separated from the other girls.*

Animated by rain, the expanse of fern seemed to grope and paw.

I'm not the kind of girl who secrets herself into the shade with young men, he heard. It was one of first things Moon Appearing had said to him on 'Ata. He looked again toward the Tamahā's compound but saw no sign of her.

He waded through the interlocking arms of ferns, knowing he'd eventually encounter this unnamed girl. He heard Moon Appearing's voice as if she were with him: *Why did you select me, and not some other?* It was the first question she'd asked him on 'Ata. He found his thoughts answering the memory of her words: *I do not select this girl, she has no connection to me, this has nothing to do with me, it's just a test I must pass.* But he had talked to Moon Appearing of tests, he'd heard her wonder aloud if she were being tested. Moon Appearing's voice again, no longer historical: *This is a test of love and mercy. To pass, one must fail, one must turn from death, one must wield the power of life.*

Not twenty paces away, he saw a figure in the green. A person was there, vision bound by a strip of tapa cloth. Her head cocked, listening. Lolohea didn't get a good look at her, but he knew she'd been trying to discern the approach of the one who'd do her harm. Lolohea didn't tread lightly, for there was no point in stealth. He glanced in the direction of his father, who watched intently, shielding his eyes from the rain. He seemed to whisper: *Do it. Don't hesitate. Act and walk away.*

As Lolohea neared the girl in the ferns, his eyes were on the Tamahā's compound—*Moon Appearing must be there*, he thought, her presence was so strong. And here was Moon Appearing's voice again, saying: *I'm the one who's being tested.* Then he was behind the kneeling girl, water tapping on her back, her ribs expanding as she drew shallow breaths. He had the illusion that Moon Appearing's mind had entered his. She thought: *I'll meet him at the cistern. Si'eta vaitupu fufū. Our secret cistern.*

How had Moon Appearing taken up residence in his mind? Why must he endure her voice, here, now, when it ran so counter to what he must do? Lolohea called out to the Tamahā's compound. "You're not being tested," he shouted. "I'm the one who must do my duty. You're the reason I must act. So we'll be free, free to change the rules, to remake Tonga, to make 'Ata ours if we desire."

The figure in the ferns tried to speak, but through a gag, her words couldn't be discerned.

His hands needed no direction to raise the club. One final task, and they were free.

I hear the clatter of water upon stone. He draws a ladle, and we drink in turn, Moon Appearing's voice said. *We quench one another. He rinses my feet with rainwater. I wash his long, wet locks. I hear the clatter of water . . .*

He wanted to stop the voice in his head as much as anything.

She's just a rural girl, he told himself. *One from a faraway island.*

Was that his thought or his father's? Or had Moon Appearing once said such a thing? He couldn't tell.

The sound, when he lowered the club, was the sound of a torn melon rind.

Call it what you will—Māhina Mate, Māhina Tō, Māhina Puli—the moon is no more.

When the sun sets, the entirety of the sky takes note, but the moon, the moon just slips away.

In considering the previous stages of the moon, we've contemplated how the moon appears to us. But how might we appear to the moon? Take, for example, the comet above. It visits once a lifetime. No person sees it twice, which means when the comet makes its eventual return, all of us have been refreshed, our footprints wiped from the beach of life. So we are eternal strangers to this object. Yet again and again, the moon glimpses our nightly labors, obsessions, carnalities, mischief-making, and avengements. Sure, by the moon's light there's some good-natured net-mending and coconut-crab hunting. But does the moon not also see which clans spark torches to illuminate the path of retribution? Does the moon not observe who rubs oil onto bodies that resist and struggle? Or which armadas quietly embark by solstice stars?

Does the moon remember? Does it tabulate the cruelty below? What harm do we do the moon simply by being human beneath her gaze? One could wish the moon died nightly, if only that she be born unburdened the next eve, free from a backlog of human depravity. No celestial order could be so cruel as to ask the moon to eternally bear witness to the hand of human suffering. Or could it? Should we hope the moon is nightly extinguished and replaced with a virginal moon, one that looks similar enough that we don't ask questions? Would we be able to identify these replacement moons? Doesn't one Fefine Girl look pretty much like another? And just as all servants appear the same and our enemies bear resemblance, we might take these different moons as one. If so, then each moonset is not a slumber. It means that *Māhina Mate* is not a metaphor. What is it to be born to die? What does it mean that we do not mourn?

Questions, questions—who has time for questions? Why ask, when the answers aren't easy? Best to simply return to our evening tasks. Down darkened lanes, in pink-tinted surf, in unlit fale or reflected in the shine of coconut oil, we carry on, agreeing to ignore the silent witness above until our deeds are complete.

Rain on a field of ferns. Drops tapping Lolohea's face.

He couldn't see the girl slumped beneath the green, but a final thought was lodged in her mind: *I learn to dance my own dance.*

He tried to drop the club, but his hand wouldn't let go.

His father, half a field away, beckoned. "The boy has earned his kava!" he called.

Lolohea began moving toward his family.

The boy actually did it, his father was thinking. *He found the strength.*

When Lolohea reached his father, the man was being supported by three warriors. Despite his sallow color and pallid features, the Tuʻitonga was beaming. "Come, let's distance ourselves from this lurid tableau. We retire to the royal compound!"

Doubts, the Tuʻitonga thought. *Years and years of doubts, vanquished with a single stroke.*

"Father," Lolohea said. "I think I'll live on ʻAta. That's where I'll rule from."

The Tuʻitonga thought, *ʻAta? What wild notion will the boy take up next? A little distraction, and he'll soon forget this latest whim.*

"As you wish," the Tuʻitonga said, smiling. "But don't direct your desires toward me. It's now Tonga's duty to fulfill your desires."

His mother embraced him. "That was difficult, but it's behind you."

They separated, and Pōhiva examined him. She thought, *His father was right, the boy just needed hardening. Hardening and a hand to steer him.*

The Wayfinder offered a wooden smile. "Congratulations," he said, thinking, *If Lolohea will kill an innocent girl, he'll kill anyone.*

Finau said nothing. He thought only, *Did Lolo not have feelings for her? Had he not opened his heart to Moon Appearing?*

Lolohea cocked his head. He looked to Matāpule Muʻa. "Just who was that girl?"

The poor boy, Matāpule Muʻa thought. *Always a step behind. It'll take more than one matāpule to manage him.* "I hereby certify the Final Test. The transfer of power will take place right now, at—"

Lolohea turned toward the ferns, his feet taking guarded steps in that direction. He saw in the distance that the Tamahā had left her compound. Two security men advanced with her through the ferns. Was he able to know other people's minds but not his own? Shouldn't he have known whether the girl before him was Moon Appearing? He began to run. *Moon Appearing,* he thought. A future with her had kept him going in the Fisian islands, a return to her had allowed him to become another person in Rotuma, Moon Appearing was the only landfall he thought of when they were lost in the storm.

Pōhiva called after him. "Come, my son."

But he kept going, club in hand, and when he reached the Tamahā, her men were each bearing a foot as they dragged away a body, obscured by green. Had he not washed those feet? Had he ever been more himself than when he was with her?

The Tamahā's eyes were red with fury. "Don't brandish a weapon at me," she said, lifting her Fan. "I can't stop you from killing girls. But you can't stop me from retrieving her, from making sure her bones make it home to her parents."

"Is it truly her?" Lolohea asked. "Have I done what I think I've done?"

The Tamahā didn't answer. She nodded at her men to continue removing the girl.

"But on 'Ata," Lolohea said, "I adorned her, I attended her."

"Faster," the Tamahā told her men.

"Don't you see?" Lolohea asked. "I could never have done this. I showed her the secret cistern. On the cliffs, we stood with frigate birds. Together, we weaved garments. I'm not the man who did this."

The Tamahā began moving backward, Fan still directed at him. "You did do this, and what matter if the blow felled one girl or another? A young woman is gone. Hold yourself only partly to blame, however. It was your parents who arranged this piece of subterfuge."

"You were the one who put this in my mind," Lolohea said. "You described the ferns, the low light. Mentally, you put the club in my hands."

"I did so to make it *less* likely that you'd go through with it, that if you really thought about what was asked of you, you'd refuse. You're still thinking you killed the wrong girl. Rather than that you killed any girl at all."

"That's Tonga's doing," he said. "Not mine."

Excuses, she thought, *suffice only for the self*.

"Let me see her," Lolohea demanded.

Even as he said this, he knew her features would be distorted by the blow.

"I've long suspected something," the Tamahā said. "And now I know it to be true."

Lolohea paused. "What's that?"

She didn't speak. But she thought, *He'll be worse than his father*.

"Worse than my father?" Lolohea asked. "My father's not a bad man."

The Tamahā's eyes went wide. "Quickly, now," she told her men. She looked to her compound, where she'd be safe.

Lolohea watched them back away. He regarded the Tamahā, how thin she was, how she adorned herself with common feathers, fanned in her white hair.

"Just tell me," he said. "Can you revive her? Are you able to bring her back?"

"Of course," she said. "I could awaken her right now. But I can't unbreak her head. In the future, you should consider killing girls by drowning or strangulation. Victims like that I can easily restore. But of course this one was special, wasn't she? This one you and your parents meant to take from me forever."

THIRTY-EIGHT

KŌRERO:
THE BRINK OF EXTINCTION

And so, Fan in hand, my people behind me, I found myself walking toward a bathing pond occupied by a dangerous man. My mother stopped us where the canopy was dense. "We need a poem from you," she told Finau. "It must speak of bravery, of monumental deeds."

"Poetry?" my father asked. "At a time like this?"

"I've got to act before I lose my nerve," Tapoto said. "What if my blessing wears off?" He wiped his cheek to confirm the soot was still there, then was horrified to see he'd rubbed some away.

Finau, confused, said, "Maybe poetry can wait till after we kill my uncle."

Tiri asked, "Didn't we assure the Tamahā that her nephew would live?"

"The lines you recite," my mother said to Finau. "Haven't you noticed they . . ."

"They what?" he asked.

"You know," I said. "When your poetry speaks of wind, a gust kicks up. When your verse evokes a whale, we suddenly hear one. It happened with flying fish and parrots and frigate birds."

"One of your poems referenced a nonu tree," my mother said. "And what was our first meal upon landing?"

"That's all coincidence," Finau said. "Poetry's filled with imagery."

"If it's coincidence, then where's the harm?" I asked.

"Humor them," the Wayfinder said. "Just get it over with."

"All right," Finau said to me. "But don't forget your pledge to kill 'Aho. You have the Fan. This is our chance."

I'll admit I'd been pondering what the Tamahā had said—about human frailty and having sympathy for the broken and the ill-fated.

"She's not going to kill him," Tapoto said. "I am. Or, I mean, not *kill* him, just defeat him. What I'm trying to say is, I'm the one who's *not* going to do the—" Here, he got flustered and quit.

To Finau, I said, "Just open your mind to poetry. Say whatever comes. But, you know, some lightning bolts wouldn't hurt."

"Fine," he said. Then he uttered a line from an ancient Tongan poem:

Ngāahi 'ūmata monosi	*Rainbows mend*
ha 'uhila tapa i langi.	*a lightning-rended sky.*

"All right," said my mother, striving for patience. "How about lines recounting an epic act?"

Finau closed his eyes, reciting:

Tetē ngāahi 'ao'ao fufula,	*Puffy clouds, drifting by,*
tamate'i e mālohi 'o e la'ā.	*extinguished the might of the sun.*

"*Puffy clouds?*" my mother asked. "That's worse than rainbows!"

"*Mother*," I said. I told Finau, "Just say whatever comes to mind."

"Fe'unga," Finau said. He then repeated these words:

'Ahi'ahi'i kotoa e foaki a mamaha,	*Having sampled all the shallows had to offer,*
foki e 'anga ki he moana.	*the shark returned to the deep.*

"Good, good," my mother said, though her face suggested failure. "That'll have to do."

"Am I the shark?" Tapoto asked.

Several people said, "No."

Tapoto looked wounded. His eyes kept going to the trees ahead, beyond which our fates awaited. "You're no shark," I told him. "Sharks are cold and indifferent. You're the one the whale spoke to. You're the one who carries his people on his back."

Sun Shower neared him. "That's right," she said. "You have a big heart and a brave spirit." She thumbed stray smudges from his face, though to others it must've looked like she wiped away tears.

The matāpule led the way. We put a fly whisk in the crimped hand of his nonfunctional arm, so his impairment might be less visible. When we broke through the trees into the open space around the pool, 'Aho was the only man to be seen. Chest-deep in water, he was attended by several lovely women. They massaged his scalp, oiled his shoulders, and plied him with pleasing, inaudible comments. More Fefine Girls—looking wary and uncertain—watched from the beach.

'Aho turned in the water to face us. "Another matāpule?" he asked. "I just got rid of one." He began wading our way, wringing his long hair and pulling it back. He was of no special height or frame, and, while he was well-built, there was nothing notably imposing about him. As he neared, he seemed to realize there was a group of us. "What have we here?" he asked.

"Where's his limp?" Tapoto asked. He turned to Finau. "You said he was injured."

"He must've gotten better," Finau said.

"You told me he could barely walk," Tapoto snapped.

It was then that 'Aho discovered the Tongan princes were before him. "You two," 'Aho said, his face lighting with anger. 'Aho began running at us, clearly intending to attack Finau and the Wayfinder. I lifted the Fan, to show 'Aho we were not defenseless, but I must've moved it too fast: there was a great crack in the sky, a flash of light, and for a moment we were blinded. I scrambled low for cover, not realizing the strike had come from me. When my sight came back, 'Aho was studying me, the ink about my mouth and chin, the Fan in my hand, and the Tamahā's sooty blessing, visible on my face.

Sweet Sun Shower started shouting at 'Aho. "We've brought a man from far away, and he's going to destroy you. Destroy you!" She pointed at Tapoto. "He's big and strong, and he's not afraid of you."

Tapoto declared, "I have no fear." Whether he believed these words or not, I couldn't tell.

'Aho kept his attention on me. "How'd you get that Fan?" When I didn't answer, he extended his hand, expecting, I guess, for me to hand it over. He said, "I've seen that Fan husk a man and ribbon his skin into the trees. Are you prepared for that?"

The hand before me was stamped with a jellyfish. It'd taken lives, broken bodies, undone spirits. And it had compensated its victims with nothing but a black forget-me-not. I wafted the Fan at 'Aho—quite lightly, for I was much afraid of the device's power. I intended only to get this ugly hand away from me. Instead, the entire man staggered backward.

"Who are you?" he asked. "Do you know the nature of the men you shield?" He pointed at Finau. "This one sealed me alive in a tomb. And the other sold my son into slavery."

I asked, "Your son, who killed an innocent girl from Rotuma?"

"Ah," 'Aho said. "I see they've been telling you stories."

Here's where I learned the value of a matāpule.

"We come with a proposition," Dead Matāpule said.

Though the matāpule was clearly alive, I'd started thinking of him as Dead Matāpule. Once you've seen someone's corpse, it's hard to think of them another way.

"I don't deal with matāpule," 'Aho said to me. "Tell these *princes* to reveal the location of my son."

I held the Fan like a knife, but that only revealed my trembling hand.

"We propose a duel," Dead Matāpule said. "Should you lose, you'll depart forever."

"You don't seem to know much about fighting to the death," 'Aho countered. "How does a dead man take his leave?"

Dead Matāpule said, "Should you prove victorious, the location of your son will be revealed to you."

'Aho said, "Tell me where my son is, and I'll leave right now."

"This is one of his refrains," the Wayfinder said. "Declaring his immediate intentions to leave. Yet he never goes away."

Dead Matāpule said, "We propose a duel that concludes not with death, but with the first drop of blood."

"Someone wants to fight me, yet emerge unscathed?" 'Aho asked in disbelief. He moved to Finau. "Is this format designed to protect you?" Before Finau could respond, 'Aho decided not. He turned his attention to the Wayfinder, who received only a snort of dismissal. 'Aho sized up my father—wrinkles about his eyes and gray at his temples—before scanning rapidly past all our older men and women. Even though 'Aho had been told Tapoto was his opponent, even though Tapoto had declared he had no fear, 'Aho strained to look behind Tapoto, as if a fierce warrior were perhaps hidden by Tapoto's great bulk.

"Don't pretend you don't recognize the man who'll defeat you," Sun Shower said.

'Aho turned his attention to her. "You look familiar," he said.

"I'd better," she said.

"We've spent some time together, haven't we?" he asked, letting his eyes roam her body. "We've had dealings?"

"You like the looks of me?" she asked. "You'll see my face for all eternity, because this is your last day."

'Aho smiled with delight. "If the duel's with her, then I accept."

"I beat you once already," Sun Shower said. "And you don't even know it."

'Aho's smile slipped away. He took a step toward her. "Tell me your name, again."

Dead Matāpule intervened. "The duel will take place here and now, and the results will be final. Do you agree to face your challenger?"

"Will my challenger face me?" 'Aho asked Finau, stepping close to him. "Are we not meant for a rematch?" Here, 'Aho reached out to Finau, perhaps to see if Finau would flinch. When Finau didn't, 'Aho fit his hand to the black jellyfish on Finau's neck. "I know you're afraid of me," 'Aho said. "Why don't we skip all this *duel* business? Just tell me where my boy is."

"He doesn't know," the Wayfinder said. "I do."

'Aho turned to the Wayfinder. "Tell me where I can find my son, and I'll depart. I'll take my girls, and you'll never hear from us again."

"You're not taking anyone," Sun Shower said. "We're not possessions."

"Aren't you?" 'Aho asked. "Don't ambitious parents willingly surrender their prized daughters? Did your parents not relinquish you to be properly trained and suitably matched?"

"Leave her alone," Tapoto said. He took a breath. "Will you fight me or no?"

'Aho's attention remained on Sun Shower. He showed her his jellyfish. "Tell me we do not match."

Tapoto stepped between the two. "I've undergone more drills than you can imagine," he warned 'Aho. "Don't make me unleash that on you."

"Just leave," Sun Shower told 'Aho. "Any girl who wishes to join you is free to do so."

"Don't you want to return to your war?" the Wayfinder asked 'Aho. "Where murder and assault are acceptable pastimes?"

"*Return?*" 'Aho asked. "Don't you get it? The war is here. It's in the food you eat, in your pleasant evenings and long nights of deep sleep."

"I have a feeling," Sun Shower said, "that when you leave, the war'll go with you."

"Just tell me where my son is," 'Aho said, "and you'll find out."

"It's not as simple as knowing his location," the Wayfinder said. "The journey to him will be no simple voyage. The rains have started, the winds reverse. At night, the stars are only sporadically visible. And the currents in the corridors you'll enter are treacherous. Plus, waiting ahead is a special nautical danger you've likely never encountered."

"And what's that?" 'Aho asked.

The Wayfinder didn't answer. Instead, he turned to Tapoto. "Can you beat him?"

Tapoto looked to us, his people. He looked into our eyes. Assured of our faith in him, he nodded.

"Agree to our duel," the Wayfinder told 'Aho, "and should you win, I'll take you to your son."

"Never," Finau said.

"Don't do it," my mother said. The anxiety in her voice revealed a truth: she believed Tapoto would lose.

"It's not worth it," I told the Wayfinder.

'Aho seemed amused by our regard for one another. "I accept your offer to navigate, except for one thing: Should it not be commensurate with the navigation services Havea offered you?"

"How's that?" the Wayfinder asked.

To Finau, 'Aho asked, "How long was Six Fists conscripted to serve your father?"

"A decade, more or less," Finau said.

"*A decade*," 'Aho repeated. "And don't forget Punake. How many years did he donate?"

"About the same," Finau confessed.

'Aho turned to the Wayfinder. "How many years did Havea give?"

"Nine," the Wayfinder admitted.

Here, 'Aho offered his first genuine smile, a true, hollow-socketed grin.

"Nine years your navigator?" the Wayfinder asked.

"Agree to that," 'Aho said, "and I'll accept your terms, whatever they may be."

I turned to the Wayfinder. "We'll find our way. We've survived adversity before. There's no need to do what you're doing. It's worse than risking your life." While I spoke, his eyes roamed the royal bathing pond, the disheveled Fefine Girls, and this, the island of his birth. "Hey," I said, shaking his shoulder. "We get a say in this. And we don't want to lose you. I don't want to lose you."

A calm resolved itself in the Wayfinder's eyes. "This is the only way."

I wanted to wake him up. For being so selfish, I wanted to slap him.

"It's agreed, then," Dead Matāpule said. "A duel will commence here and now between Tapoto and 'Aho. The victor will draw the first drop of blood. Should Tapoto prevail, his opponent will depart Tonga, alone, never to return. Should 'Aho win, the location of his son will be revealed, and the Wayfinder will become indentured for nine years."

"Such an ugly term, *indentured*," 'Aho said. "Let's just say he'll lend me his service."

Dead Matāpule asked Tapoto, "Any other terms? They've been relinquished to you."

Tapoto must've been reassured to know his blood would not be spilled, at least not beyond a drop. But harder to swallow was the notion that another might have to pay his debts. "We'll fight with thin spears," Tapoto said, and the Kohimu brothers quickly set out to strip and sharpen a pair of green branches. When finished, they looked more like skewers one would use to cook fish over an open flame. When handed his spear, 'Aho examined it in amusement, bending it back and forth before discarding it.

"Just do your best," the Wayfinder told Tapoto. "No one asks any more of you."

Dead Matāpule took the fly whisk from his crimped hand. Waving it, he signaled for the duel to commence. 'Aho asked him, "Say—aren't you the matāpule from earlier?" With a note of reluctant admiration, 'Aho added, "Even death doesn't stop you from insinuating yourself into every proceeding."

Seizing upon a distracted opponent, Tapoto advanced at full speed. He dived, tucked, and, coming out of a roll, struck at 'Aho from below, thrusting his spear upward at 'Aho's abdomen. Unfortunately, the strike came up short, leaving the tip hovering in empty air. 'Aho took hold of the spear. With a jerk, it was wrested from Tapoto's hands and cast aside. Tapoto, sprawled on his back, was breathing heavily. It was clear he'd had no plan beyond this.

"What's happening?" Tiri called out. "Is there blood?"

"To your feet!" my father shouted, a command Tapoto obeyed.

"Hands up," Mama Mānunu called, and up went Tapoto's hands.

'Aho approached him and delivered a sharp uppercut to Tapoto's gut, dropping him to his knees and lowering his hands. It was the same tummy punch Finau had landed.

Tiri recognized Tapoto's groan. "Oof," she said in sympathy.

Next, 'Aho clapped a powerful, open-handed slap across Tapoto's face. It turned Tapoto's head and closed his eyes in pain.

"No blood," 'Aho announced.

Now I understood the man's plan—a long, bloodless beating was in store.

My mother gave me a look suggesting all was lost.

"Get up," shouted Sun Shower. "Defend yourself!"

Tapoto staggered to his feet, half his face bright pink.

"Take him down," Finau suggested. "Use your weight to your advantage."

Tapoto lowered his head. He spread his arms, fingers wide, like a crab. Then he ran at 'Aho. It must be said that Tapoto's balance was off from that clap to the head. He'd not yet caught his breath. And not long ago, he'd been too sick to even stand. 'Aho easily sidestepped this attack. As Tapoto went past, 'Aho took hold of a finger, and with a quick motion, broke it backward. The event made no sound, except inside my head. Tapoto called out in pain and regarded his dislocated finger in horror.

"Any blood?" 'Aho asked Dead Matāpule, who shook his head.

"Breathe," Finau counseled.

"Evade him," my father called out. "Give yourself time to recover."

The Wayfinder watched these proceedings with disbelief on his face. Nine years.

As 'Aho sauntered toward Tapoto, Tapoto, holding his injured hand, circled away.

"Use the Fan," Sun Shower urged me. "The Tamahā gave you the Fan for a reason."

I didn't know why I'd been given the Fan, but it wasn't to slay the woman's nephew.

'Aho closed the distance. When 'Aho feigned a strike, Tapoto's hands went out in self-defense. Seizing one of these hands, 'Aho turned the palm awkwardly, wrenching the arm and twisting it behind Tapoto's back. Here, the arm—straightened and fully extended—was ready to be broken. 'Aho lifted his elbow high to deliver the blow.

"Give me the Fan," Sun Shower pleaded.

When I didn't, she ran full speed at 'Aho, hitting him square in the back and knocking him down at the edge of the pond. She landed atop 'Aho, who managed to turn under her so the two were face-to-face. She shouted for Tapoto to aid her. Looking almost amused at this turn of events, 'Aho asked, "How have you kept yourself from me for so long?"

Dead Matāpule mused on this development. "Were 'Aho to have a matāpule," he said, "that matāpule might object to a young woman joining the duel. I'd naturally counter that 'Aho had relinquished the duel's terms to his opponent. And if ʻAho's matāpule pointed out that Sun Shower was larger than ʻAho, I'd remind him that ʻAho himself was heard to desire a duel with her."

Sun Shower straddled ʻAho, whose legs were on dry land, but whose torso was enough in the pond that he had to strain to keep his face above the shin-deep water.

Tapoto scrambled to join Sun Shower, dropping his full weight upon ʻAho's midsection. Together, they had the dangerous fellow hopelessly pinned. ʻAho, who expressed no awareness of the danger he was in, looked up at Sun Shower in awe. "You're a powerful woman," he said.

"I'm from Tafahi," Sun Shower said. "There, you have to be strong. But it's a different kind of strong than you understand." She placed her palms upon his chest. "You're probably not used to women laying hands upon you."

"Tafahi," he said. "Maybe one day I'll visit. I should like to see the place that made you."

Sun Shower leaned forward, her chest, and much of her weight, now squarely above ʻAho's face.

ʻAho gazed upward. "I've always felt like I was from a rural island," he said. "One so far away it didn't have a name or any other inhabitants, a place where the only customs were my own. Do you know how hard it is to find someone to join you on your island of one?"

He searched her eyes, trying to determine, perhaps, whether she might be the kind to join him. He moved to speak, but he'd already uttered his last words.

When she bore down, so did Tapoto, forcing ʻAho's face underwater. Now ʻAho was represented by a pair of arms that, rather than fighting, seemed to be searching, like he was reaching to take the hand of someone who'd help him. At the end, when he must've been losing his air, ʻAho touched Sun Shower's face, feeling the outlines of her chin and cheeks and lips, not dissimilar from the way Tiri would trace the features of someone she wished to remember. At last, his hands dropped. This was followed by a long quiet, during which Tapoto and Sun Shower, pressed together as one, dared not move. Soon, a cloud of muddy water obscured ʻAho's face, erasing him. Only now did Sun Shower and Tapoto relent. They stood—she muddied, he bruised—and embraced without speaking.

The Fefine Girl named Kakala approached 'Aho's half-submerged body. She kicked him in the side and gasped when bubbles escaped his sunken face.

I turned to Dead Matāpule. "Is he dead? Do you certify it?"

Dead Matāpule looked at the lifeless figure before us. "He's dead."

Of the Tongan brothers, I asked, "Did we fulfill our end of the bargain?"

No one looked more relieved than the Wayfinder. He nodded.

"Is 'Ata ours?" I demanded.

"The island's yours," Finau said.

Here, I walked to the dead man. His body had seen more abuse than I'd first noticed. His legs and forearms were covered with scars. But it was the parts I couldn't see that bothered me. I kept thinking of his mouth and eyes open to the water. Of mud in his lungs and empty tooth sockets. I remembered his remote island, inhabited by a single person.

"Tapoto," I said. "Drag him out of the water."

"What? Why?" Tapoto asked.

"Just do it," I said.

I finally understood why I'd been given the Fan.

※

After dragging 'Aho's body out of the water, Tapoto began an animated retelling of the man's demise. It turned out Tapoto was a pretty good storyteller. I wanted to hear every word, but I had work to do. I went to 'Aho and crouched beside him. His dead eyes were open, pupils wide and fixed. What had he beheld, at the end?

I gave him the tiniest waft of the Fan. His eyes began receiving the world as a newborn would.

I asked, "Did you go to your island of one?"

His expressionless eyes swiveled toward me. When I wafted him again, his lips parted. "You probably assume this is a sad occasion for me," he said. "But I've died before."

"How'd you end up this way?"

"What, drowned in a pond?"

"No, as a man who harms others."

His eyes traced the tree limbs above. "My journey is one of many paths."

"I know your uncle tried to kill you," I said. "And your brother sent you to war. But you're more than what happened to you. You have a say in who you are."

"You think I chose this life?"

"Was there a moment when another path appeared, when you could've gone a different way?"

"Why'd you awaken me?" he asked.

"I'm worried," I said. "I'm worried about Tapoto. We don't believe in hurting people."

'Aho's eyes flashed to Tapoto, arms wide, voice booming, as he regaled everyone.

"You talking about the big fellow?" 'Aho asked. "He seems to be doing just fine."

"I'm worried about him for later, when it sinks in that he killed a man. If I called him over, would you forgive him?"

"For killing me?" 'Aho chuckled. "That's a good one. It's almost worth the cost of being revived. But I know how the Fan gets used around here. Men are brought back, toyed with a bit, then extinguished at one's convenience. So do me the favor—send me on my way."

"You're not being toyed with. I've got to do something, something very important, and it makes me worried for myself."

"What do you have to do?"

"We're a nonviolent people," I said. "So I've never hurt anyone."

"Who're you going to hurt?"

"You."

There was a terrible scream. When I turned to see the matter, it was Kakala. She was looking at me, horrified. "She's talking to him," she called to the others. "She brought him back to life!"

Everyone gathered around me at the water's edge.

"What're you doing?" Tapoto practically shouted.

Sun Shower looked at me, shock on her face. "You can't play around with him. Do you know how dangerous he is, do you understand what he's done to us?"

'Aho strained to see the faces of those above him. I gave him the slightest waft of my Fan, which allowed him to turn his head.

"Stop it!" Kakala called out. "Stop this nightmare!"

"I won't let him hurt anyone," I said.

I looked to my mother. Silently, she shook her head. But I had to make my own decisions.

"What would you do with another life?" I asked 'Aho.

"You can't do this!" Sun Shower shouted.

I cracked the Fan into the sky—a blinding light, a rolling boom, of which all Tonga took note.

I asked 'Aho again, "What would you do with a new life?"

He looked from me to the others. "I should not have gone to war," he said. "I should've run, at all cost. I should not have taken the lessons of the Tu'ilifuka. And my poor wife, I would never have—"

"That's your old life," I said. "I'm talking about a *new* life, what would you do with that?"

"I could never have a new life," 'Aho said. "The things I've done, there's no way to escape them."

"What if you could?"

He rolled his head to look at the black jellyfish on his hand. "I'd be recognized wherever I went."

"I could fix that," I said. "I know a man. His name is Papa Toki. He has a good life. He's a father and a husband. He does his share of labor, though there are things he can't do. Still, he's a jovial fellow and he makes his contribution."

"Yes?" 'Aho asked.

"All this Papa Toki does with only one arm."

"What happened to his other arm?" 'Aho asked.

"That doesn't matter." I called out, "Bring me a flake of obsidian. And a blade jagged enough to saw bone." To 'Aho, I said, "I've never actually removed a limb, but I've seen it done, and I'm pretty sure I can do it. Soon you won't be able to mark anyone, and without the jellyfish, no one'll associate you with who you once were. It'll give you a chance."

'Aho looked at me in disbelief. "But why—why would you help me?"

"Because it's who we are," I said. I tapped his right arm. "Feel that?"

He shook his head.

"He doesn't even get the pain?" Sun Shower asked. "You revive him, you're going to release him, and he doesn't even get to taste the suffering he caused?"

"He did get murdered today," I said. "And he's going to lose a limb."

Someone arrived with the blades, a hatchet head, and a nearly see-through flake of obsidian.

The Wayfinder neared me. "You sure you know what you're doing?"

"No," I said, and then I asked him to hold the Fan while I worked.

"You never relinquish the Fan," he said, his tone sharp. "Unless you do so forever."

I looked to him, a little shocked.

"The Fan can make the cut," he said. "And do so cleanly."

I placed my foot on 'Aho's forearm. "Prepare for a new life with your son," I told him.

'Aho looked suddenly afraid. "What if I'm bad for him? What if he's better off without me?"

"Maybe that was the case with his old father," I said. "You have a chance to be his new one."

'Aho closed his eyes and nodded.

I aimed the Fan at 'Aho's wrist.

"Wait," Tapoto said. "Papa Toki's entire arm was missing. You aim to take but the hand."

"That's where the ink is," I said. "And without a hand, he can wield no club."

"With his arm," Arawiwi said, "he could still wrap up a woman and hold her against her will."

"Yeah," Mama Mānunu said, "while his other hand plied its dark trade."

"We're removing his dominant hand," I countered.

A Kohimu brother said, "Losing two hands would truly humble a fellow."

"Take the arm at the elbow," my father said. "Nothing sinister could be done without a forearm."

The other Kohimu brother advocated taking a foot, too. "Then he'd have to hop. No one-footed man ever gave chase to a woman."

"But his power resides in his hand," I said. "That's the whole point of the amputation."

Thus began a cycle of deliberation, with various folks favoring different levels of amputation, a conversation that quickly descended into grievances over the outcomes of past discussions, with plenty of ire from those perceiving themselves to be less heard than others. Papa Mānunu suggested taking 'Aho's eyesight. Tiri countered that losing one's eyes could actually make a person stronger.

"What about his balls?" Mama Mānunu asked.

"This quickly?" I asked everyone. "Is this how fast you forget who we are?"

Almost bitterly, my mother said, "Just snuff him."

"No, Mother," I said, raising the Fan. Then I lowered it like a knife. At first it didn't seem to have done anything. There was no sound. Maybe I expected some fire or light. But when I nudged the hand, it moved independent of the wrist, a cauterized cut becoming visible.

Kakala came forward to regard the dismembered hand. Already it was losing its color. "He'll never mark anyone again?" she asked.

"Or take up a club," I said.

Heilala asked, "And he'll never return?"

'Aho shook his head.

Sun Shower studied 'Aho, who remained on his back. "I killed you," she told him. "A Fefine Girl did this to you. We can salt your sleep again."

I restored 'Aho with three wafts of the Life-Affecting Fan. He stood, looking uncertain.

The Wayfinder said, "Your son is on the island of Kao."

"The *volcanic* island of Kao?" 'Aho asked.

"Steer for the setting star Masisi," the Wayfinder said. "And beware: underwater vents make the currents treacherous. You must approach from the west."

'Aho glanced at Sun Shower. "Yes, you killed me," he acknowledged. "But death is nothing."

"You're right," she said. "It's life that matters."

'Aho turned to go, but by chance he noticed something on the ground. It was his right hand. He bent to retrieve this lost piece of himself, but stopped in shock at the sight of a handless arm reaching to grasp an armless hand. Looking shaken, and stumbling somewhat, he took his leave of us.

THIRTY-NINE

WHERE WAVES EVER CREST

A WORD ON HANDLING METEORS
AND A CAUTION AGAINST LOOKING
DOWN UPON THE MOON

Tonga's matāpule began planning for the king's death. Vaka were sent to rural islands, commanding elaborate funereal feasts for the dying Tuʻitonga, as well as grand inaugural banquets for his son. But how were hard-pressed islands to meet these demands? Fruit trees don't suddenly produce second crops. Sweet potatoes won't spontaneously mature. What were small islands to do, if in the Sacred South our own insufficient harvests were bolstered only by war?

How does the depletion of our resources connect to dominion over heavenly objects? It has to do with appetites. Why do we hunger to have the moon kneel down? From whence did we develop a desire to make the moon submit? The impulse is real. You've seen men facing east come evening along the oyster-colored cliffs of ʻEua or atop the spires of ʻAta. From these vantages, men place themselves above the sea-dawning moon. Looking down on Māhina herself, that's where men get their dangerous notions of dominion. Could men make a species extinct or a forest disappear if they didn't first see the moon as beneath them?

The next Tuʻitonga must make certain practices tapu. The handling of meteors should straightaway be forbidden. Gazing at stars reflected in the water, sailing to meet comets, and looking down upon the moon—all these should be prohibited. For only after engaging in such practices does the reduction of the earth become imaginable. Once a man hefts a chunk of heaven, once stars become but freckles on the face of the lagoon, what's left to stand in the human way?

The Tuʻitonga's entourage departed the scene of Moon Appearing's demise, heading for the royal compound, where Lolohea would become king. Unable to take more than a step or two, the Tuʻitonga finally consented to being carried. But manhandling the Tuʻitonga was no simple affair. After a hundred paces, the men lowered him so they could catch their breath and better coordinate their carry. Lolohea went to his father's side.

"Have I been duped?" Lolohea asked him. "Was I tricked into taking something precious from myself?"

"The Tamahā is to blame. She groomed that girl against us. You've been spared the worse fate: having the girl you care about become your lifelong adversary."

"But did you *know*, Father? Did you mean for me to destroy the thing I cared about most? Was this a test upon a test?"

Instead of answering, the Tuʻitonga scanned the rain clouds. He thought, *If only I could convey that whatever hurt the son hurt the father more. A father and son breathe the same breath, share the same blood, but pain, pain should belong only to parents.* "Shed your fear of death, son, and life will take its course. Death is nothing. And life, life's but a single wave crest."

"So life doesn't matter? Moon Appearing didn't matter?"

"My brother reminded me that Tonga would continue being Tonga without him. It was perhaps the truest thing he ever said. Tonga will continue being Tonga without me because of you, son. That matters."

"Those words, I heard them spoken today," Lolohea said. "About Tonga continuing to be Tonga."

"Spoken by whom?"

"When I passed by the family grave, they emanated from inside."

"Under no circumstances are you to open that tomb."

Lolohea didn't understand. "But, Father, how would you get to the afterlife?"

"Do not open that grave. When I die, just bury me on 'Ata."
"What about your eternity?"
"You're my eternity."

Inside the royal compound, the Tu'itonga was set down beside a ceremonial bowl of kava, its surface dappled by raindrops. To humble himself, he summoned a piece of char from the firepit. With this, he struck a line down each cheek. Rain, mixing with soot, made him appear to weep dark tears.

Rings of important men formed around the king. Matāpule Mu'a began a speech, the contents of which Lolohea didn't hear. Three village chiefs squeezed in next to him. One looked at Lolohea garishly, thinking, *By being the first to seize the new Tu'itonga's attention, I shall wrest back my stolen plantation.*

Another wondered whether he should offer the new Tu'itonga his eldest daughter or youngest.

The third thought, *I know Lolohea's weakness for pigeons. By gifting him the island's last flock, I shall indebt him to me.*

The Tu'itonga stirred the kava, lifting scoops high and pouring them back. Lolohea approached and knelt down. The Tu'itonga filled a coconut shell and held it dripping between them. In a subdued voice, so that others might not hear, he asked his son, "In whom will you place your trust? Your brothers, of course. Your wife, when you meet her. Eventually, your own sons and daughters. Who'll you turn to in the meantime? I've always sought counsel in the natural world. Note the frigate bird. Ever he faces the buffeting wind. This bird has no history. He does not reflect or regret. Instead, he angles himself into the next gust."

"It's not what's to come that concerns me," Lolohea said. "How do I undo what's just happened?"

"Relinquish the past." When Lolohea moved to speak, the father shook his head. "Drink, my son."

Lolohea took the shell and downed the kava, bitter like puddle water.

Seeing this, the father's face softened, not into a smile, but a look that said, *It's done.* Disturbingly, he reclined on the ground, eyes pointed toward the falling drops. "To arrive, one must depart," he said. Then he uttered the second part of the navigator's farewell. "Kuo pau ke ke nofo," he said. *You must remain.*

Lolohea neared. "Father, let's get you some medicine."

"Kuo pau ke ke nofo," his father repeated. *You must remain.*

Reluctantly, Lolohea said, "Pea ko koe kuo pau ke alu." *And you must go.*

Inside his father's mind, Lolohea found not words but images of birds, thousands of shearwaters, taking early wing across the sea and also returning late to roost. These two-going birds occupied his father's thoughts, arriving and departing, their wings tinted both by the yellow birth of morning and the evening's pink decline.

"One thing remains," his father said. "My ink."

To Matāpule Mu'a, Lolohea said, "Alert the Tufuga. The Tu'itonga will take his final ink."

"Don't worry," Matāpule Mu'a said. "Tangata will get his ink."

Tangata. Lolohea had never heard his father called by his given name, which was the humblest of Tongan names, as Tangata simply meant "Man."

When Lolohea stood, a cloak of yellow plumage was draped across his shoulders. For something made of feathers, it was surprisingly heavy. The cloak fit perfectly, proving his big-bellied father had once looked exactly like Lolohea.

Matāpule Mu'a said, "You're now Tu'itonga. Yet I'm loyal to your father." Here, he passed his fly whisk to a young man with tears in his eyes. "My son is now your matāpule. He's been briefed on your concerns."

This young man, this new Matāpule Mu'a, asked, "What's your first command?"

"The Rotuman captives will be returned to their homes, and my cousin Mateaki will be set free."

The new Matāpule Mu'a took a breath. "But, Tu'itonga, you do yourself no favor. Your cousin will not be grateful. He won't thank you for his liberty. He'll brim with vengeance for his ill treatment. He'll seek to remedy the disappearance of his father. What, other than blood, will suffice for him?"

"But he's family," the new Tu'itonga said. "He's my cousin."

The young matāpule raised a single eyebrow.

"Release the Rotumans, at least," Lolohea said.

"There'll be angry chiefs if we break a deal with them. And who'll do the Rotumans' labor? All our young men are engaged with the war or are managing foreign plantation workers."

"End the war, then," Lolohea said.

Attempting to hide his shock at this proposal, the new Matāpule Muʻa changed his approach. "We need make no decisions today. Shall I summon some dancing girls?"

Lolohea asked, "And by 'foreign plantation workers,' do you mean war captives?"

The new Matāpule Muʻa said nothing.

"Free them," Lolohea said. "All of them."

Before his matāpule could counter him again, Lolohea turned from this conversation. Right away he was confronted by a contingent of Lifukan chiefs, their minds fixed on renegotiating tribute payments. Veering from them, Lolohea was blocked by two chiefs from western Haʻapai islands, each hoping for a favorable ruling concerning a contested fishing ground. Petitioners had formed circles beyond circles, and their thoughts—demanding, insistent—filled his head.

Lolohea found his mother at his father's side. And here was the Fisian boy, Vula, who'd had little opportunity for farewells when he'd lost his true father. Now he was expected to lament the loss of a replacement.

"Mother," Lolohea said, moving toward her.

Pōhiva looked upon her first child. *Lolo*, she thought.

But then his mother glanced past him. People'd begun lowering themselves to the ground.

Turning, Lolohea saw the Tamahā had entered the compound with her entourage. Bearing her Fan, she advanced alone. Lolohea studied her face for signs of grief at losing Moon Appearing, but the woman bore no expression. She came to a halt in front of Pōhiva. "I'll care for the Fisian child in your absence."

All fell silent, to witness this exchange.

Only now did Lolohea perceive the severity of his mother's miscalculation. She'd adopted the boy because two sons had been taken from her. Now it would happen again.

"This is difficult for you, I understand," the Tamahā said. "I know what it's like to lose an heir."

His father said, "Don't pretend the boy possesses royal blood."

"By *boy*," the Tamahā asked, "do you mean your son?"

"Adopted son," the former Tuʻitonga said.

The Fisian boy looked from face to face, trying to make sense of what was happening.

The old Tuʻitonga said, "Lolohea, you must give her nothing."

Pōhiva stood. She bade the Fisian boy rise. He was reluctant, so she tugged the tether that connected them.

"You must stop this, Lolo," the old Tuʻitonga said. "Only you can clip her wings."

Lolohea made no move to act. What mattered most was that a boy was wanted, that someone would take him under wing. That's all his brothers had ever hoped for. And Lolohea saw some justice in the act. The Tamahā had helped start the war with Fisi. It only seemed right that she raise one of its lost sons.

Pōhiva ran a thumb along the Fisian boy's cheek before pulling him close to exchange breath with him. Then she removed the tether and slipped it over the Tamahā's wrist.

As soon as the Tamahā had made her exit, the assembled men set upon Lolohea again, seeking his intervention in their various causes. He maneuvered to find an exit. Almost free, he ran into a fellow who seemed to want nothing more than to stand in his way. The man thought, *So here's my new king, this boy who's spent his days judging dancing girls. I'd like to meet him on the field and see if he's made of something more than oysters and pillows and poetic allusions.*

In the rain, the cloak began smelling of the birds it was made from.

Another man crowded Lolohea. He had gifts of dried turmeric and sandalwood, which he used to distract Lolohea while other men flanked him. This man bowed theatrically before saying, "I come with a matter of utmost urgency."

The young Matāpule Muʻa forced his way into this circle.

"I must find my way out," Lolohea told him.

When they turned, a man wearing a necklace from Lifuka brazenly confronted Lolohea, saying, "What man could command war when he himself has not known war?"

Matāpule Muʻa resorted to waving his fly whisk, which brought shame to all he directed it at. Thus, Lolohea began edging from the crowd. "I need you to do something," Lolohea told him.

Embracing his role, Matāpule Muʻa said, "Anything."

"Fetch me the meteor."

The matāpule stared at Lolohea. *The meteor?* he thought. *What could he want with that?*

"Why do you question me?" Lolohea asked the startled matāpule. "Bring it."

The Wayfinder appeared, beckoning. "Come, let's retreat to my vaka," he said as they walked. "We can bring Moon Appearing back. The comet's still in the sky."

Lolohea asked, "Didn't that trip cost Havea his life?"

"Each journey is its own," the Wayfinder said. "Even if it costs us dearly, won't she be worth it?"

"The Tamahā has her body," Lolohea said. "She'd never give it back."

Speaking of Moon Appearing conjured Moon Appearing. The way she'd been half seen in the ferns somehow made her doubly seen now. Lolohea placed an unsteady hand on his brother. If he let himself feel what he'd done, he'd find himself sprawled beneath the sky like his father. Perhaps that's what his father felt at last, the weight of everything he'd done.

"Talk to the Tamahā," the Wayfinder said. "Reason with her."

Lolohea kept remembering Moon Appearing's voice, he kept feeling the blow. *I broke her*, he thought. *Perhaps her breath could be restored, but what would return her sight, her memory, her spirit, all that she was?*

Ahead was the little fishing boat the Wayfinder had steered. Still strapped to the outrigger was the girl who'd found such cheap passage from Rotuma. Her features were drained of color. Lolohea didn't feel sadness at this sight but hate, hate for the people who'd done this to her.

The Wayfinder led him to another vaka, one with a familiar red sail. He said, "We'll figure a way to restore Moon Appearing. First let's get her body back."

Why should I deserve her back? Lolohea wondered. *I, who've thrown her away.*

"Sail us to where the waves meet the cliffs," Lolohea said.

Finau joined them on the Wayfinder's old double-hull, the *Pelepeka*, the *Tamed Bat*. They stripped the landing lines, took up paddles, and just as they were pushing off, the new Matāpule Muʻa climbed aboard with a meteor.

In the lagoon, rain fell light and straight, flattening the water. As they entered the Piha Passage, however, the sea reared blue, serrated like tuna fins. Lolohea regarded Tongatapu's coast, slowly slipping past. He thought of ʻAta, a place without gruff, self-interested men, a place without people at all.

Inside the Wayfinder's mind, Lolohea found no language, only echoes of the scape before them: rain blurring wave faces, rounded clouds rooting beneath an easterly wind.

Inside Finau's mind was a memory of Punake, sweaty, chipping bird shit off a ghost vaka, weeping at the sight of shearwaters, which was how Finau had last seen him.

To his brothers, Lolohea said, "We've been told we'll inherit special powers. 'Gifts from the gods,' they say. What kind of gift is burning ink onto another? Or removing their souls?"

The Wayfinder tried to console him. "He who is spared must spare himself. That's what Havea said."

"Are such gifts not really curses?" Lolohea asked. "And aren't they paid for ten times over?"

"You did what you had to do," Finau said. "Don't blame yourself. Blame whoever blows the wind."

Lolohea asked, "What if your gift was being able to peer inside people's skulls?"

Finau, in attempting to imagine the inside of a skull, instead remembered what it was like to be inside that tomb, which meant Lolohea experienced being sealed alive in darkness.

Matāpule Muʻa offered a consoling voice. "One should expect a new Tuʻitonga to go through a period of adjustment."

"I know what the problem is," Lolohea said. "Again and again, I do as I'm told. As I ought, as I ought, as I ought."

The young matāpule said, "Memorializing your father will help with the transition."

Lolohea shook his head. "There'll be no funeral."

Matāpule Muʻa looked to Finau and the Wayfinder to see if they'd heard what he'd heard. Astonished, he asked, "What of your father's journey to the afterlife?"

"The tomb shall not be opened," Lolohea said. From the matāpule's hands, he took the meteor. He'd seen it incandesce on ʻAta, and by its roiled, bubbly form, it was clear the object had once been molten. Now the feel of its cold, burnished shoulders suggested an eternity without heat. The question of its proper state seemed far from resolved, but that was fine with Lolohea: being between worlds was something he understood.

The matāpule thought, *Advisers must be appointed, agreements renegotiated, insurrections quelled. Instead, we entertain morbid thoughts, meteors, and sudden cliff-diving trips.*

"When a rural girl dies," Lolohea asked, "one without status or rank or royal blood, do you think her spirit awakes in Pulotu?"

The matāpule shook his head. He thought, *I must remember Lolohea's been raised by a father who sheltered him. To such a young man, an average girl might be a weighty thing, weighty as a melancholy poem recited before sleep.* Matāpule Muʻa said, "Perhaps we should save our philosophical musings for the kava circle? Might we discuss instead the arrangements for your father's funeral? Dignitaries will soon arrive, tributes will be—"

"Our father's not going in that grave," Lolohea said. He might as well have been speaking about himself, as he couldn't imagine an afterlife without Moon Appearing.

In disbelief, Matāpule Muʻa said, "But the grave conducts royal spirits to the next life."

"I've been in that grave, have you?" Finau asked. "I've seen the next life."

Matāpule Muʻa said, "Might I suggest—"

"Our uncle ʻAho was right about one thing," Finau said. "The worthless nature of matāpule."

"I'm sworn to serve Lolohea," Matāpule Muʻa countered. "Serve him in life and death, surrendering my soul when he does. I'll leave it to others to measure the worth of such service."

"The u'ui crab may swap its shell," Finau said. Then he became frustrated, his face bristling with anger. "Punake isn't here to complete my couplets!"

The Wayfinder told the matāpule, "We'll need you to retrieve the body of Moon Appearing."

"I take my commands from the king," Matāpule Mu'a said.

"Get Moon Appearing," Lolohea said. "And I declare our family grave tapu. No one's to even touch it."

Matāpule Mu'a said, "But funeral plans are—"

Finau said, "I'll never allow our father, alive or dead, to enter that grave."

Shocked at this notion, Matāpule Mu'a said, "People don't go into graves *alive*."

"What're you waiting for?" Finau asked. "Go, implement our commands."

"Go?"

"Now."

The coast was veiled in rain. The matāpule looked toward the mist-shrouded reef, with its unseen breakers. "You mean, swim? If this is some kind of loyalty test, I assure you—"

"I'll finish my own couplet," Finau said, adding:

| 'Oku ala fakafetongi ehe u'ui, hono nge'esi | *The u'ui crab may swap its shell* |
| ka e 'ikai hono huhu kona. | *but not its poisonous sting.* |

Then, with a sharp heel, Finau kicked the matāpule into the passing sea.

The diving cliffs had darkened with rain. Lolohea stepped from the pitching vaka and held on to the rock wall's ancient handholds. Rain softened the edges of the sea, left everything the gray of mineral glaze. Reaching the cliff top, he sat, wrapped in a cloak of yellow feathers, catching his breath.

Knowing the contents of other people's minds left Lolohea feeling unaccountably alone. Far from garnering a sense of connection or access, he felt kinship with those whose minds would never be known because they'd never return. He thought of Six Fists, a man who'd left his family one day to go fishing. He thought of the flowing black hair of those riding the Old Canoe into the depths. He thought of his father's coconuts, in each a pickled soul. In the rain, Lolohea felt the absences he himself had left, in Fisi, in Rotuma, in a field of ferns. These memories came with the smell of wet rope, the melodies of a bone flute, the splash of a body being rolled into the sea.

He absorbed the thoughts of the rain. The rain didn't use language or deliver anything like a message. Yet, from the falling drops, he understood they'd fallen before. The cliffs conveyed notions, too, far beyond words: The first Tongans had stood here. This was where they'd sung up the sun, had bidden farewell to the moon.

Lolohea rose and walked to the bamboo, the wet foliage dripping constellations into the soil. The bamboo poles, he understood, had retained the song of the extinct pigeons that once dwelled here.

Coo-oo, ooh, went their simple call.

He removed his cloak and hung it in the bamboo. The poles' movement in the wind was as true as any poem yet conveyed, and without the feeble nature of words. The cloak shared with Lolohea a sense that he wouldn't take it up again. Someone else would wear it next. Lolohea took this knowledge with the same sense of inevitability that came with knowing human thoughts—minds were what they were and not much subject to change.

At the cliff's edge, he lifted his meteor. It hummed a single, endless note, one harmonic with the sea, the sky, the basalt beneath. It was a tone you could feel, as when a vaka's hull is given final shape by rubbing pumice along its waterline. That thrum—of lava sanding beams for the sea—could've been the sound of the first people, preparing to depart for the first island.

Diving, previously, had been an escape. But the meteor was an instrument of communion, one that had surveyed the celestial and touched the heavenly domes. It had once been liquid. It had been fire. It was freighted with all it had encountered. Falling to earth a second time, this time in Lolohea's hands, would be but an interesting diversion in its long journey, for the meteor was destined to traverse the entirety of the endless void, even if it stopped in Tonga for an eternity or two.

Gripping the meteor, Lolohea dived into the sea.

Earth, sky, ocean—unified in a single fall.

He was propelled through the water to a rock ledge below. In the past, he'd let himself drift, ambient in the current's billow. Today, he placed his back against the rock and balanced the meteor on his chest, so that he looked up to an out-of-focus surface. It wasn't like he could read the thoughts of the sea. It was more like the sea itself was of a single mind, its entire knowing contained in every surge. Lolohea understood that life consisted not of generations, but a single, unfurling state. Like a fire moving across a wooded island, life wasn't the fleeing of the animals but the tindered consumption of the flame: slow-walking, the crackling red was what we considered time, and we were but the fuel that curled in its heat. Lolohea understood there was but one voice, the ocean's, and all other utterances, from whales' and birds' to people's, were but dialects. And Lolohea understood the ocean touched all places, in all times, simultaneously cupping the moon as it rose in the east, while fanning down the western sun. By reaching out, he touched the fingers that'd fashioned the ancient handholds. Above, he beheld the dip of the first seagoing bird's beak. He felt the sting of the jellyfish that was all of human suffering.

His vision began to sparkle, it darkened at the edges. But the darkening was good. It was the dark between the stars, the dark of ocean depths, the dark release of seed inside the womb. It was the dark inside a loved one's mind, the untapped fluid suspending a beloved's self. It was the dark of your *before*. He understood that he was starting to encounter her, that in their *befores* was how they'd appear to one another. To the sea the once and future were one and the same. Lights sparkled. Limbs floated. Against his chest, the meteor's heart began to beat. The sea lapped the shores of an island called Hunga, and he could see Moon Appearing dance the tauʻolunga in the dark. The sea encircled ʻAta, and his fingers were again sticky with hibiscus pollen as he placed a yellow belt around her waist. The salt in the water communicated her wound, and he let the sea transfer this pain to him. He let the current carry forth his thoughts so she would know his mind. And thus they began the pleasure of encountering one another again, but this time with total knowledge. This time with an eternal before and, in due course, the promise of the long, long after.

Though she couldn't be seen, though he couldn't locate her, he felt her presence.

What's your plan, she asked him, *for getting that meteor back to the surface?*

She was right, he hadn't considered this problem. The observation made him laugh—bubbles of air rolling upward. He wasn't using that air anyway, not really.

What's your plan, he asked her, *for wafting a Fan underwater?*

She showed him. He felt a current ripple across his body, and he knew that she was with him.

After dropping off Lolohea, the Wayfinder set the anchor stone. Then he and Finau lay on their backs, looking up to the cliffs where their brother sat, wrapped in a yellow cloak. There was little wind, but the pulse and surge of the swells were as strong as ever. Each time the anchor line snapped taut, the vaka kicked.

"We'll get Punake back," the Wayfinder assured his brother.

"How was he left behind? How'd it happen?"

"Lolo did what he had to do."

The Wayfinder recalled the look on Punake's face when he learned he'd be left in Rotuma: surprise, betrayal, relief. Yes, *relief*. There's a moment you realize you're going to survive something. You're not out of danger, but something registers and you tell yourself, *I'm going to make it*. Maybe you didn't even know how much danger you were in. Maybe you didn't understand the nature of your peril. Perhaps you realize all this in the instant you decide you'll live. This, if the Wayfinder had to describe it, was the true look on the poet's face when he left Tongan custody. So they might want to work quickly to rescue Punake from an island where killing and war and servitude were unknown. Otherwise, the man might opt against deliverance.

Above, Lolohea rose to hang his cloak in a patch of bamboo. Then he returned to the cliff's edge, where he stood against shifting patterns of mist.

Finau raised a hand to his neck, aligning his fingers with the black tentacles.

"Does it hurt?" the Wayfinder asked. "The jellyfish?"

Finau shook his head.

"You must've been terrified in that grave. You must've thought you'd never get out."

"It wasn't death that scared me," Finau said. "It's what came after."

"The afterlife? You said you glimpsed it."

"Is Lolo going to dive, or what?" Finau asked. "It's not like we have all day. It's not like our father isn't dying. And our mother isn't being fitted for funeral attire."

"What'd you see?"

Finau shrugged. "I saw the fabled Puko tree. I saw the sacred river Vaiola. I saw the faces of the dead who'd gathered to take revenge on our father."

The Wayfinder said, "I've been sailing on nights so black you can't see your hands. In that kind of darkness, the imagination takes over. You see what you're afraid of, like rogue waves and dangerous reefs. It's not like you imagine them—you *see* coral heads, you *see* waves about to crush you."

"This was no fantasy," Finau said. "I was there. 'Aho choked me there. As I started to die here, I began to appear in that realm. As our fortunes reversed, however, as I gained the upper hand, 'Aho began to materialize there, too. We met one another's eyes. We were trying to kill each other on Tonga, but on Pulotu, we stood side by side in the purple sand. He said, *No person was able to wound me, except him that shared my blood. You're becoming one of the family.* Now I can't help thinking how our hands are the exact same size."

"You're nothing like him."

Finau looked unconvinced. "We can't let Father go there. His enemies are waiting. It wouldn't be so bad, forgoing the afterlife. A soul can live in a coconut tree. A soul can inhabit the wind or the sea."

Above them, Lolohea lifted something over his head and dove, gracefully knifing into the water.

"All right," Finau said. "He's done his dive, let's haul in the anchor stone."

"He's not done. Think of what he's going through. He may need us all day."

Finau was quiet. Then he asked, "How'd he kidnap all those people?"

Thinking about it from here, from the safety of Tonga, it didn't seem possible. "He invented an enemy. At first the enemy was our uncle 'Aho. Then it turned out to be himself."

"That's what happened to the girl he killed today. He couldn't have known it, but he turned out to be her villain. It's hard to think of Lolohea that way, as anybody's foe."

Yeah, the Wayfinder thought. *But that's how it turned out.*

"What happened to that Rotuman girl?" Finau asked. "The one tied to the canoe?"

"*We* happened to her."

"I've never even touched a girl," Finau said.

The Wayfinder let himself feel the waves below. "Me, either."

He could still see Kaniva, standing in a river of stars.

From across the waves, they heard a bird flapping. "*Nea, nea,*" it called before landing on the deck.

"So you've decided to pay me a visit?" Finau asked. "My father must've banished you again."

"*Nea*, Finau is Kōkī's firstest friend," Kōkī said. "Firstest and forever."

Finau offered the parrot a poetic response:

Ko ene toki maha pē kava	*Only when the kava is gone*
pea sīfā e kau fakaafe mali ki 'api.	*do the wedding guests stumble home.*

"*Nea,*" Kōkī said. "Kōkī come with good news. The Tu'itonga not extinct!" Here, Kōkī jubilantly spread his wings before adding, "But, *nea*, extinct is coming soon."

"Pull the anchor stone," Finau said. "We must go to Father."

"We will," the Wayfinder said. "When Lolo's ready."

"Where Lolohea?" Kōkī asked.

The Wayfinder pointed down.

Kōkī peered over the side. "Ocean make die. If Kōkī touch water, Kōkī go extinct. Lolohea not know ocean make die?"

"Lolohea can hold his breath forever," Finau said. "And the ocean, it's the way he—"

"Celebrates!" Kōkī said. "Everything worked out, *nea*?"

"Escapes," Finau corrected.

"I have to know," the Wayfinder said to Kōkī. "In parrot talk, does *nea* mean 'yes' or 'no'?"

"It mean both," Kōkī said. "Parrot talk most efficient. Like, *nea*, everything work out! And, *nea*, things almost go bad."

"Almost," the Wayfinder said. "Imagine if 'Aho was still on the loose."

"Imagine," Finau said, "if the Tamahā had managed to pass her Fan to a woman ready to use it."

The Wayfinder said, "Imagine if something had gone wrong with Lolohea becoming king."

Finau took a moment to digest that.

"There were a couple of times on our trip," the Wayfinder said, "when I thought everything would fall apart. I mean, what if we'd lost him in Fisi or Rotuma?"

"What would you have done?" Finau asked.

"If we'd lost Lolohea?" the Wayfinder asked. "I'd have beseeched the Tamahā to restore him. If that failed, I guess I'd have sailed to Pulotu with his bones. The comet's still in the sky to lead the way."

"You think that would've worked?" Finau asked.

"Didn't you hear? They say Havea brought his wife back."

Finau peered into the rain-dappled water. "How long's he been down there?"

"Not worry," Kōkī said. "Lolohea hold his breath forever!"

Finau turned to the Wayfinder. "What if you'd tried those things and they didn't work, what if you couldn't find a way to bring him back?"

"You mean, if we'd lost Lolohea, and he was gone forever? And if our parents were gone? With the Tamahā furious, and 'Aho at large?" He didn't answer his questions.

A troubled look showed on Finau's face.

"None of that'll happen, though," the Wayfinder said. He tried to calm his little brother with humor. "You're not looking to become Tuʻitonga, are you? Because you're welcome to it. I don't even like standing on solid ground."

"I wouldn't know the first thing about ruling a kingdom," Finau said. "Our father taught it all to Lolo. All I know is stupid poetry."

Kōkī squawked. "Now you know how Kōkī feel!"

"But seriously," Finau said. "What if we'd lost Lolohea, and what if you'd been unable to bring him back? What would've happened then?"

The Wayfinder shook his head. "With no one left to protect us? In a world of adversaries? I guess we'd become nomads."

"What's a nomad?" Finau asked.

"That, my brother, is something you don't want to find out."

The Tufuga's only shelter was a tuitui tree, which deflected rain for most of the morning. When its sweeping branches were finally saturated, the rain began falling beneath its limbs. Wet, the old Samoan returned home in his imagination. He inspected his root garden. He checked his daughter's bird snares. He observed his grandchildren, who, in this stage of the moon, were preparing lures for an evening on the reefs. Could they salt enough fish to last until his return?

When the former Matāpule Muʻa delivered the former Tuʻitonga for his final inking session, the Tufuga was sure the man was dead. The matāpule seemed indifferent to the way the king was rolled naked from a litter onto a wet mat. A human body couldn't look worse: the man was bloated, ill-hued, and bruised from much handling. The Tufuga suddenly knew how he'd be treated, once his purpose here was served: discarded at the edge of a Tongatapu path.

"I leave you to your task," the matāpule said. "I must attend to my affairs."

"Wait," the Tufuga said. "Is it true, is he now just a man?"

"There's a new Tuʻi of Tonga. Alas, there's a new Matāpule Muʻa."

"One more thing. I heard a rumor that the man before us possesses the purple soil of the afterlife."

"Why do you ask?"

Why had he asked? The sight of the old king made it suddenly clear that the Tufuga would never see Samoa again. All those who might honor the Tufuga's deal for his land's return and safe passage home were gone. The Tuʻilifuka was dead. Six Fists was dead. The king's matāpule would soon be dead. And the king himself was at the edge of death. How would the Tufuga make it to the afterlife if he never made it home, if his family couldn't pray over his remains and thus elevate his soul? A pinch of the afterlife could take you directly there. "No reason," he said. "Land finds land, is all."

When the matāpule took his leave, the Tufuga wasted no time in lowering the needles. Soon a traditional pattern of shark's teeth was sailing across his subject's back. While the Tufuga was inking the knobs of the lower spine, a sensitive area, the subject spoke.

"A final," the former king said, snatching a breath, "dose of pain."

Those, it turned out, were his last words.

The Tufuga had long claimed he selected his patterns based on intuitions about his subjects. This wasn't untrue, but more true was this: elite men tended to want similar ink—singular enough to claim specialness, but not too different from the men around them. So, though the Tufuga was capable of personalizing a subject's ink, in reality he ended up making variations of the same old waves, fins, spearpoints, and so on.

But what ink would he lend men if he were truly free to ink as he saw fit? It was pretty clear the man before him had become disconnected from the blood spilled in his name and the sacrifices others made in their service to him. Could the Tufuga offer the former king images of life under his rule? Could he convert ink into the sight of a Tongan armada at dawn or the feeling of a hungry family watching their snares, praying for the pigeon that would feed them?

Without giving it any more thought, the Tufuga began inking broken oyster shells across the subject's skin, followed by a string of kele'a trumpets. These would serve as warnings to all who encountered this man in Pulotu. On one thigh, the Tufuga inked an open grave. Upon the other, a ghost vaka. This lack of symmetry was thrilling! Such images required a great deal of ink, but from his subject, no complaints! Why had he spent his life inking the living, when the dead were so amenable? No need to wipe the blood. Why worry about needles sinking too deep?

The man they called Seven Fists ran up, spear in hand. Out of breath, he asked, "Does he live?"

The Tufuga shook his head.

Seven Fists took a moment to study the depictions on his former master. He must've had more pressing matters, for he was off and running again.

The Tufuga began inking an island on fire. Rising from this tableau were twin plumes of smoke, representing displacement and despair. It was then that his subject inhaled sharply and opened his eyes, taking one last study of Tonga. The Tufuga held his tools, unmoving. Then the former king exhaled long through his nostrils. His eyes fixed. His mouth fell open, hands relaxing. This time, he was truly gone.

Two security men, running from different directions, met up and began racing together down a third path. "The Tuʻitonga is dead," one declared.

"Which one?" the other asked.

"Both," came the answer.

The Tufuga regarded his work on the dead man before him. Tradition dictated every bit of skin—from navel to knee—be adorned. But this was special work, and a few splotches of bare skin only highlighted images of a frigate bird swallowing a stolen meal, and a pair of hands bound by rope. Thus, he understood it was only on this day that he truly became a Tufuga.

It was while taking this final measure that he noticed something had dropped from the Tuʻitonga's hand. It was a pigskin pouch, the kind carried by voyagers who yearned for safe returns from distant shores.

A press-gang of men ran past, carrying ropes and poles. The Tufuga asked what was the matter. One terrified man said, "We're going to open the royal tomb. Rumor has it that a living being is inside."

The Tufuga opened the pouch. There were three baby's teeth, no doubt having once belonged to the king's sons. There was a braided loop of hair, a memento of the woman he loved.

Several people ran past, bearing all their possessions, headed for the vaka at the royal landing. Power was shifting, people were taking action before loyalties were called into account.

The Samoan knew what was in the bottom of the pouch: the purple sand of Pulotu and its promise of passage to the afterlife. But when he shook the sand into his palm, it was from the beaches of Tonga. So in the end, the Tuʻitonga wished to tether himself to this place. At the last, he must have had his mind on earthly affairs, for much was the unfinished business of home.

Some of the former king's advisers and chiefs rushed past, wives and children in tow. They were heading for the vaka that would enable their escape. Several matāpule commanded them to stop, but none halted. Disobeying a matāpule meant forfeiting one's Tongan identity. Resisting the face of the king's authority resulted in complete social demotion. This meant people ran not as adherents to any cause or camp or figure, but merely as humans, trying to survive. The Samoan stood. He grabbed nothing. Despite his weak joints and tired eyes, he ran after them. He had unfinished business, too. He also had affairs to attend to. Namely, the affair of living.

FORTY

KŌRERO:
WHERE PEOPLE NEED TO GO

After confronting a tyrant at a Tongan bathing pond, I thought about something the Wayfinder said one night. We were on the deck of his waka, the swells sweeping below. People slept around us, their bodies softly rocking. Above was the comet, which had led the Wayfinder to me. It was now nearly too dim to see. I had the feeling that when it vanished, so would he. I asked how long we had left to see it.

"It's about gone," he said.

"For good?" I asked.

"Oh no, it'll be back."

"Really?"

"Of course," he said. "But to see it again, you'll need another life."

Another life, that's what I felt I was living as I headed to the Tamahā's compound, my people in tow, to return her Fan. My mother, a vocal authority on every aspect of life back home, had little comment regarding the strange workings of Tonga. Instead, she kept taking my hand in hers or pulling my head awkwardly to her shoulder.

Along the way, Tapoto and Sun Shower kept reliving the death of 'Aho. There was a righteous glow in Sun Shower's eyes. For Tapoto, it was different. Much as he was still in the thrall of his clash, his eyes flickered with uncertainty. He was unused to harm, and pressing a man beneath the water was no place to start. Plus, his own father had drowned. How could he not newly imagine his father's loss after seeing a man's underwater eyes, sensing his growing desperation, watching him struggle to surface, feeling his body jerk as he finally took a liquid breath?

I passed through the Tamahā's gates alone. A group of Fefine Girls was stacking dark stones in an effort to repair the fishponds. No one directed them, and I marveled at how such lovely girls were so industrious. I'd been given to believe they led pampered lives.

The Tamahā was by herself, working her garden. The malau birds were with her, looking for bugs in the turned soil. I extended the Fan to her. "It took me a while to understand its purpose," I said.

Her hands were dirty, her hair scattered. She looked at me differently—I had the feeling she somehow knew all that had transpired with her nephew 'Aho. She accepted the Fan, saying, "Your big friend sustained some injuries, yes? Come, there are treatments for broken fingers and cracked ribs."

She and I made our way toward a small plot, shaded by a sweeping tree. Here, we picked uhi leaves. She explained how to wrap a finger by binding it to its neighbor.

"So, 'Ata will become yours?" she asked me.

It didn't feel right to speak possessively of 'Ata. The place was still just a name. So I said nothing.

"I hope you have a fondness for birds," she said.

"The fondness one acquires after killing too many of them."

She glanced at me, to see if I was serious. "Fair enough. On the island you're from, it sounds like you'd have done some things differently?"

"Too many to name."

Her dark eyes were quite commanding. She said, "The journey to 'Ata will be a time to think about how things should work on your new island. Make some decisions before you land. Ask *yourself* what you'd do with a second chance."

I laughed. "My people make decisions by consensus, which means bickering, endless deliberation, and the hurt feelings that come with compromise."

She looked at me, registering no expression.

"Stupid ideas are entertained," I continued. "Old grievances resurface. Every last person gets a say. Do you know how maddening it can be to make decisions that way?"

"I can only imagine."

I had a feeling I'd said something wrong, but I didn't know what.

"Come," the Tamahā said. "Let me show you something to soothe the big fellow's ribs."

I hesitated. "I'm more worried about the wound up here." I touched my temple. "How'll I help him get over drowning a helpless man?"

"That's a feeling you should hope he never forgets." The Tamahā moved on, indicating various plants, naming them, offering instructions on how to fertilize and harvest each one, as if I'd be sticking around to take care of her garden. "The Wayfinder seems much changed," she volunteered.

I recalled him eating separately from us, mocking our rural practices, bossing our men, refusing to take me to our sister island. I thought of the way he arrogantly confiscated my necklace on the day I met him. Perhaps he had been changing. "What'll happen to him if he becomes king?" I asked.

"He'll likely become very alone."

That thought quieted me. The Wayfinder was already the most alone person I knew.

"The king does have one person," the Tamahā said. "Someone whose duty it is to guide him."

"Is that person you?"

"Once upon a time, it was."

Kakala shouted for the Tamahā.

What now? was the Tamahā's expression. She wiped a dirty hand across her brow and then looked at me. "You seem like a capable girl. Could you keep a man in line?"

"Are we still talking about the Wayfinder? He's been guilty of thoughtlessness, but I've never seen him out of line."

"Power changes people."

"Not if you remember what it is to be powerless."

"You'd be surprised how people forget," she said.

"Stories do the remembering," I said. "If they get told."

She scrutinized this notion. "Still, such a person would have her work cut out for her."

"What work is that?"

Kakala shouted again.

The Tamahā gestured for me to stand straight. She pulled the hair from my face. "To begin, let's ensure no harm can come to you." She handed me the Fan. "I can tell you'd be loath to hurt someone, but I assure you the day will come when you need to defend yourself or impose order. Remember: only a fool would interfere with the affairs of a woman of your rank."

I looked at the Fan in my hand. It seemed different now, almost unrecognizable.

"I have no *affairs* to interfere with," I said. "And *rank*?"

She placed a hand on my shoulder, steering me toward the others. "And you must understand," she said, "ridding the land of foolish men is no crime."

Back at the pond, a clutch of eggs had been discovered under the brush.

"Are those from the swamp herons?" Kakala asked the Tamahā. When the Tamahā didn't answer, Kakala turned to me. "The last swamp herons were killed and eaten."

The Tamahā scooped up the eggs and held them to her chest. "Those crafty birds," she said, as if they'd played an elaborate trick upon her.

※

At the royal landing, Tongan workers were outfitting two waka for our journey to 'Ata. Our people pitched in, loading provisions and hauling skins of water. My parents joined the effort, laboring with quiet resolve. I had little desire to help. For so long, I'd been focused on getting our own island. Yet, now that the time was at hand, why was I reluctant?

When Tiri wanted to explore Tongatapu, I volunteered to escort her.

We took a random path, just the two of us, and, of course, Dead Matāpule, who followed me everywhere. He made no secret of his impatience with our stroll. To best serve me, he said, he needed to know my agenda as the new Tamahā. "Don't call me that," I told him. Did I have enemies he should know about? Grudge holders? Would I mind sharing my history? *My history?* That was simple: Mending my father's nets. Satchels of dead birds. Hine and me whispering, even when no one was around. My mother pretending to cut a sweet potato into three equal pieces, even as she contrived to make mine bigger. A small mat on a small beach on a small island, where a small family questioned the sky.

A fear struck me. I turned to Dead Matāpule. "Sweet potatoes grow on 'Ata, don't they?"

His eyes closed in silent pain. His regret at pledging loyalty to me was palpable, for his life as an esteemed counselor had come to this: advising a girl and a blind woman about tuber cultivation. "I'd have to consult a sub-matāpule," he said.

We continued walking. Back home, the ocean was never far from view. Here, it felt like you could stroll all day and not glimpse the sea. And where did all these paths lead? The idea of a path that led to an unknown place was as strange as following a stranger's footprints. And I'd never encountered an unknown person on a path. It didn't take long. A woman was herding pigs our way. She must've seen how I gawked at things. "A visitor," she said. "We've not had many of those lately. What island are you from?"

"We're far from home," I said.

Tiri added, "A place we may never see again."

The woman dismissed this notion. "Your home island is here," she said, tapping her chest. "Where you live is but the sand between your toes." She studied Tiri more closely, asking me, "Has your auntie lost her . . . ?" She pointed at her own eyes.

Tiri spoke for herself. "I see farther than most," she said, patting my hand. "Only now does this girl regard Tonga. I've been looking at it since I first heard the word."

The woman and Dead Matāpule exchanged a surprised look. She studied him a moment before asking, "Say, aren't you the matāpule who was killed this morning?"

"I assure you I'm quite alive," Dead Matāpule said, and just like that, simply by being reminded of his recent murder, his spirits were very much lifted.

All paths on Tongatapu eventually led to the royal compound, which was where we found Finau and the Wayfinder. They were in a flower garden, planting coconuts. The garden was remarkable, the blossoms bright, the fragrance overpowering. "What a luxury," Tiri said, "to grow things simply for their loveliness." When I asked Finau what he was doing, he said, *Setting people free.*

"What people?" I asked.

"Not people, exactly," Finau said. "Just their souls."

"How does a soul end up in a coconut?"

Dead Matāpule said, "Not by accident."

"We've got many things to put right," the Wayfinder said. "I wish they were all this easy." He nodded at my hand. "Still, give us some help with that Fan, would you?"

What did it mean to hold the Fan? When was a girl to deploy it? Tiri said, "I don't think the Tamahā would've used her Fan for gardening."

"This isn't gardening," Finau said.

"It's life and death," the Wayfinder said.

"It's more than that," Finau added.

I looked at the Wayfinder, surrounded by his coconut project. On our voyage here, he'd been dedicated to us. Amid the vastness of the ocean, we were his only concern. He was devoted to our safety and well-being. We weren't just passengers to him, right? Some cargo he was duty-bound to deliver? I asked, "You're taking us to 'Ata, aren't you?"

He seemed to know this question was coming. "You don't need me for that. You can hold a course. The constellation Toloa will guide you."

All I knew of 'Ata had come from him. He'd told me 'Ata was ancient and sacred. That magical things happened there. That 'Ata reflected your thoughts. His descriptions allowed me to see dark canopies, rocky spires, waves of birds. The place didn't exist without him.

"It won't be difficult," he said. "I've allocated two sturdy vaka for your journey. Depart when the moon rises, and you'll reach 'Ata before sunset tomorrow."

"Why aren't you coming?" I asked.

"We've got unfinished business," Finau said. "A man has been left behind."

"We also depart tonight," the Wayfinder said. "We have some stops to make, but we'll be back when the winds shift. That's when you'll meet Punake."

I shook my head. "We'll be long gone by then."

"But you'll be back," the Wayfinder said. "You'll have to return to pick up Tapoto."

Finau must've seen the look on my face. "You didn't tell her?" he asked his brother.

"We're borrowing him," the Wayfinder said. "He's already agreed to it. We need someone to handle things while we're gone."

"You're putting Tapoto in charge?" I asked.

"Temporarily," Finau said.

The Wayfinder added, "He's demonstrated leadership and bravery."

"But he's *Tapoto*," I said. By which I meant he excelled at naps and snacks and imaginary enemies.

"Who else can we trust?" Finau asked, adding, "We'll also need your matāpule."

"And your father," the Wayfinder said. "Just for a little while."

"You've trusted them this far," Tiri told me.

"You can't spare a few days to take us to 'Ata?" I asked the Wayfinder. "I thought you wanted to show it to me."

His face suggested it wasn't a matter of *want*.

Tiri squeezed my hand. I knew she was right. I nodded at Dead Matāpule, who went to stand behind the Tongan brothers. It was clear this was his rightful position.

When the winds shift, I thought. I then gave each coconut a whiff of Life-Affected air. One by one, they cracked, and after sending down fat, white roots, up came waist-high shoots that fanned into dark green fronds.

That afternoon, we gathered at the royal compound to witness the Wayfinder becoming king. A father was necessary for the ceremony, and, having lost his own, the Wayfinder turned to mine. While my father appeared honored, it was obvious the Wayfinder wasn't close to a single man on his home island.

"The ceremony is simple," Dead Matāpule assured my father. "You merely serve him a drink."

"That's it?" my father asked.

"You kneel," Dead Matāpule instructed, "hand him a cup of kava, and offer a few words."

"What kind of words?"

"Life advice, perhaps. Or some general wisdom."

My father nodded, though he wasn't much of an advice-giver. He'd rather show you a good way of doing something, then observe you closely, encouraging you as you gave it a try. His truest moments were wordless. Like how, on chilly nights, he'd take your hands to warm them in his. Or the times, going about normal life, you glanced up to discover him looking at you, praise in his eyes.

Tongans began gathering, farmers and nobles alike. They drifted in from all paths to encircle us.

A shell of kava appeared. My father knelt before the Wayfinder and began uttering words I couldn't quite hear. Still, I knew the kinds of things he'd say. He wouldn't mention any of your flaws, like how you awakened him with sudden, crazy questions. Or how you went on and on with stories whose point you might've forgotten. Neither would he mention your mistakes, like sneaking off to another island at night or jumping off a canoe in the middle of the ocean. Instead, he'd bring up his own shortcomings, using these to show how you could never be as foolish as he, how you'd already far exceeded him. These were things he genuinely believed, even if they weren't true. A last, he'd get real, saying how great you turned out, how proud he was of you, how much you were like your mother, his highest compliment.

The Wayfinder listened to my father's words, his eyes becoming wet and uncertain. He couldn't have looked more vulnerable, and this made my own eyes warm. I could tell he'd never heard such sincere and affirming words from a father before. I'd never exactly heard such words, either. But I didn't have to. Over the years, I'd just absorbed them.

At last, the Wayfinder downed the kava, the empty shell left trembling in his hand.

When Dead Matāpule draped a cloak of yellow feathers across his shoulders, waves of people lowered themselves to the ground. The Wayfinder looked unsure as he beheld this legion of supplicated people. I'd only seen him as capable and confident. Away from water, it seemed, he was a different creature. "I've been on a journey," he said. "It was one I didn't want to take. I made no landfall at my destination. And I failed in my mission. Yet, in getting lost, I found what I didn't know I was looking for." Then he began speaking of change, of ruling in a new way, of ending the war, and of many things he'd learned from his encounter with my people. It wasn't that I stopped listening. It's that, rather than a king, I could only see the boy who'd landed on my beach. I could only remember the feeling of meeting someone *new*, someone *different*, and it mattered that it was *him*, for he was the only one in the world capable of finding me. I asked Tiri, "Are we really going to another island where there'll be nobody but us?"

Tiri closed her eyes, which was something she did when she was thinking.

I said, "Because I don't think I can go back to living alone."

"Child, we had each other. We were never alone."

"But we were," I said. "I see that now."

"Despite our problems, we were lucky. Our little island belonged to nobody but us."

I glanced at the Wayfinder, who was speaking about consensus and self-reliance. "The world is bigger," I told Tiri. "Now, when I look at the ocean, I don't see the stuff that strands us. I see a path to other places. And the stars aren't indifferent. They show you the way."

"It's not about one place or another," Tiri said. "You'd have gone anywhere, as long as *he* was taking you."

The new Tuʻitonga bade everyone rise. He removed the yellow cloak and returned it to his matāpule. He called forth Tapoto and Sun Shower. "These two have rid Tonga of ʻAho," he said. "For this deed, I give them 'hau' status. They shall keep the peace while my brother and I take a journey. Our absence will be brief, and in the meantime, they have authority to make decisions in our stead."

Someone oiled the shoulders of Tapoto and Sun Shower. They were dusted with sandalwood powder.

"Do I get to wear the feathery thing?" Tapoto asked.

Finau and the Wayfinder spoke at once. "No," they said.

The royal chef addressed the Wayfinder. "A feast is in order. Would you like eels from Fisi, parrot meat from Haʻamoa, perhaps shellfish from the Teleki Reefs?"

The Wayfinder looked to Tapoto for a response.

"I can have anything?" Tapoto asked. "You don't happen to have sweet potatoes, do you?"

"Sweet potatoes?" the chef asked, incredulous. "That's all you want?"

Sun Shower sharpened her voice. "He gave you an order," she told the chef.

A look of unmitigated joy crossed Tapoto's face. He stood shoulder to shoulder with Sun Shower, and despite his injuries, he lifted his arms in triumph. "Sweet potatoes for everybody!" he shouted.

* * *

The sweet potatoes, straight from the earth ovens, fell open in our hands. Before taking a bite of mine, I breathed its honeyed steam. Night was descending, fires had been lit, people'd gathered to eat in haphazard groups. The Tongans were full of life, laughing, sharing stories, their gestures expressive in the firelight. I wanted to know the villages they spoke of, the people they gossiped about, the unsaid things they shared with knowing looks.

Missing only was the Wayfinder. I'd gotten used to spending my evenings with him, the two of us shoulder to shoulder on a cramped deck. He was now surrounded by men who vied for his favor. They'd brought presents with which to influence him, each man awaiting the ideal moment to bestow his. One man's gift was an engraved war club. He took a risk, scrambling through the firelight, rushing forward, looking ready to attack, but at the last moment he bowed before the Wayfinder, asking if it wasn't possible to—*please, please*—secure the return of his matāpule. Others seized this moment, encircling the Wayfinder with their own appeals.

I waved at him, but he either didn't see me or . . . or he just didn't wave back. And why would he? Who was I to the king of Tonga? A souvenir from a recent adventure? An interesting anecdote in one of his tales? I was a girl about to absent myself to another out-of-the-way island, where I'd, what, spend my days staring at waves?

My mother turned to me. "Is something the matter?"

"No," I said. But then I added, "What really gets me mad are these Tongan sweet potatoes!"

"Don't you think they're wonderful?" Tiri asked.

"Of course I do," I snapped. "That's the problem." Fat and tender, these sweet potatoes were dreamy. The kind we'd been living on, I now realized, were skinny and bitter and didn't even deserve the name. My whole life I'd thought I'd known what a sweet potato was, but I hadn't, not at all.

A fruit called "banana" was passed around. One had to skin it before eating, but once it was opened, the fragrance was subtle, the flavor immediately endearing. Savoring it did nothing to help my mood. Not once did I gag, pinch my nose, or restrain the urge to vomit. No imagination was necessary to force it down. This, I realized, was what fruit was supposed to be. It also felt wrong to enjoy it, when back home people were eating grubs and seagrass and boiled bark.

In the branches above, Kōkī landed with his flock.

"Kōkī!" Finau called. "You're back—I've missed you." Finau peeled a banana and extended it Kōkī's way. Then Finau leaned to me. "Watch this," he whispered. "Kōkī'll do anything for banana."

But Kōkī kept his distance. While the red-shining parrot didn't take his eyes off the banana, neither did he near. Instead, he released a series of screeches and squawks, culminating in an ear-shattering shriek.

"What is it?" Finau asked. "What're you trying to tell me?"

"Kōkī now speak parrot talk," Kōkī said. "When Kōkī learn parrot speech, parrot memory return. Parrot-speak make Kōkī remember before you came."

"There was no before me," Finau said. "I hand-raised you."

"Kōkī remember before your people," Kōkī said. "Before your canoes, before you bring banana and cages and snares, before you began eating us."

"None of this is true," Finau protested. "Finau loves Kōkī!"

"There was a Tonga before Tongans," Kōkī said. "A place that have no name. A place that need no name."

Finau neared Kōkī, close enough to touch his feathers. "I'm glad you're free. I'm the one who freed you."

"Kōkī love Finau," Kōkī said. "But Finau the one who leash me. Kōkī must forget Finau in order to remember. Kōkī must forget banana. Kōkī must return to before." Preparing to fly, Kōkī extended his wings.

Finau looked suddenly uncertain. "Are you really leaving? Am I going to see you again?"

In parrot-speak, Kōkī said something to his fellow birds, who also readied their wings.

"Wait," Finau said. Tentatively, he asked, "Will you ever think of me?"

"Kōkī owe Finau honest. The answer to Finau question is: *Nea*."

The parrots then departed, flying in the direction of 'Eua's elusive, eastward-facing cliffs.

Perhaps to lighten the mood, two old men began to croon, each singing variations of the same song. Their voices were raw and unadorned. The effect of their overlapping lyrics was something other than harmony, something that both clashed and combined. Two Fefine Girls began dancing the tauʻolunga. No one commanded them—they just seemed to want to dance. The Wayfinder had told me that a tauʻolunga dancer must cage her eyes and execute her moves with the utmost of formality, but these girls danced as they pleased, observing one another's movements, speaking and responding with their bodies in a kind of conversation.

Tapoto stood. "That's the dance!" He turned to Finau. "That's the one you taught me." Before Finau could respond, Tapoto was dragging him into the firelight, where the two men began moving their bodies alongside the Fefine Girls. Hoots of outrage and delight rose from the spectators, none of whom could look away.

Despite his broken finger, Tapoto beckoned the women of Tonga with supple gestures. His body swayed with surprising grace, and if he felt pain beneath his purpled ribs, it didn't show in the flowing movement of his body. Finau was a terrible dancer, but his ink, a hybrid of two styles, a braiding of the earth and the sea, of Tonga and Aotearoa, was something no one could look away from.

Sun Shower rose to tie an ifi-vine ribbon around Tapoto's arm, eliciting a collective *ooo* from the crowd. Many women, young and old, soon joined in the dancing. I looked at the Wayfinder, who was standing now, lost in a circle of men who seemed intent on containing him. My mother put a hand upon my shoulder. Her look told me she knew what I was feeling. In an effort to distract me, she asked, "Shall we give it a try?"

I attempted the moves, careful to make no sudden actions with the Fan, lest I fell a tree or strike down bystanders. I stepped and turned and gestured as the others did, but I felt unrefined next to our lovely and graceful hosts. It was clear this dance was meant to be danced *for* somebody. With no one to see me, with no one to perform for, I wondered why I'd put myself in motion. Why I was on this island, in front of these people, dancing a dance that wasn't mine. I looked at the Wayfinder, surrounded by men. Why, I wondered, had I even left home?

A woman stopped dancing to speak to me. "I recognize that Fan," she said. "Does it not belong to the auntie of Tonga?"

"It used to," I said.

"And how'd you come by the Tamahā's property?"

"She gave it to me."

The woman clarified, "The Tamahā gave you that Fan?"

When I nodded, she went to the ground. Others began doing the same, and like a gust flattening a field of grass, our Tongan hosts supplicated themselves. When Sun Shower went down, so did Tapoto, and, with confusion and uncertainty, so did my parents and the rest of my people. The singing stopped. Conversation died. People's backs shone amber from the wind-stoked fire.

The men surrounding the Wayfinder went to their knees, but I stopped him before he could lower himself. He came to me, smiling. "Now it's *you* who's rescued *me*," he said.

He'd found me, utterly lost at sea. He'd come back after I'd abandoned him for a sinking canoe.

"I don't think it's the same," I said.

"Then you've never been besieged by mid-level chiefs."

We were surrounded by people on their knees, heads bowed.

"Have you ever felt utterly misplaced?" I asked.

"Only on land," he said.

"I'm not joking."

"Neither am I."

"I don't want to go to 'Ata," I told him. "I don't know who I'll be on some island I've never seen. I don't care if it's enchanting or whatever." Then I added, "I don't want you to go away, either."

"Trust me, I'm not excited about facing the men we enslaved. Or contending with those we deceived on Rotuma, not the least of which is Punake."

"Then don't go," I said. "Send someone else."

"You won't change on 'Ata," the Wayfinder told me. "*The wind against your lips—this is who you are.*"

Was I supposed to respond, *The sand between your toes—this is your home?*

"Were we just passengers to you?" I asked. "Human cargo you had to move?"

"What kind of question is that?"

"Won't you just take us to 'Ata?" I asked. In my mind, I wouldn't be going to a strange and unknown place, not if he was taking me there. "Aren't you duty-bound to take your passengers where they need to go?"

"Your people are *your* passengers," he said. "They need *you*."

"I'm no wayfinder."

"Funny you should mention that," he said. "I have something I've been meaning to give you."

When I think back upon that night, many things were about to happen. At that moment, the constellation I'd sail by, Toloa, was rising in the south, and Masisi, the Wayfinder's star, was descending in the west. There were final preparations, last provisions, the loading of pigs and chickens, creatures we had no experience with. Other significant things were to occur, though I can't remember the order they happened in. Tapoto and Sun Shower were installed as temporary guardians of Tonga. And at some point, the Tamahā appeared with Vula, the Fisian boy. Without words, he was handed over, giving the Wayfinder one more errand to run: returning a child to his home. And we were to part in the pale light of a newly risen moon. First, though, the Wayfinder removed something from his waistband.

When it was held aloft, I could see it was my greenstone fishhook pendant, the one I'd found in a grave. I'd originally seen it as a pretty adornment. Now I knew it was a symbol of great knowledge and responsibility.

He held it out, like he wanted to hang it around my neck.

"What?" I asked. "That's for navigators only."

"Anyone can learn the names of stars," he said. "Putting others first, sacrificing your own needs, valuing every last person—those things can't be taught."

"Seriously, though," I said. "I'd get people hopelessly lost."

"Getting lost is how I found you."

I shook my head. Was he crazy? "I'm a nothing-special girl from a no-place island."

"You're a rare person, from a rare place. Don't you know that? Don't you believe me?"

"Yeah, but—"

He stopped me. "Then trust me when I say that you're the one to guide your people."

"Making landfall on distant islands, that's life-and-death."

He lifted the necklace. "For now, then, just think of it as me wishing you safe passage over water."

Safe passage over water . . . the first words we'd exchanged.

I lowered my head, and he hung the pendant around my neck. I felt it against my chest, which triggered many memories. "I used to dream of being a storyteller," I said.

The Wayfinder said, "I used to dream of stories being told about me."

"I spent my time imagining a return to my homeland."

"I imagined finding new land."

I wondered when, exactly, I'd left those dreams behind.

"You know the moment my mind returns to?" he asked.

"What?"

"Brushing my finger against your newly inked skin."

"What'd that feel like?" I asked.

He extended his hand, running the pad of his index finger along my lower lip.

I closed my eyes, the touch seeming to last forever.

"Like that," he said.

Much of his hair had come loose and was falling in his face.

"You're a king now," I said. "You can't be wearing your hair like a lonely sailor."

I reached to gather his hair. To topknot it above his head, I had to draw near, so that our bodies were touching. He said, "So you'll collect Tapoto when his service to Tonga is complete?"

"If he hasn't made himself king in your absence."

"If someone tries to take over," the Wayfinder said, "I'd bet on Sun Shower."

I looked into the Wayfinder's eyes. "So, should I meet you here, when the winds shift?"

He nodded. "We won't be apart for long. You sure you won't forget me?"

"I'd probably recognize you in a crowd."

"Just look for the guy wearing the feathery thing," he said. "And what about you? You said you're afraid you'll change. What if I don't recognize you?"

"Just look for the navigator who doesn't know how to navigate."

"And if you learn the stars and currents? How will I spot you then?"

With a turn of my hand, I issued a breeze that set the firelit trees ashimmer.

"You'll know me," I said. "I'll be the girl with the Fan."

FORTY-ONE

STEALING STARS

THE STORY OF THE WAYFINDER

Of her early life, much remains a mystery. What island did she come from? Was she truly raised on famine foods? Had a blind woman really been her guide?

Some aspects of her life are agreed-upon. It's said she once crossed the sea to save a single girl. And later presided over an oceanic exodus. She'd opened graves, taken limbs, given life, and withdrawn it, all before she'd held the hand of a boy. For a time, she was the queen of Tonga. But larger destinies called. And life on solid ground lost its appeal. She took to the water, where she became known as a person who'd help folks find their way. She became known as "The Wayfinder."

Though her husband's name is not remembered, he was also a navigator. He knew the art of shaping hulls, so we can imagine the vaka they fashioned: glistening bows, crab-claw masts, sheets of reddened sail. These sails became the cloak they wrapped themselves inside. Giving birth upon the water meant making a midwife of the sea, for the swells rocked one child, and then another, into the world. Babe at the breast, another mast-bound, they weren't worried about losing a child overboard—in the waters they sailed, and if they were visited by peril, they'd likely all go down. If loss must visit a family, that's how it should be.

Did she call upon the volcanic bowls of Vanuatu? Or greet the frosted peaks of Aotearoa? No, it was out-of-the-way islands that interested her. Here were overlooked people. Women to free. Children to take in. Here were forests, much depleted. Birds in need. And countless landscapes, so denuded. Upon these things, she waved her Fan. Who else would demand an island's tribute? Who else would bid our human duty?

Reviving exhausted islands required Fan-work that took her entire body to deploy. Turning, she'd lift one leg and then kick the other, her Fan sweeping as she transferred it from one hand to the next. Sometimes a Fan must be whipped, its bearer contorting, cowls of air crackling electrical. What had a woman but her limbs, her resolve, and her willingness to grip an incandescing Fan, one that delayered the very land she stood upon? Her movements formed a kind of dance, a not-before-seen dance, one that made spectators feel the dancer's fury and ache. But the greening would occur. Roots would sink. Tendrils, buds, and blossoms rise.

Nights, her little family would lie on the vaka's deck and contemplate the heavens. Her daughters would ask about the lives of land dwellers. Did they sleep on the *actual* dirt? Did they relieve themselves where they lived? What stopped them from simply sailing away? Their hearts went out to those trapped on such besoiled, overpopulated splotches. Still, the girls were lonely. They rarely encountered others upon the sea. And when they did, it was understood these strangers would likely not be seen again.

Her family picked up a bit of parrot-talk, and freely conversed with whales, who normally had to beach themselves to engage in human speech. She discovered that if you listened to islands, really listened—to their reefs and spits and tracts of sapling trees—they'd tell you what they needed. Less and less she used her Fan. Instead, she'd confer with islanders about corrections they could make. In most cases, you didn't need otherworldly powers to help an island. There were steps that average people, thoughtful people, patient people could take.

The Fan started spending its days hanging from a peg. She knew she'd have to select someone new to wield it. Her daughters weren't likely candidates. They had other destinies. When they were ready, she hung fishhook necklaces on them, so they could make their own fates. Of course, her daughters ended up marrying land dwellers and establishing themselves as women of note on central islands. In their wake, it was just her and her husband. They could sail for days without speaking, for they were of one mind about rigging and courses and stars to steer.

At last, she embarked with her husband to find an inheritor for the Fan. Only a rural girl would do. This meant increasingly impossible journeys, to ever-remoter corners. Occasionally they encountered beaches lacking footprints in the sand, islands without woodsmoke or dwellings or stumps or latrines. On these immaculate islands, she and her husband would enter the foliage. Though mature, they weren't yet old. They'd shed their garments and garb themselves in the adornments of nature. With rainwater, they'd rinse the salt from one another. They'd loose each other's hair. In moonlight, they'd rekindle their eternal spark. And upon their departure, she'd use her Fan to steal that island's zenith star from the sky. Not steal, exactly, but coax to earth, for a while at least, with subtle pulls from her Fan.

It turned out that stars were as small as they appeared. They were cool to the touch. These stars she stored in the dark water of a fresh coconut. In this way, pristine islands were screened from human designs. Even a wayfinder couldn't find such an island again. No one would come across such a place unless they allowed themselves to become utterly, wonderfully, lost.

ACKNOWLEDGMENTS

I'm deeply indebted to Vasalua Jenner-Helu of Tonga's 'Atenisi Institute for her help with the language, culture, and history of Tonga. She helped translate the poetry in this volume and proved an invaluable resource in every regard. I'm also indebted to the University of Hawai'i's Arthur Whistler for his expertise on the medicinal botanicals of Samoa and Tonga. Over and over, Art gifted me with his deep knowledge of Pacific flora and volunteered anecdotes of his extensive sociological fieldwork. The University of the South Pacific's Paul Geraghty provided much-needed assistance with the Fijian language and the dialects of the Lau Islands. His facility with precontact Polynesian lexicons helped me navigate many complex linguistic decisions. Thanks also to Akihisa Tsukamoto of Mie University for assistance with the language and mythology of Tonga's Niua Islands, especially Niuafo'ou. Thanks also goes to Dr. Ray Harlow of the University of Waikato for his help with te reo Māori.

Stanford University has always supported my literary projects, and for this, I am grateful. Thanks also goes to the American Academy in Berlin, where portions of this book were written.

I'm eternally grateful to Phil and Penny Knight, to whom this book is dedicated, for their ongoing support of Stanford's Creative Writing Program. Their generosity has greatly enhanced the literary lives of Stanford's undergraduate students, Stegner Fellows, Jones Lecturers, and faculty members.

I'm blessed to be represented by Warren Frazier, a true friend and a prince among literary agents. My editor, Sean McDonald, believed in *The Wayfinder* from the first moment. Inordinate thanks are owed to him and to everyone on the MCD and Farrar, Straus and Giroux teams.

Most importantly, I'm indebted to my family, who supported me during the decade of this book's composition. James, Jupiter, and Justice: I love you more than you'll ever know. And as ever, Stephanie Harrell is my sun, my moon, my star and satellite.

A NOTE ABOUT THE AUTHOR

Adam Johnson is the author of *Fortune Smiles*, which won the National Book Award and the Story Prize, and *The Orphan Master's Son*, which won the Pulitzer Prize, the Dayton Literary Peace Prize, and the California Book Award. Johnson's other awards include a Holtzbrinck Fellowship at the American Academy in Berlin, a Guggenheim Fellowship, a Whiting Award, a National Endowment for the Arts Fellowship, and a Stegner Fellowship; he was also a finalist for the New York Public Library's Young Lions Fiction Award. His previous books include the short-story collection *Emporium* and the novel *Parasites Like Us*. Johnson was born in South Dakota and is an enrolled member of the Cheyenne River Sioux Tribe. He lives in San Francisco with his wife and children and teaches creative writing at Stanford University.

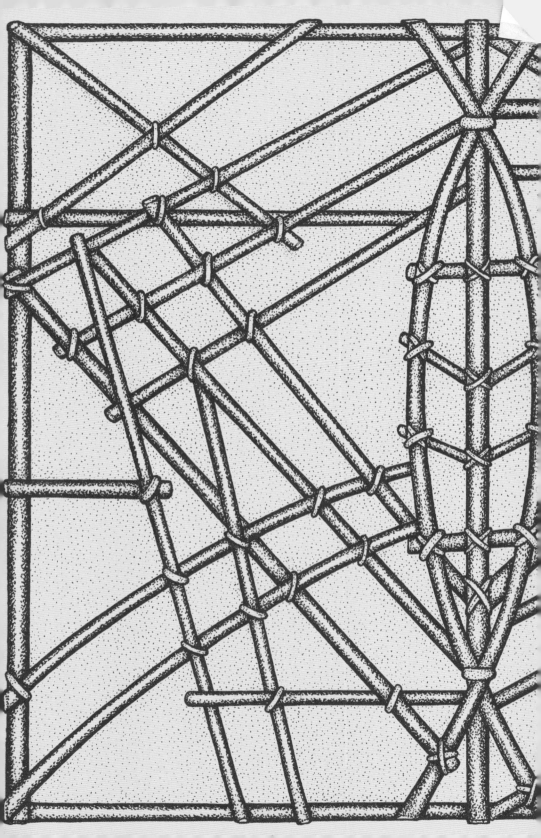